Impatient Love

When Mary Heard a quick knock at the door, her heart leapt. Then a voice cut sharply into the silence of her thoughts.

"It is Staff, Mary. I must speak with you."

Staff did not wait for words from her, but took a huge step in and closed the door quietly behind him. "I had to see you, Mary. I am sorry to come at such a dark hour."

Mary stared at the tiny throbbing pulse at the base of his bronze throat. How was he always so brown in the winter months? He had changed clothes too, and how did he ever find this forsaken room?

"Please, Staff, you must go. If anyone should find you here—"

Staff silenced her with a hot kiss. "Hush," he whispered, taking her closer into his arms. "Mary, we have waited long enough. I want you, dearest, to make up for the lonely hours, and countless advice, and worry that your kings and cursed father would totally ruin our life together. And for the wasted years. Tonight, Mary, we are going to begin catching up—and it will take a long, long time for us to be even. . . ."

Passion's Reign

BY
KAREN
HARPER

ZEBRA BOOKS
KENSINGTON PUBLISHING CORP.

ZEBRA BOOKS

are published by

KENSINGTON PUBLISHING CORP.
475 Park Avenue South
New York, N.Y. 10016

Part One

Sweet is the rose, but grows upon a briar;
Sweet is the juniper, but sharp his bough;
Sweet is the eglantine, but pricketh near;
Sweet is the fir bloom, but his branch is rough;
Sweet is the cypress but his rind is tough;
Sweet is the nut, but bitter is his pill;
Sweet is the broom flower, but yet sour enough,
And sweet is moly, but his root is ill.
So every sweet with sour is tempered still,
That maketh it be coveted the more:
For easy things that may be got at will,
Most sorts of men do set but little store.
Why then should I account of little pain,
That endless pleasure shall unto me gain!

—Edmund Spenser

Chapter One
July 16, 1512

Hever Castle, Kent

As she searched back over the span of years to where
it all began, her mind always seized upon that golden
day at Hever when she first knew there could be uncer-
tainty, yes, and even fear and pain. They were all so
young then—she but eight years, George a year older,
so baby Anne was five years that summer. The July day
spent itself in gold and green caresses for the tiny knot
garden, and the yew-lined lanes, and grassy swards at
Hever. But the reverie of that warmth and beauty always paled beneath the darker recesses of memory. Indeed, that was the first day she knew she was to be sent
away and used, and that it would make her dear mother
most unhappy.

The first thing she would recall were Anne's squeals
of delight and George's high pitched tones of command
mingled with the yelps of the reddish-coated spaniel
pups which nearly drowned the drone of bees in the
beds of roses and Sweet William. The pups were but a
four month litter from their lady mother's favorite lap
dog Glinda, but George was determined to control

them and train them to be his obedient pets.

"Stop that! Stop that! You shall bend to my will, you little whelps!" he shouted with a grown-up edge of impatience to his boyish voice as he swung smartly at them with a willow switch. They yelped sharply when the stings struck, but continued to cavort and roll about on each other, all silken floppy ears and clumsy paws.

"Cease, George! They are too young to be whipped or trained," came Mary's clear voice from the vine-woven gallery where she sat slightly apart from the scene. She felt growing annoyance from the raucous laughter and pitiful cries of the pups. "They are not hunt hounds, only lap dogs for ladies, so leave them be. Gentleness and love will train them well enough. Leave off, or I shall tell mother or Semmonet!"

The boy turned to face her, a look of disdain clouding his fine features. He put his fists on his hips and stood straight, his eyes squinting in the sun toward her shady bower.

"You shall not order me about, Mary. I am the elder, and I am the son, and I already own three hounds and two falcons. And I shall see service in the king's court long before you. Father has promised!"

"Has he now?" Mary countered, for George did annoy her so of late when he acted as though he were a lord's man or knight already and not some country lad whose father was always gone to court. "I warrant we all may stay here with mother at Hever, or maybe Blickling or Rochford, and never see the court at all," she continued.

Usually that sort of taunt unsettled George enough to quiet him, but today she hit a different mark. He advanced several swift strides toward her and, as he came into the shade of the arbor, she was startled to see the flush of his cheek and the frown on his brow. Anne trailed in his angry wake, her face curious, her raven hair spilling from beneath her white-ribboned cap.

"The fair-haired Mistress Mary with Grandmother Howard's beauty! Do not think to set yourself above Anne and me that we show the Butler blood for our dark locks and plainer faces. We are every bit as much a Howard too, and I shall be lord here at Hever someday and then you shall do my bidding, or—or I shall wed you to a poor landed gentry knight!"

The vehemence surprised the girl, for though she sometimes goaded George for his imperious ways or silently smarted beneath his overbearing attitude, he seldom responded this way. It almost frightened her and, except for Anne's large, dark eyes peering earnestly at her, she would have responded haughtily.

"I meant nothing by it, brother, and never vowed I had more of the Howard blood than you. Our lord has often told us we are all to be proud of our heritage of Irish Butler and powerful Norfolk, for was not our grandfather the High Treasurer for our king's father?"

George nodded curtly as though he had bested her and turned his attention back to the pups again. Now tired of their romp, they lay stretched into little splashes of shining bronze beside the marigold beds.

But Anne lingered, her pale yellow gown almost touching Mary's emerald skirts. The child often gazed at her older sister. She admired Mary's golden hair and clear blue eyes and lovely face, for their beauty was noticed by all, and the tiny girl sensed the import of this more than did Mary. It meant somehow that Mary was special, was different, and though George resented this,

11

the child Anne was quite in awe.

"Why can we not go into the solar to see father, Mary? He comes not much to see us. What has he so secret to tell mother that Semmonet sent us away from the house? I wish he would come out and play with us and the pups, but I know he will not."

Anne sat beside Mary on the rough wood bench, her hands folded in her lap. She looked so dainty and demure that Mary wondered anew at the quicksilver changes of temperament the girl showed. She herself felt no such feverish blood stir her moods, nor did she ever throw the noisy tantrums of which this child was capable.

"Dear Annie, Semmonet said only that father had an important message for mother and that we shall learn of his tidings later. I am certain you can manage to wait until supper, for he will no doubt stay at least until the morrow, so you may ask him then, minx."

The pale child bit her lower lip, and Mary knew another question would follow. Did she never tire of her endless probings of everything? Her mind is quick and her French and Latin may soon overtake mine, she thought.

"Mary," Anne began in her childish voice, "do you believe the king looks in true life as he does in the portrait? He always seems to look sideways at me as I come down the stairs or go in the solar. His hands are so big and strong and he looks very frightening."

Her eyes looked like wet black brook pebbles, and Mary reached out to touch her white cheek. "Well, little one, I have not seen His Majesty either, but father is proud of that portrait copy by Master van Cleve, you know, so I would guess it catches the king in truth. And

12

I agree, Annie, the eyes and the hands *do* look most frightening, especially at night when the hall lies in shadow with only candle gleams." She hesitated. "Is there anything else you would ask, Annie?"

Mary smiled at her little sister and the dazzling beauty that angered George, worried her mother, and pleased her father, simply amazed the younger child. Why could she not have golden hair and sky colored eyes and an angel's face like those in the stained glass windows at grandmother's chapel?

"I was only hoping, Mary, that he comes not back to take me to the king's court, for I should be afraid to go from mother and Semmonet and George and you. Even if father were there, I should be afraid, for father has eyes and hands like the king." Her lip quivered, and her fears, so plainly spoken, tugged on Mary's love though she herself felt no such childish worries.

"No, Annie. Do not be afraid. We are all too young to leave here now. George will surely go first and though you and I are not too young to be engaged, there has been no word of this. Maybe father comes to tell of a fine promotion above being Esquire of the King's Body. Father wishes to rise far, I know."

"Yes, Mary. And mother says he shall. Does she miss him as much as we, do you think?"

"Yes. No doubt even more. But she loves it here and has almost no desire to be at court, though I do not know why. But who would not love life at our Hever, Annie?" Mary's eyes skipped swiftly across the low boxwood hedges and the carefully tended beds of riotous marigolds, snapdragons and sweet heartsease.

"Father will soon ride back to the king's business, and we shall be safe with mother and Semmonet. You shall see," she comforted.

The child shot her a sunbeam smile and darted off, eager to follow George and the pups around the other side of the garden. Soon her lilting laugh and George's sharp tones floated through the air again punctuated by excited yelps from the litter of spaniels.

Mary grimaced as she rose, but walked away from their play. She did not want another rude encounter with George if she scolded him again. Then, too, Anne's innocent questions had unsettled her more than George's bloodless cruelty to the pups could.

Her father had ridden in hard from Greenwich and most unexpected. He did have special news for the family, that she knew. But what puzzled and bothered her the most was that he had sent the children out to play yet had summoned Semmonet. Why would his words be of import to their governess unless it concerned one of her three Bullen charges? Her heart beat slightly faster as she paced the squared outer edge of the heady-scented boxwood walk toward the house.

As she emerged from the gardens, the brightly painted ornamental facade of Hever rose up before her set like a gaudy jewel in the clear blue frame of cloudless sky. Its blonde brick walls and decorative chimneys and water lily studded moat rested in the meadows at the fork of the gentle River Eden. Mary knew well the heritage of the house, for it was the same proud heritage of her family, and she and Goerge and Annie had been taught to rehearse it well.

"Built by great-grandsire Geoffrey Bullen, lord mayor of London, who married the proud daughter of Lord Hoo," she recited half aloud. "Once a mere hunt lodge, but now the family seat of his grandson Lord

Thomas Bullen of King Henry's great court and his Lady Elizabeth Bullen.''

She went in step to her chant toward the house from which she and the other Bullen children had been temporarily banished. She crossed the now-useless drawbridge and went beneath the rusty pointed teeth of the raised portcullis. As a younger child of Anne's age, she had pictured that entry as the mouth of a terrible dragon whose jaws might snap shut in an instant and devour a fair maiden beneath. Long ago she had darted through fearful that the iron jaws would trap or crush her, but she was much too old for such foolhardiness now.

The cobbled courtyard lay silent, and the shiny leaded windows of the hall and solar glinted in the afternoon sun and gave no hint of what dark secrets might be proudly announced within. She would await the parental summons in her bedchamber away from the howls of pups or George's taunts or even Annie's childish questions. Maybe Semmonet would be in the nursery now and could tell her of the special news, for did not Semmonet treasure the happiness of her three charges above all?

One oak door to the hall stood agape. The warm fresh air of the day was a blessing in the frequently shut up house. A sunbeam-dusted shaft of light poured onto the worn oak floor inside the entry as the girl stepped inside and looked guardedly about. The low hum of her parents' voices drifted from the solar still lifted in earnest conversation. She continued to the great banister and put one slippered foot on the first stair, but halted in the huge square of sunlight as her mother's raised voice pierced the silence.

"My dear Lord Thomas, I grant it is an honor, and I am proud of your appointment as ambassador to the Archduchess of Savoy, but the other matter is out of the question." Her clear voice stopped, and Mary sought to picture her lovely mother's angry face. She had always seen her in control of herself, always calm and gentle. Surely father would not insist he take George abroad with him on this new business.

"Settle your feathers, my beautiful little mother hen," came her father's voice with its familiar edge of authority. "I have already obtained the placement. I have great plans for all three and, believe me, the opportunity is fortuitous. We dare not pass up this chance for the advancement and polish needed. Where else could the golden egg fall right in our laps and without cost to us? I had thought, of course, when the king's sister should be sent abroad to marry, the time would come, but this is even sooner than I had hoped."

Mesmerized by the voices, Mary edged closer to the huge door of the solar, set slightly ajar to seize the fresh air. Guiltily, she stared back at the piercing eyes of her king whose portrait hung in the dimness of the hall not washed by the sunlight which slanted in on her trembling body. Yes, indeed little Anne was right. The king's eyes seemed to accuse and frighten.

Suddenly, her heart lurched and her mind grasped each single word of her mother's quaking voice: "I pray you, my lord, let this honor go until she is at least in her tenth year. She is but a mere eight years and not a child fully raised yet."

Mary's slender frame leaned for support against the carved linen fold paneling of the hall. She crumpled wadded balls of her green skirts in tight fists. They

16

spoke of her . . . and to be sent to . . . to . . . where is Savoy?

"Margaret of Austria and Regent to the Netherlands, Elizabeth, imagine it. It is the highest rung of the ladder for now, and when she is educated there, it will be a finishing school second only to the French court itself. When she returns, where else is there for her but among Queen Catherine's ladies in His Grace's very eyes?"

"Yes. Where else," came Elizabeth Bullen's low voice, and Mary was hurt and shocked by the anger of it.

Mary could hear her father pacing now as he often did when he thought out a problem or gave orders. His footsteps approached the door and turned back. She wanted to flee but her knees shook and her feet were rooted to the floor.

"Not all women as beautiful as you, Elizabeth, choose to live their lives away from the power and heat of the sun, however, lovely their country homes like Hever."

"There is sun here, my lord, and beauty—and peace of mind."

"Do not bother to argue, Elizabeth, for you know my meaning and my mind. Thomas Bullen, of merchant stock—yes, let them laugh now, for they shall all be left behind as we mount the pinnacle of the realm tied to His Grace's good will."

Her mother's quiet voice went on, and Mary marveled that she should dare to answer her lord back, for none of them ever dared to argue or deny him.

"The farther we all climb, my lord, the farther we may fall. I have seen this king at close range, even as

17

you have, and I tell you he shall never be denied or the denier suffers. He never forgives and I fear . . .''

"Enough, lady. We have had all this discourse before, and to what end? Great Henry would have made you his mistress, the lovely blonde Howard beauty, Elizabeth, the Bullen bride, but you would have none of the honor. 'S blood, madam, 'tis a miracle of cleverness and flattery we recovered from the blow at all. We would have been much farther on the road than this if you had accepted.''

"And it would have been only honor to you, my lord? It would not have caused you a moment's stir that your wife was ridden abed by Prince Henry and maybe got his seed to give her babes and they of no true Bullen blood to make your name!'' She had spoken the tirade quietly, but desperate sobs threatened to well up at each word. Mary's eyes filled with tears at her tone rather than at the full impact of the meaning.

"Yes, of course I would have suffered, but it was the future king, lady, the present king. Well, it is ten years gone, but I promise you, I shall never let such a chance go by the wayside again!'' There was a long silence, and Mary put a foot out to flee.

"Brussels is so far, Thomas. She is so young, so innocent.''

Innocent? Mary pondered the fear and shock she had felt in the last few minutes, her thoughts mingling with the excitement of her new importance and the thrill of the distant unknown. She turned toward the staircase but retreated back behind the door at her mother's voice, suddenly so close.

"I shall fetch Mary since Semmonet has been sent to pack for her. The children are out by the knot garden.''

18

Her mother brushed by on the other side of the door.

"And tell her nothing of it, lady," came her father's sharp voice after her. "I would tell her myself so she will understand the good fortune of it."

Elizabeth Bullen's slender form never turned back as she raised her head and departed from the hall to search for Mary. How beautiful her mother's face and carriage, how lovely her golden hair now threaded with fine silver in the sunlight.

Mary decided to follow her and meet her as she returned. She would never know what her daughter had heard, or of her sadness. Should she say she was glad to go so mother would be comforted? Or would it hurt her to think her daughter would so easily leave her now—or ever?

Mary stepped quietly to the door and, hesitating, peered carefully into the courtyard to see that her mother had departed. It was quite empty and peaceful, beige cobbles, brick honey-colored walls all awash with sun. How she would fear to depart, hate to depart!

"Mary!" came her father's voice, nearly in her ear. She jumped. "Your lady mother said you were about the grounds. Where have you been?" He stood over her, tall and handsome and assured. His dark beard was precisely cut and his velvet-clad shoulders looked dazzling blood-red in the sun. His dark eyes regarded her carefully as he bent his head slightly. "Have you been about the hall long?"

"No, father. I was outside with George and Anne, but they went off and, well, I finally came in."

"You have just missed your mother, but I have a wonderful surprise for you I would tell you alone."

His slender, strong fingers fastened firmly on one of

her shoulders, and he gestured toward the open solar door with his other jeweled hand. She walked unsteadily, suddenly wary, her excitement mixed with childish misgivings. She could feel King Henry's side-glancing eyes pursue her into the solar. She was most unused to private audiences with her father, for he was not often at Hever. How much she loved him and wanted to please him, even as he sought to please his king!

He pointed to the scroll-work stool beneath the lead paned windows where mother often sat doing needlework. He took a step as if to pace, and then abruptly sat in the master's chair and cleared his throat. It suddenly struck her funny that this great lord of the king might be afraid to inform her of the decision that his wife Elizabeth had protested.

"You are very beautiful, my Mary, your perfect oval face, your golden hair, the promise of your slender body. You are all I could ask in a lovely and obedient daughter."

"I am glad, my lord. Semmonet declares I look as mother used to when you came new married from court to Hever."

"Perhaps Semmonet remembers much it is better not to tell, Mary. Yes, you will favor your mother greatly as you grow to womanhood. Though I pray you have a more carefully molded character and may prove more pliable to your lord's wishes. Will you indeed prove so, my little golden Mary?"

He leaned close and patted her hand as he spoke. Again, as over and over in the few hours she spent in his presence, Mary fell instantly in love with him, beyond the bounds of a daughter's ties. For he was not a father she knew, this handsome, tall king's man. He never looked on her with smiles like this, nor spoke to her privately, nor touched her trembling hand.

"Yes, my lord father. I would wish to please you, always." Her voice was a mere whisper and her curved mouth a wan ghost of a smile.

"Then we are off for the royal court of Margaret, Archduchess of Austria, Mary, I as royal ambassador and you to be with her maids-of-honor and learn the fine arts of beautiful and accomplished ladies. You shall have pretty dresses and meet lovely people and perfect your French. You would like that adventure, would you not, my dear?"

The girl raised her blonde head, and her clear blue eyes filled with tears as they met his intent, piercing ones.

"Will it be much like Hever, father?"

"No, better, all more important and splendid and wonderful. Exciting people, great castles, lovely fountains and gardens. The archduchess shall be very pleased with your beauty and manners."

Her voice quavered as she thought of her mother's loving face and nasty, dear George and Annie and Semmonet and the quiet horse she loved to ride at Hever. "Will you be near, father?"

"Yes, as king's ambassador, there whenever you would see me, child."

"Then I know I shall be happy to be there with you," she said in simple trust.

He rose swiftly and patted her slender shoulder. "Here, Mary," he added quickly, reaching toward the table behind her. "Now that you are to set out in the fine world, I fetched you a Tudor rose from the king's gardens at Greenwich. You shall someday belong to the

21

English court, my girl, so remember this when you are steeped in the luxurious beauties of the Belgian court."

She was touched by this act, so unlike anything her aloof, clever father had done before. Surely she would be close to him now, since they would be far away together. The rose was a lovely velvet red despite its slight droop from being carried so far from its garden.

"It is a wonderful rose, father," she said, but as she reached for its stem, she recoiled from the tiny stab of a thorn. She squeezed her finger and a crimson drop of blood formed.

"You must learn to beware of the hidden thorns, foolish girl," he chided. "Come, take your rose and up to Semmonet. She has been packing your things this past hour. We leave Hever tomorrow at dawn and sail from Dover on Monday. Be gone, girl."

Mary rose gracefully and, gingerly holding the flower, curtseyed solemnly. Then she heard herself ask, "And what did my lady mother say of this honor?"

He faced her squarely and looked down into her clear blue eyes. "She is absolutely thrilled that you have this wonderful opportunity," he said. "She only hopes you will be true to the aristocratic Butler and Howard blood that flows in your proud Bullen veins. Now, be gone."

The girl spun swiftly in a rustle of skirts and a whirl of golden hair. She did not want her father or anyone to see the new-learned doubt and pain stamped on her brow and hidden in her eyes.

Chapter Two
November 4, 1514

Les Tournelles, Paris

For the first time in two years, ever since the bright facade of Hever had dropped behind the massive oaks and beeches already obscuring the dwindling forms of her mother and Semmonet, George and Annie, Mary sobbed wretchedly. She had not cried one whit when her lord father had left her in the opulent but austere world of Archduchess Margaret's vast court, nor when she felt the suffocating pangs of homesickness those first endless months, nor even when the archduchess had been sadly touched to part with her at the English Lord Ambassador's sudden insistence. Even departing England again hurriedly, this time with the lovely Princess Mary Tudor, King Henry's own beloved sister, the little Mary Bullen had not shed a tear. What good were weak and foolish sobbings when no one would listen and nothing would be changed?

Indeed, she was of full ten years now, and was thrilled to serve so beauteous and kind a lady as the Tudor Rose, herself sent from her home. But Princess Mary was now Queen of France, her marriage a bind-ing seal between the two powerful nations, her body a human link between her brother England and her husband France.

But Mary Bullen cried now, finally, her sobs so swift upon each other that she could scarce breathe. King Louis XII, the English Mary's elderly husband, had ordered all the English ladies of his bride's entourage dispatched from France forthwith.

Father would be chagrined, yes, angered, but she could face that well enough, for it was no doing of her own that his master plan to have her reared at the French court and near the king's own dear sister had gone awry. The pain was rather for the slender and radiant La Reine Marie, for the sweet lady would be as good as deserted in a foreign court with an old and sickly husband-king and her dangerous nephew Francois, the king's wily heir, hungry for his throne. The sharp, wrenching pain was for herself, too. What would father do with her now? She adored the gentle French queen and was as loathe to be torn from her as she was once from her own mother.

Mary Bullen, *la petite Anglaise,* as King Louis himself had called her, had much company in her emotional agonies as she sat on a richly tapestried chair in the queen's privy chamber. Sniffles, red eyes, and irregular half-choked sobs came from Elizabeth Gray and Margaret and Jane Dorset and the red-haired Rose Dacre. Even Lady Guildford, whom the laughing maids had smugly dubbed their "mother protector", wiped her swollen eyes continually as she gave curt orders for the packing to the hovering French maids.

"Come, all of you. Dry your eyes and regain your composure before our sweet queen returns. Would you

24

have the parting be more painful for her than it already has been, for she has pleaded beyond propriety and beneath her dignity to have us stay." She turned her silver head toward the maids. "*Oui, oui,* put all the busks and hoops together. It matters not. And perhaps," Lady Guildford continued in one breath, suddenly addressing her English charges again, "perhaps His Grace shall protest this effrontery to his stubborn cousin King Louis!"

Like the other older girls, Mary rose and tried to assume a calm demeanor. She shook out her lavender velvet skirts and dashed some of Jane Dorset's rice powder on her flushed cheeks. She might be the youngest by far and a mere maid compared to the others, but she tried with all her strength to emulate the court ladies' carriage, manners and style. Even her soft-clinging lavender gown over the pale yellow kirtle echoed the ornate French fashions the English maids of Queen Mary all strove for. The tight inner sleeve of yellow satin was embroidered and slashed to reveal her soft, lacy chemise which also peeked out from above the oval neckline, and her velvet slippers and folded back outer sleeves perfectly matched her gown. And certainly, she would do much more than copy styles to please the lovely and sad Queen Mary.

The bustle of the packing ceased suddenly as the gold and ivory doors to the chamber swept open and the queen swished in buoyed by immense pink silk skirts and puffs of Chantilly lace. For warmth and elegance, the queen's dress bore a five foot pink silk train, and loops of ermine and jeweled girdle dripped from her narrow waist. Her angular headpiece picked up the ermine trim of her belt and her soft-edged pink slippers were studded with amethysts and emeralds.

How calm, how radiant and beautiful she looked, as always, the newly-awed Mary thought. If she could only be like her some day, so beloved of her ladies and her family! How her brother the magnificent king Henry the Eighth of England had beamed when he hugged her goodbye and kissed her cheek with the fine words, "God be with you, my beloved sister Mary." And she had grasped his great beringed hand, held it to her cheek and whispered in a voice so gentle few had heard except the lady herself, her royal brother and the dainty, golden-haired maid who held her furred cloak.

"You will not forget your promise, my lord, not even if I be gone for years," Mary Tudor had begged her brother Henry.

The king had answered bluntly with a swift sideways look not even regarding his sister's sad, upturned face it seemed to the Bullen girl. "No, of course I shall not forget, lady," he had said and turned away.

But that once-treasured memory of meeting the glorious Henry, King of England, while her father hovered solicitously behind her, was tarnished now by these events. And through it all, their beautifully complexioned, raven-haired queen was trying to be brave.

"Alas, my dears, my husband the king says he wishes me to be a French queen to him and not surrounded by those who would cushion me from French ways. For now," she put her graceful hand on Lady Guildford's trembling arm, "we must obey. Perhaps when he is assured of how honest and true a French queen he has, though English Tudor blood flows proud in her veins, he will relent."

"When your dear brother our Lord King hears of

this cruelty, he shall have words for His Majesty, indeed," flared the quick-witted Rose Dacre. "I shall tell him of it straightaway upon our return, Madam!"

"We must remain calm, Rose, and surely my brother will know of this . . . this problem, before you could tell him. I pray he will always remember his promised duties to his loyal sister." She smiled a wan but, to Mary, a dazzling smile.

The queen caught Mary's serious face, and their eyes held. "His Grace *did* relent one tiny bit, Mistress Boullaine, for indeed he said he never meant that you must leave, since you are but a maid and sent to his court partly for a French education. His Majesty said he never meant '*la petite blonde Boullaine*' was to be dispatched."

She held out her hand to the girl, and Mary walked the few steps radiantly aglow, despite the surprised stares of the other English ladies.

"Madam, I am so pleased to be allowed to stay." She curtseyed, then straightened. "Would that the others dearer to you might remain, but I shall do all I can to keep your company."

The graceful answer pleased the queen and seemed to soothe the others who clustered about her for a solemn farewell. There would be no grievous departure scenes in public to kindle court gossip and the wicked snickers of which the mannered elite of the realm were fully capable. Mary Bullen's goods were hastily unpacked and with long last glances and curtseys and clinging of hands, Mary found herself, for the first time, alone with her adored Mary Tudor, the lonely new Queen of France.

* * *

It seemed most natural to the queen and most wonderful to the young Mary that they were frequently together in the next two months after the English ladies were banished. The feasts, the dancing, the masques went on without ceasing, although the elderly and ailing King Louis was often too weak to enjoy them. The young queen immersed herself in the royal revelries to the growing delight of most of the courtiers who would have been obliged to feel they should diminish their frivolities because their king was temporarily indisposed. Always nearby, lurked the charming, clever, and handsome Dauphin Francois; only twenty, but ageless in wit and watchfulness. The young queen found him engaging and quite irresistible, so the young Mary Bullen thought. To her ten-year-old eyes, he sparkled with glamor, magnetism and fascination.

And the sensitive, young English companion to the French queen, who observed much but participated little because she was yet a child, idolized her laughing mistress. Yet, though the queen seemed often among the courtiers, she was never really part of them. Indeed, the fair Reine Marie seemed to wish that time would fly on swifter wings.

Often when they were alone, closeted in the queen's privy chamber, Her Grace would talk on and on of England and her dearest bluff brother Hal from days before he ascended the throne, and of the most wonderful and jovial people of the Tudor court.

"I feel I could readily name them all now, Madam," Mary admitted to her queen one night as they sat late over warmed wine and a gilded chess board, to which they paid scant attention as their talk skipped from point to point. "I feel as though I truly know our

Queen Catherine and His Grace and even his dearest companions as well, as say, Sir Charles Brandon, the delightful Duke of Suffolk." Mary Bullen laughed her lovely, lilting laugh at the thought of her father's surprise when she could show him she recognized all the important people of the court before his busy hands could even point them out. Then she stopped, suddenly unsure, for the queen had paled visibly and was grasping an ivory glided chesspiece in a white-knuckled fist.

"Charles Brandon—delightful? Why do you term him that, Mary?" Her unsteady voice sounded not angry as Mary had feared, but strangely puzzled and hurt.

"I meant nothing by it, Your Grace. It is a word you have used to describe him and I only thought to . . ."

"Did I now—delightful? Ah, indeed he is that, *ma petite*." She smiled warmly but her gaze seemed clouded and distant.

She sees him even now in her mind's eye, Mary realized in wonderment.

"What else have I said of my brother-king's dearest, truest friend, my Mary," she queried, her voice now playful.

Mary remembered well all the phrases of praise and happily recounted events, but she felt quickly shy of repeating her queen's words. The sure knowledge came swiftly to her naive mind that this woman could have loved elsewhere than her old husband the French king. Her marriage was, of course, arranged, and she had long before that been years promised to Charles of Castille, but she knew him not. Just because she was a princess and meant for a special marriage bond, could she not have given her heart elsewhere? Would not her own dear brother's best companion be often about and then . . .

"Perhaps I have often said too much to be remembered or related, Mary." Her perfect teeth showed white, and her dark eyes sparkled. She leaned forward across the wide chess board, her jeweled crucifix trailing its heavy pearl-studded chain over the marble noisily. She reached her pale hand across to cover Mary's smaller crucifix.

"God forgive me, Mary, but Charles Brandon is the dearest man in the world to me next, of course, to my brother and my lawful husband."

Tears sprang to her eyes and hovered on her thick lashes. Her grasp on Mary's hand tightened. "It helps me to have said it, Mary. I pray you will keep my secret. Only three others know of it, His Grace and I and the Duke himself." Her gentle voice trailed off and she loosed her grip on Mary's hand, seemingly surprised she held it so hard.

"You see, Mary, my lord, King Henry, has solemnly vowed that should I ever be widowed in my willing service to England as King Louis' queen that I—yes, I alone—may select my next husband!" The words were quiet but fervent.

Mary sat wide-eyed and intent, the impact of being privy to such high dealings crashing with the queen's passionate words on her ears and heart. "Indeed that is most generous and wondrous kind, Your Grace," the girl was at a loss for proper words of comfort.

"His Majesty, my dear brother, generous and wondrous kind, *ma cherie?*" A musical chuckle floated to Mary across the chess board. "Well, maybe, but there is no way to be certain, you see, for it suited him well to give me that promise at the time. And if it suits him not, should I wish to collect on the strange bargain, the rhetorical question is, my Mary, will he even remember it? Will he honor it if I am needed to wed elsewhere? I tremble with the thrill of the possibility, but with the fear of it too!''

She held out her hand, palm up, fingers extended toward the girl and indeed she did tremble, and the carved queen piece quivered in the dancing candle gleams.

Her eyes seemed to focus on Mary's earnest, lovely face. ''You must understand the way of it, Mary. You may thank the Queen of Heaven—the first Mary of all Mary's—that you are born to your lord father Sir Thomas Bullen, ambitious and clever though he is, and not to a blooded king.''

Mary's mouth formed an oval of surprise before she could hide her feelings, and her blue eyes widened honestly. Though she had been taught to cleverly mask her feelings at the court of the archduchess as well as at this witty French court, she remained somehow too naive and trusting to master the art.

''Mary, hearken now. It is this way in our world!'' With one graceful swoop of her silken arm, the queen cleared their chess board, scattering the pieces noisily onto the parquet table top.

''Forget the pretended chess rules, Mary. This is how the game is truly played. This great king can do anything he wills at anytime it suits him.'' She slammed her elaborately carved king piece down in the center of the board with such vehemence that the girl jumped. ''And here, Mary, all the little pawns to be spent at his whim to win his daily games at court or at

Parliament or between kingdoms or whatever.''

She pressed a little handful of the gaily painted and gilded marble pawns haphazardly about the loftier king piece. ''Of course, the king is surrounded by a few knights, men who deem themselves great, not quaint horses as these. But though few knights realize it, they are only pawns. And you and even I, Mary, we are pawns to go here or there as the king piece wills it.'' Her nimble fingers flicked the tiny pawns about randomly.

Finally, Mary found her voice despite this sudden strange behavior of her adored companion. ''But, Madam, you indeed are this great queen piece and surely not a pawn.''

''No, Mary. I warn that you must learn the actual rules if you are even to survive at royal courts, be they in France or Belgium or fair England or far-off Araby.'' Her lilting laughter filled the room again. ''Kings may make certain pawns queens, but be assured they are pawns yet, and their only power comes in realizing this—yes, and in accepting it as I do!''

She slumped back, seemingly bereft of the mingled passions that had stirred her uncharacteristic outbreak, her raven locks dark against the crimson velvet of the chair back. Her eyes still narrowed in thought, her face flushed, her full breasts rising and falling steadily, she stared fixedly at the bewildered girl.

''I meant not such a tirade, Mary, and you must know you have nothing to do with my desperation. I usually control it under my smiles and nods and pleasant chatter. It is another lesson you must learn, *petite Marie Boullaine.*''

''Yes, my queen. I am learning, and I am grateful to

my lord father that I may learn at your court and from your own lips.''

"It is not my court, Mary. Far from it. But, you see, I am most fond of you and would be sad to lose you, now more than ever since you have seen the real Mary Tudor and her heart's secret and act as though you love her still.''

"Yes, my queen, truly!''

"Then, my dear, I hope I may keep you near me whatever befalls as it soon may.''

"I would stay by your side always.''

"But you are only of ten years, Mary, and 'always' is a good deal longer than that. I fear and pray I may not be queen here long.''

"Madam, I . . .''

"Hush, Mary. And vow never to speak of my fears and thoughts that you have shared here tonight, to no one, especially not your father, however much you adore him. And never to the charming Dauphine. He too, waits and watches, Mary.''

Puzzlement creased Mary's brow again, but she hesitated not a moment, "I vow it, my queen.''

The slender Queen of France nodded and rose, her hands on the corners of the huge chessboard. Mary knew she was drained of energy and emotion, and she stood waiting patiently to be dismissed. But the queen leaned close to her again, and her quiet words came at Mary like steel-tipped arrows.

"You must understand you are an entirely vulnerable pawn, Mary. You are so lovely and will be more so as you mature. As I have told you, you will be the image of your beautiful Howard mother when she first came to my father's court on her new husband's arm.

All looked on her and adored her. All, Mary, for she even stood high in favor with my brother Prince Harry before he wed the dowager widow, Spanish Catherine.''

She stopped her words, uneasy at their import for her young charge, but the blonde girl faced her squarely and did not flinch. ''Your father is ambitious and would be even more powerful in the king's shadow than he is now, so remember to keep your own heart hidden and intact. Maybe you shall find some ploy to choose where you would bestow your love someday, even as I pray I have.''

Her lithe hand briefly rested against her maid's pale cheek. ''But while I can, my English Mary, I shall protect and guide you. I will do that while I yet can.''

Mary nodded and smiled, her golden curls bobbing gently in affirmation. As she curtseyed to the queen and took a few steps backward to summon the royal attendants, her mistress' voice came again.

''And Mary, we shall each keep one of these little painted pawns as a sign of our knowledge and our secret.'' The girl stretched out her perspiring palm, and the queen pressed into it a marble green and white, gilded chess piece.

''See, my Mary, a mirror piece of mine, even to the emerald and white of Tudor colors. Tudor pawns, indeed!''

Again her swift silvered laughter filled the tiny privy chamber and Mary's amazed ears as she departed the room.

Chapter Three
December 29, 1514

Hotel De Cluny, Paris

The sick and old King Louis XII had been dead for a
week. He had dropped off to eternal sleep as easily as a
rotting apple drops to the ground from the still vigorous
tree. The fruit remaining on the tree was ripe and
healthy, and the whole vast orchard of fertile France
tensed with anticipation.

The first long-expected cries of "*Le roi est mort*" soon
became the vibrant shouts of "*Vive le roi Francois!*" as
the lusty twenty-year-old nephew of the dead king ascended. Francois' wily mother, Louise of Savoy, already assembled her son's new counselors and his
clever and passionate sister Marguerite sent him a bar-
rage of instructions and suggestions. All necessary
steps were taken by the new monarch to ensure and
strengthen his long-awaited and often-doubted succession. Most importantly, the eighteen-year-old English-
bred queen, who had gone from "*la nouvelle reine Marie*"
to "*la reine blanche*" in the brief transition, was under
royal orders of close confinement in the tiny old medieval palace of Cluny.

The grieving young widow, the dowager queen, was not in any danger, but was rather being protected and sheltered by her step-nephew, the new king. But, although she was not in danger, all knew she could become a danger, and so the custom was fulfilled: she was to be kept under lock and key for six weeks to assure the new king that no child of the dead monarch would come from her body to supplant Francois on his long-desired throne.

"*La reine blanche Marie*" would remain at Cluny until Francois and his rapacious family were certain she was not pregnant, though Francois knew well that old Louis had been long since past his vigorous manhood. Still, the former queen was young and vibrant and charming. Had not he himself even wished to seduce her and put away his fat and pious wife, Claude? Perhaps there had been other men about her also, and he must be absolutely sure. Then she must be married off as soon as possible to Savoy or some well-attached French count. She must be kept in France and not returned to her brother who would no doubt use her again for a marriage advantageous to the English. She must not go to placate Francois' rival for the title of Holy Roman Emperor, the young Charles of Castille to whom she had once been promised. Then, too, she was so lovely, so desirable, so ripe for plucking, he would have her about his court for his own uses.

The widow herself was in a state of twisted tensions. She was shocked that it was all over so quickly—a few swift months of brocaded processions and twittering courtiers, his withered old hands on her body and it was over. She had written in secret desperation to Cardinal Wolsey through the new French ambassador, Thomas

Bullen, and more circumspectly to her beloved brother, for her correspondence would be carefully probed by Francois' new appointees.

She lay awake long into the chill French nights, her heart, thoughts and prayers pounding in the silence, hoping beyond hope that her dear brother would keep his promise and that she might return to London and wed with her Suffolk. She paced the richly carpeted stone floors muffled in her white mourning wrap, and peered long, watching for dawn in the gray east beyond the imprisoning square courtyard of Cluny. Grotesque gargoyles bent angularly from above her window, their demonic faces haunting her waking dreams and her racing fears. Then, more often than not, the dear little Boullaine, whom she insisted be kept with her and be allowed to sleep in her chamber, would stir and ask if she were well or if she might comfort her somehow.

"You do comfort me, *ma cherie,* just by being near at this—this most difficult time. My body aches for sleep, but my thoughts will not allow it. No one can truly understand, and that is well. It is enough you are with me. Sleep now, Mary."

"But, Your Grace, you are so dear to me, and perhaps I can understand just a little." The girl's long blonde locks were all the exhausted woman could discern in the gray dimness of the room. She advanced, still tightly encased in her ivory wrap, and sat wearily on the foot of her maid's narrow bed. She spoke in a low whisper.

"This place shall be the end of me, Mary, if I do not receive word soon. Six weeks to live in this place and but one gone already. I shall turn to the gray, cold stone around me! Does the English court not even know what has happened? Forgive me, Mary,'' she said more quietly at last. "I know your father has conveyed all my pleas."

"Of course he has, Madam, and soon a message will be here."

"Did he tell you it would be here soon, *ma cherie?*"

"I, well, I have not seen him, Your Grace, any more than usual. He is so busy as the new French ambassador, you see." Her quiet voice hung suspended in the silence and both were soon lost in their own lonely thoughts.

"I know you think often of him, of your brother, the king, and of . . . the duke, my lady. It is only seven days. Someone will come soon."

"Yes, indeed, but the one who comes soon is my loving nephew Francois, *le grand roi*. And this visit will be not for pretended condolences, but to force me to marry his mignon or submit to some other which his mother or sister have suggested. How shall I gainsay him then, Mary, without my brother's might? I fear, Mary, I fear!"

They instinctively clasped fingers in the darkness, and Mary wished so desperately to offer her older friend a thread of hope, however slender. "Surely my father will be calling again soon and you can at least ask his advice, Your Grace."

"No, sweet Mary. I would not hurt you for all the gold in France, but his advice would be that other charge I fear to obey. 'Marry wherever your royal brother could best use you for England,' he would say. Well, never! Never again."

Her fingers tightened so suddenly that they crushed Mary's hand painfully. "I must—I shall—tread this course between the Scylla of Francois' intent and the ugly Charybdis that my brother should make me wed abroad again. Never!''

She released the girl's hand and rose, a shrouded figure in the gloom. To Mary, her queen looked oddly ghostlike in white, the French color for mourning. Mary felt the tingling blood rush back into her fingers. She wished to argue with her fair Tudor princess, that surely her father could be trusted as the king's great ambassador and that Henry, too, was a fine Christian king and would keep his promise to her, for she had heard him say so herself. But she knew well that her mistress did not trust these men when it came to her desperate love for the Duke of Suffolk, and she held her tongue.

"I am able to sleep now, I believe, *la petite blonde Anglaise*. I shall not have the new king find me gaunt with gray lines on my cheeks and brows. And pray God this wretched toothache shall abate before I must face him.''

Her graceful form glided away from Mary toward the great canopied bed which already bore the fawn and white colors and the salamander badge of the new King Francois I.

"I shall tell the king that you are to remain for our interview on the morrow, Mary. It will lend me comfort and surely he will not begrudge me my only English maid. Sleep well, Mary.''

"And God watch over us both, Your Grace,'' came the whispered voice of Mary Bullen to the silent gray chamber.

Even the sunlight of December looks chilling,

thought Mary Bullen as she gazed at the slate sky over the stony balustrades of Cluny. At least she could bundle up and walk the old Roman ruins in the frozen gardens again today. "If this Hotel de Cluny were on the river, we would freeze indeed, Your Grace," she observed to her mistress as she sat stiffly in her carved oak chair awaiting the new king. Her heavily brocaded skirts with their stuffed folds looked like carved marble, but Mary knew she was no cold statue. She could see Mary Tudor's quick breathing move the tight-fitted ivory silk bodice under the folds of tulle and white crepe draped gracefully from her shoulders. Jewels winked steadily from both layers of brocade sleeves where they were slashed for decoration, and heavy girdle and rosary chains drooped to the carpeted floor by the tips of her velvet slippers.

Mary Bullen herself felt cold and colorless in her heavy white velvet and brocade gown which clung to her yet slender form which promised the full curves of a woman's body. How still the room was until her dear queen and friend spoke again.

"I fear we might freeze anyway, Mary, in our hearts at least, if we do not escape this place soon. He knows full well I am not with child. How I long to burn this colorless brocade and silk and tulle and crepe before his eyes and dance laughing at his consecration at Reims!"

Her vehemence frightened Mary, and she felt the knot in the pit of her stomach tighten. "You are only tired, Your Grace. There will be good news, and soon. How is your toothache?"

"Worse, Mary, worse and worse. This oil of peppermint and camphor helps not at all. But then, I pain all over, so who is to tell its cause or remedy?" She

40

laughed strangely, and Mary was grateful for the knock on the door. She moved carefully back against the wall to appear as unobtrusive as possible in this confrontation of her powerful betters. Her white skirts rustled surprisingly loudly.

The door glided open as if of its own volition and he was there, larger and grander than Mary had ever seen him at banquet or masque or gaming. His massive shoulders stretched the white velvet taut, and his sleek black head with the fine-chiseled features towered near the ceiling as she stared, mesmerized. In that stunning instant she tried not to gape, but his agile legs and hips below his short, white velvet, ermine-edged cloak fascinated her as he swept past and approached her waiting mistress. White embroidery, lace, delicate tuckings, and elaborate ribbings rioted across the white of his short doublet, breech, and tight stockings. Despite the fact that he, like them, was clothed entirely in white, he radiated warmth and vitality. His muscular legs were revealed in each sinewy twist and turn by the golden filigree material of his garters. He swept off his ermine cap flowing with pure white heron plumes and his golden belt, dagger, and the decorated codpiece that covered his manhood, all emanated a richness and heat that neither Englishwoman felt in her mourning whites.

Mary Bullen drew in her breath swiftly in the tiny silence of the room before anyone spoke. If her dear mistress Mary Tudor felt anything of the impact this Valois king had on her, this interview would be interesting indeed!

Francois bent gracefully to kiss both of the pale woman's cheeks and his embrace seemed to linger. *"Ma*

41

cherie Marie. How is it with you, my most beautiful queen?"

"I am queen no longer, Your Grace, as well you know. But I thank you. I am well."

"But so pale, *ma charmante*? Would that Francois could bring sweet roses to those fair lips and white cheeks."

His voice seemed of deepest velvet as the cloak he wore, and his caressing tone so intimate and personal that Mary felt a rush of embarrassment even as she saw her mistress blush hot under his intense scrutiny.

"Your Majesty, I request that my English maid be permitted to stay. She is most dear to me."

His sleek head rotated smoothly, and the fierce, dark eyes were on Mary. Unlike anything she had ever experienced, they seemed to sweep over her in a moment, probing, piercing. She remembered to curtsy.

"*La petite blonde Anglaise Boullaine. Oui.* I remember. She grows into a Venus, does she not?"

The sensual mouth under the long aquiline nose had formed the remark smoothly, and Mary's heart nearly fell to her feet. To be so complimented by the King of France! But then, she thought, he is merely being charming. What a little fool is the '*petite Boullaine,*' she told herself firmly.

The new king and old queen sat together near the window under the huge tapestry of Orpheus and Eurydice trying to escape from the black reaches of Hades. Mary perched nervously on a gilt chair in the corner and tried to pretend she took no notice of their passionate interview.

"You must have no fear for yourself, Marie," Francois' resonant voice assured her. "I shall see you are

42

well cared for always."

There was a tiny silence and the queen's voice shook when she answered simply, "*Merci*, my king."

"You know you will draw 80,000 francs yearly and have the revenues of Saintonge. You shall want for nothing. And I wish to have you loved and protected by a husband as well as by you adoring king, to remain here ever with us."

Mary Tudor's sharp intake of breath shredded the tiny calm. Although his eyes took on a new wariness, Francois du Roi held the pale woman's hand tight in his own and plunged on. "My dear, the Duke of Savoy is from my own blessed mother's family. He is honorable and true and he shall adore you."

The queen shook her head violently so her raven curls bobbed free of her white lace angular headpiece. She could not find the voice to answer, and Mary desired to run to her and throw her arms about her shoulders in comfort. But it was the muscular arm of the King of France which was about Mary Tudor's quaking body.

"No, *cherie?* You favor him not? Then one you know more intimately and who has loved you always, the Duke of Lorraine? So blond, so tall and handsome? You have laughed often with him before."

The widowed queen stared now at her clenched hand in her white lap while Francois seemed to hold the other captive. Her youthful body sagged in exhaustion and dejection, and she heaved with silent sobs, but no tears came. Mary Bullen felt rooted in terror to her chair.

"You shall have the great monies of Blois too, and live like a queen indeed! Marie, *ma cherie*, which do you choose?"

The rush of tears came then, and Mary thought she could hear each as it pelted onto her ivory satin dress making a tiny silvery print on the material. Still, the distraught woman sat staring at her hand; Mary feared for them both.

The king sat like a statue and then rose suddenly over the sobbing woman and shook her shoulders. "*Si vous plait,* Marie, Marie."

His body tensed like some marvelous great horse before it vaults. Then Mary Bullen could remain silent no longer whatever befell her.

"Please, Your Grace," she breathed, striding to her mistress in a rush of silken skirts, "she has not slept well, and her teeth ache and she is—is, so in need of a strong friend!"

She knelt at her queen's side as though oblivious to the frustrated king before them and caressed her shivering shoulder with one slender hand and held her tear-speckled fists in her other. "Your Grace, all will be well. Surely this great king can aid you if he knows your true heart, for have you not said he is the greatest *chevalier* in the kingdom? He is a true Christian king and will be most kind, my lady."

Mary Tudor looked up from her lap, her eyes wide and almost unseeing. For one tiny second Mary feared her anger at her maid's daring to urge her queen to share her heart with one she feared could ruin her only chance for happiness. Then the queen's dark eyes focused on Mary's blue earnest ones and the tension seemed to flow out of her body.

"Would that I were free to wed you myself, *ma* Marie," came Francois' voice so close to Mary's ear she almost bolted. "Then your fears would not be so

44

great."

Will he believe that my mistress loves him only and, therefore, she will not wed with his courtiers, Mary wondered. But, who would not love this godlike man?

"I do love and honor you, my Francois, but not just as you would have it. I would no doubt have loved you fully but for the duty we have owed to others and my admiration for your majesty."

Mary Tudor rose suddenly as though to distance herself from the stunned young king. She stood behind her chair facing him, her cheeks still glistening with tears. Her maid still knelt by her empty chair, and Francois stood with his legs slightly apart and his hands at his sides, waiting.

"My dearest lord, before I ever beheld your fine face or was ever promised to King Louis, I loved another. I loved him honorably from afar, and I love him deeply still, with a true heart and would love him from afar no longer. Indeed, my brother king did promise once that if I were ever widowed, I might choose my second husband with his blessing."

Mary felt Francois tense beside her. She could feel muscle and sinew stiffen, and she feared for them both again. Mary Tudor calmly stood her ground.

"And who is this most fortunate of men?" he queried.

She hesitated and then spoke his name in a rush of words and feelings. "The King of England's dearest friend, Charles Brandon, Duke of Suffolk."

The name hung between them, both proud young people, both wanting their own way. Mary Bullen held her breath, and it suddenly occurred to her that her father might be angered that she dared to so mix in above

45

her place, and to support his king's sister in her "*affaire du coeur.*"

"Then, my sweet love, your brother, King of France, shall aid you to your heart's desire!" Francois shouted a laugh and circled the chair to pull the astounded woman roughly to him. "Indeed we shall have you wed here on his arrival, for has not my cousin king wished and promised you your happiness too?" He spoke over her dark head tucked perfectly under his chin.

Mary Bullen felt suddenly ashamed that at this joyful minute all she could do was wonder how it felt to be held so tight to that powerful body.

"Suffolk comes soon with condolences from London I am told, so we shall see to it. Leave all to me."

Mary pulled her head away and gazed up into his animated face. "He comes here—and soon?"

"*Oui, ma Marie.* Then we shall change your widow's weeds to secret bridal. After it all, we shall tell the world, and I shall stand by you both. Fear nothing."

"Shall I fear not even my brother's anger, my king?"

"No, least of all that. He has given you his promised word. Does he not wish joy for his lovely Tudor Rose and his dearest boon companion? I will write him explaining all, and should he not accept at first, you shall live yet here in France at the festive court of Francois."

His dark satyr's eyes danced, and it occurred to Mary Bullen that he much resembled a tiny painting from her grandmother's home at Rochford where the devil awaited a group of lost souls at the gates of hell.

"Shall she not be a beautiful bride, Demoiselle Boullaine?" His white teeth showed when he smiled so, and

46

Mary was entranced.

"*Oui, mon grand roi!*" she managed.

"Then I shall see to it that your life shall be filled with joy, my lovely sister Marie."

Mary Bullen rose to stand, gazing in awe at the radiant pair. She smiled brilliantly at her new king believing that all would now be well.

Chapter Four
February 20, 1515

Hotel Des Tournelles, Paris

The rich Gothic city of Paris was awash with silk banners and crimson bunting. Ribbons and painted standards dripped from narrow windows and silver and white drapes swung from poles spanning each narrow street along the royal entryway. Every window was packed with common folk, and the elite of the realm peered from hackney or carriage. Every neck craned, every eye squinted into the chill wintry sun. Every heart thrilled at the triumphal entry of the newly-consecrated King Francois I into the city. Every soul believed that today was the beginning of an exciting new era for France.

The fabulous event marked the end of official mourning for the dead Louis who had gone to sleep with his sceptered ancestors beneath the aged stone floor of St. Denis Cathedral. This day was the end of his young widow, Mary's, traditional mourning. Mary Tudor and her little English companion gladly breathed the free air of Paris.

But their new found freedom from their royal

quarantine was not what delighted their hearts, and spun their lovely heads with joy so intense they were almost giddy. Nor was it the drums or trumpets or French fervor for their new monarch. Charles Brandon, the King of England's own dear friend, stood with the English women on the narrow carved balcony at the palace, and Francois had accomplished all he had promised. Mary Tudor and her beloved Duke of Suffolk had been secretly wed for two days.

"Your Grace, I can see the silver canopy over his horse," Mary Bullen shouted, quite forgetting her properly trained modulated voice in her pure excitement. "Oh, look, his horse will not even stay under it and prances about. How fine he rides!"

"Yes, my Mary. He has been a fine soldier and horseman much longer than a king." The new Duchess of Suffolk put her graceful jeweled hand on Mary's shoulder, and the fox trim of her furred sleeve tickled Mary's cheek.

"All kings ride so, I warrant," came the duke's voice on the other side of his bride's bobbing head. "Henry Tudor is the finest horseman I have ever had the honor to ride beside."

The mere mention of King Henry seemed to throw a pall of silence on the three. Mary darted a quick glance at the handsome couple. Surely they were made in heaven for each other. Both so fair of skin, dark eyes and hair, so regal, so desperately wrapped in each other's love. Certainly the great Henry would see this and wish all happiness to his dear friend and his cherished sister.

"I wish the terrible silence from my lord king and Wolsey would cease," her mistress' voice floated to her

49

ears nearly drowned by the blare below them in the street. Speaking of silence of any sort struck Mary as ludicrous, for the trumpets, drums, and shouts beneath their vantage point had become a roar like the crested sea in an autumn storm at Dover. "Can he not remember his vow to me and the love he bears us both," she shouted, leaning nearer to her tall husband so he could hear. "Thank the dear Lord we have strong allies in Francois and his queen."

The duke's eyes narrowed, their deep fires set off by his dense black hair and beard. "Time and our love are in our favor, my pet. And as for the new French king as our ally, well, indeed, he is his own ally in these dealings."

The words were spoken almost as a warning and Mary Bullen, though puzzled at their import, turned her attention to the writhing masses of people below. The king was in full view now, attired completely in white and silver. His ivory stallion was nearly lost beneath the gilded trappings and sumptuous saddle.

Mary cheered and bounced with the crowds as Francois saluted. He seemed adrift in a sea of brocades and banners and finally disappeared into the palace below their view. She wished fervently that he were returning victorious to her, blonde Mary from England, and that her beauty and clever, stylish ways would bind him to her forever. What a queen she would be for him, and her father would be so proud! She would invite mother and Annie for her coronation, and dance with Francois before all of their admiring smiles. But what foolishness, she lectured herself, for she was only ten and a poor English maid and one he would probably never look on again. She would return to London with her dear mistress, the English king's sister, and only dream of this wonderful moment in the years to come. And what would her lord father say if he knew such strange thoughts haunted her dreams?

"Mary. Mistress Mary!" The duke was gesturing to her, for he and his radiant duchess had already stepped back inside their rooms now that Francois had ended his triumphal return. "Stop your dreaming, nymph, and come in from the chill air."

She hastened to obey, for she sought always to please this virile, great man whom her princess so adored. He was a close friend to King Henry, and no wonder he was so loved by the fiery Tudors. Could she herself only find a lord so charming and loving as the duke or Francois du Roi!

Mary helped her mistress remove her cloak and noted the rosy blush on her fair cheeks. Though it was still the dead of winter, Mary Tudor bloomed with health and beauty. "My own sweet Tudor rose," Lord Suffolk often called her. Surely that glow was the look of love, Mary marvelled.

The lovers sat intimately on a pink brocaded settee, and Mary, who delighted in serving them since her mistress wished their privacy from French servants, poured them goblets of crimson burgundy. The new bride's low-cut emerald velvet gown made a splash of color as the two sat bathed in February sun.

"Thank you, sweet little Bullen," came Lord Suffolk's rich voice, though he needed not thank her for such tendered duties. "Forgive me, lass, but I find it a wonder that such warmth and trustful innocence radiates from the daughter of that fox of all politicians, Thomas Bullen."

51

He saw confused hurt in the girl's eyes, so he added more gently, "Men who serve the king must be clever and wily, Mary. I say nothing against your sire. He serves his king as best he sees it." He took a slow sip of wine, his eyes still on the attentive girl. Her slim body so daintily attired in the rosy-hued velvet gown with the deep oval neckline bent slightly forward as she hung on his words. Along the soft linen chemise which spilled from her wrists and rimmed the bodice, tiny embroidered bees and flowers and butterflies flitted and bloomed. How fresh and springlike and lovely, the Duke thought. Somehow this little innocent with the guileless face had indeed managed to be a comfort to a much older, more sophisticated woman whom he had now made his dear wife.

"Your father may be here with words from Greenwich Palace and King Henry for us soon, little Mary Bullen," he said to comfort her and break the silence of his stare. "Do you see him often now he serves His Grace, King Francois here in Paris?"

Mary's blue eyes fell to his strong fingers curled about his goblet stem as the old haunting loneliness descended on her again. "No, my lord. He is so busy on king's business and I so busy in serving my beloved princess that . . . that we seldom have time to see each other here in France." She raised her eyes to the warm gaze of her mistress hoping for the comfort and understanding support she had often found there, but Mary Tudor smiled warmly upon her husband as though she had not heard.

"Being about the business of the realm keeps us all from doing what we would most love to do, Mary Bullen. We must all be brave about it. I can see why you are a true companion friend to my dear wife.''

The girl smiled at him gratefully. She had found comfort where she had sought none. It was only then that Charles Brandon, English gentleman, and as fine a connoisseur of women as he was of horses, felt the full impact of the maid's youthful beauty and her magnetic pull beneath the naive face. Her mature looks to come would serve her well at the English court when they were allowed to return—if they were allowed to return.

"Mary, please fetch my enameled jewel box. I wish to show my lord some of my royal regalia." Mary Tudor laughed musically as though there were some clever joke spoken, but Lord Suffolk only narrowed his eyes over his glass of burgundy.

Mary knew well the three-tiered white, deep blue and gold box to which her mistress referred. Too, she knew well the jewels nestled there on peacock blue velvet, for she had often plucked one out for her queen's toilette or seen her ponder over them lately. Poor dead King Louis had popped them at his youthful queen as though they were bon-bons or mere baubles. Once, when Her Grace bathed, Mary held up a massive strand of pearls across her own newly-developing breasts covered with golden brocade, and held sapphires next to her sky blue eyes and imagined that . . .

"Thank you, Mary. Leave the door ajar so you can summon us at once should the ambassador, your father, arrive." Their dark heads bent together over the cache of jewels as Mary curtseyed and departed the chamber. She slept now in a small anteroom since they had moved in state to Francois' palace and Mary Tudor bedded with her new husband.

She picked some needlework from the chair and

gazed at it guiltily for a moment before tossing it on her narrow bed. She was much too busy lately for such placid work. What a bore it was anyway unless one could chat or trade juicy palace gossip to help forget the endless threading and pulling and knotting.

Mary settled her rose-hued velvet skirts carefully as she sat, for her mistress had ordered her this new gown and another for after royal mourning, and she intended not to have it wrinkled should she see her father when he came today. Came here, but not to see her. She readily forgave him his busy life but, by the saints, she missed him and suffered that he never sent for her, visited or even sent a gift. Just notes dashed off, notes to properly serve the king's sister and be grateful for her fortunate station at the court and be worthy of the Bullen and Butler and Howard blood that flowed in her veins. Flowed? Rather, beat passionately, if he only knew! Beat and coursed and cried for her mistress, and now that she was happy, for her, for Mary Bullen, herself!

She pushed her head back suddenly, willfully against the carved high chair back. But she adored her father so, and would above all else make him proud of her.

The low voices of Mary and Charles Brandon floated clearly to her in the silent room. Were they indeed arguing over a mirror? The Mirror of Naples, no doubt, that huge tear drop cut diamond on a pendant that sparkled like fire when it hung between Mary Tudor's two full breasts above the deep oval velvet or brocade of a bodice.

"It is yours as widowed queen, is it not? They will never ask for it. The Cardinal says such would help to change His Grace's ill temper at us for the marriage without his permission. My pet, it is a very small price to pay, and Ambassador Bullen would be the safest channel.''

Mary Tudor murmured low words of reply but her usual lilting voice was more muffled than her lord's. They must be planning to send a gift of the queen's jewel to King Henry then, and her mistress hesitated to part with it. For the favor of the great King Henry it seems a small price, mused Mary Bullen.

Three piercing raps suddenly resounded from the door in the next chamber and the girl hurried to answer it. She hoped she looked pretty and dignified and proper. It was her dear father standing tensely, his fist poised to knock again, an anxious pageboy with a lighted link behind him in the gloom of the passageway.

''Father? I am so pleased to see you.'' How desperately she wanted to throw her arms about his furred shoulders, but she stood stock still as he pushed the door open wide and entered.

''The princess and Lord Suffolk are here, Mary?'' His swift sidelong glance took in the whole room instantly.

''Yes, father. There, father, within.''

''Awaiting me?''

''Yes.''

''Close the door, girl. And announce me. Also, Mary, do not leave. I would see you afterwards. You and I have business to settle.''

Her heart leapt. Business to settle? It was obvious he was angered. At her? But he had told her to serve the princess well, and maybe now she would return with the Tudor rose to the English court. Surely that had been his ultimate goal for her.

Automatically, she closed the heavy door and slipped past her silent father into Her Grace's bed chamber. To her astonishment, her mistress had been crying, and the duke was endeavoring to comfort her. He looked up nervously, and his dark eyes squinted at the girl standing in the dusk beyond the sunny pool where they sat.

"Your Grace, the English Ambassador, my Lord Bullen, wishes to see you. He awaits."

Charles Brandon jumped to his feet, and Mary Tudor wiped her cheeks with her fingers. From somewhere, as Mary had seen her do time and again, the proud woman covered herself with composure and nodded. "We will see him now, Mary."

She curtseyed and backed from the room nearly bumping into the angular form of her father, his arms folded across his cloaked chest, his hat now held in one hand.

"Her Grace will see you now, my lord." He nodded and entered, closing the door firmly.

How suddenly familiar it all seemed, seeing him and being so formal and having to wait while he talked behind closed doors to others, like that long ago day at Hever when he told mother he was sending Mary away.

Tears came to her eyes unbidden, and she felt weak and tired and very alone. Mary Tudor truly needed her no longer, not like she had. She was glad that Her Grace was happy and in love, so why should she cry? Father was angry, and she feared his displeasure. Dreaming of Hever and mother always hurt. And how much she wanted someone wonderful and grand like the handsome French king to love her.

She fought for control of herself. She was never like

56

her mistress and the others when it came time to hide emotions. She still had much to learn before she could ever face the royal court of the English king.

She peered at her azure eyes in her tiny silvered mirror and wiped her cheeks, carefully pinching them for color. Slowly, she dusted her face with powder, resmoothed her coif, twined her side curls about her index finger and let them pop back into place. She paced and tried to make her mind a blessed blank, but her thoughts darted about the room and tried to pierce the thick wooden door behind which the great Henry's lovely sister faced the great Henry's ambassador. Surely he would be meek before the king's dear sister.

Then, he was there. His face was impassive, but his eyes gave away his tension and his anger. "Sit, Mary. I will be brief."

Please, father, stay for a while, she thought, but she sat gracefully, correctly.

"It is difficult to say how long the Princess Mary and her—the duke—will be staying here in France. When they leave, it may not be to return to the English court. And so, she has released you from your service to her, and you will join Queen Claude's household here as a maid of honor to continue your schooling in French and court ways."

Mary's face showed her dismay clearly, and she clenched her hands as though she would implore him. "But, my lord, she said she needs me and wishes me to remain with them."

"With *them*, Mary!" His voice spewed venom, and her eyes widened in terror as though he had hit her. Then he lowered his tone and bent menacingly close. "My foolish girl, there may not be 'them' unless the

57

king's blood greatly abates. The fool Suffolk has committed a treasonous act in this illegal marriage. He dares! He dares to come so near the throne in marriage! An effrontery to his lord king and to his once best and trusted friend our sovereign king!''

"But King Henry promised her she might choose her husband should King Louis die,'' Mary interposed weakly.

"Ha! His Grace promised! Promised one day, perhaps, but that is not the way the wind blows now. She is important state business, and she has ruined it all.''

"She is only a woman in love, my lord.''

"She is also a fool and will pay dearly starting with this.'' He extended his clenched fist and there lay the Jewel of Naples in his square palm. How dull and heavy it looks against his flesh, she thought irrationally.

"I will not have you go down with her, child. I thought she was the one for you to serve.'' He swallowed audibly and pocketed the great gem. "I was mistaken.''

"The new king of France favors the marriage, my lord. Surely he will help to turn His Majesty's mind.''

He reached for Mary's shoulders, and his fingers hurt. "Stupid girl. He was only too pleased to have a valuable marriage pawn out of the way of a dangerous English alliance. He would have turned bigamist himself to keep Mary Tudor from a marriage to Charles of Castile. The fond and friendly Francois helped them only to their own destruction!''

Tears ran in jagged paths down Mary's cheeks and fell off her chin. Each time she blinked, she felt the droplets plaster her thick lashes. Tiny involuntary sobs wracked her throat. Her father took his hard hands away and stepped back a pace.

"You have been trapped and used, child, and I will not have that. You are too important to my plans. I only hope the king never hears you were privy to their marriage plans and never told me. And I pray he never blames me for not having stopped them, though I could hardly have stopped the wily fox Francois from his meddling."

"Francois and Claude and their household progress toward Amboise," he went on. "It is on the Loire where they will establish their court. You are going with them on the morrow." He looked sideways at her small oaken garderobe. "You must pack immediately."

"They stay not here at Tournelles?" she heard herself ask.

"Paris is noisome and too near the church powers. It is another wise move. Needless to say, Princess Mary and the duke remain here until they can work out their difficulties one way or the other."

"You are helping them?"

"I help only my king, child." He turned to go, and she stood desperate for kinder words, for a gentle look. "And of course, the Bullens," he added at the door.

"Dry your eyes, Mary. We are blessed that the new queen will take on two young English girls. She is pious and the people love her, though much as with our own king, Francois loves elsewhere."

"You said *two* English girls, father?"

"Your sister Anne joins you this summer. I go home to fetch her when I take this bauble to His Grace. I expect you will know to take good care of Anne. She is witty and clever already, though her looks will never

59

match your Howard beauty.''

At least I shall have Annie's company, thought Mary, as he swung the door wide and the dozing link-boy jumped to attention in the hall behind. But Annie is only eight, and Annie is mother's baby.

"Anne is young, my lord, younger than I when I went to Archduchess Margaret's court.'' Now mother will have empty gardens at Hever, she thought.

"Younger, but perhaps with more sense, Mary. Remember everything the two of you do can and will reflect on me and the Bullens. Make me—and your mother—proud, Mary. Bid farewell quickly to the Princess Mary. I will keep in touch.''

The door closed. Mary sank, drained, on her narrow bed. At least she would have Annie to get to know again, to help, to mother, to love.

He did not even remove his cloak while he was here, she thought bitterly. She began to sob.

Chapter Five
June 22, 1517

Chateau du Amboise

The ponderous, lumbering Medieval castle of Amboise was a miracle of rebirth. The massive stone walls had sprouted arabesques of arches and charming pinnacles pointed their creamy fingers into the tall blue skies of the sheltering Loire valley. Rich parquet floors and spacious windows graced the once gloomy chambers and spans of fragrant foliage edged the formal gardens of Persian roses and gentle scented lavender. From fountains arched tiny rivulets of clear water and Italian tapestries and paintings caressed the papered walls in gallery and chamber. Francois' chateau stood proudly at the glowing dawn of the French Renaissance.

In the three years since the decrepit Louis XII and his ancient order had passed away, all of France had flourished under the promised hope of the new king's ascension. On Francois' badge stood the mythical salamander which could survive fire, and so far, Francois had been true to his motto: "I nourish and I quench." In the past two years, the young king had marched south conquering the Swiss and making a triumphal entry into Milan. He had been honored by the pope, had breathed the learned, artistic air of Renaissance Italy and had returned victorious to Marseilles stuffed with new plans, laden with Italian styles, and accompanied by the sixty-four-year-old Leonardo da Vinci. Francois' power and patronage gave great impetus to the new France. He both extinguished the settling ashes of the Middle Ages and nourished the glowing kindling of the Renaissance.

Transformation had touched Mary Bullen's life, too, for she was a part of the upheavals and shifting times. Uprooted from her disgraced mistress and guardian, the young widowed French queen, she had joined the three hundred ladies in waiting to the pious, ever-pregnant Queen Claude. She had delighted at the queen's belated coronation this past season and rejoiced with the realm when an heir was finally born this year after two darling but dynastically useless daughters. And finally, though she never fully understood why it had taken so long when her father had promised it three whole years ago, her eleven-year-old sister Anne had joined her at Francois' fashionable court.

"But, Mary," Anne had complained more than once since she had arrived a week ago, "why must we always be in chapel or studying Latin texts? Even the needlework is, well, so religious!"

Mary sighed, for Anne voiced the exact sentiments of most of Claude's sheltered *demoiselles du honneur*. "Her Grace is a good and pious woman, Annie, and we are her charges. She will not always keep us from the other court. We are too many for her to watch, and some of us shall be noticed sooner or later. You will see."

"The other court. Of *du Roi* Francois? *Oui, ma Marie*, but I am only of eleven years, and I doubt I shall see much *beaute* or *gallantre*. *C'est grande dommage*."

Mary put down her pettipoint on the marble sill and gazed fondly on the lovely valley with its rim of blue-green forests and its carefully etched ribbons of grape vines.

But today, Mary mused, she and Annie could actually be a part of that lovely, naturally-hued scene, for Anne wore golden satin slashed to reveal a daffodil yellow brocaded kirtle underneath her full skirts, and she herself was in the palest of green watered silk with silvery threaded trim along the low, oval bodice, double slashed sleeves, and waistline lacings. Yet, sitting quietly like this, did not Annie's golds and yellows make her dark eyes dance even more, whereas her own gentle greens just made her meld into the scene unnoticed?

"You shall go far someday, Annie. Your Latin is perfect, your French is beautiful, and you are so witty and clever already. And look at me, fourteen and still a reclusive English maid much alone—save for you, Annie."

I wish you would no longer call me that, Marie. It sounds so very childish, as though I still toddled at Semmonet's knee in leading strings. I wish to make well in the adult world now, and father says he knows my wits and charm will take me far some day."

Mary felt strangely stung by the girl's words, and she knew her face showed it. She had never quite mastered the etiquette of the disdainful mask to cover hurt or sorrow. She kept her graceful neck arched toward the window and her wet eyes on the abundant green Loire and the gentle hills. "Of course, Anne. And father is always right. As I said, you shall reach far at court whether it be Francois' or our own king's, of that I am certain."

"If I only had your face, though, Marie, and were not so thin and pale and raven-haired. And," she lowered her pleasant girlish voice until it was barely audible and Mary leaned closer, "if it were not for my foolish hand."

Mary glanced to Anne's lap where the offending fingers curled carefully under the mesh of her newly begun embroidery. As always, she had secreted the tiny stub of the sixth unwanted finger which sprang from her slender small finger of her left hand.

"No one notices it, Annie—Anne. You cover it so beautifully with your tapered sleeves."

"If anyone should ever laugh, I know I should hate them instantly, and somehow, I would find a way to make them suffer too!" Her thin, dark brows knit and her eyes narrowed.

She has much of George's temper in her and must learn to bridle it, thought Mary hopelessly. Why do we not feel closer as I thought we would when she arrived? Surely, time together here will change that.

"Marie, Anne, we are allowed to go, now if we wish! I knew we could escape postnoon duties if we just bided our time. I knew it!" The gleeful messenger was Jeanne du Lac whom Mary admired tremendously for her red-haired beauty and her popularity with many handsome courtiers. The thrilling message was that they were free for several hours to see the glorious tilt match in the gardens with the king and his beautiful friends.

They did not even stop to return their needlework to

their rooms or to get a proper head cover, for the hour was late and no doubt the festivities had already begun. Mary would see Francois again, Francois du Roi, her secret passionate fantasy since his magnetic eyes had rested on her momentarily three years ago and he had termed her a young Venus. How wonderful, how distant he was. And those that surrounded him, how blessed.

"Now, Anne, you shall see those great ones of whom we have told, and the wonders of the court," Mary promised breathlessly as they descended the great curving porphyry staircase and traversed the long gallery which linked the chateau to the formal gardens. Francois had cleared a huge expanse for the tiltyard and frequently in the warmer months came the seductive sounds of trumpets and cheers.

"Oui, you shall see the other court, the one any redblooded Frenchman would prefer to our shadowed world of the saintly Reine Claude," Jeanne put in as they slowed their pace, aware that they were in public now despite the deserted state of the formal gardens in the golden sun. Deserted except for the white-haired, bearded old Italian master whom Francois now patronized. He sat with his profile to them, his sketch pad poised on his lap while he gazed at a distant vista.

"The *Premier Peintre, Architecte et Mechanicien des Rois*, to use his proper title," explained the lovely Jeanne as though she were lecturing guests. The king says his da Vinci paints the valley here and dreams he is home in Florence."

"The king himself told you that?" asked Mary in awe.

"Well, I heard him say it to Francoise de Foix only

the other day, Marie,'' Jeanne returned nonchalantly. She turned to Mary's little sister. ''Francoise du Foix is the king's present *maitresse en titre, ma petite*, Anne,'' Jeanne added.

''Indeed, I have told Anne of her and of them all, Jeanne, though she has not had the chance to see them before today,'' Mary said.

''I understand the English king must hide his mistresses from the court. Is it true? It seems all rather uncivilized,'' Jeanne commented. Mary was grateful she need not answer, for they were at the brightly festooned galleries, and the joust was already in progress.

The crowd roared its approval sporadically and the blare of marshalls' voices broke in to announce names and titles and outcomes of each bout. Fawn and white bunting puffed then fell in the warming breeze as the girls peered over the heads of those not perched in the elevated seats to catch sight of the present fray.

''It is Bonnivet himself,'' whispered the excited Jeanne. ''I can tell by his armor and crested heume.''

''The dearest friend to the king,'' recited Anne, for the clever girl had indeed learned her catechism of honored names and titles from her sister in the week she had been at Amboise.

''And all know he adores and wishes to seduce the king's sister, Madame du Alencon, who loves her own husband not at all,'' added Jeanne as though anxious to impress with her knowledge of inner circle scandal. ''Come. There must be some seats in the pavillion where we can see better.''

The English girls followed her carefully, wending their way through the rainbow silks and slippered feet along the rows of cushioned benches. They wedged themselves in among a cluster of other unattached flowering *mignonnes* of the vast court and thrilled and applauded with their neighbors.

To Mary's deep disappointment, Francois himself had jousted first and they had missed his splendid victory over his picked opponent of the day, Lautrec, the brother of his mistress.

Both Mary and Jeanne sought to educate the wide-eyed Anne as to who were the important people, but many were too distant across the field in the facing royal gallery and some sat well ahead of them, their fine coiffures or plumed hats the only way of identifying them.

"That fine and beautiful lady there, the lively one now chatting with the king's own mother, is she not Francoise du Foix, his mistress?" asked the girl excitedly.

"No, indeed, *ma petite*," cut in Jeanne's voice as Mary began to answer, "that is the king's beloved sister Marguerite, his '*mignonne*' he calls her. The jeweled lady seated over there is Francoise, for she is not a favorite with the king's mother and sister, though he listens well to them in all else."

To be Francoise du Foix or any other lady he gazes on with love, thought Mary solemnly, how wonderful. Better that than to be his queen, fat and white-faced and always swollen with child and only bedded when another nursery cradle was to be filled. Everyone knew Francoise de Foix was his third official mistress, but she was so stunning and so gay, surely this affair would last on and on.

"I said, Marie, Rene de Brosse stares with love sick eyes at you as he did in the gardens last week." Jeanne elbowed her gently and looked in the opposite direction. "Do not look that way now, silly, or he will know we have noticed."

Mary felt herself blush slightly, but, with difficulty, she kept her expression unconcerned. "I favor him not, Jeanne du Lac, I swear he is but fifteen and he still has pimples. I would much rather have his older brother Guillaume take note of me!"

Jeanne's silver laugh floated to Mary's ears. "Guillaume, *ma Anglaise charmante*, is two years wed. Though that has stopped few dalliances of other men, with that bridegroom, the word is that he is faithful to her still."

"Marie, he is making his way over here. You are right—he is very awkward," Jeanne went on. She patted her beautifully wrapped reddish tresses. "Shall Anne and I start on ahead? I would introduce her to my sister Louise."

Mary rose with them stubbornly. She did not like the way Jeanne assumed charge of her little sister, nor did she care to be deserted with the gangly Rene.

"Do not be such a goose, Marie," scolded Jeanne. "You are a ravishing maid—all the ladies say so—and it would do your reputation and experience no harm to be escorted by a courtier from a fine family, pimples or not. Maybe you can convince him to introduce you to his brother." Her green eyes tilted up as she smiled at Mary.

"Oh, do, Mary. I shall be fine with *ma bonne amie*, Jeanne," added Anne as they turned and threaded their way through the courtiers.

Mary felt like a stranded boat on a rainbow sea of silks only momentarily, for Rene soon approached and doffed his lavender-plumed hat. His gangly body was encased in pale purple silk and even the slightly-padded, ornate doublet and the deep-cut, white velvet-lined second sleeves could not make his thin shoulders look masculine, nor could the bulky tied and jeweled garters on his lean legs develop his calves or the swells a man's legs should have. Her eyes darted behind him for anyone she might know; then she smiled and nodded and listened as he took her arm and guided her from the stands. She had not even set eyes on Francois, so the day was nearly ruined anyway. What could a walk with Rene add or detract to the once beautiful day now?

"How does our Queen Claude after the birth of the Dauphin?" the tall lad was asking. He bent solicitously close for her answer.

"Somewhat weak and sickly still, *monsieur*," she responded, wishing he did not lean so near as he brushed against her. She was suddenly angry with herself that they had left the tournament early. She could still hear the clash of lance on shield and the solemn announcements of pursuivants clearly behind them.

"You, no doubt, miss the Dowager English Queen Marie whom you served before," he chatted on. "At least she has returned to her homeland now. Did you know she had to bribe her brother, and stole some of her queen's jewels to do it, and when she reached Calais to sail home she had to hide from an angry mob? The French royalty do not make such foolish marriage vows. She is fortunate the English *roi* forgave her."

"Please, Rene," Mary cut in, "say nothing unkind of her. I *do* miss her greatly. She was dear to me."

"Ah, of course, *ma* Marie. And do you know when you blush you are exquisite? Your hair looks so golden, so adorable uncovered, and your eyes and face are that

69

of a Diana,'' he said, putting out his hand against a tall, trimmed privet hedge to stop her slow progress. "I have worshipped your beauty from across the room too long." His voice broke.

Now, she thought warily, this is a swiftly different tack. He has learned fancy court flattery well.

"I thank you for your kindness, Monsieur Rene." She hesitated on the brink of either fleeing or giggling as he moved the other hand slowly, tentatively to her narrow waist.

"Could you not learn to address me as *mon Rene, cherie*?"

Before she could step back or raise a halting hand to his chest, he dipped suddenly and crushed her lips with his. Her eyes widened in surprise, and she thought instantly that it was quite impossible to even fantasize that she could so intrigue a charming, dashing man like Francois with this whelp wrapped around her. She pushed hard against his chest, but he did not budge. Instead, he tightened his grip, pulling her full breasts against his narrow silken chest.

She turned her head stiffly away and was surprised to hear the shrill pitch of her voice. "Rene, no, *si vous plait*!"

She twisted away. They went slightly off balance and bounced against the sharp pricker hedge. She shrieked in fright and pain as he bent to kiss her throat and pulled jerkily at the low square decolletage of her dress.

"My precious Diana, I can do much for you here at court," he was saying brokenly. He sounded quite breathless.

He was from a powerful family. Perhaps her father would be angry if he ever heard she had offended a de

Brosse. And that silly Jeanne would no doubt gossip and laugh.

"No, no," she shouted, despite her fears as his long fingers plunged into her dress and brushed a taut nipple. Did he think her such an English simpleton as to lie with him here in broad daylight in the king's gardens?

"*Pardon, jeune monsieur*," came a strange crackling voice, and a huge thin hand descended on Rene's shoulder pressed close against her own now bare shoulder. Rene raised his head, his eyes wide, his mouth open. "The *demoiselle* does not wish your attentions now, *monsieur*, and it takes a wise warrior to know when to retreat, *si*?"

Mary saw it was the old, white-haired artist from Italy whom King Francois so favored. Pray God, the king himself was not about to witness this shameful display.

"Signor da Vinci," Rene responded, taking his hands from Mary so suddenly that she almost tilted into the privet hedge again. The old man steadied her elbow, and she quickly shrugged her bare shoulder to pull up her dishevelled dress.

"Perhaps midafternoon is a poor time for romance, especially in near view of the king's tournament, eh? You are Monsieur de Brosse, are you not?"

"*Oui*, Signor da Vinci." Rene looked suddenly like a huge whipped puppy. That he unhanded her so quickly and did not show anger at Monsieur da Vinci was no doubt because the whole court knew well how the king cultivated and honored the old man. It was said they often spent hours together just talking.

"Another time would be better then, Monsieur de Brosse. I shall be honored to walk your lady back to the

Chateau.''

Obviously disconcerted, but at a loss for a reply, Rene bowed, and leaned to scoop his hat from the even-cut turf. ''Mademoiselle Boullaine,'' he said curtly and disappeared around the hedge.

''I have not rescued a maiden in distress for years, Mademoiselle Boullaine,'' Signor da Vinci said quietly, musically, and she marvelled at the way he almost sang his French. ''You are the English ambassador's daughter, are you not,'' he intoned.

''*Oui*, Signor da Vinci. *Merci beaucoup* for your aid. The attentions were quite unwanted.''

''Ah, *sí*. We will say no more of that. I was just trying to see how the craigs across the valley touch the tiny cliff-clinging town on either side when I heard you. The Loire is much like the far reaches of the Arno, you see.''

They strolled easily around the hedgerow and there was the lovely fountain and opening view where the girls had seen him earlier. He had not moved all afternoon.

''I live at Cloux in a spacious house His Majesty granted me, but the vistas here are much more pleasant and, well, more like home.'' His eyes went past her, far over her shoulder and clouded beneath his bushy, snowy eyebrows.

''Florence, *signor*?''

''Sí, Firenze. But now, this shall be my home.'' He sighed and motioned for her to sit next to him on the marble fountain ledge. Pleased, she did so carefully as he picked up his discarded notebook and stick of brownish charcoal.

''Is this,'' he nodded his head toward the valley, ''a

French and Italian view only, or could it be your England?''

She gazed slowly over the misty haze of easy hills and azure sky and plunging valley. "I have seen no English view like this, Signor, but England has its lovely rivers and beautiful hunt parks. And English gardens are wonderful." Her voice trailed off.

"You see one now, a lovely garden in the eye of your heart and you could tell me every tiny petal in it, every butterfly and sunny splash, could you not? Knowing how to see, that is the most important gift from God. 'Sapere vedere.' ''

His left hand nearly skimmed over his paper now, but it seemed he seldom lowered his eyes from the stony pinnacles beyond. She watched breathless, yet wanting to ask him what he discussed for long hours with his patron Francois, and what he thought of the wonderful man.

He finished, then, and bent his head over his notebook. His huge nose seemed to point directly at the charcoal misty cliffs and forests and towns he had drawn so effortlessly. He writes backwards, she thought as he labeled the sketch, but assumed it was merely that the Italian looked so strange.

He turned to her and seemed to stare for long minutes, but she felt totally at ease. "Has Clouet sketched you?" he questioned finally.

"No, Signor. He is the court artist."

"And are you not of the court, Mademoiselle Boullaine?"

"No, Signor, only one of Queen Claude's maids of honor."

"Ah, that other peaceful and moral court," he said

and rose. "I move more in the worldly court of king's projects," he continued in lilting French. "I draw canals for Romartin, I sketch scenery for court masques, I keep my notebooks. I remember other kings and projects and notebooks. But enough of an old man's whimsies."

Mary noticed other people now meandering back across the formal gardens from the tiltyard. If only Francois himself would come along and hail his artist and then . . .

"I shall sketch you someday," he was saying. "You could be a Florentine beauty, you know, fair and blonde and azure-eyed. You show your most inner thoughts in your eyes when it is an unfashionable thing to do, but how touching and how feminine. Like la Gioconda." He smiled and his eyes were misty again. "I shall not forget you. I shall see you again, Mademoiselle Boullaine."

He folded his notebook pertly under his brown-silk arm and bowed slowly. "Remember my motto, fairest lady. At court knowing how to see can be one's very survival. *Adieu*."

He turned and walked slowly across the terraced lawn before she could reply, and she realized she had foolishly raised her hand to wave at his retreating back.

Knowing how to see, yes, indeed. And knowing how to avoid that whelp Rene de Brosse and keep Jeanne from snickering, and Annie from prying.

Chapter Six
December 13, 1518

Paris

The first two days of the visit of the King of England's ambassadors to Paris were the most thrilling of Mary Bullen's life. Her father was always rushing about the proximity of the Palais de Tournelles where Francois and Claude resided during the visit. Then, too, the ceremonies and festivities forced the newly-pregnant queen to dispense with her usual strict and solemn schedule so that Mary would be able to see the wonderful Francois at close range. Most marvellous of all, Mary had been selected as one of the twenty ladies in waiting to accompany the queen as honor attendant. As the laughing, buoyant Francois had put it, "the lovely *demoiselles* shall be a very special scenery for this glorious *fete*."

Even on the first day of the official visit by King Henry VIII's thirty hand-picked ambassadors and their privy advisors, Mary had been present to see the royal greeting. Francois was determined to match, indeed to surpass, the glittering reception his envoy Bonnivet had received last autumn at Hampton Court from

Cardinal Wolsey and his dear "cousin" Henry. And now that the one-year-old French Dauphin was married by proxy to the two-year-old daughter of King Henry and his Spanish Queen Catherine of Aragon, Anglo-French relations were much improved and Francois would allow no stinginess of gala hospitality.

All of the maidens who toted the ermine-edged trains of the king's mother, sister and wife were fair and blonde, chosen from the three hundred ladies of the queen. On the morrow they were all to be dressed in gentle golds and beiges and creamy-hued silks to complement Master Leonardo da Vinci's spectacular painted setting for the great celebration at the Palais du Bastille. But today at the Bastille, a more circumspect and regal pomp was the order of the day.

Mary, in contrast to her expensive and frivolous dress for tomorrow, had chosen a gown of mauve colored silk and delicately sculpted brocade today. The smooth lilac bodice was taut to push her well-developed breasts fashionably up above the neckline rimmed with seed pearls, and the gently rustling skirts shifted from mauve to violet hues as she walked. The full outer sleeves were lined with soft but inexpensive rabbit fur and the fitted inner sleeves dripped a narrow cuff of open weave Belgian lace.

Mary nearly floated on a cloud of tremulous joy as she and the other maids arrived at the lumbering gray-stoned Bastille with the heavy trains of the king's ladies. The French royal party would follow soon after to take up their official stances. Then on a fine-tuned cue, the English envoys would approach with their formal bobbing of heads and wax-sealed documents of greeting. But several of the peripheral English advisors were in evidence already, ascertaining propriety, scanning the vast expanse of the public audience hall, or scuttling about from the French marshalls to the self-important Ambassador Bullen and his privy staff.

To Mary's delight there was a pause in the bustlings and her father, looking resplendent in his ermine and velvet, his heavy chest crossed by a massive golden chain, motioned her to him. He stood behind a somewhat shaky portable desk with seals and wax and a disarray of paper, giving orders, questioning men who darted here and there at his will. As Mary neared him, carefully avoiding the vast length of purple velvet carpet on which the English party would approach the enthroned Francois, he ordered the desk cleared and removed. Only one young man, taller and broader-shouldered than the rest, remained in low conversation, so Mary paused a few steps distant, poised, excited.

The young man listened earnestly to Lord Bullen, his strong brown head cocked, his muscular silken legs slightly apart, and still he was as tall as her father. She had never noted that man before. He was either French, on her father's staff or maybe newly come from London. Anyway, he was in the way, for she seldom spoke with her father alone and never when he was in such a fine mood. She tapped her silken slipper in growing impatience.

Then they both stopped and glanced at her and her father extended his beringed hand. "You look lovely, Mary. Being the English ambassador's daughter has helped you to be here today, though you will look the part. Whose attendant are you to be?"

"The queen's, my lord, though the king's mother

and sister have as many bearers.''

"Fine, fine." He turned away and gestured to an aide who advanced swiftly. He seemed to forget she stood there at all and that he had not even seen her for three months. It was then she noticed the other man again, and realized he had never looked away from her nor stopped his deliberate slow perusal of her face, her figure, her mauve-hued brocaded dress. He seemed to study her, quite unabashed.

Her first impulse was to turn heel on such a rude scrutiny, but she still hoped to speak further with her father. And, somehow, she was curious about this tall man, though his frank, roving gaze unsettled her.

He wore rich browns to match his hair, but his raiment did not look as fussy or costly as she was used to seeing at the grand and glorious court of Francois. He had a rugged face with high cheekbones and not the chiseled features of a Francois or Rene de Brosse. His brows were raven dark and rakish; his jaw square and strong; his nose was well-formed enough, although it appeared he had broken it at least once, probably in some brawl or joust, she thought. She hated to admit it, but the man stood with an angular grace of easy stance and masculine charm. His mouth, which quirked up in apparent amusement or pleasure at her emboldened stare, was wry and somehow very interesting. Then he grinned brazenly and she looked away to feel the color mount to her breasts, pushed up above the neckline of mauve silk and seed pearls, to her neck, her cheeks.

"Tell the fool to see to it in the anteroom before the *gendarmes* form up," came her father's exasperated words into her consciousness. "S' blood, I shall see to it myself!"

He spun and was gone in a swirl of jade green cloak, the distraught messenger trailing after him. Mary was embarrassed to find herself standing only four feet from the staring, tall man with no one in shouting distance in the whole, vast, purple-bedecked hall.

"What good fortune," came the man's low voice in an English accent.

"I beg your pardon, sir," she returned as icily as possible and stood her ground as he took a presumptuous step forward.

"That the Lord Ambassador leaves me here as escort to his so lovely daughter, Mary Bullen."

He said her name somehow differently, and it intrigued her. "He hardly left you as escort, sir." She hesitated, not wanting to leave despite his rank impudence. "I must return to my duties."

He fell in easily beside her as she walked slowly along the edge of the velvet runway. "Please allow me to introduce myself, Lady Mary. I am here on my first visit to France, and my French is rough at best. It pleases me to find so charming a lady with whom I can converse in my own tongue. The French women seem to flit about a great deal, but I prefer a fair and honest English maid anytime."

How did we get on this tack so suddenly, Mary wondered, keeping her eyes lowered. His huge feet almost brushed the hems of her skirts as they walked.

"You have become shy, Mary Bullen. But a moment ago I was certain your fiery glance could match my own."

She lifted her head jerkily to face him and met those deep brown probing eyes again. He seemed young, yet somehow worldly.

"Are you someone's English secretary, sir," she parried, hoping the point of her barb would sting.

But he just gave a shouted laugh, and she desperately hoped that the other girls and her father could not see them or hear his rudeness.

"I am a ward and often companion to our great King Henry, Mary, whom we all serve even when we are safely esconced in the cloistered court of Queen Claude." His teeth shone very white when he smiled. It suddenly annoyed her that he could have sun color on his face in December when most Englishmen went silken pale.

"Indeed, sir, I meant not to offend, I . . . "

"But you *did* mean to offend, golden Mary. *Touche!*" He chuckled again at her, and she disliked him more than ever. How dare he gibe at her and read her thoughts. She had taken quite enough of his ill-timed wit, King Henry's courtier or not.

"Your clear blue eyes give you away, Mary," he was saying, apparently with all seriousness as she turned in a rustle of mauve brocade.

She did not look back even when his last words floated to her alert ears. "William Stafford at your service always, Mademoiselle Mary Bullen."

It annoyed her that the impromptu interview had unsettled her so, and especially that William Stafford had seen her father dash off as though he cared not at all for his daughter. Still, her father had complimented her appearance, and she knew he felt proud that she was a part of this important international occasion.

She soon forgot the annoyance at being ignored by her father and teased by William Stafford in the pomp and glory of the afternoon. The king looked more godlike than ever, and she could watch his aquiline profile clearly over the queen's plump shoulder from the screened platform in the corner of the stage. He sat enshrined on a royal dais, his silver cloak lined with herons' feathers setting off his muscular body encased in golden silk. He nodded and raised his hand in salute to the Englishmen who displayed their official papers and recited the English king's salutations in deep-voiced Latin. When it was over Francois, his advisors, and his trinity of bedecked and bejeweled women descended from the stage and retreated down the lengthy purple velvet path edged with two-hundred *gendarmes*, gilt battle axes held perpendicularly before their grim faces.

Mary shuddered with excitement. Her eyes darted proudly to see her father's alert gaze as she swept by poised on the left rim of Queen Claude's heavy train. But she fought to control a grimace when she caught the intent stare of that rude William Stafford only one aisle beyond King Henry's royal ambassadors.

The second day of the English visit continued in a marvelous fantasy of beauty, glory and grandeur. After an elaborate formal mass at Notre Dame early in the day, the crystal afternoon air resounded with the trumpet blares, crashes and rumbling clinks of a formal joust. Though Mary and the other maids of honor had not been able to attend the gay tournament, the loss was easy to bear, for they spent the afternoon in final fittings of their lovely Florentine gowns and in rehearsal for their roles at the evening banquet.

"It is the most beautiful gown I have ever had," Mary admitted to Eugenie, fair, blonde and blue-eyed like herself. "The queen said Signor da Vinci sketched each costume separately to blend with his masque scenery. I cannot wait to see it all!''

"It will be magnificent," responded the petite Eugenie as she stretched her silken arms luxuriously over her head. "I detest standing about for measurings and tuckings and . . . you know, Marie, we shall have to carry these gowns with us and dress at the Bastille. It would never do to offer du Roi a sweetmeat with a wrinkled skirt." She laughed and turned away, and Mary's excited eyes took in the tumble of gentle hued colors about the vast room: blonde beauties, all, with their silk garments of creams and whites, pale yellows and golds punctuated only by the more homely colors of the dressmakers who cleared their cluttered gear to depart. She wished desperately that the king himself might come to check on his chosen maids and that his eyes would rest on her again as they had so long ago.

She sighed and shrugged out of her dress. She was one of only three maids dressed entirely in gold and white, the full satin skirts flounced and gathered with tiny silken rose buds. They had told her that Signor da Vinci had labeled the drawing of this dress for the English maid Boullaine. She smiled at the compliment. The master had not forgotten the girl he had rescued in the gardens at Amboise more than a year ago.

The sparrow-like seamstress stuffed the dress's sleeves with cotton batting and darted off with the garment held high. Mary drifted with the others in the direction of the special hairdressers assembled for the event. She soon found, to her great delight, that the master mind of this elaborate spectacle had sent numerous sketches of hair styles for the setters to emulate on the maids. And one fine-lined drawing was of a clearly recognizable face while the others merely had the shapes of heads under the curled or upswept tresses. Mary gazed on the sketch in wonder.

"It is my face indeed," she breathed.

"It seems, Mademoiselle Boullaine, the *premier peintre du Roi* has decreed this very look for you," smiled her hair setter. "Sit, sit. I hope my art will not disappoint Monsieur da Vinci."

The afternoon swept around Mary's excited, spinning head on wings. Their carriages approached the massy Palais du Bastille an hour before the royal party, ambassadors, and the two-hundred and fifty chosen revelers would arrive. The street leading to the Bastille gateway seemed more a tunnel through a deep forest, for fragrant boxwood, laurel and festoons of flowers decorated the shops and towering narrow houses.

They were ushered into a hallway adjacent to the courtyard where the banquet, dancing, and masques would later take place. When they had been attired, they were scrutinized by the pointed stare of their steward and left on their own with warnings not to peek out when the royal persons arrived—and not to sit or lean. They stood about in beige and yellow clusters chatting, anticipating, and giggling nervously.

But then their steward was back, and with him strode the master of Francois' *fete du royale,* Signor Leonardo da Vinci. He looked fragile and more stooped, Mary thought, but somehow dynamic force emanated from his face and gestures. The girls hushed at once.

"Perfect, perfect," the old man chanted, nodding his masses of snowy hair in rhythm with his voice. "Olympian nymphs all with a Diana and a Venus too.''

Mary stood to his left, and he approached her slowly. His eyes seemed very red and tired. She curtseyed.

"Stand straight, my Diana, stand straight. *Sì*, the lines of the dress and hair are perfect. I knew they would set off your face the way I had seen it in my mind.''

He clasped his blue-veined hands tightly in approval, and she smiled at him in sincere appreciation and affection. He lowered his voice and turned his back on the hovering steward. "Would you like to see the rest of the frame for my creation, la Boullaine?''

"Oh, yes, Signor da Vinci! Would it be possible?'' She almost bounced from excitement, but restrained herself properly.

"But of course. Cannot the artist share his visions with those he created?''

He gestured toward the doorway, ignoring the perturbed steward who obviously wished none of his costumed wards out of his realm of control. The double doors to the central courtyard stood ajar, and Mary sucked in her breath as they entered. It was magic. In the broad daylight of chill December he had made the gardens at Hever or Amboise. Above them stretched a clear starlit night with the golden star planets trembling overhead in a velvet blue heaven. Tears flooded her eyes at the wonder of it.

The master's cracking, gentle voice disturbed her speechless revery. "Though you say nothing, I know you understand. It is always in your eyes, *charmante* Boullaine.''

"It is magnificent, truly magnificent.''

"It is only waxed canvas painted with stars and hung

84

with golden balls and set off with hundreds of candles and torches. But somehow it seems more, eh?'' He smiled and his thick mustache lifted. ''I did a much vaster one for Ludovico Sforza in Milan years ago, you know.''

He raised his fragile left hand and pointed. ''The queen and queen mother will sit in the lower galleries and the king and his beloved sister Marguerite there in the center.'' Her eyes took in a richly brocaded platform draped with flowers, boxwood and ivy. ''Du Roi insisted on his shield and colors of tawny and white on the walls and as the carpet. Well, it is still the heavens of Florence or Milan, Francois' salamanders or not. All is ready. I had best return you to your jailer.'' He smiled again.

''Though I have been much busy and have not seen you for, well, for a time, Mademoiselle Boullaine, I knew how you would carry your new year on your fair face. I have sketched you since we have been together, often as a chaste Diana and once as la Madonna.''

Mary's steps faltered. ''The Blessed Virgin, Signor?''

''*Sì*. Do not be surprised or deem it only an honor. You see, that Mary showed pain in her eyes too and even at His birth and adoration, she could never hide the pain to come. *Adieu, mi* Boullaine.'' He bowed slightly and drifted back toward his creation before she could thank him or say farewell or ask him what he meant, and the anxious steward immediately shooed her back into his skittish brood.

Too soon the hours flew by and they held their breath at the blare of trumpets and the shouts and bustling of the heralds and servers as each of the nine courses went to the tables of the feasters. The lilt of fife and viol came and went as did the dancers and singers. Then the twenty maids grew silent, for they knew their time had come.

Bearers appeared with flower-strewn trays of confections and sweetmeats which the golden nymphs would offer to the guests royal and honored, French and English. Mary marvelled briefly at the orange and lemon blossoms of December which lined her tray.

They stood in order, breathless. The doors swung inward. They smiled and tripped in gaily among the clustered tables, each a golden glory in the vibrant glow of six hundred candles.

The guests murmured to each other or sighed audibly, their sight again dazzled and newly surfeited as their palates had been with delicacies and fine wines. They chose their confections gingerly, and their admiring glances did not waver from the exquisite Florentine living creations of Master da Vinci.

Only after the sudden impact of their entry did individual sights sort themselves out for the excited girls. Mary's eyes again took in the incandescent magnificence of the overhanging heavens. Queen Claude and Louise du Savoy were ablaze with winking jewels. Mary could not pick out her father among the Englishmen though she scanned the jumbled faces as best she could. But Francois du Roi stood clearly before her gaze as she smiled and nodded and inclined her laden tray to the eager hands of guests on both sides.

Francois was the sun at the very core of the artificial universe as he circulated on his own course among his seated guests. He glowed in white satin embroidered with tiny dials and astronomers' instruments and mathematicians' compasses all in gold, no doubt also the wonderful work of the Master da Vinci. Mary tried to watch the king often, lifting her eyes whenever she moved from person to person or swung her tray from side to side.

"Thomas Bullen's daughter, so I hear," a robust Englishman announced to his surrounding friends.

Mary smiled radiantly at him and replied, "Though I am raised at the French court, I am true English at heart, my lord."

Several applauded and commented heartily to each other. She could not see her father to share this fine moment, and she felt it would seem foolish to ask the men where he sat. To her dismay, she *did* take in the avid gaze of the tall, brown-haired William Stafford who sat but one person beyond the man she served now. How she would like to bypass him deliberately or give him a pert remark to wipe that wide-eyed smile from his lips, but she dared not in full view of so many.

As she turned toward the spot where she would be forced to offer him his choice, several of the Englishmen about her rose suddenly and she spun slightly, hoping to relocate the king. She nearly dropped her gilded tray, for he was so close that her flared nostrils took in his musky scent, and the white and gold shining satin of his doublet nearly blinded her. The room seemed to tilt as she curtseyed.

"A goddess in gold and white to match her king," he spoke lightly in his peerless French. His eyes pierced her satins and her skirts, and her heart beat terribly fast. She could not answer. One slanting eyebrow arched even higher over his narrow, dark gaze. She began to tremble and fortunately he suddenly looked aside at the observant group of Englishmen.

"And now you can understand more fully the glories of my France," he boasted to them. His eyes sparkled and his teeth gleamed in the rampant candlelight. He extended his jeweled hand and, in full view of the avid hall, stroked her blushing cheek with the backs of his slender fingers. He towered over her far into the painted heavens and the tiny instant of time seemed to hang eternally in the stillness.

"But, indeed, Your Grace, this golden nymph is one of the glories of fair England," came a voice in halting French. "This is Mary, Ambassador Boullaine's eldest daughter."

There were a few random stifled laughs, but most trained at court held back to see Francois' reaction.

"Then I am certainly anxious for more complete French and English relations, my lords," he chortled, and the surrounding groups exploded in appreciative and relieved guffaws.

Mary went scarlet and her eyes darted from face to face, torn by fears of what her father might think of such sport. Her gaze caught and held with William Stafford's. He did not laugh with the others, but looked most annoyed.

Francois gently pulled her tray from her hands and set it on the edge of an ivory tablecloth. He boldly tucked her right hand under his arm and held it close to his warm, muscular, satin-covered ribs.

"I think, gentlemen, the English ambassador's daughter should be a more important part of this grand alliance of nations. Besides, she matches her French king better than any other lady here tonight. Our pure white and gold seem destined to make us a pair!"

He laughed again and kept her at his side as he strolled and chatted and drank in their adulation. But Mary, stunned and thrilled as she was, took in other realities under Signor da Vinci's gold and deep blue heavens: Queen Claude's condescending glance, his sister Marguerite's amused smile, and Francoise du Foix's bitter glare. Finally, when she saw her father's proud grin and curt nod, she relaxed somewhat, but she could not seem to escape the disapproving face of the impudent Sir William Stafford. And, too, she kept wondering what Leonardo da Vinci could read in her eyes if she had seen him again as she paraded under his painted waxen sky.

Chapter Seven
January 10, 1519

Chateau du Amboise

The familiar stifling silence had fallen on the queen's court again: for the fifth time in four years the twenty-one-year-old Claude was sickly and swollen with royal child. Again her young and vibrant maids whispered begrudgingly in the hallways and took care to smother their giggles and gossip. All too soon the twenty fortune-favored maids who had attended the lavish French and English ceremonies in Paris ran out of marvellous tales to relate, and life fell back into its ponderous pattern of prayers and readings and study and needlework.

But for once the enforced duties in the hush of Queen Claude's wing of rooms at Amboise seemed a welcome shelter to Mary Bullen. Claude's chambers were a precious haven before the storms of decisions and rolling emotions which surely must follow if she would be caught in the shoals of Francois' power outside the queen's influence. Jacqueline, Jeanne and Eugenie and her own dear Anne might murmur and complain under their breaths at the tightening new restrictions, but Mary was secretly glad for the respite.

It was true that the news of her glorious walk with the king at his banquet in the Bastille had done wonders for her reputation and power among the other maids. Anne had made her tell the story over and over, though she had not told any of her listeners of the ill-bred William Stafford, nor of Francois' lingering kiss on her lips as he departed to rejoin his imperious sister, nor of his quiet, deep-throated promise that he would see her again soon and in private.

It was that very thought that terrified her. She was not so unschooled in court ways to be naive as to his intent. She read his piercing gaze and felt his fingers brush her tight gold bodice as he bid her swift *adieu*. How she treasured each gilded moment with him—and how greatly she feared a future near him.

Her girlish fantasies of Francois quite eluded her now. She seemed frozen, unable to summon up the marvelous dreams she had paraded back and forth across the stage of her imagination since that magic time he had gazed on her long ago in Princess Mary Tudor's chilly room at Cluny. This was different. It was a flesh and blood Francois, and she could no longer control his longings and his chivalric manners by a mere turn of her mind's eye. She feared for her reputation and that her father and Queen Claude would disown her if she shamed them with the king. But then, was it not an honor, too, to be so chosen? She shuddered again though she sat full in the warmth of the vast hearth in the queen's anteroom.

"Are you cold, Marie? It is stifling in here in general, I think." Anne's nimble fingers halted poised above her small tapestry loom, her needle trailing a thin shaft of crimson yarn.

"No, Anne. I am fine."

"Your patience to sit about has certainly improved since your journey to Paris," Anne responded, narrowing her dark almond-shaped eyes slightly. "You used to be happy to escape these dreary chambers once in a while." She lowered her voice even more. "I think the sullen mood of Her Grace's pregnancies has mushed your spirit, Marie Boullaine."

"Do not tease, Anne. It is gloomy outside today anyway. If you need the diversion of a stroll or high adventure in the frozen gardens, Jeanne will be only too willing to go with you. I shall remain within summons to Her Majesty. Besides, the queen mother and Madam Alencon will be here soon and they always provide diversion. Really they are as much at the heart of the realm as is the king."

"Do you think much about seeing him again, Marie? How exciting that the great king truly knows you and favors you and recognizes you. Does not the sense of power thrill you?"

"His Grace was only being kind, Anne. I told you that we happened to be dressed much alike and I caught his eye. That is all."

"Coward," Anne teased and laughed. "I shall ask our father what he thought of it, next I see him."

"Feel free to leave me, little sister, if you care more for your own interpretations." Mary rose swiftly and some of her flaxen threads spilled from her full-skirted lap.

"My sweet sister Marie does indeed show the temper of which she used to accuse George and me," said Anne, widening her gaze in gentle mockery as Mary bent to scoop her threads from the footstool and floor.

She felt miffed mostly at herself, and she instinctively sought the refuge of the queen's rooms, through the open doors where she knew neither Anne nor the others would willingly follow.

The fire in the queen's chamber burned quite low and her priest had evidently just departed. Queen Claude leaned back on a chaise couch, her prayer book open in her lap, a lady in waiting on both sides of her like silent sentinels. Her bulk was already great. Mary had noticed that with each close-spaced pregnancy, she carried the child lower and seemed to swell sooner. The queen's eyes slowly moved to Mary, like dark coals on her white face. Her left eye always seemed to squint, and this disconcerted her ladies.

"Marie, *entrez*." Mary curtseyed and sat on the tiny prie-dieu near the queen's feet. "What is happening in the outside world today, *ma demoiselle?*"

"I have not been abroad, Your Grace," Mary answered simply.

"But out of the windows, are the skies still gray, Marie?"

"*Oui*, Your Grace."

"Then what use is it for me to try to let some light in here before my dear husband's mother and my dearest Marguerite arrive? I have been lying here summoning my strength for the interview." She spoke almost to herself. "They bring such vitality, you know, and I seem to have none of my own lately."

She ordered the shutters be spread inward anyway, and the room was diffused with a hazy gray light. She stood shakily and murmured to no one in particular, "And my poor Francois. How he chafes at the bit in such weather. Francois must always be active and have

93

diversions. And this terrible business of who will be the next Holy Roman Emperor—ah, I pray hourly for it to fall to my husband.''

As though she had foreseen their approach, the queen turned to the door as Louise du Savoy and Marguerite entered in a rush. Marguerite wore a flame-colored velvet gown edged and lined everywhere with either golden satin or whitest ermine with black flecks in the fur, whereas the more subdued Louise's heavier body was swathed in richest burgundies weighted with gold thread, jeweled girdle, and heavy pearls. Each woman took Claude's hand solicitously. Mary and the other ladies stepped back to the wall, for the queen never liked to be without several attendants. The royal ladies clustered together before the hearth. Though the queen sat down again and tried to hold herself erect, her back was like a bent bow, but the other two reminded Mary of taut strings ready to send out a brace of sharp arrows.

"My poor daughter Claude," began Louise du Savoy in her guttural voice, "how does this future prince you carry?"

"He stirs about and turns me blue along my belly, Mother," the queen answered her mother-in-law, and Mary marvelled at her meekness with these two.

In both Marguerite and the queen mother, Mary could see the long-nosed, dark-eyed Francois, in each the coiled spring of wound power beneath the surface.

"And how does my husband lately?" the queen was asking. "He is much burdened by his rightful inheritance of the cloak of Holy Roman Emperor?"

"*Oui, Oui*, greatly burdened," Marguerite responded in her quick sing-song French. "But if anyone can help to sway those wretched Germans who hold the important votes, it is the king's envoy Bonnivet. The Pope is already ours, Madam, but that she-wolf Margaret of Austria hates our house. I would strangle her for her meddling, if I could get my hands on her!''

Mary's head snapped up at the mention of her first royal guardian, the kindly Archduchess Margaret. It puzzled her that the dear old woman could hate Francois. She must remember to ask father someday if he would have time to explain.

''The money—the money is another problem, Madam,'' Marguerite continued, her head bobbing vivaciously to punctuate her words. ''Millions of francs and still the bankers quibble. Quibble with the King of France!''

Claude's voice came pale and listless after Marguerite's. ''I am grateful that my dear lord's family can sustain him in these court matters. I am often from the realm of his influence.''

''That is as it should be, dear daughter,'' Louise du Savoy responded. ''Your support for your lord is made manifest here, in the loving care of his children. This is as it should be,'' she repeated slowly.

''I do prefer it to other courtly duties, for what need is there of that when *du roi* has you and his Marguerite?''

Louise du Savoy nodded silently as though that closed the matter, but Marguerite began again. ''Francois is much unsettled lately, since you asked, sister. The English stance worries him and, you may be pleased to know, he has had a falling out with his 'lady' the haughty Francoise du Foix. It is long overdue that he sees that woman's true colors.''

"Marguerite, please, I hardly think our dear Claude wishes to hear court gossip in her condition . . . "

"You detest that woman too, mother, and always have," Marguerite answered, tossing her dark tresses. "The snow-goddess has carried on once too often with Bonnivet, and she shall reap her own harvest now." She laughed quickly, sharply. "Maybe it is partly the cause of Bonnivet's appointment as legate in Germany far from the lady's wiles."

"Hush, Mignonne," scolded the older woman. "Your preoccupation with Guillaume du Bonnivet much questions your own interest in the man." She frowned and shook her head.

Yes, remembered Mary suddenly, it is often rumored the Lady Marguerite has long favored Bonnivet though she is wed to Alencon.

"Anyway," put in the unquenchable Marguerite, glancing down her nose at her annoyed mother, "our *roi du soleil* is bored and unsettled, and it is hardly weather to tilt at jousts or chase the deer or boar afield."

Claude listened impassively, and though Mary could not see her face clearly, she pictured her white stare and blurry gaze gone awry.

"We must be going, dear Claude," Louise du Savoy said in the awkward silence. "I would like to stop by the royal nursery wing on our way."

"Of course," said Claude properly, rising slowly with them. "All was well yesterday when I saw them, and the dauphin can nearly speak in sentences. They told me his first words were '*du roi*.' It is appropriate, is it not?"

"Indeed, my daughter," her mother-in-law said

96

over her velvet shoulder as they approached the door.

Marguerite's falcon eyes caught Mary standing nearest the door. "Boullaine's daughter," she asked, half to herself. "But not in gold and pure white today." She laughed and was gone with her awesome mother trailing in her sweet-scented wake.

Mary fervently hoped the queen would not think the remark meant she had done anything wrong, for she had remarked kindly to Mary how lovely she and her dear husband had looked together at the feast. But Claude had sunk down in her vast cushions again and seemed to doze almost immediately. Mary sat at her feet for a soundless time, then rose to leave. Claude's voice floated to her again.

"Do not let Madam du Alencon tease, nor the queen mother frighten you, *petite* Boullaine. But have a care not to cross them either."

Mary turned and her silken skirts rustled loudly in the quiet room. "*Merci*, Your Grace."

But Queen Claude leaned as though she drowsed heavily, her bulky form outlined before the low-burning hearth.

Mary soon found she was foolish to think she could hide from facing the restive king by hovering close to the queen's well-guarded chamber. The arm of *du roi*, she learned that same day, could reach anywhere.

"Marie, Monsieur du Fragonard is here in the blue room—to see you alone," came Jeanne's excited words. She lowered her voice cautiously as she leaned closer. "No doubt, he bears a message from His Grace, Marie, for Fragonard is most intimate to royal business—in private matters."

97

Mary could feel her heart beat a distinct thud, thud. "Then I must speak to Monsieur Fragonard," she said only.

Jeanne trailed along down the narrow hallway to the reception room, one in a series of formal receiving chambers which the sequestered Claude seldom used. Jeanne lingered at the door while Mary rapped and entered.

Monsieur Fragonard had silver hair and his doublet and hose were of shimmery gray satin. He bowed elaborately and unnecessarily low.

"Mademoiselle Marie Boullaine." He seemed to breathe her name rather than speak it. "May we sit together for a moment? I have a message for you from *du roi*." He smiled smoothly and she sat where he had indicated. "A message for your ears only."

He leaned one lace-cuffed hand on his silver-headed walking stick. "Our king is still charmed by the memory of your warmth and beauty from your too brief time together in Paris last month. You, ah, no doubt, think fondly of him too."

There was a tiny silence while her mind darted wildly about for a way to draw back from the looming precipice. Fool, she told herself, was this not what you have dreamed of for these last four years?

"*Oui*, monsieur. Of course I think fondly of *du roi*."

"I would explain to you as a friend, Mademoiselle, that the king is very busy lately and bears much upon his shoulders. It would be a joyous duty to lighten his burden and give him pleasant conversation and diversion, would it not?"

"All would wish to serve the king, monsieur."

He searched her face carefully. "*Oui*. Then, I must

98

inform you that His Grace requests the privilege of your company, Mademoiselle Boullaine.'' He stood and meticulously pulled his lace shirt through the silver slashings of his doublet.

"When, monsieur?" Mary asked as she rose.

"Now. Can you not leave your duties now? The hour is long before supper or the queen's evening prayers. May I accompany you?"

He pulled the door open, and Mary half expected to see Jeanne du Lac poised on the threshold, but the adjoining rooms and hall were quite deserted. Mary took shallow breaths to steady herself. She was distinctly aware of each step she took along the gallery leading to the king's wing of the palace. At least it was broad daylight and not a summons in the night she had dreaded would mean that he had other plans for her than conversation. Monsieur Fragonard's silver walking stick made regular tap-taps on the inlaid floor to punctuate her breaths and heart beats.

"Here, *mademoiselle*," he said finally. "This is a private way to His Grace's afternoon study." He pushed open the narrow door and they came face-to-face with a tall *gendarme*, his sword at his side. Her guide merely bobbed his head to the soldier, and they went on through two tiny rooms lined with books and containing several low tables each laden with strange globes, mechanisms or clocks.

"*Adieu* for now, Mademoiselle Boullaine." His words came suddenly as they faced another closed narrow door. He rapped three times, bowed, and retreated the way they had come.

Mary shuddered as he left, not as much from excitement or fear as from a strange repulsion towards her so proper guide. Somehow, he reminded her of a graceful, silver snake.

The door swung open and Francois stood bathed in the light of the room behind him. He squinted to see her better. She had not expected him to be so close. He was dressed very informally with dark purple satin breech and hose and an open brown velvet doublet over his white silk embroidered shirt. Only his velvet, square-toed slippers, heavily filigreed in gold thread and his very large embroidered codpiece seemed blatant and ornate. Stunned, she began to sweep him a curtsey, but he seized her hands and pulled her gently into the room.

"My Marie, my beautiful golden Marie," he mused aloud to himself as he held her hands at her sides and scrutinized her.

"I am hardly your golden Marie today, Your Grace." She glanced down ruefully at her everyday dress of green watered silk with the tiny rim of lace edging the swell of her breasts above the low-cut oval bodice. "But your summons came so quickly that I came as I am."

"What more could a man wish, *cherie*? At any rate, I sent you a request, not a summons. If I summon you someday, you shall know the difference. Did Fragonard say otherwise?

"No, Your Grace. He was most kind."

"Green suits you too, Marie. Indeed, everything does. Green is most pleasant in these wretched, chilly months when there is little riding and hunting. Only business, worry and lectures from one's advisors or family."

He smiled and released her hands and Mary relaxed.

How wonderful she felt, how important to be near him. Surely since she was Lord Boullaine's daughter and under the queen's protection, he would not expect her to lose her reputation. He was much older, and kings never had liaisons with unmarried ladies that she had heard of. She smiled warmly at him.

"Now I remember," he said quietly, "why I think of you as golden Marie no matter what dress you wear." He took a quick step toward her and then turned. "Will you have some wine with your friend Francois, Marie?"

Awed by his informal manner, she took the stemmed goblet willingly and looked up, unafraid, into his dark eyes. Then the familiar awkwardness leaned on her heart again. He did not speak but studied her carefully, and the tiny flames in his eyes warned her of potential disaster.

She turned sideways from his hot stare and surveyed the room. Its walls were dark wood in layered paneling and edged with gilt. A fire crackled merrily behind a carved screen. There were books, a huge compass, maps, stuffed brocaded arm chairs and a narrow lounge bed along one wall. There was only one window, but the thin winter sun slanted across the carpet and warmed the chamber.

"Come, Marie." She looked back at him startled. "Come see the view from one of my favorite windows. I can see far down the valley from here, and the Loire is like the green ribbon in your hair."

He leaned against the rich paneling and turned his head to gaze far out across the recessed window ledge. She joined him, setting her half finished wine glass on the table, realizing too late that it was something she could have held between them as they stood so close.

He pulled her against his side in a brotherly way and put one arm lightly around her shoulders. He pointed to the tiny village on the opposite cliff face. "I shall tell you a secret, *ma cherie*. One night last summer, Bonnivet and I and a few others disguised ourselves and rode through the streets throwing eggs at windows and whatever people we saw." He laughed, and she could feel his ribs and shoulders move as he did. "A tiny hamlet, but with as fresh a supply of wine and women as any!" He squeezed her shoulder as he chuckled, then loosed her again merely resting his now heavy arm on her. "Now what the devil was the name of that little place? We shall have to do that again some time, if we live through this blasted, boring winter."

"I watched your Master da Vinci draw that view once from the gardens, Your Grace."

"Did you, sweet? Signor Leonardo is ill and maybe shall not last the winter either. A genius. He and I appreciate each other."

"It is said you have often spent hours together talking of—well, of everything, Sire." She felt a stabbing sorrow for the old man's illness.

"It is said, sweet? Then it is one of the only true rumors about the king to fly around the halls of the palace lately. Shall we give them all something new to speak of to pass the dreary months until spring, golden Marie?"

He turned her to him and his eyes went to her lips. Foolishly she blurted out, "The queen mother and your sister Madam du Alencon visited the queen today."

His eyes did not waver, and he leaned into her pressing her between him and the wall. "Fine. Then they will be busy and not bother their Francois all the rest of this so lovely afternoon.''

He bent his head and took her lips gently for a lingering moment and then with hot intensity. She kept her eyes tight shut and tried desperately to stem the trembling in her knees. She could not think of anything but the feel of his velvet chest and the hard muscles of his thighs and his probing tongue. But she must think, she must!

His hands dropped to her narrow waist and one came slowly, treacherously up to her shoulder, sliding, tugging at the oval bodice. He shifted his weight and his lips caressed her neck and kissed her throat. His thick dark hair tickled her chin. He raised his head.

''From the first moment I saw you, *cherie*, I knew we were meant to be together. You are so lovely, your eyes, your lips, your hair. My Venus, your king would be most blessed should you allow him to gaze on you, like Venus, undraped.''

She opened her mouth to give him whatever answer she could find, but he stopped her lips with a fiery, open-mouthed kiss. She wanted to say no, but she wanted him more, his warm gaze, his flattery, his praise. She knew in her head he offered her words to seduce, but she could not stem the desire for a man's touch—especially this king.

His fingers slid down between her full breasts and to her own amazement she arched up against him. His other hand descended between her back and the wall and cupped itself firmly against her derriere through the voluminous folds of her skirts. Her eyes shot open. She could feel the sudden stab of his codpiece against her thigh as he leaned into her. A man's deepest affections she desired, but . . . but this was no lovestruck Rene de Brosse in the hedges. This was Francois of France. Fear welled up suddenly.

"Please, Your Grace, please, no."

He gazed down at her, and one dark brow arched. "Afraid, *cherie*? I should have called you my Diana and not my Venus, is it not true, little virgin?"

She tried to pull gently away, but she was still trapped by his strong body. "You are still virgin, are you not, Marie?"

"Yes, my king."

"Then I shall be very gentle for now. Where better to learn the arts of love but from your king, sweet?"

He half swept, half carried her to the narrow bed with its one huge padded bolster. She thought he would pull them both down, but he turned her away from him and began to unlace the back of her gown.

"I have thought much of you since the English banquet at the Bastille, my beauty. Everyone there saw what a splendid pair we were, I so dark and you so radiant fair."

And what of your mistress, Francoise? a strange voice in her head screamed. I will be for your pleasure on only this long afternoon and then you will return to her? she wanted to ask.

Her bodice fell away, and he stood tight against her shaking back. He put his arms around her and plunged his hands beneath her silken chemise, pulling her breasts free. She had not realized the chill of the room before, nor that her body was damp. She felt shame that her nipples leapt so eagerly to meet his teasing fingers. There were hot coals in the pit of her stomach and even between her legs.

"Let me, Marie," he said low. And in one tug, he pulled her dress and chemise from her. She tried to step back but nearly tripped in the folds of her skirts as his hands held her waist firmly.

"You must trust me, my beauty. Trust me. Close your eyes and trust your Francois."

He laid her back on the bed and pulled her tangled skirts off her ankles. His eyes raked her, burned her, and she pulled up her knees slightly to hide the dark gold triangle of hair at which he stared.

"Close your eyes, Marie," he urged again. He began to pull off his breeks and hose and her eyes widened despite his orders. She wished somewhere deep inside her mind that he would just caress her and love her and care for her and not have to do this. But surely it would be worth whatever came to have his love.

He pulled her trembling legs apart gently and lay immediately between them, his massive body hovering over her but his weight on his arms and elbows. His kisses were very wet, and he turned his lips sideways and plundered her mouth with his tongue again.

She felt totally open and vulnerable to him. Then he ceased his kisses and murmurings and moved up higher on her and probed slowly into her. His thrusts stabbed and she tried to pull back, to slide to the side to escape the pain. He seemed almost unaware of her as he rose and thrust at an even, ever increasing pace.

The pain between her thighs departed, but the fire remained and flowed strangely into her loins and limbs. She closed her eyes and held on to his strong neck trying to imagine it was her wedding night and that he would love her always. Then he heaved a sigh and relaxed heavily against her.

"You are perfection, golden Marie." He raised his mussed head and stared into her blue eyes. "No tears, eh? Fine. This will be a much better winter than I had imagined. Francois will teach his little newly-broken filly how he likes to ride."

He rolled off her, and she saw he was bloody—her blood. She gasped and he followed her wide-eyed gaze.

"Ah. I have not had a virgin since Claude." He laughed. "No, lie still, sweet. I will dress and get someone to care for it. I assure you, it will never happen to you again like that."

He patted her bare flank as he rose and was pleased to find her eyes still on him. "Save your stares for the next time your king is aroused for you, *cherie*, and then you will have something to fear, eh? I had considered a second lesson today, but a little rest would give you some time to heal a bit."

He tucked his wrinkled shirt into his breeks and laughed deep in his throat. "We had best get you cared for and back to the rest of the maids, sweet. Our pious Claude would never understand your being late to chapel on any accord."

There was a sharp knock on the door, and Mary sat bolt upright. Panicked, she reached off the bed for a petticoat to cover herself.

Francois strode to the door and held up his hand to her for silence. "What is it?"

"Your Grace, you bid us to inform you if the Master Leonardo's condition worsened. Pardon, Sire, but he hovers at death's door already and would see Your Grace."

"I will be ready immediately. Wait there. No, go fetch me the wench Isabelle first."

106

"I wish I could keep Master da Vinci here longer," he said almost to himself. "I have need of him."

He threw on his dark velvet cloak. "I meant not to leave you so suddenly, Marie, but Isabelle will tend to you, and Monsieur Fragonard will see you safely back to your quarters. He awaits there."

He motioned swiftly toward the door from which she had entered. "Have Isabelle tidy your coif." He approached her sitting with her petticoat covering her from breasts to knees. He pulled it suddenly from her, pressed her on her back, and bent to kiss a soft breast.

"Remember me, Marie. I wish I were coming back for more sweets as soon as Isabelle finishes with you." He towered over her. "I will send for you soon, golden Marie." He yanked the door open and was gone.

She stared at the painted ceiling for a moment, then scrambled up and draped the petticoat over her again. Poor Signor da Vinci lay dying. What would the kind old man think of this if he knew? And Jeanne, Annie, Claude, the whole court? Dearest saints in heaven, what would father say?

Isabelle knocked once and entered with towels and water, her eyes uncurious, her hands quick and sure. As she helped her dress, Mary's mind finally began to work again and fear raged in her thoughts. If the pious queen found out, she would disown her and father would be ashamed and angry. But if she were to anger Francois with her refusals, what then? Before it all came out she had to tell her father. If he discovered it later, it would be as his anger against Mary Tudor when she had secretly married the Duke, only worse since she had no brother king to protect her. Or would Francois stand against her father for her?

She nodded her thanks to Isabelle and pulled open the door to face the stealthy Fragonard.

"I shall see you back now, Mademoiselle Boullaine, and if there is any favor I might do for you on behalf of the king, please let . . . "

"There is one I would appreciate, *monsieur*," she said bravely.

"Ask it then, *mademoiselle*."

"Would you see that a brief letter to my father, Ambassador Boullaine, is delivered? I have not seen him for weeks, and my sister and I miss his company."

"I would be delighted to serve you, sweet lady," came his smooth reply as he sharply pushed the door open with his silver-headed stick.

Chapter Eight
July 3, 1519

Chateau du Fontainebleau

A thin finger of pale sunlight parted the heavy velvet drapes and pointed crookedly across the bed. The rhythm of the king's deep breathing was unbroken, and Mary marvelled that they had slept the night through. She had never before stayed long abed with Francois after his lovemaking, but many things were different now. How forced his laughter had been these last few months, how jerky his once fluid motions, how brittle his temper. Court pressures and the fear he would not be chosen the next Holy Roman Emperor rode him cruelly, even as he rode her.

Her mind drifted to her increasing cowardice in facing him after that initial seduction in January at Amboise. The trembling she felt with him had been not only because of what he did to her body, but because her body, despite her shame and fear, seemed to respond beyond the reins of her own control.

She had actually gone so far as to hide from Fragonard one day in late February when she heard his voice in the hall and his silver cane rapping on the bedroom door of the small room she now shared only with Anne, who was in attendance on Queen Claude at that hour. She had heard his metallic voice speak to someone when she did not respond, and then, blessedly, his foot-steps had departed. No less than ten minutes later, as she had sat smug and relieved that today she would not turn to melted honey in the king's arms no matter what he asked of her, the door had banged open and the king himself had filled its fragile frame.

"Marie! What luck that you have returned. I do not like for my dear Fragonard to report to me without my precious when I sent for her. 'But, of course, she was there waiting, Fragonard,' I told him. 'Of course, she was awaiting my call for her with bated breath and only fell asleep, eh?' " He grinned at how huge her blue eyes had gone in her pale face and how poorly she hid all the thoughts and passions that passed behind that pretty face of hers. He shouldered the door shut behind him and moved with catlike grace into the room while she scooted off the far side of the bed in a flurry of sky-blue skirts.

"Your Grace—but, you never come here to the ladies' rooms! I—Fragonard—"

He had laughed low in his throat, obviously pleased at her fluster and embarrassment. "Marie, Marie, naughty little girl. You cannot lie to your king, but you shall lie with him. And now, here. I grow impatient with these flutterings."

He shot the bolt on the door behind him, stripped off his black and red striped doublet and the ruffled white lace shirt under it in one pull.

"But your guards in the hall, Sire," she floundered, her eyes on him as he peeled off his black velvet

110

breeches and his stockings held by elaborately embroidered and bejeweled garters.

"They are down by Claude's chambers, little nymph, and the whole silly court is atwitter over much more than whom I choose to bed during this wretched international mess. But," he said and laughed low at her again, "if our being caught worries you, pet, I shall oblige. I shall leave my rings on for a quick exit and you shall—well, let us make it hot and quick if you are so shy, my love."

Her face and throat went scarlet hot clear down to the low square-cut neckline of her simple, clinging blue velvet day gown. She knew it amused him to torment her like this before he took her, even as a hunter would play with a cornered doe. At that, her ire rose and she fought to calm her panic that he knew she had avoided Fragonard. She turned to face him squarely with her chin up.

But as he stalked her around the end of her and Annie's tapestry-hung, four-poster bed, his huge muscular form, naked and covered with sparse, dark hair like the paintings of satyrs she had seen, awed her anew. He chuckled and his eyes glinted when her mouth dropped open at the sight of his blatant desire for her.

"Your Grace, please, a maid's room is hardly a setting for *du roi* of France," she heard herself whisper.

"But my little filly, you know your Francois likes you different ways and places. We must hurry now. You have said so yourself—"

He lunged at her but she had not dared to flee. At first his assault seemed foolish until she realized in the onslaught of hands and his demanding mouth that he only did it to amuse his stubborn sense of adventure and sport.

Roughly, he kissed her and forced her lips apart to ravish her mouth; his hard hands tugged, then yanked her dress from her shoulders and peeled it down to expose her breasts. She almost forgot herself and hit out at his massive shoulders pressing her down when her nipples became so tender from the pinching, rubbing, and nipping, but he seized her free hand and returned to his rough seduction.

Seduction, a little voice deep in her mind taunted her, seduction again as everytime when he takes you, makes you want him, then just leaves. Seduction because you let him, seduction because you want him.

Through lips still tingling from the heat of his kisses, she murmured, "No," so quietly she was not certain she had said it.

Francois raised his handsome, sleek head so close to her. He looked misty-eyed, his features blurred with passion as always, just before he finished with her. They stared into each other's eyes one moment and the sheer animal magnetism and power of the man drowned her half-formed protest in a sensual assault far more treacherous than his mere touch.

"Oh, *oui*, Marie, *oui* and *oui*," he said through panting lips as he yanked the last laces at her waistline loose to free her full skirts. He dragged her out of them and kicked them off the bed, ignoring the fact that she still wore her torn chemise and rumpled corset which now pulled awry to thrust her full breasts up, swollen and waiting for his touch.

"You will not send Fragonard back without you when I call again, little Marie." He smacked her bare flank sharply as he leaned over her looking very much the wild man of her worst dreams of him. "On your knees to your king, little filly."

He lifted and swung her to her knees on the bed before him facing away from him before she could even reason out or protest what he ordered. He pushed her face and shoulders down onto the smooth coverlet, and he had already positioned himself between her spread ankles behind.

One arm came hard around her waist to hold her to him and the other moved to caress her breasts as he drove deep into her woman's nest of love. She was suddenly angered and frightened anew, but her struggles seemed only to urge him on as he drove repeatedly against her. The hot fire which always overtook her began its treacherous path through her limbs and stomach again despite the fact she felt he was only amusing himself at the expense of her poise and her cherished, foolish dreams he loved her. Just as she was certain she could attain some wonderful release from the agonized passion, he finished and merely pulled away without another word and with no soft caress.

Now in his big bed some five months later, she shed no tears for the foolish Mary Bullen as she had that day after he had dressed hastily and gone out. She turned her head and stared as impassively as she could at him. She stretched carefully and pulled her rampant tresses from under his extended left arm. He groaned and she froze like a hunted doe. She heaved a heartfelt sigh and stiffened again as the sleeping man murmured incoherently. Then she smiled to know that even kings had fears and nightmares, even as she and Annie.

The last few months had skimmed by, first with the

thrill and danger of the king's avid attentions and then with apprehension as he grew restive with her and sampled other sweet bon-bons at his court, bouncing back to Francoise du Foix's luxurious bed whenever his appetite waned. The bitter shredding of each girlish fancy—that he adored her only, that she could keep this handsome king forever, that he would be her knight protector—had given her months of foolish agony. Francois du roi enjoyed his Marie Boullaine under his thrusting body when the whim took him, but she was no more dear to him than one fine palfrey from a whole stable or one blooded beagle from his pedigree pack.

Sometimes she thought that she could have withstood all the disillusionment except when he left her with his cronies to amuse them in their beds. Then she was certain she could die from shame and pain. Once she had heard them laughingly comparing notes on how their pretty pack of *jeune filles* were ridden, and how each liked best to be positioned, and what cries each made when her moment of climax came. In that crashing second something sweet and vital inside her turned brown and withered, and her long tended love for Francois du roi was no more. Knowing how to see clearly could be one's very survival at court, Signor da Vinci had told her long ago. Yet she had not seen Francois clearly until she had shared his bed, and there was no way she could draw back now.

She thanked the blessed virgin her lord father knew not about the others besides the king. When she had sent to him for advice and help, he had encouraged her to share the glorious king's bed, for was not such service an honor? She prayed fervently again her father would never know how the glorious Francois offered and loaned her to his friends and had once paid a gambling debt with her. She shuddered at the thought. The winner had been Lautrec, Francoise du Foix's crafty brother, and the memory of his demanding hands and mouth and his uses of her was enough to make her draw far within herself in shame.

She pulled restively farther away from Francois in the great bed and rolled on her side, curling up her knees like a child, her back to him. An honor to be possessed by the King of France, father had said, a monarch almost as grand as King Henry. Her reputation would be much enhanced both here and at home, he promised. But Mary could too often visualize her mother's tears if she heard, Semmonet's cluck-clucking with her tongue in disapproval, William Stafford's accusing look, and Signor da Vinci's warnings of the pain she showed in her eyes. Queen Claude knew, Mary was sure, but her kindness never wavered. Better to be sick, ugly Claude than pretty, healthy and so ensnared. Dear heavens, someday she would escape, somehow she would go home and show this man who consumed her body and crushed her pride that she favored him not.

If only she could be like the lady in the small portrait by Master da Vinci which Francois had hung in whatever bedchamber he inhabited—it hung here now—the lovely lady whose eyes and lips only hinted at the smile of her inward heart. "La Gioconda" Francois called her. Mary sat to study the painting, but the sunlight had not yet reached it and it still hung in dim obscurity. But the lady sat there forever calm and let one wonder what thoughts pulsated behind her placid brow. The king could never shatter La Gioconda's calm as he crashed through the deep forests after stag or danced wild galliards or skewered his nymphs.

"Awake, golden Marie," came his deep voice behind her. He ran his warm hand lazily down her bare spine. Gooseflesh rose on her neck as she turned slowly to face him.

His eyes were languorous, heavy-lidded and she murmured a low protest as he rose only enough to cup a breast with one hand and to pull her down beside him with the other.

He took her mouth and pulled away the sheets that were trapped between their bodies. He held her tight against him, a firm hand grasping her soft buttocks. "You were not leaving, were you, *ma cherie*? I sometimes see flight in your eyes, but you must remember your Francois is a skillful hunter and loves pursuit as well as capture. Someday after the chase, I shall charge my horse across the lawn, swoop you up, and ride off to rape you on the gentle forest floor, *oui, ma* Venus?"

She was stunned to feel his erect manhood against her when he had just awakened and after their bout last night. She had once heard Francoise du Foix tell he rode her three times in one afternoon, but she herself had never stayed with him much over an hour. To her dismay he rolled flat on his back and lifted her on him. He arranged her legs so she straddled him, and she let out a little cry as her weight pushed his full length into her. She did not want him, and he hurt her, though that was nothing new.

"The king has been riding much lately, pet, and it is rumored that some ladies would like to hunt boar with their Francois. Let me see how well you ride a stallion and maybe I shall take you with me today."

He laughed up at her, his eyes ebony slits and his

teeth gleaming white in the dimness of the canopied bed. She wanted to blurt out that she did not desire to hunt with him. She wanted to dive off his strong thighs and beg him to take her any other way and have it over, but she bit her lip and complied.

He laughed and moaned, but the pace did not seem to suit him, for he seized her derriere roughly and sent her bobbing up and down to his own fierce rhythm. Despite her discomfort, a warm liquid fire began to spread through her loins, but as she felt his surging rush, he stopped and she wilted across his chest.

She moved to shift herself away but froze warily as he fell immediately into deep, patterned breathing. Her knees began to ache and she carefully raised herself.

Both of Francois' dark eyes shot open. "Which position do you favor, my golden Marie? If not this, there are many others we can try." He laughed shortly, his piercing eyes still on her face.

She tried to compose an acceptable reply, but he rolled her off him and sat up as though he expected no answer.

"You are sweet indeed, *ma petite* Anglaise, but all sweetness with no spice can be boring to a man of spirit. Now let me tell you of that witch Francoise whom I vowed I would never bed again when I knew the little slut was unfaithful to me with Bonnivet—Guillaume Bonnivet, one of my closest friends—damn her selfish little soul!"

He pulled on a white silk shirt as he spoke, then stepped into his breeches. Mary sat huddled on the bed wrapped in the sheet like a protective silken cocoon.

"After I had punished her enough with others—almost a fortnight—I decided she had been dangled in

117

the royal wrath long enough. I went to her room unannounced early in the evening, expecting to make it a fine night and to my surprise and delight she was already nude in bed. I had knocked but briefly on the door and called her name before I entered, and it came to me she might have been preparing for someone else. All the better, I thought, the little vixen will pay for it.''

He sat now on the bed, his back to Mary, and furiously stuffed the legs of his breeches in his tight riding boots. ''The bed was warm, she was most willing, and her, ah, special attentions soon made me forget my anger. Having plowed her rich, moist furrow—thoroughly, sweet Marie—I rose to leave, for I wanted her to know she was mine whenever I would have her; yet she held me not.''

He spun toward Mary and yanked the sheet off her to her knees in one quick motion. ''Even the wily little bitch Francoise knows who is master, my sweet.''

There was a silence. Mary fought to keep from hiding her face in the pillow or grabbing the covers back from his greedy hands. ''*Oui*, Your Grace.''

''Ha! Well, Marie, the best is yet to come. I had to relieve myself after all that excitement and saw no chamber pot. And, well, to show her my disdain, I urinated a hot stream into her damned laurel leaves so fashionably set in the unused fireplace. The little bitch looked shocked at the effrontery but knew better than to protest, for she knew she deserved to have me aim at her hot bed with her still in it.''

''Later, Marie,'' he leaned over her on the bed, and she feared he would lie full length on her again, ''I found she had been entertaining that whoreson Bonnivet between her legs even as I knocked at her door, and the fool had dived behind the foliage in the fireplace to hide when I entered!''

Francois roared with laughter and slapped Mary's tawny, bare flank as he rose. ''How perfect! King's justice! And that is when, sweet Marie, I decided to send Bonnivet as my envoy to wheedle or buy the damned legates electing the new Holy Roman Emperor. But blessed Saint Michael, I must be hearing any day now, for the election was four days ago.''

He combed his flat, shining hair as he talked and then jerked open the door and strode into the anteroom where she could hear a low drone of voices.

Mary swiftly pulled the sheet up and tugged it out at the foot of the bed to drape a robe. Why had he left the door ajar? Someone might come in and see her like this.

She bent to glance in the silver mirror and frowned at the tousled girl reflected there. She gathered her chemise and skirts from across the room scattered like blown leaves. There was only one entry to this chamber so she would need to wait until Francois and his faithful entourage vacated the anteroom for their usual mad pursuit of boar or stag. She had no rigid schedule here at the vast hunt lodge of Fontainebleau.

She had her chemise and petticoats on when the low buzz of men's voices, punctuated by an occasional staccato of laughter, ceased utterly. Puzzled, she padded barefoot closer to the door and stood listening intently under the portrait of Signor da Vinci's ''La Gioconda'' now fully washed in sunlight.

''News from Bonnivet in Frankfort? Damn it, coward, arise and speak to your king! Francois awaits!''

Pray God the news is not bad, Mary thought, crushing her crumpled dress to her breasts. If they should

119

all have to live in the shadow of his terrible temper, then . . .

"Your Grace, your most humble servant, Bonnivet, begs me to inform you that the electors have betrayed their promises to you and . . . and . . ." The man's muffled voice broke. "The electors have chosen young Charles of Castile, Sire."

A tiny silence trembled in the room while all held their breaths, awestruck. There was a sharp crack and a thud, and Mary jumped backwards as though she had been struck. "And why is Bonnivet not here to tell his king of his failure himself," Francois was screaming. "Well?"

"Monsieur Bonnivet is much ill and most wretched from his exertions in his king's favor, Your Grace, and was forced to take the cure at his estates on the road back."

Francois' high-pitched laughter shredded the air. "Damn Bonnivet and that she-wolf Margaret! Damn them all! Charles? The bloody bastard Charles! Get out of here, all of you, now! I said we were hunting boar and by hell's gates, we shall!"

"Francois, my dear, my dear," came a new voice in the anteroom, and Mary knew it was the queen mother. "The news then is bad with all your rich deservings, my love. Here, dearest, come and talk. There are other roads to ultimate power for one so deserving, one chosen by God to rule, my love."

"But what a blow, mother. Damn Bonnivet!" Francois suddenly sounded like a small boy being comforted. Mary darted back from her listening post as their voices came nearer. They entered the bed chamber. Louise du Savoy had her arm about the king's

120

drooped shoulders and they sat on the edge of the mussed bed together, oblivious to the nervous, half-clad Mary. Francois' head was bent over his knees, and his voice was on the edge of sobs.

"All, all ruined, mother. Three million *lire* all for nothing."

"No, Francois. We shall rebuild. Only now we must go another way to keep from war with Charles' Spain."

He put his face in his spread hands. It was then that Louise du Savoy's surprised eyes took in the frozen Mary, but she only motioned her to silence and went on smoothly.

"You have already proved your greatness as a sol-dier-king, my dear. Now you shall prove your great-ness as a statesman-king. We shall bargain with England and your dear brother-king Henry VIII for al-liance against Charles. You shall convince them you bargain from strength not weakness, my dearest love." She stroked his head gently, rhythmically, and Mary marvelled at her control over the volatile king.

Finally, he raised his head. "The English, *oui*, a grand alliance between two powerful kings and their nations. I shall meet with him. *Oui*, I shall command him to come here."

"Not command, my son. Request, even implore. For strength can come from counterfeit gentleness, *oui*?"

Francois stood suddenly, almost brushing off his mother's clinging hands. "It shall be done, mother. No wonder Francois is a powerful king, for he has a verita-ble she-wolf for a mother, eh?" He laughed jaggedly and his eyes caught Mary's. She feared his wrath then, for she had beheld his weakness.

"Be dressed, *petite Anglais*, for Francois du roi kills a boar single-handed in the courtyard today. Kills a great slathering boar and anything else that gets in his way!"

Louise du Savoy's low voice cut in. "My dear, you will not risk such foolhardiness only to kill a boar? Unhorsed?"

"*Oui*, mother. I have vowed it. It pleases me, and I do it."

"Francois, you should realize . . ."

"And so, Marie," Francois interrupted his mother's plea, "be dressed quickly and join the gallery. Mother, come, for you shall be proud."

He strode toward the door then spun around sharply. "Though Marie Boullaine serves her purpose well, I almost wish I could see the sour, busy Ambassador Boullaine standing in her place, mother. I could put him to good use today, for now I need more English than one shy maid."

His brittle laughter floated back to the embarrassed Mary as she hastily shook out her full skirts and stepped into them. But Louise du Savoy swept from the room without another word or glance, and Mary was left alone under the portrait of the lady with the smiling eyes.

Francois had arranged the amusement for the day, but the mood of the courtiers at Fontainebleau was anything but festive. Mary noted tight little groups whispering as though they were waiting for the other royal fist to strike after the initial outbreak.

Francois darted about ordering his guards to move the barriers or change the wooden poles which blocked the grand staircase from the arena in which he would confront the pawing, grunting boar they could all see freshly penned by his trappers. Courtiers jostled each other at the narrow windows for a good view, latecomers and ladies stood on the staircase behind the barricades for the best position. Mary, newly changed and coiffed, joined Jeanne du Lac there.

"Need I even ask where you have been, Marie?" Jeanne asked icily with a raised brow. "Francoise du Foix was quite incensed when she realized you were with him all night, you know. She worries her hold is slipping, and she *does* keep track of us."

Mary could feel a hot blush spread on her cheeks, but she changed the subject. "Is the word well spread of Charles' victory as the new emperor?"

"*Oui*. And I hear du roi took it violently, even slapped the poor messenger from Bonnivet." She laughed in her silvery tones.

"It is true, Jeanne. I was there."

"Well! Will you tell me all of it?" There was a little silence. "Francoise declares you only interest him because you are different—English, I guess."

"And because of her mock sweetness," came Francoise's catty voice behind them suddenly. "Any man needs a little rest from an exciting gourmet diet at times." Her clear green eyes bored into Mary's as though she were daring her to answer.

"Indeed, Madam du Chateaubriand," Mary responded slowly, turning back to the wide-eyed Jeanne. "That is what His Grace indicates, too. Yet he finds it tiresome to have to knock and announce himself so that others can quickly vacate the place where he himself would rest."

Francoise's feline eyes narrowed, and she spun

123

sharply away. Jeanne nearly sputtered in disbelief that the sweet-tempered Marie had so bested the confident Francoise.

"Marie, tell me what happened," she begged as they settled themselves behind the other ladies. "To what do you refer? Tell me!"

"Later, Jeanne. I meant not to be so vicious. I fear I just wished to strike out, and, well—she was there."

A gasp of anticipation rose from the gathering as the boar was pushed and shoved by four trappers into the crude arena. Francois appeared clothed for hunting as she had seen him this morning. He swept past the clusters of ladies and vaulted the barrier at the foot of the steps bravely, his single sword held aloft. Everyone else cheered mightily, though Mary kept her chagrined silence. It came to her that she knew how the boar felt, ensnared, terrified, about to be skewered for the king's pleasure.

How Francois had laughed at her shame and fears that time in Queen Claude's room when he had summoned her while Claude and most of her ladies were at chapel. How he had seemed to revel in her outright terror they would be discovered in the queen's bed which he admitted he never visited anymore until it was time to get poor Claude with child again.

If one of the ladies had come in to see the English Mary Bullen with the French king astride her naked hips, or if the king's mother or sister—or Claude, or worst of all, her own father had seen that!

She shrugged and shook her head, not realizing Jeanne studied her intently. How she had suffered from the knowledge that Francois did not value her except as an occasional amusement; how her hatred for him

124

grew. Fantasies that he would love her as she had once loved him—shattered, all shattered now. And in the place of girlhood dreams grew a woman's realization of a world where hurt and pain were not only possible but certain.

"He is so brave and magnificent," Jeanne said loudly to no one in particular.

The boar pawed the cobbles of the courtyard, then charged at the king who leapt from his path laughing wildly. Francois jabbed at it once, as it made a raucous pass. The sword drew a crimson puddle of blood on its bristled back. Wide-eyed in fear, it smashed the barricade before the steps and vaulted the low rubble of the crude wooden poles. Horrified, the ladies on the steps screamed and scattered as the boar smashed its way up the staircase. It slavered and wheezed and shoved past. Mary crushed against Jeanne in panic. Its terrified rush left a black smear of blood on Mary's flying skirts. She heard herself scream as Francois and six armed courtiers charged past after the boar, now loose in the long gallery of the chateau. Mary trembled with fear and disgust as other people inquired of her well-being. Then they scurried after their king, and Jeanne pulled Mary along in their wake.

"You can tell the king it kicked you and he will be most guilty and solicitous for days, Marie. Oh, look at the path of his blood!"

Mary stood silently at the back of the courtiers crowding the doorway to the lovely salon now transformed into a trampled battleground between king and victim. Perhaps Francois will be injured or killed, Mary thought suddenly, and then crossed herself hastily for the wicked idea.

The beast ran in circles now, and nearly vaulted out of corners when Francois had almost trapped him. "Stay back! Stay back!" the king warned between gasps as he chased the terrified boar. "This is king's business alone!"

The curved tusks of the animal ripped a velvet drape as it charged, and its flying hoofs spun him madly on the thick carpet and polished floors. The king's third thrust went true. The hilt of Francois' sword drove into the stretched throat of the beast and it sank to its knees impaling itself further. It shuddered and heaved over on its side, one tusk digging into the plush carpet. Francois approached dramatically. He withdrew the bloodied sword and plunged it deep into the heart where it stayed, its silver hilt bobbing merrily above the slaughtered boar.

A tremendous cheer went up for the begrimed, sweating hero. His dark eyes gleamed, and his breath came swiftly through parted teeth. All were in awe of his nerve and prowess, but Mary felt suddenly sick, queasy and weak at her knees. She leaned against Jeanne for support.

"Does the blood sicken you, Marie? I thought Englishmen were marvelous hunters, too. Here, Marie, sit here and it will pass."

Jeanne helped Mary to a carved bench in the huge entryway of the chateau, then scurried back to the room where Francois was soaking in the adulation of his mignons.

Mary leaned her head back against the carved panelling and kept her eyes tight shut until the feeling passed. How foolish. She had seen animals trapped and slaughtered before, and it would be a popular pastime

126

at King Henry's court when she went home.

Home. Home was Hever, not London. Sometimes she thought she would never go home to Hever. If only her father would wed her to some English lord who would be kinder than Francois—someone truly affectionate and protecting. Her gaze drifted out the front doors over the ruined barricade and sought the deep blue-green of Fontainebleau's vast forests.

Jeanne scuttled back and broke her reverie. "They are coming this way, Marie. We are to have a banquet and dancing tonight and eat the very boar we saw killed!"

Mary stood as courtiers trooped back through the entry and down the steps to survey the fated barricade. Several bent to touch her bloodied skirts and to praise the bravery and finesse of their king again.

Then Francois swept by laughing, his beaming sister Marguerite on his arm and a frantic Francoise du Foix following behind. He stopped when he saw Mary's white face and offered her his other hand. "Marie, they tell me the boar bloodied your dress as he charged past with the king in hot pursuit. He did not harm you?"

"No. Thank you for your kindness, Your Grace." The sweet words turned to dust on her lips, but she had said them.

"Fine. I would not wish to begin better relations with your country by harming one of their most charming treasures, eh?"

As Mary took his arm, the king's eye caught Francoise's face. "And you, Madam, may go find your damned Bonnivet and warm his bed. I am certain he shall have need of such solicitation after his miserable failure in Germany."

127

Francoise's jade eyes showed no pain or anger as far as Mary could tell. She swept her king a low curtsey, still holding her proud head erect so that her full breasts were almost completely visible above her low-cut neckline. "Better to send me to far Muscovy and let me freeze to death, Your Grace. Though in shame or disfavor, I would dwell near the sun." She smiled brilliantly at her king, and Mary could feel him waver.

"Well, then," he returned, "see that you do not get so close that your lovely dress becomes singed by the sun, or that your fair skin feels its full heat."

"I would welcome it, Your Majesty, even if it meant I would be burned."

Francois laughed in delight and responded gaily, "Well, come along all of you. We have much activity left today."

Though Mary held the king's arm on the opposite side of Marguerite, Francoise du Foix's full swaying skirts nearly pushed her away as she chatted and laughed along side her king.

Chapter Nine
June 6, 1520

Picardy

They were to call it The Field of the Cloth of Gold, a magnificent meeting of sovereigns and nations on the smooth grassy plain between Guines and Ardres. Mary and Anne Bullen were thrilled to have been given over to the care of their father for the three-week spectacle. They were among their own countrymen, although Anne thought them crude and coarse in manners next to French courtiers. Most importantly, father had promised they would be presented to King Henry.

Mary was elated to be temporarily free of Francois' fickle whims for her presence. And what wonderful diversion the feasting, jousting, and elaborate entertainments would be—a far cry from Queen Claude's stuffy court. "Unfortunately," she sighed, "there is only one cloud in the sky." William Stafford was serving as liaison between her father and the English king, and she was going to have to put up with his annoying presence.

"Why have you attached yourself to this particular duty?" she asked Stafford coldly as soon as she had the opportunity. She intended to settle him in his place as quickly as possible, so he would not bother her over the days to come. She had learned to set Rene de Brosse back by copying some of Jeanne's and Francoise du Foix's cattiness, and she meant to be rid of the ever-watchful Mister Stafford immediately.

"I have not attached myself, Mistress Bullen. It is only slugs and snails and sticky courtiers which do that. I have been attached by His Grace, though a more pleasant and scenic assignment I could not have imagined." He had his hands linked behind his back and his muscular legs spread as he regarded her with amusement.

"Do you not consider yourself a sticky courtier, sir?"

"I serve His Grace at court not by design, Mary. He keeps me about him at his choosing—for his safety, he believes. I would be a well-content midlands farmer had I control of my life. But I will tell you of all that another time."

He turned away to gather the ambassador's papers as he heard Thomas Bullen's strident voice in the next room. A farmer? She was much puzzled by such foolishness from a man who obviously had the king's eye. And she was angry with herself that she felt intrigued by what he said when she had fully intended to dispense with him completely.

She turned and smiled vibrantly at her father who bustled in with several men in his wake, followed by her vivacious thirteen-year-old sister.

"Father says we may go to survey the royal arrangements, Marie. Everything is prepared for the arrival of Francois du roi and Henry Rex on the morrow. We are even to enter King Henry's beautiful palace!"

"Settle down, both of you and get riding gear if you wish to go," came her father's voice over Anne's. "Stafford, I am glad to see you are prompt. His Grace calls you Staff, I believe."

"Yes, my Lord."

"Then I shall too. I recall you were an able privy aide two years ago in Paris. I can use you well here. Keep close as we survey preparations and keep an eye on the girls, will you?"

"With greatest pleasure, my lord."

Mary was chagrined to see that last impudent remark amuse her father who was usually so stern, but everyone seemed to be in a fine mood on this day. She hurried to get her riding gloves and a large brimmed hat to shade her face on this hot, sunny day.

Their inspection party was not so intimate as Mary had visualized as they clattered fifteen strong out of old Guines Castle and followed the narrow road down toward the sloping plain. She and Anne rode lovely palfreys brought last week from England.

"There are some forty-five hundred courtiers or servants arrived at Calais to accompany His Majesty, including two-thousand horses," William Stafford said at her side as they cantered along.

"Tell us all about it and the court and His Grace if you please," Anne said, riding on Stafford's other flank.

He laughed. "Well, Mistress Anne, I fear we have not the time for all of that now as we are nearly arrived, but I would consider it an honor to converse at length with you later."

"We would be grateful, sir."

131

Mary thought of a scathing remark, but held her tongue.

They halted in awe at the view spread before them. Striped tents, hundreds of them, looking like fluted sea shells, sprang from the plain. A huge gilded tent which glittered in the sun pointed skyward. There were tournament fields and brightly painted tilt rails and flags, flags fluttered everywhere. The entire panorama was dominated by the English king's newly finished Palace of Illusions.

"It is marvelous," breathed Mary.

"Indeed, but I would expect as much from eleven thousand Dutch workmen, Wolsey's brain, and millions of treasury pounds," William Stafford commented.

They rode down toward the fabulous palace, and Stafford helped the two ladies dismount. Mary gazed up at the shiny glass windows, the battlemented walls and the four huge towers with mock arrow slits. Four golden lions topped the gatehouse pillars and Tudor pennants danced aloft in the gentle breeze.

"They say it was all built in England and then shipped over in parts," Mary put in. "But it looks like stone."

"How things look are often not what they are, Mary," William Stafford said, close in her ear. "It is only a beautiful sham—painted canvas over stout English timber. But stout English underpinnings may serve it well."

She ignored his cryptic comments and looked about for her father. He had already disappeared inside with his entourage, and she was annoyed to see that Anne must have tagged after them.

"Should you not go inside, Mister Stafford?"

"Shall we do so, Mistress Mary? And would you not call me Staff?"

"You said the king and your friends call you that, and—well, I am neither."

"I would be your friend, Mary Bullen."

She looked straight up into his eyes, and the impact nearly devastated her poise. The look was direct and piercing, yet so different from the wily scrutinies or lecherous looks to which she had become accustomed. Her legs felt like water, and she turned away to break the spell. "The fountains are lovely," she said finally. "Bacchus and Cupid aloft."

"Bacchus for good times and Cupid to show love between the English and the French, a tenuous love affair at best. Cardinal Wolsey has temporarily jumped off his secure seat on the fence between Francois I and the new Roman Emperor Charles, but it will not last. I prefer English to English marriages myself."

"You are somewhat of a cynic, Mister Stafford," Mary chided.

"The fountains, by the way, spout white wine, malmsey, and claret. The French masses will love the English king for that alone whatever peace comes from this meeting. They have ordered the common folk to keep at a distance of six miles or face arrest, but they will swarm here. You see, Mary, I am a realist and not a cynic at all."

They walked under the oval gatehouse entry and across a tiled floor. "They will think we are dawdling," Mary remarked, and walked faster. "I would stay closer to my father."

At her words William Stafford sat deliberately on a

133

long banquet bench by the huge trestle table in the center of the great hall. "You may be certain he will never be far away the next few weeks, Mary, for he will want to be in charge whenever you are near His Grace."

She stopped and turned toward him, annoyed that he could make simple statements sound so ominous.

"Before you scold me, Mary, I shall give you something to be angry about. But I hope you will think on my words and know they come from concern and not malice."

"I have heard quite enough of your comments, Master Stafford." Her voice sounded tremulous even though she sought to put him off with cold scorn. Damn them all for traipsing on ahead and leaving her here alone with this man!

"I must find the others," she said, and turned to flee. But he was quicker than she. He darted off the bench and had her firmly by the arms before she had gone four strides.

"Loose me!"

"You will listen, Mary. Are you afraid of what you might hear?"

"I shall call the others!"

"Do so and then all may hear of my warnings of your relationship to Francois and selected others."

Her heart stopped at his last word, and she began to tremble inside.

"Your reputation has preceded you, beautiful Mary, and may be unfair, but you must realize the quagmire ahead."

She ceased trying to pull away, and he led her back to the bench.

"I will listen. What do you have to say?"

"You realize, I am sure, the French court knows you have been one of Francois' several latest young mistresses—in addition to his about-to-be discarded du Foix."

Mary looked intently at her folded hands in her lap. "Yes, I know. Secrets are hard to keep when they involve the king."

"What French court gossips know, English court gossips soon know also, Mary."

She looked up, startled. "But Amboise is so far away from London!"

"The way at court—any nation's court—is to know all the business of one's own king and other kings. Pope Leo X in the Vatican probably knows how many times Francois bedded you."

Her face went white and a shudder ran through her body. Mother could even know, but at least she was never at the English court. How could she ever face the English king now?

"But Father said," she began and then stopped, realizing what William Stafford might think of her father if he knew she had been urged to continue her affair with the king.

"I knew it! I guessed it!" His words were angry and he hit his knee hard with his fist. "He no doubt counseled you that it was in your best interest," he hissed.

She could not lift her face to him, but she wanted to defend her father. How dare he question his betters, but she could not afford to anger him further since he knew so much already.

"You mentioned others, William." Her use of his first name seemed to soften his rugged features. "I pray you will not mention the others to my father," she went

135

on. "I had no control over what the king expected of me with his friends. He gave me no choice. But, please do not tell my father."

"I promise I will not, Mary. I need not, for he has known no doubt longer than I have, or has King Henry."

She cried aloud as though she had been hit in the stomach. "You are lying. The others—Father could not have known about the others. I never heard it about the court from anyone else!"

"Then you have not only been treading on quicksand, Mary, but you have had your beautiful blonde head in it."

"He could not know! He said nothing!" Her voice rose and, angered beyond further words at his lies, she raised her hand and slapped his face with all her strength. The crack resounded in the lofty room and she shrank back from him on the bench. A red mark slowly suffused his cheek.

He reached calmly for her wrists with his huge hands and pulled her closer to him on the bench. She went stiff, but her skirts made her slide to him across the polished wood. "Did striking me help the pain, Mary?" His voice was gentle and she longed to collapse against him, to sob her shame on his shoulder.

"I am not finished. Hate me if you will, but listen carefully. King Henry, my master whom I serve closely everyday, will find you most entrancing when your father dangles you before him. What red-blooded man would not? He knows of your reputation, but contrary to what you are thinking, it intrigues him, it titillates his sometimes jaded senses and bored mind."

She stared into William Stafford's dark eyes, mesmerized. How could he speak of his king this way?

"And when he sees you, sweet, your naive beauty, your youth, and blonde innocence, he will be quite ensnared. If your father should try to bring you home to England, and I predict he will, it will be a fine path to escape the trap into which you have fallen. But go home with your eyes wide open, not to let such entrapment happen again." He reached for her shoulders and shook her slightly. "Do you understand?"

"Yes, I think so. I would wish to go home."

"Home, Mary, but home to what? That is the danger. The time is ripe for the great Henry to think he loves you. He is long tired of Spanish Catherine who gives him dead sons. His mistress Bessie Blount—blonde and fair as yourself—bore him a son last year and his interest in her is also dead. Tread carefully, sweet Mary, with both eyes open, and do not trust the king or your father."

"Then whom am I to trust?" she challenged him. She lifted her head as she heard their fellow visitors approaching, her father's voice distinct among the others.

William Stafford pulled her to her feet. "I would tell you to trust me, Mary Bullen, but I do not savor another slap when I have you aroused. Still, I promise you that you will pay dearly some day for whatever slaps or scratches or sharp words you give me. You will pay, sweet Mary, but in a time and manner of my choosing."

She blushed and sputtered, but the others were in the room now and she turned away to compose herself.

"Mary, there is a secret passageway should the king need to escape from the gallery clear to Guines Castle! They dug it underground," Anne blurted as she hurried to Mary.

"There you are, Stafford," her father way saying. "We are going to swing around by Francois' golden tent on our return. S'blood, I wish the fountains spurted wine already. It is a damned hot day. Have you seen enough of the king's Palace of Illusions, Mary?"

"Yes, father," she spoke at last. "Quite enough for now."

They returned to the tethered horses and, much to her dismay, William Stafford helped her mount. "Did you hear that, Mary," he whispered in her ear. "It is rightly called the Palace of Illusions."

"I heard clearly enough, Mister Stafford."

"Then heed what you have heard," he added, and turned away to smoothly mount his own waiting steed.

Mary knew the moment she surveyed the glittering room she would never forget the sight. The clothes and coiffures were not as grand as those of the French, but she was in the dazzling midst of the Tudor court and her exiled English blood moved her beyond belief. If only father had brought her mother, she thought, her life would be complete for this one lovely moment.

Mary wore a blue satin gown with side slashings, and one of the deepest square necklines she had ever dared. Her golden tresses were swept back and piled layer upon layer above her fair brow and at her throat she wore a single huge pearl drop which had once been her grandmother's. Anne too, looked vibrant in crimson and white, her pale skin setting off her dark, eager eyes, her long sleeves characteristically dripping extra lace to hide the tiny deformity of her left hand.

Father ushered them into the opulent, buzzing crowd

which awaited the arrival of the king. Mary recognized few faces in the velvet, gilded swarm except her Uncle Norfolk and her cousin Sir Francis Bryan, who kissed her cheek lingeringly and complimented them all. Despite William Stafford's cruel words earlier in the day at Ardres, Mary was pleased to have her father hovering so close, and she summoned the courage to ask him her pressing question.

"What, Mary?" he responded, as she began to speak, his head swiveling slowly, his eyes far past her as he surveyed the assembly.

"I asked if I shall be going home soon, my lord father."

"Why did you think that, girl?"

"I am older now than many of the girls, and I—I just wondered."

"It is possible. I shall think about it tonight, or soon."

"I should love to go home to Hever, father."

"Hever is hardly what I had in mind for you, Mary. After your fine opportunities in the French court, I hardly . . ." His eyes darted to the back of the room in the sudden hush. "The king comes," he whispered.

Mary strained to see. Trumpet blasts split the close air, heads turned and people bowed in a surging wave as the Tudors entered and moved toward their chairs. Thomas Bullen had positioned his little brood well, for soon Mary could see the tall dark husband of Mary Tudor, and then the red-blond smiling giant, the king himself.

They curtseyed low and did not rise again until the royal family had seated themselves. Instantly, Mary saw her dear friend and guardian of earlier days, the king's beautiful sister, and her eyes filled with joyous tears. Her brother-king had forgiven her and she and her beloved Henry Brandon looked radiant side by side.

But Mary's adoring gaze was mostly for the king. It was hard to believe her father had served this great master for so long. She had only seen him once when she had held the Princess Mary's cloak and heard him promise her that if the French king died, she might wed elsewhere of her own choosing. She had quite forgotten he was so well-proportioned. His golden-red beard set off his ruddy complexion and slate-blue eyes. A blond giant to overcome his rival the dark satyr king, she thought proudly. The English monarch wore silver and white silks and massy golden chains draped across his powerful chest and shoulders in perfect balance to the brawny thighs and calf muscles bulging the silk of his hose and emphasized by gilded and jeweled garters. The flagrant, massive codpiece over the king's manhood was covered with a matching gold with jewels to offset his gold and jewel-edged collar as if to call special attention to his powerful face and loins.

It was only when father urged them forward that she noted the queen, pale and heavy in dark green, with a large crucifix leaning on her ample bosom. Another Claude, Mary thought, stunned by the yawning gap in vitality between this dynamic king and his quiet queen.

Even as the three Bullens approached the dais, they caught the king's eye, and he motioned his ambassador forward, his jeweled fingers sparkling in the light. "Thomas, where in Christendom is Wolsey? He should have been here for this reception!" His voice seemed to rise and fall in each sentence. Mary stood slightly behind her father, and Anne stood apart from them both, watching.

"Your Grace, I saw him in early afternoon and he yet had much to do at Ardres. He will be back soon, I am sure, with final arrangements."

"He had better be. These are his doing, all of it, and I will not be arriving in the morn before my brother Francois does. I will not be there standing about and waiting for the arrival of the French!"

"Even the finest details have received our close attention, Your Grace. And may I say your marvelous Palace of Illusion far outshines Francois' silken tent."

"Well, I mean to show them all the power and greatness of England. And what say our young English beauties, though raised at the French court? These are your daughters, are they not, my clever ambassador? A pox on you to hide such delights from our eyes."

His narrowed gaze glittered over them swiftly, and Mary was relieved to feel no romantic lure. William Stafford was quite mistaken, she thought, as King Henry turned to introduce them to his wife.

"My dear, Bullen's lovely flowers. Bred and raised behind your moated walls at Hever, eh?"

Henry and his ambassador laughed. "They have been educated for some years at the court of Francois, Catherine," the king plunged on, his eyes still on Mary. "A fine finishing school, no doubt." Mary paled at his final words, and it was suddenly Anne who answered smoothly.

"We enjoy the French court, but of course we miss our home at Hever and all of our beautiful England, Your Grace."

Queen Catherine's lips broke into a warm smile. "I

remember your lovely mother at court when I was not yet wed to His Grace,'' she said in accented English. ''Looking at your blonde daughter, my Lord Bullen, is quite like having the years rolled back. Do you not agree, my lord? She is so fair.''

''Yes, yes, my Catherine. But the years have gone by and here stands quite another lady, fresh and on the brink of a great experience, eh, Thomas?''

''Sire?''

''Surely your Mary is old enough now to return to her home. She seems ripe for marriage. Is she betrothed?''

''No, Your Grace.''

''Then we shall make her a good English marriage before some French fop gobbles her up, Thomas. Catherine could use a lady-in-waiting from a fine family such as your own.''

Thomas Bullen bent low in gratitude, and the queen kept silent.

''I always hearken to your advice, Sire. I shall think on the possibilities. Anne, of course, should stay longer, as she is but thirteen.''

''Anne? Ah, yes, but it was Mary we were speaking of.''

''I understand, Your Grace.''

''And Thomas, though I have heard from you and my cardinal, I would like to hear about the character of Francois du Roi from the lips of one who has lived in his court recently. It may help me to deal better with him if I know how much we are alike,'' he said loudly, for the curious crowd near the Bullens had grown two and three heads deep.

''In intelligence and wit there is no comparison,

142

Sire," Thomas Bullen put in grandly. "And Mary shall be available to offer you her opinion should you desire it."

"Do not stray far, Thomas," were the last distinct words Mary heard as others took their place near the king and the voices behind them became a dull steady buzz.

"Where was your tongue, girl?" her father inquired out of the side of his mouth as they departed the press of the crowd. "Even Anne spoke. I thought you knew how to handle kings by now. Flattery and smiles and speak up sweetly. You are not to stand there like a hollow golden goddess. Your beauty will take you only so far, and he does not fancy ninnies!"

Tears stung her eyes at the sudden rebuke and a lump caught in her throat. "I was not bid to speak, father. You spoke only of me, not to me."

"At least he will probably speak to you later. See that you find a sweet tongue by then!"

"Yes, I will, father."

"Perhaps Marie was too much in awe, father. With her beauty she need not cultivate wittiness as much as I," put in wide-eyed, serious Anne.

"Yes. Well, both of you at least look your best for the Bullens today. You know your brother would give his best falcon to be here, so make us all proud. I do not intend to have Mary leaving one royal court unless it is to enter another. Do you understand, Mary? You are not going home to embroider with your mother in the long afternoons at Hever nor to breed children on some rural estate."

He sighed and patted Mary's shoulder. "Dry your eyes, child. I meant not to be harsh on this wonderful

143

evening. It is only that I will have the best for you and for Anne. I should have explained this all before, but I have been much taken with king's business. Do you understand?''

''I think I understand much more now father,'' Mary said quietly.

''Fine, fine. Now we shall just bide our time for the king to remember he wishes to talk to you about Francois. Would you like to go back near the throne and speak to your former mistress Princess Mary? You were once aggrieved to leave her, I recall. She is much in the king's favor again.''

''Yes, I would appreciate that, and she has never met Anne.''

They wound their way back through the clusters of courtiers toward the dais, and the beautiful Tudor Rose sighted Mary and her father. How lovely the king's sister looked, Mary thought. Her gown was dazzling crimson to offset the rich hue of her lips and cheeks. Golden ribbons were threaded through the slashes in the red, tight bodice of the gown, and emeralds in gold filigree rosettes hung from her slender neck and her tight, chain-link girdle. Twisted strips of fox and whitest ermine lined the puffed outer sleeves and ornate crimson headpiece, separating the dark, rich velvets and brocades from her creamy skin, like a beautiful painting set in a precious frame. Princess Mary Tudor, now the adored Duchess of Suffolk, held out her graceful hand to her old friend Mary Bullen before they had emerged from the press of people.

''Mary, my dear, how you have blossomed!'' the princess marveled. ''My lord, do you remember the charming girl who was my English maid of honor when first we wed in Paris?"

Charles Brandon's dark eyes surveyed Mary's flushed face and the warm embrace his wife offered the girl. "Of course, I remember, and she is much grown to a beauty. You have conquered the king's heart, I hear."

For an instant Mary thought he spoke of King Henry and then blushed to realize that William Stafford's words must have been true. The English court knew of her affair with Francois du roi.

"Hush, my lord," his wife put in. "Anyone would be taken with her beauty, and we need not your commentary on it."

She turned intimately to Mary and lowered her voice. "You must forgive him, my dear, for he still bears enmity against the French king and your father. I shall see you do not suffer for his feelings."

Gratefully, Mary introduced Anne to the duke and duchess. The dark haired girl handled herself with skillful aplomb, again to the pleased surprise of Mary and the avid eye of Thomas Bullen.

"Shall we see you at court? Does she return home to England now, my lord Ambassador?" Princess Mary questioned Thomas Bullen directly to warm the icy air between her husband and her brother's ambassador.

"His Majesty was just suggesting the idea, Your Grace. Perhaps if we could find Mary a suitable husband, she could live at court. She has never forgotten your kindnesses to her."

"Then we shall see you, Mary. I shall urge my dear sister-in-law Queen Catherine to consider your service in her household, or maybe, even in mine."

At that last suggestion, Thomas Bullen seemed to

hustle his daughters away, but their proximity to the throne drew the king's attention again, and His Grace rose to follow them into the crowd. For countless minutes Henry Tudor smiled, and cajoled, and flattered Mary, hanging on her every word and opinion of Francois and the French court. Mary smiled, cajoled, and flattered in return under her father's watchful gaze. The time passed swiftly and Mary could remember little of it afterwards, like a once-vivid dream that has flown by morn. All she could think of the entire way back to Guines was how William Stafford's warnings could have been sound advice after all. She noticed Anne's starry-eyed gaze and her father's smug approval not at all.

Chapter Ten
June 16, 1520

Picardy

For ten days the plain of Ardres rang with trumpets, shouts and applause. The nobility of two realms swarmed among the gaily colored tents which studded the tiny parks and bordered the tilt yards, dancing greens, and wrestling circles. The great folk of the two nations intertwined even as did the Hawthorne tree of England and the raspberry bush of France in the golden tent where the blond and raven haired royal giants had met and embraced to begin the festivities. Serious business was conducted at this entente cordiale: Wolsey met with Louise du Savoy; Suffolk met with Bonnivet; financial promises were made; and King Henry's young daughter was once again engaged to the French prince. Each side eyed the other through the haze of laughter and tried to bridle natural suspicions behind forced smiles. Banter and joviality flowed as profusely as the wine from Henry's fountains, but beneath the golden surface lay the stoney gray foundation of distrust.

For Mary Bullen, the days raced by as swiftly as the huge destriers which charged at each other along the gilded tilt rails. She mingled freely with both courts, but felt most comfortable with the English. Though she did not know them well, she made new acquaintances daily and was convinced their interest in her meant they could not possibly know of her besmirched reputation, which William Stafford had so cruelly flaunted in her face. The English king himself sought her out for conversation whenever he noticed her about, and a tiny plan began to grow in her mind. She would show King Francois how little she thought of him if she could arrange to be often near the great Henry. And indeed, if she were going back to England as had been hinted at and promised by both her father and the king, what had she to fear of reprisal?

Mary accompanied Princess Mary, Rose Dacre, and several English ladies past the tournament gallery decked in Tudor green and white on one side, and Francois' tawny and white bunting on the other toward the lawn where wrestling had been the favorite entertainment all afternoon. "My father has said that our king is a wonderful wrestler, Your Grace," Mary offered.

"My dear brother is splendid at whatever he pursues," smiled the princess proudly, "and as king he must surpass his nobles. Francois, as I recall, was most admirable, also. I thank the blessed Lord we have been able to keep those two from challenging each other at the lists or elsewhere. My Lord Suffolk jousted against Bonnivet and was victorious today. As long as we let their favorite courtiers represent them on the field or the list, I have hopes that we may keep this assembly peaceful."

But how I should like to see them set on each other

148

and Francois bested by our English king, Mary thought passionately. "It is said both kings will soon run out of champions to hurl at each other, Your Grace."

"If they do, Mary, we shall be true patriots and challenge the French king's powerful mother and sister or perhaps Francoise du Foix," the princess joked, and Mary joined her in giggles.

"But, Your Grace," put in Rose Dacre with a brilliant smile, "the Lady Mary Bullen has already challenged Francoise du Foix."

Laughter froze on Mary's lips at the barb and the princess came to her aid. "Rose! Mary was a dear friend to me when I was in sore need, and I will not have her teased for your silly amusement even though the times may be gay and frivolous."

"Yes, Your Grace. I meant nothing by the jest, Mary."

Mary's gratitude flowed out to the beautiful princess as they joined the irregular circle of courtiers around the fringe of the wrestling ring. Today she and Mary Tudor had both chosen green gowns in honor of the Tudor king, though of course, the Duchess of Suffolk's gown was much grander than what her father's allowance could purchase. Mary Bullen's gown was a willow green, simply cut and offset only by the vibrant pink satin lining of the sleeves and the narrow pink stripes along the fitted bodice. Mary Tudor's gown sparkled with sunlight glittering across the jade green sheen of the fabric and winking at the jewels that studded her delicate kid leather belt, gloves and even her square-toed slippers. Anne Bullen, in brightest canary yellow silks, standing near with some other court maidens, including Jeanne du Lac, approached the Princess Mary and swept her a graceful curtsey.

"My lord father's aide William Stafford wrestles next, Your Grace," Anne told her. "He has been very kind to Mary and me. And," she announced grandly, her eyes sparkling, "he wrestles with the brother of the French king's mistress, Francoise du Foix. It is the famous Lautrec, one of the king's finest generals."

Mary's fingernails dug into the palms of her hands as she fought to keep from showing emotion. That William Stafford wrestled for King Henry she cared not at all, but he wrestled Lautrec, the wily courtier to whom Francois had given her when he lost a bet to him gambling. What if Lautrec saw her here and remarked to Stafford about it? That meddler already knew too much to be trusted. Blurred scenes of how Lautrec had used her far into the night in his deep bed flashed through her mind, and she shut her eyes tight, hoping to stop the flood of memory.

"Sister, are you quite all right?" Anne inquired at her side. "Is the day too warm for you?"

"No, Anne, my thanks. I am fine now. But shall we sit up here in the gallery instead of standing about the ring where we might be a distraction?"

"It is much more exciting here, Mary," chided Anne, as though she were speaking to a child.

"Yes, Mary," added the princess. "We have done enough sitting around. Let us stay here—at least until my lord husband or the king spot us and make us behave." She laughed musically again as the two wrestlers came into the ring and bowed to their monarchs.

"King Henry looks grand today," Mary noted proudly. Though he and Francois sat in the shade next to their two colorless queens both dripping with jewels,

150

she thought he far outshone the dark Francois. His red beard looked almost golden, and both kings sported closely cropped hair having ended their mutual vow not to cut hair or beard until they met on The Field of the Cloth of Gold. To her delight, Henry nodded and lifted his huge hand to her, or was it to his sister Mary who stood beside the Bullen sister? At any rate, he did not summon them to join the royal party and let them stand about the ring like the other courtiers. How she wished Francois had noted the English king's probing stare and her own radiant smile and nod in return.

Wearing only breeches and a waist sash of bright green and white, Stafford faced his brawny opponent. Stafford's tanned chest was covered with dark curly hair in contrast to Lautrec's smooth paler skin. They crouched and circled about each other warily, each waiting for an opening to grasp the other. Mary could distinctly hear their even breathing, and Lautrec seemed to talk to himself in low tones. Then Stafford dove for Lautrec's thighs, his brown head butting against the Frenchman's hip as Lautrec flung himself backwards, and they went to their knees on the smooth turf. But Lautrec reached for Stafford's arm and tried to twist it behind and they spun away together, half-rolling, half-kneeling. Their breath rasped in their throats and grunts and groans came from their parted lips as they struggled and strained. Advice and cheers went up from the encircling crowd and the royal gallery, and Mary wondered if Francois *du Roi* even regretted the night he had ordered his "golden Mary" to lie between those strong muscular thighs of his friend Lautrec.

It had all started amusingly enough that night at the

gambling tables of Francois' huge Medieval redecorated castle at Amboise, Mary remembered, as her unwilling mind darted back to almost a year ago. It all started so amusingly, but in truth it turned out to be the violent end of little, golden Mary's innocent love for Francois du Roi, however crudely he himself had used her.

All evening from across the golden brocaded gaming tables Francois' comrade and military general, Lautrec, had been eyeing her strangely. Everyone knew the power and wiliness of this ally to the king: everyone knew the short, stocky, square-cut man was the hero of the Treaty with the Swiss, the Governor of rich Guyenne province—and the brother of the king's influential mistress Francoise du Foix. But Mary had never seen this man—any man here but Francois and that silly Rene de Brosse—leer at her so.

Eventually, wishing to avoid Lautrec's stare, for the rude gaze in the blunt, welted face was increasingly upsetting, she tried to concentrate on the cards and the outrageously escalating wagers. Mary sidled up to Jeanne du Lac and turned her head away to whisper, "Jeanne, do you think Lautrec has drunk entirely too much? He has never even noted me before tonight, I vow, and now—"

Jeanne's lovely face went instantly intent and her painted mouth went round in surprise. "Blessed saints, Marie! It really is you la General has been ogling all evening? I was wondering, and could hardly tell from way over here in this press of courtiers. He is not usually one for the roving eye, or so I hear from his cousin Albret. But really—he is staring again right this moment so do not look up. Oh, heavens, this is rare."

"It is stark raving nonsense and you know it," Mary hissed, but her stomach began to twist in an intricate knot at something Francois had murmured to her after dinner.

"I will send Fragonard for you by ten after the gaming," he had said, "unless that damn Lautrec gets too lucky again and insists I pay my little wager."

"Little wager?" she had inquired. She knew, everyone knew the king bet huge sums, horses, or whole estates on the gaming tables when he fancied he was bored. But surely whatever he had promised the wily Lautrec if he won at gaming today could not take all night to pay.

"Marie, I said," Jeanne whispered directly in her ear, "that Francois is boiling angry. Look, he has lost that whole pile of markers to Lautrec!"

It was true. Lautrec's ruddy face beamed at the victory while Francois rose glumly and his clustered, chattering *mignonnes* had the presence of mind to scatter quickly to avoid whatever scene would ensue. Francois never lost gracefully.

"Your night—again, Lautrec," Francois said low as Jeanne pulled Mary away toward the entrance to the great hallway.

"Come on, you goose," Jeanne scolded. "The king is livid under that apparent control, and I for one do not wish to be in his way. You can be a great ninny and stand about waiting for the back of du roi's hand or returning Lautrec's hot stares if you want, but I am for bed!"

"Yes, yes, I too, Jeanne," Mary said, and went up the vast sweep of oak painted staircase hung with heavy-framed paintings of mythological characters, to the bedroom she shared with Anne.

"*Bon nuit*, then, Marie," Jeanne turned back to say. "And take it from one who has been about this realm a bit more than you, *cherie*—do not ever flirt back at Lautrec. They say that frightening face has a bad temper and spoiled nature behind it. And—" she lowered her voice even more as she wiggled her fingers in that peculiar wave of hers— "they say he beats his wife. *Adieu*."

Mary waved to Jeanne as the lovely girl went three doors down the sconce-lighted hall to her own room. How she wished the king would not send for her tonight and she and Annie could just talk, remembering days at Hever before all of these terribly complicated relationships and entangled rumors. They say . . . they said, Jeanne always repeated so avidly.

But Mary was no sooner in her rooms wondering where Anne was and staring at her worried face in the small gilt-frame mirror, than someone knocked on the door, and she stepped, suddenly afraid, to open it.

"Monsieur Fragonard," she breathed as her glance took in Francois' favorite silvery-tongued and silvery-dressed messenger.

"*Oui*, Mademoiselle Boullaine. I am a bit early, I know. Du Roi said you must come immediately."

"Yes, but it is surely not yet ten and he said—"

"But with all the pressures of the ah—evening you have witnessed, you understand a few necessary changes here and there and you will comply fully, I know."

His words, his look made her pause even as he indicated she should follow him. Had this cold creature actually smiled when he had said that one phrase—

154

comply fully?

At a loss for words, she closed her door and swept along beside him. It suddenly annoyed her how he seemed to order her about, to know she would obey. But when had she ever given him cause to believe otherwise?

As they passed into the edge of the vast warren of halls and rooms that housed the king's retainers, Fragonard paused and knocked on a door. It was opened immediately by a serving woman Mary remembered was named Isabelle. Mary breathed a sigh of relief when the tall Francois loomed behind the woman's shoulder. Fragonard closed the door and was gone.

"Your grace," she greeted him and a quick curtsey was all she managed before Francois swept Isabelle aside with one arm and took her shoulders.

"Marie, I— You have got to get ready for bed right away. Isabelle is here to help and I shall wait until you are ready."

"But we never needed—"

"Dearest little golden English girl," he began almost poetically, but then a frown crushed his lofty eyebrows down and he began to pace. "Just do it, Marie. Go on! I have something to explain to you."

She had stood there like a wooden doll, frozen in increasing shock, panic, and grief as Isabelle's steady hands divested her of her clothes and sponged her quickly with rose water. The king's jerky words went on explaining how he had wagered much to his boon companion Lautrec—explaining what he had wagered and lost.

Mary pulled away from the startled Isabelle as she tried to dust her with powder, and a fine, white cloud of it drifted to the carpeted floor. The king's sneeze had nearly drowned out her protest at first: "No, my lord king! Not I! That is impossible!"

Francois du Roi shoved Isabelle away and she went gladly, merely draping a pure white silk gown over Mary's naked shoulders. The gown slid silkily down off her back and hips immediately as Mary stepped back and tried to pull away from Francois.

"No, you cannot mean it," she heard her voice say. But was that her voice truly, she marvelled, for it sounded so deadly calm and her insides were fluttering terribly.

"*Oui*, Marie. One night. One night only I told him. Look, sweet, he favors you, at least your blonde look of innocence and purity."

"Innocence and —." She could not repeat his words and she only stared open-mouthed at his audacity.

"Sweet Marie, do not cry. I told him you would be willing if I asked you. Do not cry, sweet, or you will ruin the eye colors on that beautiful face."

She went stone cold and rigid in his arms then as all the lies she had told herself these months about her fancied, handsome *du Roi's* love for her paraded themselves across the stage of her mind laughing, taunting.

"No," she said again and her gaze blurred the elaborately embroidered, jeweled ribbon on Francois' broad right shoulder where she stared wide-eyed. "No, you would not do this. I cannot."

"Listen to me," he said low, stooping to pick up her robe, draping it over her shoulders, then shaking her once. "You will do it for me. I have favored you, coddled you. Lautrec is a friend to me and I have given my word. He expects a frightened little innocent—it will please him, so do not think he demands anything fancy or elaborate as he might from the others if his tastes ran to that. Just go along and keep those tears off your lovely face or I swear, I will give some lurid report of your demeanor here to your precious father Ambassador Boullaine.''

Her eyes focused on his then and she hoped the utter contempt of her stare hid the naked fear she felt at that threat to tell her father.

''Never, never dare this again,'' she heard a woman's voice say as he hurried her toward the big waiting bed and pushed her between silken sheets. She stared up at the draped, brocaded, crested underside of the vast canopied bed and realized clearly for the first time she was even awaiting Lautrec in his own bed under his own governor's crest of Guyenne. She did not glance up at the nervous king again. She enjoyed his unease and did not even look his way when he began his recital of how this night would grieve him—to be away from his dear Marie and suffer the pangs of jealousy and remorse.

Finally, he stopped talking. A clock ticked somewhere and the fire crackled. Her own breathing quieted. Francois still paced in his velvet slippered feet. Like a nervous panderer, she thought. Her mind floated, somehow a blank, except for the little voice which kept urging her to shriek at him that the great *du Roi* of France was no better than a liar, thief, and a whoremonger!

The memories spun and twisted at her like the two wrestlers here at her feet, and her mind returned with a jolt from that terrible memory of her night with Lautrec.

157

The fighters were down on the grass again. This time it was the Frenchman who rode Stafford's powerful body. The Englishman's great tawny shoulder almost brushed the chalked edge of the circle. Suddenly, Mary heard herself crying out for William Stafford, whom she ordinarily detested, but how wonderful it would be to see the smug Lautrec beaten and Francois' honor diminished before all.

"Come on, Staff, you can beat him. Get up, get up, please," she heard herself screech like the lowest fish-monger on the Paris streets.

The men nearly lay at her feet and she felt an over-whelming urge to kick out at Lautrec or to shove him off the writhing form of the Englishman. "Staff, Staff, come on!" she shouted again, oblivious to the stares of the princess and her sister.

And Lautrec, this grunting, straining, powerful man who grasped and grabbed at William Stafford now, had done the same to her that night of black memory. He had gloated over her, examined her as he leered and re-marked foul things as though she were a prize brood mare. She had fought to keep her mind a blank and just have it all over with, but he had expected more than silent stoicism from the *petite Anglaise blonde*—he had wanted fear and pain. He had turned her over his horri-ble legs which Staff leaned so hard into now and spanked her until she turned and writhed and twisted and showed him the life he wanted. There had been no use fighting him or denying him his way as he had pressed her down under him in his big bed. Her body had been sore for days from his powerful thrusts, de-manding mouth, and rough hands. Yes, she hated Lautrec, but she detested Francois far more for his bru-

158

tal treachery.

Suddenly, Stafford gave a great grunting heave, and Lautrec's strong body seemed to twist off his nearly-pinned man. Stafford dove at Lautrec's shoulders and pinned him down heavily as the marshall began to count, "One . . ." Mary held her breath. To have Lautrec shamed was some vindication, though she could share it with no one. "Two . . ." Unfortunately, it had to be the meddling William Stafford who was her unknowing champion. "Three . . . Honor to King Henry and his gentleman usher, Master William Stafford."

The crowd cheered and applauded and the men rose wearily and grasped hands. To Mary's delight, Lautrec looked like a sweaty, grass-stained field hand in his ruined tawny and white. The men bowed to the royal box and, before he followed the defeated Lautrec from the ring, Stafford turned in their direction and bowed low to Princess Mary, his eyes and teeth white against his sweaty, tanned face.

Francois was obviously quite miffed, but Henry pounded him on his velvet back good naturedly and reminded him that the French champions had earned many a fall and tournament point over the last week. Yet it was clear to all that the English, though from a smaller, poorer nation, held the balance of athletic prowess.

"My dear brother," King Henry was saying in a booming voice, his arm still draped around Francois' silken shoulders, "I would try you for a fall in a friendly bout. Will you accept?"

"Oh, no, my Henry," Mary heard the princess beside her murmur under her breath, "this is not wise."

"Indeed I accept, brother Henry," intoned Francois loudly, bowing and smiling to the rapt gallery. As they stood and made their way down to the field, both queens put out their hands to detain their husbands and implore them to be seated, but the mood was set—the challenge lay there in the sun for all to see.

Bonnivet seconded his master, helping him remove his doublet and shirt while the crowd watched to see the powerful French king half stripped before them. The Duke of Suffolk hastened to assist his king, his dark smooth hair in sharp contrast to Henry Tudor's mane and beard which gleamed in the light.

"Both are magnificent," Rose Dacre said too loudly in the hush, and Mary nodded wordlessly. She hoped she never saw Francois' bare chest again as long as she lived. Like a lion compared to a sleek fox, King Henry's massive chest and arms were covered with golden hair.

The royal opponents stepped gingerly over the now-blurry chalk circle, and bowed in tandem to their nervous queens. There was no cheering or raucous advice from the crowd. It was as though all of them around the circle stood in a sorcerer's trance. Then Bonnivet and Suffolk began to shout encouragement and soon the din of voices rose. Other courtiers strolling in the area came bounding in to swell the cheering crowd, and Princess Mary wrung her hands in nervous anguish.

The English king side-stepped Francois and stuck a brawny leg behind him hoping to trip the lithe man backwards, but Francois twisted from the attempt and Henry nearly toppled over. They recovered their stances and began their stalking anew, their eyes boring into each other's. Then Francois darted forward. Henry's great arms reached to encircle the French king's trunk. Swiftly, Francois bent, then straightened. The King of England flipped over and lay flat on his back.

The screams died to nothing. Francois, too, looked stunned and froze like a statue. In the hush King Henry towered to his feet and said plainly, "I will have another bout for a fall. Now. And then we shall see."

Mary's stomach churned with excitement and fear. She longed to see the great Henry throw the confident Francois, but she knew the results could bring chaos and ruin to this lovely Field of Gold.

Amazingly, like a mirror vision, the two sisters of the kings swept into the wrestler's circle and curtseyed to their brothers. Mary had not even seen Marguerite in the swollen crowd, but she had been fully aware of Mary Tudor's anxiety.

"You were both wonderful, spectacular!" said Marguerite in her halting English to the two sweating giants. Princess Mary chose the tack of taking her brother's arm and clinging to his clenched fist while curtseying to the French king and Marguerite.

"As once queen of your nation, I was often honored to see your greatness and prowess, Francois du Roi, and I have often thought, as I did today, what a godlike match you and my dear brother king make in all endeavors."

Both Claude and Catherine had descended from their perches by this time and Catherine added the ultimate soothing balm. "Dinner is served now in the king's fair Palace of Illusions," she said in her strangely accented French, and then repeated it in English, though everyone present understood the French well enough. "Please join us all in a stroll to the banqueting hall.''

Momentarily, all focused on the tiny wrestling circle crowded now with the two kings, their queens, and dear sisters. Mary noted William Stafford across the sea of faces and wondered vaguely how much of the bout he had witnessed. Then Anne tugged gently on her sleeve, and they drifted along in the whispering waves of courtiers meandering toward the huge Palace of Illusions.

It was King Henry's turn to stuff the royal and noble masses with delicacies and wine. Each night the host king strove to offer some viand or decoration or delight to top the previous offerings. Although only three hundred elite of the thousands present at these lengthy revels were feasted each day in the presence of the sovereigns, the surprises tonight took their breath away. Not only was real gold plate used instead of the customary trenchers of day-old bread, but each diner was supplied with a spoon and fork to use at the meal, rather than making do with their own spoons and no forks. Still, the most marvelous titillation was yet to come. After the pheasant with baked quince, venison bucknade, stuffed partridges, dolphin and thirty peacocks with lighted tapers in their beaks, and numerous toasts with heady glasses of sweet Osney from Alsace, the cupbearers and servers rolled in a massive subtlety of an exact miniature replica of the Palace of Illusions with orangeade moats and huge Tudor roses and Francois' salamanders on all corners. A ripple of applause went up and King Henry glowed with pride.

Mary sat between Anne and Rose Dacre at a table of mostly English ladies. She had a clear view of the head table which was raised on a dais, and if she craned her head a bit, she could see her father at the next table with her amusing cousin Francis Bryan. Twice when she looked their way, she caught the all-seeing eye of William Stafford seated near them so she gave up looking about the vast hall and concentrated on the chatter at the table. The first time the conversation truly seized her attention was when the subject suddenly became Francois' belabored mistress, Francoise du Foix.

"Look at her standing up there at the head table, flaunting herself in front of everyone—and next to his queen!" hissed Rose Dacre. Mary *did* look. Indeed, the beauteous Francoise was leaning over Francois' chair as he smiled up at her chatting. Queen Claude looked elsewhere as usual, but the English king was all eyes.

"I warrant he summoned her," put in Anne. "Even she does not have the nerve to prance up there unbidden."

"Anne, please," Mary chided gently, amazed that her little sister could sound so worldly. Has she ever talked about me like that? she suddenly wondered.

"I cannot fathom a court so unchristian as the French. Imagine actually flaunting one's mistress before the court and queen!" Jane Dorset said, her narrow-eyed gaze riveted on Francoise. "People may know of Bessie Blount and even His Grace's bastard son, but he never displays her that way!"

"A lady of the French court—Jeanne du Lac, Anne—once told me that she thought it most uncivilized that the English king had to hide his mistresses and pretend he had none when everyone knew he did," Mary said quietly, and the beautifully coiffed heads within hearing swiveled toward her. "Though not hav-

163

ing lived at the English court, I know not for certain how things stand," she added.

"His Grace does not go through a woman a week, as we have heard the French king does, Mary," came Rose Dacre's unmistakably pointed voice. "Perhaps, since you have been at the French court, you could tell us of that."

Mary felt the color flow to her cheeks, and she kept silent. "I meant not to criticize His Grace," she offered, "and when I return home to England, I know I shall have much to learn."

"Granted, Mary, but you *do* seem a quick learner," Rose parried and, discomfitted that no one else joined their repartee, she observed, "Well, here comes Francois' *mistress en titre* now, and her charming face looks like an absolute thundercloud!"

With her head held high, Francoise approached their table, chatting and nodding to those she recognized. Eventually, she halted her glittering progress behind Rose Dacre. Mary almost wished she had known of Rose's words and had come to scold her for her impudence.

"Marie Boullaine," came Francoise's sweet voice in lilting French, "Francois *du Roi* wishes to speak with you at his table. I did not ask him the reason, perhaps some message for your father."

Embarrassed, Mary rose and stepped over the bench on which she sat. She held her tongue until she and Francoise were out of hearing range of her dinner partners and then said, "If Francois *du Roi* had a message for my father, he could easily summon him, as you well know."

A smile still on Francoise's lovely face, she answered

164

evenly, "Perhaps he intends to parade all of his conquests before the English king in order, little Boullaine. Actually, I know he only wishes to hurt and humiliate me, to bring me to heel and back to his bed a willing victim like yourself. You may tell him, if you will, that it will take much more than trying to humble me by sending me to fetch his little English slut to make me lose my spirit!" Francoise stopped then, apparently surprised at her own vehemence, and Mary ached to slap that painted red smile so near.

"I shall tell him all you have said, Francoise du Foix, now, in front of Queen Claude and my King Henry. Then perhaps I shall hear when I am at home in England of your retirement to your dear husband's chateau far from court." Mary turned away before the other woman could respond, and mounted the dais.

Francois, resplendent in deep purple velvet, contrasting with the English king's rich crimson doublet and hose, held out his hand to her. She felt compelled to take it, though the raised red eyebrows of King Henry worried her. Francois immediately fired his first salvo in hearing range of his rival king. "You must come soon to visit my golden tent, Marie. I have not seen you much of late. Do the English keep you hostage? The ceiling of the tent is the wonderful star-lit sky Master da Vinci painted for our fine banquet, when you and I were dressed alike and strolled under our own heavens. Do you remember, Marie?"

Mary nodded and offered a shallow bow in silence. As she rose, Francois began a flowery thanks to Henry for the beautiful maids of England. "I urge you to send us all you can spare, my brother Henry," Francois chortled.

Henry Tudor smiled thinly but did not laugh. Mary could sense the tangled tensions. She had never before been with them when they were together. Was the cause only the foolish wrestling bout, or more?

"Mary, of course, being of marriageable age now, will be coming home immediately," Henry said flatly.

"Indeed? I had not heard of this. I am much grieved. And whose sudden decision is this? Golden Marie, how do you feel about this command," Francois probed, his narrowed dark eyes upon her.

"I shall be happy to return to my home, Your Grace, for I am true bred English, even though your court has given me French polish. Of course, I shall greatly miss the kindness of our dear Queen Claude. She has been most considerate of me always, no matter what foolish mistakes I have made."

Her heart rose in her throat at the audacity of the reply she had so long desired to give. She tried to smile sweetly and look innocent of her motives. Francois glared but a moment and Henry's voice was lighter, almost jovial as he spoke.

"Do not grieve the loss of one of your queen's maids so greatly, brother Francois. I assure you, such beauty and wit will not be wasted. I personally shall find 'golden Mary' a suitable English husband, and she will serve at the court of her king."

Mary could see the muscles in Francois' jaw go taut and his slender fingers wrap tightly around his goblet filled with ruby wine. "I envy her husband his treasure," he said. "Perhaps, my trusted Henry, if you and I are as alike as your dear sister claimed today, after you were thrown in our wrestling bout, I shall envy you too, eh?" Francois' brittle laughter filled the air as

Mary curtseyed and turned away, though she had not been formally dismissed. She could feel the myriad eyes of the room on her, but she had had quite enough of the tense banter between these two powerful magnets of influence.

"Mary," King Henry's voice floated to her, and she turned again.

"Your Grace?"

"I am sending for your father and intend to discuss some diplomatic matters with him in a few moments. I would wish you to wait for me—and your father—in the antechamber."

"As you wish, Your Grace."

"I do not order you, Mary," came his now-hushed voice. "I only request."

She thought instantly of Francois' same words to her once—words that lied to her foolish heart before he seduced her in that tiny room at Amboise.

"I shall be there, Sire." She managed a little smile but she felt drained now, embarrassed, proud and afraid. Relieved to see both queens still turned away from their husbands in continual conversation, she stepped from the dais.

When the confrontation with Francois that she had longed for was over and she had exited down the narrow hall lined with hanging tapestries, her knees went weak and she began to tremble uncontrollably. She sat gratefully on a velvet-cushioned chair in the anteroom. In the vast hall with its vipers and sly foxes, huge bearlike Henry seemed a distant dream. She closed her eyes to gain poise and control before they would be on her again—the king, her father. She prayed God she would never see Francois at close range again, the god-like

167

Francois du roi who shattered little girl's dreams for his own pleasure and amusement—and to pay gambling debts.

"Mary, are you feeling well enough to stay, or may I take you back to Guines?"

Her eyes shot open at the familiar voice—Staff! Up close, his more refined appearance in gold velvet and heavy brocade, made him look every whit as handsome as he had while dirty and sweaty in the wrestling circle, she reluctantly admitted to herself. His huge shoulders stretched the costly materials taut and his doublet outlined the heavy muscles of his chest and tapered, flat belly as completely as his hose etched every sinew of his brawny thighs and calves. Despite the disdain she tried to show him, her eyes darted guiltily to the gold brocade-covered codpiece where his powerful loins joined. Then her eyes met his lazy perusal of her body with the usual resounding crack of energy which leapt between them.

"William Stafford, are you always about? Must I see you everywhere I look or turn? Did the king send you?"

"No, Mary. Your father did. Are you all right after your dangerous interview? How does it feel to be a little pawn tossed about between two kings?"

"I need none of your impudence, Mister Stafford!"

"I am thrilled that the fire of spirit still burns beneath the pliant sweetness. And I had hoped that after this afternoon you had resolved to call me Staff."

"Why should I?"

"Perhaps you will at least do so when you become aroused or excited, Mary. Was that not your clear voice I heard as I rolled about on the ground at your feet this afternoon: 'Come on, Staff, you can do it'?"

Mary felt herself color instantly. "Do not be so conceited to think that I wanted you especially to be the victor. I am true English, you know, and would cheer for any English contender."

"Alas, I had hoped your concern for me was of another sort." He hung his head in mock grief and she almost burst into laughter. Then he said quietly, "I was hoping your good will was truly for me and not against poor Lautrec. Has he been an enemy to you?"

"No. No, indeed, and it is none of your concern."

He flashed her an impudent smile. "Then he was something to you, but I shall console myself with the fact that you seem to detest him. You know, sweet Mary, you have never yet mastered telling lies, at least not lying and hiding it. And you still have a conscience. You had best learn to lie and to bury that conscience if you are to get on at great Henry's court, lass."

"You have no right, no right at all to counsel me. Why do you concern yourself anyway?"

"I assure you, Mary, it is not part of my duty to either your father or the king. Therefore, I must have my own motives. When you grow up a bit, from the foolish wisp of girl you are, perhaps we shall discuss my motives. Until then, you will have to wonder."

Her hand tingled with the desire to slap him again, but would he take it as calmly this time? She wanted to beat on his chest, to kick at him, to scratch and scream. It frightened her that he aroused such feelings in her when he was so obviously beneath her concern.

The dark curtains parted in the awkward silence, and Thomas Bullen darted in. "Is she quite all right, Staff?"

"Ask the lady yourself, milord. I would say her spirits are quite high."

"That is a good girl," he nodded. "What exactly did the king say, Mary?"

"Which king, father?" Out of the corner of her eye she caught William Stafford's delighted smile at her impudence.

"His Grace, of course. He said he would choose a husband for you. Did he give a name?"

"No. He said only to await him—and you—here."

"Fine. Fine. Maybe you will be returning home with the royal party."

"I should like to at least visit mother at Hever."

"Indeed if there is to be a wedding, you shall return there to prepare . . . if that is permissable," he said as an afterthought. "And what were Francois' words? Did they argue?"

She was about to recite the entire incident excluding her sharp comments, when King Henry loomed large at the curtained doorway. Her father and Stafford swept low bows.

"She was marvelous, Thomas, marvelous! She put the French king back on his heel like I never could have imagined from a mere sweet wench!" It was then Mary noticed that the king had brought with him a short, muscular man she had seen often about the king's retinue.

"Mary has been telling me that you will select a husband for her upon her return, Sire. The Bullen family is most honored at your concern."

"Not shall, Thomas. Have. I have the perfect choice—a most loving and loyal man with a proud name for himself at the court of his king." He motioned with a quick jerk of his raised wrist, and the man behind him stepped forward and bowed.

Mary's eyes widened and she was aware that behind them all, William Stafford had crossed his arms on his chest and stood with his legs spread.

"My Lord Bullen knows of the fine reputation of William Carey, Esquire to the King's Body, Mary. That is an important position at court, of course, dear Mary, for the Esquires keep watch outside the king's bedroom door at night and attend to his wardrobe and attiring, too."

He paused and Mary's nervous eyes flickered over the sandy haired, serious faced William Carey. He was pleasant looking, if somewhat round-faced in contrast to the square, strong chin Stafford sported. Oh why, she cursed herself silently, did she have to think of that wretch right now!

"Mary Bullen," the king was saying, "I would proudly present Will Carey to you as your future and most loving husband."

Mary stemmed her desire to burst into tears. She curtseyed. Henry beamed and her father's face was unreadable. And in the shadows, William Stafford looked angrier than she had ever seen him.

"Now, I know you have much to say to each other, but if Sir William will wait outside, I promise him I shall turn over his lovely fiancee momentarily. Thomas, I told him he might only walk her back to the castle tonight. You understand, I know." He turned his great reddish head slightly. "Staff, is that you? What the deuce are you doing here?"

Stafford's voice came rough and low. "Lord Bullen sent for me, Sire. I will be going. I wish the Mistress

Bullen much happiness in her coming marriage." He bowed from the waist and was gone.

"Out, out, you two! We will be but a moment. I wish to thank the lady for her clever handling of that French fox when the knave thought he had bested the English. Ha!"

She was alone with the king, but the thrilling reality seemed not to make the proper dent on her consciousness. She could not even smile at him though her brain told her to do so.

He approached her slowly and took her hands in his huge ones. "Mary, I hope the choice of husband will please you. He is a good man, patient, and his position keeps him much about court circles—and his king. You will live at court after the brief honeymoon. 'Tis tradition, you know, honeymoons. Will you like living at our court, do you think, Mary?"

"Of course, Your Grace. I shall be honored."

He bent his head nearer to her impassive face. "I want you to be more than honored, beautiful Mary. I want you to be happy. You and I shall be great friends, you know."

She lifted her gaze at last. His eyes were set deep in shadow and she could not see them though she sensed he watched, waited. Suddenly, she felt happy, relieved. She was going home to mother and Hever. And as for marriage, what had she expected? William Carey would have to be good to her if the king himself had chosen him. She would be at court and away from Francois and all the gossip.

"I am excited to be going home, Your Grace. I know it will all be wonderful. I thank you for your care on my behalf." She smiled radiantly at him, and he grinned like a boy. Why, it will be as easy to please this man as if he were that silly Rene DeBrosse, she thought, much relieved.

"You are so lovely, Mary," Henry Tudor said breathlessly. "So lovely and so dear." He raised her hands slowly to his mustached mouth and kissed them lingeringly.

I feel nothing, she assured herself. He cannot sweep me off my feet the way Francois did when I was a mere girl. William Stafford was wrong about this king's snares and traps for me.

He leaned to brush her lips gently and, without another word, led her through the lifted flap of curtain. William Carey seemed to stand at attention and her father sat on a bench a little farther off waiting for his king. The hall was greatly deserted now. Yeoman guards snapped to attention when they saw their king emerge and servants cleared the scattered remains of the feast.

"I entrust her to you, Will. I shall have two guards follow you on your walk back to Guines, for this is mighty precious cargo, eh, Thomas?" She curtseyed, William bowed, and they were out in the clear night.

She drank in a breath of fresh air and saw the vast heavens stretched overhead sparkling down on King Henry's silvery Palace of Illusions. How like a fantasy it all was, like poor dear Signor da Vinci's lovely painted waxen canvas sky.

Will Carey took her arm gently and they began to pick their way through the torch-lit lanes toward the dark castle beyond.

Part Two

Pastime With Good Company

Pastime with good company I love and shall until I die.
Grudge who will, but none deny,
So God be pleas'd, this life will I
For my pastance hunt, sing, and dance.
My heart is set on goodly sport,
To my comfort, who shall me let?

Youth will needs have dalliance,
Of good or ill some pastance;
Company me thinketh the best
All thoughts and Fantasies to digest.
For idleness is chief mistress of vices all;
Then who can say but pass the day is best of all?

Company with honesty is virtue, and vice to flee.
Company is good or ill,
But every man has his free will.
The best I sue, the worst eschew.
My mind shall be virtue to use,
Vice to refuse,
I shall use me.

—King Henry VIII

Hever Castle, Kent

The intermittent sun streamed through the oriel window in the solar, turning the floor rainbow hued. The Bullen and Howard crests, set in the skillfully leaded panes, stamped their vibrant stains on Mary's tawny skin and pale yellow skirts. It was a humid, close day and the air stirred fitfully in sudden gusts. Puffy clouds prophesied rain, but not a drop hit the gardens or gravel walkways.

Mary saw Semmonet below on the path, and she swung open the latched panes of the lower window and stuck her head out. "Semmonet. I am up here! Michael found me!"

The wiry, quick governess squinted up at the disembodied voice in the sun. "Lord Bullen is not there already?"

"No, Semmonet, just I."

"Then stay put, my girl. I shall be right up." Her voice trailed off as she disappeared.

Summoned again by father. Would things never change? At least her mother was delighted to have her home, and now Lord Bullen had arrived without even the usual warning. How wonderful these three weeks had been since Mary's return from France. Home at beautiful Hever to relax, to think, to ride the sloping hills and pick buttercups by the gentle Eden. To talk to mother and tease Semmonet and pretend that the eight long years away had never happened. To imagine all was well and secure and there was no quiet man named Will Carey to wed, and no king to take over one's life. She shuddered, for another stone-gray cloud had smothered the sun and the lovely room went leaden-hued.

"Mary, I could not find you anywhere," Semmonet shot out in her rapid fire way as she entered. "The grooms said you were not riding. Where did Michael find you?"

"I was just sitting by the sundial in the herb garden—thinking."

"About your wedding with a king's man," Semmonet prodded.

"No, Semmonet. About time."

The little wren-like governess knit her thin brows. "I thank Saint George we found you before the lord came down from doing his papers to see you. He has important news!"

"Perhaps the wedding is off, and I am free to marry whom I will choose." She could not keep the corners of her mouth from turning up. "I think Michael the gardener or Ian the blacksmith would do, for I know both of them better than Mister Will Carey."

Semmonet did not laugh at the tease, but wrung her small hands. "My sweet Mary, surely any bride feels nervous. You will love him. It is best to get to know one's lord after the marriage. A fine arranged marriage by the king! Ah, who could ask for more? You will live at the great Henry's court.''

"Well, yes, there is that. The king's sister will be there much. Perhaps we shall be friends with her and the Duke.''

"And the king favors you, little one, the king!'' She hesitated and wiped her palms nervously on her purple skirts. "Does he look like his portrait, Mary, the one in the hall? I heard Lord Bullen say His Grace might visit here before you are wed. Does he look very like the painting?''

"Well, rather more blond, I would say, but huge and intent with piercing blue eyes. But whenever I try to recall him clearly, all I can see is that picture. I guess I looked on it too much as a child.''

"A little girl's dream come true, my Mary.'' Semmonet smiled and rested her hand on Mary's shoulder.

But the young woman did not hear Semmonet's last words. It was true. She could recall the satyr face of Francois du roi and poor Claude's pasty face and that of old Master da Vinci. That damned smirking face of William Stafford even taunted her in her dreams, but to recall King Henry—the harder she tried, the more his face swam behind a filmy mask in her mind.

"I say, Mary, did that wag Michael tell you to await Lord Bullen here in the solar when he finishes? I warrant it is important news!''

"Yes, Semmonet. That is why I am here. I would much rather be out riding, you know.''

Mary instantly regretted her tart tone, but Semmonet patted her shoulder and bustled off. She thinks all my actions are a bride's nervousness now, Mary

179

thought, suddenly annoyed at the woman.

She had not ridden much in France the past years. The king had never taken her hunting as he had his du Foix, and since Queen Claude seldom rode, neither did her maids. How wonderful it was to ride at Hever and have the wind streaming through her loose hair and the secure feel of Donette's rhythmic canter under her. Donette was the foal of a horse she had loved years ago, gentle, quiet Westron, dead last year, mother said. Mary rode every day, free and happy. She would ride today if father would ever come.

Thomas Bullen brusquely pushed open the door, as though she had summoned him with her thoughts. He smiled broadly and a stab of quick joy shot through her. He had parted from her tenderly at Calais. Her good fortune still held, for he was obviously glad to see her.

"My dear girl," he said, his voice strangely quiet. He put a black linen arm awkwardly around her shoulders as she rose. "You look more beautiful than I had remembered, Mary."

"Hever is good for the soul and the body, my lord."

He looked surprised at her answer. "And a king's attentions, how are those for the spirit, Mary? I have exciting news." The glowing colors danced across his black hair and dark garments as he talked.

"The king has bestowed more honors on us than we could have ever hoped at this early stage. He gives William Carey the offices and revenues of Steward of the Duchy of Lancaster, Constable of the Castle of Plashy, and Keeper of two other great parks—I cannot even recall which ones."

He ticked the prizes off on his beringed fingers under Mary's steady gaze. "Also, as you heard from His

Grace's own lips, Carey is named Esquire to the Body so that you two may live well at court. And, it is only the beginning. Your husband and, of course, your family, will benefit mightily from your good graces with the king.''

''Then I wish you and him all happiness,'' she heard herself say tonelessly.

''And as for you, my girl, I must be certain you understand the honor. There will be jewels, beautiful clothes, exciting, important friends—and power, if we play the game well, Mary. Power.''

She could feel the distinct thud of her heart. She felt nothing but frustration at her father, Semmonet, Will Carey, yes, even the king whose face she could not picture.

''He comes to visit, today, Mary. Here, at Hever at last.''

''Will Carey,'' she said testily, knowing full well her intent to take the eager look from his eyes.

''No, girl! The king, here! He rides from Eltham where he has a fine hunt park. You shall see it soon, no doubt. It is mid morn now. They should be here by noon.''

He glanced up at the fretful sky through the leaded panes. ''I pray he is not put out of his humor by getting drenched in a sudden cloudburst.''

He rubbed his large hands together rapidly. ''Your mother has much to prepare for the royal dinner. God only knows how big a retinue he will bring.'' He strode toward the door.

''Wear your most beautiful dress and you shall walk with him in the gardens. The gold and white from the great banquet in Paris will do.''

"That is much too formal for Hever in the summer, father," she countered as he disappeared through the door.

His head popped back in. "This is the king, girl, the king himself. If you seem to forget that in any way, you shall answer to me."

"Yes, father," she replied, but he was gone. She sat stockstill and watched one blood-red pane of glass change from dull to crimson. The rainclouds *did* threaten the day. She cared not if the whole retinue drowned on their merry jaunt from Eltham. She felt it again, the slow, growing panic, the anger. She had tried to reason it out, to examine her feelings, but really, she had none. Her thoughts never got her anywhere.

She bounded up and raced to her room for her straw hat and riding gloves. She jammed her feet into boots and rushed to the door. She would clear her mind by riding Donette before they came. She could at least decide that for herself. She nearly collided with her mother as she darted from her bedroom. Elizabeth Bullen looked worried and distracted.

"Mary, you are not . . . you cannot be going riding!"

"Yes, mother, only for a little while. I must." She stood nervously facing the lovely, fragile looking woman whose azure eyes and high cheekbones she had so clearly inherited.

"I have so much to do. Your father wants to make certain you will wear a particular dress. He told you the one?"

"Yes, mother, he told me. I shall wear it to please him." She hesitated. "I will wear it if I may ride

182

Donette just for a little while, mother. They will not arrive until high noon. Father said so.''

Her mother's slender fingers stroked her arm briefly. "I do understand your desire to get out of the house, Mary, but it will not sit well if you are not here when His Grace comes. That is the way it is, Mary. We must accept."

"I will be here, dearest mother, and in the chosen dress."

Elizabeth Bullen nodded her silvered blonde head. "Then take care on the horse, my Mary."

We must accept. The words echoed through Mary's brain in rhythm to her steps as she hurried toward the stable block. We must accept—we must accept. We must—we must.

How clearly now she remembered the forbidden knowledge she had stored up all these years, that her own lovely mother had turned down this very king's invitation—the honor of being his mistress. How angry father had been, but she had weathered his anger somehow. Now she, Mary, was perhaps her father's last chance, for Anne was but thirteen, off at the French court and likely to remain there for years. She felt it clearly, coldly. She was father's golden opportunity and she dare not fail him. Even mother now counseled that she must accept. We must accept.

Donette was unusually nervous and jumpy but Mary turned her head toward the river across the meadows. She wanted to ride away from the north road, the direction from which the king would come.

The chestnut bay broke into a sweat sooner than usual, for the air was muggy. Mary would rest her by

183

the Eden in the shade of the leafy poplars. She did not look back at gemlike Hever with its painted facade set in its lilied moat. She wanted to go on forever.

The breeze had picked up and the poplar leaves rattled noisily against each other as she dismounted. Low rumblings seemed to come from the very roots of the massive trees.

"Thunder. Perhaps it will rain now, Donette," she comforted the stamping mare with her soothing voice.

Lightning etched the graying sky over the forest, and Mary counted slowly until she heard the resulting thunder. Her Uncle James had taught them the sailor's trick of counting between the lightning and thunder to judge the distance of the storm. "At least seven miles yet. Good horse. Good Donette."

How marvelous the breeze felt flapping her full skirts stiffly about her legs. She should never have worn this color of dress riding, but she had been in such a hurry. Well, the washmaids would get it clean.

My precious gold and white dress on a day like this, she mused. It is because father knows it impressed Francois that he asks me to wear it for Henry Tudor. "He hopes it will work its magic again, Donette," she shouted over the windy rustle, and Donette whinnied in return.

But that dress would always bring to mind old Master da Vinci and not Francois, she vowed. How little she had known the old man; yet it was as though she had known him always. He had asked her once how an English landscape looked. He would not like to see this scene, nature whipped and blurred. He preferred the tranquil and the balanced.

Several drops hit her face and pelted Donette's

smooth brown flanks. Mary sighed and, as she mounted, a tremendous crash of lightning splintered a tall poplar nearby. She could even smell the acrid, charred wood.

Donette reared and Mary clung to her arched neck. The reins slipped for an instant and the mare started for home at a swift gallop, cutting through the trees.

"Whoa, girl! No, Donette, no. Whoa!" Mary knew better than to be in a forest in a storm. Even if they were soaked, the grassy valley was the safest place to be. Suddenly, King Henry's face sprang before her mind's eye in his finery, as she had seen him last. She grabbed for her horse's reins and missed. Did this storm seize him as he approached? Was his reddish-blond hair sticking wet to his forehead?

A strangled cry escaped her parted lips as she seized the reins and struggled to turn Donette around. Thunder echoed deeply through the huge tree trunks as she yanked the horse to the left. She turned obediently, but went, as one drunk, through the low-limbed trees. She ducked and shielded her face as the wind whipped sopping leaves at her face and hair.

She started to laugh uncontrollably at the scene she must make, the scene she would make when she returned to Hever. Her long blonde locks hung down her soaking back, and she was bruised and cut.

They emerged in the meadow and Mary dismounted. Grasping Donette's bridle, she led her down into the tiny grassy depression they had called "our valley" when they played here as children. George, of course, always had to be the leader. George, who was in London at Lincoln's Inn obediently studying law.

Mary slipped to her knees in the slick grass, pulling

185

Donette's head down with a jerk. She rose and stood shakily as the storm surged around them. Drenched, she huddled close to Donette. Mother would be worried, but she most feared what father would say. Even her best dress could not save her now.

Swiftly, suddenly, it ended. The thunder rumbled off over the hills and the downpour diminished to gentleness. Mary mounted and carefully walked the mare toward home. She would tether Donette by the green garden and go in through the kitchens. With Semmonet's aid she would somehow become presentable.

The bricks of Hever were glazed by the downpour and iron drainpipes spouted noisy shafts into the moat. The wet leather reins squeaked as she tied them to a post. She gathered her cold, wet skirts tightly and hurried across the wooden ramp.

The kitchen door stood agape and wonderful aromas floated everywhere. The dim room was packed with servants. Even father's groom turned a spit, and wash girls stirred sauces and peeled peaches. The massive open hearth was crammed with kettles, skillets and spits, and its welcome warmth beckoned to the chilled woman.

Only a few shocked servants looked up to notice their drenched, bedraggled mistress. She hurried down the dark passageway that led toward the foot of the great staircase, and stopped. The king must have arrived early, for several strange men lounged about outside the closed door to the solar. No doubt His Grace and her parents were waiting within, waiting for her.

Embarrassed, she dared not look at the amused figures who stopped their conversation as she mounted the steps to flee. She was only a little way up when she heard a too familiar voice.

"The golden, the beautiful Mary Bullen. Beautiful and wet and cold. It was an unwise time to go for a ride, Mary."

She spun around, her eyes wide. "William Stafford! Who invited *you* to Hever?" She went hot crimson at the obvious answer to her question, and at the picture she must make for him as his cool gaze swept carefully over her. His two companions watched the confrontation with amusement. She would have to scold him later if he had dared to tell them anything evil about her.

She tried another question to break the silence, to still the rapid pounding of her heart. "Did His Grace bring Will Carey also?"

William Stafford lowered his voice, and his eyes went to her heaving breasts with the wet cloth sticking so close to her skin. "Why should His Grace bring someone as insignificant as Carey? He is only the man you will wed." He hesitated at her silence. "Are you so anxious to see Will Carey, then? I shall tell the fortunate scoundrel when we return to Eltham. We left him angrily shooting at the butts. Some wondered why he was not included in this little visit, but why should he be, when the king only came to see his French Ambassador Bullen at his charming home?"

He shrugged with mock indifference and the old urge to slap him returned with stunning impact.

"I have tolerated far too much of your sarcasm and impudence in France," she said, low enough that his two eager cronies could not hear. "Quite enough. And I shall hear none of it here!" She turned her back to him dramatically. And with as much poise as she could

187

muster, she started up the endless stairs.

"Is it so hard to admit that I was right about everything so far, Mary?" He raised his voice and she turned again, afraid they would hear in the solar. "And you will have to tolerate me, Mary, for I live at court too and as close to the king as I warrant you shall live."

How she hated him. His insinuations frightened and shamed her.

"I would counsel you to say 'no' to all their rotten plans, sweet lady, but my selfishness wants you about the court and not banished in disgrace to this moated sanctuary where I could never see you."

Her mouth dropped open at his audacity. She wanted to run, but she was frozen to the steps.

"I cannot help but fancy a wench who looks as beautiful soaked and muddy as she does on a king's arm. Only, guard well your heart, Mary Bullen."

She turned and fled. How dare he address her like that in the hall of her father's house with his lord king in the next room and two jackanapes looking on!

She had been wrong. Mother was not in the solar with the king and her father. She and Semmonet were pacing Mary's room, terrified. They did not scold her, and tears came to Elizabeth Bullen's sky-blue eyes. If she was to be scolded or lectured or hugged or whatever, there would be time later. His Grace was waiting.

They stripped Mary of her sodden garments and rubbed her skin with linen towels until it glowed. They powdered and perfumed her, for there was no time to wash anything but her face and arms. On went a silk chemise and flounced petticoats over her tingling body. Semmonet desperately tried to towel her hair dry but gave up and left it in damp ringlets and tight curls.

"No. She shall go bareheaded, Semmonet," came Elizabeth Bullen's only words as the little woman reached for a gauzy headpiece. She wore the huge single Howard pearl at her breast, just above the low neckline.

They hurried her into the hall. She went on steady legs, feeling dazed. It was as though she watched a play or some childhood fantasy from afar. It was a repetition of some little girl's dream of once loving the handsome king of France.

William Stafford still stood sentinel at the solar door, under the huge portrait of the king. He bowed gracefully to Elizabeth Bullen and opened the door for them. Surely he was not bowing to her. Well, what did it matter now?

"Ah, here are the ladies at last, Your Grace. Mary was caught in the rainfall in the gardens and insisted on changing."

Both women swept a low curtsey to the dark shadow surrounded by patterned light.

"You remember my wife, Lady Elizabeth, Sire?"

Mary rose to face her king who seemed to tower over them all. His narrowed eyes appraised her mother, then swung to her. A smile lit his strong features.

"I do remember her well, Thomas, and her service to the queen. How like her mother your golden Mary is. That is what I remember now."

The king curled his huge jeweled fingers around Mary's slender ones. He was not wet from the downpour at all. He looked elegant in his purple doublet with his ruffled golden shirt pulled through the numerous slashes. His hose were brightest blue. He was much too

189

dressed up for a mere summer ride through woody Kent.

"Now that the rain has ended, perhaps you will show me the lovely Hever gardens before dinner. There is time for a small tour, is there not, Lady Elizabeth," Henry Tudor inquired politely.

"Of course, Your Grace," came her mother's voice. "We shall wait on your return. Mary much favors the rose garden to the south." Her voice trailed off.

"Then we shall walk there. I have some wonderful news for Mary—news of honors to her betrothed and herself."

"Mary will be pleased, Sire," her father said, and she caught his tone and stare like a threat, like an actual physical shake.

She took the king's proffered arm and smiled up at him through her lashes. His wariness, his propriety seemed to melt, and his boyish grin returned. She felt a strange power over him as she had once before and her fears ebbed. Perhaps this could be fun, a challenge. "Father brought me a lovely rose from your gardens at Greenwich once, Your Grace. You must have spectacular bushes there—Tudor roses, all."

Henry Tudor laughed deep in his throat, and she could hear her father's audible sigh of relief. No, I shall not fail you, father, she thought. You will love me and be proud.

She was pleased that the nasty Stafford was not in sight as they emerged in the rain-washed air.

"You look ravishing with your hair in tiny curls, Mary. Is it a French style?"

"No, Your Grace. I was quite drenched by the rain. The truth is, I was on a horse which bolted at the thun-

190

der.''

His arm stole behind her and encircled her narrow waist. ''Perhaps you need an expert to teach you riding, sweet.''

Mary colored at the blatant *double entendre* but did not let on that she knew his intent. ''The Princess Mary often praised your sportsmanship in all things, Sire.''

''Did she now? Yes, you were first with the princess when she went to France.''

''And I was permitted to stay when the other women were sent home.''

''That damned rotting hulk of a king had the audacity to die but three months after their so carefully arranged marriage,'' Henry groused as his great paw of a hand cradled a full blown pink rose. He held the upturned face of the flower, but the scent which he inhaled was the sweet dampness of Mary's hair. ''The French all whispered that his young bride was too much for him, my spies told me. But I should think a sweet, willing young woman is good for the blood.''

He pulled her to him and took her mouth gently at first and then pressed her to him with fierce intensity. Mary yielded coolly, inwardly amazed at his boldness here in the rose garden at high noon. But this was the king.

He loosed her waist but seized both her hands in a grip which almost pained her. ''Dearest Mary, you must see how entranced I am with you. I will see that you are cared for and protected always. You have ensnared my love. You will bear Will Carey's name and perhaps his children, but I would sue for your love.''

He raised her hands to his lips and, straightening her curled fingers, kissed her open palms. ''Your king is

191

only a man in this, Mary. Fear him not. Yield yourself to him, and his gratitude will be eternal.''

Mary gazed up into his eyes and was ashamed to feel how much she enjoyed this. Francois had only taken and without such pretty words.

''Do you understand, Mary?''

''Yes, Your Grace, I believe so.''

''Will you be my love?''

She felt a nearly overwhelming urge to say ''Perhaps,'' or laugh and skip off to see if he would follow, but she dared not and father awaited dinner. ''You are so direct, so—powerful, my king. I mean that as a compliment. You are so different from . . . from men in France.''

''I am English, Mary, and the king. Yet I beseech you to yield to me. I do not order.''

The old lie again, the tiny voice in her head warned. But unless you are pleased, Sire, destruction would surely follow, she thought.

''My heart belongs to no one else, my lord king. If given but a chance, I am sure . . .''

He swept her up in a huge bear hug and his warm, masculine affections melted her reserve. She preferred this openness to his hot kisses. Why could her father never be like this? How her love would flow out to him then. What she would not do for her father if he would only love her and show it like this.

''My father has always loved to serve you, King Henry, and so shall I, though I intend not to be an ambassador.'' She blushed at her poor joke and her use of his Christian name.

Their laughter intertwined, his, boyishly loud, hers sweetly musical.

"No, indeed, Mary, we shall find some service more suited to your lovely talents. And you shall call me your Henry when we are alone, as much we shall be, golden Mary."

Her father waited on the front entrance steps all smiles, and Mary saw Semmonet peer from an upstairs window. She gave William Stafford her most condescending smile as they went into dinner where her mother hovered about the head table.

And while the Bullens ate and laughed and listened to their king through the long afternoon, another dark summer storm came to rend the peaceful landscape at Hever.

Chapter Twelve
August 18, 1520

Greenwich

The great river glittered green in the hot summer air, but here on the barge the breeze was always delightful. "A perfectly lovely day," her mother had said over and over. A perfect day for a wedding.

Mary looked down again at her hands resting in her lap and at the new gold band which glinted on her finger. She was Lady Carey now, and this quiet, solicitous man beside her was her new lord. She prayed God Will Carey would not hate her.

In the awkward silence she took to staring at her knees again, covered so elegantly and properly with the sleek ivory satin that reflected the glint of afternoon sunlight on the Thames and bespoke she was a bride. Was it a grim twist of fate that the color of mourning for the French indicated a bridal day in King Henry's England? Her skirt was a graceful bell shape elongated in back so that she pulled a five foot train when she walked. When she danced tonight, she would lift that traditional bridal train free of the floor with a clever hidden handstrap of silk the royal dressmaker had showed her. Decorative slashings in front of the skirt revealed a golden brocade kirtle underneath which also echoed in the gold linings of the loose second sleeves turned back fashionably from the fitted undersleeves edged with lace. Tiny satin-faced roses of delicate pink, rimmed her square neckline and dotted the tight ivory satin bodice which pushed up the rounded, creamy tops of her breasts to full advantage. His Grace's eyes had seemed to linger there today, but she was quite unsure of what Will Carey had seen when he scrutinized her. She tossed her waist-length golden hair, brushed free and studded with fancy ribbons and sweet flowers in the fashion of a bride, and Will shifted in his seat beside her as though he sensed she were restive.

Their barge was heading downstream to Greenwich, to the City where they had been wed; Great Saint Helen's, Bishopsgate, only an hour ago. It all seemed like some misty dream: holding Will's gentle hand and reciting the vows, her mother's tearful face, Semmonet's proud wink, George's pride to be near the king. The king had come with a few courtiers, wished them well and kissed her cheek, his loud voice echoing to the Benedictine nunnery chapel in the south nave of the church.

The king had come. Her eyes squinted downriver, but his royal barge festooned in Tudor green and white had disappeared ahead of them, around the broad bend of the River Thames near the Tower. She was grateful the king had not brought William Stafford to her wedding. His accusing gaze would certainly have ruined things. The fact that father was in France on king's business and missed the wedding, was grief enough for one day.

"Your dress is so beautiful, Mary. Had I told you so?"

"You did, Will, but I thank you again. The service was fine, and I am looking forward to our banquet."

"And to the night to come, Mary?" He put his hand carefully on her satin knee and his eyes were in earnest. "You are so very beautiful. I gained much today."

Indeed you have, she thought, revenue and lands from your king, but she said only, "I hope I will please you, my lord."

His hair looked almost reddish in the shade of the awning. His gold and ivory doublet fashionably slashed with his lacy, puffed shirt pulled through for effect, matched her colors perfectly. Despite the warmth of the August day, Will wore an ermine-edged mantle across his shoulders and an impressive, heavy gold chain with a medallion signifying that he served the king as an esquire over his chest. His flat, gold brocade hat sported a long white plume and his gartered hose were obviously new-made to match his stylish square-toed slippers.

Surely, since Will was privy to His Grace in his valued court appointment, and with all the new gifts of lands, he knew fully of her circumstances with the king. Surely His Grace had explained to him. His hand remained on her leg, but he turned again to talk to his sister Eleanor, a learned ten-year nun, a sophisticated gray-eyed woman with a high brow and thin nose. Mary felt she had almost gained two new sisters-in-law in one day, for George would soon wed Jane Rochford and Elizabeth Bullen, to George's obvious annoyance, had invited Jane today.

Jane sat near George now, who stared, tight-lipped, out over the water while Jane leaned toward him, chattering. The girl's face was pert and beguilingly heart-shaped, her cheeks and lips rosy, but her snappy eyes darted about entirely too much, as if her thoughts were on a hundred different flights at once. Her raven black hair shone in the sun but she was always tossing it or petting it with her quick little hands. Her shapely eyebrows had a most disconcerting habit of arching up entirely too much, as if everything she heard were some marvelous disclosure.

Poor George. Semmonet had told Mary that George had long loved Margot Wyatt, who had been their playmate from the manor next to Hever. Little Margot Wyatt with her freckles and skinny legs. But Semmonet said she had grown to quite a beauty. A pity the Wyatts had no title or lands which Thomas Bullen coveted.

The massive gray walls of the Tower of London slipped by, and the waves from their barge lapped at its stony skirts. The watergate guarded by the ugly iron teeth of its portcullis was nicknamed Traitor's Gate, for the worst sorts of prisoners of the crown entered there, never to return to freedom. The battlements of the White Tower peered over the walls at them. Thank the merciful Lord God there had been no prisoner's heads or rotting corpses hanging from London Bridge on the day of her wedding.

"Mary." Jane Rochford's animated face bent over her shoulder. "It was so kind of you to have me here today. And how wonderful that His Grace would come! I heard the wedding feast is his gift to you, and there will be dancing."

"Yes, Jane. His gift to me and to Will."

"Oh, of course. I pray my wedding to George is only half as wonderful."

197

"I am certain you will be as happy, Jane."

"Do you think we will have a banquet at court?"

"I do not know. George will have to speak to his father on that."

"I was thinking, Mary, that your name now rhymes, like a sonnet—Mary Carey."

Will turned his head to stare up at the Rochford girl.

"If I can be of aid to either of you, I shall be most willing. I am proud to be marrying into such a wonderful family as the Bullens." She curtseyed and turned back to George.

"I warrant everything is wonderful with that little chatterbox," Will commented under his breath. "Does she know the Careys are not a family newly arrived at court, but a venerable one of once fine standing?"

Amazed at his hurt and angered tone, Mary instinctively touched his arm. "Tell me of it, Will. Father said something of it, but I would hear it from you."

"I want you to know all of the tragedy, Mary, now that you are my wife, for Eleanor and I can share our burden with you."

At her name, his sister bent close to Will's shoulder as if to become a full member of their conversation. Her clear gray eyes seemed to have great depth as they peered down her elegant nose. "She can hardly share the full burden, dearest Will. She is not born a Carey."

"She is now a Carey by marriage, Eleanor." He cleared his throat nervously and momentarily glanced toward the grassy bank where a group of fieldworkers shouted and waved their hats at the decorated barge. "Had they seen their king pass by only minutes ago?" Mary wondered.

"There were several families of great bearing and

rank who made the mistake of taking the Yorkish side in the late civil war, Mary. The Careys of Durham were one of those families who lost vast lands and wealth when the Lancastrians were victorious. Our present king's father, our sovereign King Henry VII, had a long memory for disobedience, as does this king. Though our generation does not suffer direct persecution," he reached for Eleanor's hand, "we are given little. We are earning our way back."

"And my dear brother's marriage to you is a fine sign of our return to our proper status, though the marriage was not arranged by us."

"I see," said Mary.

"And I, of course, aspire to be a Prioress of a great order in the Holy Church. And now, with Will so near the king's influence we shall see."

"Yes. His Grace has given Will some revenue grants as well as a fine position already," Mary said foolishly, realizing they knew well of the new honors.

"Perhaps Esquire to the Body is not a fine position, Mary, but a sound beginning." Eleanor Carey nodded pertly as though the lesson were over, and she leaned back and straightened in her seat again.

She hates me, Mary thought. They feel their blueblood requires me for the status they want. She despises me.

The green swards and trees, red brick turrets and banners of Greenwich loomed into view. Fine white stone statues of the king's beasts guarded the barge landing, but Mary saw instead the tiny chess pawn Princess Mary Tudor had given her so long ago. Not griffins and lions and unicorns lined the graveled path to the palace, but kings and queens and knights and

199

pawns.

"Here, Mary." Will was offering her his hand as they climbed from their velvet seats on the barge. "Come, my wife. The king awaits."

Mary ate little of the fabulous meal, for her stomach had suddenly twisted into knots. Her detached calm was gone. She feared not, yet she had to force herself to nod, to smile, to converse. She loved bucknade and stuffed partridge, but still her food went largely untouched. George took to teasing her and eating off her plate while Jane scolded him for his rough manners.

The wine was good though, sweet and cool from the vast cellars at royal Greenwich. The king had raised numerous toasts to the young bridal couple, and even thought to give a fine father's toast in the absence of his dear servant, Thomas. The king might as well be my father now anyway, Mary thought petulantly. He sits by my beautiful mother, gives us the bridal feast and controls my life. But I wish father had the king's warmth. She took another deep drink of the wine.

When dusk descended, the servants lit tapers and cleared the tables. The musicians played from the gallery until, at a graceful handsignal from their king, their ranks swelled and they broke into a gay wedding coranto. Will seized Mary's hand, and they followed along in the tiny running steps led by the king and the blushing Lady Bullen.

Mary felt rather dizzy and soon laughter bubbled spontanously on her lips. How Annie would love this revelry here at Greenwich with the king and chosen members of his inner circle. And how proud her father would be to see it! Was he thinking of her wedding day far away at Francois' Amboise?

The king bowed and claimed her hand for the stately pavan, and Will danced with her mother. Mary felt no nervousness as she lengthened her steps slightly to match the king's long strides. He wore deepest crimson with golden trim, and his white silken shirt and broad collar made his healthy complexion glow in the candlelight. The tiny roses on her white slashed skirts and the pink ruff above the square bodice seemed to echo the louder brilliance of his colors. They turned and bowed, whirled and began the pattern again.

Mary felt less giddy by the time the faster galliards began with the sackbutts wailing and fydels and lutes lilting from the upper balcony. She turned in her hand-to-hand progress down the line, and came face to face with her new partner, William Stafford.

"I had not seen you," she shot out breathlessly as they swept through the raised arms of a silken and velvet arch.

"I had vowed not to set foot here to ruin your fine day, but I could not resist just a look at the festivities—and the bride. You look ravishing. My best wishes for your happiness—with Will Carey, I mean."

"Is it not possible for you to be civil? Must you always accuse and provoke and . . ."

"Hush, Mary, or people will notice. You are at court now. You have not yet learned to hide your feelings. I suggest here in the bear pit you try harder." The dance ended with a graceful, sweeping bow.

"I detest you, William Stafford."

"That is better, sweetheart," he said low. "Anyone gazing on that lovely face now would think you loved me well enough as any friend to your new husband."

"Staff, I had thought you were busy elsewhere to-day." Will Carey clapped the taller man lightly on the shoulder as he approached.

"I only stopped to wish you both well. As I told you, Will, I knew your bride briefly in France when His Grace assigned me to be liaison to Lord Bullen."

"Staff and I have some things in common here at court, you see, Mary."

"Indeed?"

"The Staffords are as in disgrace as the Careys. Only," Will swung his eyes about the crowded room and lowered his voice, "the Stafford treason was more recent than the War of Roses."

"Treason," Mary echoed.

"Have you not heard of the Colchester Rebellion, Lady Carey? My uncle swung from the hanging tree at Tyburn and my father, being but a lad, was pardoned. As they are both dead now, I pay for their guilt."

"Their poor ghosts still haunt the Stafford family manor, Mary," Will put in.

"Or so my elderly aunt claims. She says one or the other of the dead rebels' spirits still goes up and down the staircase at night wailing 'down with this wretched king!' " William Stafford stared fixedly into her face.

"Which king?" Mary asked wide-eyed.

"I know not, Lady Carey. I have yet to see or hear the ghost. It does not amuse it to walk about in bed-rooms during the days I am home at Wivenhoe."

Though he recited the incidents in a straightforward way, it seemed to Mary that William Stafford's mocking undercurrent was still there. "But you are not in prison as heir to their rebellion, Mister Stafford. You serve closely to the king in his court."

"Exactly, lady. She will learn fast here, Will. And maybe we should be watched. Those of us who are paying the price of some great indiscretion never fear committing the little ones," he said, his gaze still on Mary's face despite Will Carey's growing unease. "A good evening to you both." Stafford bowed suddenly and was gone, as though he had sensed the approach of the king behind his back.

"It is fair time, everybody, time indeed," Henry Tudor bellowed and the music ceased instantly. He seized Mary's hand and pulled her under one great arm and Will Carey under the other in a massive hug.

"Ladies, hasten to put the bride to bed, for we men shall be up soon and a new lord likes to find his wench awaiting him and ready!"

Everyone laughed and Henry Tudor bent his head to kiss her hotly on the mouth. His breath smelled of cloves and wine. Horrified in front of the clapping crowd, she yielded, annoyed and ashamed. She was suddenly grateful that her dear friend the Duchess of Suffolk was in childbed and could not see her triumphal wedding feast, a gift from the king. And, of course, had Queen Catherine chosen to attend, Mary would have died from shame this very moment.

"Come on, Mary, run," cried Jane Rochford as she seized Mary's dangling arm and pulled. Her mother, Rose Dacre, and several giggling women behind her, Mary fled. Breathless, they mounted the steps to the room where Will had slept these last two nights she had been at Greenwich, while she had bedded with her mother.

A waiting Semmonet had already turned down the smooth linen sheets. The younger ladies peeled Mary out of her bridal dress, and, through her own tears, Mary saw the tears on her mother's face.

"Be happy for me, mother," she pleaded quietly while the laughing women fetched her night chemise and lacy robe.

"I am, my dearest. I was only remembering my wedding night and all my dreams then."

There was no time for comfort or a hug, for Rose Dacre was telling everyone how swiftly the king liked to follow with the bridegroom as he had at this very palace when his sister Mary had formally remarried the Duke of Suffolk on English soil. "His Grace had the Duke at the door half undressed before we even had the princess in her robe," Rose continued.

"It was their third marriage then," Mary put in, her teeth chattering from her jangled nerves. "I was at her first secret wedding, and then they married later at Lent in Paris."

"That is true," Rose added, somewhat more icily, as the others turned to hang on Mary's story. "You were such a child then, you were allowed to stay."

"Oh no, the strewing herbs," shrieked Jane Rochford as the boom of men's voices sounded in the hall. "Oh no, get her in bed!"

Jane threw quick handfuls of dried lavender, daisies, fennel and tansy on the floor, and their heady scent instantly permeated the air. Four great pounding knocks filled the room, and before Lady Bullen could touch the doorknob, the door swung wide to reveal the king bent over laughing and a blushing, bare chested Will Carey.

"Husbands never need to knock, madam," Will said boldly, and then blushed deeper realizing the import of his words. But the other men seemed not to hear as they shoved him into the chamber and followed on his heels. The room seemed packed, but Mary sat calmly in bed against a puffy bolster in her robe, covered to her lap by the sheets.

"There she is, you lucky dog, ready for you! . . . I wish I were you, Will! . . . Get yourself a fine son this night, Will Carey!" The raucous laughter swelled, and Mary was tempted to cover her ears.

Then the king shouted, "Out, out, all of you vagabonds!" and, obediently, the revelers streamed out into the hall.

Mary glimpsed her mother turn and smile, and Semmonet waved. Then there were only three, and Mary feared for one foolish instant that the king would dismiss the meek-looking Carey as well. Henry Tudor's eyes devoured her, raked off the sheets, pulled at her chemise and . . .

"Good fortune to you, Carey. Use her gently. I envy you your warm bed." The king pulled his hot gaze away, turned, and slammed the door.

Will went over and shot the bolt. Mary still felt His Grace's eyes on her, sharp, powerful like the portrait in the hall at Hever. He had told her yesterday by the tiltyard that he would try to give her a week, but he loved her, so he could not promise. She felt much safer with Will Carey but, truly, the king excited her more.

"What are you thinking, Mary?" He took slow steps to the canopied bed. "You are so beautiful. I am a fortunate man. His Grace could have picked Compton or Hastings or Stafford, but he gave you to me."

"Stafford? William Stafford?"

"Of course. He is unattached and a close courtier, though I am sure His Grace considers him a greater rebel and harder to control than I."

Yes, no doubt William Stafford would be harder to bribe if the king wanted to bed his wife, she thought bitterly. So, the great Henry had explained it all to Will Carey. He understands I shall be the king's mistress, and he will accept it for his lands and monies and his hateful sister. Then, we are all to be pitied, so what does it matter? But I love no one like poor George who will have to bed with giggly Jane Rochford while dreaming of long-legged Margot Wyatt. So why not Will Carey for me?

Will had stripped off his shoes and hose and blew out several candles, leaving only two by the huge oaken bedstead. "I trust we can be of help to each other, Mary. The court can be a frightening place. I will keep my place, my beautiful wife, but you must remember, king or no, you bear my name."

He tugged on the ribbons at the lacy neckline of her robe and helped her shrug out of it. He pulled her tight against his lightly-haired chest, tucking her head under his chin. "I will try to be gentle, Mary, but on the nights when you are mine, then you are mine only. I have told myself so time and time again these last few days."

He rolled her on to her back and tugged her thin chemise up above her waist, spreading her legs and mounting her immediately. "This night will be a long one, I promise you, my little bride."

It was a long night, as Will Carey made calm, deliberate, possessive love to his wife more than once, more than twice. She submitted in body, but her heart was free as she had told herself time and time again these last few days.

But what angered her as she closed her eyes to finally sleep, was that she dreamed not of the quiet, serious Will Carey, nor of the lusty king. It was the handsome, rough face of William Stafford which laughed and stared and haunted her sleep.

Chapter Thirteen
August 26, 1520

Greenwich

Mary was swept through the next few days at the royal court on a wave of frothing excitement. She strolled, she danced, she smiled and laughed in a sea of new faces. The king took the newlyweds hunting in the blue-green forests of Kentish Eltham. She watched His Grace and his closest circle of comrades tilt, bowl on the green, and shoot at butts. The king taught Mary to gamble at Primero and Gleek and to dice for coins and kisses at the Hazard tables. The whirl of fun and flirtations from Henry Tudor went on and on. Mary was content to ride the wave of the royal affections forever.

Her entire first week at court, Mary never once saw the queen who summered with her young daughter, Mary, at Beaulieu for several weeks of respite and contemplation. It was whispered that Spanish Catherine was most pious and beloved by the people of her realm, though Mary caught the undercurrent of gossip against her from some courtiers. Though they said she used to display a winning smile and fine sense of humor, the past two years, since the sixth stillborn child she had delivered to His Grace, she had grown heavy and wore out-of-date gowns, crucifixes, and top-weighty jeweled headressses. Jane Rochford had even whispered that the poor, sad queen wore a haircloth of the Third Order of Saint Francis under her opulent clothes, even in the hot summer months. Beyond such chatter, the distant life of Henry's queen touched the laughing Mary Carey not at all.

Will Carey was kind and attentive when the king was not about, and that other Will—everyone called him Staff, and he seemed to be vastly popular—seldom bothered her. He appeared to be a fast friend to her husband, so she steeled herself to be kinder to him, since she would no doubt see him much. He was right about one thing, the rogue. She would have to hide her contempt for his outrageous actions now that she lived at such a civilized court. At first it had amazed her that King Henry wanted such a cynical man from a dangerous family around him all the time. But the more she studied Stafford, the more she understood. Staff was witty, an excellent horseman and sporter, and what better place for a king to put someone he did not trust than next to him at butts, or as the opponent on the other side of the tennis net? As far as Mary could tell, Staff was the only man who had the nerve or the stupidity to always tell the king what he thought and beat him at bowls too. She would follow her clever king's lead: they would allow Staff near, but never trust him.

Even now Staff leaned against a gilded gaming table, rakishly at ease, his eyes alternately on her and his casts of his ivory dice. Mary leaned lightly against her husband's arm as she threw her dice. A lucky seven! She laughed and scooped the coppery coins from the little painted Hazard circle.

"Will, you have the only lady I know who can make money living at court instead of losing it," Henry Norris gibed. Several others laughed, but Will Carey's mouth only forced a tight smile. "It is time the Carey fortunes shot upward, gentlemen."

"I do not worry about my husband's family's stakes at the game, Sir Henry," Mary shook her dice violently and blew on them for luck as the king had taught her. "It is my brother George I would keep out of the poor house, before our father returns and strings him from the Tower for his foolhardiness at the tables."

Francis Weston's voice came teasingly over the clicks of dice, "I would not be too hard on him, Lady Carey. I would drink and gamble the evenings away too, if I had a little magpie forever chattering in my ear. Besides, he told me when I helped him back to his room last night that he favors Thomas Wyatt's sister, Margot."

Mary rolled a ten and her streak was broken. "I would appreciate it if you would not repeat George's problems, Sir Francis." She looked up at the tall, handsome man. "It is painful to love elsewhere from where one must wed. But it is not an uncommon pain, and George should not have spoken of it." She suddenly had the oddest feeling that Weston would make a cutting remark of some kind to her. He seemed to hesitate. Would he accuse her of marrying one man and loving the king? Surely, he would not dare. Besides, he would be wrong, though she could not tell him so.

"My apologies, lady," he said, and his green eyes searched her face briefly. She was annoyed that Will paid so little attention to her conversation. George was his brother-in-law. It would not hurt his Carey pride to come to her aid.

Weston, Norris and their ladies moved to the other table and George, with Jane Rochford in tow, drifted toward the Careys. George had one hand on his sword and drummed his other fingers on the table edge as Will Carey cast his dice.

"Damn, Will, you are as ill-fortuned as I tonight. Where is His Grace anyway? He is usually in the thick of the action by now. He will not be pleased when he finds some of us are already down too many coins to take him on tonight."

Mary answered George before Will could respond. "He is with a messenger from the queen at Beaulieu, George. Why do you not wager smaller amounts? It is still early. Here, but do not risk everything on one foolish throw." She extended her palm to George, and he sheepishly took the little pile of copper coins.

"My dear, you should keep your winnings," Will chided at her side. "When the king comes, you know he likes large wagers and you are his favorite partner."

Mary blushed at the scolding and George noticed. "After all, the game is called Hazard," George said with an edge on his voice. "You have to take risks and hazard a win—as in life, Will."

Before Mary could change the subject, Jane Rochford's light voice interrupted. "I think it is all tremendous fun, and George usually does very well. He studies so hard at Lincoln's Inn, it is no wonder he likes to have a little fun sometimes." She smiled sweetly at George, who chose to ignore her support as he headed toward the other table.

"He is bent on winning back the money he just lost

211

to that handsome Will Stafford," Jane explained over her shoulder as she followed him. "I just love to see the two of them bluff each other."

"I wish George would dice with someone trustworthy," Mary muttered to Will under her breath.

"If you mean Staff, Mary, he is one of the most trustworthy men I have ever known. Besides, your brother is old enough to take care of himself. He is a full year older than you, so let him be."

"He does not act it," she countered testily. "And I thought Stafford was a traitor."

"Has His Grace spoken to you of Staff? No? Then you should remember that the way of it, with both Staff and the Careys, is that we pay for something our elders did—our dead elders. His Grace likes and respects Staff and me, or he would never have us about and in trusted positions. If he says otherwise, it is just bluff talk." He took Mary's arm and guided her away from the table. "As for your dear George, your father will settle him soon enough when he returns from France."

Mary thought of many things to say in reproach of his lecture to her, but she held her tongue. All he thought of was the precious Careys earning their way back. He had no right to look down on George and the Bullens the way he did, and as some of his friends did too. He looked on her every night with eyes full of passion, but he was always so inwardly controlled whenever he touched her or spoke to her that she was not sure if red English blood flowed in his veins or not.

To make her temper worse, there stood that foolish Jane Rochford gazing up at Staff's smiling face. There was always some woman trailing after him or on his arm. She should have known he would be a skirt chaser

212

in addition to everything else. Will was wrong. His Grace would never trust such a man. She would ask him herself what he really thought of William Stafford when she got the chance.

Edward Guildford, Henry Clifford, and a few others were slowly vacating the Hazard tables to conserve their purses until His Grace appeared. Mary tapped her foot in impatience. Why did Will have to make her so upset tonight when she had been having such a fine time? Maybe she was used to having Henry around to cheer her and keep the court hounds at bay from their rude remarks and Will from his scolding lectures. Now, if only George had the sense to quit gambling with Stafford and await the king's arrival!

Henry Tudor swept in at last, looking grand and huge as usual. He clapped his hands and summoned them all around him like a pack of spaniels.

"Wonderful news! We are to have a revel, and I have just been planning the entire thing myself. We have not had a fine one since May Day and this will be the most fantastic yet." His narrow eyes glowed and he looked so confident. Mary felt better already for his mere presence.

"The setting will be Sherwood forest. We will have a marvelous Nottingham Castle, and we shall all wear masks. Mister Cornish who helped me with the idea will teach you the knight and lady parts tonight. We have no time for gambling tonight. The masque is to-morrow!"

The rapt audience murmured at the news. A pleasant diversion indeed, and Mary was thrilled. She had seen such elaborate masques at Francois' court, but had only taken a small part while Francoise du Foix was

213

given the exciting roles with the king.

"All right, everyone to the hall to see Mister Cornish. And do what he bids, all of you, with no arguing, or you will answer to me!" Everyone laughed and trooped off behind the Guildfords.

"I need Lady Carey to play Maid Marian, so you may leave her behind," the king called out after them suddenly. Mary turned, her heart beating fast. What would Will say? "I know you will not mind," the king rushed to Will. "Mister Cornish has a lovely lady for you to partner. And when you get to the hall, tell Staff not to get in the dancing either. I have another job for him." He dismissed Carey with a wave of his hand. "So many details, Mary."

"What a wonderful idea, Sire," she smiled up at him. "Did you think of it just this evening? You said nothing of it earlier."

He took her arm at the elbow and led her to a darkened windowseat in the crook of the huge bay window overlooking the black Thames down the sloping lawns. "I like surprises, my Mary, especially for one I love. Do you approve of being this Robin Hood's Maid Marian?"

She nodded happily as he put his huge hand on her chin and tilted her head up. He bent to meet her mouth. His kiss was warm, then crushing, and his tongue probed her mouth in the French way. His other hand crept to her narrow waist, then slid up her breasts to the rim of her lacy neckline. He pulled her to him across the polished wood and slipped his hand down into the dress between her full breasts. Her eyes flew open in surprise at his bold tactic here in the public room of the palace. But it was dark and the windowseat

214

gave some privacy. He was king and he had sent them all away—George, her husband, Staff, all.

His breathing was loud and deep. "Mary, I have waited so long, willing myself not to touch you, waiting as I had promised I would. But the king is only a man in love, and he can wait no longer. You would not have me wait longer, would you, my love?"

"I was so happy when you walked into the room tonight, Your Grace. I have been so thrilled this last week at your court. I thank you for, well, for all this."

I have told the truth, she thought. Can I tell him I do not love him?

"All for me, sweetheart, the happiness, the thrill? It is not because of your new husband?"

"No, Sire. Will is kind and considerate, but the happiness is you."

He crushed her against his iron chest so tightly she could hardly breathe. His hands ran wildly over her back, down her hips, and one palm cupped her derriere smashing the voluminous skirts. "Mary, you will yield to me! Tomorrow will be the beginning of our love in truth. Tonight we must join the others and smile and dance and plan for the revels on the morrow. Then, tomorrow night after the masque, after the welcome home banquet, you will stay the night with me and Will goes home alone! I shall send him on a mission if I must. I have waited too long. S'blood, I will take you before the whole audience at the feast or on the jousting green if I am held off longer!"

Mary smiled tremulously at him as he released her. She carefully straightened her mussed clothes and hair from his fervent attack. They rose reluctantly to join the others.

"Did you say, Sire, the masque is for a welcome home feast?"

"Yes, my luscious Maid Marian. The queen returns from Beaulieu tomorrow morn. It will be her first night back at court for a fortnight, so it is all in her honor."

A tiny hurt bit at Mary's insides somewhere. On the good queen's first night at home, she would dance for her and bow to her and then become her dear husband's mistress in deed as well as name.

Mary could scarcely believe the swiftness with which the masque fell together. By the next evening everything had been assembled as if through sorcery. The framework of a great machine, which had obviously been employed for other revels, was garlanded with saplings and foliage to create a rich green forest setting which could be rolled out into the middle of the room. Another vast contraption on wheels was built from scaffolding and covered with canvas painted like stone to serve as the wicked Sheriff of Nottingham's castle where the maidens would be imprisoned to be rescued by the brave band of Merry Men from Sherwood. Costumes for the men and ladies appeared as if from nowhere. Intricate initials of H and C were embroidered on the bodices, entwined with roses in honor of the queen. In the morning the revelers rehearsed their parts and the leads practiced their few lines of speaking with musical accompaniment. The queen's retinue had arrived in the hour before noon. All was magically ready.

Everyone attended the banquet dressed in standard court dress, for they would don their costumes at a signal from the king. Once again, Mary was too excited to

216

eat, although she kept dabbing at the marvelous porpoise in mustard sauce. His Grace and Queen Catherine sat on the dais with the Duke of Suffolk alone, for the Duchess was not yet recovered from the birth of her cherished new daughter.

"How wonderful to marry for love and still be loved," Mary said aloud, instantly wishing she had not.

Will Carey had been brooding under a raincloud all day and she assumed it was because he had guessed or been told that tonight he must begin to pay for the bounty which had fallen into his eager hands. "The princess was damned fortunate the king loved Charles Brandon and that the crafty Lord Chancellor Wolsey made him realize that there were other ploys to keep England attached to both Francois and Charles of Spain. The king's whims toward women blow which ever way and when. That goes for his once beloved sister and poor Bessie Blount who bore his son hidden at a priory, and has been packed away in a swiftly-arranged marriage ever since. You would do best to remember that, wife."

Tears stung Mary's eyes and she did not look up. "I shall remember it, sir."

"I am counting on it. One day I will have you all to myself, and then we shall see!"

His bitter vehemence almost frightened her, but what did she expect? He was a man with pride, especially family pride. He cares not as much for me as he does for his Carey escutcheon being tarnished, she thought.

The queen, as far as Mary could tell, looked very pleased to be at home. She gazed on her husband often, nodded and chatted. Did he love her still? Surely he had loved her once in these ten years of their marriage, but when did love cease? She looked heavy and tired next to her exuberant lord, but she had borne him seven children and their little girl, Mary, was said to be her father's pride. But like Francois, he could nod and smile to his queen and then turn and leer at Mary from across the expanse of laden tables.

She hoped the queen would like her part in the revel of honor. They would wear masks, but they were all to unmask at the finale and be presented to Her Grace. Would she hate her when she heard court gossip? Could she ever understand that Mary Bullen had not chosen to warm the king's bed, but it had just happened somehow?

"Stop staring, foolish wench. You had better learn to be more discreet here. Our king does not parade his mistresses under the nose of his consort as did your fine Francois du Roi!"

Mary kept her stubborn silence for a moment, then said, "I was only looking at the queen. I have not seen her for a long time, you know."

"She is a fine and patient lady with her bullish lord," Will whispered. "And I do not give a whit who you are staring at, but the king obviously thinks it is at him. There, he rises. Come, let us get this farce over with. It will take us long enough to change."

Mary wanted to ask him why he bothered to participate in the masque if he thought it all foolishness, but she knew better. The king commanded, and that was that. Besides, she did not wish to cross Will while he displayed this nasty temper. She hoped he would get used to things and be more himself. If she could face up to it, he must learn to.

She donned her silken green and white dress and pinned the gauzy veil on her loosed hair. Her mask, as the king's and the villain sheriff's, was golden to separate them from the minor characters. That was the only bad point of this whole marvelous endeavor, she thought, smoothing her full skirts over her hips—for some perverse reason, the king had appointed William Stafford to play the Sheriff of Nottingham, and that meant he was her kidnapper and she had to stay wedged with him in the castle scaffolding while the other ladies were rescued first. Then Robin Hood came to personally challenge the sheriff for her release.

"At least good Robin beats the scoundrel in the end," she said aloud to comfort herself. Will had said the king chose Staff because it pleased his sense of adventure to become an outlaw himself while making the blackguard the symbol of law and order in the realm. But Mary knew better. The Sheriff of Nottingham was a wretched villain, and the king saw clearly enough to typecast the part. She had quietly told Staff that very thing at a rehearsal in the morning, though he just laughed at her and the snub gave her no pleasure.

They lined up in order; the lights dimmed; the music began. The settings of forest and castle creaked into the cleared center of the room and the dancing between the Merry Men of Sherwood and the ladies began. The steps were mostly those of a well-known pavan, for they had had little time to practice. The masks were secured by tied ribbons, but Mary's kept slipping to obscure her vision. Everyone looked strange and distant in their masks. She suddenly felt as though she had never known any of them at all. The men's hair color was hidden by their green forest caps, and the women's heads were almost completely covered by their filmy, floating veils.

In the first dancing encounter, Mary partnered the king proudly, wishing her father could see her here at Henry's court—surely, he would love to see her like this. Through the eye slits in her mask she could see little four-year-old Mary Tudor standing on a chair next to her mother, her eyes wide in awe at the beauty of the event.

The music quickened, the sheriff and his men attacked the dancing group and temporarily threw the outlaw band into disarray. Robin Hood, of course, had already departed on business into the green forest, for it would never do for *this* Robin to be vanquished, even if that had been the original story. The ladies were seized and taken to the castle with shouts and cries from the audience.

As he had done at the two rehearsals, Staff made certain that he was the one to abduct the blonde Maid Marian. The king had encouraged it, for the arch villain of the piece should take the love of the hero, so that they might fight in the end.

Mary kept her tongue while in front of the group, for she saw no way out of the situation. But each time he wedged her tightly between his strong body and the inner wooden framework of the castle, as they awaited the final challenge of Robin Hood, she told him to keep his hands to himself and off her waist and hips.

Tonight she had intended to put someone else between her and Staff while they stood, eight of them, packed in the mock castle. But her mask slipped again and, in the shadows of the inner void, he had her tight against him again. She raised her mask above her eyebrows and tried to thrust an elbow into his ribs.

"Loose me," she whispered.

"Hush, sweet Maid Marian. There is a full audience tonight and we must not ruin the king's fun—unfortunately." His voice was low, but his mouth was so close, he rustled her hair and veil when he spoke.

"I am sure this amuses you!"

"No, sweetheart, it pleases me to have you so close and my captive. It is my fondest fantasy."

She hated him for his mocking ways, but his voice seemed to be in earnest. She pushed out against him to free herself from his near embrace, but he did not budge and she felt his hard, flat stomach and muscular thighs press her back. Her heart began to pound distinctly from the strenuous dancing. He too seemed out of breath, breathing raggedly in her ear, standing close to her, touching her everywhere. His hands rested on the rough wood behind her against which her hips leaned. They stood silent while the music played on, and somewhere out there, Robin and his men searched the forest for their ladies. She wanted to threaten him, to say she would tell the king or her husband, but she did not. Her knees grew weak against his legs and she began to tremble from somewhere deep inside.

Then the music changed. The ladies and the sheriff's men spilled out of the castle for combat, leaving only the sheriff and his prisoner for the outlaw hero to find a few moments later.

Neither of them moved, although the dim empty cavity of the castle now gave them room. Staff bent his head and his lips caressed hers once. "No," she said. "No."

He kissed her again, bringing both hands up behind her head to hold her still, and his hot lips slanted sideways across her open mouth. Her head spun crazily. She was dizzy. She could not breathe in here. She would fall in front of the queen. They would all know what he had done. There was no time left, surely. The castle portcullis would swing up, the door would be opened and His Grace would see them!

He pulled his mouth away and said against her flushed cheek, "I have never envied any other man his bed before this long, long week. Now two men will possess you and neither really loves you, Mary Bullen. Think of me when you spread your sweet thighs for them!"

He pulled away from her abruptly, and she almost fell. His words spun in her head, but she could not grasp the meaning. He tugged her by her wrist to the door of the castle just as it swung wide and the king stood there, his golden sword held aloft and his mask obscuring his face. Mary thought to yank down her mask just as she followed the beleaguered sheriff into the pool of light at center stage. She stood with her hands clasped in mock fear as they parried and thrust at each other amid cheers and applause in the ring of dancers. It was sometime then, during their fierce battle, that she caught Staff's words and grasped their meaning. Undoubtedly, he did not really care for her, but was only amusing himself by chasing the mistress of the king. Surely he must detest His Grace for his handling of him all these years, even as Will Carey resented it.

The sheriff was beaten and his sword was dropped at the feet of the victor. Applause exploded and everyone bowed before Queen Catherine and the tiny clapping princess. Mary took her curtseys between Staff and the king, but none of them looked anywhere but on the smiling Catherine. Finally, she was presented to Her Grace, who said some kind words about her father and her lovely mother, and then the room emptied swiftly. Henry escorted his queen from the table, and carried his smiling, babbling moppet on his great arm.

Mary had not expected that. Perhaps she had misunderstood him. Her husband was gone and, thank the blessed saints, so was Staff. But Francis Weston was at her side taking her elbow gently. "May I escort you, Lady Carey? His Grace said he would be but a moment."

Her apprehension ebbed, but then embarrassment flooded in to think that they all knew. Weston, her husband, Staff, they all knew. She dreaded what the queen would say when someone told her about why the young Bullen girl was newly come to court.

Sir Francis said not another word, and Mary briefly wondered if he had done this for His Grace before. Maybe with poor banished Bessie Blount. Weston's own wife? She began to tremble again. She thought suddenly of another who had been sent to fetch her for a king—the cold, snake-like man in gray silk. What was his name?

"Good evening, Lady Carey," Sir Francis said with a quick glance that rested on her white face and heaving breasts. He quietly closed the door to the small room.

She leaned on the door for a full minute, her hands pressed to her breasts. The room was all linen-fold paneling and the wood seemed to glow in warm shadows from the low burning fire. There was a table and wine, three chairs—were they expecting a third? she thought irrationally—and a huge bed, high with a deep crimson coverlet. She sat in the nearest chair and leaned back on the stuffed blue velvet pillow.

William Stafford was crazy or he just meant to hurt her. Perhaps he was angered he had not been chosen to wed her and so be given the revenue and lands from the king. Perhaps, in that sense, he was jealous. How she would like to think he was jealous! She was grateful the king had not chosen him to wed with her, or deliver her here tonight. She could never have faced that.

Resolutely, she pushed William Stafford from her mind and banished the bitter, pinched face of Will Carey. Tonight she was waiting for the King of England. Father, I will sleep with your king tonight, she thought. Please come home soon, so you will see how well I am getting on.

Then a tall Robin Hood filled the doorway, his hair glowing red in the firelight, his gleaming narrow eyes upon her.

Chapter Fourteen
September 22, 1520

Greenwich

The summer weeks flitted by on butterfly wings for Mary Carey at King Henry's busy court—and in his massive bed. Will Carey's honeymoon with her had lasted but a week; this one, with the loud and laughing king, went on and on. They hunted, they rode bedecked barges up and down the Thames, they laughed and danced and sported and held hands. For Mary, it was truly the first courtship she had ever had, and she was wholly in love with being loved, if not with the effusive lover himself.

"Mary! Mary, His Grace is waiting for you under your window and half the court is in tow," Jane Rochford squealed and darted to help Mary pin her new green velvet riding hat on her heavy piled gold curls. "You had best give him a quick wave from the window if you intend to keep him waiting so patiently."

"There. I am ready, Jane, but I shall perhaps wave anyway. What a beautiful autumn day!" Mary shoved open a thick glass and leaded window and leaned her head out to wave. Her bright Kendal green riding gown and green plumed hat looked perfect for this day, she thought, as the king and several of his closest courtiers caught sight of her, waved and shouted their greetings.

"I am on my way down and I feel lucky at shooting today!" she called. They had all looked so excited and happy, like children, she thought: George standing proudly by His Grace, the king smiling, everyone eager to be off for the mounded, grassy hills where the painted bulls-eye targets were ready to be studded with their arrows. It had only been the avid-eyed William Stafford leaning on that big oak behind the king who did not smile up at her.

She hurried down the huge east staircase with Jane Rochford and several other friends trailing behind. Mary was proud of the effect of this dress that she had taken hours to select colors and materials for. This was her most simply cut dress as it was for riding or shooting. The velvet gored skirt was only moderately full and it was the long-sleeved, tight-fitting jacket with the row of molded brass buttons that set the whole outfit apart from others she had seen. The smooth cut of skirt showed off the top curve of her hips and a pleated cuff draped from the waist of the jacket. It emphasized her flat stomach and full breasts to perfection, despite the fact that the bodice styles imported from France and Spain were all rather tight with the cleavage pushed up above the daring low necklines. But, not for a morning of shooting arrows at targets, Mary thought. The king will have to leer at pushed up breasts elsewhere today!

The air was crystal clear, the sun like some cut jewel set in the blue velvet sky. She had been told England was often rainy and foggy in the autumn here along these great, rambling palaces on the twisting Thames. But today, all was beautiful in Mary's world. His Grace had even sent Will away again, probably for a week this time, so she would not have to put up with his grim looks and sour disposition today.

"Good morning, sweet Mary," the king boomed out the moment she emerged with her trailing ladies. As if, Mary thought, she had not been in his bed all last night, and as if most of the courtiers standing about did not know it.

Arm in arm despite the twitters, winks, and murmurs—and Staff's pointed stare—they strolled across the green lawns and cut through the rose gardens to the shooting range. The late summer gardens had greatly gone to riot now, and the leggy stemmed roses were making their last stands before frost time.

The king pulled his dagger and, with a flourish, cut her a full-budded white rose. "Put this rose here in your sweet bosom which that green velvet so naughtily hides, my Mary, where I may stoop and inhale its wonderful fragrance today," he said low, and shot her that devilish, little boy grin of his she so adored. "Besides," he went on as they continued walking, "I like for you to be in Tudor green and white. The king's dearest possessions, you know."

With his upper arm, he brushed her left breast firmly, deliberately, despite all the pairs of eyes, as they strolled the last yards to where squires had set up all the equipment for the shooting match. Yes, the quivers of arrows bore the Tudor colors and green and white Tudor pennants sprouted from the great, tall walls of Greenwich behind them. The king's possessions, he had said, and rightly so, as everyone, especially her father, viewed things. Only, despite her exciting days and long nights with Henry, King of all England, she never really felt he possessed her. Her body yes—he took that repeatedly, but she still felt only flattered and touched. There was something yet to *really* being possessed that she knew was missing with this generous Tudor, and even with the selfish, handsome Francois before him. And, although her name might be Carey now, poor solemn Will hardly played a part in these thoughts.

"My dear Lady Carey," the king's voice boomed at her. "Have you taken to daydreaming so early in the day?"

"Oh, Your Grace, I am sorry. What did you say?" She shot him a dazzling smile and lowered her voice for the next words. "I am sorry, Sire, but the lack of sleep at night that makes me like this today, is hardly all my fault."

He threw back his golden-red head bellowing a laugh, so that everyone who was not staring already, soon was. Henry Tudor looked overpowering in size, elaborate clothing, and the magnetic aura he always exuded. The peacock blue velvet which stretched across his muscular shoulders pulled taut when he bent to choose an arrow, as he did now. His loose-fitting back cape, which he would probably discard soon enough from the heat and exertion of his endeavors, swung easily to his gold belted hips, and his brawny-thewed legs in dark blue hose were planted firmly apart in square-cut slashed velvet slippers as he shot his traditional first arrow to signal the start of their impromptu tourney. Gloved hands applauded madly though the shot was

228

barely to the edge of the central red eye of the circles.

"S'blood, I hope the entire morn will not be off target like that," he groused.

"You are too fine a shot to even hint at such things," Mary comforted, and was rewarded with another big Tudor grin.

"True, sweetheart, but some days can bring a terrible run of bad luck even to the best of us. But how your sweet face and words always cheer me, my golden Mary." He bent to select another metal-tipped arrow from his green and white quiver, and fitted it carefully onto the string of the huge, polished oaken bow.

It was then, with a smile still on her face from the warmth of Henry's compliment and affection, her clear blue eyes locked with the direct stare of William Stafford. The look was so blatant—so intimate, even across the servants holding the quivers and bows—that it nearly made her knees buckle. Confused, angry, she stared back until his impertinent gaze dropped to go over the whole length of her body like a rough, physical caress. Then he turned away, squinted down at his strung arrow and shot. His bow whanged, his arrow thudded, but she pulled her eyes quickly away to select an arrow for herself.

"That one hit head on, Mary! Did you see it?" the king was saying.

"Yes, it—yes, it was wonderful, Sire," she replied, trying to steady her voice and her hand. The king was watching her first shot, probably others were too, even Staff. How marvelous he looked today, in darkest brown to match his hair and piercing eyes. She lifted her bow and pulled back the string. Here, the king had sent Will away and just when she was feeling light-hearted Staff, who had forced himself to be somewhat of a gentleman since the night of the masque, took to staring at her out here where anyone could see.

She snapped the bow string free from her gloved fingers, remembering to aim slightly higher than her mark as Will and the king had taught her. Damn that Stafford! she cursed silently, as her arrow thwacked the outer ring of the target.

"My sweet Mary's face looks like a thundercloud," the king teased, and she forced a smile. She refused to let Staff ruin this entire day, and she would never, never let him know he could affect her like this. She smiled again up at the king whose ruddy face watched her, suddenly wary.

"Your Grace, it has been nearly a week since I have shot and I believe I could use another lesson. Sometimes with so many courtiers all about who shoot so very well, I get a little nervous. And after all, you are such a marvelous shot, and there you are looking at me too—" She let her voice trail off, somewhat ashamed of herself for so obviously trying to manipulate him, but she had seen enough ladies handling men over the last seven years to know how to do it when she needed to. Even father would be proud of her now.

"You need another lesson from a master," the king said, and put his big hand over hers where she held her leather-wrapped bow grip. His smile was not intimate but caressing, and far more comforting than the sharp looks Staff shot at her.

"Yes, a lesson would be lovely, Your Grace, a private lesson without everyone gawking whenever I miss the mark."

"Oh, well yes, only everyone just got all dressed for

shooting at butts and now we can hardly shoo them all away after ten minutes, can we, my sweet lady?''

One of his large hands rested firmly on the small of her back as he bent to select an arrow for her bow. He squinted at it, and flipped it over scrutinizing the cut of the feathers. "A king's arrow," he said. "This one will shoot true."

Reluctantly, she placed it and he helped her sight it, lifting her left elbow slightly as she held the arrow ready. Let them all think her a poor shot, she fumed. Queen Claude's ladies were never allowed this sort of sport. Let Stafford give her those dark stares of his and the king think he possessed her when no one did. No one! Not Will, not her father, not her past, not even this great king whose bed she had shared almost nightly for a month.

Holding her breath, she released the string and the arrow pierced the heart of the target while the buoyant Henry Tudor laughed loudly. She laughed, joined by several nearby courtiers who hardly realized how close they had come to being banished from the butts range a few moments ago.

The day was back on an even keel for Mary. After all, the day was so lovely and her father had never been more proud of her. Cruel Francois had been replaced by this laughing, affectionate king, Will was not about to frown, and Staff had stalked off some where and left her alone. Alone, yes, caught up in the array of all the activities. Alone inside where no one could ever really possess her heart.

She laughed, and impudently gave the great Henry a suggestion when he fielded his next shot.

* * *

231

That night, after feasting and dancing in the great hall of Greenwich, she had bathed, dressed in a flowing golden yellow silk chemise and robe and sat at her mirrored table while her tiring woman, Peg, brushed her long, thick tresses. Mary missed her young maid Nancy, but when Will was away and she slept nightly with the king, she always gave Nancy orders to stay with her sister Megan and used the regular palace servants. And she simply could not stand to have Jane Rochford fussing around her in the evenings to gloat and simper when she left for the king's rooms. Her hair pulled and crackled now as if alive with some energy of its own in the cool September night as Peg ran the bristles through it.

Mary sat patiently awaiting the king's summons so she could slip down the side hall to his suite of rooms, close to this lovely little suite he had given her and Will. She stared at her face and form in the candlelit mirror; oval face, the even, balanced features everyone seemed to admire—aristocratic Howard features, father always boasted. Huge blue eyes with dark, thick lashes despite the fairness of her skin and the light wheat-colored hue of her long hair. A slender neck, full breasts which the tight-bodiced fashions of the day could hardly abide, a flat stomach, rounded hips and long legs. And was it all of this, this outside beauty that made people, men, kings, want her? Or, like Anne, was there something within that made them seek her out?

Mother loved her for herself, her old governess Semmonet too, but after that she was not certain if people just wanted her—or was that love? Oh, what was the use of all this foolish thinking, she scolded herself. It only spun her around in circles. Here, this very note lying right before her, a note from the King of England, said he "loved her desperately and eternally." And it had come with her lucky bull's eye arrow pierced right through a heart drawn on the note and the huge signature "Henry Rex" as if she would not know what Henry had sent it!

"Are you ready, Lady Carey?" Peg's voice broke into her reverie. "His Grace's man be waitin' outside wi' two linkboys."

Mary rose and, as a last thought, took the arrow pierced love letter with her. It would not do to leave these lying about. She always destroyed any letters Henry had sent her. She was not sure why—to be careful like father perhaps, or to protect Will from hearing further gossip, or ever seeing such a note. Maybe so that she did not have to believe it was all true.

Peg wrapped her in the blue velvet cape she always wore in the halls over her nightwear, and Mary followed His Grace's trusted body servant and one linkboy while the other brought up the rear. When they had begun this affair, Mary had asked the king to please summon her with trusted servants and not any of the courtiers who served him so closely in the treasured court appointments, however trusted they were supposed to be. And His Grace, though evidently amused to think it would ever keep anything secret, humored her by giving her her way.

At night there were always at least four Esquires of the Body within call of the privy chamber in case the king needed help with his clothes or food or someone to rail at. But she never saw them, of course, and Will was never on duty when she was with the king. The two gendarmes with their long silver poleaxes nodded to her

233

and opened the king's doors. No way to hide any king's visitors from them, but then, she could not imagine their ever saying a word.

To her surprise, the king sat at a table cluttered with missives and rolled parchments. The firelight behind him edged his auburn head and massive red and black robed shoulders with a glowing, shifting outline. He rose immediately and gave her a huge, reassuring bearhug as soon as the doors closed. He wore nothing under his robe, she surmised, because she could see curling, reddish hair down to his navel where the robe split open and his big, powerful legs were bare to his feet thrust in velvet slippers.

"Mary. S' blood, you smell wonderful, but I hope that is not some damned French perfume. Worse and worse relationships with Francois' minions, it seems. Sit here by the fire a moment. I will play servant and pour us some wine, my love."

She laid her blue velvet cape on the back of a chair facing his huge, carved one across the table. "But I would be happy to serve you, Your Grace. You looked very busy when I came in. I shall get the wine."

Like a big, scolded schoolboy, he did as she said, awkwardly covering his bare legs by folding his robe over them. She realized his eyes were on the pile of papers on the table and not her as she poured two goblets of his favorite sweet Osney from Alsace. Their fingers touched when she handed him his goblet, and he smiled up at her. Before she could move to the chair across from him, he pulled her gently toward him, indicating she should sit on his lap. Careful with her wine, she did so.

"I am afraid the wine is French, Sire, but I promise

234

you my fragrance is not. Pure English dried lavender, lilies-of-the-valley and rose petals. I store my gowns in it."

"Ah, is that it? A pity, sweet Mary," his voice wrapped around her as warm as his hand on her hip, "for we shall have to dispense with this lovely yellow silk thing soon enough." He nuzzled her silken shoulder and they sat quietly for a moment, content in their physical contact, listening to the warm crackle of the fire in this intimate moment.

He drained his wine and took her half-finished goblet from her unresisting fingers. "Sweet Mary, so beautiful and yet so untouched," he said low.

"Hardly untouched, my lord king," she chided and poked him playfully in his hard-muscled belly, but she saw then on his earnest face a fleeting mood of seriousness or sadness. She sat still to listen to what else would come.

"All the roistering about, all the gaming," he began, evidently searching to express some difficult or new thought. "Well, you know how busy and demanding it is for me, especially now that I am taking over more from Chancellor Wolsey, keeping a closer eye on him and the realm's business, as it were."

She listened carefully, thinking how often her father tried to pry from her anything of import the king might say to her in a trusted or unguarded moment. She nodded to encourage him, but really, she had no idea where this confession would go.

"I mean to say, I do not know why an anointed king of the earth's greatest realm has to be so set upon with petitioners and petty papers to read and sign, and tricky foreign realms to watch like Charles' Spain and

Margaret's Austria and your wily Francois' damned France!''

"Forgive me, Your Grace, but neither the French king nor France are 'mine'.''

"I did not mean it that way, sweet wench, really, only it galls me sore to think you were his once.''

She tried to scoot off his big lap but his iron hands held her hips against his strong thighs. "Sit, sit, madam. I meant not to rile you. We all make foolish errors, I warrant. Sit still, I say, Mary. I apologize.'' He pulled her fiercely to him, his lips moving in her loose hair along her right temple, his hands stroking her silken back and hips.

"There now,'' he crooned. "You are the last one in the world I want to turn argumentative and feisty, sweet. I meant only to tell you how pent up I sometimes get with all this business. I meant not to scold. By the saints, I need your serenity and beauty at the end of a day.''

She relaxed and shifted against his body, encircling his bull neck with her arms. There were so few quiet moments with this volatile, active man and here he was telling her he craved them. She smiled cuddled against him, savoring the warm affectionate caress Will had never given in his quick movements over her body. Peace and serenity, yes, like a little girl in her father's arms.

But the tiny, breathless moment was gone as quickly as it had come. His warm lips traced lower across her jawline; his hands began to stroke and knead her soft flesh; his hard manhood pressed against her buttocks through his robe and hers.

He stood her up in front of him on the soft Brussels

carpet spreading his knees so that she stood between them. His robe pulled away from his red-haired thighs but temporarily hid his growing desire. Seemingly impatient now, he reached up to undo the embroidered frog fastenings of her yellow robe and pulled it quickly down off her shoulders so she stood before him in only her thin silken undergown. She knew her nipples pointed through the shiny, thin material of the gathered bodice, for his eyes fastened there and his pink tongue moved to wet his parted lips. He always breathed heavily, sometimes almost panted when he looked at her, and it was then she felt a strange sort of power over this man of power—but that was hardly the love he always vowed to her.

"I adore you, my golden Mary. I love you," he was rasping low even now. He tugged the flow of cool silk down off her shoulders and then off the curve of her hips until it dropped in a rippled pool around her ankles to leave her naked in the firelight.

"Exquisite, my gold goddess. You shall always be mine. Mine, only!"

She smiled at the small lie and forgave it instantly as he pulled her a step closer and bent her forward until his mouth could fasten wetly on a full, pink, pointed breast. 'Always'—Francois had said that at first and she had foolishly believed him. Father had promised once, when she first left Hever, that he would always be nearby whenever she might need him. But she believed in 'always' no more.

The familiar warm tide of sensual pleasure washed over her from her breasts which he licked and fingered and pulled on so gently, to her belly where he stroked, to her hips and derriere he grasped, and even to her very woman's core. His bearded and mustached mouth tickled pleasantly everywhere it went.

Suddenly, in one of his quick, wrestling style moves, he stood her back again, then pulled her forward, parting her unsteady legs with his big knees. Her legs wide apart, she came down into his lap facing him this time. As he gave one quick tug to his own robe caught awry, she saw his blatant intent. Her smooth thighs grazed the outside of his hips and he slid her closer to him. He lifted her by a firm hold on her hips. She thought she would pitch backwards off the chair, but he had positioned her perfectly and her waiting warmth took him smoothly. She gasped as the rest of their bodies pressed together, her soft breasts crushed to his powerful, hair-matted chest, his bearded, panting face so close to hers.

"Mary, sweet Mary. You always do this—to me— and I can never hold back," he said between violent thrusts that pierced her to her very core. His eyes were closed now, his head back as his huge body shuddered with a passionate ecstasy which she marvelled at. This felt wonderful, yes, even exciting, but there was never time for her to reach the entire release she knew men boasted and women whispered of. It was so sweeping and powerful, but then, like now, this great king never waited for her.

He groaned and shuddered again and she felt him pulse into her. Despite the rush of passion and the hum of blood in her veins, she thought how strange that Francois, Will, and Henry, all men, ended their love-making with this wonderful climb to passion and release, and yet they were all so different: Francois, cruel and somehow degrading; Will, possessive and cold; and this giant of a man passionate but too hurried.

Stranger still it was only when Staff glowered hotly at her, and that one time he had kissed her the night of the masque, when she had thought such all-consuming passion might be possible. And that, of course, was pure foolhardiness and could never be.

"Mary, am I hurting you?" he questioned. She opened her eyes to see him slumped back against the tall carved chairback staring at her curiously. It occurred to her for the first time, as he studied her, that he was probably wondering why she did not respond more or cry out in pleasure as she knew women did. Surely, this king was used to being praised by many for everything he did.

"You never hurt me, my dear lord king, only please me again and again and again." He laughed low and his face lit like a Yuletide candle.

"That is my Mary, serene even in her lovemaking, but later, after a little respite, we shall see." He hoisted her off him and held her hips firmly until her legs steadied under her.

"What sort of riddle is this, Sire?" she asked, hoping her voice sounded light.

He stood and straightened his robe around his big girth, then put her robe around her nakedness before he led her to his eight foot square bed. "Get a little rest, my lady, and then you shall see. The king can get any advice he needs, you know, about anything, however personal." He took her robe away, pushed her gently down onto the bed and whisked the soft silken sheet and warm coverlet up over her.

"But you, Sire," she said. "Are you not coming to bed?"

"Yes, love. Shortly. Now, do not get over anxious

and do not tease about this little surprise to come. I am just going to finish these few wretched papers and hand them out to that damned ever-hovering secretary in the hall and I shall be right back. Sleep now, lovey, and I shall wake you. Do as I say now. You shall need your rest when the Tudor lion comes back to you shortly.''

She watched him move away and bend instantly over his papers. She had never seen this side of him before, so distracted, yet filled with fierce concentration. At least he had not sent her away as Francois almost always had. She yawned and stretched luxuriously in the massive bed under the carved and gilded crest of the Tudor kings. She was tired and she could feel herself slipping away. It must be nearly midnight now.

Through a fog of her thoughts she heard his quill pen occasionally scratch out his name 'Henry Rex' even as he had on that impassioned love letter. Impassioned, Henry Rex of England impassioned, passionate. Then why not I? she thought with one foot on the hazy edge of dreamy unreality.

She was full of his seed now as she was almost every night, and what would become of her if she conceived a child? But she had never conceived all those times with Francois, that one terrible night with Lautrec, and now with this proud Henry.

Proud, so proud, all of them. Never admitting they could be wrong except in little things, always having to feel masterful and in charge. A paper rustled somewhere on the fringe of her thoughts and a chair scraped back. Maybe he was coming to bed now. He had never before done work in the middle of the night, and he usually took her two or three times in quick succession.

She drifted again softly, silently through the sweet

smelling rose gardens of Greenwich, or was it Hever? No, she must be at court for everyone stood about shooting arrows at one another, laughing cruelly when someone was pierced. The king was laughing too, drawing his strong oaken bow at everyone, and then she saw her father shooting his full brace of arrows from a never-empty quiver. Arrows flew at her from everywhere—the air was black with them and she was afraid. But none hit her.

Then she saw Staff by the tree, his arrows like his eyes. He raised his bow directly at her; she held up her arms and tried to scream but no sound came. She tried to run but her feet were as heavy as lead.

His arrow whirled at her; she saw it coming and to her own amazement, she moved to meet it. It pierced her sweetly deep in her loins and a rolling wave of rapture beat in her like coursing blood. The arrow Staff had shot she now held tenderly in her hands and saw it had penetrated not only her very soul but also a note with a roughly drawn heart. "I love you desperately and eternally," the note read. "Staff." She looked up in amazement but he had turned and was walking away.

"Mary. Mary, my love. I am back with you." Two strong arms reached for her in the bed and she cuddled instantly against the strong naked body murmuring into his shoulder. Staff, she thought, Staff. She jerked away completely awake. Had she said Staff's name aloud too?

"Do not startle, lovey," the king's deep voice comforted. "You were tossing about and murmuring, lost in some dream."

"Oh." She tried to relax against him. "Did I say

241

anything?''

"A lot of mishmash, sweet. Was I—was I in your dream, Mary?''

The dream flooded back to her in an overwhelming rush, and she felt her whole body go scarlet hot. How dare her sleeping mind play tricks on her like that, she fumed silently. Mooning after Staff, mixing him up with the king and longing for him. But then, she had had other foolish dreams.

"Mary?''

"No, Sire, you were not there and that made it a bad dream. You see, everyone was shooting but not at the targets on the butts—at each other. And then it got all mixed up after that.''

He hugged her close, silent for a moment. "But you are happy here with me, Mary. Are you not?''

"Of course, my dear lord king. The love note you sent me today, it was in the dream.''

She could almost feel his proud smile in the darkness of the deep bed. "Ah, my sweet, sweet, golden Mary, I have never loved a woman more than I do you. Never. Not Catherine, not—anyone. And I want you to feel it too, that desire I have for you everytime I look at you. I know ladies do not feel it the same way as a man, but I have heard enough boasting among my comrades. By the rood, I have done enough of it myself to know women also cry out and are—swept over in a thrill of passion. Here. Here, my dear, relax and let me show you. Let me touch you here.''

She frowned in the dark, and tried to fathom the full intent of his words. He had been talking to some of his friends and they had told him women showed much more passion than she evidently had been showing. But

242

did not women only show what they truly felt and did not she only feel the beginning stirrings of passion for this big, affectionate man? By the holy saints, if he had said anything to Weston or Norris or George or Staff, she would strangle him!

"Mary. Mary, love, lie still, I say. Let me feel you, stroke you before I mount you, love. You are like a fractious filly now. Lie back here."

She let him pull her down. She knew what he intended now. Francois had done it often to please himself more than her, she was certain. His hands would search, his fingers probe that secret, hidden, private part of her between her legs until she cried out that she could bear no more. Now this king would take her, even as Francois had while she cried out love words she could never mean, only to be cast aside and disappointed. What then if Henry boasted to Staff or all of them the next day the way Francois and his cronies used to trade tempting tidbits about riding their pack of "jeunes filles"? Then her heart would be pierced indeed with the arrow of shame!

She forced herself to tolerate his insistent fingers and his mouth, teasing a pink nipple to new life. People had always told her she was a terrible liar, she thought. All had told her she could never hide the truth, but it seemed so important to keep intact and separate that part of her Francois had abused, that she must try this.

"My dear lord—Henry—the moment you look at me too, the moment you touch me, I desire you between my thighs. The way you have loved me this past month—I thought you knew that."

His hand between her legs hesitated and she managed to move slightly away. "Is it true, love?" he demanded.

"Have you not seen how happy I have been this last month with you? You seem so all wise about things, especially women, that I thought you knew."

He propped himself up on one elbow, trying to see her face in the dim shadows with only distant fireglow lighting the room. "So, you would want nothing different in bed than the way we have been to make you completely happy?" he asked suspiciously.

Only time to myself off at Hever, Will forgiving, and father not angry, the little voice in her head taunted, but she said only, "Indeed, my Henry. Only, perhaps it is a little worrisome to a lady if her love sends her to bed alone while he bends over his papers instead of her ready body."

He stared down at her shadowy face one minute more before he threw back his big auburn head and shouted a laugh. "Who is to say the lovely, blonde Bullen is not the cleverest wench in the land, eh? She keeps her king faithful and happy," he said much too loudly as he crushed her to him and pushed her back against the deep, down-filled bed bolsters to make lightning quick love to her once again before he slept.

Chapter Fifteen
October 14, 1521

Whitehall

A brightly clad bevy of court ladies trailed after Mary as she left her apartment and went out into the crisp autumn sunshine. As at Greenwich, the swards at Whitehall slanted down to the river though the once clear vista was now cluttered with tilt yard, archery range, and the close-cropped alley of grass for bowls, and a tall maze nearer the river. The crowd clustered on this clear afternoon at the newly built tennis courts of which the king was so proud. Whitehall was the newest palace given outright as a love gift—a policy gift, Staff called it—by His Grace's Lord Chancellor, the Cardinal Wolsey, who had moved his busy household upstream to his country palace Hampton Court. Mary favored Richmond and Greenwich of all the palaces, but on a day such as this, who could not love Whitehall?

"His Grace was anxious for you to come to see him play against my Lord Francis," Joan Norris said for the second time, hurrying to keep pace with Mary's strides. Mary had learned to walk and dance faster, much faster, in the year she had been the energetic king's mistress.

"Actually, I believe he promised he would beat Sir Francis soundly," joked Lady Joan, and Mary forced a laugh.

"Your Lord William is much from court this past week, Mary," observed Jane Rochford tagging close behind.

"Yes, Jane, but it is Father sent him this time and not the king. As you know, Jane," Mary said, turning her head to the girl, "Father asked Will to accompany him to visit the Bullens' new revenue posts at Essex and Nottinghamshire. They are due back today. Are you quite certain you have enough to occupy your time without George before the wedding?"

"Of course I do, Mary, now I can be with you every-day. Lord Bullen is pleased, too, and I do so wish to make him happy."

"So do we all, Jane," Mary shot back quickly and then regretted the sharp tone to her voice. No wonder Father and George had had a tremendous row over the Bullen-Rochford betrothal a few months ago. George had evidently been forced to see the wisdom in the marriage, but she could hardly blame him for his impatience with the meddling little Rochford. But George's sulkiness had worsened since, and he seldom came to court now that Jane was here to attend Mary. Jane Rochford saw Lord Bullen as her protector and deliverer. If only the wench knew the salvation of her coming marriage had nothing to do with herself and all to do with her family title and lands, who knew what she would say or do then.

Several young men tilted at the quintain on the joust practice grounds trying to learn the timing and placement of the thrust of the lance from a moving horse. The wood and leather mock opponent twirled and spun on its pivot as they made passes at it. They were so confident, so awkward, and Mary remembered George, gangly and skinny at Hever years ago. She favored stopping to watch their serious antics, but she had been summoned to the tennis courts again.

The archery range where she had shot at target with the king only yesterday was nearly deserted. Her aim was much improved and it annoyed her to have to wear the proper lady's half-gloves when she shot. Henry was much pleased at her progress since the last contest, but she did not tell him that both Will and Staff had given her lessons while he was in council.

Despite the brisk river breeze, she felt warm in her fawn-colored pelisse. Still she wanted to wear it over her dress whenever she was in public where someone might notice her slightly expanded waistline. Soon someone would see, then everyone would know, and the king would put her aside as he had Bessie Blount. He pledged eternal love and had been relatively faithful for over a year, but Mary was no country-bred wench who trusted in men anymore. And her greatest fear—the thing that kept her awake nights when His Grace or Will rolled over and went to sleep—was that there would be no way to truly know who had fathered the babe.

"I am sorry, Jane. What did you say?"

"I said, the cheering from the courts is so loud that they must have started the match without you."

"Well, that is fine. They last a good long time anyway."

Jane had taken to brazenly flirting with Mark Gost-

247

wick but, except for pitying poor George even more, Mary ignored it. She was relieved when Jane excused herself and went to sit with him on the far side of the court.

"I must warn you, there is a rumor that the queen will appear this afternoon, Mary," Anne Basset whispered to her as they waved to the beaming king and his opponent, Norris. They sat on a padded bench which was quickly vacated for them. Mary self consciously draped her pelisse closer about her. This canopied area was much too warm with the courtiers packed in like this.

"I do not believe she favors the embarrassment when she knows the blonde Bullen is about the area," Mary replied carefully, "though she always handles the encounters beautifully by smiling and nodding and, if she must speak, inquiring sweetly after my father and mother."

"She knows His Grace has given you his heart. All she has now is half a daughter. And, with the king's illegitimate son being raised so royally, she fears."

"She has always been gracious enough to me, Lady Anne. She is not here, so we will let it rest, please."

Anne Basset nodded, but her eyes showed her dismay at never being able to taunt Mary Carey enough to get some bit of information for gossip. Was the woman also so sweet and tolerant in the king's arms? What was it like to bed with the Tudor stallion? She had wanted to ask Mary in private, but her blue eyes seemed distant again, lost in some reverie in the midst of the crowded court.

The king played tennis with much power and verve. But then, so did Norris. Henry grunted and threw his huge body several steps into the court each time he served, and he often cursed loudly or flailed the air with his racquet if the leather ball did not land where he intended. She had watched him play for hours in the closed courts at Greenwich. Only last week he had played a two-hour game with Staff, winning only in the last set to the deafening cheer and applause of the assembled crowd. At least in that interminable game she had had Staff to study. His lithe body was angular and lean compared to the king's, although his muscles bulged across his back and chest. He was there across the court with that fawning Lady Fitzgerald at this very moment. It annoyed her the way the raven-haired woman clung to him and brushed against him all the time. Well, what did she care? She pulled her eyes away and forced herself to refocus on the game.

Tennis players always wore white on the Tudor courts, pure white, a fashion begun by the king, she supposed. Henry hated to play up to the net and was content to stand firm on the back line, smashing drive after powerful drive into his opponent's court with his quick, rapid thrusts. She smiled and hoped no one noticed how her thoughts always went to her face no matter how hard she tried to look indifferent. That was exactly the way the king made love. Quick, powerful thrusts and then it was over before his passionate kisses or fierce caresses could work the magic on a woman of which a man was capable. And Will was so self-disciplined, even in bed, she could not imagine the babe that grew within her could be a Carey son. Her throat constricted in fear again. If the baby looked like the king, whatever would she do? At least Will and His Grace had similar coloring, but the Tudor hair was a deeper red. If the king sent her away from court, she would be lost. And father might even turn against her.

She was making herself sick from worry. It was too hot in here. All the people so near, looking at her and the king. But her cloak was her protection. She wiped her damp brow again and shifted nervously in her seat. Who was winning? She must put her mind on the game.

Worst of all, Staff was sauntering over, and he could always see right through her. She valued his advice about others in the intricately woven web of courtiers, but she needed none of his lectures on her own behavior now. Besides, there was an unbreakable magnetic pull of attraction between them of which he had long teased her, and she had stopped fighting with him on the point. When he brought it up in jest or in earnest, she raised her armor of silence, but he knew he had won.

She remembered, particularly last month, when Will had been suddenly summoned by the king. She, Will, and Staff had been together on a crisp, clear evening drinking hot mulled cider in front of a fire in the Carey suite of rooms. Will had scurried away with a brief peck on her cheek and a quick word to Staff about the good fortune to be summoned by the great Henry more frequently now that the Carey rise to power had begun.

"I shall just sit a few minutes with Mary, Will," Staff had called after his retreating friend and then waited until the door banged shut to add, "and then head home to my lonely little bed while sweet Mary sleeps alone tonight." He had given her a forlorn, doleful look, his hand over his heart and she had burst out laughing instead of scolding him.

"More mulled cider, sweet?" he asked, and leaned

over to pour her from the metal flagon before she answered. She held her mug out for him, annoyed that her hand shook a little.

His next words startled her. "I swear, your husband is as blind as a bat and as foggy as the Thames marshes, sweetheart." He turned toward her, "If I were Will, I would not let you out of my sight around a ravenous blackguard like myself."

"Oh, Staff," she said, trying to sound amused. Then, foolishly she turned to smile at him. The impact of his gaze, his very presence made her insides tilt.

He jerked his head away first, staring wide-eyed into the fire, then downing his cider in several huge gulps. "I have to leave now, Mary, before I do something very, very foolish. And, considering with whom you sleep when you are not with Will, damned dangerous, too."

"Must you go?" she had said before she could stop herself.

He looked at her again, the firelight edging his rugged profile and dusting his black velvet shoulders with a rosy glow. "Yes, Mary, I really must. The time is not ripe yet, as they say, though heaven knows I would almost hazard it all for one sweet—"

She leaned forward, entranced by his words, unaware of how lovely and vulnerable she looked in the golden glow of firelight. "For one what, Staff?"

He rose and moved away from her, walking around the backs of the three chairs facing the hearth as if he were afraid of being near her. "For more than one kiss, that is certain, love. This little game you and I play is a serious one and do not ever make a mistake about that, Mary. Let us just say I would almost risk it all for one sweet, little—more than you are willing to give me right now. I think you know how I feel and what I want from you, lass. Goodnight, then.''

The door had closed on him and disappointment instantly overwhelmed her. Why did he have to run like that when they had some quiet time together? Did he fear the king's spies as he had mentioned once? But his last earnest words echoed in her mind: she *did* know what he wanted, and the prospect thrilled her. Suddenly, the delicious sweet cider had turned very sour and the firelit room had gone very cold.

She no longer feared Staff would do anything to hurt her. Besides, she was well-protected by her relationship with her husband, who was one of Staff's best friends, and to the king whom he served. He had not touched her for an entire fourteen months, but to take her arm, since that foolish Robin Hood masque. He knew his place now, so she could usually relax and genuinely enjoy the time he spent with her and Will. At least he had had the kindness to fob that vine-like Emily Fitzgerald off on Edward Courtenay and not drag her over here.

Ignoring Anne Basset's eager gaze, he bent over Mary's shoulder from behind her. ''Will you walk with me briefly? His Grace will not mind. He is winning and we will tell him you did not feel well. You do not, do you? Come on. Excuse me, Anne,'' he added to the Basset girl.

''Oh yes,'' she breathed, smiling up at him. ''Shall I come too? I would be pleased to help if Lady Mary does not feel well.''

''Thank you, but she only needs a bit of fresh air,'' he answered.

The girl's breathy sigh greatly irritated Mary. She

rose to join Staff. "Has she been in your bed, too, Staff?" she inquired more icily than she had intended.

"Too, Mary? I am sorry you cannot mean in addition to yourself, so to whom are you referring?"

Her head was beginning to hurt and he was intentionally annoying her when she needed his support. If she could only tell him of the baby. He had been around the court enough, and knew the king well. At least she could listen to his advice and take it into consideration.

"Lady Fitzgerald, of course," she answered after a long pause. "And, no doubt, others."

"You cannot expect me to live like a monk while I am waiting for the king to toss you out and for you to realize you love me, Mary." He turned his head and looked straight at her. His brown eyes were suddenly flecked with tiny shards of gold. It frightened her how much she loved to have him talk so foolishly. She lowered her eyes to her hand resting on his blue velvet arm.

"This is a surprise. Silence and smokey stares have become your favorite weapons against me, but never when I speak of loving you. No tart words? Let us face the truth, sweetheart. You have two men at your beck and call, so why should I be celibate?"

"Why do you not marry then?"

"The truth? I cannot afford it and I cannot hope that His Grace would see fit to drench me in revenues and lands as he does my fortunate friend Will Carey. And why should I wed someone I cannot tolerate when it is so easy to bed others I can?"

Mary could feel the color mount to her cheeks at his words. She had heard others speak and jest bawdily at court, but the truth, plainly spoken from Staff, often

253

embarrassed her. They were almost to the privet maze. She had not realized they had come so far from the tennis court. Surely he would not take her into the lover's maze in broad daylight.

"Imagine a lover's maze shaped like a cardinal's hat, Mary? Well, the esteemed Cardinal Wolsey has had lovers and a wife, so I should not be so surprised at it. Do not balk. I am not foolish enough to take you in, although there is little I would like better right now. Neither of us needs to be banished from court, at least not now."

They sat outside the maze on a turf seat encircled by a bed of orange marigolds and yellow chrysanthemums. The shouts from the tennis area were distant and she suddenly felt tired and drowsy. The river glinted silver through the distant golden beeches and tall ashes.

"It is lovely here," she said to break the silence.

"Does it remind you of Hever?"

"Yes. Some, but it is so peaceful there and here it is usually so busy and confusing."

"I know. Mazes. Masks hiding masks, all more intricate than the crazy hedges in this cardinal's hat." He fingered a loose strand of hair on her shoulder and took his hand swiftly back. "Will and your father should return today, I would guess. Whom will you tell first, Mary? Your father, Will, or the king?"

Her heart lurched. "Tell them what?"

"About the babe you carry."

She raised her head wildly, her eyes wide in shock. Then she felt them fill with unbidden tears that coated her lashes and spilled down her flushed cheeks. "But I . . . is it so obvious, then? Dearest God in Heaven,

254

everyone will know.''

He scanned the area and then covered her clenched hands with his big one. ''Of course everyone will know, Mary. This is the court and you sleep with the king. Do not cry. Everything will turn out for the best one way or the other.''

''How can it? He will banish me like Bessie Blount and take the child away to raise.''

''Maybe not. He has proved he can father a living son already. Bessie Blount was unmarried when she was unfortunate enough to conceive. You have a husband. It is only a question of the king's continued affections which are at stake. He has never returned to a favorite after she bore him a child, damn it.''

''But you said it would please you if he would put me aside.''

''Not if he sends you and Will off to some impoverished castle on the Welsh border!''

Before she could stop herself, she smiled at his impassioned words, but he was staring off in the distance, frowning. ''I—Will and I—could always go to live at Hever with mother.''

''That is entirely unlikely, Mary. If the king casts you off, your father will too.''

''That is not true! My father loves me. We have never been closer than when he came home from France. I will not have you speak of him that way!''

''I do not mean to hurt you, sweet, but of course he acts loving to you now. Through you, come preferments, power and little goodies like new stewardships at Tonbridge, Brasted, Penshurst and another big promotion which is probably in the wind about now.''

''Stop it! I will not listen to your slanders. Just because my father is successful and you . . . I will not listen to your jealous lies!" She put her hands to her ears.

"I think you had better get control of yourself, Mary Bullen. You are acting like a spoiled little girl. We will have to go back now. Dry your tears and listen carefully."

"I do not wish to listen to you at all."

He reached for her arm and shook it like he would a rag doll's. "I said listen, and I mean it! Or I shall take you into the maze and you will listen there."

Her eyes widened and she stared at him, the blue of her eyes melding with the azure October skies behind her golden hair.

"Do you know who is the father of the babe? Well, do you?"

"I am not certain."

"All right. When you tell Will does not really matter since he will see the import of it all. Tell your father as soon as you can do so. He will be upset, but you must weather it out. He will probably ask you to keep it from the king until His Grace publicly announces that he is to be appointed Treasurer of the Household at New Year. That way the king will be hard pressed to rescind the position even when it gets around that you are pregnant and will be leaving court—only for a while, hopefully."

"But the king will see me and he will know. You did."

"I am a confirmed watcher of beautiful blondes with sweet faces and nasty tempers. No, I promise you it will be a while before His Grace notes your condition, if you are careful. I doubt that he will even notice that your monthly flows have ceased since he beds others lately."

She blushed hot that he would dare to mention her monthly flow. Was there nothing the man did not think, or would not say if it suited him?

"It does not hurt you, Mary, that he sometimes seeks out others?"

"Not really. Well, it hurts my pride a bit."

"But you do not love him?"

"You notice everything about me, private or not, Staff, so you tell me," she challenged.

"Ah, there is my old Mary, sweet faced and sharp-tongued."

"Only to you. You anger me beyond belief sometimes."

"I know. That pleases me, and to hear the truth from those tempting lips so much more than I used to. And since you were honest with me, I will tell you. You do not love the king. You loved another king once. He used and hurt you, and Mary Bullen decided never again. Come on, lass, we must go back."

They walked slowly toward the green and white canopy covering the tennis courts. "And do you love Will Carey?" he pursued.

"In a way," she drawled slowly.

"If you do, 'in a way' you do not." He stopped. "I shall not return you to your seat. It is enough that we walked off together. Say only that you dressed too warmly and needed fresh air. Smile that fabulous smile and all will be forgiven. Your servant, Lady Carey." He bowed to her with a rakish teasing smile lighting his face and paced quickly toward the ruddy-bricked, turreted palace.

The swelling sound of the cheering crowd had not abated when Mary re-entered the tennis grounds.

257

Henry was beet red and gasping and Francis Norris looked gray and exhausted, but the game plunged on. Few heads turned to note her arrival and Mary breathed a sigh of relief. Perhaps it would be possible to keep the knowledge of her pregnancy from the court, at least for a while. Lady Guildford had taken her vacated seat, so she watched from the cluster of people behind Norris' side of the net where she was sure the king would notice her. She could tell him that she moved to be able to see him better. Norris dove for a ball which bounced along the corner line and missed. Henry switched sides and served again, his sharp grunt of exertion was heard throughout the crowded area. Norris whacked a clean return, and the king returned it.

"This is for game point," Mary heard someone behind her say, and she was glad it would be over soon. She hoped the king would win, for when he was beaten he was quite out of his humor for the rest of the day. Surely Francis Norris would have the good sense not to defeat Henry Tudor in front of such a crowd. Whack, thump, still they volleyed. Then Norris missed a shot right in front of Mary and the hushed crowd exploded. The king embraced Norris at the net, beaming with joy. On the day I finally do tell His Grace I am pregnant, she thought, I shall be certain he has just won at tennis.

A gentleman usher held the blue and purple velvet robe the king donned after heavy exertion. Nodding and bowing, he plunged through the press of courtiers, heading straight for Mary. The sense of thrill and power returned with stunning impact. The king, Henry Tudor, sought her out from the masses of adoring subjects.

"Did you see that last serve, sweetheart?" he bellowed over the noise. "I never was in better form than today!"

"You were marvelous, Sire. Atlas himself could not have bested you."

"Nor that sly Francois, eh? But that rogue Norris was good. He was excellent," he admitted grandly, brandishing his racquet like a sword. "I had to be at my peak to beat him today!" He put one big arm over her shoulders, and they slowly strolled back toward the palace, acknowledging the compliments from groups and individuals. For once, he did not walk too quickly for her to keep up easily, and she kept her cloak wrapped firmly about her body.

"Gads," he said exuberantly in her ear, "if we could only go to bed now, I would show you how a victorious athlete behaves after a game like that one."

She laughed along with him for his boyish boast, and he grinned down at her. "There is your father, sweet," he said suddenly and pointed with his raised racquet. "I do not see Will Carey anywhere. Thomas, did you find all well in my kingdom?"

The king grapsed Thomas Bullen's shoulder in a rough masculine greeting as Thomas arose from his bow. He beamed to see Mary under His Grace's other arm and kissed her warmly on the cheek.

"And where is my man, Will Carey?" Henry asked.

"All is well in the realm, Your Grace. The commons love you. That was always obvious to Will and me. Will brought his sister back for a stay from the priory at Wilton, Sire, and he wanted to get her situated before he reported to you. The ride much tired her. And how is my beautiful daughter?"

"Well, as you see, as sweet and charming as ever, Thomas. Whatever services you lend your king, this is the dearest prize you could have given. See you have not come to take her away," he laughed.

"Never, Your Grace. Mary would be desolate should she be taken away. The Bullens are only too honored to be able to share with our king who has blessed us with so much."

"Then I shall trust you with her while I change for dinner. The queen shall attend the meal, I believe. Be certain, Thomas, you keep my golden Mary safe from my wily courtiers who lurk about. Especially the renegade Stafford needs a watch, eh, Mary?"

He turned and was gone in a cluster of men, slapping Weston on the back and recounting the match.

She took her father's offered arm, and they drifted away from the bunches of people toward the river landing. Instinctively, she grasped her cloak tight again. Staff had told her to tell her father as soon as possible. If she told him out here but within earshot of others, he could not possibly berate her too long or too loudly.

Thomas Bullen broke the jumble of her thoughts. "How are you getting on with His Grace? He has not been near that Woodstock wench again I hear."

"You are well informed for only having just returned, father. No, I think he has not seen her. He has been with me . . . at night, I mean."

"Fine, Mary. I was hoping that would be one result of my taking Will away for a while. Your husband was only too glad to see lands and stewardships he hopes will bear the Carey name soon enough, though he never ceases to tell me that the return of his beloved lands at Durham are the final Carey dream. I am sorry you will have to put up with that sour sister of his for a while. Do not feel you have to take any of that snobby preaching on the greatness of the Careys from her. She ought to be smart enough to realize from where her bounty flows, but she seems terribly one-minded. They are both obsessed with their family name. Let me know if she bothers you."

"Yes, father. I will."

The barges rocked gently, rhythmically at the landing, gilded and brightly painted though now sadly stripped of their bunting and banners. Their feet made hollow sounds on the landing when they mounted it. The river rustled by calmly and gave the illusion that the sturdy landing was adrift in the currents.

"Now what is this gibing about wily courtiers lurking about, and especially William Stafford? Has he been bothering you? You must guard your position carefully, girl. Do I need to warn him to keep off?"

"No, father. His Grace was jesting. I took a little walk with Staff during the tennis match today, because I felt ill, rather faint. Stafford is only a friend of Will's, so leave him be."

"And I know damn well you have better sense than to care for someone of his questionable reputation and rank, so enough said. His Grace cares a great deal for him, or he would be out on his ear a poor country squire of a stoney farm on the borders somewhere." He leaned on the painted rail along the landing and faced her squarely. "You say you were ill? Are you better now? Or is the illness just a clever ruse to keep Will Carey away from you?"

Mary looked out across the stretch of green water and his eyes grew wary. She was almost tempted to let

261

him guess. She knew she was a craven coward when it came to crossing her father. But he loved her and he needed her now that she was in the king's goodwill. There was strength in that.

"I am not exactly ill, father. I am . . ." She gripped the carved rail in front of her. "I am with child, my lord."

It had not been so frightening to say it. The green depths swirled into gray ones under the rail. She looked up through her lashes. The explosion did not come, but his face grew livid under his mustache and beard.

"Damn, I knew it had to happen. How long?"

"How long?"

"How long have you been pregnant, girl?"

"Around three months, I think. I was hoping I was wrong, but it is certain now."

"Well, it had to happen. Judas Priest, why did it have to happen now? I had hopes when you went a whole year without catching it. Could it be His Grace's child? Well?"

"I cannot figure it, father. Yes, it could be, but Will was at court that month, so how am I to be sure?" Tears came to her eyes again. Why must I cry so easily, she scolded herself angrily. What good did it ever do to cry in front of father?

"At least you have made it more than a year, and that is a good bit more than the Blount woman lasted."

"Bessie Blount was not married, and I am, father."

"Yes. I am pleased to see you have been reasoning out what we must do to protect our interests, Mary. Yes, she was not married, nor did she have a family or father to stand behind her as you do. We must protect the family at all costs. Do you understand?" He swung about, bending over the safety rail with his long arms leaning stiffly on the wood. He looked sideways at her. "I said, do you understand, Mary?"

"Perhaps I do not. Perhaps you had best tell me what to think." She could see it coming already, the gleam in his narrowed eyes. She felt strangely betrayed that Staff had been right when he had said her father would ask her to hide it from the king for his own ends.

"On or about New Year's Eve, Mary, His Grace will make me Treasurer of the Household. As you may know, that position entails power as well as grants. The Bullen name has never risen so high as that, and we must protect that position. I have hopes that if I hold that favored position, His Grace will return you to court after you bear your child, and you may be able to ensnare his heart again. I can tell from the way he greeted me today that he does not know of your condition. Am I correct?"

She nodded, peering at the leaden reflections of clouds on the dull jade surface of the river.

"Then I would ask you to keep the news from the king until he makes the announcement of my new position. It should be soon. Thank God, we do not have to wait until the appointment is final in January, or we would never make it."

"Do you not think, father," she inquired sweetly, "that His Grace values your service so much that he would still appoint you whether or not I am handy to warm his bed?"

He grabbed her wrist in a vise-like grip and jerked her hard up to his velvet and silken chest. "Damn it, girl, I am depending on you to handle this properly. However much fine service I give His Grace you are the important link right now, and I do not appreciate the implication. Have you been about this clever court so long you forget who got you these honors in the first place?"

"No, father, I have not forgotten. Please. You are hurting me. I just get frightened and homesick sometimes."

"For Hever?"

"Yes. For Hever. And for mother."

"Well, you can stop that now, for the odds are good you will go home to bear the child since it will be more natural and will cost His Grace no extra coinage, as did the Blount wench." He patted her drooping shoulder awkwardly. "I meant not to hurt you, Mary, and I realize you must feel afraid sometimes, for the stakes are high. But I am back to stay for a time now, and you can rely on me for support. I ask you to keep your secret only for a little while. The announcement of the advancement must come soon. You will help, will you not, my Mary?"

"Of course, father. I always have."

"And do not be sad, Mary. Times are bad with France, so I intend to fetch Anne home on the excuse of George's wedding. Then when His Grace calls you back to court after the child is born, you will have George, Anne, and Jane Rochford about to keep you company, as well as Carey and me. That will help."

"Yes. It will be wonderful to have Anne home, but that Rochford girl can drive me to distraction at times."

"Really? I think her a rather good soldier. She knows her place, and she is fond of you, Mary. I appreciate her. She often tells me what is going on. She will help to settle George down and help him forget that foolish Wyatt girl.''

Mary pressed her lips together tightly. He guided her up the path toward the tiltyards. "Let me see you without the cloak. Here, just hold your arms out." He bent in front of her and peered at her waist and stomach as though she were a filly for sale. "Quite flat yet. We are in luck. No one has noticed, have they?''

"I would say I am much too small, father, for just anyone to notice.''

He squinted into the sunlight at her face. "Good. Then everything is settled. I imagine we can at least tell Will the news. Perhaps the Careys will rejoice at the prospect of an heir, and at least he will have the brains to hold his tongue until it is time for our next move. After all, you could be carrying the king's son. There might be fine possibilities in the years to come.''

They did not speak again as their footsteps crunched the gravel of the slanting path that linked the green-gray river to their king.

Chapter Sixteen
April 6, 1522

Hever Castle

Another crunching pain seized Mary's belly and shot jaggedly along her spine. She clenched her hands and wrinkled her brow. It passed as swiftly as it had come.

Anne bent her sleek head toward her sister, but did not touch her. "Mary, is it time? Shall I summon mother or Semmonet?"

Mary shook her blonde head slowly, her loosed hair sliding along her back and shoulders. "I am certain it is just another false pain. I will not be put to bed, and the midwife called again for nothing. I felt so foolish. I can feel the babe has gone lower now. Perhaps soon." Tiny tears trembled on her thick lashes but did not spill. "If only this wretched waiting were over, Anne, I would be so happy."

"I can understand that, Mary. If I were in your exciting place in life, I would want to go back too. It is just too silent here—no dancing, no banquets, no *chevaliers charmants* to twist about one's little finger for mere amusement."

"I did not mean that I was anxious to leave Hever,

Anne. Have you not longed for home while at Francois' court all these years?"

"Oh, at first, when I was young, I suppose."

"But you are only fourteen now."

"Almost fifteen, sister, and old enough to long for the excitement of Amboise and Chambourg. Fortunately, this boorish exile shall not last long, for father has promised I go to the English court to serve the queen. They say in France that she is quite stuffy, mopes and wears haircloth under her unfashionable dresses, Mary. Is she truly another Claude?"

"She is not well loved by her lord, Anne, so she has that to share with the French queen. Only she seems to me much more tragic, for she was loved once, and she must have the memories of the loss to torment her. The king chose her, you know, though it is said the marriage was his father's death bed wish. I doubt that Francois *du roi* ever cared a whit for poor Claude. And then, there are the babes. Her Grace has had six dead babes, Anne, and the man she adores gone from her too." Mary put her hands on her huge stomach protectively.

"I am sorry I made you talk of dead babies, Mary. I did not mean to upset you." Anne had long ago dumped her pile of embroidery on the turf, and she munched handfuls of the last of the winter walnuts as she spoke. "Truly, Mary, what is it like? I am old enough to know now."

"To carry a child?"

"No, silly goose. To belong to Caesar, to share his bed, to have everyone defer to you—and, well, to have his child."

"This babe is my lord Will Carey's child, Anne. I

267

have told you that before."

"Father says it can just as well be the king's and that we are to keep mum on it outside the family, and let them wonder."

"Father is not birthing this child, and I do not wish you to have Will hear such talk." She reached out her hand to Anne's arm. "Please, Anne, try to understand."

"I do, Mary, truly. It is no wonder both Francois and His Grace desired to love you. Even when you are so, well, *enceinte,* and heavy at the waist, you are still beautiful, sister. I wish I had your Howard looks." She leaned her slim body back on the bench and stretched her arms over her head. "Then I warrant I could have a new courtier every week."

"Anne, you sound so heartless! You have become a real flirt. You have been about Francoise du Foix too long."

"At least I came back a virgin from France, Mary, though Francois du roi was beginning to give me those soulful, dark-eyed stares when Father called me home." She giggled. "Besides," she added when she saw her older sister's hurt expression at the reprimand, "Francoise du Foix is quite out of favor and has been these last six months. Anne du Heilly is the light of the king's life now. She is blonde and blue-eyed like you and was quite an innocent when *du roi* first noticed her."

"You have changed, Anne. You are much older than your years. Soon you must think seriously of marriage and of motherhood."

"I hope not immediately. Some perfectly proper marriage father arranged would probably bore me, and

I do not care if I never give birth." Almost uncon-
sciously, her slim hands went to her flat stomach. "I
shall never be another Claude or even, like mother, to
have the heirs and be shifted off. Will you not just die,
Mary, if you are not summoned back to court—after?"

"Will has some lands now and a manor house I have
never seen. Besides, Father says I shall be called back.
My husband serves the king, so we must live at court."

"You are the one talking like an innocent, Mary. Father says he can only hope you will be returned to
court. And I am sure Esquires to the Body can be
changed. But I would so like us all to be together at
court especially with George. George needs consolation
and diversion. He always did favor Margot Wyatt and
now he has had to wed with that chatterbox Rochford.
Father had best not try to arrange such a marriage for
me, though I would consider it if it would mean I could
live at court."

Mary shifted her bulk and felt the child kick as hard
as he had these last few months. The little fellow kicked
and punched at her insides so hard sometimes that even
Will could see the movement. At first it had frightened
her that someone else had taken control of her body,
but then it delighted her. Now it filled her heart with
foreboding of the hours of pain to come. And Will was
still kept at court. At least he should be here when the
Carey heir was born.

"What did you say, Anne? He is moving, see?"

"Yes. Well, I was saying I wish you would tell me all
about the king from your point of view. I am certain it
would be more exciting than hearing it all from father's
lectures."

"I shall, Anne. I promise, for I wish someone would

have told me the truth before I got involved in it all. There was only one who told me much about it, and I was too stubborn to listen to him."

"Who? Will?"

"No, not Will. A friend of Will's, William Stafford. He was an aide to father in France. Do you remember him?"

"Vaguely. Tall and brown haired with that roguish look?"

"Yes. That is Staff." His face drifted through her mind as it often did, no longer jesting and taunting, but concerned and warm. She had not seen him for almost five months. Too often she found herself wondering if he still cared for her and would watch her from across the room and kiss her fondly on the cheek as he had when Will had taken her to Hever so long ago to await the child. You are really quite a fool, Mary, she told herself firmly. He is probably reveling in Lady Fitzgerald's bed or even that clinging Anne Basset's, and hardly giving his pregnant friend's wife a moment's thought.

"Why are we speaking of William Stafford anyway? I would like you to tell me about some important, exciting people, please. Personal things, not political things, like father always does."

"I promise I will, Anne, but I am very tired now and just want to sit awhile before mother makes me go back to bed. The gardens at Hever are so restful. I can almost pretend nothing outside even exists."

Anne's eyes grew wide with sudden knowledge. "Are you afraid, Mary? You mustn't be, you know. You are young and strong and everything will be well."

"Thank you, Anne. Those sweet words mean much to me just now."

"I meant not to tire you. Shall I fetch mother? She always knows what to say and do."

"Yes, please, but do not hurry. I would like to be alone for a moment."

"Semmonet said you are not to be alone."

"Just walk slowly then, and that will take a little time. I will not be really alone."

"All right. And we shall talk of the court and king to-morrow." Anne bent her lithe body and scooped her embroidery from the grass. She swept down the gravel path, her head held high as always.

Yes, the girl would go far. She was so poised, spirited and clever. Even her needlework made Mary's look crude by comparison. Anne's stitches were tiny and delicate even though she secreted her deformed hand beneath her work. If she ever really dared to stand up to father when he chose to wed her to someone she did not favor, Mary would like to be there to see the scene. Anne had much to learn about many things, including their father.

Mary sighed and stood slowly. If only the child would come. If it could only be over! How she would like to mount Donette and ride like the wind across the meadows to the Eden and lie on her back under the beeches with her hands behind her head. Perhaps if she were not summoned back to court . . . but Will could manage to keep his position, she could just live here with mother and raise her son here.

She walked slowly around the patches of mint and dill which encircled the stone sundial. Sky blue morning glories clung to its fluted base. It was noon, dead noon, and the iron finger set to tell the time threw no shadows. Time, time. Another minute, another hour, another sharp shadow on the face on the stone dial. Five months away from court, two years away from France, so far away from safety, security and peace. The king had sent her a tiny enamelled box and one garnet necklace in those five months, but what did that assure? He might never want her back. Father had said they could arrange her return to London, but she was not certain of that. Will had made only four visits in five months. His sister Eleanor stayed on at court and he would probably rather be near her than his wife anyway, since her Carey blood is not from some forced marriage.

The April sun gave a warm embrace, but she wandered a bit off the path into the shade of a skinny-leafed weeping willow near the little pond. How she would love to stoop and pick those tight clustered violets, but she could not. This time next year, pray God, she would have her babe in her arms, and could stoop to pick them.

A branch rustled behind her and she spun her head sharply. "Oh, Michael, you frightened me. What are you doing here?"

The thin, gangly boy smiled shyly at her. His front teeth gapped wide, and he seldom smiled outright. He reminded her of George years ago, before France, but his hair was flame-colored and masses of freckles dotted his long face.

"I didna' mean to scare you, Lady Mary. I was jus' walking through and I thought to see you be all right since the Lady Anne left you."

"I appreciate that, Michael. And I have wanted to

thank you for the cuttings of forsythia and pussywillow during the rains. They lightened my dark room and cheered me tremendously.''

He smiled again, his felt hat held nervously in his awkward hands. ''I was tellin' my mother it is too bad the Lady Mary has to come back to visit in the winter months, for she always loved the gardens best of all the Bullens. I try my best to keep them nice for the lord and lady. The lord, he ne'er sees them, but Lady Elizabeth, she loves them, an' I know you do too.''

''We all appreciate the fine work the gardeners do, Michael. I am glad to see you so grown. Will you wed soon?''

''There be no one I fancy now, lady, but if I find someone, I will ask my mother and Lady Elizabeth for permission, and wed with her gladly.'' He took a step closer in the spotted shade. ''I remember the day we had to look for the lost spaniel in the box hedges, lady. And I remember best the day the king came to Hever and walked in my rose garden.''

Simple pride shone on his face, but Mary did not miss the fact that his eyes dropped swiftly, accusingly, to her rounded belly. Even the servants knew and whispered that the child the Lady Mary carried was the king's.

She turned away, suddenly terribly hurt by his simple face and gentle gaze. What honor could there be in bearing a bastard to the king if honest servant's eyes accused? Even peasants who worked the gardens with their hands were free to choose whom they wed.

A stab of pain gripped her at the waistline and spread swiftly downward, crushing the breath from her. This was no agony of guilt, memory, remorse or a false pain

273

of birth. This was different. Her knees nearly buckled and she leaned heavily on the tree trunk. "Michael, fetch . . . my mother."

"I can help you to sit, lady. I will fetch her."

He grasped both arms above her elbows. She would have shouted at him not to touch her, but the next wave of pain staggered her and she toppled against his grimy chest. He backed carefully out onto the gravel path holding her up by her arms. Her legs followed wobbily, draggingly. Tears of fear and pain coursed down her cheeks, and she bit her lip.

If I were a true bred court lady, she thought crazily between pangs, I would ask this gardener to take his hands off me and show no pain on my face at all. He half sat, half leaned her on the bench where she and Anne had been, and raced off saying something back over his shoulder. What had he said? Another pain seized her, and she heard herself scream. Truly, this was it, this was her time. Where were the men in her life when she needed them? Her father should be here for the birth of his first grandchild. Was Will on his way? This baby was not early. He should be here, too. Damn the king! Damn him who could send maids five months from his court just because they conceived and their waistlines no longer suited his roving hands.

The next pain swept over her like a huge wave and her ears rang, drowning out the garden sounds and all thoughts. Then mother, Semmonet, Michael and some other man were there. They carried her into the dark house and to bed.

It seemed she had long drifted on waves of pain and exhaustion. She screamed for them to take the bedclothes off and begged them for cool water to drink. Her body was not her own. She tried to hide from its strange revolution in the corner of her mind, but the agony pursued her, and she screamed again. There were two midwives, mother and Semmonet. Father had said two midwives. There must be two to make sure the child was delivered safely. How she hoped the child was a girl and had the identical look of a Carey to spite her father. How many hours on the sundial in the garden? Why could the tearing pains not end?

They told her to push, and she did with all her might. It helped, but the pain swept her back, so what did the tiny respite matter? How could women do this all the time? Claude. Poor Claude and the Spanish Catherine! All those dead children after so much pain. Please, God, do not let my baby be born dead. "Mother! Mother! Water!"

Elizabeth held the goblet to her lips and she drank greedily, spilling half the water down her chin and neck. It felt good. The only thing that felt good. "You are doing fine, dearest Mary, just fine. Push harder next time."

She bore down as hard as she could. When she dared to open her eyes again, she could have laughed at the crazy sight of her legs spread and the midwives peering at her intently, if another pain had not washed her laugh away. What was it that Staff had said to her that night? When you spread your thighs for the others, think of me.

"It crowns, lady. Push harder, hard," the voice came to her.

Crowns, who cared about crowns except Henry and father? Push hard, push, push!

A huge black wave rolled over her, and she felt herself break in two jagged pieces. Then there was a loud cry, and she no longer felt the need to scream. Would they leave her alone now? She was so exhausted.

"Mary, Mary, everything is fine." It was mother's voice, mother crying and shaking her shoulder.

She opened her eyes. They had let light into the room, and it almost blinded her. But there in her mother's arms lay a child. Her child, with a tiny red face screwed up to a pouting circle at its mouth and one balled up fist against its cheek.

"It is a son, Mary, a beautiful, fine son."

Mary smiled in her mind and opened the fingers of her hands as Elizabeth Bullen placed the tiny bundle next to her on the vast bed. She touched the little hand. "Father and Will decided his name is to be Henry, mother. Henry Carey." She wanted to hold the babe to her, but she drifted off, floating on the bed in helpless exhaustion.

The utter joy which coursed through her with the milk which suckled the babe was unbelievable. She held him carefully to keep him secure and to be certain he would not break. He had little reddish-golden fuzz on his head and his eyes were the clearest blue, although mother said all babies looked so for the first weeks. It would please father and probably Will, too. The babe's coloring could be construed to be pure Tudor, but was not so far from the Carey looks. So let them wonder.

Will Carey and several other riders came pounding into the courtyard the morning after the baby was born. Will looked so in awe of the tiny bundle of reddish gold that Mary felt a jab of guilt for cursing him for his absence. The king, no doubt, the king had kept him. George had come, Anne said probably just to escape his wife's flapping mouth for a few days, but father would follow later in the day. The king had sent his good wishes and a silver christening spoon. Mary enjoyed the proud comments and pleasure of George and Will, and then she slept again with the baby's cradle next to her bed.

She was famished that afternoon and downed a huge bowl of frumenty while Anne sat by the bed and repeated all Will, George and their comrades had been telling her of life at court.

"George is so unhappy, Mary. I tell you, if father tries to marry me to someone as silly as Jane Rochford, I shall run all the way back to France! Oh, by the way," Anne added as she took a swift peek in the cradle on her way out, "that man you spoke of, the tall and charming Will Stafford came with Will. You are right. They are fast friends. See you when father arrives."

Mary put her spoon on her emptied pewter plate. Staff here with Will? However did they both get away. Would he come to see the baby or think it was only for the family to see? Suddenly, for the first time since the birth, she thought of how she must look. Her stomach was so much flatter but, even tightly bound, she had a long way to go to get back to her normal waistline. "Mother! Semmonet!"

"Mary, are you all right? Hush, sweet, or you will wake Mister Henry Carey," Semmonet scolded lightly as she bustled in. "Still hungry? Your father has just ridden in."

"Semmonet, I need a mirror, comb and rice powder. I must look terrible!"

277

"You must not do too much so fast, dear. You just look a little pale. Here, look in the mirror."

"Rosewater, too, please."

"Maybe Lord Bullen will be more interested in the baby than in how you look, child. Or, is this for someone else?" She narrowed her eyes in mock suspicion, but Mary ignored the stare and Semmonet darted out again.

Indeed her hair looked like a Kentish haystack, but her face was not too pale. Somehow she thought she showed good color. And she knew the robe looked well, for it was the lovely lace and ribboned one from her wedding night.

George appeared, then mother. Then father swept in with a broad smile. Perhaps he had heard the child had the king's hair.

He bent to kiss her forehead and gave her hair a quick caress. He studied the baby at length leaning close over the cradle. "A fine son, Mary. I know Will is proud." The statement hung there, and he said no more.

"We shall unwrap him for you to see, Father," Mary said with a nod to Semmonet.

"Let the lad sleep, daughter." He clapped his hands together loudly as if to silence all the little conversations in the room. "The Bullens are fortunate—again. Mary bore a fine son and still looks beautiful, which is another blessing because in June Will is to fetch you back to court. The king himself told me he misses your golden smile, my dear, and," he lowered his voice, "no doubt, he would like to catch a glimpse of little Henry, too."

George chortled deep in his throat, and Anne's

278

shapely eyebrows arched up as if to say, "I knew it all the time." Mary said nothing, but she *did* feel relieved. It was not that she would see the king again or even that the news pleased her father so much. Perhaps she had missed the excitement of life at court.

"Mary." Thomas Bullen leaned both palms on the bed beside her so firmly that she almost rolled against his arms. "I know you are tired now, but this is a wonderful day for the Bullens. No one has gone back into favor like this before, but I had faith we could do it. And, as I promised, Anne and George will be there too, so you have absolutely nothing to fear. All right?"

She smiled in the direction of the cradle although she could not see the tiny head from where she was. "All right, Father."

"Excellent. Now, one more fortunate piece of news. Anne, His Grace has been thinking of your happiness as well as Mary's."

"Yes, Father?" Anne stepped forward near the foot of the bed with her hands clasped to her breasts and her dark eyes dancing in anticipation.

"His Grace has set a most favorable match for you with a fine title and estates. You will come to court with George next week, serve the queen and be wed, in the autumn, in Dublin."

Anne looked stunned. Her eyes glittered and then hardened dangerously. "To whom have I been promised in Dublin, Father?"

"To James Butler, a fine match. He is heir to the entire Ormond estates. You will live at Kilkenny Castle on the Rive Noire. He is handsome, red-haired, an Irishman of course, and you will be a fine lady."

"Should I not have been consulted? At least Mary

279

gets to live at court. I should like to also and not for just a few months while preparations are made to ship me off to some man I have never seen and do not wish to wed.''

"We shall talk further of this honor, this royal command, Anne. Later.'' He glanced down eagerly into the cradle as if the subject were closed, but Mary saw clearly that it was not.

"I have only arrived from France, my lord, where you sent me to be schooled and groomed to return to the English court, and then, perhaps, marry some landed Englishman. I do not favor being sent to the barbarous Irish in some dark castle I have never seen to breed red-haired sons for some lord I cannot love. If you will not listen and I must plead with the king directly, I shall do so!''

"Elizabeth, settle the girl down. I should have realized it would be too much of a surprise and she would need time to think.''

"No, father, I need no time to know what I think. George has married Jane Rochford as you ordered, and he pines away for the girl he truly loves. Mary is wed to Will Carey, but,'' she lowered her voice ominously as though Will could hear from the solar below, where he waited, "she beds with His Grace and somehow bears sons to them both.''

"Anne, I warn you . . .'' Thomas Bullen's voice came low and he motioned to his wife to take Anne from the room.

Great tears came to Mary's eyes. Anne's words hurt. They were thoughtless, brash and cruel, but they were true. George looked stunned. Anne turned and fled before Elizabeth could get to her, and George followed the women through the open door.

Her father studied Mary's face briefly. "I am sorry to have this happen here to upset you, Mary. It is a wonder the boy still sleeps after that screaming. Anne will be all right. I shall see to it."

"Anne is right, Father."

"Right about what?"

"George is desperately unhappy. Anne has only returned. She is but fourteen and she wants to live here, to experience court life for herself."

"She will, Mary, she will. The wedding is not until autumn and she will have you to set her a good example. It is just that she is the youngest, and your mother has spoiled her. The lad is beautiful. May I hold him later?" He turned and strode from the room without waiting for her answer.

The door stood open, and she felt a desperate urge to call for Semmonet. She must hold the baby and rock him to set right all the conflict and unhappiness. But she did not wish to see any of them now. She only wanted her baby close to her, away from Anne or George or even mother.

She lifted the sheet and carefully slid one leg over the side of her bed, then the other. The cradle was so near. This would be easy. She slid her hips off, her feet touched the floor and she stood. A spinning hit her and swept her around so she could not even see the cradle. She put her hands out to break her fall, but strong arms caught her and lifted her high.

"Foolish girl," came the low voice in her ear as she was laid back on her bed. She opened one eye slowly and looked up at the tilting ceiling. Staff leaned over her, serious concern stamped on his face. "Shall I call your mother? Are you all right now?"

"Yes. I did not think it would be so difficult to stand. I am glad you came." She put one arm over her eyes to stop the rushing whirl of the room.

"So am I, Mary Bullen."

She realized how she must look to him stretched out under his gaze on the bed in her thin chemise and lacy robe.

"Will said I might come up to wish you well. I saw the door stood open with no one about, and you, ready to topple over," he explained as if to apologize for his sudden appearance.

"You just missed a fine display of Bullen family politics," she said grimly with her eyes still covered.

"I did not truly miss it, sweet. It was quite discernable from the front stairs."

Her eyes shot open and stared up into his. "Did Will hear?"

"I think not. The solar door is closed. Here, you had best get back into bed before someone comes in and wonders." He pulled her to a sitting position, plumped the bolster behind her back, and covered her legs with the rumpled sheet.

"Thank you for your care," she said. "You would make a fine bedroom nurse."

"Anytime you want someone to help you into your bed, remember me then."

"Really, Staff," she scolded lightly unable to keep the smile from her face that he would still tease her so. "Now tell me, how is everyone at court?"

He pulled a chair close to the foot of her bed, carefully avoiding the end of the cradle, and she thought foolishly how far away he felt now. "If I told you about everyone at court, lady, it would take hours and I would have your governess on my back, so I will be brief. The king has gone through three quick romances in your absence and he misses you. If your father tells you he has set up your return, do not believe it. His Grace misses his golden Mary.''

"And how many quick romances has Will Stafford gone through in these five months?''

"And does he miss his golden Mary, do you mean?''

She felt herself blush under his steady stare. What had gotten into her to encourage him like this?

"Well, since you ask directly, sweet, you shall have a direct answer. I long for you to come back and tease me and insult me. If there were room for three men in your busy little life, I am afraid I would be most insistent on where you spent your time and at least some of your nights.''

She pulled in her breath sharply. He dared to imply that he wanted her for a lover! It was madness. She should be insulted and tell him his place the way she had often before, but she was so glad to see him.

There was a lengthening silence and raised voices came from somewhere down the hallway. Coward, she ranted at herself. Say something. Tell him the truth. "Would you like to see the child, Staff? I was trying to get him to hold when I . . . fell.''

"I have found in my experience that babies all look alike when they are born, but I hear this one is special, with Tudor-colored hair. So let's have a look.''

She meant to protest as he bent and handed her the bundle, but he seemed to do it expertly. "In your experience, Staff? Do you mean to tell me you have children hidden somewhere about the kingdom?''

283

"Not a one," he replied, "but since this lad is so fine looking, I might be interested in ordering one myself from the same, ah, manufacturer." He grinned rakishly at her and reached out one finger to touch the babe's tiny curled hand which grasped eagerly.

"You see, Mary Bullen, babies know whom to trust."

"Babies may, but how is a poor wench supposed to know?" she prodded dangerously.

"Why, ask anyone, anyone but the king or your father." He straightened and backed away several steps. "Will is waiting. I hope to see you before we depart on the morrow, Mary, but if not, remember that the one thing which does not change for you at court is William Stafford. Remember that, lass." He bowed and his eyes went over her briefly. He nearly collided with a wide-eyed Semmonet as he turned into the hall.

Chapter Seventeen
June 19, 1525

Hampton Court

The entire court was in an uproar the day after the king's blatant move against his lawful queen and his daring elevation of those forces which could cause her harm. Ignoring his six-year-old daughter, Mary Tudor by Queen Catherine, the king had invested Henry Fitzroy, his six-year-old illegitimate son by Bessie Blount, as Duke of Richmond and Earl of Nottingham and Somerset. The boy was assigned a vast household of his own. The chess move was clear to all observers who knew the rules. Bessie Blount's son was being groomed as the next Tudor king. And in that elaborate investiture ceremony, a spate of other courtiers were advanced who were the current rooks, knights, and pawns about the great Henry. To allay the alarm of Thomas Bullen, who knew the proper moves as well as any, the king bestowed a viscountcy. Mary had expected her father to be in an expansive mood from the honor and was hardly prepared for the irate display he was giving in Will Carey's suite of rooms as she made ready to answer a summons from the king.

"But you are Viscount Rochford, now, father, and the diplomatic missions are a great honor and responsibility His Grace gives. You have never shown a care for the queen's feelings before. I cannot see. . . ."

"No, you would not. Will, can you teach her nothing of political intelligence, as close as she has lived to the seat of power these five years?" He turned back to Mary and slapped his palms down on her little oak dressing table so that the bottles, mirror and enamelled jewel box jumped and shuddered. "Damn it, Mary. You too have a son who could be His Grace's flesh and blood just as well. Do not protest, Will. You know it. Baby Catherine—well indeed, she is yours, for the king was obviously in a wandering mood those months, but the boy is Tudor through and through."

"Little Harry is not so far from Will's coloring, and you know it, father."

"Bessie Blount came and went in a season like a single, pretty flower, but you, Mary, you are yet his favorite who blooms anew after five years. Bullen stock is of better mettle than the Blounts!"

"If Harry should be His Grace's son, my lord, you must admit that Henry Fitzroy was the first born," Mary shot back.

"Whose side are you on in this struggle, girl? You have always been too fond and sweet, accepting and content. Do you have no ambitions for your son or for you and Will? Have you ever advanced the Carey cause to which your husband is so dedicated?"

"Yes, my lord, I have spoken to her of it often," Will put in.

"Rightly so. Mary, must I do all your thinking? Must I tell you every move to make? The diplomatic missions keep both me and George away from court more than I would like, and I fear you grow too headstrong for Will to handle." He ignored Will's fidgeting and growing annoyance as he berated his wife while she sat stonelike at her dressing table.

"Have you heard a word I have said?" Thomas Bullen demanded. He pulled her to her feet facing him and suddenly the wall she had learned to build against him crumbled and she feared he would strike her.

"Yes, of course, I hear you, father. Only . . ."

"Only what?"

"I have done . . . I will do what you say, but I will not risk little Harry by insisting or even hinting as you would have me do that he is His Grace's child."

"Risk him! The king has only two living sons, madam, and you bore him one. The Fitzroy boy is a weakling. Anything is possible."

"Please, father. You are hurting me. Will, please help me to . . ."

Her father dropped his hands from her arms, and she stepped away from him.

"We had best tell her what we have decided and be done with these foolish arguings, Will. The king's boating party to see his new gift from his dear Cardinal Wolsey will not wait for one silly woman."

"Tell me what? What have you done? Will, tell me!"

"Mary," Will stepped forward and put an arm around her shoulders. She froze, waiting. "I have told you that this court is no place to raise a son."

"He is not even four years old and he needs us, Will. He stays."

"You have won that bout before, Mary, but not

287

now."

She shrugged his arm off her shoulders and moved several steps away. "Harry stays here with his parents, my lord father, or the king is likely to hear hints that the boy is indeed Will Carey's son and no other."

Thomas Bullen clenched his fist, and she knew he would hit her, but he restrained himself. His long face was livid and a huge vein throbbed in his neck.

Will's agitated voice broke the thread of passion between the Bullens as they stood there frozen. "You must not gainsay your father on this point, Mary. We are agreed. You know you wish for a fine education for our son, and it is long overdue to begin. Next month the boy joins the household of the new heir to the throne at Hatfield House. He will have playmates there, a fine tutor, and we can easily ride to see him often if you wish."

"And he will be where he should be, daughter. Close to the heir and sharing Fitzroy's education should it ever happen he needs it. Wipe those tears. The king will want a happy face on his jaunt upriver."

"You do not take Catherine! She does not even say her sentences yet. She is still in leading strings." Her voice was pleasing when she meant to be so strong. She was afraid to threaten father as she did Will. They were all she had to love. Well, almost all, but the other was impossible.

"Of course Catherine stays, Mary," her father reassured her, trying to pat her arm, but she recoiled from his touch. "Her position is hardly at stake. And, Mary, I am trusting you to be wise in this with His Grace. There are others to whom he has turned and can turn again, you know."

"Why do you threaten me with that? It frightens you more than it does me, father."

"I am not threatening you, dear Mary. Only warning. Your own sister, for example, seems to have much influence over him. Not only has she had her marriage promise to the Ormonds rescinded, but she has been brought back to the king's good graces after that foolish Percy affair. Anne is bright and smiling and is much about, so dry those tears. No doubt, His Grace's retinue gathers at the royal barge now, so be quick." He clapped Will twice on the shoulder and strode from the room.

Mary sank onto her bench, leaning her elbows on the dressing table. Even when she tried desperately to erect barriers to keep herself from hurt, she failed. Failed to hold the king's attentions, failed to please Will, failed to communicate with Anne, failed even to protect her little son.

"Mary, your father is right. We must hurry. You will have to remake your eyes. Come on now. It is all for the best. You will greatly disappoint the king, your cousin and Staff, whom His Grace put in charge of this tour today."

She said nothing. Mechanically, she began to reapply her eye colors.

Mary felt like a wooden doll that little Catherine had dragged through the gravel or stepped on, as she joined the gathering group of courtiers. Jane Rochford greeted her gayly with a swift hug, and Anne waved brightly surrounded by a little cluster of men including Weston, Norris, and their tall cousin Sir Francis Bryan. William Stafford came up from behind with the lovely fair-haired Maud Jennings on his arm, and Mary felt another sharp twist inside.

It suddenly annoyed Mary that she and the Jennings woman had both chosen gold for this barge trip to Hampton. Really, Mary thought, and glared at Maud through slitted lids, anyone who knew anything about fashion at court knew the king's mistress Mary Carey often wore gold as her color and, out of deference, chose others. Mary's gown was a particularly elaborate satin and brocade one she had worn only once before. Her filmy, short veil set far back on her small, jeweled headpiece rustled in the river breeze as she tossed her head to pull her gaze away from the flirty Maud Jennings.

But her eyes had taken in the girl, and Staff with her, all too well. Maud's dress might not be as expensively made or as fashionable, but Mary had to admit it showed the maid's flagrant charms to best advantage. She had a most annoying habit of swishing those velvet and brocade covered hips entirely too much when she walked or leaned into Staff as she did now.

Of course, he was probably encouraging Maud's display of tasteless possessiveness in front of them all, Mary fumed. His huge chest and shoulders were finely encased in perfectly fitting, almost iridescent peacock blue which melded to green when he flexed those big muscles as he did now. His white lace and linen shirt showed slightly above his V-cut doublet to emphasize the bronze coloring of his face and throat. As Mary darted a glance at Staff to drink in his face, lithe body, and brawny legs displayed in the same bright blue, to her dismay, she saw that they were approaching. How dare he drag his latest little minx over here by me, she

290

thought, but she nodded politely enough to them both. Maud gave a little sigh when Staff halted by Mary, but the girl did not see Staff's gaze so swiftly, but completely, over Mary Carey.

"It is somewhat cloudy for the outing, but His Grace is so happy, he will not even notice," Staff observed. Maud's other hand rested possessively on his arm. She almost clung to him. It amazed Mary how angry and hateful she felt toward Staff for his smiles and his obvious attention to the young maid who was newly arrived at court. She herself had no one to cling to—no one but a sixteen-month-old daughter, and how long would they let her keep her?

"Are you well today, Lady Mary?" Staff inquired, searching her face.

"Yes, quite," she returned icily. She refused to look into those eyes which always pretended concern. "Which barge are we to ride on, Will?" she asked her husband, turning her back on Staff.

Staff answered the question. "Will, His Grace has asked Francis and me to ride the royal barge since he sent us to Hampton to be certain the Cardinal had vacated his household for this visit, so would you do me the great favor of escorting Maud on the second boat? I promise I will take her off your hands when we arrive." Maud laughed musically and squeezed the arm she held. "The king, of course, will want Mary on his barge and, since I can see him coming now, we had best get on. My thanks, Will."

"I am used to partnering court ladies, Staff, but none so sweet and new to our court as this," Will replied graciously.

Mary turned away and strode toward the gilded

291

barge decked in green and white banners and awnings. Staff had her arm before the boatman could help her in.

"What ails you, Mary?"

"Do not touch me, please. I wish to sit with the Duchess of Suffolk."

"You will sit with His Grace, unfortunately for me—that is, unless your little wren of a sister tempts him to take her away from the string of admirers she always flaunts."

"At least Anne is happy now. When the king and the Cardinal took Harry Percy away from her, I doubted she ever would be again."

"I am not so certain she is truly happy now. She seethes inside, Mary. But she is adept at putting on a happy face while you never seem able to manage it lately. Did your father berate you that your son was not given a title yesterday with Fitzroy?"

She turned to look fully into his face for the first time today. His eyes were in shadow, but he looked perfectly serious. "Are you a spy, William Stafford? Why does it seem you always know the business of the Bullens?"

"When will you learn that it takes no spying, sweet Mary? It is all so easy to read."

"Not to me. But then, who would expect such a foolish woman to understand the goings-on of the great world outside her empty little head?"

"I have told you not to let your father get to you like this."

"Take your hand off me. The king is here. Go back to your fair-haired, cow-eyed Maud!"

"I hope we can talk later, Mary, without Will or the king." He half turned away from her and bowed low with the rest of the courtiers on the royal barge as the king, Duke and Duchess of Suffolk mounted the barge. But he said out of the side of his mouth before he left her. "I do not love Maud Jennings, Mary."

Carefully, Mary composed her face and, when she caught sight of the Duchess' warm smile, her own joy was genuine. "Mary, it has been two days since I last saw you. Is little Catherine's fever abated?"

"Yes, Your Grace. It passed in but a few hours. I prayed that your Margaret would not catch it."

"I keep her out of the night air, and she is healthy as a pup. My dear Charles dotes on her, though I know he wanted a son. Now, if we can just get through the summer without anyone catching the foul sweating sickness, I shall be able to face anything."

"What do I hear?" the king boomed so close in Mary's ear that she jumped. "We are about to go on a fine outing to see my new palace at Hampton, and I hear mention of the damned sweating sickness. Pray God, it does not strike the court this year. Besides, ladies, we shall all sit it out safe hunting at Eltham. Charles, sit with your lady there behind me and do keep her off such vile topics, or I shall personally toss her into the Thames." Everyone laughed and Mary went through the motions. "Mary, here with me. I cannot wait to show you how magnificent my Hampton is. We shall move the court there soon, though I may let Wolsey use it from time to time when we are elsewhere."

Mary sat obediently at his left and carefully arranged her stylish dress fold by satin fold.

"You look lovely, lovely as always, Mary. I have just the pair of topaz earrings which would set off your eyes in a color such as that. The color of golden sunlight, eh?'' His narrow eyes caressed her openly.

"Thank you, Sire. You look spectacular today."

He beamed like a schoolboy and Mary returned his smile willingly. As usual, he did indeed look impressive in Tudor green and blinding white to match his barge and, probably, the pennants which would mark this new palace they would visit.

"Where is that little minx of a sister of yours, Mary," he asked, suddenly craning his huge neck. "There she is! Next to an unmarried courtier, of course, flirting. Staff! Here, to me!"

Neither Anne nor Staff missed a chance to be with someone young and flirtatious, Mary thought as she smoothed her skirts and gazed out over the water. She would not give Staff the pleasure of thinking she had time to listen to him. She lowered her eyes as he approached and stared fixedly at the glint of reflected sunlight from the river surface as it danced along her gold skirts.

"Yes, Sire?"

"Staff, are you certain that everything was fully in order? Sir Francis told me the cardinal had a huge gilded bed in his privy chamber with golden cardinal's hats on each bedpost."

"It is true, Your Grace. But he did remove that bed and one vast desk. Everything else stayed. You will be pleased, I know.

"I would never want the common folk to know of it, Staff, but I know he kept a string of women to share that gilded bed, and that he hides a wife besides!" He lowered his voice and Staff leaned closer over Mary to hear. "In other words, under that mountain of fat draped with scarlet robes, and all that piety lurk a nor-

294

mal, lusty man, eh?'' The king and Staff laughed loudly enough for most heads to turn their way. Mary folded her hands demurely in her lap and sat stockstill, as though she had not heard.

"I warrant the sweet Lady Mary has been about me enough that she does not even blush at jests such as that." The king covered her silken knee with his hand and squeezed it playfully. Mary turned to him ānd forced a smile.

"And while we are on that delightful subject, Staff, how do you find little Jennings?" Henry guffawed and Staff shifted from one foot to the other, a set smile on his face.

"I find her a bit of an innocent, Sire," he said quietly.

"Still, Staff? But she has been at court three weeks already. I would never have imagined I should have to give you lessons." He snickered again and Staff bowed and backed away although Mary could not see that he had been dismissed.

The king was in a soaring mood. He mingled with everyone on the barge and waved to those on the following one. He threw coins to onlookers on the riverbank when they got close enough to shore. He chatted incessantly to Mary, kissed her and pinched her as though he were trying to lift her spirits too. He recounted at least twice the marvelous investiture service by which his son had become his heir and her father had become Viscount Rochford. He inquired how her little sister Anne got on and which of the courtiers she truly favored in her heart.

Wolsey's massive Hampton Court Palace glowed almost rosy pink in the diffused sunlight. Its twisted sets of chimneys and crenellated roofline pointed toward the graying clouds. They disembarked and strolled parallel to the moat, through the watergate toward the huge house. Even as they approached, His Grace told stories of the times he had feasted here and recited some of the improvements he would make.

"One night a group of us invaded a banquet my lord cardinal was giving—do you remember, Norris?—disguised. We picked out the prettiest wenches there to dance with and unmasked after it was all over. Were you there, too, Weston?"

"Yes, Your Grace. What I recall best was that you immediately chose the most charming wench for yourself before the rest of us could even get into the room." Everyone within earshot laughed in unison.

"Now, seriously, everyone, I mean to tell you we shall be on a progress to Hampton as soon as everything can be assembled and this great brick barn sufficiently prepared for a royal visit. Sir Francis, I meant to inquire about the jakes. Are they quite in sound shape? Wolsey built the place here on this stretch of river upstream from the City because it is the healthiest place around in the pestilent summer months—and closer than Eltham or Beaulieu. We shall summer here and the sweat shall never find us at all. Sir Francis?"

"Yes, Your Grace. The lackeys spent a week swabbing the jakes and priveys after the cardinal's huge staff vacated. Besides, the palace has private water closets in each of the principal three hundred bed chambers, an elaborate sewer, drain system and fresh water brought from Coombe Hill three miles distant."

"Ah, yes, Francis. I meant to tell them of that. It

seems our busy Lord Chancellor was even more skilled at building than at doing the king's business which was given over to his care.''

Mary saw her cousin Francis color slightly as he realized his exuberance had made him overstep his place. Everyone kept his peace wondering what marvels His Grace would point out next. Mary walked on his arm as they entered the great courtyard. She kept her eyes on Henry's proud face, for she did not want to be caught by Staff stealing a glance at the way his demoiselle innocent draped herself against his body as they walked.

The king had now entirely taken over the tour himself, as though he had designed and built the monstrosity. It was typical of the king's ebullience and acquisitive nature, and they were all used to it. Staff and Sir Francis, whom the king had ordered to organize the jaunt, dropped further back in the group as they paraded from room to opulent room. There were close to one thousand rooms in the palace, but they traipsed through only the principal chambers. Rich damascene carpets virtually littered the floors. Gold and silver plate encrusted the massive oaken hutches and sideboards. Tapestries from Flanders draped the walnut carved walls and mullioned windows lent a golden glow to the myriad hangings of gold and silk. Their eyes could not take it in, they who were well accustomed to the opulence of the king's palaces.

''It seems the Lord Cardinal overstepped his place as a man of the cloth and a servant to the greatest king in the world,'' Mary heard Anne say distinctly at the king's elbow, and she held her breath at the tactless remark. There was a sudden silence as they stood under the heavy tapestry of Daniel in the lions' den. Anne had hated the great cardinal ever since he had forced Harry Percy, the young son of Northumberland, whom Anne loved desperately, to renounce the Bullen wench and submit to the arranged and proper marriage his family had set with Shrewsbury's daughter. Anne carried the bitter resentment against the cardinal in her heart, Mary knew, but to dare to voice it like this to the king was dangerous.

Henry Tudor's voice sliced through the quiet. "Lady Anne is quite right, but the cardinal has learned his place with his king. This palace is the palace of the monarch, not of his servant, and he willingly bestowed it as a gift. The cardinal knows full well his lord is a hard taskmaster, and if he should forget again, we will remind him. Hampton Court is king's court now, my Lady Anne."

Anne's dark head bent as though in acquiescence to his power, and when she lifted her face to him, her smile was brilliant. Mary was stunned at the fine line of tangible magnetism that crackled between the king and her little sister.

"We had best see the gardens before it rains. I have magnificent plans for a pond, tennis courts, a tilt ground, and a huge lovers' maze which I am sure you will all have memorized by this time next year. Come, come."

Mary felt him pull back and hesitate when Anne strolled by, as though he wished to disengage her arm and seize Anne's. She lightened her arm against his instinctively, but he chose to move on. It was graying outside as they drifted out, and the lovely gardens seemed subdued and silent. The group splintered off in pairs or clusters, and Mary smiled to see the Duke and

298

his beloved Duchess walk off toward the knot garden arm in arm, as the fondest lovers. But when her eyes took in the bright blue of Staff's doublet as he led Mistress Jennings toward the rose beds, her smile faded and she bit her lip in anger at herself.

"Well," the king intoned smoothly, "if everyone is pairing off for a garden walk, that leaves us, sweet Mary." He bent to kiss her lips, but stopped poised above her, his eyes darting off into the distance. "Your little sister can hardly practice her French-learned wiles on your Will, sweet, and that appears to be the only victim left to her."

Mary turned her head slowly and saw Will seated with Anne in earnest conversation on a marble bench surrounded by a riot of lilies, cornflowers and broom. The scene reminded her of a painting that hung at Francois' Amboise of a pair of Italian lovers in a flowered frame.

"Damn! But I should have seen to it that Will had someone to be with. Where has that little Jane Rochford gone?"

"Jane Rochford is another sister-in-law to Will, Sire, but I will admit it does seem strange to see Anne unattended by at least two gentlemen."

"Yes—yes. Perhaps you had best stroll with Will just for a while. She will talk the poor devil's ear off, though I do not wonder that it is witty talk. Will! Mistress Anne!"

Mary felt nothing but amusement at the situation. Nineteen-year-old Anne had caught the eye of the restless king. She had seen it happen before. He would spin off for several days in a romantic whirl and she would have a small rest until the conquest was complete and he returned to her. Each time father had seen it happen, he had been in a tizzy of worry. Mary nearly laughed aloud as Anne and Will sauntered up to them. Her father would be trapped because both of the ladies in question were his daughters. And His Grace—well, there was obviously no way this little passion for the sleek Anne could be satisfied, since the whole civilized world knew the king had bedded Mary Bullen for five years now, as his favored mistress.

Mary gladly took Will's arm as the king offered his to the radiant Anne. Anne made a sudden move to lift her left hand to wave as they turned away, but Mary saw her catch herself and jerk her fingers down into the folds of her dress. Never, since Anne had been a very young girl, had she nearly shown her tiny deformed finger. The situation must indeed be a heady one for the girl.

"I pray she does not get herself in this too deep, Will," Mary observed quietly as they strolled in the opposite direction and heard Anne's lilting laughter float back to them.

"She trapped him this time, the little fool. She insisted we sit right there on that bench where we could watch His Grace."

"Oh, no. She cannot be taken with him."

"I think not, but did you catch her comment against the cardinal in there?"

"Who could have missed it?"

"I think she has some half-hatched plan in that pert little head, to have revenge on the cardinal through the king for taking Percy away from her."

"That is too far-fetched. That was almost three years ago and . . ."

"Why else would she question Staff and me about how His Grace regards the cardinal, if anyone else has power over Wolsey and so on?"

"Silly girl, I will talk with her, Will. We do not speak much lately and I did not know. She will get into quicksand if she has thoughts like that. And if she meddles, father will have her head on a platter."

"Perhaps, Mary. Or else the little nymph realizes that if she has Henry Tudor's ear, she need fear your father no longer. But it never works to try to use this king. You might warn her of that, Mary. He is the user." Will's voice was bitter. He pulled her arm and held her close against his ribs. "I would not have you angry with me, wife, over sending Harry to Hatfield. I truly believe the lad needs sound schooling if he is to go far, and we can see him much there."

"Even if your motives are pure, I know father's are not. He did not coerce or bribe you to get you to agree with him?"

"I do not buckle to the Bullens, Mary, least of all to your father. If I seem to agree with his tactics, it is only when the Careys will benefit too."

"I should know that by now."

He turned and carefully eyed her impassive face. "See that you remember that, madam."

"And when His Grace goes on to someone else as mistress *en titre,* will the Careys mourn with the Bullens, or will there be a parting of the ways?" she heard herself plunge on, and all the frustrations of this long day made her voice shake with anger.

"I serve His Grace, separate from any bargain you may have with him, lady. I have my own ties to him and I will not hear you imply otherwise." He stopped and faced her squarely. His face was as cloudy as the sky behind his head.

She drew in a quick breath and the scent of roses nearly overpowered her. She pulled her eyes away and there, across the tall arbors and through a whitened trellis decked with yellow roses, William Stafford crushed Maud Jennings to him in a passionate embrace.

"I am speaking to you, Mary. Your father may think what he damn pleases of the Careys, but I will not have the mother of my children against the Carey cause!"

Mary stared at his chest, her eyes burning with unspilled tears. "I meant nothing by it, Will. I only, well, I only wish you would stand against my father with me when he threatens me or little Harry." She had to get away from this garden. She would not put it past Staff to seduce the wench right there on the grassy turf.

"My sister and I have worked hard for what we have now, and we intend that the Careys shall be even further restored in the next generation. You birthed them, madam, but they bear my name. And I am lord of them even though I cannot, at times, control where their mother makes her bed."

"Will, please. I do not need your reprimands. I need your love and understanding."

"You have my duty, wife. After that, things get most difficult. The barges wait on the other side of that hedge, beyond the roses. Since we undoubtably ride back on different boats anyway, I am certain you can find your own path when you are finished crying for your little Harry and what the Bullens will say when they hear Anne walks at Hampton with Henry Tudor in place of golden Mary.'' He mockingly bowed to her and spun on his heel.

Mary's first impulse was to throw herself flat on the grass and scream and sob. His anger and bitterness astounded her. He kept it tightly bottled most of the time but when it exploded . . . He *did* hate her. He had finally admitted it. She crumpled weakly on a carved bench under a bewinged marble Cupid. The tears which would help release her agony did not come. She felt drained, totally enervated, and she dreaded raising her eyes again to the trellised arbor where Staff made passionate love to that woman.

She breathed hard in great quivering gasps drifting between outrage and desolation. Perhaps she was beyond crying ever again. She felt the urge to run away and hide, to flee like a child playing hide-and-seek in the gardens. They would wonder where she was, they would search, but they would have to return to the palace without her.

She craned her neck and looked at last. Staff and Maud had disappeared. Or maybe they were sprawled on the grass. She heaved a deep sigh. The garden was so unutterably beautiful, and she was so wretched. If anyone noticed her here alone, the gossip would be all over the court. The blonde Bullen sits alone and her husband and the king desert her. She thought to laugh at what father would say to that, but she heard a few huge raindrops plop on the gravel path and watched them bounce the green rose leaves. She tilted her head up to the pearl gray sky and blinked as a drop drenched her thick lashes. She moved to stand under the enclosed arched trellis and saw Mary Tudor and her Duke of Suffolk run laughing along the path to the watergate.

She must go back. They would all be coming now, but she stepped back hidden in her tiny shelter in the rose garden.

She saw him then and instinctively took another step back into the thorns. He was so tall and the peacock blue of his garments stood out clearly in the riot of pinks and whites and greens at his back. But he was going the wrong way, not toward the barges. What had he done with his little paramour, Maud?

Mary watched him silently as he walked farther away from her. When he spun back, he caught sight of her and strode in huge steps through the rain to her. She thought to run, to lead him a chase through the gardens, but she was frozen in anguish and fascination. He put a hand on each side of the little enclosed bower blocking her in.

"It is going to pour, Mary. Why did you not come back with Will? He says His Grace chooses to take the little Bullen for a walk."

"Yes. Will and I had an argument and he preferred not to enjoy my company either. Did he tell you that? I am returning to the barge now. Please do not concern yourself. I know you have more important people to look after. Let me pass."

"Stop this nonsense. Everyone will be coming back soon and we have not much time." He took a step closer to her in the cool protection of the sweet-scented bower. "They will not notice us here, and we will return separately in a moment. I should take the few minutes we have to give you one of my educational messages about being careful not to scold the king about his attentions to your sister, or doing something foolish like pleading with the king to restore little Harry to you, but

I need this time for something far more important.''

He dropped his hands to her waist, and she took a step back, pressing closer into the leaves, blooms and prickers. He reached again and pulled her gently to him.

"Do not dare to ever touch me again!" she spat at him. "Go caress your Maud, go kiss her in the roses!" A little sob tore from her throat, and the stubborn tears sprang to her eyes again.

He loosed her waist and took one of her hands firmly in both of his warm ones. "I am in your bad graces, sweetheart, and rightly so. I did not know you and Will stood so close in the garden."

"I am certain it would not have made one tiny difference to you if the cardinal himself would have stood there watching!"

His teeth shone white in the dim bower as he smiled and the rain splattered down around their protective arch of leaves. "I am elated that my attention to other ladies displeases you."

"I could not care less what you do, William Stafford!"

"Really? Fine, because I am going to kiss you and if we had the time, I would carry you to one of those three hundred silken beds in that great pile of Wolsey's bricks and make hot love to you whether you were willing or not. I told you I do not love the little Jennings, Mary, and I told you true. You know whom I *do* love, do you not, sweetheart?"

His voice was so low and caressing, his dark eyes so mesmerizing in the regular patter of raindrops that she almost relaxed against him. His strong hands went to her waist again, he gave a little pull and she leaned

305

full on him as his lips descended. She went limp and her thoughts and fear subsided as she returned kiss for searing kiss. Her arms stole up his back, and she pressed her open palms against the iron muscles through the velvet doublet. He shifted his weight and tipped her back a bit in his encircling arms. His lips traced fire down her throat, down to where her breasts swelled above the tiny lace rim of her decolletage. Her head dropped back on his shoulder as his fingers tugged the golden satin and slipped one breast free. She startled but did not protest as his lips descended again, this time on her taut nipple. His tongue teased it back and forth while her breath came in strange little gasps over which she had no control.

She closed her eyes desperately against the rampant assault on her senses. Her legs were like jelly and her brain threw pictures at her of her on the ground beneath him, her bare legs spread, inviting him, begging him to take her. A low flame burned in the pit of her stomach; yet a chill raced up and down her spine.

"Sweetheart, my sweetheart," he repeated along her bare flesh. He pulled her up straight against him, almost brutally, and kissed her again hard on the mouth. She felt her wet nipple and breast crushed to his velvet doublet and the sensation thrilled her. She could feel everywhere he touched or looked, distinctly, intimately. He kept her pulled hard against him and his voice shook when he spoke. "We have to go back or we will have them beating the bushes. And if we stay any longer, what they would find is you flat on the ground under me with your skirts up in the rain." He released her and, reluctantly under his burning gaze, she covered her breast and shoulder with little shaky tugs at the cloth.

"I truly meant to only find you and bring you back to the landing, sweet, but when I saw you here alone, I could not help myself. It has been so many years I have longed for the forbidden fruit, Mary, and I am not really a very patient man. You were angered with me today for kissing Maud, but years of smiling and laughing with you and breathing in your sweet scent and seeing that luscious face and body near me and then bidding you a curt goodnight as you go to Will's or Henry's bed is pure hell." He reached over to smooth her hair. "I tell you, Mary, whomever I have slept with these past five years, I have dreamed it was you or, if not, your face came back to tease me—to haunt me—soon after. Do you understand?"

She nodded, her eyes wide. It was like a dream and she wanted to be hidden away with him forever. Then she heard her own voice say in a rush, "I rely on you above all others, my Staff, even though I try not to admit it to myself sometimes."

He put his head out of the bower and looked both ways, then came back towards her and kissed her swiftly on the lips. "I want more, much more than your reliance, Mary Bullen, and I will have it. But we must be careful, very careful. I will not have your safety or our chances to be together at all, ruined by one passionate mistake."

He pulled her gently from under the arched trellis after him, and she was amazed to feel the rain had almost stopped. He held her arm so tightly it almost hurt.

"Perhaps there will be some day soon, some place where we will have time to finish what we only started today, sweet. I see no one on the path. Go back along that way. I shall come from another direction in a few moments. Go on. Now!''

She turned on wooden legs and hurried down the crunchy wet path toward the line of trees that hid the boat gate. Her heart pounded, and she forgot to lift her sodden skirt hems in her excitement. Let the king cast her out, let Will hate her, and her father storm. There was one who loved her and whom she could trust. She glanced back quickly but he was gone as though he had never been there at all.

She darted from the overhanging yews toward the barge landing as the rains began lightly again. Her seat by the king awaited her, although he had put Anne on his other side. Will gazed off at the far Thames bank while pretty Maud Jennings had her lap full of roses.

Chapter Eighteen
October 17, 1525

Eltham

All during that summer, while the dreaded sweat stalked the narrow streets of Tudor London, the great herds of roe and fallow deer fed and grew among the leafy boughs of Eltham forest. At morning and evening some became bold and walked the orchards and green swards on their spindly, graceful legs. Unknowing, they awaited the bow and the packs of the king's hounds and his nobles who would hunt them bloodily, lustily in the months the court hid from the sweating sickness in the Kentish countryside.

King Henry had been at Eltham for nearly a week on this trip, stalking deer, riding merrily to the horn, and feasting off the groaning tables under the massive hammerbeam roof of his rebuilt hunt lodge. The queen was absent, sequestered as she had been throughout the long, dangerous summer at Beaulieu, but the gentle slopes of elm, ash and beech rang with shouts of His Grace's favorites.

Mary rode to the hunt in the king's private party as did the ever-present and laughing Anne. But each time

His Majesty dispatched a huge roebuck or cornered a brow-red doe for the kill, Mary recoiled more into herself and the lusty scenes of blood no longer excited her. At first she had believed her queasiness meant she was with child again, but she knew it was not true. Her revulsion at their lusty killing of the gentle deer was somehow tied to the fact that Will Carey grew increasingly cold to her and that the king no longer sought her bed. Mary and the whole court knew full well that Anne kept tantalizingly out of the king's reach and bedded with no one. Mary told herself she was glad to have Henry Tudor gone, but her feelings of oppression grew.

The day was brisk, very brisk for a mid-October sunlit day. Mary was content to ride sidesaddle far back in the hunt party where she could see Staff's green cap and broad shoulders several riders ahead. His powerful body rose and fell rhythmically as he rode his huge stallion, Sanctuary. "A strange name for a horse, but a wonderful hunter," Mary said aloud to comfort herself. Thinking of the hunt two days past when Staff's catch had been far greater than the king's, she added. "Only he would dare."

"Dare to flaunt Anne that way with you here too, Mary?" Jane Rochford asked, and Mary was instantly annoyed that the ever-present girl had heard her and thought she was speaking of the king.

Why are you not tagging along behind Anne? Mary wanted to taunt, for even the wife of her brother could see the way the royal wind blew toward the younger sister. But she said only, "Why do you not ride with George today or with Mark Gostwick, Jane?"

The slender woman seemed to tense at the mention of the man she now favored openly. "I thought, per-

310

haps, you needed my comfort and solace since none of your men have paid you the slightest attention lately. Do not tell me you do not fear for your position, dear Mary, or fear your father's wrath at the trends of the times."

Mary wished she could strike Jane's smug face as they cantered close together, to shove the ingrate, Rochford, from her horse, for her continual gossiping and mock concern drove both Bullen sisters to distraction. But Jane spurred her palfrey ahead and wedged into an opening near Mark Gostwick in complete defiance of what the Bullens thought. At least George did not care. He rode far ahead with His Grace and his beloved Anne.

Mary cantered beside Thomas Wyndham of Norfolk now and his new and starry-eyed bride Alice from the vast Darcy family. Another rare love match—fortune had blessed them since their parents had long ago arranged their marriage, yet they truly loved each other. "I do not belong next to them or anywhere here," she said half aloud to her chestnut mare Eden, a gift from His Grace last year whom Mary had named for the gentle river near her home. Only Eden heard, and flicked her alert ears sharply in understanding. Then she heard it too, the horns, the baying of the pack, and their canter accelerated to a gallop through the half-bare trees. The clatter of forty horses' hoofbeats seemed to echo thunder off the huge trunks of the deep woods.

As the pursuing party spread out in the heat of the chase, Staff turned his head swiftly for a glimpse of her. She caught the movement and smiled broadly though he was too far ahead to tell she had noticed. He did care. Always she saw signs of it in his calm or teasing

311

words if they had a fleeting moment alone. How she wished they could be really alone with no servants to stare, Will far away and the king himself gone, gone forever. But he was right to be safe and secure, though she herself would throw caution to the winds whatever wrath befell them. She shifted her weight forward on her horse. Like all women, she rode sidesaddle, though unlike most of them, she had ridden astride unseen by others at Hever and she liked it far better. That would shock them all. That and her knowledge that the great Henry really intended to bed the younger sister of his five-year acknowledged mistress.

The yelping and baying of the hounds was much louder now. Perhaps they even now surrounded their terrified prey cornered or disabled. The king would be first to the deer, and his steaming bloody knife would drip with the blood of the kill.

She reined in and dismounted in a cluster of stamping, snorting horses since those ahead of her had done so. It was good to stand on firm earth, to feel solidity and not the rhythmic constant swaying in the saddle. She dropped Eden's reins and stepped forward around Weston's huge stallion. Staff came from nowhere to take her arm firmly at the elbow. She smiled tremulously at him at the impact of his sudden proximity.

"I have not seen Will, Staff, not for a long time. And do you know why we got such a late start this morning?"

"No and yes, lass," he said in her ear over the shouts of the crowd nearest the action. "One thing that never ceases to amaze me is how your sweet female minds dart about with at least two or three concerns at once. It quite tires me to attempt to keep up with you."

"Please do not tease, Staff. I am not in the mood. And I have never noticed that I tire you."

He leaned even closer. "If I ever get my way with you, my love, I promise you I will not tire—ever. And I meant not to upset you. I know times with Will, your father and even your dear little Annie are tense. For some strange reason, Will has attached himself to your brother this morning. And as to why we got a late beginning, I cannot say except that His Grace had some kind of personal business. I am afraid it may have had something to do with the little ice woman with the looks of fire—your sister—but I may be wrong. He can hardly attempt to bed her with you and Will about, and evidently still in favor."

She did not answer, though months ago such advice and words about her sister, brother, Will or father would have drawn her anger. They stepped high over the crushed thicket as they approached the cluster of people. The smell and sounds of death permeated the chill air.

Staff loosed her arm, and they moved separately around the groups of standing courtiers. The king with his boon companions, Norris and Weston, behind him had slain three deer and their slender bloodied limbs still convulsed in sporadic shudders. The great Tudor stood astride a massive twelve-point buck, his crimsoned hunt dagger raised aloft while the crowd applauded and cheered and murmured. The other two were does, much smaller, both turned away from the slaughter of their master-buck as though they could not stand to see his sleek brown body on the leafy turf.

And then Mary's eyes took in the import of the whole scene—Anne standing stiff between George and Will

Carey and His Grace offering her his victorious dagger the way he had offered it to Mary Bullen these past five years. But Anne shook her head, took a step back, and the king turned to stone. Then he half-motioned, half-shoved Will aside with quick words and turned his back on the obviously dismayed man while the circle of observers waited and studied their sovereign's every move. The huge reddish head bent to Anne again in earnest conversation. He ignored George, poor discomfitted George, as though he were not there.

It was like some play on a trestle stage with a dark forest setting, or some terrible nightmare come to life. Anne's slender cloaked form was blocked out by Henry's massive back, but Mary instinctively feared for her. Something was very, very wrong. Anne had evidently refused the offer of the dagger, a foolish affront before the court, no matter what private disagreement she had with her king.

Will Carey suddenly grabbed Mary from behind and pulled her several steps behind a gnarled tree trunk. His face was deathly pale and he could not speak at first. Mary turned her head to stare at the king disbelieving that Will could have come away so quickly. His fingers bit into the flesh of her arm.

"Damn your little bitch of a sister," he groaned. He glared at the rough bark behind her head and pushed Mary against the tree. "She will ruin everything. She will be the end of us all."

"Please, my lord, what is happening?"

"You fool. You cannot mean you do not know. Why did you not head her off? She has taunted and flirted and led him on these months for her own selfish ends. And now, when she reaps the obvious rewards of such sluttish behavior, she draws back, she refuses." A strange, strangled sound came from deep in his throat and he raised his wide eyes to her shocked face at last.

"His Grace has asked Anne to bed with him," she got out in a half choked voice. "Here? At Eltham" With me along?" Her knees began to tremble and she felt as though she still rode the bouncing Eden careening along dark forest paths to some bloody destruction.

"He asked her first last night and told her to think about it until this morning. He just offered her the dagger of his kill and she refused it thinking it would be as good as her compliance later in his bed. Her father will kill her! Or if he does not, perhaps I shall."

Their conversation was no longer private as others of the hunt party streamed back to their grazing mounts whispering and shaking their heads. Over Will's shoulder Mary noted the smirk on Jane Rochford's face as Mark Gostwick helped her up astride her palfrey. Mary caught Jane's sharp eye and turned away as she nearly dry-heaved with the sudden impact of reality. Many hated the Bullens; she knew that. Even Jane and maybe Will, ashen faced and grim-lipped before her.

Then the stunned Careys saw Anne and George ride by only a stone's throw from where they stood, as if transfixed. Anne had taken to wearing tiny bells on her saddle and bridle, and the gentle tinklings drifted foolishly in the chill air.

Will glanced around the tree and pulled his head back jerkily. "I knew it. Doomed, doomed. He stands there, livid with his fist clenched and Norris, Weston and Stafford stand around like great wooden dummies at the quintain. We had best flee. I will not face his narrow-eyed wrath again for the stupidity of a Bullen wench, any Bullen wench.'' He strode off, and she wondered if he meant to leave her here alone.

She took a few steps in the direction in which she had left the untethered Eden. To her surprise, it was Staff who held her horse as she crunched through the crispy brown leaves, and Will was nowhere in sight.

''I thought you were with His Grace,'' Mary said, as though nothing had happened.

''I was. Will has gone to fetch his horse. I think, Mary Bullen, the time is finally come for your graceful exit from the king's august presence. I only hope that somehow, through Will's tenuous position or your father's craftiness, you are both able to come back.'' He seized her waist and hoisted her to her lofty perch above him before she realized the full impact of his words.

''Leave court? Leave Eltham, you mean. Is Anne to stay? Is she in disgrace?''

Staff's dark eyes swung swiftly in a wide arc around the clearing in which they stood, she astride, he leaning his chest against her knees as if to reassure her shaking limbs. ''I am afraid I mean leave court, Mary. Has Will not told you? That foolish slip of a sister of yours has overstepped and badly. She led him a merry dance, and then hit him square in the face with a refusal. Twice. She is no innocent. She knows better than to tempt a rutting boar, and then try to ward it off with a child's stick. And, unfortunately, you and Will—and I—must suffer, Mary. I had not thought it would happen this way. By the blessed saints, he ought to just rape her and have done with it, but he has never had his pride stuck full of lances by a lady he desired before. He is hardly a mortal man in that respect and his wrath may fall on you all out of proportion.''

"And has some lady stuck your masculine pride full of lance points?" she heard herself ask foolishly, as though they were just passing a sunny afternoon and in no danger at all.

"Some lady used to, but I think she has come to see the error of her ways with me. If it ever comes to it that I can ask her to be mine after all these years and she tries to gainsay me, I shall force her to my will. She owes me too much and in such circumstances she would never escape me."

Mary opened her mouth to reply but the words would not come. They stared deep into each other's eyes, unblinking, and her pulse began to beat a nervous patter which no danger from the king or even her father could ever bring on. "Staff, you must know that I . . ." She jerked her head up at the crashing approach of a single horse through the nearby brush.

Will emerged and walked his nervous steed close to them. "Where in the devil is your horse, Staff? You said you were coming with us."

"Yes, Will, I ride clear to Richmond with you," Staff said, never taking his eyes from Mary though he addressed her husband.

"Richmond? Clear to Richmond—today?" she asked in the sudden hush of the forest.

"We can hardly stay here where we will bump into His Grace, of course," Will said while Staff turned away to get his horse. "Thanks to your sister's meddling, we may have to leave Richmond, too, and hide out for a time at my country house. Poor Eleanor will take this very hard."

Damn Eleanor, Mary thought. "His Grace said we are to go?"

317

"He told all the Bullens to get clear from his sight and he shoved me out of the way as he said it. His passion is for Anne, not you, Mary. We have to face that now. Staff thinks if he pursues Anne, you must necessarily be put out of his path as a stumbling block to Anne." Will turned away as he saw Staff canter from the path behind them. "I am sure His Grace would have no real objections to bedding with you both, mayhap together," he concluded bitterly, half to himself. But she heard and the words stung.

How stupid she had been, she realized, to once believe this king would be her escape from the lust and cruelty of Francois. Staff had been right, always right. He had seen the dreadful face behind the jovial mask when she had not. She began to cry soundlessly, tearlessly, for herself and poor Will and for her little Catherine who depended on her, and for five-year-old Harry who could well be the flesh and blood of this fearful king. And for Staff whom she loved and would never have but for stolen moments which just made the pain of pretending all the worse.

"Buck up, wife," Will's words floated back to her. "We must pack quickly and be in Richmond before nightfall. We will take Staff and two grooms with us. I hate to admit it, but we need your father's crafty skills before we decide what to do. I cannot wait to see his face when he hears that this time the wench who draws his king off from his golden Mary is his own Anne! I cannot wait to see him try to worm out of this predicament! And when he hears she refused him before half the court and that she and George are banished to Hever and all the Bullens are to keep out of his sight, ha!"

His shrill laughter pounded on Mary's ears and caused chills along her spine. She dropped back slightly to ride abreast with Staff, for that was her only security now. She detested Will and feared the king. And the coming interview with her father made her grow numb all over. She turned her face to Staff as they clattered swiftly toward the wooden facade of Eltham set among the dying brown leaves of the Kentish weald.

The pounding of Mary's tumbled thoughts and the pounding of the horses' hoofs on the long, bleak road to Richmond were as one. The golden forests of the weald and the clear sunshine on Eden's flowing mane could not lift her spirits or comfort her. Perhaps Anne and father would get what they deserved, for Anne had dared to believe she could lead the king on and then throw him off at her will. Yet, the girl had only wanted power as she had been taught—power to fill the void of a lost love, power of revenge through the king over the hated cardinal who had sent her lover away to marry someone else. And father—well, he was as he was. Over the years, through the pain her love for him had caused, she had come to see him clearly. He loved his children only as a prideful possession, as his means up the royal ladder of riches and influence from which others whispered his mean birth would keep him. Now the Bullen dream was over and he dared not blame his daughters as much as himself.

The closer they got to Richmond through Weybridge, Chertsey, and Staines, the further her security of her love for Staff slipped from her grasp. The closer she came to exile with Will to his country lands she had never seen, the more the pain of loss and separation cut

319

like broken glass in the hollow pit of her stomach. She tried to sit erect in the hours of the hurried ride, but her shoulders slumped lower and lower as did her heart.

They rested once at a tiny thatched inn near Chertsey for bread, cheese and hot wine. She wanted to throw herself into Staff's arms and never see the court again at all, but she sat properly wedged in against the wall by a silent Will Carey. Little Catherine waited at Richmond with their servant Nancy and, for Catherine, she would ride on.

It was late dusk when they clattered into the vast stable block at Richmond. Will helped her dismount, and she stretched her weary, cramped limbs gratefully. They hurried up the gravel path past the formal railed gardens where the massive new marble fountain sprayed its tiny flumes into fluted basins. Mary and Will went to their rooms while Staff went to inquire on the whereabouts of Lord Bullen.

Nancy was surprised to see them, but Will sent her off to sleep in the common hall without any answers to her earnest questions, and Mary went directly to see Catherine. The child slept soundly, curled up crushing her pillow to her to replace her lost doll, Belinda as though the world would quake should she not have the ragged face beside her in the dark. Mary kissed the untroubled forehead and smoothed back the golden curls. The regular sound of the child's breathing comforted her greatly. She would make Catherine her life away from court, away with a husband who did not love her, away from her family and from Staff.

"Staff is back already, Mary. Your father has not returned from visiting Wolsey at Lambeth, but he took a barge and as it gets pitch black soon, he should be back

320

any time. We left word for him. He will be here directly when he catches wind of all this." The triumphant laughter was gone from Will's weary voice at the thought of his father-in-law's anger. He threw his cloak on a chair and went back into the sitting room.

In the dimness of the bedchamber, Mary washed her face and smoothed her tousled hair. She peered at her face in the gray mirror, a face they said that had never learned to hide and dissimulate, to pretend indifference or joy as was proper etiquette at court. What was it the old Italian master of the French king had told her about pain in her eyes? Old Master da Vinci and Staff—they had always seen things clearly.

"Mary. Is the child all right? Are you coming out here? There are several things we must discuss before we face your father. I will not have him badgering me."

She went out immediately. And what about his badgering me, my protector husband, she wanted to demand. "You will wake Catherine if you do not keep your voice down," she said only.

Neither of the men moved at her words. Staff and Will sat at the large oaken table, Will slumped over it, Staff leaning back with his long legs stretched out under the table. Will's back was to her. She took the chair that Staff offered her without rising. He sloshed red wine in her cup, and she drank it straight down.

"Maybe we should all be drunk when he arrives," Will observed impassively. Staff grunted. He poured Mary another cupful.

"I wish we could go to Hever," she said quietly.

"Home to mother," Will jibed. Then he added, "That is out, totally out. We are about to become *personnae non gratae* with your father as well as the king, just as though we had never been the Bullens' bread and butter for these past five years."

Mary no longer felt the urge to argue such accusations. "I know we cannot go to Hever, Will. I just said I wished we could."

"And," Staff put in, reaching his arm for more wine for himself, "it is very likely that His Grace may pursue Anne there, and it would hardly do for the lovely sister and ex-mistress to be under foot."

"He will never pursue Anne further," Will countered. "Did you not see the livid look on his face and the hatred in his eyes this morning when she stood up to him? When Thomas Bullen figures it out, he will probably hope that Mary can win back His Grace despite our banishment. The little ice goddess Anne will have none of her king in bed, and His Grace knows it. He will glut his prideful, lusty maw with the first pretty face and body he sees tomorrow, mark my words."

"Perhaps, Will, but when he slakes his thirst that way, what then? Boredom sets in. You know him. He is a hunter and relishes a challenge, even the distant danger of defeat. That is the only reason he puts up with me on the tennis court or at the butts. Unlike some, he gets truly bored with sweetness and compliance." He gave Mary a warm glance when he saw Will staring down into his goblet. "Unlike some men, he may be entranced by the little witch, for to some, stormy days are more loved than clear, golden ones." He moved his muscular thigh gently against Mary's leg under the table, a tiny caress, then took it back. His face was impassive when Will looked up from his cup.

"Will you tell Lord Bullen of your thoughts, Staff?"

"Only if he asks directly or threatens to dangle Mary in front of the royal nose again. She has had enough and is well out of it, Will."

"But suppose it is necessary, Stafford," Will said, his voice taking on a new edge. "Your family position is not involved. That is fine for you to say. Or," his fingers drummed loudly on the table, "do you have other interests in this? You are not the only one who observes the behavior of other men, you know."

Mary's fingers tightened around the metal stem of her goblet. Surely Will had never seen them alone together. They had never been alone enough for Will to suspect, and there had been no consummation of their love.

"I have an interest in this, Will. For a friend I have had for years and of his wife, whom I care for too." They stared long at each other across the narrow table, and Mary held her breath.

"I am sorry, Staff. It is all getting to me. That damned George asked me to stay close to him and Anne today without telling me why and it was me, not him, His Grace shoved out of the way when his temper snapped. It is a hard thing, to work so hard for favor, and have it ruined through no fault of one's own. Eleanor and I had such hopes."

Mary drained her wine cup and put it down hard on the table. Staff said slowly, "You care too much, Will. Do not let His Grace's quicksilver moods ruin your chances for happiness."

"And you, friend Stafford, do you care for nothing? Is it so easy for you to let go of a dream?"

Mary's eyes filled with tears, and as she poured herself more wine, she interrupted shakily. "I only want you to promise me one thing, Will, please.''

Will swung his eyes from Staff's calm face to her impassioned one, hardly guessing the real cause of her tearful look.

"I want you to promise me that you will not allow my father to use our son as a bribe or wedge on His Grace. Keep little Harry out of it."

"And you, madam, do you wish to be kept out of it, if your father insists?" he probed.

"I can try to fend for myself against him, Will. Our son Harry cannot."

"When have you ever fended against your father, golden Mary?" Will asked coldly. "We shall see."

"I think we shall see now, Will," Staff interrupted and rose quickly to his feet. Hurried footsteps sounded in the corridor and a fist rapped twice on the door.

Will stood slowly and Staff retreated, with his cup, to a chair along the wall. Mary swung open the door and curtseyed.

Her father and Uncle Norfolk burst into the room bringing a draft of chill air, as though they had come straight from outside. "Well, the rumors are at Wolsey's door already, and I am certain the grand cardinal was pleased to think that the upstart Bullens could fall through the foolishness of a mere girl. I brought your uncle. This mess may take more than my head to put right." His still-gloved hand lifted in the direction of Staff. "I see you are here with them, Stafford. I sometimes think you have observed His Gracious Majesty as well as I. You may stay. Perhaps I can get straight answers out of you if my own family is as wayward as usual."

He sat in Staff's vacated seat and threw his hat into

the middle of the table. Norfolk draped his furred cloak over the back of Will's chair and sat against it silently, his eyes darting from Will to Mary, who closed the door.

"Well, where is she?" Lord Bullen demanded. "She refused him, they say. Where did he send her? Is she back here with you?"

"Anne and George have gone to Hever, father," Mary said behind him, and he swiveled in his seat to stare up at her grim faced.

"And I suppose you were not even on his arm, or were sour faced and sad to be near His Grace as you have been the past year. You lost him, girl. You let all this happen."

"Mary held him for five years, my lord," Will responded quietly, and Thomas Bullen shot him a frown.

"Well, obviously, that is all water over the mill dam now, Carey. So we must regroup and go on from here. He said he wanted all the Bullens to get out of his sight?"

There was a silence and Mary could tell that Will was hesitating to tell him of the shove the king had given him, which he clearly interpreted as the banishment of the Careys with the Bullens.

"Well, Stafford?" Thomas Bullen swung his gaze to the tall man sitting against the wall. "I knew I could not depend on rationality here when we are so desperately in need of it. How did you interpret it? Can Mary stay? To try again?"

Staff strode to the table and leaned his hands upon it, towering over Bullen and the avid Norfolk who had not yet spoken a word. "I shall tell it to you as I see it, my lord. Mary dare not stay, at least for now. If Will complies with the implication of His Grace's meaning, they should retire for a while, and they may very well be welcomed back later as part of the court. I think the king feels no enmity towards Mary and will not unless she becomes an embarrassment to him if he decides to pursue Anne further.''

"Ah," Bullen let out breathlessly, before his eager eyes became impassive again.

Stafford paused as though to let the possibility sink in. "Anne is the cause of the unrest, my lord. The king is hurt, but I believe the hurt may turn to challenge. It is not impossible that the king may choose to hunt a doe in the quiet gardens of Hever as he did in the noisy forests of Eltham." Staff straightened as though the lecture were complete. "He has done so before, I remember."

Norfolk's deep voice broke the pause. "Then, Thomas, there is the possibility of Anne. I cannot believe Anne could hold him over Mary's beauty, but we have seen it—His Grace is bored all the time now, with the queen, with his future."

"And Anne can be made to see the error of her ways," Thomas Bullen intoned. "Damn the willful wench to lead him on and deny him in public. It is worse than the nightmare of Elizabeth's refusal."

Mary shuddered at the outright mention of the family secret she had heard her parents discuss so long ago, when she was first sent away from Hever. Will stood impassive, and Staff retreated against the wall. Unheeding, the two men huddled over the table in earnest conversation, as though there were no one else in the room. Mary strode over to Staff and drank from his cup. She had had much wine, more than usual, and she felt dizzy, but she did not care. She did not care about anything as long as they left her children out of it and she did not have to return to the smothering arms of the king.

The low buzzing of their talk ceased. Will was the only one close enough to hear what they had been saying and he stood frozen, like a statue, near the table.

"You think Carey may come back to court after a time?" Bullen questioned again, turning to Staff and speaking as if Will were not standing only five feet away.

"Yes, milord. Especially if they get away before his return."

"But if Anne should come back to court?"

"Will's position as Esquire should not be in danger, even if Anne should return. The king will only promote a Gentleman Usher to do the work while Will is away. I think I can see to that. And why should the king's new mistress not ask for her sister to come back to live at court if worse comes to worse? It will not touch His Grace's scruples, and it will be as though Mary were never in his bed. You have seen it, Lord Bullen. You know it to be true."

"Exactly. Then I am off to Hever tomorrow to deal with the foolish baggage who has caused all this upheaval. Damn it, Norfolk, her mother always did spoil her and cling to the girl as the last of the brood. She said she would never live with me again if I sent Anne to France younger than I had Mary. It is the only time I ever gave in to the woman. I waited over two years past when Anne should have been at Francois' court with Mary."

Norfolk nodded as he spoke. "Yes, Thomas. Mary

has always been as sensible as she is beautiful. But I have hardly known Anne since that crazy Percy affair. Something broke in her then, I think. I wish you God's help in dealing with the sticky situation."

Thomas Bullen rose to go, as though all were settled, then spun back to Will who still seemed dazed by it all. "See that you are gone before the retinue arrives, Will. To Plashy, I think, since the house is better there than the one in Lancaster."

"I had thought Plashy. If you can use your influence, be certain my household position awaits me when we come back." Will's voice was strangely forlorn, not bitter or taunting as Mary had expected when he faced her father. He had not seen Thomas Bullen as crushed by the news as he had hoped. He is astounded at the Bullen resiliency, she thought.

"Then I will contact you there when it is safe to return. And, Will," Thomas Bullen added as he and Norfolk turned at the open door, "do not fear for your precious position. I have the surest feeling that your friend William Stafford will hold it secure for you until your return. And then there is always the child if His Grace does not forgive Anne her foolishness."

Mary's head jerked up from her cup. "Father, wait." Staff reached for her arm, but she was too quick for him as she moved unsteadily toward the two men.

"If Anne is wise and strong enough to stand up to your counseling as I have never been, then I am all for her. That is a battle she must fight for herself. But if she will not be your pawn as I have been so faithfully all these lonely years, then I tell you now, sensible little golden Mary will never allow you to use her son to buy favors with the king. Never."

Thomas Bullen's dark eyes widened suddenly and then narrowed to slits of blackness in the dim room. "I spare you my anger, Mary, because exile and the loss of those things with which you have been surrounded are hard to accept. Go off to Plashy with Will, think it over and remember to keep your tongue. I want no silly letters to the king. You have been a good soldier, girl, but admit it. Your rewards have been great. Good night, Mary."

"I may have been a good soldier to you, father, but to me, I have been a damned fool! I hope Anne tells you to go to the devil! You wanted to send her away to Ireland. You stood there while she was ripped apart from Harry Percy. You married George to that treacherous Rochford woman." Sobs tore at her throat and tears coursed jaggedly down her flushed cheeks.

Staff was the first to reach her as her father grabbed her arms and shook her. He shoved her against Stafford, but his toneless voice addressed Will. "Your wife is drunk, I think, Carey. You had best calm her hysteria before she gets on the subject of her own marriage of which I was hardly the cause. See to her."

The door slammed behind him. Mary seized Staff's arms and pushed her wet face against his soiled velvet chest as Will stood silent, watching his impassive friend comfort his sobbing wife.

Part Three

A Lover's Vow

Set me whereas the sun doth parch the green,
Or where his beams may not dissolve the ice,
In temperate heat, where he is felt and seen;
With proud people, in presence sad and wise,
Set me in base, or yet in high degree;
In the long night, or in the shortest day;
In clear weather, or where mists thickest be;
In lusty youth, or when my hairs be gray;
Set me in earth, in heaven, or yet in hell;
In hill, in dale, or in the foaming flood;
Thrall, or at large, alive whereso I dwell;
Sick or in health, in ill fame or in good;
Yours will I be, and with that only thought
Comfort myself when that my hap is naught.

—Henry Howard, Earl of Surrey

Chapter Nineteen
December 28, 1527

Greenwich

The single narrow window in the bedchamber Mary shared with Will looked over the stretch of lawn to the now deserted bowling greens and beyond to the gray Thames. She was grateful her friend Mary Tudor had allowed that little Catherine could share the spacious royal nursery with Margaret, the love child from her beloved Duke of Suffolk. Mary turned, leaned against the window ledge and surveyed the irregular, cramped quarters wedged in the far northwest corner of maze-like Greenwich before the kitchen block began. Isolated quarters were a far cry from the fine chambers that were theirs when she had been the king's mistress. And a far cry from a year ago during the Twelve Days of Christmas at lonely Plashy in Northampton.

Mary sat again at the small drop leaf table and balanced her hand mirror against the wine jug. There was no room here for an elaborate dressing table with its rows of cut glass bottles and polished framed mirror. Father had said that, because of Will's reinstatement as Esquire of the Body, they would probably be given other quarters later, but she did not really believe it. Except for Mary Tudor and her mother, who was here as companion to Anne, she had seen no one of importance since they had arrived late last night. And tonight at Christmas revels she would have to hold up her head and face them all—proud Anne and the king who forgot everything so easily. And Staff. She bit her lip hard to keep the tears from welling and ruining her newly applied eye color. Surely Staff would be there with some adoring woman on his arm.

She saw it all then—not the small chamber at Greenwich to which they had returned—but the wood-beamed hall of the modest manor house at Plashy only a month after they had fled the king's wrath. Staff had ridden to Northampton to see them, and she had fought to control the ecstacy she felt to be near him again. He had supped with them so close across the trestle table and told them all the news of how the prideful king had bedded three ladies of the court in quick succession. Then he had turned restive again and had ridden off to Eltham to hunt. But Eltham was only a morning ride from Hever as well they all knew. His pursuit of a Bullen was on again, but Anne had held her ground firm, against her father's counseling.

Still, it was hardly the news of her sister or the king she had cherished that sunny day more than a year ago when William Stafford had visited Plashy. It was the sight of his rakish smile and the smell of his leather jerkin when she poured his wine.

But Will was watchful and not to be fooled. He saw her love for Staff on her face and in her eyes when he rode in that second time. He was cold to Staff and bitterly cruel to her. If it had not been for the fact that he knew his friend held his position safe for him in his absence, and had he not trusted Staff's lack of ambition to advance himself through it, she was not sure what he might have done to her. So through the months she lived at quiet Plashy with an embittered husband and a growing daughter, she guarded her face and hid her aching love deep in her thoughts.

Will had stopped bedding her after that. He moved to another bedroom down the narrow, crooked hall on the other side of baby Catherine's room and fed his mind's eye on his frustration for the ruin of the Carey cause. He blamed Mary's failure to hold the king. He left once for three weeks to visit his beloved sister at her priory, but Staff had given up visiting and she had no way to send for him and no way to guess at how long her husband would stay away with the only woman he truly loved and trusted.

So the days without a visit from Staff or word from court had dragged into weeks and months, and her well-tended love turned to doubt, frustration and then anger long after Will had returned and spring and summer had fled. They awaited the word from her father that they could return. She agonized in her lonely bed at night over Staff's desertion. She dreamed of him kissing Maud Jennings in the rose garden at Hampton, Staff making love to the raven-haired Fitzgerald, Staff laughing with others . . . and loving others.

"I said, Mary, are you ready? Your sister sent word that we might stop in her rooms before the revels, and I think we should. Your father is there. I expect he will know about our other accommodations and my position. I would at least like to be informed before I have to face His Grace. I have not seen your dear friend

335

Stafford anywhere today, but he assured me the position was mine when I—when we, actually—returned."

The ever-taut edge was in Will's voice, but she had given up the inward shudders she felt at his cold stares and indifference. "Yes. I am quite ready, Will."

"Whatever there is lost between us, Mary, I am pleased to see you still make a fine appearance. You are a little pale and wan, but your fabulous face and body never fail you. Your clever little sister may be quite put out and banish you again if you dazzle her by comparison, you know."

"I have no fear of that, Will. It is said she has splendid gifts from him, the best suite in the queen's wing of the palace, notes from him daily at Hever, and his Tudor heart to trample on if it pleases her."

She swept by him in her sky blue dress and opened the door to their room herself. Even the archway to the main hall was narrow and she made certain that she carefully gathered her full skirts with their silken ribbon catches and slashes as they passed through. The dress was last year's fashion, with a tight and low square-cut bodice which came to a point at the waist, but Mary Tudor had assured her that it was still stylish enough to wear. The matching blue silk slippers were slightly soiled from romping galliards long months ago at Whitehall. It was an endurance test for slippers to dance all night with the king, but she figured no one would notice if she danced with Will in a crowd tonight.

Will led her through the weblike corridors of Greenwich to the queen's wing and to Anne's spacious suite. The first thing her eyes saw when the painted door swung wide for them, was Jane Rochford hovering over Anne and stroking her black tresses with a gilded hairbrush. Anne's dark eyes caught Mary's in the huge polished mirror she faced.

"Mary, dearest!" Anne's face was alight with excitement and her eyes sparkled. "Now the holiday is perfect. You have seen mother this morning, I hear. We are all back together. And what fun the revels will be tonight! I am to be the lady with the Lord of Misrule, and you know who always takes that part!"

They embraced, almost formally, and Anne turned to kiss Will on the side of his cheek. Anne looked wonderful and words spilled from Mary in a rush. "Yes, Anne, I have seen His Grace play that boisterous part many times. Once," she said almost to herself, "he stumbled and his whole arm flopped in the Wassail bowl."

"I remember that," Jane Rochford put in merely nodding to Mary and turning back to finish Anne's coif.

"Will thought father would be here, Anne." Mary stood aside and scrutinized Jane's fussy ministrations over Anne's headpiece and jewels.

"Oh, he is, somewhere, Mary. He is never far away, as you can imagine." Anne giggled and her eyes sought Mary's in the mirror again. "He was livid and fumed for days, sister. He threatened to beat me, but he never did. Not when he saw His Grace still cared, even if I held the cards."

"And do you hold the cards still, Anne?" Will queried.

"Wait and see for yourself, Master Carey," Anne teased. She bent to pick up her pomander ball on its velvet ribbon and added, "There are jewels and notes and flowers and great promises and I control father

337

now—wait and see, Mary, if you do not believe me—and still His Grace has my refusal to share his bed and my word that I have only come for Yule festivities. I shall go back to Hever afterwards and await my next move however much father fusses. Wait and see."

Your next move, Mary thought hollowly. But Anne, she wanted to cry, you are acting and talking exactly like father. She pictured again the tiny green and white chess pawn Mary Tudor had once given her which she still had in her jewel box and had stared at so often in the long afternoons at Plashy while Catherine played in the orchard outside the window.

"Here you are, Mary, Will. You look fine. It is good to have you both back." Thomas Bullen patted Mary's shoulder and shook Will's hand. "Yes, you look well, Mary, as always. A little thinner perhaps."

"And older, father. And wiser."

He eyed her face carefully and turned to survey Anne. "Black and red for Yule, Anne? The slashings on the gown are very deep."

"I am not ready to be seen in Tudor green and white, father. I think the dress looks perfect with my dark hair and eyes and so does Jane."

"Yes, Jane would." He spun to Will and Mary noted the new massive golden crest on the heavy chain her father had draped across his velvet and ermine doublet.

"Will, the position is yours. Fear not about it and, of course, the lands and parklands from His Grace will remain quite untouched. As you know, you have Stafford to thank for holding the appointment and freely returning it to you. The man's cynicism and lack of court ambition when the king so clearly favors him, never ceases to astound me. Anyway, I offered him several hundred pounds a few months ago for holding the position for you—gambling money I told him—but he would take nothing. A rare, but foolish knave and evidently a trusted friend to you."

"Yes. Evidently," Will said so ominously that Anne looked up from her mirror. Thomas Bullen narrowed his eyes, and Mary held her breath.

"Let's be off. We must not keep the Lord of Misrule waiting. Come on, come on." Thomas Bullen waved his jeweled hand toward the door and shooed them into the now crowded hall as if they were chicks from the hen yard at Plashy.

Mary marvelled at his calm, expansive mood. She had expected a raving fury. Maybe Anne was taming him and was truly in control of her situation. Yet as Staff had once said, no one controls this king. He himself is the user.

Fifes, lutes, fydels, drums, and sackbuts wailed from both of the musicians' balconies overhead. People stood about in vibrant colors tapping their feet, but no one dared to dance until the king arrived. Mary wondered if Queen Catherine would appear tonight. Despite His Grace's constant neglect and his elevation of his bastard son over her dear little daughter, the queen had always come for Yule. Mary caught a small, heartfelt glimpse of her infinite, patient agony as she continued to live in the palaces of a husband who no longer loved her. Then she caught sight of William Stafford across the crowded hall.

She stood frozen and the whole room receded. Music played on distantly but the bustling and restive room packed with courtiers, died away to nothingness. Will pulled her arm and her feet moved. Staff stood far across the torch-lit bedecked room with a beautiful woman on either side of him, like silken sentinels. Will propelled her directly toward them. It all flooded back then, the pain after he visited them no more at Plashy. He had not come for five months of endless days, and she knew he must have forgotten her and was teasing and loving someone else.

"I do not know why the handsome devil does not marry, do you, wife? I cannot imagine he would be so foolish to pine away from something he can never have."

She felt wooden-legged and her feet seemed to drag on the floor. She saw the kind face of the Duchess of Suffolk as they passed and she nodded, but the smile she sought would not come to her lips. She did not care if they were all thinking, here comes the king's discarded mistress back to court after her shameful exile. Let them envy Anne and pity her. Let them all pity her, for she would never have the only man she had ever truly wanted. Let them all think her crushed that she had lost the eye of their terrible king.

Stafford and Will clapped each other on the shoulders and she stood rooted to her tiny piece of floor. As far as she knew, he had not even glanced her way. The two crimsoned-gowned women smiled and stood at attention, apparently waiting to be introduced. Mary felt lifeless and fought to keep her face calm, to keep from wadding handfuls of her azure gown into her tight fists.

Staff looked absolutely resplendent, and the impact of him so physically close to her after all these months nearly swamped her senses. He wore a deep burgundy velvet doublet with gold lining to match the short cape

340

over his broad shoulders. Decorative slashings across his hard chest revealed more rich, gold material, but the heavy leather belt studded with glinting metallic pieces around his flat stomach allayed any impression that he might be a mere pleasure-loving courtier. He looked bigger than she had remembered him, his cloth-covered thighs stretching the crimson hose, the crimson and gold codpiece mounted between his thighs, a fierce reminder of what she would never have from him.

"Mary," Staff said finally, and stooped to kiss her cheek, a mere brush of his lips. "She looks as beautiful as ever, Will. And is there no other child to come after the long stay at quiet Plashy?"

"No, and not likely to be," Will said pointedly. "Two is enough. Let her sister have the children now."

Staff raised one dark eyebrow. His eyes flitted over Mary's face and seemed to take her all in. She felt totally naked before him. He always read her perfectly. He would know of her wretched love for him and would probably tease her for it.

He pulled his eyes away and turned to Will again. "His Grace is most willing for you to resume your position. He tried to give it twice lately to George Bullen, thinking it would be another gift to Anne, but she wants George to be the messenger back and forth between Hever and the court. And, as you will soon see, what the Lady Anne wants, she gets." He lowered his voice to Will and Mary could barely hear the next words. "The little fool insists she is not here to stay but returns to Hever with her guardian mother soon, and I know for a fact the royal stallion has not had her. The wench's daring does boggle the mind."

Staff and Will stood apart now and there was an awkward silence. "Lord and Lady Carey, permit me to present Eleanor and Dorothy Cobham, Lord Sheffield's fair daughters from Derbyshire fresh come to court to serve Her Grace. Also," he lowered his voice conspiratorially, "they are appointed through Bishop Rochester and not through the king, though I assure you they have been since duly noted by His Majesty."

Will laughed, although Mary could see little humor in the remark. He pulled her away with some other whispered words to Staff, and as they traversed the long floor, she dared not look back.

Trumpets sounded and Queen Catherine entered with several ladies. Her women were all in black, as was Catherine. She had not changed. The huge, heavy golden and jeweled crucifix swung across her stiff bosom still. But how her daughter, Mary Tudor, had grown. His Grace must be in an expansive holiday mood indeed to allow his cast off daughter here at court with her mother. The girl's hair had gone from reddish hue to quite dark and she was tall, thin, and serious faced. She held her head erect and proud among all the whispers and her black skirts swished by near Mary. Mary wondered if their drab clothes were a sort of protest, a dark blot in the shifting sea of beautiful, colored silks that clustered around the dance floor. Wait until they see Anne, she thought then, Anne in her shining black silk with her blood-red slashings.

The trumpets sounded again, and her thought was fulfilled. His Grace entered, masked as the Lord of Holiday Misrule with a masked and laughing Anne on his arm and a veritable parade of costumed giants with huge steaming wassail bowls in their arms. Draped mummers with myriad ribbons hanging from their elaborate costumes and spiced cakes on silver trays followed. Eight lovely maidens skimmed by in striped garments holding wicker baskets laden with sprigs of mistletoe which they tossed to the crowd in quick handfuls. All bowed to the queen and princess, who finally managed a smile, and then the mummers circulated through the press of people passing out their cakes and ale and mistletoe.

Mary stared long at Henry Tudor and her sleek and giggling sister. She felt nothing. She could not summon up the tiniest pang of grief or remorse at the loss of her lover of five long years, and who would ever believe her? Maybe Staff would have once, but he hardly cared now. And Anne was making her own way now alone, even without father. Of course, she and Will would have to live at court but, except for being near her friend the Duchess of Suffolk, the thought terrified her.

At least starting tonight as he resumed his duties as Esquire in call of the king's bedchamber, Will would often be gone from the narrow bed they had been forced to share last night. There was beautiful little Catherine to care for, to love. Above all, to keep her sanity, she must avoid William Stafford and try to forget the women she would see him with as, even now, he stood so close to Dorothy Cobham across the room.

Will had gone in the wake of the king when His Grace departed the hall after hours of dancing and revels, leaving Mary to find their distant chambers in the far reaches of bricked Greenwich by herself. She once thought she knew the palace well, but it was only the royal apartments and larger chambers of the courtiers she had known, not the cramped quarters of this wing, back by the tiltyards and sporting fields. Weary, she found the room after two wrong turns, and pushed the door open to find her faithful Nancy waiting, warming her mistress' robe over a charcoal brazier, since there was no fireplace in the chilly room.

"I am glad to see your sweet face, my Nance," she said to the girl. "Tomorrow night I shall have you wait outside the great hall to help lead me back to this hidden den."

"The lord says surely your rooms are to be moved, Lady Mary. A lord and lady of the king can hardly stay in this cold hovel." She pulled her woolen shawl closer and hunched up her shoulders. "I left little Catherine about an hour ago. She was so excited she could hardly sleep. I think she misses her little room at Plashy, but she and the Lady Margaret take well to each other. Margaret gave her a wee leather-faced doll and she fell asleep with it in her arms." She began to unlace Mary's dress as she spoke.

"She is young and adaptable, I pray, Nance. Maybe that doll can replace the one she dropped from the fishing boat into the pond. She cried three nights over the tattered mite." Mary stepped quickly out of her chemise and wrapped her furred robe around her body. She was so warm from dancing that she hardly felt the chill. She would be in bed and sound asleep before the icy cold crept into every corner of the room in the long hours until dawn.

"Will you be quite well, lady, since the lord sleeps in call of the king? I could stay."

"Thank you, Nance, but I will be fine. I am exhausted and really need the time alone after the bustle of the move and the ride over the muddy roads to

London. I *do* depend on you greatly, you know, but I need to be alone.''

"Yes, lady," Nancy nodded as though she truly understood. "I be in the common hall with my cousin Megan if you should need me. I dare say you could catch a linkboy to fetch me." She opened the door to the dark hall and a noticeable draft swept past her. "If there be any linkboys in such distant reaches of this cold palace," Mary heard her murmur as she closed the door.

She warmed her hands for a moment near the charcoal embers, then brushed her hair listening to the crackle of the brush through her long gold tresses. She could feel the chill now. It was creeping into her. Maybe when Anne left to return to Hever those rooms would be available. She laughed aloud at the foolish thought. "Those rooms are in the queen's wing, silly," she said, and her own voice in the now silent room startled her.

At least when they progressed to Whitehall or Richmond or wherever, Will, as Esquire, would be certain to get her a room with at least a fireplace. "This room is as cold and sullen as the look His Grace gave me tonight with his fake 'welcome back, dear Mary' speech," she accused the cold chamber.

When she slid her feet into the icy sheets she wished desperately for a warming pan to dump the charcoal embers into and run between the smooth linens. She lay there curled up stiffly for a moment and got up to don her robe again. It was then she heard the quick knock on her door. Her heart leapt at the sharp sound in the silence of her thoughts.

"Who is there?"

"It is Staff, Mary. I would talk with you."

She pulled the robe tight around her hips, but her feet would not move.

"Mary." He pushed the door slowly open and his shoulder and head appeared far higher up the door than where she stared. She had forgotten to shoot the door bolt. She had forgotten he was so tall.

He did not wait for words from her, but took a huge step in and closed the door quietly behind him. "I had to see you, Mary. I am sorry I startled you."

"At least you still remember my name," she heard herself say shakily.

A swift grin lit his features. "I remember a good deal more, Mary Bullen."

She turned away so he would not see the fear on her face, the longing, the bitter anger. "My name, as you well know, William Stafford, is not Bullen nor has it been for a long time. I believe my husband, Lord Carey, is a dear friend of yours." She looked down at the tiny mirror she had left on the drop leaf table.

"I did it all for you, Mary—for us, holding his position like that."

"How considerate and noble." Her voice caught as though she were on the edge of tears. She spun to face him and was terrified to see he had come much closer. "How considerate, just like all the visits you paid us at Plashy the last five months we were there." She stared at the tiny throbbing pulse at the base of his bronze throat. How was he always so brown in the winter months? He had changed clothes too, and how did he ever find this forsaken room?

"When I saw Will's bitter suspicions for our feelings," he went on, "I knew it was foolish to cause you pain when I was there and much worse pain after I left.

346

I knew he would take it out on you, and it was the only way I could protect you, even a little bit. I missed you, too."

"I did not say I missed you."

"You did not have to, sweetheart." He took another step forward and, like a coward, she pressed back against the rough plaster wall next to the window. "I was so happy when I knew His Grace would allow you to come back. And when I saw you with Will tonight, I thought, what for? For the delicious torture of seeing you daily and not being able to touch you, to make love to you?"

"Please, Staff, you have to go."

"I will. Later. Then I thought, I have to forget you and marry as the king wants. . . ."

"The king wants you to? Whom?"

"One of the Dorset lassies he wants to come to court. I have only seen her once. But then, I realized I cannot forget you because I have desired you ever since I set eyes on you in the dusty old Bastille in Paris and knew that the blonde beauty with the smothered fire in her eyes was for me. And I have loved you almost as long as that, Mary." He leaned close to her, not touching her tense body but placing his hands carefully on the wall on either side of her tousled head.

She closed her eyes treasuring his words, his soothing voice she had thought she would never hear again and had desired so desperately in the long hours away. She felt tears squeeze through her lashes. He was so close she could smell sweet wine on his breath.

"I kept Will's position for him, Mary, and I stayed away from his wife whom I love and he does not, damned fool that he is, and now he owes me. He owes

me that I can be near you and I will be, I will be." He
nuzzled her hair and bent to kiss her throat. A little stifled cry escaped her as he leaned gently against her. He
raised his head and stared down into her wide eyes. His
lips descended upon hers. He was so warm and strong.
All the loneliness and pain flowed out of her as she returned his caressing, probing kiss. His kisses deepened
and she felt his breath hot against her cheek. She forgot
she was pressed to a cold wall in the slums of vast
Greenwich and that her husband did not love her and
she had fallen far from the good graces of her king.
Here was all that mattered.

She lifted her arms to his broad shoulders and
pressed him close in return, arching up against him.
Her robe fell open but she no longer needed its furry
warmth. He moved a half step away, parted it slowly
and put his hands to her waist, covered only by the thin
chemise. The span of his hands nearly encircled her.
His thumbs moved slowly over the tiny swell of her
belly. He lifted her, his arms like metal bands around
her. The heavy robe dangled straight down from her
shoulders to the floor. He laid her in its warm folds on
the bed, strode to the door and shot the bolt. His boots
thudded on the floor beside the bed and he yanked his
doublet and shirt over his head as though they were one
garment.

"Staff, we cannot. Will might . . ."

He silenced her with a hot kiss, and his hands went to
her waist again. "Hush, love. Will is thinking of the
king and the Carey name. None of that has anything to
do with us."

Her limbs felt like water, and a hot pulse raced low in
her stomach. She wanted this so much. She wanted him

348

and had for years. She went limp as his hands crept up to her pointed breasts and his knee rode intimately across her legs.

"I told you once that I was not a very patient man, Mary. I—and we—have waited quite long enough, but if you choose not to submit, I shall take it on myself, and you may blame me in the morning. I want you, sweetheart, to make up for a lot of lonely hours, and countless advice, and worry that your kings and damned father would totally ruin your life, and for a lot of your own tart words. And for the wasted years. Tonight we are going to begin catching up and it will take a long, long time for us to be even."

His voice mesmerized her and the low flickering flames, dancing in his dark eyes, entranced her. She struggled away from him. He let her sit up only to tug the robe off her arms, tumble her over him, and pull the chemise up to her hips.

"No," she said once, but she almost laughed at her lie, for she wanted him so badly.

He pulled the fur robe over them as the cold air bit at her naked body. His mouth covered a rosy nipple, and he kissed and teased it while one hand fondled the other breast. He stretched the ruffled chemise up to her chin and then over her head. His hands were everywhere. This was far different from Henry Tudor's rough caresses or Will's swift, cold possessiveness. Instinctively, she arched her back and parted her knees. This was madness. How often, how many years in Henry's vast bed or in Will's narrow one, had she fantasized that Staff would seize her and take her, force her to lie with him, crush her beneath his thrusts as he rode her passionately and told her he would love her forever. And now it was real.

He stripped off his breeches while she smiled deep inside for the pure joy of having him look on her that way. "Your eyes are smiling, Mary, though I would not put it past your lips to tell me a foolish 'no' again." He shifted his body and his full bulk hovered over her like a warm protecting roof against the cold world. He slipped his knees between her legs and she reached up and encircled his neck with her arms. His face was so close over her, and he hesitated for only a moment.

"Your face is always beautiful, love, and that is why men desire you. But it is honest, too. Honest and so clearly lovely within. That is why this man has loved you and desired you all this time. Until the late winter dawn I am going to make love to you, and I will watch your face and know you love me too. You are mine, Mary Bullen, from this time on, no matter what befalls."

He poised himself over her and slowly drove deep inside, his dark eyes never leaving her face. He began full, hard thrusts, and fell to his elbows, kissing her, then pulled his head up to watch her again. She knew she was blushing with fierce embarrassment. No, that was not it. She was hot all over, and her limbs were not her own. She felt no shame as she had with Francois, so long ago, and no anxious desire to have it over with as with her Tudor king, not even the tender patience she had felt with Will when she had been his bride.

"Yes. Please. Yes. Staff, I love you, I have wanted you so," she heard her voice say, muffled against his warm neck, and he grinned broadly, even as his jagged breathing deepened and his fierce rhythm increased its pace.

She wrapped her legs tight around his back, and her arms grasped his neck so hard that she pulled his head down to hers, and he kissed her fiercely. Tears coursed down her cheeks and a huge surging wave shook her and turned to flames in her stomach and legs. He crushed her hips down into the soft bed. She lost control of her breathing and panted in little gasps as he plunged deep into her again and suddenly held still, shooting an incredible warmth into her to soothe the heat of her loins. He lay collapsed against her, sweating in the chill of the air. Then he raised his disheveled head and looked down into her languorous eyes only inches away. He smiled rakishly.

"I would almost have to say that that few minutes was worth seven years of hell, sweetheart." He reached down, pulled her discarded fur robe over their perspiring bodies and lay against her with her head tucked under his chin, and stroked her hair gently. Her free hand, rested in the curly hair of his chest.

She sighed. "I have never felt so safe and content. But I am old enough to know that the real world is outside there, outside that door."

"Yes, my Mary. But there are many doors in His Grace's palaces, and some day we may have a door of our own." His voice broke and he hesitated. "Some day."

She snuggled closer against him. She felt incredibly happy. She would not care if the king, her wide-eyed sister and screaming father beat down the door. Now she had more to live for than a son she was never allowed to see and a tiny daughter who grew too swiftly.

His voice broke into the silence. "But for now, as I told you, love, it is only a beginning. And that was only a tiny downpayment for seven years.''

His hand rode along her hips and ribs to tease her breasts again. The embers in his dark eyes fanned to flames while she stared deep into them. She started to smile as his mouth descended, but she was soon lost in the trembling of their fierce embrace.

Chapter Twenty
April 27, 1528

Hampton Court

The weeks, days and hours were precious now and not to be dreaded as Mary had feared: each meal, each walk through the wood paneled and tapestried halls of Greenwich, Whitehall, Nonesuch, or Hampton—any moment she might see Staff.

Their times together were often fleeting and bittersweet, but Mary treasured each in her heart. The stares, rude barbs, and effronts to her as the king's now-cast-off mistress bothered her not at all. Anne's self-centeredness, the lack of her father's goodwill which she had once coveted—what did that matter now that William Stafford loved her and she belonged, body and heart, to him only?

They had become as clever as the king's court spies, Staff teased her. Sometimes Mary's trusted maid Nancy went between them with information about when one of them was unexpectedly free or where to meet, but usually they managed unaided. When Will, as Esquire to the body, fulfilled his duties as royal valet and companion to the king by sleeping within call of the royal bedroom, Staff sometimes dared to come to her, but often they met in the dead of night in some unoccupied bedroom or other empty chamber in reach of whatever palace the court visited. Staff seemed to know everything: Will's schedule, what rooms in what halls were vacant, when to dare much, and when they must go endless days not chancing a tryst. Mary trusted Staff completely, as completely as she desired and loved him.

But it had been almost a week now, the longest they had not dared, and this chilly and damp late April day here at Hampton Court was starting to seep into her bones. After each time they had been together, she fed herself on warm memories of each embrace, each passionate caress, living his tender touches over and over until the memories cooled and she burned with desire for new lovemaking with him.

Mary leaned her flushed cheek on the cool pane of the leaded window overlooking the vast stretch of roofs at Hampton abloom with twisted brick chimneys in the early morning rain. This room was not a bad one really—spacious with a fireplace and a tiny sitting room attached. How the Carey living quarters had improved since they had returned from their year long exile only three months ago! Their bouche too, the daily allotment by rank of candles, bread, wine, and beer sent to the hundreds of courtiers' rooms, had increased. Probably the result of some comment of her sister to the Great Henry rather than His Grace's true estimate of the Careys' worth. But today, the red bricks of Hampton were glazed with chilly rain and a gray fog drifted in from the river with cold, clenching hands to dampen her precious memories.

She heard her maid Nancy come and she turned to

see the girl's arms full of the laundry she had gone to fetch and a bolt of shell-pink satin. "Good news, Lady Mary," the sweet-faced, brown-haired girl beamed at her mistress as she laid the pile of goods carefully on the table. "The washer women had the linens all done and—look at this!"

Mary gazed with awe at the thick bolt of pale pink satin Nancy extended toward her. She hated to admit it, but she had longed for new gowns after a year away from court while her own sister's growing influence over king and courtiers had changed the styles gradually until her older clothes looked much outdated. Long, tapered sleeves dripping with lace were now the rage and a more bell shaped sweep of skirt than the padded ones Spanish Queen Catherine still clung to. Mary did not care for her own pride so much that some of her clothes were several years out of style from the heyday of the king's bounty to her, nor for the terrible family pride her father espoused. But she did so want to look beautiful and fashionable for Staff and, of course, she could take no gifts or money from him or her penurious husband, whose wealth went for Carey causes, would know.

"It is so lovely, Nance, and such a delicate color."

"Enough for a May Day gown if we get after it fast enough, m' lady. Let's see—it be but four days away, but if we work at it and I get my sister Megan to help us a bit on all the fancy tuckings and embroidery—"

Mary slid her tapered fingers along the rosy and silvery sheen of the material. Even in this muted light it came alive with shimmering highlights when it was turned or moved. "But, Nance, where in the world did it come from? Not my Lord Carey, I warrant, and

355

Lord Stafford does not dare."

Tears of excitement flooded the maid's hazel eyes and she nearly jumped about in her desire to tell. "By the saints, Lady Mary, I was waiting for you to ask me and you just keep staring wide-eyed in wonder at it all. Your lady mother has come to court with your sister for May Day and she brought it for you."

"My sister?"

"No, your lady mother."

"Why was I not told they were coming? I should have known the king would insist Anne be here for the May revels, I guess, but, oh, why do they not tell me anything anymore? And mother should not have borne this great expense for me. Father does not give her a very big allowance for Hever anymore as she and Semmonet are the only constant householders now." She sank into a chair at their little table with the bolt of shimmery pink satin spilled over her knees.

"Saints, Lady Mary, I thought you would be dancin' on the ceiling for it and you look like the gray sky outside. Lady Bullen said to tell you that she will see you as soon as she and the Lady Anne get settled and after she talks to Lord Bullen."

"Good luck to her on that," Mary said grimly.

"M'lady, I been thinking," Nancy began slowly and then charged on in a rush of increasing speed, "since striped and inset bodices be all the rage, we could cut pieces of ivory satin out of your wedding gown you been wanting to make over, maybe even line the low-square-cut bodice of this May Day dress with the tiny pink roses off that old-fashioned, slashed wedding skirt."

Mary smiled broadly at the slim girl hovering over

her and wiped a threatening tear away with the back of one finger. "Yes, Nance, a wonderful idea. My dear mother should never have done this, but I think she knows how poorly I get on here except for—well, she could know nothing of Lord Stafford." She and Nancy grinned conspiratorially at each other as if the empty chamber were simply brimming with spies.

"Let's do it then, Nance. This will lift my spirits on a dreary day."

"And you will be the best dressed lady, as well as the most beautiful as always," Nancy chortled and gathered the washed linen from the little table to give them working room.

"Saints, m' lady, we will never manage to lay and cut this out on this little table, and we sure cannot put it on this floor. Shall we go down to the great hall or some larger table to do it?"

"No. No one wants to see Mary Carey about cutting and sewing her own dresses down there. It is just not done. Here, help me move aside these chairs and this table. This rug is clean and we shall have to be careful. If my mother should appear—which I doubt, since she will probably send for me to Anne's rooms—she will certainly understand."

"And Lord Carey?"

"He said he was to be about when the king receives the French ambassadors so I have no idea when he will appear. Right now at least, my Lord Carey is the least of my worries."

"Yes, mi' lady," Nancy said solemnly, studying her mistress' face for a moment before they bent to heave and slide the heavy, carved furniture to the corners of the room.

On their hands and knees, they crawled around the edge of the rippled pink sea of material spread between them, measuring, cutting. They studied the cut of earlier dresses and Mary even lay down on the edge of the satin so they could judge the tapered sleeve length before they cut. The rain beat down outside, glazing the windows and occasionally plopping into the ashes of the hearth. Their backs, shoulders, and arms began to ache as the pink cut pieces piled up on the bed.

"There, Nance. And look. Enough for a dress for little Catherine, I am certain. It does not always do for her to be wearing last season's clothes in such close proximity to the Duchess of Suffolk's little daughter Margaret. Now we will cut those strips from the wedding gown and snip off those lovely roses. You should be a seamstress and designer of ladies' gowns, Nance. What a wonderful idea to cut up this old one like this!"

Alight at the praise, the girl beamed at her mistress' words, her sweet, honest face sprinkled with faded freckles. They had worked over the eight-year-old wedding gown but a few minutes when a knock sounded at the door. Still on her knees, Nancy swung it open and an astounded little boy neither of them recognized stared down in surprise at the two women on the floor over a pretty dress they were cutting to shreds.

"L-Lady Carey?" he stammered.

"Yes. Do not be afraid to speak your piece. I am Lady Carey."

"I be Simon the linkboy from the east hall down there," he said, and pointed off down the corridor.

"Yes, Simon?"

"The Lady Carey's presence is requested by her lady mother, Lady Bullen in this place, m' lady. See

358

here, one a the king's gent'men wrote it down for me.''
He extended to her a tiny square of parchment which
he had evidently bent and wrinkled in his hot little fist.

Mary rose and took the note from the boy. "Thank
you, Simon. You may tell my mother I will attend her
immediately.''

The boy grinned. "Yes, m' lady, but I am not
'sposed to go back there. The gent'man already give
me a copper for it.'' With that, he was gone.

"Imagine paying linkboys to deliver messages these
days,'' Mary said as she unfolded the little piece of paper. "They used to do that *gratis* as well as light the halls
after dark.''

The note said simply, "Your mother and Anne have
come to court. Since they are busy and you are not, I
suggest you visit your horse in the east stable block
nearest the herb gardens now. Ignore the rain. Eden
misses you.''

Staff, of course. Had he gone stark mad sending her
a written missive like this? But, of course, it was not
signed. Now, the note said. Did he mean right now?

Her heart began to hammer as she bent toward her
little mirror. She saw her cheeks were already flushing
pink in anticipation. "Nancy, get out my green riding
dress and a shawl and hurry.''

The girl darted up and pulled the outfit from the
huge coffer at the foot of the bed. "Going riding in this
fog and rain, Lady Mary,'' she protested gently as she
shook out the skirts. "Saints, lady, this is a wrinkled
mess. Your mother and the Lady Anne want you to go
riding in this weather?''

"Please, Nance, hurry. I will help you with the May
Day dress when I come back, all night if we must. And

if my mother or sister send for me, only tell the messenger I am out and will attend them presently."

Nancy helped her mistress change clothes quickly. "But that note," she sputtered and then her face broke into a huge grin. "Oh, *that* mother," she laughed and winked and they hugged before Mary hurried out the door into the long, oak paneled hall. It was only as she went down the twisting, enclosed back stairs toward the east stables that she realized she still held the little note clasped tightly in her sweaty palm.

The rain had let up somewhat. 'Ignore the rain,' he had written. Yes, she could do that now and gladly. But surely there would be others about the stables, grooms or squires. It did not matter: if they had to just pet Eden and whisper love words over the mare's back, that would have to be enough for today.

She covered her bare head with the dark woven shawl and skirted the herb gardens which would soon burst and bulge with green rows of well-tended asparagus, parsnips, peas, onions and beets. The red brick stable blocks loomed ahead a brighter red in the rain. The Tudor arms inset in stone were over the center door, but she took the gravel path around the side and darted under the overhang to flap clinging raindrops from her shawl.

She entered the warmth of the huge stables and thought instantly of the stables at home. Ian, the blacksmith, tended Hever's small stables proudly despite their meagerness, for when father was away and George gone too, there was no need to support the large number of horses they had once kept there.

The king loved his horses and his hunt hounds, and both were well cared for under this vast roof. It smelled

360

damp here, but fresh—straw and malt all mingled with leather and punctuated with the wheeze and stamp of snorting, shifting horses in their stalls. She glanced down the long rows and saw no one. She had visited her mare Eden here before and her stall was much farther down.

"Excuse me, lovely lady, but are you wanting to ride any mount in particular? Might I be of some help? Do you think you could handle a large, eager stallion to-day?"

She whirled to face Staff where he stood at his ease between two tall destriers which knights rode at the tilt rail. She would have rushed to him to throw her arms around him, but he held up one hand, and she smiled in obvious wicked anticipation.

"Staff," she whispered. "It looks empty here, of people, I mean."

He grinned rakishly at her and raised one eyebrow. "I know, sweet lady. Most of His Grace's men are in the Great Presence Chamber and the women are all aflutter over your sister's arrival."

"But you—how did you manage to get away?"

"I lied," he said low and came toward her in the aisle between the stalls where she stood. "I told them I have heartburn from that wretched orgy of rich food His Grace dined those Frenchies on last night. Actually, it was not that much of a lie, lass, only to tell true, the cause of my burning heart is hardly His Grace's highly seasoned food."

She giggled in sheer delight at his tease, despite the way he glanced quickly up and down the aisle and firmly took her elbow.

"Have you missed me?" he said out of the side of his

361

mouth as they strolled between the two long rows of horse croups and tails.

"Of course. It has been a whole week, my Staff."

"I know, sweet, and I hate to send for you like this at the oddest times and weirdest places."

"But we decided we must do that now to be together."

"Yes. Yes, shh. It is only that I wish so desperately that I could give you your own house and stables—and bedroom. What were you doing when the boy came with the note from 'mother'?"

"You rogue! Actually, if you want to know, I was cutting my old wedding dress to shreds."

"So it has come to that, has it? Making a new gown from it, I suppose you mean. Mary, I have told you before and I shall tell you now again. You are without exception the most ravishingly beautiful woman at this court whatever you wear—or do not wear."

A lump caught in her throat at the verbal caress. When he talked to her, even looked at her, it was always as though he touched her all over, stroked her bare skin, even thrust his love keep within her.

"If you think we have come here for a mere stroll among His Grace's ponies, sweet, you are in for a bit of a surprise, and I hope a pleasant one," he was saying. "I have told you that I am not a patient man and I am afraid you are about to see the results of that. In here, Mary."

She followed him trustingly through a small door in the back of the stables. It was a low, long, narrow room with a row of pallets covered with deep straw. There was a small table with a bench, a braided rag rug on the floor, and several open grates along the outside wall to let in air and light. Still it was very dim in here. Stafford shot the bolt on the door behind them and then shoved a heavy bench to rest against it.

"The man in charge of the grooms stays here, Mary, and he owes me a favor. He knows I have a lady with me, but he will keep himself and the grooms clear for a while. They are busy enough with all the French mounts in the west stables anyway. The straw is all fresh on the pallets, love. I hauled it in myself from the loft this morning. See, over here."

She stepped forward and saw three of the low wooden pallets on their sturdy, squat legs had been shoved together, piled with deep straw and covered with his big, black velvet cloak. She knew he was watching her intently, one hand still lightly touching her elbow.

"You know, my dear Lord Stafford," she said low trying to keep her voice from trembling, "you can absolutely ruin good velvet in the rain. I am so glad you found a warm, dry place for that cape. And I love the feel of velvet on my back."

They came together in a crushing embrace, their hands on each other's backs and hips, their kiss searing, their tongues darting, probing. He started to undress her almost immediately, and her hands lifted to unlace his white linen shirt and pull it over his head when he bent over for her. His hands were so sure on her riding habit and voluminous underskirts.

"Put your arms down at your sides for a moment, love," he said, and she realized that the way she was clinging to his neck made it impossible for him to divest her of her chemise. She lowered her arms obediently and he pulled the lacy straps of her chemise off her shoulders, down her tingling arms to where the lace

363

edging scraped sensuously across the pointed nipples of her breasts, then skimmed down her hips as he knelt to brush the ruffled circle of linen and lace clear to her ankles.

He stayed there a moment kneeling in front of her as she stood naked before him, his head at the level of her stomach. His hands lifted to her rounded buttocks and he pulled her a step to him, showering little kisses across her belly, hip bones and down her quivering thighs.

She put her hands on his head and stroked his thick hair. How crisp it felt, how clean. She moved her hands to caress the strong nape of his neck where his hair fell over warm, taut skin.

The trembling in her legs spread like a flaming brand into the pit of her stomach. It was always, always like this with Staff, she marvelled—not fear-tinged awe as with Francois, nor tender calm as with Will and Henry. This was mutual, rampant, flowing, devouring— She moved her legs apart willingly when he nudged her knees and plundered between her thighs delicately, expertly with his insistent fingers.

When she could not control the shaking in her body, any more than the cascade of love words which spilled from deep inside her, he tumbled her back onto their soft straw and velvet bed. She parted her knees and reached for him, her face rapt, her eyes languorous in the overwhelming rush of ecstasy.

He leaned so close over her, as if memorizing her face, that she smelled wine and sweet cloves on his breath. Every long, dark eyelash, the deep brown eyes with floating yellow glints like a brook in the sun, his strong nose—he looked suddenly so serious now.

"Tell me what you want, my love," he rasped through parted lips. "Tell me now."

"You, Staff, you. Forever and always. Please."

"Only Staff?"

"Yes, yes. Please, my love. Put out the fire."

"But first I have to fan it brighter," he said low, and moved into her instantly.

She felt the straw prick her bare back and buttocks through the soft velvet as he crushed her down. She felt the hard strength of his long, lean body, his thrusts in her deeper, deeper. The fire in her did turn to hot, quenching liquid then, but she only loosened her tight grip on him when the gentle rains came to cool the raging torment of their love.

May Day dawned glorious and golden at Hampton Court on the springtime banks of the broad River Thames. All morning the air had been split with the racket of workmen putting up the May poles and wrapping their twelve foot lengths in alternating strips of Tudor green and white. Trestle tables were being laid outside and covered with long white tableclothes soon to be laden with food for over a thousand May Day revelers. From two newly-installed temporary fountains at the edge of the rose gardens, streams of the king's two favorite wines, Osney and Compolet sprouted in noisy trickles awaiting the thrust of goblets or parted lips of thirsty imbibers.

At eleven in the morning the greens, gardens and the elaborate maze would burst with the light-hearted, laughing courtiers who now kept to their rooms to dress and primp and prepare for this extravaganza to welcome the onset of spring and the temporary return to court of the Lady Anne Bullen. The eternally repeated topics of how many lands or titles or preferments the Lady Anne would get and how long she would last with the king on this one day, took second place to the scuttling whispers of fashion and merriment.

"The dress is perfect, just perfect, Lady Mary," Nancy crooned as she sat back proudly on her heels to admire their four day creation. "I warrant even the Lady Anne shall not be as talked about and noted to-day!"

Mary pirouetted slowly as Nancy held their only small mirror so that she could catch at least a sideways glimpse of herself. She had to admit the gown was lovely. The shimmery blend of delicate shell pink and ivory in the bodice set off her milk and peaches complexion, and the light blonde tresses arranged so carefully. The press of the taut bodice pushed the creamy tops of her graceful, full breasts up over the lace and rosebud edging of the low, square-cut gown. Rustling satin skirts belled out in the graceful French style everytime she swayed her hips slightly. Her full outer sleeves over the tight fitted ones dripped Belgian lace plundered from the wedding dress also, and a silver belt with clinking, delicate links which had once been a long neck chain, dangled from her tiny waist. They had even covered a pair of old, worn white dance slippers in the pale pink satin. They both knew grass stains from the dancing on the lawn would surely ruin the slippers, but for today it was worth it.

Will stepped in from the hall dressed in his best beige doublet, matching hose and white lace and embroidered shirt and his mouth dropped. "A new dress, Mary? Is there a secret admirer, or did your avaricious little sister send you down a cast-off bolt from her coffers?''

"Will, I do not need your snide remarks today. Mother brought me this pink satin from Hever when she came last week and if you had been anywhere about these last four days, you would have seen Nancy and me personally slaving over it."

"Well, it is lovely. You look fine. That will set them back on their heels when they see how Lady Carey looks, eh?"

No thanks to you, she wanted to say, but she did not intend to ruin this beautiful, exciting day carping at Will.

"You are evidently ready then, wife. Yes, you and Nancy did a very pretty job here. Those little roses at the neckline and hairpiece remind me of another gown you had once, but for the life of me I cannot think which one. Let us be off then. It is almost eleven and it will not do to keep His Grace waiting. I did tell you I am to go with John Ashton, Thomas Darcy and a small contingent of guards to fetch the Princess Mary for her father later this afternoon, did I not, Mary?"

"No. No, you did not, my lord." She took his offered arm as they went out into the hall increasingly full of courtiers heading downstairs. "But she is at Beaulieu, Will. You cannot possibly get back until tomorrow."

"True, madam," he said tight-lipped. "See what you can make of the respite then."

She darted a sideways look at him through her thick lashes, suddenly afraid. Could he know about Staff and her? But no, since things were bad in their marriage, he had probably meant that she would not miss him. Besides, he said no more about it and Staff and she had been so careful.

Still, she felt the first tiny stab of guilt for a long time. The moment he had told her he would be away, had not her first thought been to somehow tell Staff?

The sun dazzled them as they stepped out the big back doors facing the pond garden on the south front lawns. Mary blinked and squinted until her eyes adjusted. Courtiers were streaming in their springtime pastels like gentle trails of ribbons down to the burgeoning tables and waiting May poles on the river. The poignant fragrances of boxwood and sweet lilies-of-the-valley permeated the air everywhere here.

Her eyes skimmed the clusters of chatting, strolling people for Staff. He was always ridiculously easy to pick out, of course, because he was so tall, but she saw him nowhere here. Perhaps the king had attached him to his retinue at the last minute, and the big, brazen sovereign had hardly put in his appearance here yet among these still somewhat subdued courtiers. Do not panic and do not show dismay, Staff had warned her, when you see I am escorting Dorothy Cobham and Isabelle Dorsey. It would look most suspicious for me to attend May Day like a single stag among the does, only to shoot soulful looks at the married lady Lady Carey all afternoon. She knew he was right. At least there would be two women with him, she breathed, and that was infinitely better than one.

"Well, wife, steady yourself for the onslaught," Will was chuckling and Mary's eyes foolishly searched the path for Staff with his two females in tow until she realized Will could not possibly know of that. Then she saw what he meant: in an elaborately ruffled and embroidered gown of light green and pale yellow, a laughing Anne Bullen pulled Henry Tudor decked in blinding white and gold down the path directly behind them with the rest of the Bullen family in their broad wake.

Will took Mary's arm firmly and they both bowed low as the royal entourage approached. Anne giggled; George nodded and tried to shift away from his clinging wife, Jane Rochford; Lady Bullen clasped her hands in delight and nodded at Mary over the perfection of the dress. The king and Thomas Bullen both stared wide-eyed at Mary.

"Well, well," the king's voice came to Mary's ears uncharacteristically raspy. "Thomas, you rogue, how did you ever do it? Two beautiful, ravishing daughters. Lady Mary, my greetings this fine May Day and to you Will, of course, whom I see more often." His eyes, in shadow, went deliberately over Mary, but Anne's head jerked toward the king and she possessively took his white-satin covered arm.

"My dear lord king, everyone awaits," she said, and tugged his arm. He pulled his eyes away from Mary like a guilty schoolboy caught cheating at sums and with another mumbled word and quick backward glance, went on.

Thomas Bullen dropped behind the departing king and spoke first to Will, as if Mary were not even there. "Did you mark all that, Will?" he demanded low. "I would advise you and your lady here to patch things up and put on a good front. Anne seems so willful and nervous I never know what she is going to do next. You *do* look spectacular, Mary dear. See to her, Will."

Mary stared at her father's retreating back through slitted eyes as he hurried to catch up with the king. "Do you have anything to say, madam?" Will probed the minute they were all out of earshot.

"About what, Will? My father's cryptic comments of His Grace's greedy eyes?"

"Do not raise your voice out here like that, Mary. I was referring to how your father knew things were— well, unsettled between us."

She started to walk toward the festival green and he had to hurry to keep up. "Honestly, Will, you ought to be used to father's knowing everything by now. It can hardly be a secret at court that you bed elsewhere but in the Lady Carey's room."

His hand shot out and seized her wrist, whirling her around to face him. "And you, madam?"

She faced him squarely, calmly, fighting to keep panic and disdain from her face. Over his shoulder she caught a glimpse of Staff in a tawny and gold doublet on the path a little way behind Will. Staff—with a lovely woman on each arm. If they approached Will and her while Will probed so suspiciously, she would be lost for certain.

"Will! Will Carey!" Will turned away and squinted into the late morning sun. It was Sir Francis Weston in the most incongruous yellow for such a masculine sporter and soldier, and quite out of breath. "Will and Mary! His Grace has asked me to fetch you to his table directly. He said the entire Bullen family should be together today to please the Lady Anne."

They set off across the path at a good clip, and Mary could feel Staff's eyes boring into her from behind. To please the Lady Anne, in a pig's eye, Mary thought grimly. She had been the king's mistress off and on for five years and she could still read his thoughts well enough. He had ogled her but briefly on the path and now meant to use her either to set Anne back on her heels a bit, confuse her father's wily brain—or, or . . . No, the other possibility could never be that he had looked on her with real interest for himself after all this time. No. Never that again. She would run away first, drown herself in the muddy Thames despite this new dress! Later, in the dancing, she must somehow get to Staff. Staff always knew what to do.

"Mary, are you all right? I did not mean to ruin this happy day. And here, the Careys fully back in His Grace's goodwill! Eleanor will be so pleased when she hears."

Mary only nodded, tight-lipped as they were seated down the table from the king. She could not see Staff, as he no doubt seated himself somewhere in the swelling crowd behind them.

The May Day sun slipped on golden slippered feet across the blue, blue sky as the day wore on with feasting and dancing. A new May queen and king were chosen each year. Mary watched as Isabelle Dorsey, whom Staff had once said the king had wanted him to marry, was chosen to serve with the youngest Guildford son. She remembered, as if in a distant dream she had been selected for the honor her first year back from Francois' gilded court.

She danced around the May pole with many partners, weaving, then unweaving the ribbons each pair of cavorting revelers held while following the simple running and bowing patterns of the dance. Will partnered her first, then George, then Weston, then Norris, even the king—then, finally, there was Staff.

One hand was firm on her back, his other grasped hers and their ribbon as they moved together around the circle. "Will is leaving for Beaulieu," she whispered.

"I know. You look absolutely ravishing, Mary, like a spring angel I could find in the gardens, if there was such a thing as spring garden angels."

"How much wine have you and your charming little ladies had, my lord?" she asked. They were both out of breath. Oh no, she thought, the musicians are stopping. It was over too soon. Everyone around them was applauding and laughing. She knew her disappointment showed clearly on her face and here Staff dared to grin down at her like that. Only a few moments with him, and he looked so happy to be going back to squire that insufferable Dorothy Cobham and the flightly May queen about the gardens or into the lover's maze.

"My beloved, sweet Mary, will you never learn to hide your feelings?" he was scolding low with a distinct glint of devilment in each dark brown eye. "I said I know Will is leaving. As soon as he does and you can hie yourself away from your loving family and avid-eyed king, do so. Only, do not go back to your own suite and do not get entangled with the sticky Bullen clan for supper later. Come to Lord Aberganny's rooms on the third floor directly under the south turret. If you turn your lovely head, you can see the windows to the room now. It seems," he ended his whispered recital of instructions, "Lord Aberganny's father has died in Yorkshire and I promised to watch their rooms while their household is away this week."

"Oh, Staff!"

"I said, do not show what you are thinking, madam.

It is not yet the custom in brash Henry's wild court to make hot love to one's lass under the May pole while a crowd looks on. Go back to Will now. I shall be waiting."

She tried to walk calmly back to her seat, to remember to nod and speak without screaming her joy to people she had known for years. Tonight tonight, rooms of their own, a place of their own, a bed of their own, her heart sang. Suddenly, this so beautiful, precious May Day could not be gone swiftly enough.

She cuddled next to Staff in the big, soft bed that night, all night, without the pressing worries of dressing hurriedly to scamper back by a certain hour. Staff had aired the room and filled it with vases of sweet-smelling wild flowers and they had enjoyed a long, leisurely meal together before bed. It made it so much easier to pretend this was all theirs, Lord and Lady Stafford, properly and prosperously esconced at court, but, of course, all of that could never be.

She sighed and moved the sole of her foot slightly against Staff's bare, hairy leg.

"Mary. It is early, love." His voice came out drowsy and warm and moved the hair at the nape of her neck where his mouth rested. "Not sleepy?" he asked, and moved his big hand under the covers to slide up along the curve of her bare hip to skim her waist and lightly cup her breast as she lay with her hips cuddled in his lap in what he called spoon fashion. His other hand pressed under her until both of his hands hung suspended not really grasping her breasts but with the taut nipples barely touching the center of his palms. Her breasts pointed instantly against the light friction as he moved his open hands gently in little, teasing circles, first one way and then the other. She felt that tiny touch clear down to her stomach. Desire stabbed so sweetly between her thighs that she groaned and shifted her hips back into him.

"Not sleepy?" he asked again, and chuckled low.

The wretch, she thought. If he meant to do this to her and then go back to sleep, but then—she knew better. She could feel the hard thrust of him pressing her buttocks, and his hands became more urgent.

He rolled her onto her back among the soft pillows and bent over her, controlled and gentle once again, touching her, kissing her full breasts and flat belly. He began to kiss her eyelids but soon ran his slick tongue down the smooth skin of her throat and much farther until she arched up at him as if begging him to take her, and still the delicious torture. His face glazed with passion, he did as she asked and she thought she would surely die from the pain of such exquisite joy. And when they slept, exhausted, wrapped in each other's arms again, she dreamed only of golden days alone, hidden in his love.

Chapter Twenty-One
July 21, 1528

Hampton Court

"The dog days" they had always called them, the long and muggy summer months of July and August when the royal and noble fled to country refuge and the poor of the towns and populous cities prayed that they would be spared. The dreaded sweating sickness hung ¹ .e a curse over Tudor England as it had many summers since it had first broken out among Henry VII's victorious troops at Bosworth Field. Now this curse, this quick seizing death, was the only thing which terrified the present powerful king on whom his father's power had been bestowed—save for the fact he had no true and legitimate male heir with whom to leave his kingdom. His Grace and chosen courtiers hid from the long reach of the sweat in the deep forests of Eltham.

But Eltham was a smaller refuge than long-armed Greenwich or sprawling Hampton Court or great walled Windsor. Only a fragment of the massive court could bed and board at the beamed hunt hall for the weeks the palaces nearer the city might be unsafe. So nobles of the court with country homes had taken to them in haste, and others shifted as best they could in the nearly deserted cavernous halls of the palaces. Tensions and terrors were great, for it seemed that control of one's own life was in the hands of some grim, invisible spectre.

"Damn it, Mary. Six months of my patient work and now we are left here because His Grace still cannot bear to have you around. I know that is it. I have seen him look at you. He thinks your presence here helps to keep his darling Anne away even though everyone knows he has given her a promise he will forsake all others for her if she will yield to him."

"You know that is not true, Will. We are not here because I keep Anne from him. It does not matter to Anne that I am here. She thinks if she would come to live at the palace the walk to the royal bed is too short. She fears she would lose him then and her power would be gone."

"We all fear that, dear wife. And now all my careful planning, my work to earn the Carey way back has gone for nothing thanks to the meddling of the greedy Bullens!"

She wanted to hit out at him, to grab that constant bitter look from his face and smash it, but she controlled herself and touched his slumped shoulder. "I think you are over-reacting, reading too much into the fact His Grace did not choose to take you to Eltham for the summer. He only took one fifth of the court and only four of ten Esquires. Does that mean that the other six are all in disfavor? I think not."

"I think not," he mocked. "Is that your clever reasoning or Staff's?"

"Please, Will, try . . ."

376

"I am trying, madam. But he took Stafford, did he not? He took six of the twelve Gentlemen Ushers, our dear Staff included. The king is unwise to favor him because he is a fine sportsman and it amuses him to have someone who will challenge him, stand up to him at tennis or butts and tell him the truth."

He shrugged her hand off his shoulder and rose to face her across the tall-backed chair. "When I heard that His Grace had said he would take Staff, I told myself that it is because Staff is dependent on him and has no country seat to flee to, as do others. But Stafford told me he inherited a farm and manor at Wivenhoe near Colchester from a great aunt while we were rotting away at Plashy last year. It is that terrible little place with the ghosts, I think. So you see, he has a place to go and one not so far at that." He squinted to see her clearly even though she stood so close. The hour was still early, but he had managed to work himself into a heavy sweat. "Did you know that Stafford has lands now, Mary?"

She sat in the narrow windowseat and leaned against the protruding wooden sill. "He told me."

"Yes, he would have. How foolish of me to ask."

"The king knows we have Plashy to go to, or even further into the country to the parklands if we really thought to flee London by a good distance. And, Will, everyone knows that Wolsey built Hampton here on this stretch of river because the air is so healthy and the water supply . . ."

"Is that why four died here of the sweat last July? Everyone knows that well enough. Oh, you have no worries, I realize. Little Catherine is safe at Hever with your mother and Anne, Stafford is off at Eltham, though I am certain you will miss his company, and you—well, the Bullens live charmed lives anyway. That is rather obvious!''

She sighed and her eyes stung with tears which did not fall. Yes, she missed Catherine, but she was old enough to visit her grandmother at Hever. She and Anne had always treasured their visits to Rochford Hall in Essex. But she was deathly lonely without Staff, their talks, their joy, their lovemaking far into the long nights whenever they could steal time together.

''I will not flee to Plashy, Mary. It would be like being in wretched exile again, and I will never admit defeat by going back there. Plashy came from my clever marriage to a Bullen. I admit that. But our lives are here now. When the Carey name is restored, I shall have other fine lands on which to build a manor. Someday the manor at Durham may be mine again. It was never this damned hot at Durham!''

''Times change. People change, Will. Perhaps we can never go back to what was.'' She lifted her gaze to the distant gardens greatly gone to riot in the heat and not well tended by the unsupervised gardeners during these dangerous times. It reminded her of the wild gardens at the north edge of Hever across the stone wall where the flowers bloomed totally free and uncut.

''Anyhow, we are not going to Plashy and we are not going to Hever to live off your father's funds and be near that scheming sister of yours. Little Catherine can visit, but we are not going and that is final. I have been thinking, however, we can visit Eleanor at Wilton if only for several weeks. We would be within close call should they return here unexpected and, besides, I need to talk to Eleanor. She understands.''

378

Mary bit her lip to keep from a sharp retort. Eleanor, Eleanor. If only there was no such thing as incest between a brother and sister, Will could marry his beloved Eleanor. Perhaps, when the Careys earned their way back, they could ask for a royal or papal dispensation and marry each other. Then she would be free to go off with Staff. How desperately she wished for it!

"I do not plan to go off to Wilton, so if you must go, I shall remain here," she said when she could trust her voice.

"I decide where we go or do not go, madam!"

"I am not going, Will. Go if you must."

"You would like that. You would like to have me away. Perhaps you could ride alone to Eltham then, alone and unencumbered, to your dear father. Maybe the king would be glad to see his golden Mary you are hoping, not to mention Stafford. Staff would be there waiting, Mary."

"Leave me be, Will! I am sick, sick to death of your bitter hatred. I did not choose this marriage! I am not the one who chose to desert our bed at Plashy. I did not even choose to be born a Bullen, but I am. Please, please, leave me alone!"

"I suppose you did not choose to love Stafford either, Mary, to light up like a torch when you see him, to laugh at his jibes, to smile at him across the room." He put his hand to the door latch and hesitated.

She stood and the morning sun from the window behind her made her mussed blonde hair appear to have a strange halo around it. "No, my lord. God forgive me, I never chose that. It just happened." She faced him squarely across the room, her chin held high. There was a strained silence. Still he hesitated at the door.

"Then God forgive you, Mary, but the Careys never shall." He went without looking back, but he did not slam the door as she had expected. It stood ajar and the dim hall was all she could see beyond.

The morning wore on and she did not stir from the sequestered room. The brick walls kept the heat out until late in the afternoon even though the window faced south. If Will had not been in such a heated rage, he would have realized it was cool here and not fume so about the heat of the day. She and Nancy sat talking and she embroidered while the girl darned the silken stockings she could no longer afford to give away when tiny holes appeared in the heels. They ate some fruit for lunch and drank a bit of tepid malmsey. The afternoon stretched on peacefully, and she did not think anything of Will's long absence until his man, Stephen, came looking for him.

"But you say his horse is here yet, Stephen?"

"Aye, milady. He threatened to go to the priory at Wilton, but he has not done so, unless he thieved a horse. I shall find him along the river perhaps, though it is not like him. But who can he find to talk to around here, since the queen's household be at Beaulieu and the king's at Eltham?" He nodded his sandy head and backed through the door with his cap in his hands.

He probably intended to punish her by staying elsewhere, she thought. He need not. She regretted her words and actions already, but that could not change the truth. Perhaps if she were not here as though she were awaiting him, he would come back sooner. "Let's sit out by the fountain for a bit, Nancy."

"But it be turned off now. Remember? Anyhow, my lady, we might get overheated and you know that is one

380

sign. There be plenty of myrtle and rose leaves in the drawers, but we have no sapphires to stem the start of it if the curse should come here."

"I know, Nance. But we are far into July and a good stretch from pesty London. I forgot the fountain is off. We shall just sit in the shade. Maybe there is a tiny breeze off the river as yesterday."

"At least the river flows toward London and not from it to bring the stench of death. Hundreds are dyin' the drovers say."

They had only begun their slow stroll under the trimmed yews when Stephen's voice floated to them in the still, stifling air. Already she knew the day was much too warm, and they would have to turn back.

"It's Stephen, lady, yellin' and wavin' at us." They both squinted down the lane of sunsplotched yews.

"Come on, Nance. He wants us, yet does not come to fetch us. I warrant my lord has come back in a huff."

The closer they got to Stephen, the more disturbed Mary became, and she picked up her skirts and ran even though she felt the beads of sweat begin to trickle down her temples and between her breasts. When they had nearly reached him, he turned and loped ahead throwing the words back over his shoulder.

"The lord, Lady Mary. He got overheated, I think. But the thing is, lady," he blocked her as she reached for the latchkey to their chamber, "though he be sweating, he has the shakes bad, too."

Mary's heart lurched. "Dear God! No!" Nancy drew back with a little gasp. Mary quickly shoved the door open as if to push away her growing dread.

Will sat slumped, curled over the table drinking wine in sips. His ragged breathing filled the quiet room. He stared at her almost unseeing, his eyes glazed.

So great a change in such a little time, she thought, panicked. It cannot be. "Will? Do you have a bit of a fever? Please, Will, get in bed, and I will sponge your face. A little sleep and all will be well. You are overtired, and your anger has exhausted you." She touched his arms to help him rise. His shirt was sopping wet and stuck tight to his clammy body.

"I am not going to bed. I need rest—here—and some cooled wine, not this hot stuff. Tell Stephen to see to it in the cellars."

Stephen snatched the pitcher and was gone before Mary even looked up at him.

"Yes, my temper got the best of me," he got out between pants for breath. "I should have gone to Wilton. The thing is, I have stomach pain too, and it would be too hard to ride with it. I shall go to Wilton tomorrow." He clenched his fists around the empty goblet and groaned. "I may ride to see our old home at Durham again. I would like to see Durham."

Mary wrang out a cloth in the washbasin and sent Nancy to fetch fresher water. "Tell no one anything," she whispered to the frightened girl and squeezed her arm in warning.

"Is it the sweat indeed, lady?" she mouthed.

"I pray God it is not. Go on and hurry!"

"Will, come on. We must get you to bed where we can care for you so this, this fever, will pass."

"Yes." He lifted his tousled head weakly from his hands. "Yes. I feel suddenly exhausted. I have worked too hard for His Grace. But, Mary, you must not let me sleep. People who sleep never wake up again when they have the sweat. Only this is not, cannot, be the sweat. I have not been in a city in weeks."

He leaned on her and his weight was tremendous. How foolish she had been to send Stephen and Nancy on errands. She staggered toward the bed nearly dragging him, and they fell on it together. She sat only to rise immediately, but he grabbed her wrist.

"Just because you love him, Mary, you will not let me die?" His wide eyes tried to focus on her face but they wandered and everything swam before him.

"You will not die, my husband. I will not let you die." But his head had already dropped back on the pillow and he panted in short gasps with his mouth open.

She swung his feet up onto the bed and covered him with a thick blanket from the chest. She stood frozen for a moment. Her mind raced pouring over the advice and remedies she had heard discussed in whispers these past years. This was impossible. It could not be happening to Will.

She pulled her fur robe from the storage chest and scattered crushed lavender leaves, in which it was entombed for summer storage, all over the floor. The person must be made to sweat the poisons out, to sweat profusely, she remembered. Where were those servants?

With deadly outward calm she began to bathe the sticky sweat off his face. Dearest God, it was the sweat indeed, for he smelled of old closed up rooms. That was one sure sign Lady Weston had said, the smell of old closed up rooms, like death.

Nancy was back with fresh water and fruit and Stephen tiptoed in with wine and sticks of wood under his arm. She remembered instantly. "Yes, Stephen, we must have a fire. We must drive out the poisons. And when you get it going, you must see if there are any doctors who remain, though I heard Her Grace took the last with her. Hurry, Stephen.''

"But he is asleep already, lady. We must not let him sleep," Nancy's voice came from behind her.

"I think it is early yet, and he will need his strength.''

"My sister said once they sleep they never wake, lady.''

"Hush, girl, and fetch the myrtle and rose leaves for the sheets.''

Mary marveled at her own control in the next hours. She was sharp with the servants, but as the room became an inferno in the late afternoon sun with the fireplace roaring, they all dripped sweat and spoke no more. She kept Will awake as best she could, but he wafted in and out of consciousness even though his stomach and head pain increased.

"The whole room is spinning,'' he whispered dazedly. "Is Eleanor here yet?''

A new fear grew in her like an ugly gray mushroom. "Eleanor, my lord? No, Eleanor is not here yet.''

"You have not sent for Staff to marry, have you?'' he nearly shouted, then fell back on the bed exhausted.

Tears coursed down her face. "No, of course not, my lord. Rest. Do not fret. I am here. I will care for you.''

The stench of the room enveloped them now, smothering the sweeter scents of the medicinal myrtle, rose, and lavender from the fur robe in which she desperately wrapped him. He sucked the special powdered wine hourly through a goose quill Stephen brought as the night wore on. Yet he sweated out all the liquid and never had to urinate. She sent Stephen and Nancy to sleep in the corridor within call and kept the fire burning herself. Maybe they could escape from the smell and they would not hear his tortured ravings of his lost name and his accusations of the Bullens and his wife. In the waves of heat, she stripped to her soaked shift and began to bathe his face again when his eyes shot open and he seized her wrist weakly.

"Is that His Grace calling me? I have to go. He is wanting me to come to him." He feebly tried to move aside the heavy covers but could not. "Is it night, Mary?"

"Yes, my dear lord. It is night." She gently sponged his forehead.

"Then he must be calling for me. It will anger him if I do not come and we will lose everything, my dear love."

"You must rest, Will. I am here. I will not leave you."

"Oh, my dearest Eleanor, we will lose everything we have worked for!"

Tears flowed down her cheeks to mingle with the sweat which already stung her eyes. His love was for his sister and his cause. He had never loved her and it was her fault. She had been a terrible wife to him. He could have loved her. He gave her two beautiful children. She had hurt him so with five years of shaming his treasured name with the king while he was sent here and there on trumped-up missions. And now, with Staff, whom he had once trusted and even idolized a bit . . . Was that her fault too?

"Dearest God, I have sinned greatly," her lips said and she bowed her head in utter exhaustion and hopelessness. They said the sweat was sent as a curse from

God to sinners. But why Will and not the sinner?

"You look beautiful, Mary."

Her eyes opened and she stared at him through a heavy mist.

"In dresses for revels or in your shift, so beautiful. Maybe the king will summon you to him tonight and not me." His trembling lips tried to smile. "Then you can try to save the Carey lands again." He made a weak attempt to clear his throat of its roughness, but only wheezed. "Is Eleanor here yet?" he asked again. "She will want to go to Durham with me, even though you do not."

She gave up fighting to keep him conscious, for the pains increased in his head and stomach and shot him wide awake when he tried to doze. She sponged him still, and held his fluttering hands in hers, and quoted Bible verses to him for her own comfort as much as his, but he constantly interrupted and asked for water or his sister.

Near dawn she called to Stephen for more wood and in utter terror at Will's shallow pained breathing, sent the disheveled Nancy for a priest. The girl could find no one of the cloth, not even at the friary outside the grounds, which served the royal chapel. She returned breathless and teary eyed as the first glimmer of light permeated the gray room.

"There is no one, lady, no one. I am sorry. Everything seems so deserted."

Will stared up at the new voice and managed a wan smile. "I knew she would come. I knew she would come if I called her."

Mary pressed his trembling, cold hand between hers. "Yes," she choked out, "yes, she came, my lord. Rest

386

now. All is well."

He narrowed his eyes and they seemed to focus momentarily on Mary's bent head. "I am sorry, Mary," came the quiet words. His head dropped back suddenly, and his eyes stared beyond her.

"I am sorry too, my dear lord. Can you not forgive me?"

She raised her hand to sponge his forehead, but the words went unheard. With the first light of the new day upon his face, Will Carey died.

Stephen and some husky groom had put the wrapped corpse on a table board and carried him to the chapel yard for burial after a stunned Mary and silent Nancy had washed and reclothed him. Victims of the sweat must be buried immediately so their decay would not send the rampant poisons into the air, especially in the summer months when it was most virulent. There was no one to give them permission to bury him on chapel grounds, but Mary sent Stephen and two others there to dig the grave anyway.

The next day Nancy found a kind, old chaplain on the outskirts of Kingston to come the five miles to recite over the grave and give the last rites posthumously, as was allowed for any plague victim. They stood in a tiny circle around the sunken fresh grave two days after his death. Mary still felt it was unreal. She felt nothing but a vast, gnawing emptiness.

"Perhaps we can ask the king to have him moved later and buried at Durham Priory where he would have wanted. Perhaps we can get the money for a fine brass monument so he can lie with his forefathers there," she had said over and over that day to Stephen or Nancy or the old priest.

Now he was dead three days and she insisted on lying on the raw ropes of the bed which had supported the mattress on which he had died. They had burned the mattress and robe and all the bedclothes in a bonfire in the courtyard. There was no one left to panic but the deserted servants of nobles who had fled and no one to comfort her but Stephen and Nancy. She wanted no one. She felt dead too, and she stared at the whitewashed ceiling that had seen him die for hours on the third day.

It seemed to her she had slept in the evening, but she could not tell where her waking and dreaming thoughts began or ended. Nancy was strewing fresh herbs on the floor she had scrubbed. How dare other people go on about their duties so calmly when poor Will had died and his God-given wife had failed him so miserably. She had turned against him all the months he had needed her understanding. She had reveled in her power over the king at her husband's expense and, when she could not care for the king, she had turned to another. She had loved another man desperately with her whole heart and slept with him willingly, gladly, while her poor husband sought to earn his way back with his king. Earn his way back for himself and for their children too.

Mary thanked God again that Catherine was safe at Hever. Explaining to Catherine would be terrible, but their seven-year-old son was old enough to grasp the impact. She had sent word to Will's poor Eleanor ensconced in her priory at Wilton. That will be the death of her dreams, Mary reasoned through the mist of her exhaustion.

She still wore her funeral clothes. She had no black, but she would get a mourning dress somewhere, even though they had no ready coins. She had a white dress though. In France widows wore white for a husband's death. Perhaps some of the king's gifts to her could be sold, or one of the parklands His Grace had granted Will on their marriage. She would just lie here forever doing penance for her sins until they all came back to court in the autumn and found her here, laid out just like this. Her heavy eyelids closed again.

Then a bird's song somewhere outside the window pierced the darkness of her thoughts, and it came to her in a rush. She must go to Hever!

She sat up instantly and a terrible dizziness assailed her. She felt weak and panicked instantly. "But no, I do not sweat. I do not feel the slightest bit hot or have any stomach pain besides hunger," she assured herself aloud.

"Lady, are you up? You feel better now? I have watched you sleep these many hours, and I knew you were still healthy," Nancy said bending close and still holding the herbs in her gathered apron.

"Yes. Yes, I am better now, Nance. I must have food and drink and get my strength back now."

"The Lord be praised," the girl recited solemnly, crossing herself.

"And then we must walk in the gardens before nightfall and get a good night's sleep. Tomorrow, as soon as we can pack some things, you and Stephen and I are going home, Nance. Home to Hever."

"We cannot travel the road clear to Hever, the three of us and you so obviously a fine lady. It is too unsafe and especially in plague times, lady. There be robbers

389

all over the roads. Stephen will tell you so.''

"I cannot help that, Nancy. I will go in disguise if I must. We cannot hire anyone to ride with us as we used to. And we are going tomorrow, so you may tell Stephen while I eat. Go on!"

The tall girl opened her mouth as if to protest, but instead dumped her stuffed apron on the table and strode out the door.

"Yes. One hard day's ride and we shall be at Hever. Home to mother and Catherine." She rapidly began to eat a peach.

Mary slept much later than she had meant to, and was immediately angered that Nancy had let so much of the morning go by without waking her. "I do not intend to stay in some house or inn before we get there," Mary scolded Nancy as she donned her brown riding dress. She had considered the idea of disguise, but had no men's garments to fit, and she could not bear to put on any of Will's things even if it *did* mean she could ride astride instead of the bothersome sidesaddle, for the long trek. Since they would travel without a single packhorse, no one would think they had anything to steal anyway.

She had told Stephen exactly where to bury her jewels in the rose garden. They were safely hidden under the turf in the trellised bower where she and Staff had found shelter from the rain, Will and His Grace so long ago. She bit her lip hard. All that was behind her now and she had much penance to do. The Carey cause might be dead with Will, but she had his children to raise and care for. She must put her own foolish longings aside.

The door opened behind her as she stuffed the two dresses she would take into the saddle sacks. "Did you bury them where I said, Stephen?" she inquired tautly not turning. That was the last of the packing. They could go now and leave everything else behind.

"Mary."

The voice was deep and soft and it terrified her. She spun wide-eyed to face William Stafford. Her new-won resolve fled from her face, and her strength went from her knees. He was beside her, pulling her gently to him, her face nestled against his black linen chest.

"Thank God you are safe. I am so sorry to hear about poor Will, despite my feelings for you."

She stood for endless moments pressed to him like that, not moving, not thinking. Then she stepped back and her hips hit the bed behind her. "How did you know?"

"The messenger you sent to Wilton stopped at Eltham on the way back. The word has rocked the court—and frightened them that the sweat would come again to Hampton and claim one of their own kind. His Grace regrets he had no doctors to leave behind when he fled. He had sent his last spare one to your sister, and he did not believe Will would really remain here when he had a country manor."

"A doctor to Anne? Is she ill? But Catherine is there!"

"Not ill, I think. It is only that the king worried that he might lose her in any way. I warrant your blonde moppet is quite safe at Hever with your mother and the royal doctor hovering about." His sweeping gaze took her in from hem to hair. "You are thinner, sweetheart, but as beautiful as ever. I know it must have been awful for you."

She turned her back on him slowly and took a deep breath. "That is what Will said before he died, you know. He said that I looked beautiful. Oh, Staff, I have failed him so, and I have to make it up somehow."

"Failed him? What are you talking about? Much of what he had that he valued he owed to you. It was his own decision to turn bitter, to cast you adrift where you might—well, be susceptible to other emotional ties." He put both hands on her shoulders, but did not turn her to face him.

"He was delirious, and he said other things. He accused me of sending for you and the day he fell ill, we argued and I admitted I loved you. He took that with him instead of the love I could never give to him. Now—and now, I cannot bear it." A little sob wracked her. He pulled her slowly against him and rested his chin on the top of her head.

"Death is hard to bear, but the living must not feel guilty to go on living, Mary. Yes, Will Carey was a good man in many ways and the snare he found himself in with the Bullens was not of his own making. He was the king's pawn, love, but he agreed to that. He reveled in it until he saw the price did not suit his family pride. But then he took it all out on you and not on the devils who make the rules to such games."

"He needed the king to earn his way back."

"This king can be denied on such matters if one is careful. And I meant to accuse your father as well as the king for all the dirty dealings where you and Will were concerned."

"Anne is being careful in refusing the king and getting away with it in fine style. Is that what you mean?''

"I spoke of myself in refusing marriage when His Grace wills it, Mary. I will never marry the Dorsey wench now and the king will accept it from me. Wait and see.''

A quick irrational joy shot through her that he would not marry. She had privately grieved that he would these last six months since he had told her the king's wish. But it must not matter to her now. She must be strong against him.

"Your girl Nancy says you are riding to Hever,'' he began on another tack in the awkward silence. "I can understand your wanting to go home to your mother and daughter, but Lord Bullen will not fancy having you underfoot when the king rides over to court the Lady Anne.''

She pulled away from his hands and her voice was piercing. "I will go! You and Stephen and Nance together will not stop me! If His Grace comes I shall hide in my room or ride my horse to the forest and hide there. I will go home! I make my own decisions now, William Stafford. And do not think you can placate me with your patient smiles,'' she added, her fists on her hips.

"I am only pleased to see the fire has not gone out, lass. It is fine if you make your own decisions separate from your father from now on, but separate from me— well, that is another matter we have much time to discuss.''

"I have no time for you, my lord. I am leaving.'' She tried to skirt around him but he pulled her into a chair and sat facing her so close in another, that their knees touched.

"Your girl says you have been warned that the roads are unsafe, especially with so many bailiffs and sheriffs ill and the towns in general disarray. Prancing off in that tight-fitting dress with only a serving maid and one lad does not seem like a very wise independent decision to me." His thick black brows covered his brown eyes, and she wanted to scream at him and kick and scratch.

"You are mine now, Mary, mine in our mutual love as I am yours. You will do no such foolish thing. I have had to handle you with kid gloves these past years for, legally and otherwise, you were not mine. All that has changed now. I will not have you hurt in any way by anything including your own dangerous plans."

"Let me go. I am Will Carey's widow and not your wife."

"No, but you are my woman and you will obey me until your pretty head clears enough that you can see what you are doing—and what you want from life now that you are free."

"No," she shrieked, more afraid of herself than of what he might do. She scratched at his wrist and stood to flee. He yanked her sideways into his lap and his iron arms tightened around her, pressing her head against his warm neck. She thrashed her legs under her heavy skirts and struggled in his smothering embrace. Angered beyond belief, she went limp but his words, "Let me know when you are willing to listen and stop behaving like the spoiled little Bullen I used to know," infuriated her further and she bit hard on the taut sinew at the side of his neck.

He cursed once and spun her away. She raised her hands to slap him, but he pulled her forward. She did not fall to the floor as she had expected, but found herself stomach down over his spread legs with the palms of her hands flat on the carpet. His hard hand descended once on her rear, but the heavy riding skirt took much of the blow. She clawed at his legs and tried to wriggle upright but stopped in fear as her skirts whooshed up over her head and she felt his hand smack her with only her chemise to pad her. She lay still while the blood rushed to her head and she fought the urge to scream out her love for him no matter how he handled her.

"Are you ready to listen now, Mary? I much prefer kissing you to this. It is all that I thought of on the road back from Eltham and I have not done it yet. I do not blame you for fighting another man's control over you or for the guilt you feel. Only this man loves you, sweetheart. Why not trust that and later we will decide together if we should be together permanently? I will never force that decision on you."

He helped her up and she sat back on her own chair looking stormy but resigned. He leaned back not touching her as he talked.

"I will take you to Hever, lass, since that is where you are so set on going. I cannot blame you for wanting to leave Wolsey's vast brick pile with its unhappy memories for you. But we shall get you some men's clothes, pull your golden curls up under a cap, and . . ."

"I cannot wear anything of Will's. I cannot!"

"No, nothing of Will's. I will get you some small breeks and a shirt and jerkin. No one will notice the boots are a woman's. And since we are getting a late start and you are so high strung—and mostly because I have been without you too long and am a selfish man and far stronger than you if you choose to argue this—we will stop midway at a little inn I know at Banstead and spend tomorrow there together. Then we will go on."

His eyes searched her face and marvelled at her quiet acceptance. "I will deliver you safe to your mother and little Catherine at Hever, for Anne comes soon enough to court as unwed queen, and I warrant she will bring you with her. Your father will be much too busy with her concerns to bother to marry you off again for a long while, if ever, and, when you come back, I shall be waiting. Then we shall learn to make joint decisions, my sweetheart. You shall see."

He rose and bellowed for Stephen at the door. The lad bounded in dressed for riding. "Mistress Nancy told me you were here, my lord. I be glad of it. She says you will take us to Hever."

Mary's head snapped up. So he had decided to deliver her to Hever and it had nothing to do with her desire.

Staff looked at her evenly. "You see, Mary, it is a fortunate coincidence that you and I are making the same decisions already."

She tried to glare at him, but he turned to Stephen and sent him to fetch some clothes for her and Nancy from Lord Aberganny's servants in the other wing of the palace. He poured them both a glass of wine after Stephen had darted out. "If you want to take that dress you have on, lass, you had best take it off and stuff it in my saddle pack. I have little of my own. Take anything else you think my stallion can carry."

"I will wait until Stephen returns with the garments before I disrobe. Nancy can help me change."

"As you wish. As you wish for now, anyway.

Banstead is a most beautiful little town, Mary. It will do us both good to rest there a day. We shall send Stephen and your wench on ahead to Hever and tell them we are a day behind. Let your father wonder. He does already I warrant. He accused me of wanting you for myself when I refused to take his bribe for keeping Will's office for him while you were at Plashy. As careful as I tried to be maybe I showed it on my face. Our love, I mean. The way you do show it now."

"I do not now, Staff. Things are different."

"As I said, we shall see, lass. My lass. I expect at least one tiny kiss before we go, payment for taking you safe to Hever if nothing else moves you."

"I shall not kiss you for your rough handling of me. And you might have had the decency to stop by Will's grave at the chapel. He was once your friend, you may remember."

"I asked Nancy to show it to me before I came in, Mary. I am grieved for his death and the loss of the children's father, though I cannot pretend it changes my love for you in the slightest."

She kept her silence, ashamed that she had accused him of such callousness. But she must guard her heart against him and make him take her to Hever without a stop at an inn where she would face him alone. She loved him far too much to handle that.

Stephen knocked and entered to break the jumble of her thoughts. "Will these do, my lord?" he inquired, holding up brown breeks and a sky blue shirt.

"Good, Stephen. They will suit her just fine. The shirt will match the cloudy blue of the lady's eyes."

Stephen grinned broadly and went out to find Nancy. Staff rose to fetch the horses.

Chapter Twenty-Two
July 26, 1528

The Road to Banstead

By late morning Staff had hired a horse barge to ferry them to the south bank of London where they would take the Great Kent Road toward Hever. The shimmering July sun had already sucked the heavy dews from the fields along the river and the heat of the day was upon them.

"The London streets are likely to be deserted," Staff said to Stephen. Mary and Nancy listened intently. They were afraid that he dared to take them into the very city where the sweat was said to have slain folk in the tens of hundreds this summer. But Staff had claimed it was the quickest and safest route. So Mary relented and held her fears in silence. She could not have stood another bleak night in the palace in the room where Will had died with accusations on his lips.

That morning few farmers worked the fields and tiny vegetable gardens which stretched down to the Thames. Occasional travelers along the footpaths glanced up in interest to see a ferry headed toward the city with four horses and six people, but there was scant traffic on the usually busy river and, in general, nothing stirred. The barge drifted past the turrets of deserted Richmond. Its vacant windows stared like great hollow eyes reflecting the sun, its landing docks, tilt yards and bowling greens silent. They spoke little on the barge as the river pulled it relentlessly toward troubled London.

Then the city loomed up from the field with its solemn church spires and clustered thatched roofs huddled in the beating rays of the noon sun. Staff made them drink the first of the wine and eat the fruit they had brought, for he intended to set a hard pace when they were on the road. Mary tossed her plum pit into the murky Thames and saw it instantly disappear into the depths. She wiped her sticky fingers on her breeks as she had seen Staff do and a smile came to her lips.

"It may seem strange to be in breeks, Mary, but it has advantages, you will see. Besides, I think you and your Nancy both make handsome lads—right, Stephen? And the swords add the right touch. I think you had better get the stray curls up under that cap. It will make for a dusty neck on the road, but I have no intention of attracting rogues or ruffians with wench bait."

Stephen laughed at his words, but Staff was tight-lipped. Mary noted to her dismay how much Stephen seemed to hang on everything Staff said, to follow him about to serve his every whim. He had never been so puppy-like with his own lord.

"Is there much danger then?" Nancy asked timidly. "Stephen says so."

"Stephen is wise to be prepared, lass. We shall set a good pace to Banstead, and I warrant no one will bother four quick riding men."

The once bustling wharfs and quays were deserted and Staff had the bargemen put in at the landing under London Bridge. Houses and shops clung to both sides of it like barnacles, but their mass provided shade as the four led off their horses to dockside and Staff paid the boatmen. They were eager to be away to leave the cursed city behind, and they shoved off for the upstream row to Hampton as soon as they had their money.

"I cannot say I blame them for their haste," Stephen said. "I never thought I would be visitin' plagued London."

"The sweat is hardly the plague, lad, though it is bad enough. You will no doubt see the crosses on the doors though. Keep a stout heart. We will leave the city behind soon for the free countryside. Besides, I was here one summer in the sweat season and nothing happened to me."

The servants seemed to treasure this bit of comforting information as they mounted. If Stephen and Nancy are impressed by that, so be it, Mary told herself. It sounded like pure foolhardiness to her. Surely there were a lot of things she would learn about William Stafford that would make it easier not to adore him.

There were abandoned carts in the streets of Southwark as they passed, and pigs rooted and chickens scratched unhampered. The central gutters of the narrow streets were a stench of rotting vegetables and human wastes which steamed in the sun. As they rode swiftly by, huge Southwark Cathedral stood silent sentinel to the devastation. Crude wooden coffins piled for burial in the already-crowded and walled graveyard

400

huddled against the church's outer walls. Tears bit at Mary's eyelids at the sight of the stacks of human sorrow. At least they had buried Will right away. Staff was crazy to bring them so near to unburied plague bodies. They would all catch the sweat and be dead before they even reached Hever. There was nothing he could do to her to make her stay with him in some little inn in tiny Banstead. She would insist on riding on with the Carey servants.

Southwark was a terrible part of town and she had never seen it so close, for usually traveling parties of noblemen skirted far around its worst haunts. The dingy bawdy houses and taverns which sailors of the merchant vessels and king's fleet visited were crammed together. No doubt the sweat ate its gluttonous fill here, for people were so packed in that but a few dead would mean destruction for all. Bloody colored crosses stained the dirty wooden doorways here and there. It was like a ghost town with only a few stragglers or faces peering curiously from a second or third storey window. Ordinarily, there would be a vast bustling swell of traffic into the city on this highway to the south, but there was almost none. They rode on at a steady clip and their horses' hoofs echoed off the nearly abandoned streets.

Soon, but not too soon, the city was behind them hovering above the fields with the hazy sun on it like some giant pall. The gardens and apple and peach orchards of Kent stretched ahead of them. Mary took deep, free breaths now, for she had tried to breathe shallowly with her hand over her mouth in the reaches of the city. Let him smirk at her if he thought she was foolish.

"I am not laughing at you, Mary. I was only thinking you make the best damned looking boy I have ever seen and, unlike some of His Grace's fine courtiers, I do not usually find young boys at all entrancing.''

She could not help smiling back at him. He had not spoken since they had left the barge and his voice was somehow comforting. "Then I see no need of your spending a day and night with a boy at Banstead,'' she threw at him. He raised one rakish eyebrow but turned his face to the road again.

As they got further out, they passed occasional drover's carts, farm wains, or painted chars, and Mary relaxed as the scene became more normal. Mother and Semmonet would be pleased to see her despite her tragic news. And little Catherine would squeal and throw herself into her mother's arms as she always did, even when they had been parted but a little while.

They were nearly to Croydon before their hard taskmaster let them dismount under huge oaks along a stream. "I would love to lie here on the bank and sleep,'' Mary said wistfully, stretching her cramped muscles. Her thighs ached terribly and the sword was always in her way. She had never ridden so far astride before. It must take some getting used to and she could tell poor Nancy was suffering as she moved her legs awkwardly and leaned wearily against the trunk of a massive oak.

"Sore, sweet?'' Staff asked as he offered her another swig from their wine canteen.

"Not so bad that I shall not make it clear to Hever today, my lord,'' she returned tartly. The wine was warm but good on a dust-caked throat.

"If you tried to make it clear to Hever today, lass, you would not walk for a week. As it is, you will be most

402

comfortable resting on your back and not walking about somewhere.''

She turned her head to give him a pointed stare at his gibe, but he was looking away straight faced and evidently meant nothing by it.

''I am thinking of keeping Nancy and Stephen in Banstead, too. The lad would make it well enough to Edenbridge by night but not the girl.'' He rose, evidently not expecting her to have any part of the decision about where her servants stayed or went. It irked her, but she let him help her mount. It would help if Nancy were about if she were forced to stay at Banstead the night with him. That way she could insist the girl sleep with her.

Orchards and wheat fields gave way to patches of beech and elm, and Mary began to sense the look of home. Then the single stands of trees became the deep blue-green forests of the Kent she knew, and she relaxed until her eye caught the weather-beaten sign pointing its ragged finger to the west off the Kent Road—to Banstead, it said. Staff reined in his wheezing stallion and the others halted their horses around him in a tight circle.

''How do you feel, Mistress Nancy?'' he inquired jauntily as though they were out for an afternoon's ride at Greenwich.

''Tired, my lord, and a bit sore. I shall make it, though.''

''Good lass. But since the hour is probably on three, I suggest you and Stephen ride with us to spend the night at Banstead and set out for Hever early on the morrow. Lady Carey and I will probably be there sometime in the next day, or the one after.''

Nancy's eyes went wide and her mouth dropped open. Had she not seen what he was implying before, the simple wench, thought Mary. Well, at least she understands his meaning now and she will be my ally when we arrive at his precious inn. And now he dared to hint that they would stay more than one day as if he thought she would run off with him when her lord husband was dead only five days!

"Yes, milord," the girl said. Staff nodded and they turned their horses' noses toward Banstead two miles to the west.

The village was quaint and charming; Mary had to admit that much. No horrible crosses defiled the doors and people wandered about normally at their daily tasks. A Medieval steeple dominated the view, its darkened stone and slender Gothic spires distinct in the sunlight. Across the central town green which stretched at its feet, a few cattle grazed. The village inn stood out plainly among the clusters of other white washed and black timbered walls. The inn curled itself in an L-shape around a garden gone to summer riot of late roses and splotches of blues and golds. "The Golden Gull" the frayed sign read with its proud painting of a wheeling sea gull upon a sky of clearest blue.

She pulled one sore leg over Eden's lathered neck and let Staff lift her gently to the ground. Her legs nearly buckled on the cobbled courtyard, and they shook as he led her by the elbow to the inn door which stood silently ajar. The huge common room within was dim. It trestle table was set for supper, but no fire burned at the hearth and no one scurried to welcome them.

"Whitman!" Staff deposited her on a bench, and

Nancy sank wearily beside her, after nearly tripping over her unwieldy sword. Staff went to the steep stairs which disappeared to the second floor. "Whitman, you old sea dog, come out of hiding and now! You have guests, man, paying guests!"

A door slammed in the depths of the house, and feet thudded quickly up the steps from beside the fireplace. A great red-bearded face appeared and Mary's mouth dropped to see how much the man looked like the king—huge and red and ruddy, but much shorter.

"Stafford, damn yer eyes!" came the explosion and the man pounded Staff on the back rather than bowing as he should have, she thought. "I never thought to see you hove to in these parts. You have not forgotten the coins I owe you for dicin' with me, is that it? Come to collect yer due?"

"I thought maybe we could settle that once and for all staying in your fine hostelry a night or two, my man. This is Lady Carey and her servants Stephen and Nancy. Can we find anyone in this deserted place to care for us and our horses?"

"A course, my lord, and proud of it." His deep-set eyes took in the tired party and lit to see such a beauty in men's clothes as Mary's long locks spilled from under her linen cap.

"There be fine rooms for all of you upstairs. Will three do, one large and the other two wee ones? There be little business at Banstead, but we do right well for those that come through. A little traveling fair is in town now, but those kind a folk stay out in their own tents. Allow me to show you to yer rooms. My wife, she be back soon after she spends all my money at the fair, eh? We have two little ones, milord. Life is good here

405

since I left the *Mary Rose* these six years when my sire died an' left me the Gull.''

They trooped up the stairs, and it was only then that Mary's eyes took in the elaborate rigged ropes and ship's tackle along the walls of the room and stairwell. "The *Mary Rose* you said, Master Whitman? His Grace's fine ship the *Mary Rose?* You have been a sailor in the king's navy then?''

Staff laughed aloud at her deduction, but Whitman's beaming face was serious. "Aye, milady. For fifteen years I be a sailor for this king and his royal father afore him. We protected the channel on the *Mary Rose* where I met his lordship on some a' his voyages to France. And afore that I sailed on the *Golden Gull* where, if'n I can say it, I had a much kinder master, eh, milord?''

"We shall tell the lady the whole story after she has rested, Whit.''

"I sailed on the *Mary Rose* once,'' Mary said to them as they paused on the tiny landing from which several crooked doors departed. "I sailed on her with Her Grace, the Princess Mary, when she went to France to wed King Louis. It was a very long time ago.''

Master Whitman regarded her closely. "I was on that voyage, my lady, but I canna' say I remember you. The princess was the lady for whom the ship was named well enough. You musta' been a wee child then. But the ship I loved best was the *Golden Gull*. It stands for freedom you see, an' not having a cruel and heartless man for a master even if he be handpicked by the king himself, eh?''

Master Whitman did not bat an eye when Staff put Stephen and Nancy in the two tiny rooms and guided Mary into the larger chamber and, after a few words about supper, firmly closed the door. To Mary's shame, Stephen accepted it, Nancy looked jittery despite her exhaustion, but Master Whitman only twitched at one corner of his bearded mouth. Mary held her tongue until his footsteps died away outside the door.

"This is entirely unsuitable to me. I will bed with my girl since you so obviously intend to sleep here."

"I think you had better wash your grimy face, sweetheart, and I will get you a bath after we have eaten. I am starved."

She stood uncertain as he peeled off his shirt and dug into the saddle sacks he had deposited on the floor. "A dress would feel better than those breeks I imagine, though you do them justice well enough." He looked up sharply. "Where do you think you are going?"

She paused with her hand on the door latch. "I told you. I am staying with Nancy."

"Look, Mary. I am filthy and tired and hungry and so are you. In short, I am just in the mood to put you over my knee again if you do not stop this arguing."

"I would scream and everyone would hear."

"I assure you that would amuse John Whitman immensely and it would mean I have to send Nancy and poor Stephen on ahead tonight so you have no one to run to."

"You would not do that!"

"Really? Shall we try it?"

He faced her across a narrow space, his face dirty, her brown riding dress dangling from his fingers. His hair fell in disarray over his tanned forehead and his eyes pierced her as always. Her legs still trembled as though she were still cantering in rhythmic motion on

Eden's back.

"No," she said. "I will stay for now. I know you will not force the widow of your dead friend to bed with you if she declines. And I will not be the cause of my servants being mistreated by someone who obviously does not care about them." She took the dress from his hands and turned to pour water from the pewter ewer to wash her face and arms.

The food Master Whitman put before them was simple fare, but they devoured it as if it were the finest feast at court. To Mary's great relief Staff stayed in the hall talking with the Whitmans and Stephen while Nancy helped her bathe in the bed chamber. She had not expected such manners and restraint from him considering the way his eyes caressed her, and she began to relax somewhat. Her servants were nearby, and she had been with him all day and he had not attempted to kiss or fondle her. Surely he understood her position and would not make it hard for her.

Dusk descended on the little Kentish hamlet and she and Staff stood in the cobbled yard of the inn stretching their weary limbs as tiny star points began to pierce the darkening sky. Such starry nights always reminded her of Master da Vinci's velvet painted ceiling. But even the old man had not had the humming of locusts and crickets under his close-hanging heaven. Staff stood behind her, not touching her, but she felt his presence like a physical caress. His tall head and broad shoulders threw a long shadow from the lanterns in the hall across the stones and into the rose bushes. Inside, Nancy chattered to Master Whitman's wife, Margaret, and Stephen dozed by the low fire.

"Will you walk with me by the pond, Mary?" his voice came quietly in her ear. "There is a little fish pond just behind the inn."

Despite the fact that she should have told him no, with the stars burning so brightly and the three quarter moon just rising over the thatched rooftops, she nodded and walked on ahead. The earth smelled fresh, as though it had just rained, and she felt very much at peace with herself despite her burden of guilt. Hever would do this for her too, this calm inside, this deep calm.

The little pond was as still as glass and the patches of oval water lily leaves cradling their pure white blossoms looked like stepping stones across its surface. She leaned pensively against the trunk of a trimmed willow tree. Trimmed, no doubt, to keep the view of the pond from the windows of the inn. The willow arched over them like a protective parasol. Fireflies studded the dark grass along the edge of the water.

"Am I to understand that you mean not to bed with me now that poor Will is gone and you are truly free to do so with a good conscience?" he asked low. The question hung between them and, though she had the proper answer composed in her head, the words would not come. "I will not have you come to detest me the way you did Francois, nor be indifferent as you did with His Grace for his ownership of you. I love you too much despite the way my foolish loins ache for you to be spread beneath me."

Her pulse started its thump, thump in the silence. She blessed the dark that he could not see her face.

"They were kings, father approved, and it just seemed I never had a choice," she heard herself say finally. "And Will was suddenly my God-given husband."

"King-given husband rather," he put in.

"But, you see, my father has always pushed or pulled me and if he has not, others have. Now I can make my own decisions."

"I approve, Mary, really. I cannot tell you how desperately I have wanted to hear something like that from you. Only, if it means you will choose to do without me, my first impulse would be to kidnap you for myself and never let you free." He heaved a stone into the pond, and it skipped four times in the moonlight before it sank.

"Then it would be just like always, with some powerful man making my decisions for me," she reasoned aloud.

"I know. I know, damn it!" He turned to her and pulled her gently away from the willow tree. "But the difference, my Mary, is that I love you, and I believe you truly love me. Do you deny it?"

"No," she drawled slowly as memories mingled with the griefs she had felt without him at Plashy and the joys she had felt so often with him. "I think I do love you, Staff, but, you see . . . well, my life has been so confused, and I have been so unhappy with Will and His Grace and so, maybe I . . ."

He gave her a rough shake and she stopped speaking. "I asked you once if you loved Will and you said 'I think I do'. I told you then that if you think you do, you do not. Do you remember? I do not want you to 'think' you love me. I will have you and your love, lass, and you will know it is love or I might just as well marry at the king's whim or bed some court lady who catches my

410

moment's fancy."

Tears came to her eyes, and the tiny hurt grew that always came when he spoke of bedding others. The grip of his hard hands hurt her arms. She smothered the desire to tell him how much she loved him.

"I know it has all been a shock to you, Mary, and I trust you to reason it out, if you can keep out of your father's clutches long enough. But since you are a little muddleheaded now, and since we have always had to seize our moments together as we found them, I will tell you how it is going to be between us while we are here."

She stared at his white shirt open at the neck. It seemed to glow in the dark as did the lilies, fireflies and stars.

"I will not force you to submit in bed if you do not choose to. But you must know a man in love wants more than that from you. We will have this night and tomorrow morning together after Stephen and Nancy set out. And then I will take you safe to Hever as I promised. But until then, we are close, and there can be much healing in that. Come on."

"Where?"

"I thought we could take a row in that little fishing skiff over there," he said pulling her toward the bank of the pond. "It will be a gentle ride after four hours in the saddle."

She traipsed after him holding his hand. There was a flat bottomed boat shoved high on the bank. He pushed it backwards into the water and held her elbow while she lifted her skirts and stepped in. As soon as she was seated on one of the two rough boards which served for seats, he shoved off and the boat rocked under his

411

weight. He rowed several strokes and let the oars hang at the side in their wooden locks. The pond was so small that the boat floated nearly in the middle of it, adrift among the lilies on the silent surface. The boat was short and their knees touched, his long legs spread and his feet under her seat on either side of her skirts.

"It is a beautiful night," she ventured in the quiet between them. "Drifting at night on a pond—it seems unreal."

"Yes, sweetheart." He sighed. "Can you imagine having all the time in the world here without the king calling?" His voice drifted off as though he regretted his words.

She remembered how Will had thought His Grace was calling before he died. Did the king dominate all of their lives so much then? She felt suddenly terrified that they would never be free from him.

"This little boat must be a far cry from the *Mary Rose* or the *Golden Gull* for John Whitman," she said eventually. "Does he miss the sea very much, Staff?"

"He misses the beauty and freedom of it, but he had a hard master, one he could not tolerate on the *Mary Rose,* and when he saw his chance for a life he could control, he took it. He may never see the channel or the ocean again and not be so very poorly off for it."

He stretched his arms and leaned forward on his knees, and that brought his face much too close.

"May we pick some lilies?" She turned her head to the side. "They are easy to spot even in the dark."

"Yes. They are." He wheeled the boat about to bring them closer to a small floating carpet of them, and she reached gingerly for a stem.

"Oh, they are slippery and they go down forever,"

she observed as she yanked one free and lifted it, dripping, over the side of the boat. "It does not smell, see?" She extended it toward him, but he did not even try to sniff at it. He only closed his hand around her wet wrist, pulled her further toward him and leaned over to meet her lips with his. The kiss was tender and warm. She felt balanced in space with him, floating in a trembling moment which she dared not lose. The kiss deepened and his other hand stroked the slant of her cheek and moved softly through her loose hair. When he pulled back, she stared into his eyes lit by moonlight. She thought she saw his lips tremble, but it must have been reflections from the water.

"Do you want a few more slippery, unscented lilies, then?" he asked. "We shall give them to Mistress Whitman and call it a night. I think we are both exhausted."

She pulled two more from their watery beds. They went into The Golden Gull's deserted common hall and tiptoed quietly upstairs to their room.

When he turned her back to him and began to unlace her as he had often done before lovemaking, she did not protest. She seemed to be better protected from his power while she kept her quiet calm, but the kiss of a few minutes ago still lingered on her lips. She stepped out of the dress, shivering as she did so, but he had turned away, stripped off his shirt, and poured himself a goblet of wine from the table.

"Wine, Mary?"

"No, thank you."

He tilted back his head and downed it. The bed covers had already been turned back for them. Nancy or Mistress Whitman? They were all thinking of her sleeping with him tonight; they would all believe it of her. But if she could only get through the night without throwing herself into his arms, maybe her sinful failure to be a good wife to Will could be forgiven. She would beg him not to touch her if he broke his word.

He blew out the cresset lamp, but the room seemed almost flooded by daylight. His boots hit the floor, and he padded over to the bed and lifted the covers. "Will you sleep next to the wall? I have no intention of lying on the hard floor nor of bedding with Stephen. Do not be afraid. There is plenty of room. You do not wish me to touch you, so I will not."

She stared up at him. So easily accomplished? Then she hated herself for wishing he would force her. She got in, quickly pulling her chemise down to cover her knees while he watched, seemingly impassive. When he got in, the bed sagged and she almost spilled toward him.

"Goodnight, my love," he said. "When you are in your bed safe and alone at Hever, I hope you will not have to curse these wasted hours as much as I shall and do. But if you need the time untouched, so be it."

They lay there in the awkward silence, weary, quietly breathing. Her limbs began to ache anew from being tensed up on the narrow strip of mattress where she held herself rigidly away from him. The moonlight from the window traced its print across the bed onto the wall and still she did not doze though his deep breathing told her that he was asleep at last. Her rampant thoughts would not let her relax. The memories that tortured her were not of Will or his accusing words in his delirium, but of the passions she had felt with Staff and the hours she had treasured in bed with him, in his arms, anywhere, the past six months. An unfulfilled fire burned low and torturing in the pit of her stomach. She had only to touch him, to say his name, and awaken him she knew and all this terribly agony would be over. But she would never be free then, free to know that she loved him and could control her own life. The rectangle of moonlight continued its relentless path up the wall next to her. Watching it through her tears in the quiet of the inn she fell asleep.

Staff was gone when she woke in the morning, and she was sprawled on her stomach half on his side of the mattress. She sat up, immediately wondering if she had moved this far over when he was still abed. No, surely that would have awakened her. Sunlight flooded the room making the moonlight of last night a pale memory. She quickly dressed and went to find Nancy to tie her laces. The door to the girl's room stood ajar as did that where Stephen had slept. They could not be on the road already!

"Yer friends are gone an hour already, my lady," came Mistress Whitman's voice from Stephen's room. Mary peeked around the door to see her making one of the two narrow beds in the room. " 'Tis best they be early on their way, for the bands of thieves around Oxted prey on later travelers. May I help you dress, then? Your lord be having breakfast with my John. They be always talking old times on the *Mary Rose,* though I know yer lord was not a sailor. Sailors are very easy to spot in a crowd." She laughed sweetly as she finished the laces.

"He is not my lord," Mary thought to say, but she only thanked the kind woman and descended the narrow steps holding to the ship's rigging with its intricate knots they had strung for a makeshift banister.

Staff's eyes lit to see her. He was in a good enough mood and did not seem to hold the past night against her. Ashamed of her ravenous appetite, she nevertheless ate hot porridge, stuffed partridge and fruit, and washed it all down with ale. That amused John Whitman, and he joked that she ate like a seaman who has just come back to land. She was surprised to learn that it was nearly mid morning and scolded Staff for not waking her earlier.

"Why did you let me sleep so late?" she asked again as they went for a walk toward the heart of the little village.

"You needed it, Mary, and besides, I had the distinct impression that it would have availed me nothing to have wakened you while I was still there."

She blushed, but laughed a bit when she saw he was teasing. She found it hard to believe that this passionate, often impatient man whose bed she had so hotly shared could have the restraint to leave her untouched as he had done. She was not certain if she were relieved or hurt.

The double doors to the little Gothic church stood open, incongruously bordered by a blacksmith's shop on one side and the village stocks on the other. The graveyard stretched away to the side with its crooked turfy stones pointing to the sky in imitation of the tall spires so close overhead.

"May we go in, Staff? I would light a candle and pray a little while."

He nodded and they both entered, awed to silence by the perfection of this little jewel set in the center of the

416

crude town. Stained glass windows threw their myriad colors on the floor and the crucifix was studded with heavy semiprecious stones. Mary lit a candle, knelt at the confession rail and was amazed that Staff knelt beside her, his elbow touching hers. She prayed fervently for Will's soul, for herself and for her son so far away. Who would tell him gently of his father's death, and comfort him if he cried? Then the thought came to her. Perhaps on his way back to Eltham, Staff would stop at Hatfield. But dare she ask for favors when she gave none? When she finally turned her head and looked at him out of the corner of her eye, he was staring at her and a priest stood behind them.

"We are pleased to have strangers here to worship," he said low. "Perhaps there is a special need? I did not see your horses." His crooked smile lit his face.

"We are staying at the inn, father. We are en route to Edenbridge and stopped to see my old friend, Master Whitman."

"Ah, yes. Not many travel the east-west road anymore. This chapel was once a pilgrim center for those on the road to Canterbury, but no more, no more. The times have changed. Bands of robbers dare to plague our roads to the south. I fear that the summer curse on London and these parts is God's judgment on us all."

Mary was grateful he did not ask their names or their destination in Edenbridge. If he assumed they were married, all the better. She would be ashamed to tell a man of the church otherwise. No doubt he would ask Master Whitman about them afterwards, and then he would pray for their sins. If only he knew her husband was but five days dead of the sweat, he would think she were on the road to hell indeed.

Staff left some coins in the church box, and they strolled into the sunlight leaving the curious priest behind in his exquisite little chapel. The traveling fair on the green was pitifully meagre after the grand ones she had seen at Greenwich and even near Hever. They walked among the shoddy booths, and she did not object when Staff's hand rode familiarly on her waist or touched her hair. She continued to look over her shoulder for her disapproving father or bitter Will. The freedom of being where no one knew them was awkward and heady at the same time.

They watched a morality play put on with puppets and drifted past the fortune telling booths. "Would you like yours read, sweet, or do you prefer to make your own now?" he asked.

"Yes, I do prefer to make my own now, Staff."

He smiled broadly. "That is fine. Only, keep in mind that I prefer the same. Take that and how I feel about you into consideration when you make decisions, Mary Bullen."

She scarcely looked at the piles of scarves and trinkets the hawkers had spread upon their littered tables, but Staff bent and pulled a shiny hair net from among the heap of colors. "A golden snare," he said as he dangled it in the sunlight making its thin woven links glitter and gleam.

"I will take it, man, for the lady's hair," he said, handing the eager fellow a coin.

They began to stroll back, slowly, going nowhere in particular. "However free you think you are, Mary, remember this when we are apart. I like to think that I am free too, but I am not. You have ensnared my heart as surely as this net will catch the wayward tendrils of

418

your golden hair.''

She looked at him and tears filled her eyes. "Thank you," she said, and no other words would come. She fingered the net carefully. It was very fine. How had it ended up at that wretched little country fair? What story had it to tell of its earlier owner? She wanted to share her thoughts and feelings, but she was afraid to trust her voice.

His hand went around her waist as they entered the cobbled yard of the inn. He leaned briefly against her and kissed her cheek. "Come, my golden Mary. We are off to Hever Castle," he said. They stepped into the dimness of the hall beneath the frayed inn sign.

The Road to Hever

The pace they set to Hever was not the rapid, pounding one of yesterday. They had only a three hour ride.
They chatted and pointed things out to each other
along the way. Staff was clearly loathe to have it end
and to lose her again. She accepted that fact willingly—
happily. She had asked him to stay the night at Hever
before he set off for the court at Eltham. Of course, he
would have to stay the night, she reasoned, for it would
be dark soon after dinner and the roads would be totally
unsafe. And then after dinner, she would ask him to
please visit little Harry at Hatfield and to explain the
loss of his father, of the father he had not seen for weeks
and would never see again.

Mary felt better rested and her head clearer than it
had been since Will had died, maybe the best she had
felt since the whole court had vacated Hampton and left
her there with Will. Although the day was hot, the forest path and lanes were cool in their deep shade. Except
for the cleared fields surrounding little Oxted just
ahead, they would be out of the burning sun until they

420

reached the gentle valley and water meadows of the Eden—all the way home.

They did not stop to rest at Oxted, a feudal hamlet almost untouched by modern times. Skinny hunt hounds lay in the shade of the few houses switching flies with their tails, and few people were abroad.

"I wonder if they even know here who is king or about such things as the bad feelings toward the French since the Cloth of Gold?" she said to Staff over the clatter of their horses' cantering hoofs.

"I doubt it, lass. They are still grateful in these parts that The War of Roses had not caused devastation to their fields. Is this on your father's title rights yet?"

"No. Not until five miles past here. There is a clear marker on the forest road."

"Of course, there would be. If this land were in fealty to Lord Thomas Bullen, it would say so clearly somewhere." They laughed together at all his comment implied, and left the scattered clearings of Oxted far behind.

Mary was unfamiliar with this stretch to Hever for, whenever she had traveled, they had kept to the main road and not ridden southeast from out-of-the-way Banstead. She had been on this route, but she hardly remembered it at all. The forest was thick here and there was a damp chill in the air. More than once, startled deer feeding near the lane raised their liquid brown eyes in fear and darted from their sight. And then, around a small dip in the road it all happened suddenly. There were three tree trunks across their path, and although Staff's stallion Sanctuary took the first two in one great vault and easily leapt the other, Mary's Eden jerked, shied and nearly threw her over her arched

421

neck. Staff wheeled about and, when he saw Mary was still ahorse, drew his sword noisily. Instantly, the narrow space exploded with many horses and men, and Mary heard herself scream in frightened surprise. No, there were only three men and two horses. Staff slashed at one lout holding a terrible broad sword against his one thin-bladed one. The man on foot grabbed for her reins and she screamed again as Eden reared, knocking him back.

The man dashed forward and yanked at Eden's bridle before Mary could turn the mare, and the horse's head bent low. It was then she remembered she wore a sword and that she was supposed to be a lad, but with her foolish screaming they would know she was no fighter now. As she tried to draw the sword, the burly bearded man with eyes and hair as black as coal grabbed for her waist to drag her from the horse. Mary scratched out at his face with her nails and shuddered in terror as she felt them dig into his eyes and face. He cursed and loosed her to cover his eyes in pain.

It seemed all one tiny instant since she had seen Staff, but as she glanced up again, the scene had totally revolved. Staff's attacker lay on the ground and he fought the other horsed man sword to sword spurring Sanctuary forward. He wore no spurs, but he backed the robber's mount toward the logs in the road with hard kicks of his boots on his stallion's huge ribcage. That was all she saw: then a cruel yank threw her into the bloodied man's arms.

"No!" she shrieked at him, "No!" She flailed out as they hit the ground together. She heard her sword thud behind her. Her hair cascaded loose over them both.

"A wench," he grunted, "a yaller-haired wench!"

His hands roughly grabbed at her breasts through her shirt while she writhed and kicked at him. He rolled her on her stomach and pinned an arm behind her. She cried out in pain as the clanging of sword on sword ceased utterly. She thought she would be trampled then, for Sanctuary's thudding hoofs came at her. She closed her eyes as she tasted the gritty dirt of the forest floor.

The agony was suddenly gone from her arm and back. She lifted her head and pulled her hair aside in time to see a dismounted Staff swing his crimson sword at the black-bearded man. Blood spurted from his ugly neck and shoulder and the terror in his eyes imprinted itself in her mind. She half rolled, half crawled away from Staff's thrusts and the man's screams while Sanctuary stood placidly by, glad to have the weight gone from his back.

Staff was obviously in control, though he seemed to totter and weave as the man collapsed at his feet. She glanced swiftly behind her. Of the two on horseback, one had fled, charging off into the depths of the forest from which he had come, and the other lay in a dark heap over a log, one leg caught in the stirrup of his nervous horse. She ran to Staff. He leaned heavily, his back to her, against a tree. His boots nearly touched her would-be attacker who lay face down in a cluster of squat gray mushrooms and damp leaves.

"Staff, I am sorry I did not help. I forgot I had a sword."

He did not turn to face her, but bent over exhausted. Would he be sick to his stomach at the killing? She was the one who felt she would vomit, but she felt such relief at their deliverance from the gang, she steadied herself quickly. She reached around him and tried to turn him gently to her, but her fingers felt wet and warm. She darted around him and bent over oblivious to her sticky, red hand.

"Staff, you are wounded! Is it bad? Let me help. I did not know."

He sank to a sitting position against the rough bark of the tree and she saw clearly the spreading black stain on his dark jerkin where his shoulder joined his massive chest. She knelt, nearly touching him.

"Thank God, it is my left side," he said. "But it burns like the very devil and I think it is bleeding too much already, Mary. You were a hell of an asset in that fight . . . but then, I did not choose you to be my soldier." He closed his eyes against a flash of pain and then opened them to stare at her frightened face.

"Do not look so awful, sweet. I can ride and you will soon be home. You must help me stop the bleeding. If I even turn my head a bit, it pulls terribly. Do exactly as I say and be fast about it. I do not think that bastard who escaped will bring aid, but I want us out of here."

"Yes, Staff, yes. I can make a bandage."

"No. A bandage would only soak the blood. I need all I can keep. Get some moss, damp moss with the soil still on it, a big piece. Then cut my shirt away and press it to the wound. Go on, lass."

She scurried a little way into the gloom of the forest, keeping Staff in sight. He sat collapsed beside the body of that horrible man who had seized her. Yes, moss grew everywhere here. She dug and tore at a large round piece with her fingernails. Black wet earth clung to its underside. She dashed back to him.

"Cut the shirt and jerkin away with my sword. I cannot lift my arm.''

She shuddered as she lifted his sword from the dirt. It was encrusted with dried blood. She could not control the cut of the blade by holding it on its heavy handle, so she bit her lip and held it farther up its filthy blade as she cut away the two layers of cloth over the wound and tried to peel them off.

"Pull them, Mary. Be quicker. I am all right.''

She peeled them away from the slash mark and her eyes filled with fear and tears at the sight. His eyes watched her face steadily, and she tried not to show her revulsion. The wound, massive and twisted, grinned redly at her.

"Do not try to dab at it. The dried blood will help. Just press the moss on it, green side up.''

She did so and he grunted at the pain it caused. "Now see if you can wrap it tight with something.''

She ravaged her saddle sacks for her silk stocking, her only good pair. Why does someone not come along to help? she wondered distractedly. Please dearest God, do not let him be badly hurt. Oh dear God, do not let him die! Do not punish me again, please. I cannot help that I love him.

She tied the stockings tautly over the living bandage of moss, one reaching under his armpit, the other stretched tight around his neck on his right side. He put his good arm over her and leaned heavily on her while he stood and whistled for Sanctuary. The huge horse came obediently and stood stockstill. She tried to boost Staff up, but he mounted mostly of his own accord. Sweat dripped from his face from the pain and the exertion.

"Get both swords, Mary,'' he groaned out as she put

his reins in his right hand. He hunched over the horse's neck.

She grabbed both swords, and he put his back in its scabbard. Replacing hers awkwardly, she mounted. They walked their horses carefully around the fallen logs, no doubt all part of the robbers' dire trap.

"Go at a fairly good gallop, Mary. Sanctuary will follow Eden's lead." Then she heard him speak the last words he would say until they were at Hever: "I hope to hell His Grace's doctor is still there to tend the Lady Anne."

Within an hour the forests dwindled to scattered stands of oak, elm and beach as Eden scented the waters of Hever and pricked up her ears. Tears of relief flooded Mary's eyes at leaving the dreaded forest. Staff still rode slumped over without a word, but conscious. She would care well for him at Hever. She owed him so much. Only when the house was is sight did she begin to tremble at the impact of it all—attacked by thieves, Staff wounded, Will dead.

They cantered into the courtyard and Semmonet, Stephen, and Michael the gardener were instantly there to help. The two men carried Staff into the hall and upstairs at Mary's orders.

"Who is the handsome devil, and what happened to you? Where is Will? Why are you out riding in men's clothes?" Semmonet hissed at her in broken whispers as they deposited him in George's bed. She ignored the questions, for her mind was only on helping Staff.

"Is the king's doctor still here?" she asked sharply, bending to untie the crude bindings of the wound.

"No, Mary. Anne was much recovered so . . ."

426

"Anne was ill? Are mother and Catherine well?"

"Yes, and you see . . ."

"Then send for mother. Michael can fetch the apothecary in the village. Mother will know what to do. Hurry!"

Semmonet scurried off. Mary bent over Staff, stretched on the bed. She took his dirty hand in her even filthier one. Dirt was encrusted under her long nails and her hair straggled down to almost cover his head in a golden curtain.

He opened his eyes a crack. "If I get a fever from this, Mary, do not fear. Infected wounds often breed fever."

"Yes, my Staff. I will stay by you. I will not be afraid."

"Do you love me a little bit, Mary?" His voice was very weak.

"Yes, my lord. I. . . .I love you a great deal."

"Then I think I shall have to be ill for a very long time." He tried to smile, but his face contorted in pain.

"Do not talk. All will be well, Staff. I promise."

"All, sweet? I pray so." He seemed to doze instantly on the last word.

Then Lady Elizabeth was beside her and swept her wordlessly into her arms.

It had been four days since they had returned home. In a way, the longest four days of her life, she thought, but wonderful too. Staff was slowly healing and so was she. She had spent hours by his bedside, watching. When they first returned, despite mother's pleas for her to get some sleep and Anne's words that she was foolish indeed to wait up since he was obviously unconscious, she had sat and watched all night. She would occasionally pace to the next room to cherish the sound of Catherine's gentle breathing, but then she would return to stare down at Staff's wrinkled brow as he slept fitfully.

They all wore mourning for Will Carey now—all but Anne, who was content to wear only a black sash tied to her sleeve. Mother had even sewn Catherine a dark dress. It made her look terribly pale and Mary detested it, but it was right that the child should wear it for a month. Father and George were still at Eltham with the king. They must have known of Will's death for a week, but there was no word of comfort or condolence from Eltham. Today was a fine day though. It was not humid and the sun shone. And Staff sat erect in his bed against several pillows for the first time.

"Do I get some kind of kiss this morning, madam?" he teased Mary. She smiled broadly to hear the amused tone returned to his voice.

"For what?" she returned with feigned naivete. "You owe me for doctoring and linen bills, my lord, and my last decent pair of silk stockings."

"I will buy you more than silk stockings, if you will let me, sweetheart. And I will gladly give you all the kissing you may think I owe if I can get this stubble off my face and get us out of the watchful gaze of your guard dog governess."

Mary laughed. "I would shave you, but I fear you have no more blood to spare for nicks and cuts. There is a lad here who used to shave George before he had his own valet. I shall fetch him."

"Sit awhile, lass. There is time enough."

She sat back on the edge of the wooden chair. "There is something I have been wanting to say all the while you were hurt and sleeping, Staff.''

"Tell me." He looked as expectant as a little boy about to open a package.

"I want to thank you for saving me when we were attacked. I was no help. I let them know I was a woman and I screamed. I am sorry." She hesitated.

"But you *are* a woman, Mary, and had never been so abused before. I would not expect you to act differently. You are hardly trained to wield a sword. Besides, you were a tremendous help to me afterwards. Is there anything else?"

"Yes. I want you to know I appreciate—I treasure—our hours and our talks at Banstead. And, well, thank you for being so restrained."

"You are welcome. Do not thank me too much. I doubt if I could ever do it again—the restraint I mean."

She expected him to grin at her but he was serious. Her heart leapt and began to beat the quickened rhythm he could always arouse. Their eyes held. She was trying to summon her courage to give in to the magnetic pull she felt to sit on the bed and kiss him when Anne glided in humming.

"Good morning, Lord Stafford. You look a great deal stronger but a shave would help, you know."

"Yes, Lady Anne. Indeed I know." He flicked his thumbnail across the stubble. "Mary and I were just discussing it."

"Oh. Well, do you feel strong enough to tell me how things truly were at Eltham when you dashed off? Father's missives are so political and His Grace's notes are of far another sort." Her dark eyes danced over him in some sort of challenge, and he returned her gaze

429

steadily.

"I would be pleased to tell you whatever you would choose to know, Lady Anne, but right now I am famished. I intend to try to move around a bit this afternoon, so perhaps at supper this evening there will be time."

Anne lifted her sleek head to stare at Mary. "Well, of course, I know you have been unwell. It is only that I am dying to hear someone tell me the way it truly is, you see. George is kept much away these days. Perhaps at dinner." She raised her slender right hand to Mary and was gone.

"Why did you tell her that, Staff? You are hardly famished after that stew and biscuits."

"Maybe I want to be alone with only you, Mary, and she *did* interrupt us. And then, maybe it gives me perverse pleasure to put her off since everyone falls all over her these days, and it is likely to be worse when she returns to him this autumn. The time will not be long when it will be completely unwise and unsafe to put off the Lady Anne."

"You predict she will become his mistress? She says she will never do that."

"I am afraid I am starting to believe her. I think His Grace is stirring his pluck to send Queen Catherine away from court for good, and then we shall see the Lady Anne's next move. She must be a hell of a chess player, as much as you must be a bad one, love."

"I hardly think you need to bring me into this. I . . ."

"Rest assured, I prefer a poor player at that game, Mary. One I can teach and beat if I have to. The other thing is," he went on, "His Grace is not truly content

430

with having the Fitzroy boy his heir. Bessie Blount's son is no match—nor is the queen's slender, serious daughter—for a legitimate son."

"Catherine is healthy enough, although she will bear him no more children," Mary argued quietly. "He is far from being a widower."

"That is what I mean about the next Bullen chess move, Mary. We shall have to wait and see. And I do want to sit in the gardens and perhaps stroll about to get my riding strength back. I had best have that shave since we are talking only of unimportant things and not of our future. I have to be able to ride. I do not intend to be here when your father returns to claim Anne or if His Grace should suddenly appear."

She stood to fetch the boy to shave him. "I refuse to be afraid of either of them anymore," she said bravely.

"Not afraid, perhaps, sweetheart, but always careful."

She gave his good arm a playful caress as she left the room. He made a grab for her but missed. She laughed.

"Teases always get what they deserve, Mary," he called after her. She laughed again at having him sound like his old self again.

In the afternoon she and Catherine walked with Staff to the stableblock to visit Sanctuary. Mary had assured him more than once that Ian was tending the horse lovingly, but he had to see for himself. Staff walked in slow steps and she knew he still had a headache and was weak as a babe. But she was so glad to see him up! Little Catherine walked between them, holding on to both of their hands. The child had always favored Staff and remembered him from her earliest days when he would visit her parents in their chambers and tease her and make her laugh. Mother had told her that her father was dead now and that meant he had gone away forever. At least now her tall friend Staff was here with them. It would make her very happy if he would decide to stay here with mother, grandmother and Aunt Anne. She was certain it would make mother very happy too.

And now he was taking them to see his big horse. She and mother had seen him ride it in a joust one day. The king was there too. That was when she sat with her friend Margaret to watch. Margaret's uncle was the king.

"Will Santry remember me, do you think, my lord?" the little girl's sweet voice asked him.

Staff and Mary smiled at her attempt to say the difficult word. "I am certain he would never forget a beautiful lady like you, Mistress Catherine," Staff said seriously.

"Did he get hurt when you and mother did?"

"Just a little cut. It is much better now they tell me. Just as I am."

"I do not think you need to overestimate your strength whatever vows of full recovery you have made to Catherine or me or Sanctuary, Staff," Mary warned.

"Yes, nurse," he mocked gently. "I am willing to do anything you say."

"Then hush and do not tease," she threw at him and looked down to see Catherine staring intently at them.

Sanctuary stamped and snorted in his stall to smell and hear his master. Staff patted his neck and flanks with his good hand and talked low to him. Mary hoisted Catherine up on the rails of the stall so she could see and pat the huge animal.

"He is much bigger than Eden or Donette, mother."

"He has to be much bigger than my horses, my angel. Staff is much bigger than I am."

"Staff is much bigger than father, too," the child said as she stroked the sleek chestnut hair of the steed.

Mary glanced at Staff, her unspoken thoughts on her face. The child did not really understand. She had never lost anything but her beloved rag doll and that had been replaced soon enough.

"If I begin to ride Sanctuary tomorrow as I plan, Catherine, I shall take you for a ride around the moat," Staff was saying. "Would you like that?"

"Yes, of course! Can we do it in the afternoon? I think I have to sew with grandmother and Semmonet in the morning. But you always sleep late anyway."

"I have been lately, my moppet, but not anymore, since I am fast healing."

"I hope you will stay here with us, my lord. Mother is much happier now that you are better."

Staff grinned at Mary over Catherine's curly golden head and she guiltily returned his smile.

"I warrant the lass could give you lessons on how to see things clearly, Mary. Come, sweet Catherine. Run back to your grandmother in the garden. I will see you later." He lifted her down with his uninjured arm.

"You will not ride him now, without me?" she questioned.

"Not without you, lass. Tomorrow I said."

She ran several bounding steps and turned back to them. "Where did you get Santry's funny name, my lord? What does it mean?"

"It is a long story I will tell you later, miss, when I take you riding—tomorrow."

She grinned at him and darted off waving to them from near the door.

It was cool and dim in the stables and it smelled like fresh oats and straw. Ian was a very careful groom and blacksmith. Staff put a booted foot on the lowest rail of Sanctuary's stall, blocking Mary when she made a move to follow her daughter's departure.

"That child will break hearts—like her mother," he said low. "She is a miniature of you for certain."

"Unlike I, Catherine will be raised without a father to totally control her life. I pray she will be the happier for that."

"Do not hate your father too much, sweetheart. Hatred would get in the way of your dealing with him firmly enough to handle him. And why must the lass be raised without a father? Her mother is still fair, young and desirable, I assure you."

"Thank you, my lord, but her mother is twenty-four and sometimes feels a good deal older than that. Catherine will be raised without a father. Her father is dead."

"At least you are being more realistic than you were at first," he said, changing the dangerous path on which he had considered treading. He stroked Sanctuary's neck and spoke gentle words of comfort much as he had to Mary when he had first arrived from Eltham at Hampton Court.

"Why does the horse have that name, Staff? Such a serious, strange name."

"I never did quite tell you the whole story of my family's unfortunate past, Mary."

434

"Only that your uncle was hanged for rebellion against His Grace's sovereign father and that your father was pardoned since he was so young. Is Sanctuary named for something in your past, then?"

"Yes. Right, Sanctuary? In 1486, after he had won the country by force of arms in the civil war, King Henry VII was riding on a progress to solidify the north. Humphrey and Thomas Stafford—my uncle and my father—raised a band at Colchester and tried to take Worcester back for the York cause. The king immediately raised an army headed by the Duke of Northumberland and rode south to put the rebellion down. The Staffords took sanctuary at Culham near Oxford—holy, inviolate sanctuary at the altar of a church, Mary—but the king's forces battered down the door and arrested them for high treason claiming that such guilt could not be morally sanctuaried."

He turned slowly and leaned his back against the horse's stall. "Some say the king later suffered grief for such a impious act, rebellion or not, but by then Humphrey Stafford of Grafton had been hanged at Tyburn and twelve-year-old Thomas sent home to an aunt at Wivenhoe near Colchester where the trouble had all begun. But the king never forgot to mistrust the Staffords after that, and took Lord Thomas' first born son to raise at court."

"And that son is you?"

"Yes. Our present king simply inherited me and the continual duty of keeping an eye on my potential waywardness."

"But you would never do such a thing—raise a rebel army!"

"No, of course not, and His Grace knows it well

enough. The problem is, he really likes me, though I think he is a little afraid of me too. He cannot grasp the fact that I neither hate him nor worship him for his favors as do the others who swarm around him. He can never understand there is another world out there that I have always cherished.''

"Your family lands at Wivenhoe that your great aunt left you when she died?''

"Wivenhoe, yes, but more what it represents—freedom from the snares of politics and court intrigue. True 'sanctuary', Mary.''

"Like your friend John Whitman has found for himself in his little inn off the beaten path and far from the cruel master of the *Mary Rose*,'' she mused half aloud.

"Exactly. Like Hever is to you, I guess. And like you are to me, Mary Bullen.'' He gave her arm a little pull and she stepped toward him, carefully turning her cheek against his good shoulder. He stroked her hair and Sanctuary snorted and pawed in his stall.

"Sanctuary needs to be free too. He needs a skillful rider who cares for him, and he will respond beautifully. I am planning for things to be the same for us,'' he said.

Her arms went around his waist and they did not move. "Now I understand that Sanctuary is a good name, Staff. Has His Grace ever heard it? I would think it would take the wind from his sails if he understood.''

"He has heard it. I have made certain of that. Now the only thing that has been puzzling me is how I am going to explain to your golden haired moppet what 'Santry' means.''

She began to laugh but he lifted her chin with his

436

hand and covered her mouth with his. The kiss was neither passionate nor gentle, but determined, both giving and demanding. He finally raised his head and stared down into her half-closed azure eyes. "We had best join your mother in the garden as we promised, before it is too late. I am certain they would notice the straw in our clothes and hair, and anyway, your sister would probably come poking about to ask how things 'truly are at court'. I would much rather tell her than show her. Come on."

Her laughter floated to Sanctuary's alert ears as they left the stables. It is so wonderful, Mary realized, to have Staff here at Hever.

Lady Elizabeth Bullen had spent an hour each morning and each afternoon in the room where William Stafford was recuperating since he had ridden to Hever with Mary. The first days she had talked low to Mary while he slept, and the last two she had talked to them both. She took Staff's hand each time she entered or left the room. And Mary, who could never recall similar actions from her mother with any other visitor, was puzzled. She had decided it was because he had saved her daughter from rape or death at the hands of the brigands in the forest. But now she was coming to believe it must be more. Perhaps it was like an instinctive trust, whereas she herself had disliked him when she had first known him and trust had come later.

Mary watched them through her lashes as they spoke low to each other on the bench in the rose garden. Catherine threw a leather ball back and forth to Semmonet on the other side of the hedge, and Anne dared to sit and read the bawdy *Heptameron*, authored by no one less that Marguerite du Alencon, sister to King Francois of France. It was even rumored that now the king's poor Queen Claude had been dead three years, he showed more open affection to his sister than he had before, and that some of the heated passion in the text of the book was flamed by that love. Mary was not sure she even cared to read it if some of Francois du Roi's passions were laid out for all to see. But Anne, clever, witty Anne loved French things.

"So I am hoping the king will let Anne marry soon," Lady Elizabeth was saying to Staff. "Perhaps her old friend Sir Thomas Wyatt would be a good match, but her lord father does not show any interest in the lands adjoining Hever, which the Wyatt lad is heir to."

Anne's dark eyes darted up from the pages of her book. "I can hear what you are saying, mother. I do not believe I will be getting married, at least not in the near future. Anyhow, if father had cared a fig for the Wyatt estates, he could have easily married George to his long-desired Margot Wyatt." She bent her head to the book again. "I hear she is in childbed with her first child to Pierce, Lord Edgecome from Devon, anyway, so that is that. Oh, it is too hot to read out here, even in the shade. There is a good deal more shade at Eltham, I warrant."

She stood and her green skirts swung in a gentle arc as she paced in a circle around them. "Perhaps I should join you when you ride back to Eltham, Staff. Then father would be shocked, His Grace would be elated, and you could save me from several bands of thieves with rape on their minds on the way back to break all this boredom of waiting, waiting!"

Mary thought Anne looked like a slender, lovely

flower among the rest of them dressed in black. But she was so pent up with hopes and schemes she would not share but only alluded to—much like father. Yes, she was getting to be more and more like father.

"Mother, Staff promised me he would catch me up on all the news at court and you and Mary virtually keep him your prisoner, though a willing one, I grant you." She spun toward Staff and her skirts belled out in a perfect graceful cup. Her voice was teasing. "You never did tell me, for instance, how you coerced His Grace into letting you leave Eltham when you heard poor Will Carey was dead? You told him you wanted to bring Mary back here and he let you go at once? 'S blood, I would have liked to have seen that."

"Anne, sit and cease this foolishness," came Lady Elizabeth's voice as Staff was about to answer. "Thank God, His Grace *did* let Lord Stafford go or Mary would not be here now, one way or the other."

"Perhaps, Anne, the king reasoned that Staff could then see how you are behaving and report back to him," Mary put in, hoping the tone of her voice would make Anne stop her insinuations where she and Staff were concerned.

"All right, I will sit in stony silence, if I must. I do not need all of you teasing me, or I shall have to seek my desolate room alone!"

They all laughed at her, for her buoyant mood beneath the testiness was contagious. Mary stretched her legs, smiled in Staff's direction and stood to join Semmonet and Catherine. But then Michael, the gangly gardener, came striding across the grass followed by a stranger, and she sat again.

"This be Lord Bullen's lady wife," Michael said to

439

the man and they both bowed to Elizabeth. The man presented a folded parchment to her outstretched hand and bowed again.

"Nothing from father to me?" Anne asked sharply.

The messenger scanned the group, and bowed a third time to Anne. "The king's man be hard on the road behind me, begging your grace, my Lady Anne. He ha' told me he bears a message from the king and a gift." He stood about awkwardly until Lady Elizabeth summoned Michael to take the man in for refreshments.

"Our lord is coming home two days hence," she read with her head still bent over the letter. "He hopes that Mary is well settled here and will return in her sister's retinue in September when Anne goes to live at court as 'she has so wisely promised His Grace she would do'." She glanced up at Anne who sat impassive, hitting her knee with her now closed book. "That is really the import of it. Two days hence. For how long this time, I wonder."

"Not long, lady," Staff assured her. "As soon as the first span of cooler weather hits the city, the court will be back in full swing, and your Lord Thomas will be at the center of things. And the Lady Anne." Through the whole speech, his eyes focused on Mary, and she shot him a dazzling smile despite Anne's sharp stare.

"And I promise you, before I even tell my father, Staff, that I shall bring Mary back with me as he asks. Imagine you and our father wanting the same thing." Anne giggled despite her mother's pointed glance.

"Although the company is most beautiful and the conversation here a definite, ah, challenge, ladies, I shall take Sanctuary for a bit of a ride tomorrow to test

440

my strength. The next day I must set out for Eltham and I promise to stick to more heavily traveled roads—that is, unless the Lady Anne actually *does* fancy an adventure such as Mary had." He leaned forward on his knees and peered around Lady Bullen at Anne. "I cannot promise to be wounded and bleed for you though, Lady Anne. I am sure you can understand that blood shed for one Bullen lass is quite enough."

Elizabeth Bullen regarded him closely while Anne suddenly narrowed her eyes, uncertain if she were merely being teased or quite put down.

"Anyway," he continued evenly, "I intend to ride to Hatfield House to see Henry Carey on my way back to Eltham. Mary wishes the boy to be told carefully of his father's death by a friend of the family, and to deliver Will's crested neck chain. It is his heritage now."

Anne swung her book from her right hand as she took several steps away. "Thank you for the offer of the sport, my lord, on the ride to Eltham, but I truly think you prefer gentler game. And as for my nephew, Henry Carey's, heritage, who is to know if His Grace may have need of him someday? They say Henry Fitzroy is a weakling. Unless, of course, our king should take it upon himself to get a son through some other means after the Queen Catherine is sent into exile as he has publicly promised father and me." Her musical laughter floated back to them in the sunny air.

"Mary and I will miss you greatly, my lord," Elizabeth Bullen put in gently, "as will our little Catherine who dotes on you it seems. I was hard-pressed to keep her from bothering you those first days when you slept so much from blood loss. I *do* hope I will see you again and soon. I appreciate an honest man, king's courtier or not.''

Staff bent over her hand and kissed it. ''I promise you will see me again, my lady, and it must be here since you will not come to court.''

''No, not at court, unless something very big and unexpected happens, and I pray it will not. The Bullens' lives are already complicated enough as it is. You are always welcome here. Is it not so, Mary?''

''Yes, mother. Of course. Staff knows that.''

''Then I hope he will include us in his future plans,'' the silver-haired woman added as she rose. Both Mary and Staff stood with her. ''Please do not let Anne's sharp tongue turn you away from her. She needs friends, and she will need her sister's gentler influence, though I will be loathe to part with Mary when she goes back.'' She smiled at her daughter and Mary's eyes filled with glistening tears at her love for the slender woman. Mother, Catherine and Hever—with Staff here to please them all—it was nearly heaven. But now he must be going back. They would both go back to court.

''I shall miss you,'' she said to him across the tiny space of garden that separated them after her mother had left.

His teeth shone white against his bronze face and his eyes darkened with pleasure. ''But I shall be here a whole day and a half yet, wench, and we shall see what we can make of that.''

She nodded her head slowly as Catherine's squeals of delight permeated the golden afternoon.

Chapter Twenty-Four
August 1, 1528

Hever Castle

The day and a half Staff had promised her he would stay at Hever before returning to court became the most fleeting hours of Mary's life. His wounded chest and shoulder seemed to heal rapidly; he ate enough for two healthy men; and the vitality of his temperament, body, and desires returned. On the first sunny afternoon after they had managed to shake off Anne's continual questions, Mary and little Catherine had taken Staff on an extensive walking tour of Hever: the rooms and courtyard, the gardens, orchards, meadows, even St. Paul's Church down the long, winding lane where the forests started again.

That evening they sat after supper in the solar, almost as a happy little family, Mary thought, chatting and playing a friendly game of Gleek where Anne insisted she be Staff's partner and managed to hold all the cards too. But the restive Anne soon flitted off to get her beauty sleep and Lady Bullen bid them a quick and smiling goodnight.

Staff and Mary, at the big oak solar table they had

used for cards, both sat a moment, drinking in the silence and the sweet August air laced with cricket calls that drifted in through the oriel windows, set ajar.

Staff was studying her as usual, not moving but for the rise and fall of his big chest, still wrapped with a heavy linen bandage under his white shirt unlaced halfway down to reveal brown, curly chest hair. His muscular legs were encased in informal breeks and black stockings to match the mourning dress Mary wore.

"A penny for your thoughts, Staff," her voice came low in the quiet.

"I cannot see selling my thoughts for a mere penny, lass, when the Lady Anne seems to value them so highly. But then, for one of your sweet kisses I have been greatly longing for lately, and which seem to be now in short supply, I would consider it."

She felt little butterfly wings flutter in her stomach. "Agreed."

"Come here and pay up then. You can hardly expect a near invalid to chase you around the room, Lady Mary."

His voice had that old teasing tone but he did not smile and she marvelled at the shift in mood he seemed to have undergone from the chatting, cordial man of a few moments ago at their card game.

She scraped her chair back and went to stand over him. He was sitting almost a foot from the table, but his arms were so long he had reached the cards easily. He lifted his handsome head and his probing brown eyes reflected the glow of the big cresset lamp on the table. She bent down, leaning close, her breath coming through parted lips as her soft mouth met his hard one. His lips opened immediately to caress hers, moving

444

against hers, tasting her, his tongue running deliberately along the moist, tender insides of her lips before the kiss was over. He had not touched her otherwise. Was he really so unsure of her reaction after that night last week when she had not let him make love to her at Banstead? she wondered.

She started to straighten, but his uninjured arm moved quickly to stay her and he said, "Kiss me again, lass. I have two thoughts I think you would like to hear."

Inches apart in the drifting lamp glow and sweet scented aura of the room, their eyes locked. She almost swayed into him at the impact of her desire for him, but she steadied her hands on the arm of his chair and lowered her mouth to kiss him once more.

You have fallen in love with him all over again, a voice deep inside whispered to her. Again since he rescued you after Will died at Hampton, again at Banstead, again at Hever, again this very moment.

This time his kiss was not so controlled. He pressed harder, slanting his mouth across hers possessively and darting his tongue madly over, around, and under hers. His hand loosed her arm and lifted to the back of her head where his strong fingers entwined in her loose tresses to hold her lips to his. He nibbled at her lower lip, then returned to his deeper probing of her tongue and teeth and the inside of her cheeks as if he would devour her.

She could not breathe. He was making her so dizzy! But the minute she tried to pull back he allowed her, moving his hand to steady her again. "You—I," she stammered closing her eyes to stop the tilting of the room. She did not want him to know he could still do this to her so easily when she had tried so hard to hold him off last week. "I just did not want to fall against your bandage and hurt you, my lord."

It angered her that he seemed so totally composed after that kissing, but his smile was gently teasing again and she stood to move away from him around the corner of the table.

"I appreciate your concern, sweet. If I were allowed to make love to you and if we were bedding tonight, I warrant we would have to work out something very special so I could keep my weight off this arm and shoulder."

"Staff, really—"

"Think about it, Mary. The lady involved, I believe, would have to be on top and do all the—ah, moving—herself."

She felt herself go hot, then shaky under his perusal. Was this some sort of challenge? Or was he showing his hurt or anger this way, for her refusal to lie with him at Banstead?

"You have not told me the two thoughts I just paid for, my lord," she said, trying desperately to sound in control.

"You just heard the first one, love. I was thinking how much I desire to have you, but that you would have to do most of the work."

"The work! Staff, it sounds like gardening or something!"

He threw his big head back and laughed heartily while she blushed to the very roots of her hair. "Well, you know how it is, sweetheart," he got out, "ploughing deep furrows, then planting seeds and—"

"Staff!" She moved away farther around the table,

and he finally stood and moved after her. He turned her to him with one hand on her shoulder.

"Now, do not get huffy or sulk like your spoiled little sister, sweet," he said gently. "I meant not to make fun of you and the thought was true enough. I cannot help wanting to tumble my beautiful Mary as such desire is a very old habit with me, and—I think you want me, too." He lifted her chin up with two fingers and stepped warm against her. "Is it not so, lass?"

"Yes, Staff. Oh, yes. It is only that I need time to sort everything out."

"Fine. Only, I intend to be in the sorting when all is said and done, love. And do not look so forlornly at me with those huge, pond-blue eyes as though I would dare to take you here on this padded solar bench. Your mother and little sparrow of a governess would not approve of Lord Stafford half so much if they ever caught us, I warrant, although your bothersome little sister might like to know how it is truly done."

Despite his outrageous comments, she grinned and put her head against his good shoulder. "I know it is late and we are both tired, Mary, but I do not want today to end because then there is only one more before I leave."

Her voice came muffled against his soft linen shirt where her cheek rested on the familiar crisp, curly hair under the base of his neck. "I know, my Staff."

"Let's go outside and walk along the moat just for a few minutes, then. We will go out through the kitchens and herb garden." His warm fingers curled around hers and she went willingly, realizing he had not asked her if she wanted to go. Despite the scent of healing herbs on his bandage, his chest, his clothes, his hair

447

smelled so good, some unnamable magnetic masculine aroma she could never quite place.

The kitchen was cast in melded grays, the vast cavern of the fireplace on the far wall gaping darkly with no embers burning on this warm night. Somewhere in the dim kitchen a dog stirred, growled low and rolled over as they passed through. The door to the gardens stood ajar and the intoxicating aroma of mingled marjoram, mint, basil, fennel and other herbs swept in with the warm, alive night air. The grass felt damp against her slippers and smelled unutterably sweet. She followed him along the fringe of the garden on the grassy path until they turned around the corner of the house by the edge of the inner moat. Across the narrow stretch of water, the overpowering scent of roses wafted to them on the balmy night air.

He stopped, still holding her hand. "There is a little stone bench farther on if you want to sit," she offered.

"No. This is fine. Anne's bedroom window is not anywhere above here, is it?"

"No, Staff."

"Then, this is just fine. Just the frogs the crickets and us," he said. "Mary, my other thought, which you so sweetly paid me for was that now that you are free—unmarried and marriageable—and since I do not trust the king or that cat-eyed sister of yours not to marry you off to someone they fancy for their own gain—" He paused and stepped closer in the darkness. "Mary, I just could not bear to lose you again after all the waiting, now that we are so close. I cannot—I will not let another man have you. Ever!"

She moved against him and stretched her arms up around his neck. "They will not, my lord. They cannot. I am a new widow and just because Anne rides so high in His Grace's favor now, does not mean they can marry me off to just anyone. If someone even suggests it—my father even—I will tell them no!"

He rocked them back and forth gently, holding her to his lean, hard body with one hand firmly on the small of her back. "Ah, my sweet Mary. Have you been through so much and still think things are so simple, then?"

"Not all things, my Staff, but how I feel about you is simple now."

He stopped rocking them and pulled her body closer to his so they seemed to melt together. "I thought maybe you had forgotten the words, Mary. Hell's gates, do I have to be bleeding all over the bed before you will tell me?"

"I do love you, my lord. I love you desperately and I have for a very long time."

"I do not want tears and that quivering lower lip, Mary. When I go away the day after tomorrow and when we both get back to court this autumn, we are going to have to be very careful and very strong. Now tell me again."

"I love you, Staff." He moved to rest his chin on the top of her head and she marvelled again at how her face fit so perfectly, comfortably cuddled against his warm throat. They stood that way, pressed together a very long while. Then his words came low, rustling her hair along her forehead. "If I could have one more good-night kiss, lass, I would tell you one last thought I had about taking you, Nancy, and Stephen on a picnic across the water meadows tomorrow. I have got to get Sanctuary exercised and ready for the long ride he has coming.''

''A picnic? It sounds wonderful. Could we not take little Catherine?''

''A romantic picnic, Mary, a private picnic. I thought we might go a good way off and be gone all day. I shall take the moppet for a turn or two around the grounds before we leave, but I would like us to have the day alone before I go.''

''A private picnic with Stephen and Nancy?'' she teased. She saw his teeth flash white in the darkness when he grinned at her.

''You have noticed how they gaze moonstruck at each other, have you not, my sweet? Surely you recognize the look. I was thinking of giving them their private picnic and we shall have ours. Will you go? And maybe not wear black on our last day together for who knows how long?''

You have to be careful not to give him everything he wants, anything he asks, she chided herself as their lips met gently. It would be like her kings and father all over again. But no, that was not God's truth. Staff had said it; there was a vast difference. Staff truly *did* love her with all his heart and she tried to show him, in her warm embrace, that she was his alone whatever happened to crush their precious haven.

The four of them clattered out of the courtyard on their horses the next morning with Lady Elizabeth Bullen standing on the front door steps waving a handkerchief in one hand and holding Catherine's hand in the other. Although it was nearly ten o'clock and the hazy, warm sun had lifted above the slate roofs, brick chimneys and honey-colored stone towers of Hever to

450

peer into the courtyard already, the Lady Anne had not stirred from bed to bid them goodbye. It was just as well, Staff had whispered low to Mary, for he did not put it past Anne to insist on coming, and chattering about King Henry and his court the entire day.

Mary had honored Staff's request about not wearing the same black mourning dress he had seen her in these last five days, and she had spent a good hour with Nancy this morning selecting one which would be light weight for the weather, attractive to Staff, and yet still proper for the circumstances. It was wrong of her, she knew, to love Staff so completely with Will only newly gone. But her marriage seemed like years ago—forever since she had really been Will Carey's wife in more than name.

"No sour, sad looks today, my Mary," Staff said to her as they cantered side by side ahead of Nancy and Stephen on the road due east past the limekiln along the edge of the beech and poplar forest. "And I *do* like the dress. You should be able to ride, run, climb, or take advantage of whatever comes up in that."

She had chosen a light brown riding dress that she had not worn in years. The bodice and full, loose sleeves tied onto the simple skirt for effect. She and Nancy had considered lacing on a pair of gayer sleeves, but after black, this brown and yellow seemed quite festive enough. Then too, the tight bodice was edged in yellow scallop embroidery and she *did* wear yellow ribbons to hold back her full, flowing hair. The only danger was, she reminded herself, that she must be careful to keep out of this sun for long periods, or her fair skin would burn and she would never hear the end of it from dear old Semmonet.

451

Staff wore the same low-laced white shirt and black breeks that he had last night. She knew his good riding outfit had been ruined with blood when they were attached. He was certainly much too big to wear anything of father's or George's, and he had brought only this change of clothes in his hasty departure from Eltham and then offered her all the room in his nearly-empty saddle packs for her own clothes.

"My Lord Stafford," she said, almost before she knew she would speak, "you are very good and kind to me and take very good care of me, and I should like to thank you."

He looked surprised, but then a big smile lit his rugged, bronze face when he saw that no tease would follow. "I appreciate those words, my sweetheart. And, I promise you, I shall yet this very afternoon take even better care of you."

She blushed and managed to grin at him, both amused and thrilled by the remark. They turned north toward the gentle River Eden, twisting its way across the water meadows carpeted with purple ironweed and nodding daisies. Their horses' hooves thudded hollowly as they crossed over the river to the north bank where Staff reined in and the rest clustered around him.

"A rest already, milord?" Stephen asked. "Your shoulder is not hurting you, milord?"

"No, lad, no. But we will take a short rest here while Lady Mary and Nancy divide up the food that the cook has so nicely packed for us in the Bullen kitchens. I propose the Lady Mary and I ride on a little way ahead and you, Stephen, keep a watch over Mistress Nancy somewhere about here until we come back, say, about four or five hours from now."

Stephen swallowed hard and looked wide-eyed at Staff. "Yes, milord. An' certain, if—if that be suitable to Mistress Nancy."

Mary had to bite her lower lip to keep from grinning at the excitement the two servants tried to hide.

"Oh. Oh, yes, indeed, my lord," the girl breathed and nodded to Staff. "Stephen and I shall get on fine until you return."

Staff and Stephen whispered suspiciously, holding the horses a little way off while Mary and Nancy unpacked the two saddle bags of food and divided everything. The maid bent over her work with a vengeance, her sure hands moving quickly, her sweet, freckled face intent.

"Nance, you are not upset, are you?" Mary whispered.

"No, m' lady."

"I know Stephen cares for you. I know it seems like rather different circumstances than working for Lord Carey and me, but just be firm if you feel uncomfortable about anything."

Nancy tied a napkin around the divided fruit and quickly cut the block of cheese in half. "Please, Lady Mary. I am not such a green girl to not know the way of things. My sister Megan has talked to me a great lot about men. Only, if you knew Lord Stafford and Stephen was planning this, I sort of wish you would have whispered it to me."

Staff's voice boomed out in a laugh and Stephen strode over to help repack Sanctuary's saddlebags. Stephen was eighteen or nineteen, Mary judged, tall and lanky with reddish brown hair and a habit of cocking his long, friendly face to the side whenever he listened intently, as he always did whenever Staff spoke. Mary squeezed Nancy's arm reassuringly and moved to mount Eden.

"Mary, let's both ride Sanctuary. He will not mind the little extra weight and it will get him in shape for the long haul tomorrow. Is there anything in your saddle packs you need?"

"No, I—well, all right." Staff boosted her up ahead of him on the big saddle and mounted carefully behind her so her shoulder would bounce against his uninjured side. Behind them, near the wooden bridge, Nancy was waving wistfully and Stephen was pulling all three horses back toward the river bank.

They rode on, following the curving blue river eastward into the late morning sun. There were no villages along this bank, few travellers, and so, Mary hoped, no highwaymen to jump out from behind fallen trees. But Staff did not seem a bit worried, and he even whistled a bawdy tavern song as they slowly jogged along. They saw slender, reddish deer along the river arching their graceful necks down to drink, then looking up with startled, liquid eyes. The sun sifted through the trees and the jeweled peace and beauty of the surroundings awed them both to silence.

They finally selected a stretch of shady bank, grassy and slightly slanted with huge trunked oaks and shagbark hickories shivering their leaves overhead in the breeze. Staff helped her down with his strong arm, then unpacked the food from one bag and his short black riding cape from the other. "It is hardly May Day feast on green and white spread tables at court, but I warrant we shall enjoy this much, much more," he said.

To break the solemnity and tension of being here

alone with him, she teased, "I know I shall. I never *did* like May Days where everytime I looked up from my food all I could see was Dorothy Cobham draped on one of my lover's arms, and that simpering Isabelle Dorsey on the other."

"She does not simper, Mary."

"Oh, really? Go ahead and defend her then, and see what that gets you this afternoon here—with me."

They both laughed and she flopped back on his cape joyous and free, while he watered Sanctuary in the stream and put their wine jug in the water between two rocks to cool. Four or five hours, Mary kept saying to herself, hours here alone with Staff. Birds twittered in the leafy boughs overhead and she hugged herself in a rush of pure happiness.

"Mary, the water feels fabulous. Want to wade?"

"But your boots are all wet, my lord. You did not even take yours off!"

"I will if you will. Come on. I am almost done with Sanctuary now and can spare you a little bit of my time."

She had her boots off before he had returned from staking the stallion a ways off to crop grass. She stood almost shyly on the grassy bank trying to decide if the river bottom would be muddy or sandy.

"I hate this dressing and undressing with one hand," he said. "Might I use your lovely shoulder to lean against, sweet madam, while I struggle to pull off these boots?"

"Of course," she said grandly. "But them, if you just sit for a minute, I shall get them off for you in a wink, Staff."

He grinned and sat back while she knelt and pulled

off one soft Spanish leather boot and then the other. "I favor your handling of me far over Stephen's, beautiful lady," he said. "If I decided to go swimming, would you help me get ready for that too?"

"You are such a tease, my love." She held his hand and they waded in ankle deep together, giggling. "Oh, it is muddy here," she squealed.

"Can you swim, sweet Mary?"

"No, my lord."

"Then I shall teach you some sunny afternoon like this when I have you all to myself at Wivenhoe."

"It sounds wonderful. Will it be hard?"

"Swimming, my lass, you will take to like a little fish. Getting to Wivenhoe—well, that may be a trick."

Staff hiked her skirts up around her waist, baring her legs to her knees, and fastened the whole brown linen bulk with his belt. They chased silver slivers of minnows, laughed and splashed each other. They kissed, muzzled and teased away an hour until the sun stood straight overhead and Mary's nose and cheeks began to turn a warm pink. Then they clambered out and sat on the riverbank to eat.

Mary pulled her skirts up to her knees to dry her legs, then proceeded to arrange the food around them: cold partridge, cheese, bread, peaches and grapes, and moist little honey and walnut tarts. Staff came back with the chilled wine jug and she had just leaned over to slice the bread and cheese when—"Oh, Staff, oh, on my leg! Look! What is that horrible thing? Oh, get it off!"

He bent closer and grasped her knee to look. "It is a black leech, Mary, a bloodsucker. Do not panic, love. Here, do not look. I will get him off."

But she did look as Staff grasped the horrible thing and pulled while a tiny puddle of blood appeared on her leg where it had bitten her. Staff threw the leech off somewhere on the grass behind him. "There, my love. William Stafford, Gentleman Usher of the King, at your service. The leech is dead," he finished grandly.

"Do not dare to laugh at me! I think they are awful. Oh, do you suppose there are more?" she shrieked and pulled her skirts up to mid thigh turning her legs and staring down them wide eyes. "Oh, Staff, look. There is another!"

Again he pulled, then smashed the offender, his eyes on her bare thighs more than what he was doing.

She darted up and began furiously unlacing her skirt from the waist of the bodice while he watched, surprised. "Why did you not tell me those ugly things were in this river?" she scolded as her quick fingers untied her laces. "Sanctuary could be covered. You might be too!"

"I looked when I came out, Mary. They seem to prefer your sweet flesh, and I must say I really cannot blame them. They do not get much blood and no permanent harm is done, you know. I love it when you undress for me, sweetheart, but what exactly *are* you doing?"

She glared at him sitting there, cross-legged with that rakish grin and one eyebrow lifted. "If you were a gentleman, Lord Stafford—I mean, I realize Gentlemen Ushers only take visitors in and out to the king and stand about like dummies at the quintain all day to fetch anyone he wants to see—but I do not have time to go hide in the bushes and you could at least avert your eyes."

Her skirts dropped in a pool around her ankles and she kicked them away, past the waiting circle of untouched food. But the laughter faded from his face when he saw she wore no underskirts or chemise and her bottom under all those brown skirts had been merely covered by a thin, clinging pair of what the stylish French termed *lingerie* and the more plebeian English called panties.

She pivoted slowly for him trying to ignore the look she knew so well which sprang to his eyes and made his bronze skin go taut on his cheeks and chin. "Please look and tell me if you see any more, Staff."

"I warrant I am looking, Mary. But how do you know they are not up under the silk and lace panties there between your legs, love? I know that is where I would hie myself for. Or could they have crawled up under that lovely tight bodice there? If you have as little on under that as under the skirt, the little devils will have a feast."

"All right. If you insist on laughing when I detest those ugly, awful things on me, I shall just go off in the bushes and look for myself."

His big hand seized a slender ankle before she could move. "No, sweet, I shall look. I do not mean to tease. Hold still now."

He knelt beside her. "Relax, Mary. Spread your legs just a little and I will check." His hand crept up between her soft, silken thighs. She twisted her head around and saw he was biting his lower lip. Had he just wiped a huge grin from his face again? Despite her revulsion at the thought of those slimy, black things all over her, her breath caught in her throat when his fingers ran boldly under the lacy hems of the panty legs

458

and traced torturingly along the inner most edge of her thighs.

"Mary," he breathed, but stopped, apparently astounded again as she began to unlace her bodice stays.

"Staff, are there any more?" she asked, her voice shaky. "Could they really have crawled clear up here?"

"Mary, my love," he began slowly, his voice controlled, his hand cupping one full cheek under the silk panties he had pulled awry. "They do not crawl—at all."

"What?"

"They only attach themselves where they can make contact with flesh in the water, and unless one little lucky bastard was clinging to a drop of water we splashed, they could not possibly be much above knee high on you."

Her embarrassment turned the bridge of her nose and her cheeks from pink to scarlet. "Oh. But you— you let me—" she sputtered.

"I really cannot apologize, sweetheart," he said gravely. "I have been on fire for your beautiful body for almost a week now, with little to assuage the flames, and I will be damned if I am going to stop you from disrobing for me."

"For you! And all this time you have been laughing at what a silly fool I have been! Let go of me!"

With his good arm he pulled her flat on his cloak among the spread food and held her down while she thrashed and sputtered. Despite her shame and anger, he skimmed her panties off and finished unlacing her bodice before she too began to giggle, then laugh aloud at the situation.

He bent to kiss her on her flat belly, then traced his slick tongue up across her still-heaving rib cage to the undersides of her full breasts. His hand replaced his darting tongue as he lifted each breast to meet his waiting lips; she drew in a breath and caught her lower lip in her teeth to keep from crying out her excitement as he leisurely nibbled, kissed and pulled on each taut peak of desire.

"Staff, out here on the river bank like this, I think we—"

"Sh, Mary." His hot mouth descended on her parted lips even as he spoke, a kiss that gave as much as it demanded. His tongue darted, probed, caressed until she met his urging in the sweet darkness of her mouth surrendering entirely to him with an utter abandonment of sanity.

Here, naked in the cool, luscious shade pressed to him like this, all her senses thrilled, vitally alive with the touch, taste, and sounds of his fierce lovemaking. His big hands grasped her soft, firm buttocks, pulling her closer, closer to the heat of his loins. She tugged his shirt from his belt in back, her hands racing over his hard muscles there, kneading and slightly digging her nails into him as though they had a life of their own.

"Help me, sweetheart. Undress me and let me finish what we have started," he rasped out as she arched into him, twisting and caressing him through the rough material of his breeks along her smooth hips and thighs.

They sat up swaying, clinging together in the dizziness that swept them deeper into desire. "Yes, my love, here, but if you can touch me all over like that, I hardly think a few clothes should be a problem to you." She was entirely out of breath as she lifted his shirt over his head then, shaking with anticipation, struggled to divest him of his breeches.

His body was so strong, she thought fleetingly before he pulled her down again. Such long legs and powerful thighs. The white bandage across his chest made his hard, flat stomach and muscled upper torso look so brown in contrast. His curly, crisp body hair tapered so perfectly down to his lower belly reaching toward his loins. As if he could read her desires, he pulled her roughly to him and thrust a strong thigh between her legs to open her more to him.

She crushed herself against him full length as they clung together facing each other on their sides. She revelled in the secure but thrilling feel of him like this, pressed so closely to her when she was open and vulnerable to him. She trusted him entirely, as completely as she desired him, she thought. No one could ever hurt them again now. Never!

She began to rain little nibbling kisses along his temple and jawline. She blew and licked into his ear and bit the lobe ever so gently, feeling the rolling shocks of her assault on him in her own loins as fully as she felt his own touches. His hard hands were tracing little, torturing circles of ecstasy all over her and following that assault with tiny bites and kisses. She lifted her hands over her head in the luxury of his touch and felt her little pile of peaches break and roll away.

"The food, Staff, all this food," she murmured incoherently as his fingers between her thighs worked their wicked magic again.

He raised his handsome, passion-glazed face and laughed only once more. "My love, damn the food. I am only starved for you!"

And then, so that he would not hurt his wound, he lifted her astride him. His passion pierced her completely and she loved it as she put her hands on both sides of his head to lean over him while his hot mouth clung to the tips of her full, bobbing breasts so close over him.

Through a mist of flowing desire, one thought returned to her with crystal clarity as he urged her on with fierce, demanding love words: she was in control of this overwhelming love for him today and forever. No one forced her, controlled her, ordered her. She wanted to be here like this with him or under him, on him, meeting his hard thrusts like this always.

In a rush the words broke from her panting lips to mingle with his own. "Oh, Staff, I cannot—I cannot bear more! I want you in me like this so much, even when I just look at you. I love you so. Ah, I—oh, Staff! Please, I—"

The huge sweeping rush of river water and the whole airy weight of azure sky crashed into them at one time, and rolled them over together up and down into a soundless, silky whirlpool. Her liquid limbs, entwined with his, floated in the tidal currents of their love. Together, suspended, they washed up on the shore of a perfect, golden rapture.

Chapter Twenty-Five
February 22, 1530

Whitehall Palace

Mary stood in the gallery with the long sweep of windows fronting the Thames. Her view was partly obstructed by the legs of stonemasons perched on ladders chiseling laboriously at the upper stone facings which dangled from the outside cornices. For three weeks from morning to night they had picked away at the gray stone all over the palace, whatever the weather. They were chiseling elaborate H's and A's entwined with Tudor roses. Some carved the falcon heads of Anne's new badge. His Grace's King-at-Arms had discovered an elaborate pedigree for Anne stretching back to twelfth century England, so by necessity, George and Mary shared the proud new heritage. Anne had declared that their family name was now to be spelled and pronounced Boleyn, a French spelling and much more suited to a future queen of the realm than the plebeian "Bullen" from the rough north country of England. Mary knew her father had been rattled by the name change, though he held his tongue. Indeed, Anne had Thomas, Lord Boleyn, at her beck and call even as she did the king. He had come to see the perverse wisdom of his younger daughter's not bedding with the Tudor stallion, as much as he had seen the wisdom of Mary's place in the royal bed for five productive years.

Mary touched the thick window glass to see if it were cold. It seemed as mild today as it had been the last week. That was fortunate, for Anne and her ladies would take a barge upriver to Westminster to the king's court for a banquet this evening. It could get terribly cold on the river, being rowed from His Grace's court at Westminster or Bridewell to Whitehall, which he had so graciously given Anne for her London residence until the divorce was approved and they could live together.

It must be warm outside despite the gray of the sky, she thought again listlessly, for the workmen do not stamp the ground and snort like noisy cold horses as they do when it is biting. So much change. So much change for the Bullens to become the Boleyns in such a short time.

"My lady, I thought to find you gazing at the river somewhere along here. Does it make you feel closer to her?"

Mary lifted her head to see her maid Nancy wrapped in a woolen shawl, her nose still red from the cold that had plagued her most of the winter. "I was not pining for Catherine this once, truly, Nance, nor for Lord Stafford, though by your look I warrant that you do not believe me. I will see them both tonight. I *do* miss Catherine terribly, but she is better off to be with the Duke and Duchess' Margaret in the lovely royal nursery with a fine tutor. What could I ever give her here when I cannot even afford to clothe myself well? The child can easily, and with pride, wear the Lady Margaret's handed down dresses, but I can hardly inherit my slender sister's cast-off gowns even if they are in the tens of tens.'' She fell into step beside Nancy and they strolled toward the wing where Mary had a chamber and sitting room, within call of Anne's spacious suite.

"Maybe Lord Stafford will bring the sweet lass for a visit again the way he has afore,'' Nancy encouraged.

"Do not worry about me, Nance. I am resigned to it, really I am. I only regret that I cannot afford to keep you well clothed either. Thank God Stephen was so willing to go into service with Lord Stafford. But I *do* fear your sniffles and colds will turn to the blains if we do not care for you better.'' Mary reached over to pull the girl's shawl more tightly around her thin shoulders.

"Do you miss Stephen too, Nance?'' Mary teased, lightly knowing the girl much favored the lad.

"Yes, acourse, lady. But we had best be gettin' on the subject of what you shall be wearin' tonight.''

"It hardly matters, I think. All my gowns are out of style.''

"Lady Rochford!''

Mary turned in the hall in the direction of her name. It was so difficult to become accustomed to her new title.

"Lady Rochford, you have a visitor who craves an audience.'' The messenger was one of Anne's fine new servants, and Mary was not even certain of his name.

"Who is the visitor, sir?''

" 'Tis a Madam Carey, my lady. She is a holy lady and all in gray.''

"Will's sister Eleanor,'' she said aloud. Nance and the messenger both turned to stare at her troubled face.

465

"I will see the lady now. Lead the way, if you please."

Eleanor rose as Mary entered the small room. They embraced stiffly and backed several paces apart.

"Sit, please, Eleanor. I am surprised to see you."

"I must call you Lady Rochford now I understand," came Eleanor's slow voice. "The king has elevated your entire family again; your father to the Earldom of Wiltshire and Lord Privy Seal and your sister, they say, is the Marquise of Pembroke with greatest status in the realm. The Bullens are still very fortunate and—blessed."

I see your informants have not told you that we are now the Boleyns, Mary thought, but she said only, "Please sit, sister. It is kind of you to stop to see me on your way."

"I came specifically to see you, Lady Rochford. Perhaps you never thought to see me again after poor Will died, but now that all the lands are lost to the family, there is something I would ask of you."

"So you know of the loss of my son's inheritance, too. The lands are still in the family in a way, for His Grace gave most of them to my brother and sister after Will died. But the manor at Plashy went to Thomas Cromwell, a new advisor of the king. And the wardship of my son . . ." Her voice trembled but she looked squarely into Eleanor Carey's clear gray eyes, "went to my sister until the boy reaches his majority. So I am sorry, Eleanor, but if you wish funds, you must believe me that I am quite without means, quite destitute."

"I never would have believed it. But your family, your father—do they not support you? Then your influence with the king is gone? Will had known that would happen some day, you know. If he were here today, he could make his way quite alone in His Majesty's good graces."

Mary felt an urge to strike back at this woman she had never thought she would see again, but she did not. In memory of poor Will's delirious calling for the only woman he truly loved as he stood on the dark step of death, well, for that she would hold her tongue.

"The favor is hardly for money, Lady Rochford. I have been a holy sister these many years and have no desire for things of the world. *'Semper transit gloria mundi'* is my motto, and has been since the Careys lost Durham and all that went with it."

"Then, what aid did you think I could lend?"

"There is a struggle in my priory, lady, a very important one. I have worked long to be the prioress of Wilton—you never visited me there with Will, I believe. You were always too tied to the court."

"I never saw Wilton, sister."

"Will knew the importance and influence of Wilton as a priory in its area and it is a rich house—in relics and artifacts, I mean. Will would have told you that."

"Yes."

"There is to be a new appointment—the old abbess is dying and the appointment should be mine. I know in the eyes of God it is meant to be mine!"

"And you had wanted me to ask the king to help you. I am sorry, Eleanor, but I never even speak with him anymore. That is just the way it is. You must believe me."

"Oh, I do believe you. Only, you have the obvious connections yet. Your sister could ask him for you. They say she gets whatever she will have."

"Dresses and palaces, perhaps, but she can hardly

467

tamper with political or church business.''

''But Will said she hated Cardinal Wolsey since he took her first love away. You see, that would attract her to my cause. The great Cardinal Wolsey puts forth his own candidate in competition to me, not that he even knows about me, but the other woman is from his favored abbey at Salisbury. She cares nothing for Wilton and her appointment would be so unfair! For Will's sake, for the Carey children, please say you will aid me!'' Her long fingered hands smoothed her gray skirts over her knees. ''Besides, Lady Rochford, I have heard the Lady Anne, Marquise of Pembroke, does involve herself with things political and still she rides high in his favor. Can you help me?''

''The most I could do is tell my sister, Eleanor. What she or His Grace will do, I cannot say. That much will have to suffice.''

Eleanor Carey breathed an audible sigh of relief. ''That will be of great aid in a righteous cause, I assure you. I knew this chilly trip would be worth it.''

''Will you stay here at Whitehall the night? I am certain it can be arranged.''

''No, I would not wish that. I have long been uncomfortable in secular surroundings. I shall visit with the sisters at the Abbey near Westminster and hurry back to Wilton.''

''I remember you used to stay weeks with us at the court at Greenwich,'' Mary smiled, then wished she had resisted the temptation to goad her.

''Will and I needed time together,'' she returned icily. ''We—he had such fine plans. And now his lands are taken from his son. How strange the king would take a father's lands from his son . . . if the boy is indeed the Carey heir, lady.''

An angry knot twisted in Mary and she gritted her teeth forcing herself not to shout at this cold, gray creature who sat, leaning forward, her stony eyes trying to pierce her thoughts. Mary returned her stare and feared her long pent up anger would show on her face. ''She has hated me ever since her poor brother took me to his bed,'' she thought wildly.

''His Grace and your dear dead brother would both tell you the child is a Carey heir, Sister Eleanor. Henry is raised with His Grace's only son at Hatfield as a companion. My father and Will arranged long ago for the child's education.'' Mary rose, afraid to trust her voice further, afraid to show the contempt which swelled within her. It was like seeing Will again and feeling the frustration and anger she had carried toward his bitterness. Maybe she had idolized Will too much in her mind after his awful death. Yes, Will had never really loved her and his sister's stone-gray eyes brought it all back.

Eleanor Carey stood in a rustle of skirts. She swung her dark full woolen gray pelisse around her shoulders and turned to regard Mary calmly from the doorway. ''I fear I am the last of the Careys with the burden of Will's dream. Do not fail me in this, I pray you, Lady Rochford. Penance can be salvation.''

Mary stood wide-eyed, gripping her fists in helpless tight balls as the door closed behind the woman. All the anger she had buried since Will's death spilled out against Eleanor Carey. She sobbed and beat feebly, futilely on the door. She had never cried like this over his death, hardly cried at all. This release of pent up hatred was the penance of salvation perhaps, her salvation with Staff. Yes, she would ask Anne for the favor, but that would be enough. Then she would be free of the Carey curse of guilt that always lay between her and Staff, even when she felt the comfort of his unquestioning love stronger even than his arms around her.

"Your eyes are red, lady. What did that woman dare to say to you? She has no right to bother you and never did!" Nancy stood up from the bench under the window in their room.

"No, Nance, calm down. I am fine. She only asked me for a favor. The tears are of my own making."

"Well, you had best get them off your cheeks and comb your hair. His Grace is here and quite unannounced." The girl's face glowed at the news.

"Here? Where?"

"In a barge to see the Lady Anne acourse, but the thing is—Lord Stafford is here too. I saw him from the window and *he* hardly came to see the Lady Anne." Nancy came closer and stared intently into her mistress' face. "You do not look too happy at the idea of seein' him, Lady Mary. I cannot understand you. I just do not understand sometimes."

"Of course I will be happy to see Lord Stafford. And if you intend to scold me or try to read my mind, you had best leave me now."

She instantly regretted her words as Nancy wrapped her ever-present shawl tightly about her and flounced from the room. It was hard to hide her emotions from the girl, but she was not at all certain she could face Staff after that interview with Will's sour sister. As ever, Staff would read her thoughts and he would know she had agreed to help Eleanor when she had him

470

nearly convinced she was free of guilt over Will's death. Damn, why had His Grace not waited to see Anne until their appearance at his court tonight?

Mary had hardly bathed her face and dusted her cheeks with rice powder before there came the familiar tap-tap on the door. She smiled and opened it carefully.

"His Grace was longing for his Lady Anne, so I am here. I assure you that if I were the king, the royal barge would have been here at eight of the morning, and not to see the tart-tongued Anne." He bent to kiss her and she yielded her lips coolly. "Not a very warm welcome for such a pretty speech, sweetheart. Are you all right?"

"Of course, only . . ." He might as well know right away and not have to pry it from me, she thought. "Eleanor Carey was just here to ask my aid in getting her the position of prioress of Wilton." She waited, but he said nothing and bit into an apple from the wooden bowl on the table. "I told her I could do no more than to mention it to Anne."

"You should have told her to get what she wants by marrying someone the king favors, as her brother once did. You might have told her I am available for marriage since the lady I favor, evidently does not want me." He laughed with his mouth full and almost choked on his apple.

"She made me remember the unhappy times with Will," Mary plunged on, ignoring his last teasing remark. "She made me think that perhaps you were right—I have been unrealistic about his death."

"Then I thank the lady heartily for her visit." He looked quite serious as he tossed the apple core in the fireplace. "I do not think Anne will give a tinker's damn for who runs the priory at Wilton though. Nor His Grace either. Between the two of them, they are most likely to ruin Wilton along with the rest of the religious houses if the pope's Campeggio and fat Wolsey do not get this divorce rammed through. The queen is gathering her forces and, since the Holy Roman Emperor Charles is her nephew, it will be harder going to get a papal divorcement bill.''

"Actually, Anne may be interested in this, Staff. You see, the other candidate for the post is touted by Wolsey.''

He whistled low. "You are right, sweet, though I am afraid you are getting to think like a courtier. Yes, Anne will go for the bait if she can best Wolsey by it.''

"I really think that is why she wanted Whitehall, Staff. She has ordered the cardinal's hats effaced from all the windows—you know there are hundreds of them—and her initials engraved with His Grace's.''

"I know. We stopped to admire them on the way in. Now, so much for His Grace and the Lady Anne Boleyn. I would know how fares my Lady Mary Bullen when she has not seen her love for two days.'' He pulled her against him, and she willingly rested her head on his chest under his chin, where it fit so perfectly.

"Is Catherine all right, Staff? Have you seen her?''

"I see her for a few minutes almost every afternoon. Her Grace, the Princess Mary, has seen me there more than once and she asks me about you if she has not seen you. She looks at me with those clear, dark eyes and she knows I love you, Mary.''

Mary lifted her head. "You did not tell her so?''

"I did not have to.''

"She once told me that perhaps I could find a way to have the man I would choose to love as she had chosen the duke. Only, I have not found the way. They would all go straight up through the roof of Whitehall or Westminster or wherever, and forbid us to see each other again."

He bent to kiss her nose though she parted her lips in readiness. "Suffice it to say you have found the man, lass. We will yet, and soon, find the way. If they should marry indeed and then have a son, I would ask the king direct. He might be glad enough to have you off their hands, only your sharp sister and her dearest ally Lord Boleyn would never allow it if they caught wind of it. It worries me that if you were sister to the queen, they would think you suited for some foreign dynastic marriage."

"But that would be foolish!"

"Not to them, Mary. Perhaps you are too close to them right now to see how out of touch they are becoming. The people curse Anne in the streets as a bawd, the king's 'Great Whore'. The masses love their true queen. Sweetheart, there is much trouble ahead and sometimes I think the only way to keep you well out of it, is to desert the court, kidnap you to Wivenhoe and ask their forgiveness from there."

"Staff, you would not dare!"

"They would hardly throw us both in The Tower, you know. And would you not like being my prisoner in my little castle? Remember when I played the Sheriff of Nottingham and seized you prisoner in my castle at the masque?"

"Of course, I remember. You brazenly stole a kiss on the night of the performance."

"A poor substitute for what I really wanted to do, lass. But the king was waiting as he may well be now. But tonight I am not on call at his bed chamber, so I will be back; rain, sleet, or hail. Stephen and I will row over as soon as I can get away. See your door is unlocked and you have a warm drink and bed awaiting me." He kissed her hand and released her. "Damn, I nearly forgot. I have a gift for you."

He dug into his small leather pouch and pulled out a long chain dripping with garnets. They looked shiny black against his velvet chest.

"My lord, it is beautiful, but you must not bring me gifts." She looked at him, but made no move to take the necklace.

"You will not accept my money, sweet, nor will you take even a bolt of silk I offer you. I will not have them looking down on you because the Bullens—Boleyns or whatever they call themselves these days—are too damned stingy to see that their Mary, who got them where they are in the first place, is dressed suitably."

He dropped the necklace in a noisy little pile on the table. "Wear it or not, as it pleases you. It belonged to my lady aunt. If you think it is meant to be a bribe for my possession of you tonight or ever, you are wrong. It is a love gift meant to catch the cherry color of your lips in candlelight. I will see you at Westminster tonight. And think to guard your face if you see me with other ladies. Until we decide we shall tell them, I will not have your dangerous sister banish me or separate us somehow on one of her catty whims." He nodded to her, opened the door, and was gone.

She scooped the necklace from the table and examined it in the pale February sunlight. It was a fine piece, square-cut garnets strung along the thin golden links. She would treasure it, and she had hurt him in her heartless acceptance of it. She would let him know how she valued it and his love. She would show him tonight, for she would wear her crimson gown whether or not it was a three-year old style. She would wear it with the golden snare in her hair from Banstead and this garnet necklace from his beloved Wivenhoe.

Mary was grateful that the night was so mild for February, for she had no warm robe or coat to replace the one they had burned after Will had died. She had cherished that robe once, for Staff had first made love to her on it. But that was long ago and this green pelisse would have to do for now.

"Are you warm enough, Mary?" George's face came around her shoulder like a beacon of light in the gray dusk.

"Yes, George, I am fine. How are your other charges?"

"Anne is nervous and my dear wife is as nasty as always. Not that I give a damn, about Jane, I mean. Let Mark Gostwick have her if he wants her. Anne has him sent from court to annoy Jane, but I really do not care what she does. I would not put it past the little bitch to side with the queen against us."

"George, you must not talk like that no matter how much she vexes you. She is your wife," Mary scolded as gently as she could.

Completely misunderstanding, he said only, "She might support the queen's side, Mary. Our own Norfolks have split over it and our foolish aunt dares to champion Catherine's cause. I think though," he lowered his voice though no one could hear them, "the true cause of the rift is that everyone knows dear Uncle Norfolk prefers the hot bed of his children's laundress, Bess Holland, to the icy sheets of his lady wife." George chuckled and Mary spun to face him.

"Then you had not heard the latest family scandal, Mary," George pursued. "Father told Anne and me, and I thought he would have told you."

"I almost never see him, brother, though I know he is as much about Whitehall these days as he is Westminster. He is avoiding me, I think, since I intend to ask him for some financial support and he knows it. I can hardly send to mother. She has only money for household items, and I will not have her pawning jewels for me. Since Will died and His Grace saw fit to give the Carey lands, benefits and the raising of the Carey heir away, I am quite destitute. You might tell him that when you see him, though I warrant he knows it well enough already."

"Mary, I am sorry, truly I am. Anne is too. If I get some extra money dicing, you shall have it." When she did not answer as he had expected, he plunged on, "But you look magnificent tonight, sister, absolutely beautiful as always. The golden net in your hair is fine and the necklace looks new."

"Thank you, George," she said, refusing to give in to his gentle hint for an explanation of her net and garnets.

"I *did* hear though," she said to change the subject, "that the Duke and Duchess of Suffolk are arguing over the situation also. The duke, of course, sides with his friend the king, but I cannot fathom my dear friend the Princess Mary taking Her Grace's part. She has al-

476

ways been a promoter of love matches and she will ruin her happy marriage if she persists in this. I hope this will not mean that little Catherine must be taken from her daughter's nursery."

"Yes, as you say, she will ruin her precious love match. But that marriage was a freak anyway, admit it, Mary. The both of them far gone in mutual love and the lady picks the man she marries! Ha! A rare miracle and not to be believed. And the king's sister and his best friend at that! Most marriages about the royal court are made in hell, not heaven. I can attest well enough to that. Well, I see we are almost there. I had best get back to escorting Anne as His Grace sent me to do, or she will be put out. See you later, Mary."

"Yes, dearest George," she whispered to herself. Poor George, trapped with a woman he detested who would never bear him children while Margot Wyatt played wife to some strange landowner in the north. And poor, bitter Anne still haunted by ghosts she could not exorcise. Mary was certain of it now, for Anne had leapt at the chance to help Eleanor Carey become Prioress of Wilton when she had seized on the thought that it would discomfort Wolsey if the king refused his candidate. To be so eaten by hatred of Wolsey after all these years without her Percy lad. If only Anne truly loved the king now, all this would be so much easier to accept.

Mary rose and walked steadily across the width of the still-rocking barge and from the little party awaiting them, Henry Norris gave her his hand. He looked well, she thought, for a man whose wife had died in childbirth only a few months ago. Anne strode off far ahead toward the palace, her gauzy silver jeweled headpiece floating across her black tresses and winking in the torchlight on the landing. She walked between George and father, the only Boleyns who really mattered anymore. Staff was right. She and mother would never be anything but Bullens despite the royal rain of titles on them. Bullens from Hever and proud of it, thought Mary as she lifted her head and smiled up at Norris.

Mary did as Staff had bid her when she sighted him with the beautifully gowned Cobham wench across the room. She kept a smile on her lips and chatted with her cousin Francis Bryan as the court assembled for dinner. After all, she had Staff's gift around her bare throat and she could feel its metal weight along the swell of her breasts. And tonight he would be in her bed, not in flirty Dorothy Cobham's.

"It is in the wind that there will be another Tudor visit to the court of Francois *du roi* now that the sticky situation with France improves somewhat," Francis was saying. "I have a wager on that the king will take Anne with him. Personally, I think it might be His Grace's plan to test the waters to see if he can get support for the marriage elsewhere in case he does not get aid from Pope Clement."

"Really, Francis," Mary said low as her eyes went over his shoulder to her father, who was in earnest conversation with Anne and George on the royal dais awaiting the king's entry. "I think we had better forget the divorce if His Holiness does not grant it. It may mean Wolsey's utter ruin, but the king can hardly circumvent the pope."

Francis' eyebrows raised in unfeigned surprise. "Then you are less in the council of Anne and your fa-

478

ther than I had imagined."

"What do you mean?"

"The king has a new advisor now to whose dark, sly voice he harkens well. See the short, square man in black by the dais—the one who entered with your father?"

"Yes, I see him. Who is it?"

"Thomas Cromwell, once a clerk, now a wily lawyer. And he will be more—much more. He has been Wolsey's henchman and now he reports directly and only to the king."

"So that is Master Cromwell. The king gave him the manor at Plashy, the Carey manor, you know. But I have never seen him about the king socially. Come, Francis. Do not coddle me. I have been through enough to handle whatever you have to say about the king's Cromwell."

"I know that, sweet Mary. Cromwell counsels that His Grace can have his divorce without the Holy Father's word. All the king has to do, you see," his hand swept through the space between them as if he were brushing a pesky fly away, "is become the head of the English Church in place of the pope, and do whatever he damn pleases about the divorce."

"So that is what he meant to imply about Anne and His Grace ruining Wilton," she breathed, remembering Staff's warning of this afternoon.

"Who implied? And who mentioned Wilton?"

"Someone I used to know, dear Francis. Here comes the king."

"Hail to our next pope," Francis whispered chuckling close to her ear.

Before the blare of trumpets had even died away in

the crowded room, the king had cut a straight course toward the radiant Anne and was slapping George and Thomas Boleyn on their backs in some huge private jest. Then he and Anne began to circulate slowly through the crowd with George and the Duke of Suffolk on either side like stone bulwarks against the press of people.

"I wonder where the duchess is tonight?" Mary observed. "I had hoped she would go up with me to the nursery to see the children."

"Weston told me they are not speaking over the 'King's Great Matter'. They are always such turtle-doves, I would not believe it of them, but they may not even be bedding together. This mess has certainly divided the court and is likely to get worse unless Wolsey can pull off some sort of miracle. It is nice to be related to the Bullens—ah, the Boleyns—in these days, for no one ever asks me how I feel or what I think about it. They assume they already know."

"And do they, my lord Francis?" she inquired sweetly.

"I always keep in mind, my beautiful cousin, that appearances can be deceiving."

"So do I, Francis, though it is a lesson I have learned rather late."

"Do not look now, Mary, but here comes trouble."

"The king with Anne? I did not think she would dare to drag him over here," she said low without turning to look.

"No, lady. I am referring to your father. He looks like the worst winter storm I have seen in a while."

Mary's heart lurched as she pivoted slowly to face Thomas Boleyn. Perhaps I should give him lessons in hiding his feelings from the court, she thought when she caught his grim expression. Had Anne blurted out her plan to help the Carey woman already, and it had unsettled him so?

"Good evening, Francis," her father nodded. "Daughter, I want to speak with you. His Grace is busy and no one dares to sit until he does. Will you walk with me?"

"I think you are poorly informed, father," she returned calmly. "It looks to me that Anne and the king have made as much conversation as they please for now, and will sit to eat. I would be pleased to walk with you now though, if you wish."

"No, no, I must go back then, but I will see you after the meal. See to it that you do not go skipping off to see your child before I talk to you."

"I will be looking forward to our interview, my lord. It is so seldom I am able to find time to see you." She smiled up at him and dared to hold the look while his dark eyes narrowed dangerously.

"You will not be so pert when you hear what I have to say," he threatened low so Francis could not catch his words. Then his head jerked up sharply as the royal trumpet fanfare blared again. "Judas Priest," she heard him say and his face turned ashen. "It cannot be the queen. She would not dare come here where she is not wanted." He darted off toward the dais bobbing and weaving on his swift path through the astounded crowd.

It was indeed Queen Catherine and four of her ladies, all dressed in black like harbingers from hell's gates. The king went red and looked as though he would choke from anger, and Anne's ebony eyes blazed

481

defiance as she held her ground at the king's elbow. The hiss of whispers dulled to a low buzz as the fanfare ceased.

"But she does dare!" Francis Bryan said at Mary's side. "She does dare!"

The queen bowed low to the king, ignoring the haughty cluster of Boleyns and their supporters perched at the king's side on the dais. "I have missed my husband," her clear voice rang out with its unmistakable Spanish accent. "I have missed him sorely and our daughter Mary misses him also." She gathered her heavy skirts and mounted the two steps to the dais. She sank slowly into the huge chair to the right of the king's, where Anne would have sat, and two of her women hastened to arrange her skirts and move the chair closer to the table.

The king stood stockstill, a frozen statue of pent-up rage. He spun his vast back to the hushed crowd and bent low over the gold and silver laden table in front of his wife. If he meant his words to be low enough that no one could hear, he failed utterly.

"Madam," he said distinctly, "you are not bidden here, nor have you been announced."

"But I never see you otherwise, my husband," she returned bravely. Mary's eyes caught Anne's for an instant as they swept the crowd helplessly. Mary read the controlled panic in them.

The king's voice went on, dripping with venom. "The king will see you when he chooses, madam, and he does not choose so now. You have your own household and you may go anywhere you want within it, but . . . not here!" His back shook and his piercing voice seemed to echo off the rafters of the timbered hall.

Mary's nails bit deep into her palms and she was amazed to find herself so torn for this proud queen who had lost the man she had loved and whose desperation made her brave enough to hazard all. Mary tried to summon up her natural sympathy for Anne, but she was bereft of feeling for the slender, dark haired girl who stood so straight between her father and her king. No wonder others risked all for the queen's cause in the face of His Grace's wrath and ruin of their dreams!

There was a grating scrape as the queen slid back her chair and rose unsteadily to her feet. "I was not truly hungry for the feast, my king, just for the sight of you. I will await you in the privy chamber and after you are finished here with your—friends—we shall talk. I shall be waiting." She nodded slowly to the crowd. She looked so tiny on the dais, especially next to His Grace and the clump of Boleyns on his other side, two forces tugging at the power between them.

Queen Catherine descended the dais, and Mary's eyes followed her black-covered head as she exited behind the huge metal screen set to stop the winter drafts. The exit was quite near where she still stood with Francis Bryan, the doorway which lead to the king's privy chamber off the Great Hall.

Everyone sat awkwardly, silently at the head steward's signal and Mary noted the king apologizing profusely to Anne, who suddenly smiled no more. The meal was interminable and Mary could not even catch a glimpse of Staff from where she sat. She and Francis made hushed conversation about everything trivial as did the rest of the feasters until, gratefully, they were released to stream into the long gallery for dancing.

Mary rose and stretched, her eyes quickly scanning

the crowd for Staff and for Norris to whom she had promised the first dance. Before she was even in sight of the doorway, though, her father was at her elbow again. "Let us step into the hall," he said bluntly. "Everyone else is hurrying the other way. They will not miss us for a moment."

"I doubt that they will miss me at all, father," she told him as he propelled her behind the screen into the corridor through which the queen and her ladies had left so dramatically.

"Look, Mary," he began as they stood in the dim hall, "I can understand some bitterness and jealousy that the king will marry Anne, but you have to buck up, girl. Stop this testiness and, well, this disrespect I have sensed lately."

"Anne and I are on the best of terms, father, as are George and I."

"I meant to *me,* Mary, and well you know it. I cannot help it that His Grace saw fit to dole out the Carey lands to others. They were his to give; they are his to take. He leaves little Harry safely with Fitzroy at Hatfield, so be grateful to him. Some people think it means he refuses to let the lad inherit the Carey lands to show that he is not the son of Will Carey. Maybe he will give him more later—royal grants, Mary."

"Whoever says such things is quite mistaken. Harry is Will's son, make no mistake about that, father. If such rumors to the contrary are circulating, I shall set them right."

"If you do, I shall have you out of your sister's good graces on your backside in the street!" He bent menacingly close to her.

"Please understand me, father. I wish I did not have

484

to beg for your money like some poor distant relation, but I am an embarrassment to your fine Boleyn family, if you want to look at it that way. My newest dresses are two years old, and I own no stockings without my maid servant's darning stitches all over them.''

"Let me tell you something else, my girl,'' he interrupted ominously. "I understand that William Stafford much fancies you and rows the murky Thames at night to visit you. See what you can get from him. No doubt a lusty man like that is enough to warm the blood in winter, eh? Will you be foolish enough to get nothing else from him for your sweet services just as you came away from His Grace after five years empty-handed?''

Mindlessly, Mary flung out her hand in the direction of his leering face and felt her palm sting as it struck him. She recoiled instantly and, far down in the depths of her mind, began a silent scream as he threw her back into the wall and her head hit hard. As she started to crumple, his quick hands seized her above the elbows and pinned her flat against the carved wood behind.

"Now listen carefully, Mary. Play the whore for Stafford if you will, for I trust him to be too clever to be caught. I care not about how you amuse yourself. Only, keep your mouth shut about my grandson. Your sister has had the brains and pluck to rise far, and you will not misbehave to harm our chances. You will serve her and our family and do it prettily or you will deal with me. And, as for your wardrobe, Anne went to His Grace with the request that I support you, and so, I shall do so. When Anne becomes queen, you will receive 100 pounds a year. Until then, you will have your new dresses and trinkets from your father's purse. That must satisfy you, girl. And next time you need funds, do not get His Grace involved. See me directly.''

"I never see you directly anymore, father. Please understand that the money—it is not for trinkets. I do not often dine with Anne, you know. The money is for food and candles as well as clothing.''

"Spend it where you will, only be certain to look presentable. We shall have to find you a husband sooner or later and, thanks to your sister, he may be a fine one. If so, you may pay me back then.''

"I think I have already paid you many times over, father,'' she said recklessly, still jammed tightly against the wall. "Loose me, please.'' To her amazement he did so, though she continued to lean against the wall to support her shaking legs.

"Do not think, Mary, just because His Grace bid me support you and I agreed that you are somehow back in his favor. One of the reasons this trial has gone so poorly for him is that the queen's damned lackey Campeggio has been citing the Leviticus exhortation against bedding the sister of one's wife. We can all thank His Grace's lawyers that they have proved what is incest for a brother's widow, as Queen Catherine, does not hold for a concubine as you were. Remember that.''

He leaned one hand on the wall beside her head and bent closer. "I am trying to forgive your terrible actions,'' he ground out. "I know it is difficult to lose a husband and king both and see your sister mount the pinnacle of the realm. Be grateful you have a strong family around you and never—never—dare to strike me again!''

She glared at him. Tears stung her eyelids and began to spill down her cheeks. "I want you to understand,

486

my lord, that I am crying for a little girl who is long dead and who trusted and loved you once. Now she fears and hates you and, oh, God forgive her, she loves you still!'' A sob wracked her body and her shoulders heaved. He stood narrow-eyed staring at the wild display.

"Get hold of yourself, Mary," he finally said quietly. "I cannot stand here while you carry on like this. Anne may have need of me. This has been a horrible night for her with the queen crashing in like that. Think of poor Anne. Dry your eyes and go upstairs to visit your daughter if that would help, but steer clear of His Grace's willful sister if you see her. She has deserted us and the king's side too. I shall send the money over in the morning. Cheer up now. When Anne is queen, there will be many fine dresses for you and little Catherine. You will see."

Unbelieveably, he was gone. Thankful no one was in the hall, she leaned into the linen-fold paneling and sobbed wretchedly, silently until she could hardly breathe. Damn her foolish heart, she loved him through all the hate. Her father was the slayer of happiness. He was a thousand times worse than Francois du Roi who tortured little girls who trusted and loved! She could never face Staff tonight after this. But she loved Staff. There was nowhere to flee but into the circle of his strength.

There was a gentle rustle in the hall and Mary glanced up, horrified through a blinding veil of tears. It was the queen! Mary curtseyed crookedly, her hand for support on the wall. Two of the queen's ladies stood behind her peering around their mistress' angular headpiece with concern on their faces. One was old Lady

Guildford.

"It is the little Bullen girl, Mary, Your Grace."

"*Si*, I know," Queen Catherine's quiet voice floated to her. Mary nearly sank to the floor in utter terror, and the queen's gentle hands rested on her shoulders to raise her. "You must let us help you, my dear. Nothing is worth this many tears. Believe me, I know. Come, come with me. My lord king did not come to me as I asked him, so we were going upstairs. It is all right. I knew he would not come. I only hoped. Is it so with you, my dear?"

Mary nodded wordlessly, afraid she would become hysterical again if she dared to speak. Then she feared that Her Grace would misinterpret her acquiescence.

"Not that I grieve for His Grace, Your Majesty. My father . . . well, my father is very angry with me."

The queen's dark eyes flashed. "And I am very angry with your father, so we are allies, no?"

Mary felt the overwhelming desire to laugh—to laugh and shout at the shock of having the queen be kind to her, a Bullen and a mistress to the king for so long.

They walked slowly down the corridor which ran parallel to the now deserted banquet hall. Lilting murmurs of pipes and drums reverberated through the walls from the dancing gallery beyond. The queen held Mary's hand, and Mary's love flowed out to her in gratitude. If Father could see her now, he would absolutely die of anger, she thought.

"Really, Mary Bullen, you and I have much, much in common. We have both cared for His Grace and lost him. Yes, yes, I know it is true. I blame you for nothing, not for several years now. We both have daughters

488

we adore and they are, of necessity, away from us much, eh? But, then, you . . . you, Mary, have a son, also. We shall talk much while they dance. It is too late for me, but you are young and beautiful and can bear a man many sons." She turned her head away from Mary's rapt gaze. Her dark eyes glistened with unshed tears.

"Shall we stop by the royal nursery to see your little girl and my sweet niece Margaret on the way? They will be happy to see their queen. I think you are too, Lady Mary."

"Yes, Your Grace. It is true. My eyes are glad for the sight of your smile."

"I could tell that, dear Mary. Your feelings are clear on your face. Then we shall sit and talk of our daughters. My loyal sister-in-law will be there. That will be good."

Mary thought of Staff's anxious face as he scanned the dancers to see that she was not there. He would understand when she told him later. Father and Anne would never understand, but then, she would not tell them.

"Yes, Your Grace," Mary smiled at the ponderous black figure at her side. The queen's jeweled crucifix swung from side to side as she walked, and it caught the light from each separate sconce in the long hall. "I would enjoy that very, very much, my queen."

The nursery was ablaze with candles and Princess Mary looked up from a game of child's chess smiling with the two little girls as they entered.

Whitehall Palace

Mary could hear Anne's piercing laughter before the guard even swung wide the door for her. "She screamed for me to bring you, lady," Nancy panted at her elbow as they rushed down the hall. "They are all there and everyone is laughing—just like that." A squeal of raucous delight shredded the air as they entered the mad scene. Anne cavorted, still in her court dress, for they had returned only moments ago from Westminster where a masque had been held for the Lady Anne, Marquise of Pembroke. George and Anne held hands like wild children and whirled around each other leaning back against the spin. Their father laughed aloud at their antics and downed a huge flagon of drink. And Jane Rochford hit at the whirling Anne and George with a down pillow, sending great puffs of fine feathers into the air. Mark Smeaton, Anne's new and very talented lutenist, strummed a quickstep galliard from a sitting position in the middle of a fine polished table.

Mary stood aghast for an instant. She could not

fathom what might have transformed them so quickly from the dour company who had only just left Westminster. Queen Catherine had long since been banished to More House and her retinue cut from hundreds to a mere twelve. Even that glorious occasion for the Boleyns when the king had finally deserted his queen at Windsor to ride off hunting with Anne and George had not caused such an explosion of joy.

"Mary! Mar—eee! Come on! Dance and sing with us!" Anne threw herself at her sister nearly knocking her off balance and hugged her hard.

"Anne—what is all this?" Mary smiled from the pure joy of their exuberance. She had not seen this sort of foolishness since the old days at Hever. "Has the divorce gone through? But surely His Grace would have been more buoyant tonight if that. . . ."

"No, silly goose! The best news yet! We are free. He is dead! The dear, fat, old cardinal is dead—and,"—she reached far over to slap a guzzling George on the back who spilled wine all over himself and came up snorting—"he no doubt stands at the very gates of hell this moment. His Grace has probably heard the delightful news by now. Perhaps he will join us later. If he does," she added, winking conspiratorially at her amused father and grabbing George's goblet from his hand to drink herself, "we shall have a fine masque ready for him, finer by far than the one he gave me tonight."

Anne again threw her arms around the stunned Mary and turned to address them all. "Yes, a masque showing how the very Vicar of Hell who has dared to plague us all these years dies and finds he has been appointed guardian of the jakes of hell. Yes. Perfect. Music, my Mark, music suitable for an entry into hell!''

Mary stood stock still as Anne released her and strode energetically about the room yanking back chairs and her embroidery frame to give them open floor space. Dear Saint George, the girl is serious, Mary thought. The poor old man is dead and her hatred of him still possesses her after all these years. Mary shuddered and felt her father's eyes calm and cold upon her, just watching. He grinned on one side of his taut mouth, but somehow the other side drew down into a grimace.

''Besides the poor cardinal's sad fall and demise, Mary, I think you should know that the cause of all this unabashed delight is that when Wolsey was arrested to be brought back and tried for treason against the state,'' Anne lectured her, suddenly more calm, ''he was arrested by none other than the long lost Harry Percy, Eighth Earl of Northumberland—my once dear love whom the cardinal has abused so badly. If you cannot rejoice for my cause, think of the fact that Wolsey's choice triumphed over poor Eleanor Carey when we had asked to have her be made Prioress of Wilton last year. Think on that rather than Percy if you must, to get into the spirit around here!''

''Anne arranged for Harry Percy to arrest the sick, old cardinal?'' Mary asked her father quietly as Anne turned to chatter to George again.

''No, girl, it just happened,'' he answered low. ''My messengers were waiting here with the news when we returned from Westminster. His Grace no doubt has his own informants on the matter. It was evidently the king who sent Percy to do the dirty work.''

''I can hear every word you are telling Mary, father,

but say on, say on. It is all music to my ears sweeter than dear Mark's well tuned melodies. Can you imagine it, Mary? That old man had fallen so far from his pompous power when he dared to tell me whom I would not wed. I love it! He dared to separate an insignificant lad and lass in love—eventually, that lad arrests him for treason though, coward that he is, he catches a chill and dies on the road to his trial—and the trivial, foolish girl is the next queen!" Her voice rose to a high pitch, and tears of pity flooded Mary's eyes.

"At least you can look happy with the rest of us, Mary. I think I had best make you Cerebus, the terrible dog who guards the gates of hell in this playlet if you cannot look happier than that. The Boleyns are well rid of him, Mary. Harry Percy is justified and His Grace takes me to France—not Catherine. I shall be queen of England and the fat, hateful cardinal shall rot in his grave." She whirled back giving orders to Mark Smeaton while Jane Rochford hovered behind them bending to hear their words.

Thomas Boleyn set down his empty flagon and took Mary's elbow firmly. "I know it is a shock to see her so wild with joy, Mary. I like it not either. I prefer the sleek, calculating little Anne, but this has been pent up in her for a long time and is best exorcised before His Grace sees such a display. He is so openly jealous, he might misinterpret it as still-harbored love for Percy. Go along with the foolishness and maybe she will calm down. I depend on you to be a sobering influence. By the rood, George and Jane are hardly any help to me in that."

"All right, stand over here, Mary. Here. George, do you not think it would be wonderful if father would play

Satan, to pass the final words of condemnation, I mean?"

"Sweet Anne, I hardly think. . . ." Thomas Boleyn began, as George and Anne dissolved into laughter. Mary could not smother a smile at last.

"There, you see, George. I knew Mary would see the fun in the whole situation!" Anne shouted. "Besides, I truly think her sour looks lately are caused by the attentions of a certain handsome man, whose name I shall not mention, to that ravishing Dorothy Cobham."

"Enough of your teasing, Anne." Mary raised her index finger as though to scold a naughty daughter. "I will not have you going on like this."

"See, George, we got her attention at last," Anne giggled. "At least that certain rogue is one man to be trusted by both His Grace and me, so fear not we will send him into exile at his house at wherever it is, sister. He at least, unlike the butcher's son of a cardinal, always knows his place. I am convinced Staff never plans to climb so high as others around the court."

Mary turned fearfully to look at her father. She had worked so hard the past year to do as Staff advised her, so her family would not suspect they were in love. Yet she knew her father had spies, many spies. He had told her in a fit of anger to play the whore for Stafford if she wished. He would never understand their love, so let him think what he wanted. Only Anne was right, too. She was very upset at her lover's avid attentions to the beauteous Dorothy Cobham lately. Tonight at the masque he had gone much too far. Perhaps she was just moping for herself or was hurt by Anne's terrible revenge, but Staff's actions annoyed her just as much as

Anne's tonight.

"All right. Now who in hell shall we get to play Wolsey himself?" Anne asked and laughed uproariously at her own pun.

She seemed on the verge of a crying jag, Mary thought. Her face looked happy, but her glassy eyes and piercing voice gave away an inner desperation.

Before the laughter died away, there was an echoing knock on the door. They all froze like thieves caught with booty. Thomas Boleyn held up his jeweled hand for silence and motioned to the guard to open the door. Mary could see several guards in the hall and Nancy's serious face beyond as she pressed against the wall in the corridor. Yet no one stood at the door to enter. Surely the king would not come to tell the Boleyns the news of the cardinal's death himself. But if he did, Staff might come too. She would like to give him a piece of her mind after his display with Dorothy Cobham tonight! She cared nothing for all of this Wolsey nonsense compared to that.

She heard Jane Rochford's swift intake of breath as a dark-cloaked Thomas Cromwell stepped past her father into the room. His black eyes swept over them all like a bowshot. He bent stiffly to Anne and nodded to Lord Boleyn. "How perfect he will be to play Wolsey in hell if my hysterical sister has the nerve to ask," a small voice in Mary's head told her. If Wolsey had many friends like this viper, no wonder his enemies got him in the end.

"I come with a sad message from His Grace for you, Lady Anne," his voice came distinctly at them. He always spoke in a dull monotone, but people everywhere hung on his words. Even when the meaning was pleasant, his voice dripped venom—and power.

"I hope His Grace is as well as when we left him but an hour ago," Anne's sharp voice answered him.

"His Grace is well and sends his love anew, lady. The news concerns my late master the Cardinal Wolsey whom, as you know, was to be arrested and brought back to London to stand trial." He hesitated. "Do I sense that the tragic news has preceded me, Lady Anne? Perhaps your father's, ah, messengers have told you the news?"

Staff is right, Mary thought. A cold fear bit at her insides, not in concern for her family, but at the fact that this man knew everything. She thanked the good Lord that Thomas Cromwell favored the Boleyn cause.

"We have heard somewhat of the news, I must admit, Master Cromwell, but we would be pleased to have it from your lips. It is good to hear the cardinal so gently remembered by one who worked for him so closely and yet gladly left his service," Anne taunted carefully, just on the edge of accusing Cromwell of traitorous behavior.

"As I have heard you say many times, Lady Anne, we all serve the king here. Am I not correct?" He pivoted his square face slowly and his dark gaze touched each of them in turn properly, politely.

"Have I interrupted some family revel?" he probed again. His thin lips formed a knowing smile.

"Mere amusement and foolishness after too much sitting and drinking all night," came Thomas Boleyn's amused voice. "You understand how it is, Thomas, for you work much too hard yourself lately." Lord Boleyn strode several steps toward the king's advisor and clapped him on the shoulder. "Will you stay the night with us before going back? I am going there myself at dawn."

"I am sorry. I must decline the kind offer and head back. There are plans to be laid for the royal conference with the French king at Calais. And, as we both well know, my friend, there is no duty, task or price too great when one serves the king. No price too great."

Cromwell bowed low to Anne. His eyes, well hooded by his thick brows, swept over Mary appreciatively as they always did when they met or talked. It was as though he had some sort of dire plan for her. She nodded slowly to him and had the strangest impulse to cover her breasts and cross her legs for protection. That was what she always felt near him—the fear that he wanted her, that he undressed her with his piercing eyes. But that was foolish. He would never dare.

"Since I see my news has preceded me, I shall save time and be on my way back to Westminster before high tide. And to your question, Lady Anne, I did serve His Eminence the Cardinal closely and carefully. Indeed, before I came to know His Grace as well as I do now, the wily cardinal taught me everything I know of how to deal with dangerous problems. Good evening to the Boleyn family." He bowed and was gone.

The door shut behind him. " 'S blood, that man can throw a pall on a party faster than anyone I know. I always thank God in my prayers that he is on our side," Anne said quietly. The wild look was gone from her eyes and Mary was silently grateful for that.

"I think we had best remember," Thomas Boleyn said, pouring himself another goblet of dark, red wine, "that Master Cromwell and men like him are on the side of no one but themselves."

It takes such a man to recognize one, Mary almost said, but she held her tongue. She and her lord father had kept a truce of silence since the terrible row they had had at Westminster on the night the queen had rescued her. If the Boleyns had known of the gentle Catherine's kindness to her, and if they had ever guessed how she pitied the poor queen the loss of husband, position, and the right to raise her daughter, she would never have heard the end of it from any of them.

"Well, the masque in hell was a fine idea, anyway, Lady Anne," Jane Rochford put in as she sat back in a velvet chair.

"I only thought His Grace might come himself as he did to tell me I would go to France with him. I thought it might amuse him. Could it be he still harbors some concern for the vicious, dead, old cardinal?"

"Wolsey served the king well and for a great while, Anne," their father said and he sank slowly into the chair next to Jane's. "Again, it would do the Boleyns well to remember that the cardinal also taught His Grace much of what he knows of rule and authority— and ultimate power."

"Ultimate power, father?" Anne giggled and leaned back on her hands on the huge polished table near her now silent lutenist. "Shall I show you ultimate power? I can have the king here at this door, at my bidding in the time it can take some poor simpleton to row the river twice."

"And for what, Anne? What do you give him when he comes?" her father challenged. "Some silly little play about Wolsey? How long before you run out of pretty trinkets and sweet sayings and promises of sons to come? For five years you have dangled maybes and hopes before a starving man. I think . . ."

"You will not lecture me, Earl of Wilton! Earl of Wilton thanks to my power over the king! I would not be queen and merely the second Boleyn mistress if I had listened to your counsels long ago!"

The words stung Mary, but did not seem to faze their father who sat motionless, his goblet perched on the arm of his chair. Mary stood mesmerized at this confrontation between her father and sister. For, although George had told her of the increasing frequency and intensity of their arguments, Mary had never beheld them herself.

"I am wiser, child, and know this king better than you. The miracle is that you have had it your way this long. But I tell you, I have seen him turn on those he loved when it suited him. When his beloved sister Mary wed in France with the duke, he . . ."

"Stop it! No one knows this king better than I, or is closer to his heart. He can never go back on me now. He is committed. He dissolved the church for me and they will all stand behind him, all the men who bow and need his goodwill. *I* go to France to meet with the French king, not Spanish Catherine, his incestuous sister-in-law who rots away in some dusty house in the country! And I will marry him, and I will bear him sons!"

"I pray God that will be the way of it, Anne," he answered and downed his wine. "Now that he cannot go back, I am only counseling that you begin to share his bed before he doubts the sincerity of your promises—and passions."

"And then," came Jane's voice as pointed as her face, "suppose you do not bear His Grace a son as soon as he wills it. Suppose he grows impatient. George and I have no son, so . . .''

"You stay out of this, Jane Rochford!" Anne glared at her sister-in-law who merely shrugged at the words. "You bear no son to my brother because he loves you not, and I doubt if such cattiness as you show would breed anything but cats, or . . . or snakes! I am sorry, George, but it is true.''

Anne paced swiftly to Mary and her slender hand grabbed her sister's wrist in a tight grasp. "Mary bore a son, even as our mother did before us. Our heritage for sons is good, and His Grace knows it well. Maybe Mary's son was even from His Grace, so I have no fear of not bearing him sons. That is the least of my concern right now."

Mary felt the urge to snatch back her arm. Anne's words always hurt and she seemed to have lost all sense of the verbal cruelty she inflicted more and more on those close to her. Staff was right. It was as though some terrible demon seized the girl's tongue at times, as though she feared something. But she knew Staff was wrong about one thing. Surely, Anne did not fear the king's bed the closer she got to him in lawful wedlock. Surely that was what Anne had been striving for all these years.

The slim, raven-haired woman still held her sister's hand although her eyes darted about somewhere past Mary's head, and she said no more. Lord Boleyn motioned George and the stormy-faced Jane to leave. Then he pointed toward the door to the wide-eyed Mark Smeaton who obeyed instantly, tagging behind the Rochfords. Still Mary and Anne stood facing each other and Lord Boleyn's eyes swept carefully over them.

"You do understand? You do believe me, sister?"

Mary could not recall a question. It seemed such an interminable time that they had stood there. Anne's dark brown eyes still gazed into space behind Mary's head. "Yes, of course, Anne. It is all right. Everything will be fine. You are tired now and we had both best go to bed. You are going falconing with the king in the morning, remember? It will be great fun."

"And you are going with me to France and will stay very close, Mary. Promise me. If the French king will not receive me, I must have my own retinue, and a fine one. Father, Mary can have more funds, for dresses, can she not? She must be well dressed to show them that the Boleyns are not an upstart family, father."

Their father moved silently to stand behind Anne. "Yes, of course, Anne. And Mary is right. I shall call your women. You need to go to bed. I did not mean for my words to unsettle you. It is important to us all that you be rested and lovely and happy in the morning."

Anne released Mary's wrist at last and pirouetted to face her father. "Do you think I am lovely, father? Lovely like Mary to hold the king over the years? I know I have not the Howard beauty of mother and Mary, but I shall hold him. I shall!"

"Yes, of course, you shall, my Anne," her father comforted and patted the girl's shoulder awkwardly. "You are of a different beauty than your mother or Mary, but a beauty indeed. And you are clever and talented. After all, you have the greatest king in the world chasing after you. That should end this discussion. Besides, neither your fond mother or your sweet sister have risen to the heights you have. You are the only one who has truly seen the possibilities and acted accordingly. A daughter after my own mold, a Bullen indeed!''

Anne stared at him oddly for a moment and did not answer. Then she turned tiredly, slowly toward her bedroom door. "I wish you to remember that our name is Boleyn now, father, and times have changed. Please go now. Go somewhere and serve your king." Anne gestured to Mary with her right hand. "Please stay, sister. Please stay until I sleep."

Awed at the strange and touching request, Mary followed Anne into her bed chamber without another glance at their father. Anne's bed was huge and square, almost as great in size as His Grace's bed, probably because he had at first expected to share it with his dear Anne when he had granted her vast Whitehall Palace. She hoped Anne would not ask her to sleep here or in call, for it was possible that Staff would pay her chambers a night visit.

Then her own world rushed back to her. Yes, she wanted to be there waiting for Staff. He would not find a sweet, compliant lover breathless for his hurried arrival as he was accustomed. She would show him a true Boleyn temper for his over fond treatment of that Cobham wench, and if he would dare not to come at all, she would know he was with the woman. Her thoughts would take her no further. He was all she had but little Catherine. She would die if he should change his love for her.

"Do not be so grim, Mary. I do not know where our festive mood went so fast. It was that viper Cromwell ruined it all. I really meant to put on our own family revel in honor of the cardinal's leave taking of us all.

My prayers are continually answered, it seems. Cromwell would have made a fine Satan, you know. I would like to talk Henry into getting rid of that little, shifty-eyed man.''

''I think you had best not dabble in the king's power when it comes to Cromwell. Besides, father likes him.''

''And is that your recommendation for the man, sister, that father likes him?'' Anne teased. They both smiled as Mary helped Anne shrug out of her tight satin bodice. ''Rather a condemnation, I would think. I know you agree with me now on how to handle father. We shall be great allies in France.''

Anne lifted the covers and got in ignoring the hairbrush Mary would have used on her long tresses. She pulled the covers up to her chin like she used to do when she was a little girl to ward off night goblins outside the comforting stone walls of Hever. Mary felt suddenly touched and she cherished the feeling since she had been so often angry with Anne's growing petulance these last months. She opened her mouth to say something comforting and wise, but she was not sure what would do. If she could only think of something their mother might say now.

''Mary, forgive me, but I would ask you a question—a personal one.''

''Yes, Anne.''

''Will you tell me truly and not be angry?''

''Yes. I promise.'' Unless you would ask of my love for Staff, little sister, Mary thought. But she smiled and crossed her heart the way they used to do when they had some deep secret to share.

Anne smiled up from her ivory silk pillow suddenly radiant. ''I had forgotten that, Mary. How silly we were then. What I wondered was whether His Grace is very demanding when he . . . when he possesses a woman's body.'' Her smile faded from her lips and she sat bolt upright clutching the sheet to her small breasts and leaning close to Mary. ''You see, Mary, he has begun to make love to me many times and he is so strong and big. I mean, not just in kisses and caresses, but he has pulled my dresses down to my waist and feasted his eyes and hands and mouth. And then, too, he nearly took me standing once and lifted all my skirts and yanked off his huge codpiece and would have . . . have gone inside me right there had I not become hysterical from fear, and he thought he was hurting me and he apologized all over himself for at least half an hour. And then, lately, if I sit on his lap, he puts his hands up between my legs and strokes and probes and I have to pretend I like it, Mary. Please tell me if he is gentle when it comes to it. I seem so very small and he is so . . . so big, Mary.''

Her wide eyes glistened with unshed tears, and Mary's love went out to her. She felt deep shock that this little sister, this Anne she had known to flirt and tease and scream like a fishwife at a man, could know fear. But then, somewhere inside, there must still be the little girl with all the questions.

''Anne, Anne, it will be all right. Yes, everything will be all right. The king loves you and it is obvious to anyone who sees him with you.''

''But there are things they do not see, Mary. It becomes harder and harder to hold him at bay.''

''You have said you are certain of his love and that he is yours indeed now and would never go back on that.''

"Yes, I said that."

"Then he will marry you as soon as he is able. He is ridden hard by the passions you stir in him, Anne. You cannot blame him or fear him for that."

"Why cannot he not control himself as I can?"

"Foolish little Anne. His Grace is a man—the most powerful man in the world perhaps." In the momentary silence Mary beat down the memory of herself in Francois' demanding arms so long ago, entranced, ensnared, but frightened. "He is hardly used to waiting for anything he wants, Annie."

"Is childbirth so terrible then?"

"Are you . . . but you have not?"

"No, Mary, I said no. Only I know children will come if I submit to him. You screamed horribly for hours when you bore little Harry at Hever."

"I had forgotten, truly, Anne. The joy of a child is so great that after, well, after the pain and troubles, the thought of the bad part goes away. You will see."

"Yes, I suppose so. Well, it must be done." She pulled back slowly from her closeness to Mary. "Father is right, I fear, though I do not like to hear it from him. His Grace needs something extra from me romantically now. The dreadful divorce and all this nasty business with dissolving the pope's wretched church is depressing him more and more. He cannot see the happy end of the road as clearly as he used to."

"The forest for the trees," Mary thought aloud.

"Yes. Exactly. I must sleep now. We are going to fly my new gerfalcon in the morning. He can hardly rape me with our falcons on the wing, you know." Anne smiled impudently and Mary returned the look warmly.

505

"Fear not, little sister. 'The dark outside the window is never so dark when you go out,' dear old Semmonet would say if she were here. I tell you true, Anne, when His Grace gets right down to possession, he makes short work of it. That can have its rewards, but then it can mean tragedy too—if you love him."

"Of course I love His Grace, sister," Anne returned heatedly.

That sounded more like the new Anne. The mood of intimacy and warmth was broken. Mary rose slowly.

"Mary," Anne's voice floated to her as she blew out the cresset lamp and moved toward the door. "You were not speaking of love for this king just then, were you—about love having its rewards? Nor Will, I warrant."

"Please, Anne, let it be."

"But will you tell me some time what true passionate love is like? To really feel the desire to lie with a man?"

Mary felt stunned anew. Anne had lived all those years in the bawdy French court a virgin and now kept private company with Henry Tudor as she had with Harry Percy in secret, and still sounded like an ignorant child. "It will come, Anne," Mary said quietly, framed in the light of the doorway. "You will come to know all the answers and joys when you wed with His Grace and bear his children." Liar, Mary thought to herself, liar, tell her now. She hesitated to turn back into the room, and a large black form of a man blocked her path in the dimness and shot his arm around her waist. She gasped and her heart crashed against her ribs.

"I am sorry I gave you a start, girl. I wanted to make certain you had settled her down. I am proud of the ad-

506

vice you gave her. It will help," her father said quietly in her ear. She relaxed against his arm, and he squeezed her gently. How different this was of him, the caress, the gentle thanks.

"We must keep her calm. She panics the closer she gets to consummating her bargain with His Grace," he went on. He released her waist as though he was surprised he still held her against him. He motioned her silently toward the hall.

"I will send Lucinda Ashton in case you need anything, Anne," Mary turned to call back. "Good night."

There was no answer. Her father closed the door quietly behind them. His eyes searched Mary's face, and she stood still under his scrutiny. "I was thinking tonight how much you look like your mother when I first knew her, Mary. Would that Anne's wily little brain had your beautiful wrapping."

"I do not care for the implication that I am nothing but pretty wrapping, father. There is a thinking person in here, too."

"I did not mean it that way. I know that only too well, but I meant that you are more gentle, yet wayward from the cause lately too."

She felt her anger rise. "The cause? I assume you mean the Boleyn cause. I have not heard that phrase since Will died and left his precious Carey cause undone."

"Do not get your hackles up. I would have us be much closer than we have been these last few years, Mary. You are so good with Anne and I appreciate it."

"You mean, of course, that you would like to use me to keep her in line."

"Damn it, Mary. Can we not have a civil conversation? She needs your quiet influence. That is what I meant."

"To this lofty point on the ladder, father, you and Anne have done quite well without me. I see you so infrequently that I hardly feel I know you as a person, only as some powerful force pulling this way, pushing another."

He stared at her tight-lipped and the avid look in his eyes hardened.

"By the way," she plunged on, "am I to assume that you stood at the door while Anne got undressed and then listened to all the private things we had to say to each other?"

"That is enough. You are exhausted and testy, so you can take to your bed too. And you are accompanying your sister to France when she goes. I will not have your denial of that obligation."

She turned away and started toward her room. The hall was deserted except for the usual sentries who stood stonelike as though they heard nothing on either side of Anne's door. "Obligation? It will be an honor and I shall go gladly, but only because my sister asked me to go, father. It has nothing to do with your ordering me to do so. Goodnight."

She turned the corner in a rustle of skirts and breathed a sigh of relief. She was exhausted and drained. At least he had not dared to scream at her or shake her. If he thought a little hug would bribe her to start trusting him again, he was a fool. Yes, Anne did have more brains than she did, for Anne had learned to distrust their father far younger than her older, blind sister Mary.

She pulled the latch on the door to her chamber expecting to find Nancy dozing by the fire, but the girl was not in sight. Indeed it was late, but it was not like her to leave before her mistress was safe abed. She sighed and shot the bolt. She stretched her hands to the low flames at the hearth. The fire took the chill from the brisk October night, but not from her thoughts. Then something moved in the dark.

"I was about ready to fetch you myself even if I had to tangle with your father and Cromwell." He sat up on her bed. His shirt was open to his waist and his eyes glowed strangely golden in the firelight.

"Staff!"

"Were you expecting someone else?"

"That is not funny."

"I would have joined you when I first arrived, but I hesitated to interrupt the Boleyn revels at the happy news of Wolsey's death," he went on.

"It made me sick to see them cavorting around like that," she admitted. "Anne was absolutely jubilant. But I imagine you were having your own revels tonight, since you mention it."

"I hardly hated the old man the way your sister and father did."

"I meant with sweet, cow-eyed Dorothy Cobham, of course."

He swung his long legs over the side of the bed and sauntered toward her. "Oh, of course, especially since I have loved Dorothy Cobham for some ten years now and visit her bed in Whitehall whenever I can, despite the danger and the damned cold weather," he mocked. He bent to kiss her and she turned swiftly sideways to him evading his mouth and hands.

"I know full well of your attentions to her. Everyone could see at the masque—the public nuzzling, the hand holding, her rude giggles which everyone heard."

"I have no doubts your sister embellished the details well for you on the barge on your way back tonight. Perhaps since the grand Lady Anne was watching me so closely tonight I allowed Dorothy to put on a show for her." Mary bit her lower lip guiltily and was glad it was too dim for him to see her face clearly.

"Or did your father tell you how I spent the afternoon riding with His Grace and that Dorothy was one of the women who went along? Well, whoever told you, I am pleased to have you jealous." His hands crept to her waist.

"I am not jealous of that little twit." She pulled from his grasp.

"What happened in Anne's room tonight? Did they say something to hurt you?" he inquired.

"No more than usual, and I am pleased to say I handled my father rather well. He had more plans for me, you see."

His voice came taut and hard in the low dancing firelight. "Like what?"

"To keep Anne calm and to accompany her to France."

"Is that all?"

"Yes."

"I thought you meant with His Grace or a marriage. The trip to France will be fun. I am going too."

"And that is supposed to make it fun for me, or did you mean for yourself? Is little Dorothy going along? You surely do not think I relish seeing you fawning all over her whether in France or here, do you?"

"That is quite enough of this foolishness and your temper, sweetheart. The wind on the river was cold and I have missed you."

She walked over to the table and sloshed wine in a goblet. "Did you hitch a ride with that dark raven Cromwell?"

"I would not ride with Cromwell if my life depended on it, lass. I will not have him know I visit here, though the man seems to breed spies and might know already. While I am in His Grace's favor, I fear him not. Did Cromwell say anything to you?"

"About what?"

"About anything personal. I can tell by the way he looks you over every time he lays eyes on you he desires you, though I cannot blame him there."

"Desires me? You think so?"

"Yes. The man would like to have you in every sense of the term, love, though I give him more credit than to actually ask for you as some sort of reward from your father or the king. He is clever. He does not openly covet advancement the way others have. Poor Wolsey's riches pulled him into the mire as much as this damned divorce or the Boleyns."

She felt icy at the thought of Cromwell's eyes on her, so coldly, so completely. She drank her wine. "Did you send Nancy to bed?" she inquired while pouring another glass of wine.

"No. I told her where Stephen was awaiting me, and she went down to see him. She misses him. We really ought to find a way to merge our two meagre households so they could be together." His arms came around her from behind and he nuzzled her neck.

"I do not intend to be so easy for you when you are

so sweet on that Cobham wench," she said evenly.

"And I do not intend to take long rides on the cold Thames and be turned out of the bed of the woman I love," he returned, and his arms tightened.

"You may have the bed. I shall sleep elsewhere."

He turned her to him. "My temper is right on the edge, sweet. You have seldom seen my temper and you would not like it. Turn around and I will unlace you."

She began to tremble at his tone, but she was angry. What right did he have to order her into bed with him? Anne was lying down the hall thinking that William Stafford was the fondest, gentlest lover. And her father still meant to use her for whatever suited his desires. Play the whore for Stafford if you must, he had told her once. She did not belong to any of them to order around like this!

She felt his hands on the laces at her back and she pushed out hard against him. Startled, he dropped his arms, and she darted from his grasp toward the fireplace. She was instantly grabbed off her feet and plopped down on her back in a tumble of skirts and her own loosed hair.

"Take your hands off," she began, but he turned her face down into the pillows and she felt his hands on her back again. She kicked but there was nothing to kick but her voluminous skirts.

He pulled her up to a kneeling position on the bed face to face with him and kissed her hard. She fought to turn her head away, but he lifted a hand and held her chin still.

"Maybe you will like it rough, love. Then we could have tussles like this frequently. You have never really seen me this way, but you are asking for rape. Will you

512

settle down now and give me the sweet caresses I was dreaming of all the way to this blasted place in that rocky boat, or shall I just do things any way I will? The prospect excites the hell out of me. Your body is so beautiful and so inviting. I can understand Cromwell's tortured lust for you.''

He held her to him so close that their noses touched and his dark brown eyes gleamed with tiny flickers in each. His warm breath caressed her parted lips. He would not dare force her here at Whitehall with people all around and her sister's guards within shouting distance. Everyone would find out about them then, and he would never allow that. He was bluffing.

She shoved out hard against him, and it was the last thing she could remember consciously doing for a long while after. She tried to resist at first, but everything happened so fast. He had pulled her skirts off over her head in an instant while she tried to flail and kick. When she righted herself, he was naked and she tried to dart backwards away from him on the narrow bed. But then he had one big hand over both of her crossed wrists and he slid her toward him. Her chemise rode up to her hips and she kicked out at him when he tried to raise its hem.

"Wildcat," he said low and she felt her first stab of real fear as he slowly tore the thin material from her body in one long rip. She found herself flat on her back with her arms up over her head and pinned there with his left hand while his lips descended to her mouth, her neck, her shoulder, her taut nipples, her stomach and lower.

"No, no, please," she started to plead, but he silenced her with a searing kiss. And she had thought

Anne foolish to be afraid of the bed of a man she said she loved!

She bent her knees tight together to try to ward him off, but he suddenly seized and parted her legs with his hands and raised her ankles to his shoulders while he sat on his haunches staring down at her with flaming eyes. He gave a low chuckle and bent slightly over her with her legs locked against his chest and her hips nearly in his lap. Her hands and arms were useless. She felt his hardness probing her thighs and she tried to squirm sideways. He pushed himself inside her moist warmth and the depth to which he went seemed incredible.

"Wiggle all you want to now, love," he murmured, as he rocked rhythmically against her. She tried desperately to hold herself taut and unwilling against his lean body, but all she felt in place of the ebbing anger was a slow, building ecstasy at every touch and look. He spread her legs wide and came down against her full length whispering, "I love you, I love you, I love you" hot in her ear. Her arms stole around his neck, and she held him to her in their mutual thrusts.

When it all ended, her cheek was tight against his and her lips rested in the short hair at his temple. She began to laugh, happily, crazily against him, and her body shook under his heavy warmth.

"What is it, my dearest love?" he said low.

"It is not only you who are too strong for me, my Staff. It is my love for you."

He kissed her gently, lingeringly, his mouth slanted open across hers and his breath still ragged and hot.

This was the one man in the whole world she wanted to possess her, to use her, she thought deep in the swirling mists of her emotions. But the difference was

514

she chose to have it so.

As soon as he stopped kissing her, she would tell him. She would tell him of her love and that she would choose to wed him as he asked whenever he would have her.

Chapter Twenty-Seven
October 24, 1532

Calais Castle

Although the quaint coastal town of Calais, France
was wrapped in clear blue skies and sunny days that
October, inside the great white castle on the cliffs the
weather was sharp and dark. Anne Boleyn raged and
stormed for almost an entire week at what she termed
the greatest effront and most cruel desertion she had
ever had to bear. Her ladies cowered or fumed beneath
her nasty temper or, if they secretly yet championed
Queen Catherine, they smirked behind their hands.
None dared to walk within the boundaries of Anne's
thundering wrath—no one but her sister Mary who understood full well the agonies of politics when they
clashed with the agonies of a woman's heart and pride.

"How dare they? How dare they?" Anne repeated
for the hundredth time in the five days since Henry Tudor and the men of his English retinue had ridden off to
hunt and carouse with the French king's all-male entourage. "I shall be Queen of England and we shall see
then if they dare to snub me the next time we meet! I
will have the French in the dust at my feet for this!"

"Anne," Mary's voice came low in the lull of passion, "Francois' new Queen Eleanor is Queen Catherine's niece. She dare not welcome you for her family pride. Despite it all, you can see that."

"Francois should have made her come here to greet us. And that is no reason his too fond sister Marguerite should not have come in the queen's place. Does Marguerite grow so bold now that she is Queen of Navarre? She knew me when I was here. She loves Francois far better than any queen of his anyway. And to think I read her damned bawdy book to discuss it with her!"

Anne flounced by Mary and her full skirts swished as she turned to pace again. "The wily French never sent Henry word that there would be no ladies of their court to visit us in this—this prison. I have a good nerve to throw all my trunks of new gowns off the castle parapet and let the fish wear them. Then Henry would know how much this meant to me, and he will be sorry!"

She was past tears now and stared sullen eyed at Mary. Mark Smeaton had long ceased his gentle strumming on his lute as the tirade swelled, broke, and passed into a hushed stillness. They sat, as they had these last long days, in Anne's fine bedroom perfectly transported over the English Channel from Whitehall for her comfort, and some thought, for the king's too. Her woven tapestries of Roman goddesses graced the stone walls of ancient Calais Castle and the flowered plush carpet stretched from hearth to bedstead. Draped in ermine and gold, the coverlet of the massive eight foot square bed bore Anne's new falcon and rose crest. The polished furniture and golden plate in the chamber seemed to dance with hidden light within while the wall sconces had burned tapers lent a soft glow to the entire scene.

"I would ordinarily be the last one to say this, Anne, but I think you would do best to heed father's last whispered words to you."

"Oh? What? 'Buck up girl and smile His Grace all the way out the door as he goes to meet Francois'?"

"Yes. And to have this huge place elaborately decked and ready to entertain your two kings when they return from the hunt and the conferences."

"Conferences! Pooh! They are having the time of their lives—probably dancing, gambling, and having bawdy masques every night besides fine hunting in the French forests just outside the English pale where we cannot follow. Do not forget I knew Francois too, Mary. His idea of a great amusement is to go in disguise to some little fishing village or vineyard-decked hamlet—I am certain little Calais which lies below the cliffs would do quite well—and throw eggs at the men and rape the women. There! Did you know that of France's precious *du roi*?"

"He told me something of the kind once about some little wine town across the Loire valley from Amboise. He could not remember the name of the place but said he would have to go back again some day."

"He could not even remember the name of the place! How like him, Mary." A tiny smile crept to Anne's pouting lips and Mary found the courage to smile back.

"He shall probably not remember my name either, Anne. But my pride for such treatment has gone long ago. I cannot say I miss any of it."

Anne regarded her sister sideways through her black lashes. "And I cannot say I fully believe you, Mary, though I know your thoughts are hardly on the lusty

French king. 'Tis more like you miss your Stafford.''

Mary kept her tongue. She had learned weeks ago to refuse to rise to the tease as she too often had, and lately Anne had taken to amusing herself by wondering aloud in Mary's hearing how true passion would feel on the body and the heart.

"Well, so much for that topic. You are as testy as I am, Mary, only you have the sweet disposition and you choose to suffer in silence. You are right to spout father's fine advice to me like a dutiful daughter, and I shall be a dutiful daughter in return. I have won His Grace and others before and I shall do it again. They are only men. When they clatter up the winding road to the postern gate and see what awaits them, they will curse the day they deserted the next queen of England to ride sweaty and dirty after boar or deer or the sluts in some French village. They will find far lustier game here.'' She motioned impatiently to Smeaton who immediately broke into a romping galliard tune. Her dark eyes dancing with plans, she flounced out her skirts and began to pace again in little quick circles around Mary's chair.

"Listen well now, Mary. I need your help. I could not possibly stand Jane's simpering face right now, and some of the others are not to be trusted. I may have Catherine's—I mean the newly declared Duchess of Wales's—royal jewels in my coffers now, but she still has some of their hearts and well I know it. Now, we will have the most elaborate banquet this old place has ever seen—hundreds of French delicacies and some English. I shall visit the kitchens myself to see that the French dishes are prepared properly. You could check those too, Mary, for you ate at Francois' royal banquets as long as I. We will have dancing, masked I think, and a wonderful mime, maybe some charades. Yes, how appropriate. Something about the loving French and English relations, though that is a wretched lie. Some mimes from mythology. I know! We can hang these tapestries in the banquet hall instead of the silver and gold arras which are there now—we shall use those for table cloths—and put on mimes of every tapestry scene!''

"It sounds wonderful, Anne. I will help you anyway I can."

"In anyway? Remember you said that, Mary." Anne whirled and clapped her hands together once. "Can you see it all now, Mary? A feast and fun, yes, but revenge pure and simple on all of them, not the least on their foolish women who choose to let their French lords go gallivanting off to visit the English king's latest concubine. We shall show them."

Mary stood to stop Anne's nervous pacing. She took a step into her swirling path and touched her sister's slender arm. "Just what kind of revenge are you thinking of, Anne? It is one thing that they will miss the festivities and the chance to meet the English king and his future wife—that loss shall be theirs whether they know it or not—but you seem to be implying another."

Anne smiled devastatingly at her taller sister. "You had best get the ladies assembled for rehearsals for the mimes, Mary, while I care for the other orders. Do not concern yourself now with the minute details."

Mary's fingers tightened slightly on Anne's arm. "Anne, I think you had better tell me what you are thinking. There is something you have not said, of revenge, I think. I can see it in your eyes."

"Can you, sister? I thought I was rather good at hiding what I would hide. Then I shall tell you since you have no way of stopping me. The sweetest revenge shall be this. Let the pious ladies of this fair realm stay away from contact with the English King's Great Whore! Oh yes, I know what they are thinking now they do not come as they are bidden. Their husbands and sons will all go back to them awed and humbled by their evening here with Anne Boleyn—and they will all go back having been quite unfaithful to their pious little snobs." Her voice broke in anger. Smeaton had long given up playing and sat stock still listening to their heated exchange.

"You had best consider this again, Anne. You are starting to sound like you are opening a brothel. His Grace will never permit it."

"Which His Grace, Mary? Well enough you know that Francois' court has no scruples about a quick conquest of any lovely, willing lady, and I have brought enough of those—single and beautiful women with dazzling dresses. Add that to wine, dancing and a man away from his home and wife and we shall see." She yanked her arm from Mary's grasp and began her rapid pacing again.

"As for Their Graces, sister," Anne went on with an increasingly sharp edge on her voice, "you and I shall see to them personally. How perfect—it will certainly amuse father. Two kings in bed with two Boleyns at the same time, though maybe not in the same place." She smothered a giggle.

Mary felt a stab of hurt deep inside, but the great waves of disgust overwhelmed that pain. "Anne, how dare you think and talk so to me. Seduce your king if you will. Heaven knows he has wanted you long enough and has done overmuch to earn your love, but I shall have no part of Francois!''

''Do not speak to me that way, Mary. He is your old lover—oh, yes, I knew of it at the time though I was young and pondered it and wondered ever since. He must be magnificent in bed. You have no one now but William Stafford, and he is so obviously beneath you that I cannot believe that affair is serious. Francois is the king, Mary, and he deserves to be humbled. It can be your revenge for his casual handling of you. Think of the fun we shall have together laughing about it after.''

''Your anger and fears have gotten the best of you, Anne. You should rest and I will see to the plans for the banquet.'' Mary fought an urge to reach out and shake the girl, but she was obviously sick and distraught— poisoned by revenge. Wolsey's death and Catherine's fall had not yet appeased her. ''Please, Anne, sit and I will call Lady Guildford.''

''I do not want that old watchdog here! She is still loyal to the Spanish princess. And do not patronize me, Mary. I know father thinks you are here to watch me, to calm me as if I am not responsible for myself. Well, I am responsible for the rise of the Boleyns and you had best not forget it! Both you and father must do what I say now, for I shall soon be queen and you must do what I say then. Be gone and see you hold your tongue about my plans. And that goes for you too, my lovely lutenist. You are much too much of a gossiper.''

She patted his cheek and spun away. The smooth faced Smeaton gazed up at her slim back adoringly. ''Yes, my dear Lady Anne,'' he said only.

"Go on, Mary," Anne prodded with her hands, then pressed them to her slim hips through her voluminous yellow skirts. "I will have no more of your lectures. You are hardly one to warn me of traps and indiscretions, sister."

It was like a final slap across the face. Mary almost feared her, feared for them all. She turned swiftly as tears stung her eyes. If only Staff were here, but he was off riding at the king's elbow somewhere. She nearly tripped as she hurried from Anne's sumptuous chamber. She threw herself down on the narrow bed in her own small room, but the tears she thought would overwhelm her would not come. She kept thinking over and over how strange it was to wish for father to be here to stop this revenge-ridden foolishness, this mad precipice to which the laughing Anne pulled them all.

As the messenger had promised, the kings and their men rode into Calais before dinner on the next day. The watchmen had shouted their arrival throughout the waiting palace as the Lady Anne had bidden and the well-rehearsed ladies scurried to their appointed stations along the great staircase rising from the courtyard. Mary had kept to her room during most of the hurried preparations, and it had only been in the last hours of the frantic practices for the evening's mimes that Anne had insisted Mary join the others. Mary could tell by the ominous narrowing of Anne's almond shaped eyes that she was angry with her older sister. Let her know how I feel, Mary had thought vehemently, as she had walked through her given parts in the tableaus of Greek and Roman scenes. Now perhaps Anne would drop her crazed plans or at least leave her well out of it. Mary smoothed her lavender skirts which rustled in the still October breeze on the cliffs of Calais. Her eyes quickly scanned the laughing bunches of men for Staff.

Anne swept down the center of the steps in her stunning striped dress of Tudor green and white with white puffed sleeves and slashings of glittering gold. She walked under a green-boughed arch at the bottom of the staircase and bowed low to the beaming English king and the wide-eyed Francois du Roi. Mary squinted into the sun and spotted George just dismounting. There was Norris and Weston and—yes, there he was standing beside her cousin Francis Bryan and not looking her way at all. Then the king's dark raven Cromwell blocked her view of Staff as he dismounted, and she silently cursed the king for dragging that man along to always hover nearby and stare.

Whatever pretty snares Anne was weaving for the two tall monarchs, they looked well pleased to be stepping wide eyed into them. Now as the men streamed up the stairs, the English women joined them taking a proffered arm here, bestowing a kiss there, and laughing, laughing. At least Anne had allowed the women who were married to men of His Grace's court to walk with them, Mary noted grimly. She would wait for Staff to come by and take his arm no matter what they thought if she lagged that far back. She stiffened her knees to stop their trembling as Anne approached holding on to both the kings, Tudor and Valois. Francois had aged and the magnificent physique had faded. She had heard he had been to war and held a prisoner, but there was so much change in so little time. Still the face was the same—and the piercing eyes which bored into Anne's dazzling smile. He was speaking to them. His fine French floated to Mary's ears: ". . . so as I say, Mademoiselle de Boleyn, my advice to my dearest brother Henri du Roi was to wed now and then—*voila!*—see what the Pope and Charles of Spain will do afterwards, *oui*, Henri?"

Mary moved back a step in the cluster of silken skirts about her and curtseyed low with the rest. She kept her eyes on her sister's golden slippers as Anne lifted her emerald skirts and they climbed the stairs. Anne's tiny feet halted.

"You do remember my dearest sister, Marie, Your Grace?" she heard Anne's lilting voice say in flawless French. "She is a widow now, and I am pleased to bring her back to see you again as one of my ladies *d' honneur*."

There was a silence and Mary stood unwillingly, her long nails biting into the palms of her hands.

"But of course, the beautiful, golden Marie. How wonderfully these twelve years grace your face and form since I saw you last, Marie."

Mary swept him another low curtsey, but she could not force a smile to her face. Henry Tudor cleared his throat and tugged gently on Anne's arm behind Francois.

"My sister has been anxious to see her French king again," Anne added directly at Francois. "Tonight, after you are rested, you will see much of each other." She lifted her foot to the next step as Henry Tudor began to recount for her the skills of the two kings on their fine hunt.

"Charmed, *ma* Marie, charmed," Francois *du Roi* repeated as he turned away from Mary and went on up

525

the vast stairs.

Mary loosened her fists. She could have killed Anne. What possessed her to embarrass her, to hurt her like that? She should have believed Staff as usual and not defended Anne to him. The girl was dangerous and her whims were to be feared. She would never argue with him on that point again.

Mary could see Staff now and she held her ground although he was still far down the steps and most of the English women had attached themselves and climbed to the reception in the Great Hall. In her room she had hidden brief notes to both Staff and her father in case she had not chance to explain to them exactly what Anne intended in the way of final entertainment for the French flies in her fine spider's web of revenge. If she had to send someone else to fetch the notes, there were only two she thought she could trust.

She smiled to acknowledge George's hello to her as he hurried up the steps in a crowd. His Jane had already draped herself on the arm of a much improved Rene de Brosse who, Mary remembered uncomfortably, had tried to undress her one afternoon at Amboise. At least George could not care less what Jane did, Mary reminded herself. He might even approve of Anne's plan for massive seduction if it meant Jane would bed elsewhere. She turned to scan the remaining men for Staff again and saw her father making straight for her.

"Mary, walk with me. Did Francois remember you after all this time?"

Her voice went instantly cold. She suddenly feared father would not rescue her from the dire plan if she told him of it. "Yes, father. But he is much changed."

"Well, of course. So are we all, Mary, and you

would be the first to tell me so. But now, to it—how did Anne snap back so well after her temper tantrum when she heard there was to be no visit from the queen's court? She looks fabulous and she is spouting enticing plans for the evening. Do I have you to thank for her fortunate recovery of spirits?''

"I was with her much, father, but I do not wish to claim any responsibility for her plans.''

He narrowed his eyes as he caught her tone. "At least she saw the wisdom in my advice to her to buck up," he said.

"No, father. To tell you true, she saw revenge in this path. She has every intention of getting even with the French ladies who declined to come to Calais.'' She watched his face to see if he caught her meaning. Staff hovered near on the other side of her cousin watching her, but she dared not rush to him as she wished. His dark head turned away in earnest conversation with someone shorter.

"Go on, Mary. You are afraid. What sort of revenge?'' She faced him squarely but kept her voice low in the buzz of noise around them in the hall.

"After dinner and the entertainment, then mass seduction if I understand her aright.''

"Judas Priest!'' he said, and Mary's eyes widened with shock as his serious face broke into a grin. "That would set the French bitches back on their pretty heels!''

"Father, please, she cannot just . . .''

"Mary, hush. Tell me this. Does she include herself in the scheme? Will she at long last bed with His Grace, I mean? Well?''

"It seems so.''

"In that case, I do not give a tinker's damn if she has the whole lot of them hung up by their thumbs outside her window. That is what I have been urging. If this brought her to it, so be it." His eyes refocused on Mary's distraught face. "And you, Mary?"

"I think it is horrendous, and I am ashamed to my very soul that you seem to approve!"

"I meant, what role does Anne see for you in all this?"

Mary could feel herself color under his scrutiny. She would lock herself in her room and say she was ill. She would have no part of it even if they cast her off from the family forever. She would tell Staff and they would flee into the countryside to live in exile from England.

"Has she suggested that you, ah, entertain Francois?"

"I have said enough. I am sorry I thought you would wish to speak with Anne for her vengeful actions. I will be in my room. I am quite unwell."

He seized her wrist tight while he turned and smiled at someone behind her. "I will let you go now to compose yourself, Mary, but do not make me fetch you for dinner. Everyone is starved. They will be washed and eat very soon. And now, I intend to talk to William Stafford, so you need not greet him. Go straight to your room."

He let go of her wrist, and she had no choice but to lift her head and walk from the hall. She did not even dare to glance in Staff's direction, and her father clearly meant to cut her off from any aid Staff could give. She prayed that he saw their confrontation and would somehow get to her to ask what was amiss. If the feasting and banquet began, she might never tell him of

528

her plight until it was too late for his interference with Anne and her father—and the sloe-eyed Francois du Roi.

In her room she shoved her note to Staff in her bodice and tore the one to her father to ragged bits. She cast them into the swirling chill air outside her tiny window. She could clearly hear the surf pounding on the rocks far down the cliffs to which the vast white castle clung. Screams of sea gulls pierced the wind as it whistled around stone corners and into lofty crevices. She took a huge gulp of fresh air to clear her head. Whatever they did to her, she would not bed with the French king or give him one moment to think she would.

The thoughts came distinctly to her now. She and Staff must not wait to be wed hoping for some miracle. She was deeply ensnared by who she was and her ties to the Boleyns, but he had loved her and waited for her all these years despite the danger. A secret wedding it would have to be, but they would never dare to wrest it from them once she was his wife. They might send them to exile from court—so much the better. She would be a manor wife at Wivenhoe the rest of her days and be well quit of their treacheries and traps. Little Harry might be lost to them if they were not careful, but he seemed almost a stranger to her now. At least, thank God, he did not see the other Boleyns either, tucked away at Hatfield. And little Catherine must be taken with them. The rewards of two loving parents would be rich compensation for the loss of plush royal surroundings and a tutor shared with the king's niece. If they could only flee tonight!

Two quick raps sounded on the door. She slammed the tiny window shut and dashed to yank on the latch.

"Oh! Master Cromwell."

He bowed his close-cropped sleek head, his hat held in his big hands. "Lady Mary, I apologize at having startled you. Maybe you were expecting someone else. Your father asked me to fetch you to dinner." His quick eyes went past her, surveyed her little room, then scanned her from slippers to bodice. Suddenly, Mary wished she had not chosen the dress so carefully. Cromwell's gaze flickered over her once again and snagged where her full breasts revealed deep cleavage above the taut thrust of her bodice.

"Are you quite ready, Lady Mary?"

She stood woodenly facing him with her hand still on the door latch. "Yes. I guess I am ready."

He did not budge for a moment as she made a move to leave her room. "You look most ravishing, but that is hardly unusual," he observed in his quiet monotone, and his eyes darted over her again. "Your father said you might not be feeling well, but I am pleased to see no such evidence. If you were ill, I should feel obliged to sit with you until you were strong enough to go to the hall."

Her throat felt dry and she was suddenly hot all over with foreboding. Reluctantly she closed the door behind them. "I am certain your king would miss you if you did not appear at the feast, Master Cromwell."

He flashed a smile at her and, to her terror, took her arm above her elbow, his fingers scorching through the tight fitted satin of her sleeve as though her arm were bare. "Surely there must be some rewards and compensations for my loyal service to His Grace, even if it is just to accompany the most beautiful woman of his court to dinner."

The hair along the nape of her neck rose as a chill swept over her, but she could not stop her words. "But His Grace gave you my husband's lands at Plashy three years ago."

His face did not change but a tiny flame sprang into each flat brown eye. "I pray you do not hold that grant against me, sweet lady. If it would not anger His Grace, I would gladly give it back to you for your kind thoughts and, shall we say, your good graces."

She instinctively pulled her arm from his hand. "I meant not that I wished you to give me the lands, Master Cromwell, though I am certain the king would give you anything you could want to replace them." They were in the hall now among other faces she knew and she almost dashed away from him to hide—anywhere. But instead, she stood pinned by the probing stare of those small hard eyes.

"If the king would give me anything I want, Lady Rochford, I would be a happy man indeed." His gaze dropped to her low cut square neckline and she turned away abruptly.

"Here, Mary, sit here," he said, calmly taking her satin covered wrist firmly. "Your sister, the Lady Anne, wishes you to sit near your family so when the masque begins, you will be close." He pulled out the carved chair and bent over her as she sat. "You look faint, Lady, and I should not like to have to carry you to your room. Or at least, I should say, your father and the Lady Anne would not like that."

Mary's thoughts darted about in her brain, but she could find no way out. Damn her father! He knew she would not stand still for his orders, but he gave her into the care of this man. Did Cromwell know he was being used too, with her as bait? He was to coerce her into obedience and in the bargain he could sit with her and eye her hotly and touch her. What further had they promised to him? Surely he would not dare to think that the sister of the future queen could be for him!

"The room has been beautifully decorated, has it not, Mary? And would you not call me Thomas, please? I would wish to be an aid to you and a friend if you would ever permit me. It is difficult I know to be a woman alone in the vast court even when one's people are the premier family."

"*Because* one's people are the premier family, more likely, Master Cromwell," she heard herself say point-edly. She slid far back in her chair as she felt his knee brush her skirts.

"The first course looks lavish and massive, does it not, my lady?" he said as though she had remarked about the food. He leaned close to her again. His eyes feasted on her face and shoulders as she sat tensely coiled like a spring ready to jump from her chair. "I only ask you not to forget that I have given you a sincere and heartfelt offer of help at any time, Mary. You are very afraid of me it seems, and I am sorry for that. I would rather have things otherwise than that between us—not here, perhaps, but after all of these fine go-ings-on when we are home."

She refused to answer him and stared down into her dull gold reflection in the polished plate before her as Francois du Roi lifted his first toast of the long banquet to his dear Henri of England.

Mary felt exhausted after the dinner, dancing, and the elaborate charades. Cromwell did not ask her to dance and seemed content the rest of the evening to sit back and keep a steady eye on her as she danced with Norris, Weston, her brother and even Rene de Brosse. She considered trusting George with the note for Staff, but he raved incessantly about the fabulous job Anne had done with all the plans, and she was afraid. Then Francois claimed her before them all, and she dared not refuse the dance. Besides, she had not seen Staff since the lengthy dinner had been completed. She had so hoped he would get to her in the dancing as he had so often done. She wondered desperately if they had dared to lock him away to be certain their plans were not foiled. Her mind skimmed numerous escapes and discarded them as impossible. Her best defense, if it came down to facing either Francois or Cromwell in some awkward situation, would be her simple refusal. She must hold to that.

The pantomimes of mythological subjects were riotous and even the crafty Cromwell laughed a bit. Anne played the damsel in distress to King Henry's rescuing knight, and Mary played Venus emerging from the sea made by other nymphs flapping blue and golden bedsheets before her like the rolling waves of the ocean. Francois and Henry re-enacted their spectacular meeting on the Field of the Cloth of Gold of twelve years ago, but some half drunk Frenchman asked for a replay of the fated wrestling match where the French king threw his dear friend Henry, and Anne suddenly stood to end those revels. To Mary's utter relief, her father took her arm and Cromwell bowed to them both and disappeared in the noisy crowd.

"How dare you set him on me!" she began the minute they were out of the press of people.

"Calm down, Mary. You are getting as nervous as Anne used to be. Let him have his little rewards for serving the Boleyns. He is a good ally to have. Any fond dreams he may have about you will amount to nothing. Be nice to him. I hardly gave him permission to bed with you, so do not look so outraged."

"Hardly gave him permission!" She was so beside herself, she sputtered her words. "Get away from me. I am going to my room to spend the night alone. If you even entertained the slightest thought of asking me to visit the chambers of Francois du Roi, you can go to hell, and take Cromwell with you." She spun away and ran for the safety of her room gathering her full skirts as she went. To her profound dismay, couples were strolling the branching halls of the old castle talking low and laughing, stopping in the dimness between wall sconces to kiss and nuzzle.

She yanked open the door to her room and scanned the small chamber quickly before she entered. The hearth fire had been lit, and fresh wine and fruit in a gleaming silver bowl sat on the small polished table. How desperately she wished she would find Staff sitting on her bed with his rakish grin, but she knew deep inside they had sent him somewhere. She shot the lock on her door and leaned against it. Whatever messengers they sent to ask her to go to Francois, even if it be the greedy-eyed Cromwell or Wolsey's ghost in its winding sheet, she would refuse.

She pulled her gown off her shoulders and breasts and shrugged out of it. She and two other ladies shared a maid, but she would not need her services. She would be deep in her bed before the girl came to help her undress. She twisted the gown around her waist so she could see the laces and untie them herself. She stepped out of the masses of brocades and satins and layers of petticoats and wrapped herself in her black satin bed-robe, bought with father's money, unfortunately. From now on, she would go naked and starve first.

She downed some wine and was amazed to find it was as fine as what she had been drinking at the feast. How unlike the wine and ale that had been left in her chambers the last week while the men were away. To-morrow she would find Staff early and tell him every-thing. She would also make him believe that not only did she fervently wish to marry him as he had asked, for she had told him that clearly enough before, but that she would wed with him as soon as possible.

She poured more wine but slopped a considerable amount on the table when her hand jerked at the knock on the door. She held her breath, but she could hear her heart beat in the quiet above the low crackle of the fire. She pulled the black silk tighter around her.

"It is I, Mary, Jane. Will you not open the door?"

Then Jane was not with Rene de Brosse, Mary thought jubilantly. Could she trust Jane with the note to Staff? She and Anne had never gotten on, especially lately, so perhaps . . .

"Mary, I know you are in there."

Mary shot the bolt back and opened the door. Jane Rochford stood there, indeed, but the velvet arm of Francois du Roi was draped over her half bare shoul-ders. Mary's eyes grew wide and she almost slammed the door in their smiling faces.

"See, Mary, I have brought you a wonderful pres-ent."

"*Merci, merci beaucoupe, cherie,*" Francois said in

Jane's ear and bent to kiss the white skin of her shoulder. She giggled. Francois' hand went to the open edge of Mary's door. "I came to reminisce about old times, golden Marie," he said with a wink. "Be gone, be gone, *madame charmante*," he ordered the starry-eyed Jane and slowly pushed Mary's door back towards her as she stood like a statue.

"May we not recall old times tomorrow, Your Grace?" Mary heard herself say smoothly, and she fought to force a smile to her lips. "It is late and I am rather tired." She was aware that Jane had halted but a few yards away in the dim corridor. If only there were someone else about to call to.

Mary either had to fall backwards or loose the door, for Francois leaned the weight of his bent arm hard into it. He wore a black velvet robe intricately etched in silver filigree. He strode close past her into the room, but she staunchly held her place at the door.

He surveyed the room and then turned back to face her. "See, my sweet, we match again, *oui*?"

"What, Sire?"

"Just like the evening we first met when the genius da Vinci dressed you to match your king. At the Bastille. Do you not remember?"

"Yes, I remember, but that was not the first time we had met."

"Really? I could not have forgotten another." He smiled and she did not.

He raised a graceful arm to her chamber. "Then do you not recall a little room like this one where we used to meet on chill winter afternoons? Close the door, *si vous plait, ma Marie*. You are letting in a terrible chill and, if you are so tired, you had best take to your bed."

Still she did not move. He approached slowly and swung the door closed himself. It thudded hollowly. "You are shy after so many years, *oui*? It has been long. I have missed you."

Mary smiled then, for the lie was so bold she could not resist. Suddenly, her fear left her. This man could do her harm, no doubt, but not in the way he once had. She went instantly on the defensive.

"I was sorry to hear of Queen Claude's death, Your Grace. I hope you are happy with your new queen. My sister was disappointed she could not come to meet us."

"*Oui*, of course. But it is a tiny problem that she is Henri's ex-queen's niece." He hesitated. "What is it they call Catherine now?"

"The Princess of Wales, Sire."

"Ah, *oui*."

"So that means you are on the former Queen Catherine's side of family necessity," Mary continued.

"Well, my sweet, family necessity can be bent where one's own heart is involved."

"Exactly, Your Grace. And tonight I must explain to you that the family necessity which has me here in this room with you must be bent. I am sorry if there have been misunderstandings, Your Grace."

He came closer and stared warmly down at her. "You are talking in riddles, my golden one. Still so beautiful after a husband and a child."

"Two children, Your Majesty."

"I thought there was only the lad your king spoke of."

Mary felt her pulse quicken.

"And let us face the truth, Mary, you held the Tudor for five years, though now he is the heritage you leave

537

your sister.''

"My relationship with Henry Tudor, Your Grace, was truly none of my doing, except for the fact that I used to be a frightened little pawn of my father—and my kings.''

"Ah, this is another Marie indeed, but one so gorgeous still, so tempting, just as your goddess rising from the foam of the sea tonight, my Venus. I pictured you then without your garments, and I remembered the lovely days we once spent together.''

She moved to step aside, but he was too quick for her. His long hands darted to her silken waist. He bent to kiss her lips, but she turned her head. "Please, Sire, I cannot know what Anne or the king or even my father has said to you. The memories are one thing, but I wish for no others. Please, let me free.''

His arched brows descended suddenly over his deep set eyes. "Why would you deny me?'' he asked directly.

"I loved you once, Your Grace, or thought I did, but no more. The years have changed me. Please, I ask of you, Francois du Roi, to . . .'' Her hands darted to tug at his wrists as he suddenly parted her robe. "No, Your Grace, I . . .''

"Love, my Venus, has nothing to do with what joy we can give each other in the privacy of this room tonight. I have chosen you from all the women here. Whomever you fear, they need not know.''

His hands still held desperately strong by Mary's own lifted to her full breasts and cupped them. She stepped back away into the carved bureau and he pursued, his eyes steadily on her. She turned to straighten her loose robe, but he pulled it down her arms and

538

yanked the thin chemise off one shoulder and a breast freed itself from the gauzy covering.

"Perfection, still perfection," he breathed and leaned into her full length, pinning her against the heavy wood furniture behind them. He covered her mouth with his and his other hand massaged the curve of her hip. She bit his lip and tried to twist away, but he cruelly raised his knee into her and forced her legs open against him.

"Damn, petite vixen," he said against her hair as he tasted his own blood from his lip.

"I cannot help what they have told you or promised, Sire," she repeated. "I will scream and everyone will come. Everyone will know the Great Whore's sister who was the English king's mistress before her sister, does not wish to lie with Francois du Roi!"

He stood suddenly stock still against her. She felt smothered by his weight, and he had such a stomach and great chest on him that she could hardly draw a breath where he pressed her bosoms flat. Then he stepped back and she feared he would strike her. She raised her chin, brazenly, for anything would be better than his caresses.

He yanked her from the tall bureau several steps after him into the room where the firelight fell on her. In one sharp tear, he jerked her chemise from her and kicked her black robe away from where it lay at her feet. She stood straight facing him, afraid to dart back toward the bed.

"It is obvious to me, Marie," his voice came coldly, "that it is *you* who are the whore as well as your dark haired little sister. Only she is a clever whore and you are a foolish one."

"I was foolish once when I played the whore for you, Sire, but no more. Say what you will and then be gone to make your complaint of my actions to my sister or my father or whomever you are to report to."

His jeweled hand came at her and she crashed to the floor. She tasted blood in her mouth and her cheek stung terribly. He knelt over her and her eyes widened and she saw his desire for her as his robe opened. "Let me tell you what should happen to you, my beautiful little slut. I should tie you to the posts of the bed and show you how a Frenchman uses an English whore. You would cry and beg, Marie. Yes, they would all hear, so we could invite them all in. And then I could announce to them all what I really think about kings stupid enough to love whores, especially Henri du Roi! Let us make a devil's bargain, since you think you are so high and mighty now that your sister plans to sit upon a throne by only cooling the king's lusts on a moment's whim, as you used to do for me."

He stood towering over her and his slippered foot kicked at her derriere twice. "You keep the secret that I think your whoreson king is a damned fool to marry a mercer's girl and ruin the holy church in the process, and I shall keep the secret that the blonde Boleyn whore refused Francois du Roi her sweet body to plunder as he used to."

He turned away from her and wrapped his huge velvet robe around his girth. "I will amuse brother Henri and his concubine tomorrow with an elaborate tale of how well you served me anyway I would have you, eh? They will be very pleased with your performance. Goodbye for now, naked Venus."

He turned at the door and his black eyes raked her

540

nude body again. "Maybe I should get a few friends and come back. If Henri du Roi were not enjoying his Boleyn whore, I could bring him with me."

He shouted a strangled laugh and the door slammed. She lay stunned at his words, but she felt totally free of him. She did not believe his threat to return. Let him ruin her reputation with her family or his amused and jaded cronies, for her good name had been long trod upon in the royal dust of France and England too. It only mattered that Staff must know the French king told lies, terrible lies.

The chill of the castle and her thoughts snatched at her and she rose to stride nude to her wash basin and ewer. She dashed the cold water into the bowl and proceeded to scrub her skin until the tingle became a rough ache. She would have no touch of him on her. She belonged body and mind to William Stafford only, and she would die before anyone else touched her ever again. Her chemise was ripped beyond repair so she cast it into the fire and it fumed and smoked as it burned. She kicked the black satin robe out of her way and donned her crumpled mauve and beige gown not even stopping to put on undergarments. She would find Staff wherever they had sent him or maybe even locked him. She would find him. She smoothed her mussed hair and her trembling fingers closed around the silver fruit knife lying on the polished wood of the table. The fruit and the fine wine, of course, were for the French king. The whole thing had been calculated by her dear sister. The dull pain in her stomach twisted sharp again.

The knock was so quiet on the door that she hardly thought she had heard it at first. Not even the sneaky

Cromwell would knock that quietly. Perhaps her father had found out that she had failed the Boleyns now and would tell black Cromwell he could claim his prize to punish her. The knock came again. Maybe it was only the foolish maid. "Isabelle, is that you?" Her voice quavered in the room barely discernible over the low snapping of the hearth fire.

"Lass, it is I."

Half fearing a trick, she cracked the door and peered out, her knife poised just out of the visitor's sight. It was Staff's voice, but perhaps that was another trick.

"Staff. Oh, Staff!"

She was in his arms the moment he closed the door behind him and leaned against it. Cold still clung to his garments and skin, but he felt wonderful against her.

"Come on, sweetheart. You and I are going to hide out for the night in a place they will never think to look," he was saying. "Your dangerous little sister has some sort of dire plan for you, I fear, and we had best get out of here before it happens."

He craned his head to survey the hall through a cracked door. When he turned back to take her hand, his eyes widened in surprise as though he were seeing her for the first time. "What the hell has happened," he shot out. "Are you dressing or undressing? Why the knife? Cromwell? Francois?" Anger stained his tanned face livid and he took the knife from her unresisting fingers and hurled it behind her. "I shall kill your father."

"No, no, my love. Everything is all right now, truly. Francois was here, but I denied him and he left in a huff."

"In a huff? And what did the royal bastard do before he left?"

"Please, Staff, do not look so awful. He, well, he said some terrible things and tried to seduce me, but I dissuaded him."

His eyes widened further. "With a fruit knife?"

"No. With a refusal—and the truth. It hurt his pride."

"And did he hurt you, my little tigress?"

"He tried. I fear him no more, Staff, though he did threaten to tell the Boleyns I submitted to his every whim."

"I am sure he will and probably believe it himself rather than ever grasp the fact that he faced a real woman tonight and she saw him for the whoreson bastard that he is. Swear to me he did not hurt you. Did he try to pull this dress off?" He tugged the still loosened gown slightly off her shoulder.

"I was in my robe then. I was just getting dressed now in a hurry to come see where they had sent you. I knew my father meant to get you out of the way somehow."

"Yes. Lord Thomas Boleyn sent me on a king's errand to see if the royal party could visit the flagship of his navy on the tide tomorrow. I doubt if they really mean to visit, but I had no choice. He even walked me to my horse and watched me canter away." He struck his head slowly out the door into the hall again.

"Where are we going?"

"I do not know what will happen now that you have set Francois back on his royal heel, but we had best stick to my original plan. No one is ever getting hands on you again unless it is a certain William Stafford, love. Who knows if your father shall send someone else to your door?"

"But where will we hide? Did you find some place outside the castle? The gates are secured by two armies."

"Hush, love. Come on."

He tugged gently at her wrist and she followed him willingly. She would follow him anywhere he led her, though she be half dressed as she was now or even naked. The halls were greatly deserted and Mary was surprised to see no guards at the door to Anne's rooms as they approached. Instinctively, she tried to draw back from him as he swung open the door.

"Sh," he said low. "She beds with the king in his chamber and all the guards are there."

The vast room where Mary had spent so much of the past week listening to Anne's desperate tirades glowed in a strange half light. The fire was low, but two large cresset lamps threw their circles of light near the hearth.

"Are you certain she will not return?"

They stood on the flowered light blue hearth rug when he loosed her wrist. "She has finally taken the plunge to submit her precious body to the king, Mary. I think you would agree she will have enough political wile to stay at least the night no matter what discomforts or terrors befall her in the lion's den."

He squinted in the direction of Anne's huge dark curtained bed. "This bed will be comfortable enough for us, I assure you, love. We shall remake it carefully when we go at dawn."

"No, I cannot."

His strong brown hands slid up her arms. "Cannot what, sweetheart?"

"I will not sleep in her bed. How could you do so?"

"I see. Well, lass, I have no respect for the Lady

Anne Boleyn's bed."

"I have no respect for it. Only contempt." She heard her voice break, and he pulled her a step forward into his arms.

"I am sorry, sweet, but I though it would be the safest harbor for us this night. I take it that this dire plan to seduce the French and Francois was her doing?"

"Yes," she said muffled into his velvet jerkin.

"She is far more stupid than I thought," he said against her disheveled hair. "Then we, my lady, shall spend the night right here on this hearth rug, and I shall build the fire up a bit." He pulled her down gently to sit on the plush rug in the protective crook of his arm and she leaned securely against him. Moments passed. He moved away and threw two logs into the dying flames. She sat on her haunches studying the muscle bulges on his back and the lean angles the firelight etched on his face. He turned to face her three feet away.

"What are you thinking, love," he asked.

"That I have done with everything except my love for you and that if you still want me for your wife, I will marry you whenever you will have me and go with you to the ends of the earth if you ask."

His eyes glowed dark and his lower lip trembled as though he would speak. The tiny muscle on his jaw line moved. "Then you will be my wife on the first instant we can manage to escape their snares when we return. And though we may have to travel to the ends of the earth when they find out, I will wager the manor at Wivenhoe will be place we will live the rest of our days together."

Their smiles met wordlessly across the tiny firelit space between them and the whole room seemed to recede and drift away as it often did when he gazed upon her rapt that way and her limbs turned to warm water. It was as though they were afloat on this blue, blue rug in a boat of their own making. The waters of time were held in abeyance for only them as when they had drifted on Master Whitman's tiny pond behind the inn at Banstead. The loomed flowers were the water lilies and the light wool pile the surface on which their little boat sailed. There was nothing that could ever hurt them now and the golden fireflies of night danced in the darkness of his eyes.

Part Four

The Bargain

My true love hath my heart, and I have his,
By just eschange, one for the other given.
I hold his dear, and mine he cannot miss;
There never was a better bargain driven.
My true love hath my heart, and I have his.

His heart in me keeps me and him in one;
My heart in him his thoughts and senses guides.
He loves my heart, for once it was his own;
I cherish his because in me it bides.
My true love hath my heart, and I have his.

—Sir Philip Sidney

Chapter Twenty-Eight
February 22, 1533

Greenwich

The shouts and boisterous laughter of people in the cobbled courtyard caught Mary's attention only for a moment. She was far too nervous and excited to watch her brother and his cronies, including the once re-strained Weston and Norris, throw snowballs at each other and duck guffawing in white icy breaths behind the glazed marble fountain. She was grateful that the snowfall was only two or three inches deep—enough to keep the courtiers outside for a while but not enough to stop a rider on the roads on an important mission. Her warm breath clouded the pane of glass through which she stared, and she turned back into the hall to continue toward the new queen's apartments. It had been a chilly, blustery day much like this one, she remem-bered, that His Grace had wed Anne secretly here at cold Greenwich in the early hours of the morn—wed her hurriedly only two days after he had learned that the Lady Anne was pregnant.

But all that was hardly of consequence to Mary. Fi-nally, there was a glimmer of hope she might escape the treacherous maze of duties and involved relationships and spies—Cromwell's spies, Staff said. Today the long-treasured plan to leave the court and her family to secretly wed William Stafford and have a few days at Banstead before they must return to duties and the masks of pretense could become reality.

She nodded curtly to the yeomen guards at the double doors to the queen's suite and they swung them wide. Staff had gone to Wivenhoe three days ago, but now awaited her arrival at a London inn. Everything hinged on her being allowed to leave the palace for a few days. Everything she had lived for these last hard months, even these long, long years since she had loved him, depended on Anne's letting her go.

Anne sat in her massive curtained bed leaning on satin pillows each embroidered with her new crest. Her hair was loose and long and, though she looked pale, her eyes glowed with confidence and were no longer haunted with the fears of desertion and possession by the Tudor king she now knew to be her devoted servant. Jane Rochford sat in the corner doing nothing in particular and several ladies sewed on standing embroidery frames about the room. The languorous Mark Smeaton perched on the far edge of the bed playing almost pensively on an elaborately gilded and painted lute.

Mary curtseyed slightly and Anne nodded without a smile. Her eyes looked large and luminous framed by her dark brows and lashes. "Are you feeling better this morning, sister?" Mary asked.

"'S blood, no, Mary. That is why I am not up yet, obviously. I take it that all the shouting is another game of ducks and geese or a snowball fight. Is George out there?"

"Yes, and many others. There is a new dusting of snow on the ground."

"What a time to have the morning sickness for the babe. I never feel well until nearly noon and His Grace has a fit if he thinks I get up too early. Oh well, it will be well worth it when he is born. And," she added as a smile lit her face, "it makes the whole court wonder if the queen is indeed with royal child already. I hope the French spies have told Francois and his snobby queen. It amuses me to tease them all, but soon everyone will be able to tell for certain anyway. I have made it clear to my sweet faced lutenist that if he tells all he know, I will have him strung up on the ramparts of the Tower." Her slender foot kicked out in Smeaton's direction under the covers and she shot him a smile.

"I will tell them nothing, Your Grace, nothing," he sang back to her in tune with his strumming.

"I am glad you told me this terrible nausea and dizziness when I rise would not outlast a three month span, Mary. I could not have managed it otherwise. And I can feel my fine slim waistline fast going." She looked down at her barely rounded belly. "But the son for the throne, he will be worth it."

"It is of a son I wished to ask, Your Grace." Mary resisted the impulse to wring her hands and tried to keep her voice calm.

"My son, Mary?"

"No, Your Grace. Henry Carey, Will Carey's son and mine. You see, I almost never see the lad and he grows so fast. And since you keep to your bed in the mornings and see His Grace much in the afternoons, I thought it might be a convenient time for you to let me

551

visit him at Hatfield." Anne's almond shaped eyes fastened on her blonde sister's face. "It is sad for a child to be without a father and mother too."

"I hope you do not mean that as another of your pious suggestions that the king's illegitimate daughter Mary be allowed to visit her Spanish mother the Princess of Wales just because she is so ill this winter."

Mary could feel her heart pounding, vibrating her velvet bodice. "No, of course not. I meant nothing by the remark yesterday. I am speaking only of my son and your legal ward. Please Anne, Your Grace, it would mean much to me to see him even if for a day or two."

"Well, if you are not gone long, I am certain I can spare your services. Sometimes, sister," she said leaning toward Mary and lowering her voice, "I am not certain whose side you are on, although the Boleyns have quite vanquished the treasonable forces of the Spanish princess. And, as His Grace and I have said, her stiff-necked daughter will be allowed back to court only when she will bow her head to the rightful heir to the throne after he is born this autumn. Indeed, after I am crowned at the Abbey in June as His Grace has promised, no one will dare to doubt who is queen or whisper 'there goes the king's concubine, his whore' in the streets."

"You have many loyal followers and more to come, sister," Mary comforted.

"Yes, Mary. Father, the king, and Cromwell shall make certain of that. Only, it would help me to know that you are one of my most loyal subjects and not only my sister." She sighed and her slender hands smoothed the silk coverlet over her legs pensively. "I can see why the court is more boring for you now that your paramour Stafford has gone off to Wivenhoe." She raised her hand and pointed her finger at Mary as though she were warning or scolding a child. "See that you do not accidentally stray to his little manor after seeing your child."

Mary took a deep breath and fought to keep the alarm from her face. "I go not to Wivenhoe, Your Grace. Indeed, I have never even seen the place."

Jane Rochford approached the bed beside Mary and offered Anne a golden goblet with spiced wine. "Could you not hear well enough where you sat?" Anne inquired tartly to the short woman, but she took the wine. Jane said nothing.

"Fine, Mary, go if you will, but do not tarry there. And as to your friend at Wivenhoe, His Grace intends to marry him to the Dorsey wench this summer. As sister to the queen, you, of course, will wed much higher than that."

Mary almost shouted for joy. It would be too late for all their plans after tomorrow. She backed quickly away from the bed and curtseyed. She would be gone within the hour and join Staff to ride for Hatfield, and tomorrow would see their wedding at Banstead, free, free from them all for a time.

"Our sister Mary is journeying out in this terrible weather," Jane noted sweetly to Anne, and Mary could have slapped her for her meddling. "Does you father approve then, Mary?"

"I think," Mary began, but Anne's sharp tone interrupted her.

"Hush, Jane, and stay out of Mary's and my business. Lord Boleyn is not king here or queen either. It is

my decision that Mary shall visit Will Carey's son and
so she shall. Tattle to father if you wish, but keep well
from me if you do. And I will tell Cromwell myself so he
knows where she is. I hope, dear Jane, it will not choke
you to have to keep juicy information quite to yourself."

Jane opened her mouth to answer, but bent in a jerky
curtsey and backed from the bed to her chair in the corner again without a word. Anne's smile of triumph and
Mary's obvious relief hung between the sisters.

"I thank you, Your Grace. I shall not forget this
kindness."

"See you do not, Mary. And say best wishes to the
lad. Maybe I shall have him appointed to the Inns of
Court to learn royal service at the bar when he is ready.
He would be eleven now?"

"Yes. Almost twelve."

"Then he could serve my son as advisor or companion some day perhaps. You would like that, Mary?"

"The Carey children would be honored to serve the
king's family," Mary said low. Her legs began to tremble. Could she not get away? He would think she had
failed to convince the queen she should go. He might
not wait for her or come back here. "May I leave now,
Your Grace? The morning rest would do you good."

"Yes. I dare say, I should keep up my strength, for
the fact I am carrying his babe does little to dampen the
Tudor ardor at night. Goodbye, then."

Mary spun and forced herself to walk slowly from the
room. The raucous shouts still permeated the courtyard, and she was relieved to see few people in the corridor. His Grace was probably closeted with his Cromwell, for he was content no longer to let a chancellor run

554

the government unbridled as Wolsey had done all those years. She would be on her horse and off with Stephen and the grooms before anyone missed her.

Nancy's face lit like a torch when she saw her mistress' smile. "She is letting you go, then?"

"Yes and she set no real limit on the time, Nance. Is everything ready? Here, help me get this gown off."

Nancy unlaced and peeled off her dress and helped her into the brown riding gown. The girl knew her lady was going to be with Staff, but neither she nor her Stephen knew anything of the intended wedding.

"You will kiss the lad for me then, lady, when you are at Hatfield? Will he remember me, do you think?"

"He was so young when he was sent away, Nance, but I shall tell him your kind words anyway. And, as for the kissing, when last I tried it two years ago, he wiped the kisses off his mouth."

" 'Tis like a young lad I know, lady."

"Not Stephen, I hope, Nance," Mary teased and Nancy's face broke into a huge grin. Mary hugged her maid from sheer excitement as they left the room and headed for the stable block. Thank heavens, Anne had not thought to inquire which grooms or guards she took, for Staff had hand picked them all and his own man Stephen was in charge of the small party.

Eden stood waiting and snorting at the excitement of a run in the chill air as Stephen helped Mary up on the mare's back and wrapped her heavy cloak and skirts about her legs. The two other men mounted and Stephen stood awkwardly near Nancy fingering his linen cap for a moment.

"Kiss the maid goodbye, then, Stephen. We are off for the city," Mary urged, smiling down at the pair.

"Yes, milady," Stephen said seriously. He mounted, Nancy waved, and they left the warm confines of red-bricked Greenwich for the snowy river road to London.

The narrow thatch-roofed inn Staff had chosen for their rendezvous was called "The Queen's Head" and it sported a dirty sign which was evidently meant to bear a likeness of Queen Catherine's face which stared down into the crooked street. The Queen's Head stood with its eaves crowded in by other two and three storey buildings nearly in the shadow of The Tower on Cooper's Row. The only part of the sign that could resemble Anne if they ever had to change the face, mused Mary as she dismounted, was the staring eyes.

Her nose was so cold she covered it with her gloved hands and blew warm air into them as she had on the ride. Her cheeks burned and her toes in her boots felt numb, but nothing mattered except that tomorrow would be her wedding day—a wedding day she had chosen and so desperately desired.

"Here, milady," Stephen said and guided her in the door under the sign. It was dark within and her eyes swept the dimness for his tall form. The room looked deserted. Stephen swung the door shut behind them and the draft of cold air ceased.

Staff jumped up from his reclining position on a bench near the glowing hearth. "Mary. Sweetheart. Thank God!" He enveloped her in the warmth of his huge arms and led her to the fire. She drank warmed ale from his cup and stripped off her gloves to stretch her fingers to the low crackling blaze. He watched her wide-eyed, his hand resting gently on the back of her

556

waist.

"She let me go with no trouble, really, love," she heard herself tell him in a rush. "Foolish Rochford tried to intervene, but Anne would have none of that. Once she makes a decision these days, there is a great tempest if anyone tries to cross her. You are so quiet, my lord. How did you find Wivenhoe?"

"Snug and fit and awaiting its mistress Mary Bullen should we ever get to live there. I was thinking of that on the road into town yesterday—scrapping this plan and being wed in Colchester and sending them word when we were well settled at Wivenhoe. Maybe we could tell them it is haunted and keep them all away." He pulled her still cold hands into his and warmed them by gently rubbing them with his fingers. "I wanted to do that so much, my sweet, but I knew I could not or all hell would come crashing in around us." He looked down at his booted feet. "It is the first thing that has made me want to turn rebel in a long time."

"Please, Staff, do not talk like that."

"It is all right, lass. I do not mean it, only the desire to have you away from their prying eyes and greedy hands is enough to make me very careless sometimes. If it is not that damned Cromwell ogling you, it is your father's veiled hints to me that he has marriage plans for you, just to keep me under his thumb."

She turned to face him and lifted her hands to his lean, handsome face. "Staff—look at me."

He raised his dark eyes and smiled. "That is an order I will gladly follow anytime, sweet."

"I am serious. Listen. There is nothing we will have to fear from them anymore. They cannot separate us after tomorrow. We will be wed and no other husband

557

would dare accept me then. If we have to face their anger, we shall do so together. And if they send us away in disgrace, so much the better, for I would love to live at Wivenhoe.''

He stared deep into her blazing eyes. ''This Mary I will take to wife is a far stronger woman than the one I first desired. Whatever happens, sweetheart, you will live at Wivenhoe and soon. I promise. And we had best be on the road to Hatfield so that at first dawn tomorrow we shall be heading Sanctuary and Eden for Master Whitman's inn and that little church. But first I will claim a kiss from my intended, since it seems her red lips have quite warmed to my taste by now.'' He pulled her very slowly against him and put his hands under the heavy folds of her cloak. The kiss was warm and tender, then deep and probing. When he lifted his head, she saw the familiar look of passion in his eyes.

''Come on, my lass. We are off to Hatfield or else this dirty little inn will have to serve for our nuptial chamber.'' He grabbed his black cloak and hat and they strode hand in hand for the door.

By the time the early dusk turned the clean snow to evening gray, they had reached Hatfield and Mary had spent two hours with Henry Carey. He was lanky, freckled, auburn-haired, polite, and achingly adoring. He recited Latin and Greek verses for her and told her of his good relationship with his tutor and with His Grace's son, Fitzroy. He expressed his fervent wish to see his aunt the new queen whom he could not remember from his early days at court and reminded her twice that he was to be remembered to his dear grandsire. Something awful twisted deep inside Mary when the boy spoke of his grandsire the second time and, quietly, she pursued her fear.

"How often have you seen Grandsire Boleyn, Harry?"

"Oh, quite often, mother. Two weeks last. He brings fine presents and talks for hours of the court, and he promised me I shall go there some day. He has told me I might rise high in His Grace's favor with his help, and I will not forget that."

"No, of course not. Now that your aunt is queen, you can attain a favored position. She mentioned to me that you might be a companion to her children when they should be born."

"But Grandsire told me I would rise high long ago, mother, even before the new queen took the place of— well, became queen."

Damn my father, she thought distinctly. He never told me of any of these visits. But, of course, he would not want to me to know he has been long poisoning the lad's mind. When I return, I shall tell him he will stop or else I shall tell His Grace what my precious father most fears I will tell him. He will not use this child as his next plan should his other power schemes go awry!

"Mother, you look so angry. Are you all right?" His pale, earnest face bent close to hers.

"Yes, of course, my Harry. Now enough talk about the court. It is far enough away from here."

"Only twenty miles, Grandsire says, mother."

"Well, yes. Now tell me more of the geography Master Gwinne has been teaching. They used to think the world was flat, you said?" And, the words echoed in her mind, I used to think my father was to be trusted. He has bent children's minds before in his hail-fellow-well-met mask, and he will not do it again to Harry. If only Anne were not Harry's guardian now!

"Are you listening, mother?" He smiled at her, his beautiful golden-haired mother with the blue eyes and troubled face. And she had been so happy today when she first came to see him. Had he said something amiss to her? Did she think he should be further in his studies?

"Yes, my dearest, I am listening. Say on and then we should eat and go to bed, for by morning light I must set out."

"Shall I recite the lineage of our dear king for you instead mother," he inquired, his earnest eyes still on her face.

The thatched roof of The Golden Gull glittered as though it were strung with chains of diamonds in the afternoon sun. It had taken them longer than Staff had calculated on the stretch from the Kent Road west to Banstead, for a sifting of new snow had fallen and they had to keep the horses under tight rein because of hidden ruts on the covered road. Despite the biting air, they chatted and stopped to kiss and admire the powdered white beauty of the evergreen forest and the brown iced etching of the lonely trunks of elm or beech while Stephen and the two grooms dropped further and further behind.

Banstead lay silent but for the thin lines of smoke trailing their fingers into the winter sky, and few human footprints marred the untouched carpet of snow. The Whitmans had been awaiting them, for Staff had sent word days before, and soon the roaring hearth thawed out their hands and feet.

"Be the place as you remember it, then milady?" Master Whitman asked seeing her scan the room repeatedly.

"No, Master Whitman, much more lovely than I remember it," she told him. "I am looking carefully so I am certain to remember all of it."

"Aye, one's weddin' day is a special day to remember," Mistress Whitman put in. "My John brought me from Dover the very next day after our weddin', but I recall and well the little inn we stayed in down on the waterfront. There was a real feather bed in the next room, though ours was straw, and I recall that well, too." She blushed as she caught her husband's warning eye and Staff's grin. "Well, I do so recall it, and I shall tell it if I want too, John!"

"But 'tis their weddin' day, and they do not want to sit here and be told of yourn," he growled back.

Staff's voice cut in to settle the potential spat. "Now, John, we have been here long enough to warm up, so I wish us to go. Are you certain the priest will be there?"

"Aye, milord. All afternoon 'til you come, he said."

"Then if Mistress Whitman would help Lady Carey change dresses, we will be off to the church. The winter nights come early and I intend to catch all of this one, eh, Mistress Whitman?"

She laughed as she and Mary climbed the stairs. "I know yer teasin' us both, milord," she called back over her shoulder, "an' I will not rise to the taunt."

Mary unpacked her ivory and pink May Day gown with tiny roses and shook the wrinkles out of it. She had wanted to have one made especially for today, but there was no unusually fine court occasion in the near future and she was afraid someone would become suspicious.

Staff himself had requested this dress, she thought, as Mistress Whitman laced it up for her. She missed Nancy's sure hands on her hair, but her tresses were badly tangled by the wind, so on a whim she left her hair long and Mistress Whitman brushed it out for her. The golden snare he had bought for her here in Banstead so long ago has no place at this wedding, she thought, for she was freer today than she had ever been before.

His eyes lit when he saw her. He had changed to a velvet ivory and yellow doublet which matched her gown beautifully. He put the warm cloak around her shoulders. Holding her skirt hems from the snow, she let him lift her onto Sanctuary's back. The Whitmans trailed after them as Staff walked the horse the short way toward the Gothic spires which dominated the little village. They stamped inside and Mistress Whitman took their cloaks away while Master John went off to find the priest.

"You look the most lovely I have ever seen you, my Mary, and I have studied you and dreamed of you for long years now." He brushed her lips with his and straightened. "I never despaired that this day would not come, but to tell you true, now that it has, I can hardly believe it."

"You are not sorry?"

He put back his head and gave a short laugh. "You are the one who will be sorry, my love, if you try to put me off one more minute from what has always been mine since I first was swept under by that beautiful face. And, when I found there was a beautiful woman trapped behind the face, I was lost forever."

"That is a strange way to put a compliment, Staff."

"Shall we argue, then, love?" He pinched her arm gently and grinned down at her. "Here comes the priest."

"Father Robert, milord and lady," John Whitman said awkwardly.

The priest's eyes showed recognition when he saw Mary. "Yes, I believe I remember that you passed through in the terrible summer of the sweat," he said. "We spoke briefly, did we not?"

"Yes, father. I remember. You will marry us then?"

"Gladly, gladly. And, may I inquire if the lord and lady are from the court in London? You are from no family hereabouts and yet choose to be wed in little Banstead."

The statement was a request for information about this curious wedding. Staff's voice came in the stillness close beside her. "We are from London, father, and for sentimental reasons wish to be wed today. Will you comply?"

"Indeed. Then you will both vouch that there be no impediments to the union?"

"None, father."

"And the lady?"

"None, father. My lord and I are both free to wed and will have it so."

"Then, come, come, my children." They strolled slowly up the narrow central aisle between the few chairs and benches which graced the very front of the vaulted church. The colored windows stained their clothes and faces in vibrant hues. "By what names shall you be called and registered?" Father Robert inquired quietly as he turned to face them holding his worn black prayer book.

563

"I am William Stafford and this is Mary, Lady Carey," Staff told him before she could answer. Staff took her hand and faced the priest squarely.

"Then we shall begin," the father said simply, and he began his recital in Latin.

Mary stared hard at the golden crucifix against his black garments. It looked like one her dear friend Mary Tudor had worn so long ago in France, but she must not think of that now. And it was not quite as heavy as the one which used to swing from the ample bosom of the now exiled Queen Catherine who had been so kind to her when there was no need to be.

She turned her head and found Staff's eyes warm upon her. She looked down at their clasped hands as he slipped the gold band on her finger. Of course, she would have to hide it somewhere. Not on a chain around her neck, for it would show with the low cut gowns Anne had made quite the style at court. Poor bitter Anne had had her secret wedding too. But now she would bear the king a child and be safe no matter if his ardors cooled as they had toward Mary so long ago.

Staff leaned down to kiss her. They embraced each other and then the beaming Whitmans. It seemed like a dream. She was his wife and little Catherine had a loving father, though it might be months before she could be told. They could never take Staff away from her the way they had her first born, her pride and even her body. Now, now it was all hers to keep!

They signed the huge parish registry as lord and lady and sat in the tiny room which served as an office while Father Robert inked in their names on their official marriage parchment on a shaky table.

"I fear greatly for the holy church, my lord," the

priest said directly to Staff in an abrupt change from the small talk he had been pursuing. "Do you understand? Is there anything you could say to reassure me?"

"I am sorry, father," Staff answered, looking directly at the pale man. "The latest act of Parliament forbidding direct appeals to Rome is only a first step. I am sorry, but you no doubt read the times rightly."

"Yes," he said only, and bent his head to his lettering. Then he added under his breath, "I have prayed that these terrible happenings might be an indication of our Lord's Second Coming, but I fear our earthly king is only misguided and hardly the Antichrist. Is it true the one they call 'The King's Great Concubine' has so besotted his soul that he would kill the Holy Church to keep her? Spanish Catherine is queen anointed and true church folk know it well."

Mary gave a tiny gasp, and the priest's eyes sought hers. "I am sorry, Lady Stafford. I did not know where your sympathies would lie, and I should not have spoken so. But I am only a priest of a small village and, therefore, I am not afraid to say what my soul would have me say."

"You are fortunate then, indeed, Father Robert, and I wish you safety in the times ahead," Staff said.

"Thank you for your concern, but that is the Lord's business. I shall tend the relics and pray over the graves and nourish the little flock and leave the rest—including our king and court—to Him. That is the Lord's business too."

"Yes, Father. It comforts me to think of it that way," Mary said honestly. "And you may be assured that the king is not the Antichrist."

"Perhaps not, lady, but some sort of evil is coming

565

for a fall. Mark my words, evil only corrupts itself ever-lastingly and it will be rooted out." He stood with his thin hands on his little desk. "Go your way now and *pax vobiscum.*"

"Thank you, father," Staff said and left a bag of coins on the rickety table which nearly tottered under his touch.

The setting winter sun was etching great black shadows on the church as they left. The graves of the village forefathers looked like snowy miniature houses, and the first touch of eventide wind whistled in the carved entryway. Rows of icicles dripped from the carved eaves like jagged teeth of a stone monster waiting to devour whomever ventured within. Mary turned to imprint the little church in her memory, but it suddenly loomed behind dark and lonely, and she turned back wrapping her warm cloak about her.

Though the Whitmans had planned to serve Staff and Mary a fine wedding supper in the privacy of their room, the newly married couple insisted that they eat with the Whitmans at their hearth in the hall. They raised many toasts, laughed and reminisced and the four Whitman children sat wide eyed by the blazing fire, in wonderment at having so fine a lord and lady eating at table with their parents. Mary cuddled three-year-old Jennifer on her lap, remembered little Catherine at that age and dreamed of the children she would bear Staff some day, but not, hopefully, until they saw fit to tell the court and her family of their marriage and could go to Wivenhoe. She never wished to attempt to raise a son or daughter in the emotional confines of the court again.

"We will make this last toast, then, to a sound night's winter sleep," Staff was saying with his goblet aloft again. He winked at Mary and, to her dismay, she could feel a blush spread over her neck and cheeks. The fire was entirely too warm and the wine lightly touched her face and mind with laughter.

They mounted the stairs together, and she turned back shyly to wave at the beaming little family of Master Whitman. She felt every bit a first time bride even though she had been possessed by far too many men, and the Whitmans would be shocked to know of her unhappy past.

"I much prefer this to the screaming and running and undressing at court," she observed quietly as he swung open the door to their room.

"You will never know how much I suffered that night, lass."

"What night?"

"The night you were wed at court. I heard them all tearing through the hall laughing, and I went to the stables and got raving drunk with the grooms and stable boys. Lost a good bit of money gambling, too."

"Did you, my love? You never told me that."

He closed the door and shot the bolt firmly. "There are many things I never told you of my suffering for you, sweetheart. But that is all behind us now and, pray God, things will always be better for us in the future together."

He smiled a deep, lazy smile and pulled her gently over to the fire. The room smelled of fresh herbs and clean rushes rustled on the wooden floor. Deftly he unlaced her dress and it fell in a pink pool at her feet. His arms encircled her and they stood in the warmth of the

567

fire and their love.

"Wine, my love?" his voice came quietly in her hair.

"I think I have had quite enough wine, my Staff."

He picked her up in his arms in one fluid motion before she even sensed he would do so. "I think you have had quite enough of everything except me and the loving I intend to give you, Mary Bullen, Lady Stafford." He laid her gently on the bed and stood to undress. His voice came muffled from under his shirt and doublet as he pulled them off at the same time. "I promise you, sweet, if you *do* lie on this bed awake half the night it will not be with longing that I would touch you and force you to submit as last time we were here."

Her mouth dropped open slightly in surprise. "But you were long sleeping, Staff. How did you know of that?"

He laughed deep in his throat as he bent to strip off his breeks. "I told you, golden Mary, there are some things of my longings for you you do not know. You had best make a careful study of me over the years, and perhaps you will learn what I mean."

"I intend to, my lord. If only we could live together openly!"

"We will, sweetheart. We will, somehow and as soon as we can manage it. If Anne should bear him a son, I will ask him outright, but enough of that other world. This one is ours."

He lay beside her. The bed sagged in his direction and she rolled against him. He covered them with the huge comforter. She started to tell him again how happy she was, but his mouth descended on hers and his big hands pulled the chemise up past her knees, her hips, her breasts. She raised herself to help him get it

568

over her head, and her heavy wedding ring glinted gold for an instant in the distant firelight. She would wear it on a chain perhaps around her waist where no one but he or Nancy would ever see it. His hands were on her waist now and his knee rode intimately between her thighs. The whole court, the whole world could fall apart and she would not care.

She gave him a tremulous smile as he skimmed the backs of his loosely curled fingers across her lips already tingling with the sweet friction of his kisses, then ran them lightly down under her chin, along the satin arch of her throat where they flickered delicately, torturingly across her pulsating nipples. He moved his fingers now in little velvet circles around each pointed peak until tears squeezed out between her lashes at the pure rapture of it. Then his fingers continued down her ribs and slid along her lower belly while she drowned in his eyes glazed with tenderness and passion so close to hers. Finally, his hand trailed its touch of unbearably beautiful torment across his hipbones, through the silky tangle of curly, warm hair, and then between her thighs which she parted for him with a low moan.

"Mine, Mary, all, all mine, finally, my love," he breathed as his lips returned to demand the deep and plundering kiss she surrendered him dizzily even as his hands began their unrepentant stroking at her very liquid, fiery core.

"Staff, Staff, I cannot bear it—I mean, I—" she got out once, but he stopped only long enough to move her legs wide apart with his between and crush her sweet and incoherent love words with another blazing kiss.

When she got her breath and his hands moved over her again, her tongue darted wildly in and around his ear and she rained kisses across his warm temples and down his strong jawline and throat until he moved even closer between her legs. At the last tottering instant when she thought she would surely scream out her pleas for the sweet, piercing ecstasy of their final union, he put his huge hands under her soft buttocks and lifted her up slightly to meet him.

"This is our world now," he was saying low as he thrust into her waiting, trembling warmth. It went on and on forever, this creation of one body, the incandescent flowering of their passion like a deep, glowing, crimson rose bursting to bloom. Together they slipped down into the red, silken petals and around and around in the depths of its sweet and overpowering center. And all night long, their love encompassed them.

Chapter Twenty-Nine
March 17, 1534

Hampton Court

It was the earliest spring Mary could remember and the mazelike gardens were newly alive with tiny nubs of purple and yellow crocus, and the thin branches of forsythia stirred with new life in their golden buds. She gently stroked her flat belly against the mauve velvet of her gown. It gave no sign yet, but soon enough she would begin to swell with the growth of Staff's first child. They had waited a year for this and now she would tell him. He would be somewhat alarmed, for he knew that the babe would eventually necessitate their telling the king and queen and asking to be dismissed or allowed to live together at court. But they were so happy, whether they had to meet in secret or not, that they could weather even that.

She inhaled a deep breath laden with the aromas of moist spring earth and sat on the marble bench in the deserted rose garden near their hidden bower where they often met during the afternoons when they could slip away. Married more than a year, she mused, the smile on her lips again. If only the Boleyn fortunes had not been so shaky lately and Anne so hysterical and distraught, they would have told them long ago.

Mary glanced up at the wing of the nursery which directly overlooked these gardens. The six-month-old Princess Elizabeth no doubt slept or played beyond those windows—the child who was to have been the prince Anne and the king's astrologers had promised him. It was a white-faced, red-haired child whose christening at Greenwich the king refused to attend. The Boleyns had huddled behind Archbishop Cranmer as he blessed their best hope to hold the crown. And worst of all, Anne had newly miscarried of a pregnancy. Now the Boleyns were in fear and disarray and even father showed desperation in his darting eyes. This was no time for them to be told of a new marriage or pregnancy of their black sheep daughter Mary. But if only the king would cease to look elsewhere as he had lately with various mistresses and would bed with the queen, Anne could conceive again. Then they would surely tell them, and then. . .

There were quick footsteps on the gravel path, and she ducked back into their little bower. The interior was not so hidden with its leaves and flowers yet to come, but the vines and briars were fairly thick. Staff was here, his head and shoulders blocking out the garden beyond.

"Stephen tells me his Nancy says you wanted to see me, sweetheart. Is anything amiss?" He took a step toward her and his hands went to her waist.

"Not amiss, love, but I wanted to tell you something. Did you have difficulty getting away?"

"No. His Grace is with a messenger from his sister in Suffolk, and Cromwell is closeted with your father.

Cromwell has taken to giving me one raised eyebrow lately and wishing me a good night's sleep, so I assume he knows or suspects how much I see you."

"But he could not know we are wed!"

"Sometimes I do not know what the man knows or thinks. But I *do* sense that he is amazingly protective of you, for His Grace obviously knows nothing of us. It seems to have cropped from the king's realm of interest what I do, although he always wants me about on the sporting field. At least he has given up on that foolish Dorsey match for me." He smiled rakishly and took a step deeper into the bower. "I do not fancy *two* wives to please."

She pushed out her lower lip in an intentional pout. "I am starting to believe you do not deserve to hear what I have to tell you at all."

"No? It is important then? Tell me!" He gave her waist a little squeeze.

"Well, my lord, it is only that we are going to have to weather the storm sometime in the near future and tell them we are wed."

"Your sister would go right through the roof, sweet, and His Grace has been continually on edge since he signed his friend Sir Thomas More's bill of execution." His face changed suddenly and his eyes widened. "Why did you say we must tell them in the near future, love? What are you telling me?"

She smiled up at him and her arms went around his neck. "My dear Lord Stafford, you have always known everything about me without my having to tell you. Have you so changed? Has marriage so dulled your senses?"

He stared down incredulous. "Mary!" He picked

573

her up and tried to spin them, but her feet and skirts caught in the wooden trellis and the briars pulled at their clothes.

"Put me down, Staff! You cannot do that in here!" They both collapsed against each other weak with laughter.

He seized her hands in a powerful grip against his red velvet chest. "You are with child, my love?"

She nodded wide-eyed drinking in his wordless joy.

"How long? Did you just discover it?"

"I did not just discover it, my lord, but now I am certain. In late September or early October I would judge. An heir for Wivenhoe, my love."

"Yes, an heir for Wivenhoe and for freedom away from court and all their damned intrigues. But, lass, unlike some, I will be happy with a beautiful daughter that has her mother's eyes." He bent and kissed her gently as though he were suddenly afraid she were fragile.

"I will not break, you know, Staff, not even when I begin to swell. I would not want you to think that you have to . . ."

"Have no fear of that, my sweetheart." He bent to kiss her again, but raised his head and listened. "Now who the deuce is shouting like that at such a momentous time? I am so happy for our wonderful news, Mary."

"Did you think it would never happen? Thirty years of age is hardly past childbearing years, you know." She gave him a playful poke in his midsection and he grinned like a small boy. Then she heard it too, a call from far away in the gardens. Nancy's voice calling her name?

"Oh no, not a summons to Anne's chamber. I cannot bear her ranting and raving, Staff. She is utterly beside herself. It is worse than that week in France when you all rode out with Francois and she stormed and screamed for five days. I know she is desperate and frightened, but any words of comfort she just rips to shreds."

"Yes, it is Nancy, sweet, and Lady Wingfield. Go on now, I may be late tonight, but I will wake you if you are asleep, and we will properly celebrate our good news then." He kissed her quickly and disappeared in the direction of the river opposite from Nancy's approach. She suddenly wished she had waited to tell him when they were really alone with no interruptions upon their joy. But, then, this place had its own beautiful memories, and she had always planned to tell him here when it happened.

Mary flounced out her skirts and hoped Lady Wingfield would not notice the tiny pulls in the materials from the mad spinning against the rose vines. She raised her hand to Nancy as the two women caught sight of her strolling toward them.

"I was trying to call loudly for you, my lady," Nancy assured her with a conspiratory wink.

"Thank you, girl," Lady Wingfield cut in. "You did indeed know where your mistress likes to walk in the afternoons. Lady Rochford, the queen is calling for you and unless you come quickly with me, the others will bear the brunt of her temper."

"Then we shall go directly, Lady Wingfield. Do you know the cause of the summons?"

They hurried across the spring gardens, somehow changed by the fact that Mary had to go back to Anne's

575

dark, vaulted room where she had only two weeks ago borne the dead child.

"The cause, lady? Hurt, and vile temper, and fear, but I beg you, do not tell the queen or the little Rochford I said so."

Mary glanced at the sweet-faced, gray-haired matron as they climbed the stairs. "No, lady, I will not tell her that her dear companion can see things clearly."

"I know you do also, Lady Rochford," the woman whispered to Mary as they wended their way among the small crowd outside the queen's chambers. "You are somehow different from the others."

" 'S bones, where have you been hiding, Mary?" came Anne's sharp voice from the depths of the bed, even before Mary could see her pinched white face staring out at them all.

"In the gardens, Your Grace. I did not know you would be requiring me again or I would not have strayed."

"Dreaming you were home at Hever, I suppose. Well, you had best stay closer in the future. As it is, both father and I wish to speak with you."

A tiny knot twisted in Mary's stomach. She and her father had hardly been on speaking terms this last year since she had argued with him about his secret visits to her son at Hatfield. He had even taken to sending Cromwell as go-between if he wished to ask her a question or give an order.

"Sit here on the bed, sister," Anne motioned with a slender jeweled hand. "I get rather dizzy with everyone standing about or moving around the room all the time."

Mary sat gently on the foot of the bed. Anne's body

had fully healed from her miscarriage, but she seemed unwilling to rise from her bed despite what the doctors said.

"First, I would have some of the truth, and I know I will not get it from the simpering faces around me. Jane Rochford tells me—at my insistence—that my husband the king has been visiting others at night. I know that if he is seeing them at night, he is bedding them. I have long known there are various court ladies who are greedy little sluts enough to let him do as he will. Is that true, what Jane says? Is it come to that already? Tell me, Mary, for I would know. Cromwell, father and George are lying to me. Is it true?"

"I seldom see the king, sister, as you know. And I am not there to see . . ."

"Is it true, Mary? You may not be there but Stafford is about, and I know you two still see each other. Well?"

Mary held her breath, then let the words out in a rush. "I have heard that your information is correct, Your Grace."

"Then I must arise and get my strength back. Father is planning something drastic and it does not include me. I must get my looks and laughter back and then we shall see who holds this king! I can conceive again, Mary. This child was ill-formed and it was not my fault. They whisper I am the cause of it, but it is not—it cannot—be true. They say I bewitched him and my sixth tiny finger shows that I am a witch!" Her voice broke and Mary pressed her thin hand between her own.

"Who has told you these vile rumors, Anne? Jane Rochford?"

Ignoring her question and comforting touch, Anne plunged on, "The Boleyns have fine healthy children like Elizabeth, like your Henry and Catherine. I shall have another—a boy!" The queen struggled to the edge of the bed and dangled her legs still under the sheets. "No, get back all of you and leave us for a while. My sister will help me. Rochford and Lady Wingfield may stay. Everyone else, leave me!

"Here, Mary, let me lean on you. In a week I shall be back with him and there shall be no more fly-by-night whores in his bed. I shall get the names and if any of them are my ladies, they will be banished." Anne's eyes refocused on Mary's worried face and she seemed to calm somewhat. "Here now, sister, I had something to tell you of your little Harry. His Grace is sending Elizabeth in style with a full household of her own to be raised at Hatfield, so Henry Fitzroy and your son will be sent elsewhere for their tutoring."

Anne rose with Mary's help and walked a few unsteady steps. "Really, Mary, do not look so distraught. You must not expect the lad to stay with Fitzroy much longer anyway, since Bessie Blount's illegitimate son is older and should be sent to the law courts soon. Your Harry is only nephew to the king by marriage."

"Yes, Your Grace, I understand. Where will he be sent?"

"I am not certain. Cromwell is deciding a good place. I cannot fathom that I could feel so exhausted from but a few steps."

"Cromwell? Cannot *you* decide, Your Grace?"

"Yes, of course the final decision in mine. Cromwell only works for me, you know."

"Rather like, he serves the king," Mary replied before she could stop her thoughts.

"And what do you imply by that? Help me back to bed. I do not wish to have your pious lectures about anything, including that the little bastard Mary Tudor should be allowed to visit her Spanish mother. She must be made to serve as Elizabeth's handmaid and companion. Do not look so grieved. It will be a good lesson to her. She and her wretched mother must learn who is queen and who is only princess of the realm now. I could also appoint your Catherine to live at Hatfield since the Duchess of Suffolk has been so ill and at Westhorpe unable to return to court. Elizabeth should have her little cousin with her. You would like little Catherine to be well provided for, would you not?"

"Yes, oh yes. Thank you, sister." Tears of relief sprang to Mary's eyes, for she had worried over Catherine's future as she had heard daily of the worsening health of her dear friend Mary Tudor, beloved Duchess of Suffolk. All the court knew the king's sister had hovered at the very door of death these past weeks.

"I thank the saints you are not queen here, Mary. Your spine and heart of jelly would hardly do the Boleyns any good. Though I am strong and will not bow to their whims, the people and court will come to love me when they have their prince. And—they will have him from my body as soon as I am well again." She collapsed weakly to a sitting position on the bed. Mary lifted her legs and covered her with the sheet. "Tell Jane to fetch Cromwell."

Jane's face appeared beside Mary's as though she had heard every word they had shouted or whispered. "I will fetch him, Your Grace," she said, and darted back from the bed in a swift curtsey.

"And tell him nothing, Jane. Just fetch him and do not tell His Grace you do so," Anne added, her eyes still on Mary.

"Then I should go to see what father wants, Your Grace," Mary said bending slightly over Anne after Jane had departed.

"Wait, wait! Sit again. There is something else." Mary did so.

"I promise you I will take care of your two children and that I will continue to ignore your little liaison with William Stafford, at least until His Grace and I find you a husband, but you must be my friend, Mary. You must!" Her fingers gripped Mary's arm hard.

"I *am* your friend, Anne."

"Then you forgive me for making you sleep with Francois in France?"

Mary bowed her head and the huge ruby on Anne's thumb winked bloodily at her. She knew Francois had told them his lies as he had vowed. She hated the memory of that night now that she felt clean and whole as Staff's wife. What good would it do now to deny it all?

"Mary, you forgive me?"

"Yes. Of course."

"And you will help me? Vow it!"

"I do so promise, sister, unless you have some other plan for me to sleep with, wed or love elsewhere than I would choose for myself."

"You will marry where the king and I bid you, but for the rest, yes, I promise. When you wed, we shall surely find you someone you can love, as they say. And as for sleeping elsewhere, that is what I do not wish you to do. You see, Mary," her voice dropped to a bare whisper and Mary had to lean closer, "I heard father

580

talking to George about how beautiful you still are and how you seem to have bloomed anew lately and I fear that . . . well, I know father so well, I fear he may try to get you to hold the king for the family.''

Mary's body jerked back and her hands went to her open mouth. Anne's dark eyes pierced Mary's wide one. ''Yes, Mary. I am glad to see you knew nothing of it and he has not asked you yet. But I fear he will and you must vow to me to have no part of it.''

''Your Grace, Anne, how could you ever believe I would do such a thing? Besides, it is over long, long ago for me with the king, before his heart was yours. I would never do such a thing even if father threatens me.''

''I thought as much. But I have seen you bend to him before against your will and, unlike me, I know you love him still.''

''I do not, sister. That, too, went long ago.''

''Do not lie to yourself, Mary. I can see the grief in your eyes when he hurts or uses you. And do not let him try to bribe you through your children or Stafford. I am queen here. And, Mary,'' her hand shot out and grabbed the folds of Mary's gown, ''you must vow to tell me if he even asks you to do so. I can only handle him if I know his plottings against me.''

''Anne, father would never plot against you. You are his dear hope and well he knows it!''

''But, you see, Mary, you were his hope once and, when the strings to the king's heart dissolved, he dropped you. Can you deny it?''

''No.''

''I have always learned by your example, sister. Go on now. You must see him and then tell me what he says.''

"I wish not to be trapped as a spy between you and father, Anne. I have been in too many snares already and I wish it not."

"Then, on this one thing only, as you have promised me, Mary. I need your strength. Please."

"Yes. Yes. I understand."

"Go now before Jane comes back with Cromwell in tow. I am not sure what I shall tell him." She turned away from Mary on her side and sighed. "I only sent her on the errand to rid us of her prying ears. Still she may be useful to me in this." Anne's voice faded away as though she would sleep, and Mary rose carefully from the bed. Then she turned back.

"Anne?"

"Yes?"

"You might talk with Cromwell about not sending Harry too far away. He should have some companion to be educated with. I would not have him be a solitary monk."

"All right. We have a bargain, but you might tell Cromwell yourself, you know. He much covets your good will. Hurry, Mary. Then come right back and tell me."

Mary assumed she would find her father in his massive suite just down the hall. He had spread his secretaries and clerks out into George's room too, now that George was appointed Commander of the Cinque Ports and spent much time at his new gift of Beaulieu Castle ninety miles from London. It was just like a party for Anne when their brother returned from each trip or mission. If only George were here now, he could calm Anne and help her to regain her strength.

Cromwell and Jane sailed out of the door to Lord Boleyn's rooms as Mary approached. Cromwell doffed his black velvet hat and stood firm in his tracks to bow to her. Mary managed a smile, for she sensed that this cold, square-shaped man could be of more help than harm to her in the days to come. He wielded much power with both the king and queen, and she and Staff would need every ally they could muster when they told them of their marriage and the babe.

"You were just going to see your father, Lady Rochford?" Cromwell always put his statements in ominous sounding questions, Mary had long noted.

"Yes, Master Cromwell. And you are going to see the queen?"

He smiled and his eyes went quickly over her as they always did, though she no longer trembled at the possibility that he would take the next step of intimately touching her. "Perhaps I shall be back to see you while you are still closeted with Lord Boleyn, then," he said smoothly. "The queen's interviews last briefly lately, though I am certain she will make every effort to be up and about now the lovely spring is here. I see you have been strolling the gardens."

Her face showed surprise. Had he seen them? Had his spies reported to him already?

"You have ripped your gown on a briar and have grass marks on your slippers, lady," he explained. "If only I did not have to work so hard inside the palace, I would love to accompany you outside sometime. We could discuss where your son Henry shall be transferred on our walk perhaps? Good day. Lady Jane?" He nodded to Mary and swept off down the hall with Jane Rochford in his smooth wake.

Mary knocked on the door, wondering why the guards were not about. If only she could see Staff before she walked into this lion's den, she would feel more secure. Yet, she was stronger now. She was changed. Surely, she did not love her father and could stand up to anything he dared to propose.

Both guards and a messenger stood with her father at his huge desk when another man opened the door for her. He did not see her until she approached several steps wondering if his alert eyes would also discover she had been walking in the gardens.

"Mary, come and sit. These men were just leaving." He shooed them away and seated her. She felt, with great alarm, the deep irrational happiness which always bubbled to the surface when he centered his attentions on her.

"No," she thought distinctly to herself. "Protect yourself. Do not trust his mask of smiles and love."

"We have hardly talked lately," he began. "You have been such a help to Anne in the loss of this second child. I was about to send for her mother, but I think she is snapping out of it a bit."

"Yes. I have just seen her and I am certain of it. She wants to get her strength back, and I am sure she will soon. When His Grace sees her smiling again, she will be back in his good will soon enough."

"Let us be realistic about that, Mary. The light for her has gone out of his eyes. I have seen it happen before."

"Yes, father. So have I."

His eyes narrowed nervously. "Yes. Well, we must do everything to see that Anne at least has other opportunities to bear the Tudor son who will rule after His

Grace, whatever his relationship may be to her in the future.''

Mary sat stock still and stared at him until he glanced down at his folded hands. ''His Grace, as you may or may not know, daughter, has been on a bull's rampage bedding court ladies since the unfortunate loss of this second child. The women are all without principle and would hope to lure the king away from his rightful wife.''

''In other words, father, nothing ever changes.''

''Hush and listen, Mary. This is serious business for the Boleyns—and that includes you and your two children.''

''Will Carey's and my two children.''

''We will not argue that again, girl.'' He stood and began to pace back and forth before the oriel window which flooded the room with warm light and cast his shadow across Mary as he passed. ''He can stud as many of the little bitches as he wants for all I care, but there is one different, one who threatens. Anne has her here as lady in waiting now at His Grace's request, though I do not think Anne suspects her at all.''

''Of whom do you speak?''

''That simpering, smiling Jane Seymour from Wolf Hall in Wiltshire. Her family is full of overprotective brothers and so far she refuses the king and that can breed disaster as we have all seen. Now, either Jane Seymour must be eliminated, or the king must be lured away. Do you follow me?''

''Cannot Anne send the little Seymour back to Wolf Hall?''

''I fear that would be a foolish move. It would be like taking the target away from the king at butts or break-

585

ing his favorite tennis racquet. The repercussion might be, well, unpleasant.''

"Then that leaves the other option of luring the king away from the girl,'' Mary said calmly, but she knew her eyes and trembling upper lip betrayed her nervousness.

"Yes, Mary, exactly.'' He ceased his pacing and stood facing her, leaning hard on his cluttered table.

"This reminds me rather of chess, father, and I have never been good at the game, though I do know well enough the role of pawns.''

"What? Look, Mary, everything hinges on His Grace's good will, and you know well how to deal with that.''

"Do I? His ill will, rather, since I have long outlived my usefulness to him and to you, father. I will be going now before you say something that will cause a permanent rift between us.''

"Sit, Mary! You will do this for Anne, and George, and your mother and me.''

"Do not dare to bring mother's name into this, or Anne's either, for that matter! Let us go to Anne's chambers and discuss this with her if you believe it is for Anne you act like a brothel owner—like a pimp!''

She saw him clench his jaw muscles, and his eyes glared at her. Still he held his temper and his voice came low. "Anne is distraught and cannot see things clearly of late. We must do this for her without her knowledge.''

"The mood she is in these last days, she would put us all on the block at The Tower, family or not.''

"Anne's power goes to her head sometimes, but she will do as she is told if it comes down to it.''

"The answer is no, father, absolutely no. I will not help you or abet your nefarious plans."

"Do you still fancy you love Stafford? You will comply or I will have him sent away or married off. Cromwell is my ally, and he is just now ready to assign your little Harry to some abbey or house to finish his education. Would you really like that place to be clear to the Welsh border, madam?"

Mary stood but leaned the backs of her knees on the chairseat from which she had risen. "Try any of that and I shall tell the queen, father. Cromwell is the king's ally first and foremost as I have heard you yourself say. And little Harry is Anne's legal ward until his majority. Besides, if you really sent him far away, he would not be so available to have you pour your poison of his false heritage in his ears. You will raise no rumors or rebellion behind my son, father, or the king will hear of your secret visits to Hatfield all these years."

She nearly ran to the door and turned back as she reached it. "Do what you have to do, father, but keep me well out of it and leave my children untouched."

He sat calmly at his desk as though he had not heard her outburst. His voice came coldly at her back as she put her hand to the door latch. "I really ought to give you to Cromwell to tame, Mary. He has wanted to possess you for some years now and I am starting to think you deserve him. You misuse your beauty and that lush body on that renegade Stafford when you could have the king or some duke at least at your beck and call. How I have wished over the years that you had half the cleverness and brains of your sister. You have never even learned to hide the fear or love you feel when it is of dire necessity to do so."

587

"And if I have not learned to hide my revulsion o
you, my utter contempt of you, father, I am so sorry!"

She yanked the door open. "By the way, daughter
your dear friend Mary Tudor, Duchess of Suffolk, die
yesterday at Westhorpe, so perhaps we could arrange
match for you with the duke. The duke, of course, i
most grieved, but I warrant he will be rewed within th
year. So much for true love."

She stood in shock with the door half open. He
beautiful friend dead. So young and the little laughing
Margaret without her mother, and Catherine there i
that house of death.

"Cromwell plans to send for your daughter with ar
escort. His Grace will no doubt be in mourning for
month so, hopefully, that will put a damper on his amo
rous activities for a while. He loved his sister over well
to forgive her two foolish indiscretions. He only las
month sent word by Suffolk that he forgave her for he
stubborn stand for the Spanish princess he was duped
into marrying when he was only a boy."

The flow of words went right through her and she
could grasp none of them. The raven-haired Mary
dead. Mary who went to France to wed the old king so
she could have her beloved Suffolk. Mary frightened
when Francois locked her for six weeks in dark Cluny to
be certain she was not with child. Mary who looked so
radiant on her wedding day to the duke long ago in
Paris. Mary, cold and dead.

"Are you going to stand there all day, girl? Your
daughter will be back safe tomorrow. Cromwell intends
to tell Anne she will have to wear mourning for both her
royal sister-in-law as well as the dead baby, so you need
not run to her with the news. Go to your room now.

You look terrible.''

Mary did not even glance back. Her desire to scream her hatred at him was gone, burned out and wasted in her grief for her friend who first showed her how to love someone the world said she could not have. No, she thought, as she walked woodenly along the corridor with its convoluted carvings and intricate tapestries, the grief is not only for Mary Tudor. She felt grief for the entire family that they were brought to this danger- ous and horrible point: Anne, Queen of England, a frightened, bitter shell; George, besotted by his new toys of lands and position; mother, alone as always at Hever; and father. . . . Her mind would go no fur- ther. She shoved open the door to her room. Nancy was not about, but that was well. She needed to be alone now.

She rummaged in her wooden jewelry box under the crimson garnet necklace, the huge Howard pearl drop and the other gifts from Staff's dead aunt she had stored there which she dared not wear among the gossiping courtiers. Her fingers seized the tiny carved pawn from that chess game in France so long ago. She stared at it unblinking and held it tight in the palm of her hand as she sank down on the floor against the velvet draperies of her bed curtain and began to sob.

Chapter Thirty
June 9, 1534

Whitehall Palace

As her baby grew and Mary's waistline swelled, she withdrew more and more from the court around her. That was easy enough lately, for the king and queen had been on a leisurely summer progress through the green midlands of England. His Grace had even cancelled an important diplomatic trip to France to take Anne on the journey. It was commonly known that the queen was with child again and that Henry Tudor had given her one last chance to produce his heir. But now, the king and queen had returned to Whitehall and this happy retirement of Mary's would soon be over one way or the other. Either her sister would need her enough to keep her about when she knew she was with child and married to a man not of her choosing, or she would be banished or worse.

Staff had been forced to accompany the royal party, for the king favored his attendance in whatever martial or sporting endeavor he undertook. The three weeks had dragged by for Mary. She had spent the time walking, thinking, and talking to Nancy and to the Boleyn

ousin Madge Shelton whom their father had brought
o court as one of Anne's new ladies-in-waiting. The
irl was winsome and lovely with a perfect oval face and
urly blonde hair almost as light as her own. Madge's
reen eyes danced with the excitement of being at the
ourt even though its royal lord and lady had been gone
hese last weeks. The king had wanted to take the new
nd charming Mistress Shelton along on the trip, but
ad given in to his wife's refusal when he discovered
hat the queen was beginning another pregnancy.

Mary felt somewhat guilty that she liked the seven-
een-year-old girl so much, for the whole truth was that
Mistress Shelton had been brought to court by Thomas
Boleyn to hold the king's attentions for his petulant and
ncreasingly nasty Queen Anne. In one fell swoop, as
Thomas Boleyn had planned, the green-eyed Madge
ad become her royal cousin's maid and the king's lat-
st mistress. Mary hoped fervently that the three week
abbatical and the new pregnancy would soothe Anne's
ile torment of the girl. Mary also prayed that the joy
ver the new child would allow Staff and her to tell
Anne of their marriage and ask to be retired to
Wivenhoe.

It had been almost a half hour now since the huge
oyal entourage had clattered into the courtyard of
Whitehall, and Mary began to pace in her room wondering how long it would take Staff to free himself and
come to see her. When he saw her waist, he would
know the time of secrecy had passed for them, for nei-
her cloaks nor dresses with high waistlines could hide it
now. She glanced down at the completed and pains-
akingly written letter on her table under the sunny
window. She began to skim the words, though she

knew them by heart and the old haunting feeling returned. It was like guilt, hate and love all mingled together in a crucible of pain.

The door sprang open and she turned, half expecting to see Nancy with another report on the returned travelers since she had heard no footsteps in the hall. But it was Staff, so tall and handsome, grinning, and he had come back to her.

"My love, I was waiting and waiting . . ." she began, but he smothered her words with a crushing kiss. Then, with a look on his face of more awe than concern or worry, he put his hands on her shoulders and stood her armlength away.

"Lady Stafford, I believe the whole world will know you are pregnant now as well as your sister. We can delay their being told no longer. That is obvious. Who has guessed or asked? I did not imagine three weeks could make such a difference, but indeed, sweetheart, the child has blossomed and that means a certain end to our secret. I thank God they are in a fairly hopeful mood because of the queen's new pregnancy. Does your father know of our child? Cromwell?"

"I have not seen my dear father, Staff. He has been about and Madge has seen him, but he stays well out of my way."

"Then Madge must know. You have seen much of her then? I am not sure that is wise, for the sharp edge of the queen's wrath may yet fall on the girl."

"Really, my love," Mary said, looking up into his concerned face, "the girl is my cousin, though I have not seen her for years before father hauled her into this mess. But she is new here and alone, and I remember how terrible that can be in a vast court."

Staff sank down on the bed, and pulled his boots off and sighed wiggling his toes. "I applaude your sweet motives, lass, but the wench is hardly alone. In her first week at court this spring, the king bedded her, the queen screamed at her, and Norris continues to make a fool of himself over her whenever His Grace is not around. Just be careful you do not stand too close to her if the queen's axe should fall. I would have to bet that Her Grace will have little Madge Shelton, cousin or not, out of here in a week. So anyway, Madge has no doubt guessed about your babe. And Cromwell?"

"I have seen him twice, but I wore a pelisse each time. He has been very busy with the king gone, but he approached me in the gardens by the river once and I dared not run away as I wished. We walked for a little while."

"I assume he behaved himself, except for his beady eyes, that is, which try to caress you every time you are in view."

"Do not be angry, Staff." She sat beside him on the bed. He draped his arms over her shoulders and pulled her gently to his side.

"I am not angry, love. I only hate myself every time I think of you left behind here with the vipers. Lately, my Mary has taken quite good care of herself, but I hate not having you and the babe out of here and safe."

"But now we must tell them, so then we shall see."

"Yes, sweetheart. Then we shall see. I am exhausted, Mary, and had best be back by supper. Will you lie beside me here?"

They cuddled in the middle of the bed, Mary on her back and Staff on his side facing her with his arm under her head. She put his open hand on her belly. "See, my

593

love, he moves about more than ever now.''

"Or she," he said sleepily. "I still would not mind a miniature of your Catherine. Is she well at Hever? I know how much this summer will mean to your mother having her there again."

"She is quite well. But all men want a son, Staff."

"Yes, and I also. But there will be time for at least another child before you begin hobbling around on a cane," he teased. He opened one eye then the other and stared at her fine profile. "Is there something else besides having to face them that is troubling you, Mary? Have you not come to terms with your father's last wretched scheme to use you as bait?"

"No, Staff. It is not that. But there is something that has been haunting me. I have dreamed of it, Staff."

"Tell me." His eyes were wide awake on his tired face.

"While the court was away on progress—the first week you were gone—word came here that after Sir Thomas More was beheaded on Tower Hill, the king's men put his head on a pike on London Bridge and gave his family only the trunk of his body for burial."

"Look Mary. It is only another indication of how terrible the times are and how far the king has sunk into the mire of treachery. Sir Thomas More may have been His Grace's loyal advisor and friend these years, but the king turned against him completely when More dared not to sign the Act of Supremacy declaring the king head of the new church. I do not doubt that the king or Cromwell told his henchmen to make a clear example of More. Fear not for his body being separate from his head. The Lord God has need of men with the moral strength of Thomas More on resurrection day whether their heads be buried with their bodies or not. You must put the whole awful thing out of your mind."

"I cannot. How can I? You do not, and I know you blame yourself that we all signed the document like sheep. But that is not all."

"What more?" He sat up cross-legged on the bed facing her, leaning over her, intent.

"After his head had been there on the pole a week, for they say it was guarded that long and by then the crows had been at the eyes and . . ."

"Mary, do not torture yourself with this."

"I must tell you, Staff. After a week, it hardly looked like a man's head. But then, when the guards dispersed, his eldest daughter Meg Roper . . ."

"Yes, the tall girl. She married a lawyer in the king's household."

"Staff, his daughter loved him so much that she went out at night in a boat to London Bridge and bribed the keeper of the bridge to drop his head to her. She took it in her skirts and carried it home in her lap to bury it with his body. She loved him so much, she did that!"

Staff's big hand reached out and curled around hers, clenched at her side. Her tear filled eyes still haunted by the wonderment of her own words of Meg Roper sought his face.

"I am sorry, Mary. It is a fearsome thing, but you must not carry these thoughts around with you. For the babe's sake, at least."

"I have prayed for Meg Roper, Staff. I have written to her, too, telling her that I admire her courage and her love. I apologized that the Boleyn family had any part in bringing her the loss of her dearly beloved father."

"Lass, you cannot go about the kingdom trying to gain forgiveness for the Boleyns. Do not put that burden on yourself. You are not a part of them and will be well rid of them soon. Your mother we shall keep close. The rest will be most difficult to hold over the years. There is always some sort of disaster brewing on the horizon around your father and I will have you and the child well rid of it."

"Where are you going?"

"I have changed my mind. This is no time for sleeping. They have returned from a triumphant trip through the central shires and even testy Anne is in a good mood. The prospect of a child has returned the glow to her cheeks, and she was hardly booed at all along the way. His Grace has dreams and hopes of a legitimate son again and has sweet Madge to serve his every whim while he waits for the heir's arrival. We shall tell them now before supper, before someone sees you and all hell explodes." He began stuffing his breeks back in the tops of his boots.

"Still, I will send the letter to Meg Roper, Staff."

"Fine, love. Send the letter. But you must cease to carry guilt around with you for your family's actions or your disappointment in the father you love. Fetch a pelisse to cover yourself. I will not have your sister screeching at us before we can present it to them calmly first."

Though the day was warm, Mary wrapped a loose blue pelisse around her shoulders and arranged its folds carefully. Staff kissed her and sent her on ahead, through the crowded halls to the queen's privy chamber and said he would be along to join her shortly, after he had told the king and begged his indulgence. "If you can keep from discussing it with your sister until I arrive, do so. Do not play the heroine, for I want to be there. And if the king walks in with me, do not panic," Staff had instructed her moments ago. His last words went over and over in her mind. Do not panic. I will be there.

The walk to Anne's chambers was not long, but it seemed an eternity. The time had come. Time always thrust things swiftly upon one and then one had to act. Time would bring her to the labor bed to birth Staff's babe; time would bring Anne's next child; time had brought death to a beloved friend; time had brought separation from Hever; time had brought a daughter who loved her father so much that she would carry his poor bloody head home in her lap.

Anne's bedchamber was full of hovering Boleyns and, worst of all, the king was there and in a rage. Mary nearly fled in alarm, but the yeomen guards behind her had closed the door and stood against it. At least Staff would be here quickly when he did not find the king where he sought him. Only the impassive Cromwell is needed to complete this scene, Mary thought, but no one looked impassive here. She wrapped her pelisse protectively about her and lurched back against the wall as the suspended tableau before her exploded.

"Am I to understand, madam, that this entire trip where you had me prancing through Derby and Rutland and Shropshire was a cruel hoax, a deception?" The king's ruddy face went increasingly livid as his voice rose. "No child! Am I to believe a woman who has borne a child and been pregnant yet again cannot tell when she is with child! You misread the signs? S' blood, madam, the whole thing has been a typical Boleyn trick. My people are right when they shout 'Witch! Witch!' "

"Please, my lord, the signs were there. And if I am not with child, I can be soon again. Our trip was so wonderful, so placid and jovial and we . . ."

"And I touched you not and you were well content of it, madam, so how you plan to get with royal child is quite beyond me!"

"Does not the fact that the queen did not encourage Your Grace to bed her indicate that she truly believed she was with child and was afraid to harm her delicate condition?" Thomas Boleyn said low in the angry hush in the room.

Henry Tudor swung his great head toward the voice and glowered, but his quick mind was working and he hesitated.

"Indeed, my lord, that is true," Anne said, "for it is only now the riding back to Whitehall brought on my monthly flow and all my hopes were crushed. I did not know, Your Grace. In my supreme joy to believe I was carrying your child again, I did not know. I am grief-stricken to my very soul."

"And well you should be. I put off an important state visit to Calais for this . . . this charade!" He sat hard on the chair near Anne, but when she reached out to touch his shoulder, he recoiled.

"Are you certain the blood was not a miscarriage? You were not far pregnant?" he asked low, staring at her taut face.

"I am certain. I am sorry I have failed you, my dear lord. I will truly conceive now. You will see," she said and forced a smile.

"Perhaps the rest without a child growing in her womb will lend the added strength necessary, Your Grace," came Thomas Boleyn's soothing voice again. "First a fine daughter—true Tudor indeed with her red-gold hair—and then a fine son."

"I tell you this, madam," the king said quietly, apparently ignoring Lord Boleyn's words, "there had better be a son soon and a live one. I have a son in Henry Fitzroy and perhaps others, so lack of sons is no fault of mine."

Mary's pulse began to race at the implication of other unlawful sons the king could claim, and she glanced fearfully at her father's rapt face. Evidently, they had not even noticed her entry, for their attention was all bent toward the center of their universe.

"So, indeed, if another child be lost, it is obvious where the fault—the sin—lies. I am going riding now. Eat with your own little court of Boleyns and Rochfords and Norfolks. I am tired of it all."

He rose and his short purple cape swept in an arc behind his massive shoulders. His eyes bored into Mary's wide azure ones as he approached the door.

"Your Grace," came Anne's well-modulated voice behind him, and he turned back to his audience as he stood near Mary. "I will do everything I can to ensure Your Grace a fine heir—as fine as Elizabeth in whom you rightly place such fatherly pride. I will do whatever Your Grace would bid, but I would ask one small favor from you in return."

"Well?"

Anne glanced to her father's worried face and then said quite clearly, "I would beg Your Grace to send my cousin Madge Shelton from court back to her parents in

Essex. It bothers me to have her always about and not a friend to the queen much as other of my ladies who are not loyal to me.'' She stood erect, poised, and faced the king across the endless space of rich Damascene carpet.

From where she stood behind him, Mary could see the sinews in his bull neck swell, and the muscles on his huge forearms seemed to jerk. She drew in a quick breath and braced herself against the wall.

''You may have been made queen, madam, but be confident that is no assurance you may tell your lord king how to behave. You will learn to bear such things, as . . . as your betters have done before you.''

The guards opened the double doors at the king's approach, and Mary moved from the wall to keep from being crushed. The king nearly collided with her and put his hands out to roughly move her from his path. Staff's face appeared in the whirl somewhere over the king's shoulder as his strong hands set Mary back into the room.

''You see, madam,'' the king ground out to Anne through clenched teeth, ''your sister bears live sons. Look to her example. Stafford, come with me.''

All the eyes in the room focused on Mary left standing at the open double doors with Stafford standing half behind her. Everyone stared—George nervously, her father bitterly. Jane Rochford could hardly smother a simper at the whole scene of the Boleyns' dismay, and Anne merely whirled her back to them. Staff broke the spell by whispering in Mary's ear as he turned to follow in the angry wake of the king.

''Keep your cloak tight. I will calm His Grace and only tell him we are wed and ask to go to Wivenhoe. The rest is not safe now. I will hurry back. And I will somehow send Cromwell for your protection."

"No, not Cromwell," she started to say, but he was gone on a run and she ached to follow him.

"How nice that all the family could assemble for that dressing down," Jane Rochford said in the quiet of the room.

"Shut your mouth, Jane, or I will have you out in the street with the rest of the cheap gossips and tat tales," Anne shot out without looking up. "It is enough I had to bear your company these last three weeks, though at least your dear Mark Costwick kept you occupied enough for some respite."

"Do you intend to let your wife be so spoke to, George?" Jane prodded.

"Stop this foolish bickering," Thomas Boleyn's voice cut in. "Jane, you will take whatever words the queen gives you or cease to serve her and be quit of here. We all need to stand together on this."

"We have long ceased standing together, father, if indeed we ever did," Anne shouted. "You brought doe-eyed Madge to court. Now I am telling you to get rid of her if you do not wish to see that damned skinny Fitzroy on the throne in place of your own grand-child."

"That problem, I am afraid, is yours, Anne. I can-not help you there."

"No, father, You cannot help me at all. At least George and Mary are still faithful in this mess. George always, and you must admit Mary stood up to that last desperate plan of yours to have her seduce the king. And, as for the cow-faced Seymour with the big inno-cent eyes, I shall have her out of here soon enough."

"You dare not, Anne."

"Dare not? Get from my sight, father. The queen is telling you to leave."

"I am going, daughter—Your Grace—to give you time to get yourself together and to realize that time has altered your influence here. As I said, you dare not touch the little Seymour. You can only vie for the royal bed and hope to God you conceive a son. I will be back later. See that when His Grace returns from the hunt you look ravishing and greet him in the courtyard. Fight hard for him, Anne. That is your only chance now."

He strode to the door and Mary moved far out of his way. "Did you mark His Grace's interest in your son, Mary?" he said as he passed.

The characters in the room rotated positions again with the other powerful protagonist off stage. Anne sank in the chair the king had vacated and George stood at a loss for words first on one foot and then the other. Jane hovered watchful in the wings. Anne motioned for Mary to join her. Mary made her entrance with her pelisse still draped around her.

"It is good to see you after three weeks with the same faces, sister. Do not look so frightened. I am not, I assure you," Anne said tonelessly.

"I admire your courage, Your Grace." Mary sat in the nearby chair Anne's jeweled hand had indicated.

"It comes from having everything to lose rather than nothing. It is only the ones with nothing to lose who are afraid to act. Well, that is my new credo, anyway. Have you heard from Hever? Is mother quite well?"

"Yes. All is well there. My Catherine will keep mother occupied for the summer. Semmonet has arthritis, but she is managing. It has only slowed her down a bit."

Anne leaned her head on the back of her chair and closed her eyes. "Ah, quiet Hever, where no one shouts, gossips or demands." Her eyes shot open. "But did you only come to welcome us home, Mary? You came for a purpose, did you not? When I do not summon my dear Mary, she usually chooses not to come."

"Yes, sister. I have come to ask you a great favor. I feel I have served you well and I would always be your friend. I am in dire need of your love and blessing."

"What? Say on." Anne's eyes went instinctively to Mary's covered midriff, and Mary felt her courage ebb.

"As you well know, Your Grace, the Lord Stafford and I have been in love for some years."

"Lovers, you mean. That was the gift I gave you after you lost everything, Mary. I know he visited your room almost nightly. I am glad you have been happy, but do not ask me to let you wed him. You are the sister of the queen now and not just some penniless widow of a poor esquire. Do not look at me that way, Mary. I am sorry, but I have problems of my own as well you know. I will not propose to His Grace that the queen's sister marry far beneath her."

Mary stood and backed a few steps away from Anne's chair. Jane Rochford was listening so intently that her mouth hung open behind Anne, and George looked anxiously from one sister to the other.

"I am sorry to disappoint or anger you, my sister, but I have never loved anyone as I love Staff, nor shall I ever. Like the king's own sister, I married once at the royal bidding to serve the king as he would have me do. When I was cast off, I began to live my own life and

603

make my own decisions even as you have, Your Grace. I am proud to inform you that Lord Stafford and I have been wed for over a year now. I have never been happier and I regret no moment of my decision or my marriage."

For once Anne was speechless. Her dark eyes glittered then narrowed. "After all I have done for you," she said low, "you dare to repay me this way? Your son well cared for with a fine allowance and tutor by my hand. I went to father to get you enough money to replace the rags on your back after Will Carey died and you dare—you dare—to wed the rebel with the farmlands at God-forsaken Wivenhoe, wherever that may be?'

"His Grace has long-favored Lord Stafford, and he has served the king well. The Bullens have only risen so high recently by hanging on your skirts, sister. I feel I am eminently suited in class and birth to be Lady Stafford."

"You damn fool! Mary, I have loved you, but you were always a fool. George's marriage was one thing. That was long before the Boleyns—not the Bullens any longer remember, Mary—ascended. George's marriage was one thing, but this from you? You could have at least had a duke. Norris has always favored you."

Jane Rochford's voice interrupted. "I think Norris favors your cousin Madge Shelton now, though his competition is somewhat stiff. I applaud Mary's backbone. Stafford always was a handsome stud and he is obviously wild for Mary. I cannot wait until Lord Boleyn hears the news."

"Get out of my sight, you she-ass," Anne screamed turning to throw the empty goblet at Jane. "Bray your

604

gossip in someone's else's ear. Go! Never set foot in the queen's rooms again!"

Jane darted sideways to miss the flying goblet and was nearly out the door as the metal vessel thudded to the floor. She almost collided with Staff who looked immensely relieved to see that the curses and goblet were directed at Jane and not Mary.

"Confession time all around is it not, George?" Anne said over her shoulder as she saw Staff on the threshold.

Staff strode in and bowed low. He dared to stand only several feet from the seething Anne while Mary stood her ground further away. "Your Grace, Mary has told you of our news? I have told the king."

"And?"

"And, to put it true and blunt, Your Grace, we have his reluctant blessing."

"I wish he had sent you to The Tower as well I may yet, Stafford. However did you manage his blessing at all? He favors you, I know, but I would wager his motive is intended to be more punitive towards father and me—a sign that the Boleyns cannot rise so far as they think to rise."

"That was my assessment of his reaction exactly, Your Grace."

Anne took a step closer to Staff, and he stood stock still towering over her. "You always did tell the blatant truth, Stafford. What I like best about you is that you are the only one I know who can somehow keep the king off balance—now that I no longer have the power to do so, that is. That is what amuses me, Stafford. You have always had some kind of power over him where there was none given."

605

"I have been and always will be full loyal to the king and he knows that well."

"Really? It seems to me this clever little marriage move on your part shows you are quite the rebel still, my lord. But a rebel who favors gentle game. Too bad. Too bad. Did His Grace say anything else?" she probed.

"I spoke to him of my love for Mary, Your Grace. There is quite a romantic in him under all the gross power."

"Oh, yes. I remember well his version of romance. Letters, lockets, passionate vows, promises of eternal love. But there is no such thing. It is all another of the world's lies."

"Eternal? Maybe not, sister," Mary said, coming to stand by Staff's side, "but quite enough for a whole lifetime as far as I can see."

"And now I shall ask you the next touchy question, Lord and Lady Stafford. Why have you now decided to tell us this? Why have you tarried so long? Did you ask His Grace to let you go to live at your country farm because you are sick to death of the reeking atmosphere of the palace and my marriage or, indeed, was there another compelling cause?"

"I did ask His Grace that he let us retire to Wivenhoe."

"Say on."

"He said we might go for a time, but he could not spare us permanently. I was grateful for that much."

"And, further?" Anne prodded, her voice nearly breaking as her tone rose dangerously. She stared hard at Mary and her clear brow creased into a severe frown.

"Yes, sister," Mary said quietly, standing tall beside

her husband, but not reaching to touch his arm for support as she longed to do. "Yes, I am carrying a child."

Anne whirled away and yanked a tall backed chair after her so that it spun crazily toward the stunned George. A sob tore her throat and she swung her fist catching Staff on the jaw. He stood stock still until Anne recoiled and sprang toward Mary. "Let me see your sin!" she screamed, clawing at Mary. Both George and Staff darted forward. Mary sprang back behind Staff whose strong arms went around Anne before George could reach them. He held her to his chest as she thrashed, screamed, and sobbed.

"How dare you!" she cried over and over against his shirt. "It is not fair! Damn you both!"

"No, it is not fair, Your Grace, and I am sorry for that," Staff said gently against her raven hair as Mary and George stood still on either side of them. "You deserve another child, Your Grace, and surely you shall have one. If not, you have a beautiful and clever Tudor daughter who is pure English unlike the Spanish Catherine's girl. Keep calm. Do not be afraid and all can yet be well."

Anne stopped struggling and screaming and leaned against him for a silent moment. Then she lifted her tear streaked face and looked long at Mary. Staff released her.

"When will the child be born?" she asked tonelessly.

"In the autumn, sister. I love you, Anne, and I would wish your blessings."

"I cannot give you that, Mary. No, I cannot. You have deceived me terribly when you said you were my friend and I trusted you. It is enough I let you go away. Does the king know of the child?"

"No, Your Grace," Staff said low.

"You may rest assured George and I will not tell him," she said and her eyes went jerkily over Mary's shoulder toward the door. "But perhaps Master Cromwell will."

Cromwell glided toward them across the carpet. "I am sorry I could not come as soon as you sent me word I was needed, Lord Stafford. I was leaving by barge and had to be rowed back to shore. What service may I give?"

"The question is, Master Cromwell," Anne said, moving a few steps to face him, "what have you heard already? What did you know of all this long ago? I warrant you knew as many of the details as Lord Stafford himself."

"Of their liaison, Your Grace?"

"Of course! Did you think I spoke of archery practice or jousting?"

"I have suspected for sometime that Lady Stafford was with child, Your Grace, though I knew nothing of the marriage."

"For conversation's sake, I will assume that is a truthful answer," Anne replied. "Then you two are to be congratulated. You gave Cromwell's army of clever spies the slip. That is almost amusing, is it not, Cromwell?"

When he did not answer, the queen's desperate control shattered again. "Get them out of my sight, king's man! Banish them, get them well on the road before my father or the king hear of the pregnancy—not for the daughter whose very being depends on it, no, but for the beautiful daughter with the Howard looks and simple heart who bears live sons! Get out of here, all of

608

you. I have much to do!''

Mary wanted to hug Anne farewell, but she felt crushed and exhausted, not terrified as she had expected. She curtseyed and backed away, but Anne had turned to the window and George, dear loyal George, put his hands to her shoulders, and they were still standing like that unspeaking as the doors closed.

In the hall courtiers still clustered around the queen's threshold as though awaiting favors. There will be no favors today, Mary thought grimly, as she took Staff's arm and they wended their way through the maze of people behind Cromwell. Jane Rochford darted up from nowhere, no doubt lagging about to hear the rest of the screaming through the door.

''Lord Stafford, Mary, I am so happy for you!'' she gushed.

''Thank you, Jane,'' Mary said low. ''Please, please do not goad the queen so, and try to be a friend to her.''

''George is friend enough for her and that pretty musician Smeaton,'' Jane replied tartly. ''I do not see that George left with the rest of you.''

They walked on leaving the girl behind, but Mary could still hear her petulant voice speaking to someone else. They were nearly on the road to Wivenhoe now, and soon there would be a great distance between them, gossip and the court. They would be on the road to freedom from all of this and, God willing, they might be able to stay away a very long, long time.

''You lead a charmed life, Stafford,'' Cromwell finally spoke when they were out of the crush of eager faces in the hall by Mary's room. He smiled at them, but his voice was as cold as usual no matter what the words. ''It is a rare man indeed who can flaunt authority and propriety and walk away unscathed. Will you need a contingent of guards on the road?"

"Thank you, no, Master Cromwell. Mary and I have four servants between us and that shall suffice."

"Then let me only say," Cromwell went on, his eyes shifting to Mary's face, "that I shall be your ally and not your enemy should you have the need of aid even at little—where is it now?"

"Wivenhoe, near Colchester, Master Cromwell."

"Yes. Maybe I shall visit you sometime. I would like to meet your ghosts." He pivoted stiffly to face Staff. "Let us say it plainly, Lord Stafford. You and I have always been clever chess players. You are one of the few who have even beaten me. Now you are off on an adventure which greatly intrigues me." He glanced at Mary again. "The Boleyns, all of the Boleyns, may need friends, and I am simply volunteering. Do you believe me, Stafford?"

"Yes, Cromwell, for various reasons, yes. Only remember that I am quite through having my wife be a pawn in anyone's chess game ever again. I will die first."

"Then we understand each other perfectly, as I thought we always did. Good luck to you both. If you wish to know the winds of the times, you have only to write to me."

"Thank you, Master Cromwell," Mary said and forced a small smile. "If you have any influence on my sister, sir, please counsel her to curb her temper and the king can be hers again."

He stared squarely into Mary's wide eyes. "We can only hope for that, I think, Lady Stafford, and hope is often a last resort." He bowed to them in the deserted hall and was gone.

"We are going to Wivenhoe, girl," Staff told the sleepy Nancy when they entered Mary's room. "The whole world knows your mistress and I are wed and will soon enough know of the child. Pack several dresses and we will have the rest sent after us. The day is getting late, but we will not sleep under this roof tonight."

"Oh, I am so glad!" Nancy hugged Mary and turned back to Staff. "Are you in disgrace and banished then?"

"More or less," Mary answered, yanking open the top drawer of her wardrobe. "Come on, Nance. We will talk on the way."

"You see, lass," Staff teased as he felt the tremendous impact of their sudden freedom assail his brain, "Stephen is going, too, and with the tight accommodations at Wivenhoe manorhouse, your lady and I would be most grateful if you and he could see fit to share a room. And, though I fear your betters have not set you a very good example, we would prefer that you wed with him first, if the two of you would do us so kind a favor."

Nancy's face went from incredulous, to stunned, to joyous, to embarrassed.

"Staff, did you have to tell her that surprise now? You are just like a little boy who cannot wait for dinner," Mary scolded. "Nancy, you must keep packing or we will end up in a dungeon somewhere and have to rescind the suggestion." She smiled broadly at Staff as the girl bent to her packing and stuffing with a vengeance.

Within an hour the Wivenhoe party clattered away

from Whitehall along the river and soon turned eastward with the sun warm on their backs. Thomas Boleyn had not appeared to scold or stop them as Mary had feared he would. She was glad not to see him, but somehow it only said he did not care. She thought again of brave and loving Meg Roper with her father's head in her lap as they left The Tower behind and cantered through Whitechapel and Spitalfields. Staff's great stallion, Sanctuary, snorted as though he already scented the far distant Wivenhoe, and Eden kept well abreast of the huge horse as they rode side-by-side toward Colchester.

Wivenhoe Manor

It had been the most marvelous summer Mary could remember. Now the trees and shrubs and flowers of Wivenhoe flaunted their riot of autumn colors, and she wondered how long the sequestered beauty would dare to last in her life. She was heavy with child, but the joy she felt with her husband and daughter about her in their new home made her almost forget the agonies of her heart. Despite the peace of Wivenhoe, her thoughts went often to London and she prayed that her sister would find peace and love and bear her husband an heir. And too, she prayed that Anne would forgive her this secret marriage and the child—forgive her as Will Carey had not, for the love she bore Staff. When her prayers turned to her father, no words would come— only rattled hopes and jagged emotions.

"Do you really think today will be the day, mother?" nine-year-old Catherine asked for the third time in the last hour. "It is so exciting, and you promised I could help care for him after he is born." The girl's eyes darted up from the sampler she was stitching and she smiled.

"Yes, my dear, you will be a tremendous help. But remember, the babe may well be a little sister."

"Somehow, mother, somehow I just feel it is a boy. We never see Harry much, so it will take his place."

"One child never really takes the place of another in a parent's love, Catherine. You will understand that some day." Mary tried to sit erect on the stone bench in the herb garden, but her back ached so it really did no good. She would have to lie down or get Staff or Nancy to rub it. It worried her that she felt so tired when she was surely on the threshold of labor where she would need all her strength. It had been nine years since she had delivered a child.

"But if the queen bears the king a son, it will surely replace my cousin Elizabeth in their love, mother," Catherine was arguing. "Then she will be most sad when she grows up that her father will love her not. Brennan told me . . ."

"You must not listen to Brennan so much, my love," Mary chided gently trying to keep the scolding tone from her voice. "Brennan is only the cook in a small country manor and knows nothing of London and the court. Besides, Elizabeth will grow up to be a fine princess of the realm at the very least. You must keep her spirits up and be a friend to her should the queen send for you to live in the princess's company as she has promised she would."

"Maybe the queen is so busy that she forgot, mother. I have been here a whole two months since I left grandmother at Hever."

"Well, let's not speak of that now, sweet. Run and fetch Nancy for me. Staff is out making some sort of bargain with his threshers in the grain fields and he will be back soon. I may take a little nap."

"But it is not your time, is it?"

"No, my lass. Now go fetch Nancy."

Catherine scurried off, her flying feet on the gravel path making a rapid rhythmic crunching. She ran behind the stone fence and Mary could see only the top golden curls of her head bobbing along before she disappeared into the kitchen entry. The ivy draped walls of the house reflected in the fishpond and the stark contrast of whitewashed walls and dark patterned wood made an image of a second Wivenhoe in its calm watery surface. Mary treasured Wivenhoe, as she always had Hever, for the calm and peace it gave. Then, too, there were gentle water lilies floating endlessly on this tiny pond as they had at The Golden Gull in Banstead. Even the manor's ghost disturbed them not, though Mary had heard the stairboards creak at night and sensed unrest. Staff told her it was her own unrest and that the spirit visits had never yet occurred when he had been in the house. It was only the senile ravings of his old maiden aunt, he said. But Mary thought otherwise.

Once at supper, she had forced him into a debate over who the strange visitor might be who creaked the stairs. "My Aunt Susan always insisted it was my Uncle Humphrey, since he was the one hanged at Tyburn, and everyone thought a ghost must have a violent death," he had said.

"But what do *you* believe, my love," she had prompted.

"I reason that if there is any such thing, my Mary, it is my own father," he had admitted. "You see, this manor was his birthright and Humphrey had Stone-

615

house Manor nearer to Colchester before they lost that as a result of the rebellion. Then too, my father died of fever in this house and, as far as I can tell, the ghost never acts up when I am in the house. Though my mother died here giving birth to me, the ghost never came until my father died. It is almost as if,'' he concluded, his eyes growing distant and his voice softer, "as if my father is unsettled when I am at court in the hands of the king so to speak, and rests quietly when I visit, and especially now that we reside here. It is only a theory if I am to believe any of my old aunt's tales and warnings. Perhaps the stairs just creak, for I have seen nothing of it, despite the old lady's stories of furniture moved about and doors ajar. If it comes now at all,'' he had teased, "it will surely be to see what a beautiful wife and daughter I have brought to Wivenhoe. But you had best not tell little Catherine the tale. And do not worry yourself, for it is quite a friendly ghost.''

"How can you be sure,'' she had probed, still nervous about the possibility of a haunted manorhouse.

"He fears not to creak about in day as well as night. Now the best folk tellers know that no evil ghost would dare that.'' She had not been certain in the end if he were teasing or not, so she had let the matter drop. It was her own haunted mind, he had said, and well, maybe he was right.

But there had been no ghosts upon their joyous arrival here to live at Wivenhoe, she recalled, and a smile lit her tired face at the memory. Staff had carried her, dirt-stained and road-weary as she was, across the threshhold shouting for his shocked staff to assemble to greet the lord who so seldom visited and his new lady they had never seen. Safe at last in the oaken and stucco arms of charming Wivenhoe, Staff, Mary, Nancy, and Stephen had laughed and hugged each other in a raucous self-welcome. The eight member household staff had stood in troubled awe at first to hear their new mistress was sister to the Great Henry's Queen Anne Boleyn, but soon enough they had accepted and grew to like her too.

Proudly, bursting with enthusiasm, Staff had shown her the trim and lovely manorhouse of three gabled storeys. On the ground floor a solar, dining hall and kitchen rooms including pantry, buttery, and bolting room where all the storing and sifting of flour took place. Up the carved oak staircase, the master's bedroom and sitting room and four other, smaller bedrooms. Above, under the high-peaked rafters, the servants' rooms and extra storage. The house lay in a huge H-shape surrounded by garden plots, orchards and this lovely pond where she sat now.

The furnature inside consisted mostly of big, carved Medieval pieces Staff promised her they would replace over the years, but Mary had loved it all instantly. So like Hever in the rich, polished patina of the oaks, maples, and cherry woods; so open to the fresh smells of the gardens, yet so warm and cosy within. And best, she loved their tall dark oak bedstead with the carved tendrils of vines and flowers twisting up the four heavy posters which supported the intricately scrolled and crested wood canopy overhead. Even now, as autumn began, she could picture the crisp winter nights to come when they would pull the beige embroidered bed curtains closed and have their own safe world away from Cromwell's spies and the sudden summons of the king.

"Little Catherine says you would take a nap, lady,"

Nancy's voice broke into her reverie.

"Oh, yes, Nance. You gave me a start. If you would just come with me up the steep stairs and help me into bed, I would appreciate it. It is getting to be a dark day, is it not? The lord should be back soon. If it rains on the grain crop so near harvest time, he will be in a black mood."

"Have you pains yet, lady?" Mary shook her head.

They went in through the narrow open hearth kitchen and Brennan looked up from kneading a huge wooden trencher of bread dough. Her eyes widened at the sight of Nancy helping Mary toward the hall.

"No, Brennan," Nance answered the unspoken question. "We need not send Stephen for the village midwife yet, but just stay about in case we need boiling water."

"She is a fine cook, Nance, but somewhat of a gossip." Mary observed as they left the kitchen. "Jane Rochford would consider her a dangerous rival of scandal mongering if we took her to court, I warrant."

The parlor lay silent and dim off the narrow front entry hall as they ascended the steps. Although the oak staircase was dark and gloomy since no sun streamed through windows today, the stairs were well built and never creaked under even Staff's weight. That is one indication that the Wivenhoe ghost truly *does* walk here, Mary reasoned nervously.

Their bed was a tall, square one and the carved walnut cradle for the new baby stood ready at its side. Mary sat and Nancy swung her feet up. "No, no, do not cover me. It is warm enough. And if the lord comes, do not let me sleep long."

"Yes, milady." Nancy pulled the heavy curtains

over the two diamond paned windows and turned to go.

"Nancy. I have not been too short with you lately, have I?"

"No, Lady Mary. But if you were, I would understand with the babe comin' and all."

"And all. Yes, it is more than just the babe, Nance. I so often think of the queen unhappy and far away. It seems terribly unfair that I am here with Staff and things are so peaceful. You and Stephen are happy, I know. I can see it."

"I have never been so happy, lady. Perhaps I shall bear my Stephen a son in God's good time. I told him to stay close today and so did the lord. He can go for the midwife any time, lady."

"Yes, Nance. Thank you. Go on now and get me up for supper if I fall asleep." Nancy closed the door to the room quietly.

The manorhouse was very silent. Staff's groom, Patrick, had probably taken Catherine for her afternoon ride as he did when Staff was looking to manor business or spending the afternoon with Mary. And Brennan kneaded bread and Mary needed Staff and Anne needed a child. She got so tired some afternoons that she almost dozed sitting up, and her waking thoughts merged into her inner voices. It was like that now, floating on the soft mattress where they had so joyfully made love before her size and bulk had made it impossible lately. Palaces and castles be damned, I will live and die at Wivenhoe, she was thinking. The room swam in dim light and sleep would come in an instant here. Maybe she was asleep already, but then she would not know the babe kicked at her from within. It had dropped so much lower now, that it must come soon. An heir for Wivenhoe to take the place of the rebel Humphrey who was stolen from sanctuary and hanged, or perhaps to make up for Staff's father's early death at Wivenhoe, here in this room.

The sharp creak scratched at her drifting mind and her eyes shot open. "Nance!" she heard herself say, and her heart quickened as though it knew something her mind could not. The door to the room stood ajar. But had not Nancy closed it? A floor board moaned near the bed. She sat bolt upright. She felt icy cold, but the day was warm, even sultry, and no breeze stirred through the closed curtains.

"No," she said aloud and heavily moved herself toward the far side of the bed and swung her feet down. She stood unsteadily and paced slowly in a wide arc around the room staying near the wall. She dared not look back as her hand touched the door handle. It was very warm to the touch and she pulled back. She heard her sharp intake of breath in the silence, and pulled the heavy door open further by its wooden edge. In the hall she leaned on the carved banister at the top of the stairs and opened her mouth to call for Nancy or Staff or anyone. The staircase stretched downward, calmly deserted. Then it happened. She distinctly felt a warm touch between her shoulder blades and she meant to scream. But it was gone instantly, and she spun wide eyed against the wall. There was nothing, nothing, but the blur in her own eyes and that was tears.

Fear left her then. Why had she meant to shout to those working below? She felt calm and warm, for the touch had been gentle and the feeling had been love. "It is Staff's father," she whispered or thought. He had

620

only wanted to see her and touch her, for she loved his son and maybe he knew that a Tudor king had ruined her life, too. She would tell Staff later, though he might think it was all in her worried mind again. Perhaps she had dreamed it in her exhaustion. No one would ever believe the fantasy that a dead father could be warmer than the reality of a living one.

"Lady, are you all right? Why are you standin' here? Your face looks like . . . well, I was comin' to tell you your brother has ridden in."

Mary stood stone still as her wandering mind tried to grasp Nancy's words. "George here? With what news or orders, I wonder. Is Lord Stafford back? I must comb my hair." She went back into the bedroom with Nancy trailing behind. The door latch no longer felt unusually warm, if indeed it had ever been warm at all. The bed was as she had left it and the covers clearly showed where she had scooted across Staff's side to get up. Nancy seemed not to notice as she fixed the heavy curls of her mistress' hair.

George's face lit in a broad smile when he saw her and he did not hide his surprise at her changed appearance. "I had forgotten how you bloom when you are with child, Mary," he teased. "It was not since you were pregnant with little Catherine at court that I saw you like this. It becomes you so. And I never saw you in your first pregnancy with Harry at Hever."

Mary warmly kissed George's cheek. "Does it seem to you I spend a great deal of my life in exile from the court for some indiscretion or the other, George? But I have never been happier." She motioned him to a chair in the parlor and they sat close together. "Perhaps you had best not report that I am so content here. Tell father, for instance, I have never been more wretched and maybe he will leave me alone.''

"You are still bitter, Mary, though I do not blame you. You have never learned to just accept the inevitable the way I have, nor do you ever attack him as Anne does."

"Have you always accepted the inevitable, brother?"

"Ever since I had to marry Jane and I saw that the fact I wanted Margot Wyatt more than anything, was nothing to him. Yes, Mary. Since then I have taken my pleasures out of sight of them all and be damned to them. Except for mother and Anne, of course.''

"Are you telling me there has been someone else to fill the void Jane could never fill in your life?" she prodded, intrigued.

"Not really someone like Staff is to you, Mary. Several someones over the years, you might say. There is a certain woman living at Beaulieu now, and she is content to await the few days I can seize to spend there. Anne knows, of course, but I warrant father and Cromwell have missed this one." He grinned like a small boy who has gotten away with stealing chickens from the farmer. "Beyond that, I am much busy on king's business. Speaking of that, I understand you correspond with Master Cromwell.''

"Yes, we do. Is that the nature of your business here, to tell us we are to lose our last line to the court?''

"No, of course not. I wanted mostly to see you and know how you are faring. It is a small manor, but a productive one, I would judge.''

"Do not try to put me off, George. I have been around longer than you and know how things go. Did

Cromwell or father send you? I cannot dare to hope it was Anne."

"I am sorry, Mary. It was not Anne. Truly, Cromwell sends his fondest greetings. Do you actually trust Cromwell, then?"

"My Lord Stafford is not such an innocent to trust Cromwell, but they have made some sort of bargain to work together it would seem. George, will you carry a letter I have written to him? We usually wait until he sends a messenger and then just return a note with the man."

"I shall take it back for you. You alone wrote this letter? Is it secret?"

"Not secret, but I want him, and anyone he would care to tell, to know what it is really like for me now. Anne has not forgiven me, and I am grieved for that, but I regret nothing. It is there on the mantle. If you will get it, I will read you a part. Thank you. I do not want it to be secret, George. It is my letter to the world, if you would call it that."

She began to read from the parchment, "You see, Master Cromwell, the world sets little store by me and My Lord Stafford, and I have freely chosen to live a simple, honest life with him. Still, we do wish to regain the favor of the king and queen. For well I might have had a greater man of birth and a higher, but I assure you I could never have had one that loved me so well, nor a more honest man. I had rather beg my bread with him than be the greatest queen christened. And I believe verily he would not forsake me even to be a king."

"I should like a copy of that, love," came Staff's voice behind her chair. "It is most beautiful and likely to be wasted on the silly ears at court." He leaned over her chair and kissed her on the cheek. "George, you are welcome here to Wivenhoe. Did you come to see if you are an uncle again?"

They shook hands warmly, and Staff sat on the hearth bench near Mary's chair. He had been working hard at something, for his hair was windblown and there was rich, dark mud on his boots. "Then you have a message?" Staff's eyes bored into George's wary ones.

"I think you are the sort of man with whom it is best to come straight to the point, Staff," George ventured.

"And I think you will find that your sister is that sort of woman, George. Say on, but realize that anything which concerns Mary is now of utmost importance to me."

"Yes, of course. I bear a request from father."

"He could not come himself?" Mary asked sharply.

"Hush, love," Staff said. "Do not goad George, for he is only the messenger, not Thomas Boleyn incarnate."

"Things are as bad as I am sure Cromwell has told you," George began slowly. "Anne does not conceive of another royal child, although the king has bedded her off and on all summer. He goes from mistress to mistress as he has long done, but father fears that he is increasingly under the influence of one lady and her rapacious family."

"Jane Seymour still," Mary thought aloud. "Does she still hold him off? Then it would seem she has taken her ambitions and tactics from the queen."

"Exactly, Mary. That is exactly what father says. The Boleyns must hold the king, pull him from the Seymours until Anne bears the heir. Or, if she cannot, father fears Elizabeth will never get to the throne. It will be the bastard Fitzroy or . . .'' His words hung in the air, and Mary feared as she had long ago learned to do when father sought her help. Staff and Mary said nothing and George cleared his throat.

''Sister, do you not remember how the king referred to you as the woman who bore live sons the day he discovered Anne was not really with child and they argued so terribly?''

''Yes. I remember. It was an awful scene. If this has to do with my son Harry, George, tell father to forget it. The king knows well, and has for some time, that the lad is not his flesh and blood.'' She rose awkwardly to her feet. ''Father's secret trips to Hatfield to fill the boy's head with dreams were quite wasted. Whatever he is thinking, the answer is no. No, no, no!''

Staff rose to stand beside her and rubbed her shoulders as if to tell her to keep calm. ''I am fine, my lord, truly,'' she assured him, but her voice quavered.

''I think you are wrong, sister,'' George pressed on. ''I have seen the boy a few months ago. He looks Tudor through and through.''

Mary took a step toward George, ignoring Staff's gentle touch trying to push her back to her seat. ''He is a Carey through and through! He resembles Will Carey!''

''Then that just goes to show how people can disagree over it, but not be certain, sister. The lad is tall and healthy and clever, and Fitzroy is skinny and often weakly. His Grace will leap at the chance to declare Harry his own, if only you will say so.''

''Mary,'' Staff's voice came low at her, but she could not stop the flow of feelings.

"I will not keep calm and be silent, my lord. I cannot!" She tried not to shout, but she could not control her voice. "Tell your father that Harry is William Carey's son and would have been his heir if His Grace had not taken the boy's lands and birthright and given them to his love Anne Boleyn and his henchman Cromwell."

"Some believe he took the Carey possessions to show to the world that the boy was not Will Carey's son, Mary," George pursued doggedly.

"I have heard that argument before, and it is a lie. If father even suggests to the king that Harry is his son, I shall walk all the way to London if I must and deny it to the king's face! Tell father that. Tell him that some day he should try to love someone when they can do him no service for his dreadful lust for Boleyn power! Tell him that he should go back to Hever, for our foolish mother loves him still, though how she does I can never fathom. Tell him . . ."

Staff's arms were around her in the next moment, almost in the same instant in which she felt the first stabbing pain. It surely was the child, but she was so beside herself with anger and hurt that it could have been her mind playing tricks on her again.

Staff carefully picked her up in his arms when he saw the pain on her face. George stood by, clearly distraught as Staff carried her from the parlor and up the silent stairs.

"I saw the ghost. He touched me," she said to Staff between the waves of pain. Staff shouted for Nancy from where he stood and bent over her, untying her long linen sleeves from her bodice. "Did you, sweetheart? Today? Where?"

She meant to answer and to tell him how warm and comforting the memory was, but a sharp pain swept her words away. Staff was removing her shoes and telling her how much he loved her when Nancy's face appeared close over her. "Stephen has gone for the midwife, Lady Mary. I will not leave you."

"Can we send for my mother, Staff?" Mary heard herself ask suddenly. "Send George away and tell him to bring mother."

"I shall ask him, love, but I think he must return to court." Concern was stamped on Staff's strong features, and she gripped his hand tight in the next wave of pain. "We shall send Stephen to bring your mother for a visit after the child is born as we discussed, all right?"

"Father will not like her to come here to Wivenhoe, Staff."

"Then your father be damned, my love. Lady Elizabeth will come."

Nancy and Staff had her into a clean loose frock now, and she felt much better, and not so tired. But surely the Lord in Heaven would give her strength for this trial. She was no longer afraid.

"You do not fear to have the child here, do you, Mary?"

"Here at Wivenhoe, my lord? Of course not."

"In this room, I mean. Did you think you saw the ghost in here?"

"How did you know, Staff? Did I tell you?"

"No, sweetheart. I guessed. Nancy said you were standing wildly in the hall, and when you told me you saw the ghost . . ."

"He opened the door and came in to see me when I was resting," she interrupted his gentle question. "I

627

heard him on the stairs and then he touched my back. Then I was not afraid any longer, Staff, and I am not afraid now.''

"That is fine, my love. That is as it should be.''

"Do you think I am dreaming or lying, Staff? Tell me you believe it!''

"Of course, I believe it. Did I not tell you he would want a good look at my beautiful wife?''

She started to laugh at his tease, but the dark hands of pain descended on her again. She bit her lip to stop the scream. Then Nancy shooed Staff from the room as Mary began the hours of labor to bring forth a child for Wivenhoe.

A son was born nearly at midnight and they called him Andrew William as they had decided. They wanted the child to have his own freely given first name and not be named for someone in high position as were Henry and Catherine. William they gave as a middle name in remembrance of Staff's dead father and for Staff's own first name. Mary whispered the baby's name over and over on her lips and wondered, as she finally fell asleep, if the watchful ghost would come to see his namesake. Staff was beside himself with joy and pride. Nancy told her later that he had even wept, and Stephen had been sent to fetch a whole keg of precious wine from the cellar in celebration.

The next midmorn, George came to see the child before he and his man set off on the road back to Greenwich. He looked nervous and bleary-eyed to Mary, as though he had not slept. "George, I am sorry you must be the bearer of news back to court, not only that I will have none of his nefarious plot to dupe His Grace into

628

believing Harry is his, but that you are the one who will tell them that Staff and I have a son when one is desperately needed elsewhere.''

''Coward that I am, sister, I may lie low on that news until Cromwell tells someone, though Anne could hear it best from me perhaps. She needs me more and more now, Mary. I try to cushion her pain as best I can, but she gets wild sometimes and no one can stand her actions or the things she says.''

''Every woman needs a man to cushion her pain, George.'' Mary reached out and took Staff's hand.

''Jane rants and raves about the time I spend with Anne, of course. It is almost as though she were jealous, but I know that cannot be, since Anne is only my sister and not some paramour.''

''I resented Eleanor Carey once in much the same way. She and Will were somehow soulmates, and I resented that. I can understand Jane's unease.''

She thought George meant to argue the point, but he suddenly blurted, ''Forgive me for upsetting you so, sister. I fear it brought on the child.''

''No, George. All is well. The child came in his own time.''

George nodded and shuffled nervously to glance at the sleeping newborn babe again. ''Well, there is no red hair on this one,'' he observed foolishly, but Mary did not let the words upset her. ''I will be on the road, then. Thank you, Staff and Mary, for your hospitality. It is wondrous quiet here at Wivenhoe. I am not sure how I would do here after a while.''

''It is that calm and quiet we love, George. Farewell,'' she smiled weakly up at him.

George bent to kiss Mary's cheek and shake Staff's

hand. Staff walked him out of the room and down the stairs. Their voices faded away and the room was suddenly silent again. No boards creaked and she began to doze.

Staff came back just as the babe started to fuss for nursing. He lifted the brown-haired mite into Mary's arms and lay down carefully next to them. He watched while his son suckled greedily and Mary felt her love flow out to them both. When the child slept again, Staff said suddenly, "I wish to thank you again for our son, my love. Catherine is quite beside herself with joy, and it will be a battle to keep her from picking him up all the time. She wants to cuddle him like a doll."

"And so do I, my love, though he is more—much more. My first love child, though the Lord above knows I cherish the other two also. But I would die for this one."

"I pray that will never be a necessity, sweet, only that you change the toddling clothes, wipe the nose, and untangle the leading strings."

"What else did George tell you in private after I made my dramatic exit, Staff?"

He reached over and lazily stroked her loose golden hair as he spoke quietly. "Your little cousin Madge Shelton is to marry Henry Norris, for one thing."

"Anne never managed to be rid of Madge? She could not accomplish even that?"

"No, though His Grace beds no longer with the girl. As for the other gossip, there was not much to interest you."

"What else did he say of the Boleyn fortunes and the queen, Staff? Please, I would know. I will worry less then, truly."

"Remember you are here with me and safe, sweetheart, but things are bad and getting worse. Unless Anne can somehow conceive, the dire handwriting is on the royal wall."

"Meaning?"

"Meaning the king is more desperate than ever for a son as you can guess from George's little visit to us. If Anne can give him none, he will try to get one somewhere. As usual, your wily father reads the signs correctly when he thinks to pawn little Harry Carey off on His Grace. But the king wants a true heir, a legitimate son."

"But if there is only Elizabeth, and the queen cannot bear him a son . . . what then?"

"It boggles the mind. The Boleyns have risen so high they can never really retreat, only somehow be pulled off the lofty perch."

"Do you believe he would dare to divorce Anne as Catherine before her, claiming that their marriage is cursed for their dead children? No, Staff, he cannot. He would look most foolish after the ruination of the church and the killing of a raft of friends and advisors such as Sir Thomas More."

"That is my reasoning exactly, sweet. Indeed, what can he do? It will be something calculated and desperate, I fear. Clever Anne sees it too. George said she came upon Jane Seymour perched on the king's lap last week in the queen's chambers and threw a raving fit for two days."

The babe suddenly stirred fitfully in her arms, and Mary rocked and shushed him. "He senses the times are bad, Staff. And now his Aunt Anne will hate him through no fault of his own, for she hates the mother who bore him even more."

"You must not think so, lass. Anne cannot help herself."

"I know. I know. I forgive her, but how I wish she could forgive me. I feel sad and guilty that I bear this beautiful child now when her whole life depends on a son."

"You had best not feel guilty about my son, Mary, no matter what the times are like. Sweetheart, you must cease to be haunted like this for Anne or your father or the king. You are no longer their plaything but a woman of your own—and mine."

She turned her face into his hand, which caressed her cheek as he spoke. She kissed his palm. "Are you saying I have ghosts in my head, Staff? Can you deny you carry much of the cruel past about with you? The rebellion? Your entrapment by the king all these years when you would rather have been here? Perhaps you only do not show your ghosts as much as I, my lord."

He sighed and lowered his hand to stroke Andrew's velvet cheek with one bent finger. "You are right, Lady Stafford. You know your lord quite well now, and I think you love him still."

"Still, Lord Stafford? I love him more each day than I ever knew possible. But I would sleep now, too. Would you put your son back in his cradle?"

Staff stood and lifted the child carefully, the span of his two hands running the entire length of the babe's body. He put him in the cradle and covered him. "I had best go down and see how the reeve is doing with his accounts, love," he said leaning over her on the bed. "Will you sleep well here alone?"

"Of course. But I am not alone even when you are

not here. There is Andrew and the other. I am not afraid here, Staff. I think it is rather my favorite room.''

He kissed her lingeringly on the lips and straightened. ''That is good to hear, madam, for one way or the other, you had better plan on spending a lot of time right where you are now.'' He grinned and left the door ajar behind him.

She smiled at his familiar impudence. Yes, she was thrilled with the child, guilt over Anne or not, for her sister may be now lost to her forever. But she was so tired and she must sleep before the babe woke again to demand feeding. If she heard the stairs creak she would not fear at Wivenhoe for the atmosphere was free and good. If only she could smother her desperate thoughts, then only outside the sanctuary of the manor and Staff's encircling love would there be real ghosts to fear.

Chapter Thirty-Two
February 2, 1536

Wivenhoe Manor

Mary's two-year calm at Wivenhoe raising her son and daughter and being the beloved wife of one of the shire's leading landowners was shattered quite suddenly one mild winter afternoon as the icicles on the eaves dripped in random beats upon the sodden flower beds. The crisp note from Master Cromwell brought by the usual messenger said only that the king's chief minister himself would arrive by noon on the morrow with important news. Mary showed the note to Staff who had scooped up the toddling Andrew in his arms the instant he had entered the parlor.

"Master Cromwell himself," Staff said coldly and handed the crisp paper back to Mary. "I do not think we can hope that he merely desires a respite in the country."

"Now that the queen is with child again, maybe she forgives us and wants us to come back."

"I doubt it," Staff said, grinning at the delighted Andrew as he bounced the child on his knee. "She is barely three months pregnant. Forgiveness might come after an heir is birthed, but probably not before.'' He turned his head toward Mary's concerned face. ''Do you still grieve so much over Anne's cursing you when we left? You have not mentioned it for a long while, and I had hoped you had come to terms with it. If the queen wishes to see you, would you go?''

''I would like to see her, Staff, but I would not wish to stay. Wivenhoe is my home. And I would not venture to court without you, even to visit.''

''Especially not with that dark raven Cromwell in tow, you would not.''

''I thought you and he had a bargain these past years.''

''The bargain is there and well enough kept on both sides, I think, but that does not mean I do not see the man clearly.''

''Yes—'to see things clearly', Master da Vinci tried to tell me that in France ages ago.''

He eyed her strangely and forgot to bounce Andrew until the child began to shout, ''Horse, horse, papa!''

''You had best tell Brennan and Nancy then, sweetheart, for he will surely bring several men and we must ask him to stay the night.''

''Yes.'' She turned back to him at the doorway. ''Perhaps the queen has finally remembered her promise to have Catherine educated with the Princess Elizabeth at Hatfield.''

''I doubt if Cromwell tromps clear out to Wivenhoe for that tidbit, Mary. No, I think we had better brace ourselves and try to hang on to all we hold dear together.''

Mary hurried toward the kitchens to find Brennan and Nancy as Staff began to bounce their sandy-haired toddler on his knee.

"Motherhood and fresh country air has enhanced your beauty, Lady Stafford," Cromwell said as he bent low over her hand.

"Motherhood and Wivenhoe have quite enhanced my happiness at any rate, Master Cromwell," she answered calmly.

"Stafford, as always, you look in charge of life," the stocky man observed as they escorted him into the parlor for wine and fresh cheese. "A lovely retreat," he said as his eyes swept the room.

"A retreat in a way, Cromwell, but a home indeed. Mary and I have no wish to permanently return to court," Staff said, immediately on the offensive against the smug, closed face of the king's closest advisor.

"Then we must all hope that will not be necessary, Lord Stafford. But I *do* bring very sad news that needs a warm response from the queen's sister."

"Sad news? Is Anne all right? Not the babe!" Mary's voice came in a strangled tone.

"Yes, tragically, the queen has miscarried of her child, and . . ."

"No, no, it cannot be!" Mary shrieked and Staff bent over her with his crushingly strong arms around her shoulders.

Cromwell's small, piercing eyes drank in the emotional scene. "I am sorry, lady, but there was no gentle way to give you that news. It seems the early delivery was brought on by a wretched accident to His Grace. In the queen's fifteenth week, the king was riding in heavy armor in the lists at Greenwich. When he became unhorsed by an opponent, his stallion fell full weight on him. The court was paralyzed with fear, for he lay unconscious for nearly two hours and we thought he might die.''

Mary sat away from Staff's chest now, her teary eyes fixed on Cromwell's face. ''When your Uncle Norfolk carried the tragic news to the queen she went into premature labor and was delivered of a dead child. It would have been a son.''

''Then God help us all,'' Staff murmured and Mary could not find the words to say anything.

''When His Grace recovered and heard of the dead son, he stalked into the queen's chambers and screamed that . . .''

''Yes, Cromwell, we can quite imagine what His Grace might have said,'' Staff cut in.

''Ah, of course. And that terrible scene took place on the very day that The Princess of Wales, Catherine of Aragon, was buried. The king had previously found Queen Anne and her ladies cavorting dressed in gayest yellow when they had heard of her death at Kimbolton, and he blamed the queen for witchcraft after she lost their son. He has told many courtiers it was God's judgment on him for being so bewitched all of these years.''

''How dare he talk to her that way after he chased her like a lustful bull all those years!'' Mary said vehemently. ''Witchcraft! Does he take his cues from the ignorant common folk who spit at her on the day she was crowned and shouted 'witch!, witch!'?'' How dare he!''

Cromwell leaned forward, one elbow on his knee as though to observe her passionate outburst more closely. ''It is well known, despite the fact the queen tries to

637

hide it, lady, that she *does* have a tiny sixth finger on one hand—the devil's mark folk would have claimed years ago.''

''Master Cromwell, if my lord and I thought you believed this horrible rubbish for one moment, we would have to ask you to leave our home no matter how kind you have been to us over the years.''

Cromwell smiled and slowly held up a palm as if to ward off her anger. ''Please, sweet lady, calm yourself. I am here on a personal mission to help your sister and to fulfill a request she has made of me. The king hunts winter boar at Eltham and does not know I am on the queen's errand. Will you listen further now?''

Mary only nodded, but Staff's eyes bored into Cromwell's face, and he held tight to Mary's hands.

''Whether or not people believe the rumors of witchcraft from a foolish and greedy court is not my concern. My duty is to serve my master the king, and therefore, what the king wishes, I must enact. But I owe the Boleyns much, for it was through acquiring the great divorce that I first came to serve the king. And, then too, your father has helped me quite as much as I have helped him over the years.''

An involuntary icy shudder shot through Mary's body, and Staff put one arm around her shoulders. Cromwell watched her closely as he spoke.

''The queen has begged me to fetch you to her at Greenwich. She promises you your safety and prays you will come to her in her great hour of need. She bid me tell you that time is slipping fast away, and she would see your sweet face. She asks you to trust me as her messenger, for she was afraid to send anyone whom you might not believe. George and her closest allies:

638

Norris, Weston, and Brereton must stick close to the king at Eltham, of course.''

"When does the king return to Greenwich, then, Master Cromwell?'' came Staff's low voice in the jumble of Mary's thoughts.

"He is quite erratic these days. I cannot promise you he would not suddenly return. He has taken to staging elaborate masques and jousts even though the weather be biting chill, so he may be back to Greenwich soon on a whim. In short, I do not know. But the queen has great need of you and no one else can comfort, it seems. Surely the Lady Mary would be quite safe going for a brief visit to her royal sister.''

"I go with her, Cromwell. You would understand that?''

"Of course. It is good to have a larger party on these roads in the winter.''

"And the queen would have to understand that my home is here with my husband and the two children I raise. I could not stay. Would you tell her that?''

"Yes, lady. Be assured.''

"Then, shall I see Nancy and begin to pack, my lord?'' She looked up at Staff's impassive face. He continued to stare unblinkingly at Cromwell.

"Yes. Fine. And I shall stay behind now with Master Cromwell. He needs a small tour of Wivenhoe before we eat an early supper and retire to rest for the journey. Nancy must stay behind with Andrew, of course.''

Mary rose shakily. Her knees felt terribly weak as though she had ridden clear to London in a hard bouncing saddle already. As she left the parlor, she heard Staff say to Cromwell, "Tell the rest of it to me now, Thomas. I would know it all or the queen's sister stays here with me and you return quite alone.'' She halted in the dim hall and held her breath. The terrible secrets of her parents' argument so long ago while she eavesdropped at Hever came back to her hauntingly.

"The rest of it, Stafford?"

"Though you do not say so, I sense this is your last favor for the poor queen. You feel you owe her a little something and this is the final payoff."

"Really, Stafford, you read in far too much. The queen, whom I have served so faithfully as adjunct to the king, desperately wishes to see her sister. Exactly why, I am not certain, for she would not say."

"But we know whom you will serve next week or next month if he decides to rid himself of her. It is obvious there could be no divorce. This queen would not be shuffled off to some deserted country house with few servants or permanently forbidden to see her daughter. How will you manage it for him, Cromwell, since your very being will depend on it?"

"Anne Boleyn is still Queen of England, Lord Stafford and, as king's chief minister, I cannot listen to such insinuations. Will you show me your charming Wivenhoe or shall I only await our early morning departure in my room? I have brought dispatches and parchments to tend to."

"I will show you the little farm I love, Master Cromwell. I will show it to you so that you may think on its peace and security when some day you shall need such as the poor, desperate queen does now."

Mary darted toward the kitchen as she heard the chair scrape on the floor, for the sudden plans meant much work for her and the servants. She nearly stumbled over Andrew's blocks of wood strewn about the red-bricked entryway as she hurried away from Cromwell's droning voice.

The last part of their journey to the court at Greenwich was by horse barge, which Cromwell had arranged to wait for them under London Bridge in the City. Through occasional flakes of snow, Mary stared up at the stony supports of the bridge and remembered that this was where the brave Meg Roper had retrieved her father's head. It was still mild for February and the only river ice was the brittle, fragile kind which clung to the shallow shoals near the banks. The gray Tower glided coldly past and massive Greenwich appeared from behind the bare arms of the trees. The memories staggered her: she had come here as Will's bride; here the king had first seduced her; here Staff had first kissed her; here Staff had proved to her his undying love when they had returned from Plashy. Here . . .

"Mary, are you all right?" Staff's voice came low in her ear.

"Yes, my love. All right when I know you are near."

"I shall be, Mary. You will have to go to the queen alone, but I shall be near."

Cromwell hurried them along the path toward the queen's wing. "Will we see her immediately, Master Cromwell?" Mary questioned, suddenly realizing it was all rushing too fast towards her.

"I shall first announce that you are here, Lady Stafford, while you and your lord take a moment's respite and have some heated wine."

"Will my father be about, by chance, Master Cromwell? I did not come to see him."

"I realize that, lady. Do not worry. He sticks close to

641

the king these days and is at Eltham.''

"And Jane Seymour?''

"Seymour, lady?''

"Yes. Is she at Eltham, too?''

"I believe she was invited and declined. She is at Wolf Hall with her family and will not be back until the king acknowledges he will insist no more on her forbidden affections. She seems to be quite the Boleyn ally lately.''

"Hardly that! I am no wench new brought to court, Master Cromwell. That only means she plays for high stakes and you and my lord know it well enough. Do not think I am so untutored.''

"I apologize, Lady Stafford. It is seldom that such a stunning woman thinks in a—well, in a political way. I see you have learned to do so.'' He opened a door. "In here. Rest by the fire and ask my man for whatever refreshment you would have. I shall return shortly.''

They took off their cloaks. Cromwell's servant poured them wine and scraped the mud from their boots. "Can you not feel it, my lord?'' she said low to Staff as they sat before the blazing hearth.

Behind the servant's back, Staff held a quick finger to his lips and shook his head. "Feel what, sweetheart?'' he inquired smoothly.

"Well, just how familiar it all is.'' She had wanted to tell him how the palace was oppressive and terrifying to her. How the very walls and heavy tapestries smothered her after the plain stucco and rough beamed walls of Wivenhoe. But, indeed, Staff was right to urge caution. Cromwell was well known for his spies, and she and Staff had talked late last night planning how careful they must be if they chose to walk among the snares of

Cromwell and the court in such unhappy times.

Cromwell was back almost immediately. "Her Grace is ecstatic that you have come and awaits you now, Lady Stafford. Will you follow me? Your lord can be summoned from here if the queen wishes it."

Mary touched Staff on the shoulder as she followed Cromwell from the room. The strength she sought, the love she would give in this interview would be her own, nurtured by sanctuary at Wivenhoe, but it would come from her dear husband too.

Only Lady Wingfield was in attendance on the queen when Mary entered the chamber, and Anne dismissed her with a wave of her hand. How barren the room looked without the familiar clusters of ladies sewing or talking. Not even the ever-present musician Smeaton sat on table or chair or the corner of the queen's vast bed as he often had before. Surely the king would not dare to diminish the queen's household in his anger, nor would Anne's temper make them all desert her in her hours of need.

"Sister. Mary. Come here. I am so happy you have come to see me. It has been long."

Mary's eyes narrowed to pierce the dimness of Anne's curtained bed. The drapes of the room had been drawn and several candles burning low littered the huge table next to the bed.

"Sit, sit here with me so I might see you. You are not changed, not at all changed, Mary."

"I am changed inside, Your Grace. And I am much grieved to hear of the lost child, sister."

"Speak not of that. It is over. It is all over now." Anne looked thin and her face was long with dark shadows under each almond shaped eye. How those eyes

643

used to dance with flirtation and fire, Mary remembered. She took Anne's delicate hand in her own warm ones.

"I was so happy that you sent to see me, Your Grace. I have missed you these two years and have thought of you often and prayed for—for your happiness."

"God is not answering Boleyn prayers lately, Mary, though I thank you for your loving words. And will you not call me Anne today? George does when we are alone. He told me of your child and your home. I made him tell me all about you. It sounds rather like a little Hever there, but then you would like that."

"Yes, Anne. I do like it."

"And you are very, very content there with Stafford? And he loves you still?"

The pitiful eagerness of Anne's voice and face frightened Mary. This kindness, this desperate reach for love was somehow more terrible than the ranting and raving she remembered and feared. A single tear traced its lone path down Mary's cheek.

"Yes, I know. Do not be afraid to tell me. You have a man who truly loves you and two sons besides. I have accepted it all now, Mary. Do not be afraid to be here."

"You have Elizabeth, Anne, and Cromwell says she is beautiful and His Grace loves her well."

"He can hardly help loving her, for she is clever-witted and as red haired as himself. But daughters do not really count in the royal scheme of things, so that is that. Princess Elizabeth will live and die a princess if the king has anything to do with it. But now, here, you and I have some business to take care of before we just enjoy talking. Can you fetch me that document right there? I am guilty of long neglecting members of my family who need my love in return for the good service they have always rendered me.''

"Have you forgiven me then, Your . . . Anne? I have longed for that these years."

"Yes. Mary, do not cry. You have always let your heart and feelings leap to your face, though I warrant at little country Wivenhoe you need not hide them as in this viper's nest. This document gives back to you the rightful guardianship of your son Henry Carey upon my death, and . . .''

"Your death? Please, Anne, you need not . . .''

"Stop and listen, Mary. The queen is used to having people listen to her—courtiers, spies, whatever— everyone except her husband, of course. His Grace is getting desperate, and I am quite in his way now.''

"Please, do not speak of death, Anne. You are young.''

"But I feel very, very old, Mary. Now, until the event of my death, the lad's annuities shall continue equal in value to the lands which His Grace gave away at the time of the boy's father's death." Anne's eyes lifted from the paper to Mary's intent face. "I was proud of you when you told George to get father out of your boy's life, Mary. I assure you, I had George report to father exactly what you had said.''

"What did father say of it?''

"I believe he dismissed your message as the ravings of a woman in the throes of childbirth, but it rattled him greatly. He must have thought you would be properly chastened after a year's exile away from this mess. Now, the other thing about little Harry is that you and Stafford may have him to Wivenhoe or wherever for two months a year.''

"Oh, Anne, I thank you so! It is the most wonderful gift you could give me!'' Mary put her arms around Anne's stiff, slender body and trembled to know how thin she was under her silken robe. Anne put her arms slowly on Mary's back.

"Loose me, Mary,'' she said after only a moment. "The other thing is your daughter Catherine. The princess is three now, and would benefit from a part-time companion at Hatfield. Then, when her father sends for Elizabeth to come to court, Catherine could go to you at Wivenhoe. She would have a good allowance and a better tutor than she ever had when she was in company of Princess Mary's little Margaret.''

"My lord and I cannot thank you enough, dear sister.''

"Here, you must keep these documents in case father or anyone else tries to give you an argument should I not be near. There is one last thing. Fetch my jewel box. Behind that carved panel there where I used to keep it.''

Mary grasped the heavy box and put it on the bed next to Anne. "Would you believe it, Mary, that this is only one tenth of my things, not counting the crowning jewels? The others are kept under lock and key, but I shall have them sent to me in little bits in the near future. There are some things he will never have back to grace that skinny neck of Seymour or anyone else. They are by right Elizabeth's after I am gone. Do you understand?''

Mary nodded wide-eyed wondering what Anne would dare to do and whether Staff would allow her to be a part of it. Mary Tudor had once taken a jewel from

Francois and had paid dearly for it when she was discovered.

"Several things I have sent to mother to keep for Elizabeth's majority and she has vowed not to tell father. I would like to have you keep several for her too, and this piece for little Catherine." A heavy rope of pearls as big as chick peas dripped from Anne's slender fingers. "I know I can trust you to preserve these few things for my child should I be unable to for some reason."

"Yes, of course."

"Cromwell must not know. Can you put them down your dress? No, no, I shall give you this little pomander purse. Purses are quite in style now and no one will think a thing of it."

"I hardly know what is in style or out at court, sister."

"Cruelty and treachery are in style, Mary, but then, they always were. I have heard, by a note from father at Eltham, that the king returns for one of his extravagant jousts on the morrow and I wish to attend. I must show no fear or he will eat me like a little rabbit. Will you stay that long and go with me? Staff too? It would give me much strength to face all of their snickers after the, well, the death of my little son. Please, Mary. His Grace will quite ignore us, so do not fear him. Will you stay with me, Mary?"

"I would gladly walk by your side, Anne."

"Go on then and hide those jewels somewhere. Tell your lord to put them in his boots or something. He was always very clever and he feared father and the king not at all. I shall not either."

"You should not, Your Grace. You are the queen."

Mary bent to kiss Anne's sallow cheek. It felt cold, as though the sparkling life and vitality that had long warmed it had gone out.

"Come back for supper with me, Mary, and bring Staff. I shall send Lady Wingfield for you later. I trust her. She is not one of Cromwell's lackeys."

"But Cromwell has served the Boleyns, too, Anne, though of course he serves the king first."

"Cromwell serves Cromwell first, my sweet and foolish sister. Do not believe otherwise."

Mary wanted to give more words of comfort to the slender woman who sat facing her along in the huge bed under the Boleyn and Tudor family crests, but words would not come. She curtseyed quickly and opened the door into the hall. Surprisingly, it was crowded with courtiers now, but she could not spot Staff or Cromwell in the clusters of people. She held the silken purse Anne had given her tightly and began to thread her way toward the room where she had left Staff. Suddenly, Norris and Weston sprang up before her in the crowd and, as she smiled and swept them a short curtsey, the king loomed up behind them. She stepped quickly back toward the tapestried wall. He looked massive, taller and much heavier than she had remembered. His jowls were hard and square, and his blue eyes sought her own. She hastened to curtsey again. Her back hit the wall behind her as she saw his booted feet halt. His large jeweled hand shot out to her wrist. He raised her to stand before him.

"At first I thought it was just a pretty ghost from the past," he began, and the voices around them hushed in rapt attention. "Have you been summoned back to court, Lady Mary?" he asked directly.

She raised her eyes to his, hooded with thick red brows and sandy lashes. "Only for a day or two to visit my sister, Your Grace. My lord and I will be returning to our home very shortly."

"If you have come to give the queen advice on breeding sons, it is quite too late, madam," he growled. Then he pivoted his head to take in the circle of courtiers. "Come with me, Lady Stafford," he said low. "I would speak with you."

Mary caught George's worried face as she swept after the king through the crowd. This would surely alarm Anne if he told her—and Staff. She clutched the corded purse strings tight in her hand. The king had always taken long strides, and it was quite impossible to walk apace with him. She had no choice but to follow, to try to keep calm and to bluff it out if need be. She prayed he had no dire designs on sixteen-year-old Harry who was now being educated at Lincoln's Inn Field not so far away.

The privy room to which he led her was close to the queen's wing—the room in which he had put her to await him after the masque for Queen Catherine when he had first seduced her while his wife slept nearby. Surely he would not . . .

"Would you sit, lady?" he asked bluntly when he had closed the door on Norris' and Weston's faces.

"If you wish me to, Your Grace," she said, and remained standing.

"I only ask, not order, lady. Suit yourself." He sat on the edge of a huge carved chair and, as she looked at him squarely, his head appeared to be in the very center of the small bed in the chamber.

Ironically, she thought, she and the king were

649

dressed in the same colors even as they used to do years ago on foolish whims: and both wore traveling gear and riding boots. The bulky muscles of his chest and shoulders swelled his brown Spanish leather jerkin over doublet and hose of dark burgundy hue in echo to her own warm gown of the dark wine color.

"The queen sent for you, you said, Lady Mary?"

"Yes, Your Grace."

"You are still very beautiful. You have hardly changed over the years."

"I am much changed in truth, Sire, only the changes are inside and do not show."

"Are you so changed? A flagrant affair and secret marriage with Stafford under my nose all those months. And before that, I recall you served Francois du Roi in your bed at Calais quite to his utter satisfaction."

She gripped her fists tightly around the purse strings. "Francois du Roi lied to you and the queen, Your Grace. I refused his advances and he left cursing me and the English—and vowing he would tell you I had done everything he asked."

A strange grin lit his face and his eyes shifted. "Do you swear it? Francois lied?"

"Yes."

He laughed sharply. "I knew you would never bed with that wily jackal after you had been mine."

The words hit her like a blow in the stomach, but she stood still fighting the desire to flee.

"Did you tell him you loved another king, lady? You still love your king, do you not?"

"All good and loyal subjects love their king, Sire, and I have always been your good and loyal subject."

His open palm cracked hard on the table. " 'S blood, Mary! Do not be clever with me! Yes, you have changed. All of Boleyn's clever children change and for the worse. Sit, madam. I do not wish to knock you down, for it is surely another I would strike at. Sit.''

She looked behind her, then sat slowly in the chair on the other side of the table instead of the one nearer him.

"Pretty women about the court are a plague. See that you are gone by the morrow.'' His voice softened suddenly. "I would have you away and out of danger. You are innocent still, compared to the rest, and have done me no wrong.''

"Wrong? I do not understand, Sire.'' Surely, she thought, he refers to his dead son and blames Anne for that.

"How does your son, Mary?'' he said calmly as though he had read her thoughts of sons.

Which son of mine? she wanted to ask impudently, but she knew which one and would not risk his wrath on that. "He is a fine student at Lincoln's Court, Your Grace. He is tall and a good athlete. He is nearly sixteen and one half, Sire.''

"I know how old the lad is, madam. They say,'' he said, leaning forward to watch her face closely, "that he has red hair.''

"It is somewhat reddish, Sire, with auburn touches, much as Will Carey's, you remember.''

"I do remember, golden Mary. I remember much, including that your father has implied off and on that the lad was not Will Carey's child. I trust him not, so I will have it once and for all from your lovely lips, madam. Was the boy Will Carey's son indeed? Will Carey was no fine athlete and not so clever either, and if the boy has those traits . . . well, I would have you tell me the truth.''

She fought to control her voice and face. This was the moment that could save or condemn Harry. Father would be forever grateful if she would only tearfully vow to her king that the child was his. Then the Boleyns might sit more secure in the dangerous saddle of the king's volatile affections. Then a birthright to money and power would be assured, especially now that the ailing Fitzroy was so desperately ill.

"I would certainly have told Your Grace if the child was yours. I would have told you long ago, for the boy's sake and yours, Sire.'' She held her breath and stared deep into his eyes. She must convince him now, before he somehow cast the Boleyns adrift forever and kept her son to please his own vanity and passion for a live and healthy son as he had done long ago with poor Bessie Blount's boy. If he ever guessed the lad could as easily be his as Will's and that only Staff knew that truth, he might throw caution to the winds and keep Harry as his own.

"That is as I thought,'' he said finally. "I tried once to reckon it back to see if we had bedded then, and we had. But I was much about with others then and Carey was home those months, and, too, you would have told me.''

"Yes, Sire. I was with Will and you were much about with others then.''

"I will not have your recriminations, though you were always more sweet and understanding than your sister. Her recriminations are unending.''

"I meant no recrimination, Sire.''

"And now you have another son by Stafford?''

652

"Yes. Andrew," she offered in the empty silence.

"Why were you not the Boleyn who held out, Mary, instead of that sour and bitter sister of yours? Well, what is past is well past. You were well worth the bargain before all these—these complications set in." He rose, and in one step towered over her and pulled her to her feet, trapped between him and the table and her chair.

He placed his huge hands on either side of her head and stared down at her alarmed face. "You will bear no sons for Henry Tudor, Mary, but some lovely lass shall, as sweet and fair as yourself. Take that rebel husband of yours and be gone on the morrow, for I do not want you about the queen and her people. You will thank me later for that. Go and hide your pretty head at Colchester and bear him sons, but do not forget that once you belonged to your king." His face was almost touching hers and his hot breath smelled of cloves and mace. "Go from this room now or I shall take my first sweet revenge on the Boleyns in a way I had never dreamed. Sweet, sweet revenge. But, then, I have no quarrel with your Lord Stafford." Still he held her head in a vise-like grip staring down at her, his mouth poised inches from hers.

"Please, Your Grace."

"Yes, go on before I force you to that bed and we relive our first night together here, so long ago. Do you remember?" He bent to kiss her lips, but she wrenched away and backed off in a half curtsey.

"As you ordered, Sire, I shall be going." Her voice sounded choked and she wobbled on her legs. Still facing him, she pulled the door latch. "I shall remember you to Lord Stafford," she heard herself say. "He will always be your loyal servant even as I shall.''

He stood staring at her, somehow suspended between anger and awe. She tried to force a smile but could not. Gripping her purse strings in her cramped fingers, she turned in the hall and saw George and Staff hurrying toward her, far down the corridor. Ignoring the anxious faces of Weston and Norris, she walked unsteadily toward Staff.

Though she and Staff had decided they could not gainsay the king to stay beyond the next day, they went with Anne and her entourage to the joust the next morning planning to leave directly from the tilt fields on their awaiting and packed horses. Norris and George were to be part of the joust, as was the king. They were settled in their seats only a moment when one of Anne's servants elbowed through the press of people and whispered something in the queen's ear. Anne's face went stark white, and she motioned Weston to her side. Mary sat next to the queen and Staff was on his wife's other side, so Mary could hear the desperate words clearly.

''It is of Smeaton, Your Grace, as you had asked,'' the girl whispered, her wild eyes darting to Mary's face behind the queen's.

''Yes, Joan. Did they find him? Where has the rogue been?''

''He went to Master Cromwell's to dine yesterday after Cromwell returned with your sister. Then Smeaton disappeared.''

''Mark Smeaton was asked to dine at Cromwell's?'' Anne's hand grasped the girl's wrist in a cruel grip. ''There is more! Tell me the rest!''

The girl's face turned pouty and she began to whimper. "Stop that and tell me, or I will have you thrown under the horses!" Anne hissed at her. "And keep your voice down."

"Cromwell's men took the poor boy to The Tower late at night. A guard was bribed to admit that Cromwell was questionin' the poor boy under torture, Your Grace."

"Torture? Sweet, gentle Smeaton? Thinking he will tell them what? Oh, go on! Be gone and hold your tongue." Weston looked almost green with fear. Anne turned to Mary's wide-eyed stare and saw that Staff had heard too. "Did you mark that? Cromwell is desperate indeed if he has to hurt my little lutenist to get information of my supposed spying or plotting or whatever His Grace is so desperately trying to concoct. But a desperate Cromwell is dangerous, and bears close watching."

The king sat encased in armor on his huge destrier at the end of the field, and Anne waved bravely to him as though they were the most intimate of lovers. He merely nodded and, as they turned to watch George in the first matchup, Mary's eye caught her father who had just seated himself behind them. He was so much older, older than the two years that had passed since she had last seen him.

"Do not gape so, Mary," Thomas Boleyn chided low. "I am pleased to see you back with the family where you should be." He raised himself slightly out of his seat to watch George's first charge. "You and your country lord are a little late to help though. There is something dangerous afoot, Your Grace," he said quietly, turning his face to the back of Anne's head.

"The king has ordered out a triple number of yeoman guards."

"And that two-faced Janus, Cromwell, does me a favor one day and then kidnaps and tortures my musician the next. I shall have his head for this!"

"I think not, Anne," their father replied. "I am afraid Cromwell has shown his true colors by all this, and he will help the Boleyns no more. I have sent for your Uncle Norfolk. We need a conference and quickly. Damn, I wish George were a better jouster, and I do not know what in hell's gates is taking Norfolk so long to arrive!"

The stands cheered the victor who had defeated George Boleyn and the tired horses trotted off the field while the battered tilt rail was realigned. "I had heard the king ordered you and Stafford to be gone today, Mary. You could hardly expect him to welcome you with a big smile."

"We are leaving, father, but Anne wished us to accompany her here as she ends her retirement."

"I see. Then it is back to the country to desert her here to face God knows what in this wretched atmosphere."

"I have urged them to go, father. They have a lovely home and a young child to return to. Leave Mary be!" Anne ordered sharply without turning her head.

Anne rose at the beginning of the next match, smiled and waved to the strangely subdued gallery. On a whim, she pulled a golden ribbon off her puffy satin sleeve and threw it to her champion, Henry Norris, who doffed his heavy silver helmet in mock salute. As he and Lord Wingfield plodded away to take up their position, the queen's stands suddenly exploded with yeoman guards in their red doublets and hose brandishing their ceremonial axe-head pikes before them. Several ladies screamed in shock, and Staff pulled Mary back tight against him on the bench. Across the jousting field, Sir Anthony Wingfield had doffed his helmet and was staring mutely at Norris' being surrounded by guards who swarmed onto the field. Still, beyond it all, Henry Tudor sat stock still on his horse staring at them all.

Anne stood and took her father's proffered arm. "By what authority do you disturb the king's games?" her voice rang out clear and strong.

Then their Uncle Norfolk elbowed his way through the guards and Mary breathed a tiny sigh of relief before Staff's whispered words came terrifyingly clear in her ear. "That Judas!"

"Uncle, I am pleased to see you," the queen was saying. "May I ask the cause of all this array of force?"

"I fear you are the cause, Your Grace, and some of those with whom you conspire."

Anne's sharp unbelieving laughter shredded the air and her father's words came hard at Norfolk. "Look man, this is a terrible scene. Does the king actually demand . . ."

"I am sorry, Thomas, Lord Boleyn, but here is the signed writ and order of arrest for the queen to be legally questioned concerning her crimes."

Thomas Boleyn went white and looked as though he would double over in pain. "Crimes! Crimes! What crimes? Name them!"

"Not here, please, Lord Boleyn. The masses will know soon enough. Please come with us, Your Grace."

"Come where, Uncle?"

"To the palace today and The Tower tomorrow. For questioning." He handed the writ to the stunned Thomas Boleyn, and the pain was etched on his face for all to see. "I act not of my own desires, Your Grace, but the king commands. No, my lord, you shall not accompany her now. Her own answers are wanted." Norfolk blocked Thomas Boleyn's way with his gauntleted arm.

"May I go with my sister, then?" Mary heard herself ask, and she stood on Staff's arm ignoring his warning look.

"No, Lady Mary. You and Stafford had best hie yourself back to Colchester and be well out of it." Norfolk nodded to Mary's shocked face and then to the rows of guards who closed ranks to cut off the departing queen and Weston from the rest of the crowd.

"All will be well, dear sister. This is mere trumped up foolishness, and you may write that down, uncle." The queen's mouth was curved in a derisive laugh, but her eyes were wide and wild. As she turned to go, her voice floated back to them, and all Mary could see of her now was the veil of the pearl-studded red headdress which graced her raven hair. The joust field was suddenly deserted and the king had disappeared. Fervently, Mary wished she would never see him again.

"There is nothing you can do here now, Mary," Staff said low. "You will get on your horse with me now or I shall carry you? This way. Come on, sweetheart."

But Mary looked back at her father's incredulous, shattered face and hesitated. He raised his blank eyes to Stafford and then to Mary. "It says here," he read, his voice suddenly old and quavering, "that the Queen of

England, Anne Boleyn is arrested for treason and adultery with Smeaton, her musician, and Lords Norris, Weston, and Brereton, and with her brother, George Boleyn, Viscount Rochford. Smeaton has already confessed and Jane Rochford has given sworn testimony of her husband with the queen.'' His voice trailed off and Mary realized that she had screamed.

Instinctively, she reached for her father's arm, but he recoiled, crumpled the document and threw it down. ''Lies! Lies!'' Tears made jagged tracks down his wrinkled face and his lip trembled.

Staff loosened his firm hold on Mary as she moved like a sleepwalker toward her father. The horror of what the paper said, her mind could not encompass yet. But her father was crushed and in pain, that she could feel deep inside. She put one hand on his shoulder, but he stared into vacancy as though she were not there.

''Father,'' she said gently. ''Father, I know you are thinking of all your dreams and of George and Anne. Go home to Hever and mother. They will comfort you.''

His eyes fastened on her tear-streaked face. ''Leave with your husband, Mary,'' he said as though exhausted. She could barely discern his words. ''I am staying. The king has ordered it, but something must be done to save it all. Surely something can be done. I only have to think about it now.'' He turned away, stooped, and her hand fell off his shoulder as he went. She fought the urge to chase after him and throw her arms around his thin neck, but Staff's hands were on her again and he half pulled, half carried her down the far side of the gallery, gayly decked with Tudor white and green. He took her, unprotesting, through the gardens to the stableblock. It was only when he lifted her on Eden's back and she turned to glance back at the palace, that her calm became hysteria, and Staff had to carry her before him on Sanctuary until they reached the outskirts of London.

In a little inn on the edge of Lambeth, he held her on his lap and let her sob. While the grooms and Stephen hovered nervously with the horses in the street, he made her drink wine and eat fruit and cheese. "Can you ride, my love? If you do not think you can, Sanctuary can handle the extra weight until we reach Banstead."

She turned her swollen eyes slowly to him. "Banstead?"

"Yes, lass. I can fetch our son from Wivenhoe after we make it to Hever. I want us far away from here and I do not care if we never see His Grace's fine palaces again. Your mother has need of you and you of her. We can make it from Banstead to Hever by noon tomorrow."

Mary nodded slowly. Her head hurt terribly, and she was certain she would be sick if she had to get on a horse. "I can make it to Banstead, my Staff. If you are near."

"I will be near every step of the way, my love," he comforted, his mouth pressed close in her hair.

What will happen to George and Anne? she wanted to ask him, but she was afraid he would tell her the truth and not what she so desperately wanted to hear.

"We are off to Banstead and Hever, then." He swung her into his arms and strode for the door. "And never fear that our dreams will crash about us like that, my sweetheart. Our dreams are quite a different thing.''

She looked up dazedly into his worried face. Pain etched his forehead and wrinkled his firm brow.

''I shall remember that, my lord, no matter what befalls,'' she said, and he shouldered open the inn door to put her on the waiting Eden's back.

Chapter Thirty-Three
February 5, 1536

Hever Castle

Hever stood cold and bare against the gray Kent sky
as they approached. The ivy cloak of the castle was
gone for winter and only the clinging tendrils of brown
vines etched the walls. The forest's trees stood stark
and straight, and the eyelike windows reflected only the
flatness of the threatening sky. Mary's tears were long
gone and a steely calm held her rigid on Eden's back.
She felt on the sharp edge of jagged screaming fits, but
they never came. Surely all the terror and agony would
dissolve when she saw mother's face. If only she could
pull herself awake from the smothering nightmare safe
in her bed at Wivenhoe!

The horses' hoofs echoed hollowly off the inner
courtyard walls, and they drew to a halt in a ragged circle to dismount. Mary's swollen eyes scanned the upper
windows for a familiar face—of mother, or Semmonet,
or a well-remembered servant. Then the central door
under the proud Boleyn family crest opened and her
mother rushed out dressed in velvet black.

"Mary! Staff! I prayed you would come. Thank you,

my lord, for bringing my Mary home.'' She darted between Sanctuary and Eden. Her slender arms were tight about Mary, and the tears came flowing free from them both.

"You know, mother, you already know of Anne's arrest," was all Mary could manage as she pressed her cheek into her mother's silvery hair. It began to snow tiny, random ice flakes, and Staff urged them both inside.

Semmonet stood bent and more crooked than ever, leaning on a carved staff at the entry, her face a mask of shocked agony. Mary embraced her tenderly then desperately, and the Boleyn women helped the old governess into the solar, as though she were one of the family, while Staff gave orders to his servants. The portrait of the king stared down unblinking on them all as they passed.

"Sit here, Semmonet. I am so pleased to see you on your feet. Mother had written that you keep much to your bed," Mary said, amazed at her own small talk when all the eyes of the room were fastened hard on her.

"I only forced myself up today after the tragic message came from Lord Boleyn that the Queen was arrested yesterday. No one else was here who knows both our George and our dear Anne so well, and my Lady Elizabeth needed to talk.''

"Yes, of course, I see.'' Mary sat on the arm of her mother's chair and leaned into her with her arm around the fragile woman's shoulders.

"You see, my children," Elizabeth Boleyn began, holding up her hand for quiet as both Mary and Staff began to speak, "I have been awaiting some tragedy

663

for years and years now, ever since I saw the king my-self, and the king offered to make me his mistress—he was only Prince of Wales, then, you know—and when I refused because I was new wed and in love with my lord, the king was angry. Well, I could understand that, but when my Lord Thomas was even more angry with me . . . indeed, something inside me died, and I knew from then on the Bullens would live in danger. The king said so quietly, 'I do not command, I only request,' but I could see clearly what he meant and that to serve him was danger. But I never thought it could be this terrible. No, Staff, wait. I would say more."

"The Howards were never like the Boleyns have been, not in the old days at least. But soon I had the children here to love and raise—George first, then Mary, and baby Anne." She dabbed at her wet cheeks and eyes and continued to sit erect and neither Mary nor Staff nor Semmonet dared to interrupt, even with attempted consolation. "All was golden in those years for me at Hever because my lord had only his own skills to barter and he was happy as he rose high and proud and tasted the possibilities of power. But then, he took Mary and used her far away in France and then back at the English court . . . and then Anne and George and . . . he, oh, dear God in heaven, he has ruined all his children's joy and now will murder two of them, and I love him still!"

She sobbed gaspingly on Mary's shoulder, and Mary's own tears wet her mother's head. Then, amazingly, Lady Elizabeth sat ramrod straight and said, as if to Staff alone, "You see, my lord, when Mary's sister became the queen, I dreamed that perhaps, perhaps we would be safe now, for there was no higher place for my husband's desires to climb. But I was wrong. Nothing stops this king—not love, not gratitude, not marriage —he just pulls them all down at his feet and tramples them.''

"A legal son is the only protection any woman or family shall have from him, lady," Staff's voice came almost breaking. "But I believe he may not be capable of a healthy son. If so, there stands your little namesake, the red-haired princess. Now, if you would listen, Mary has some things she wishes to tell you." He nodded to Mary and she searched her mind for the words and phrases she had rehearsed on every jog of the road between Banstead and Hever.

"When I saw Anne the two days we were at Greenwich, mother, she was much changed, resigned, inwardly strong and not afraid. We must hold to that. And she was warm and kind to me, so kind. She has arranged for my oldest son to be my ward should . . . should the queen die . . . and that Staff and I may have him to Wivenhoe for visits, and I promise you he shall come here also if you would have him. And Catherine is to be raised with the Princess Elizabeth and to visit us whenever Elizabeth goes to court. Anne gave me some jewels for Catherine and Elizabeth to give to them . . . if . . . well, when they are old enough to understand. But, if the king takes his terrible revenge, who shall ever understand?''

"But that is what I was thinking, Mary," Elizabeth Boleyn returned, her voice warm and strong. "If the king pulls them all down, and if he dares to imprison or harm Anne and George, if these false charges should be published, they will all poison little Elizabeth's ears over the years. But we—all of us, especially those of

665

you who are younger than I—must tell the child the truth of the good things of her mother and family. That is what I have been thinking over and over all this long morning since the messenger came.''

''Yes, mother. And Harry and Catherine are old enough to be told the truth, and they will not forget. They will tell Elizabeth. Little Andrew will know some day too. Staff will ride to bring him here tomorrow, for we are staying at Hever a while if you will have us.''

''Have you? Yes, my dearest one, do not leave me. My pretense of strength is over. You must tell us truthfully, Staff, what will happen. You have always told the truth here, I think.''

Staff's worried brown eyes sought Mary's for comfort and returned to the steady blue-eyed gaze of his mother-in-law. ''There will be a trial, Lady Elizabeth, and the king will try very hard to rid himself of the Boleyns so that he may marry elsewhere. At best, Anne and George may be exiled and . . .''

''Oh, do you think it a possibility, Staff?'' Elizabeth's thin hand gripped Mary's wrist in excitement. ''Anne would love to live in France if she escapes this. We could visit there someday.''

''It is a possibility. But I think, with Anne's inner fire and backbone—and the fact that she will believe she has nothing else to lose but her life if she agrees to exile—she will cling to being queen and make him take it from her.''

''She is innocent of all his charges!''

''Yes, lady. Mary and I and most of the court know that, but His Grace wants to convince himself otherwise to clear his wretched conscience.'' Staff continually gripped and wrung his hands. Mary had never seen

666

him so distraught, though his face appeared quite calm.

"That bitter-cruel Jane Rochford has helped to cause all this. She dares to swear false unholy charges against Anne and her husband! But then, it is the poisons of their forced marriage coming out at last. My lord must answer to that too. The only thing Anne and George were ever guilty of was love of power, and that they learned at their sire's knee. Tell us, then, Staff, for Mary can bear it and I shall too—what is the worst that might befall?"

"The most ominous sign I see is that the king is so desperate that he is willing to let two of his closest friends, Norris and Weston, fall with the queen. And the crazy charges of witchcraft he allows his henchman Cromwell to drag out of the closet show his unbending attitude. The worse, lady, is that the innocent shall be declared guilty and shall pay the king's price for his own sins. Thank God Mary and I are well rid of him!" Tears stood in Staff's eyes, and Mary crossed the little space of carpet to touch him.

"Well, my children, spring is coming and spring always comes to Hever with beauty and consolation. I have seen that many times. You must rest now. You have not even been to your room. Semmonet and I shall await you here, and I shall order food and wine. I wish to talk some more to Semmonet."

They stood awkwardly and Mary resisted the impulse to embrace her mother since she seemed suddenly so in control of herself. They went up the broad staircase to Mary's old room. The doors to all three of the children's childhood bedrooms stood ajar and Mary wondered irrationally if ghosts lurked there or ever would. The servants had been about and their clothes were on the bed and fresh water and linen towels waited on the massive bureau. Staff leaned on the ledge and gazed out the window toward the bare gardens while Mary quickly unpacked the purse of Anne's jewelry and unfolded the legal parchment promising her control of her children.

"She did not ask you the next question, Staff."

"No. She already knows the answer to that."

"He cannot dare to behead his own queen!"

"That is why he will try to prove she is not his legal queen. He will use the witchcraft or the fact that you were once his concubine or whatever moral arguments he has, to to rid himself of a legal, God-given, and crowned queen."

Mary walked slowly to him, the stiff parchment roll clasped to her breast. "He would never order me to come back to testify that we were lovers so that he can cite his own incest."

"I have reasoned it out and I think you are right. He does not dare to do that since he has charged your brother with that same heinous crime. Oh, Mary, I do not know. I am so sick at heart and soul of it all!" He pulled her roughly against him and the parchment in her hands rustled against his shoulder. "I am so exhausted from trying to out-think him and protect you and keep us untouched and at Wivenhoe."

His admission of weakness and fright terrified her, for she had never really thought that the confident, assured, and sometimes cynical man she loved could be truly tired or afraid. "But I am here and you may lean on me, my love, always," she said low. "Whatever befalls the Boleyns, it is partly of their own making and it is a far different thing from our dreams." Her arms went around his waist and she hugged him hard.

"I seem to have heard those words before, sweet Mary. You are my strength now, you and Andrew. So we shall help your mother and get through this somehow."

"Our strength shall be that we are together," she murmured against his chest, and they stood for a very long time at the window.

The messengers came and went from Lord Boleyn over the weeks of Anne and George's imprisonment and the days of their trials. At Hever they despaired when the three commoners whom the king had raised so high and Anne's little lutenist were declared guilty and condemned to die. And their hopes rose again when they heard of Anne's fine defense of George and herself at her trial. Both Jane Rochford and their cousin Sir Francis Bryan had successfully survived the dreadful storm of accusations by totally disassociating themselves from the Boleyn family which had originally been their making at court. Their Uncle Norfolk sat, with continual tears in his eyes, it was reported, as judge of the proceedings, so his desertion of his blood relatives was complete. Mary had asked that Staff burn all of Cromwell's letters to them from the past two years when Staff returned on one of his biweekly visits to Wivenhoe, for Cromwell was both artist and architect of the disgusting cruelty and despicable charges in Anne's court of justice.

After Anne's condemnation, they still dared to hope, for the king had called a special court to declare that Anne Boleyn had never been lawfully married to Henry Tudor since she herself had made a pre-contract with her long-lost love Harry Percy. But even the court's assurance to the king that he had never been legally married to the witch queen was not to be Anne's salvation. She was condemned to be beheaded for treason, incest and adultery on Tower Green where she had been forced to watch her former friends and her brother die the day before.

Anne's death day dawned clear and fair that May and, unsleeping, Mary rose to watch from her bedroom window the sun sift its earliest rays upon the spring gardens at Hever. She was not certain she had slept at all, and she knew Staff had dozed only fitfully. They had both paced the room or gone next door to watch Andrew sleep. Once Mary had met her mother at the nursery door and hugged her wordlessly.

Staff rolled out of bed and padded barefooted with only a robe on, to stand behind her at the window. "I was wondering if it makes it easier or harder to die on such a day, Staff."

He stood warm against her back, and he pushed the window wide ajar and breathed the sweet, fresh air. "I think it would make it easier, like something special to take with you," he said quietly. "She takes your love with her, Mary. She knows that. Were you trying to send your thoughts and strength to her again?"

"Oh, yes, my love, yes!" she cried and turned to bury her face against him as she had in her weaker moments these last two months. "Please, please hold me, Staff. Please love me."

"I love you, my golden Mary. I have always loved you." His voice faltered. "Yet I am not certain saying 'love' is strong enough to tell it all—all of how deeply I have felt for you over the years. The dear Lord in heaven knows I would have killed the king if he had touched you that last time we were at court—when Anne sent for you." He paused again, then his voice came rough and hard, "As well as I could have broken Francois' damned royal neck with my bare hands for his brutal treatment of you."

Mary's hands darted to her throat involuntarily and her thoughts jumped from Francois to Anne again. Anne's slender neck would be broken by a sharp headsman's sword, and on such a sunny day!

"Sweetheart." Staff's hands were warm on her waist. "Come away from the window. I did not mean to speak such violence. There has been enough killing," he said against her hair. He lifted her in his arms as sure and strong as he had that first time in the vast reaches of Greenwich when she had been Will Carey's wife and had thought that her life ahead would be all darkness. He laid her carefully on the sheets in the morning sunlight which streamed through the window. He lay beside her and pulled her against his body. She sighed and clung to him desperately, trembling, but no tears came as they had over the long weeks of Anne's trial, the long weeks of waiting for George and Anne's deaths.

She pressed her face into his shoulder to stop the thoughts of Anne and George on the scaffold. But her eyes shot open as she pictured the poor girl, Meg Roper, receiving from the cruel pike her father's terrible head and cherishing it tenderly in her arms. Sir Thomas More had been beheaded at the king's cold command as Anne had today. And now, surely, Mary's own father was somewhere on the road to Hever.

They lay there, unspeaking, and the bird warbling from outside washed in with the sun and mingled with their quiet breathing. She stared at the white plaster ceiling that had watched her as a girl and it all came flooding back. Father was taking her to Brussels, but she was afraid and only eight years old. Then he took her away to France, and after she went, George and Anne still laughed together in the summer gardens and it was not fair. Had any of the Bullens loved each other enough along the way, knowing that they loved and cherished each other? But it was different with her and Staff. And for her children, it would be even better. She would spend the rest of her life making sure of that.

Rapid knocks rained on their door and they both shot upright as Nancy's voice came to them from the other side. "Your lord father has ridden in, my lady. He is in the solar. Little Andrew is with your mother. Shall I come in to help you dress?"

They were up and Staff had his breeks on and his shirt half tucked in when she finished talking. Mary dashed to retrieve her chemise and to brush her hair. "Yes, yes, Nance, and hurry."

Nancy dressed her and would have set her hair had not Staff stood ready and had not her heart pounded so to see her father. He was here at last, come home to Hever, but he had come too early to have stayed for Anne's beheading. He had failed to save his world, but he had come home to them at Hever.

Nancy helplessly left her mistress' hair long and loose and gave it a last quick brush. Mary descended the stairs on Staff's arm. She began to tremble uncontrollably. She was terrified to hear the news he would bring and terrified she would see no understanding in his eyes even now. And the cold, hard stare from the king's portrait at the bottom of the steps.

"Do not fear, my love," Staff said and pushed the door open.

Her father paced in broken lines before the unlit hearth and her mother sat slumped back in a chair near him. The morning sun made the room strangely bright and cheerful and stained patches of the carpet and walls red or blue through the stained glass windows.

Thomas Boleyn stopped, and his narrow eyes took them in. It seemed to Mary he had shrunk inward and his gaze seemed to come from deep inside some dark space. "You cry not, Mary. How often I have seen you cry, but not for Anne?"

"I have cried and prayed for my dear sister and brother for two long months, father, when you were not here to see. Now the only tears I have left are inside."

His eyes focused hard on her and he began his rehearsed words. "The queen is dead by now—murdered by the king—as was your brother yesterday. George died bravely they told me, and I know the queen must have too. I could not stay to hear of that. Anne was quite magnificent at her trial. Be that as it may, they both wished to be remembered to you, Mary, and Anne to your husband also. I had a note from Anne to you somewhere, but in my departure, I seem to have misplaced it. It will arrive packed in with my things somewhere. Anne bid me tell you to relate her love—and the truth of her unjust death—to the Princess Elizabeth when she is old enough to understand. She wanted both you and little Catherine to be sure to look to that."

Mary left Staff standing behind her mother's chair

with his hands on her shoulders and took two steps closer to her father. "I shall see to it as a solemn trust, father. Anne gave Harry Carey into my keeping also, though there are other monies for his education."

"Yes, she told me so." He said nothing else and continued to regard her awkwardly as though she were a person he did not know.

"And you, father?" She reached out carefully and rested her fingers on his tense arm.

"I, Mary?" He pulled away and began to pace again. "I have failed, failed completely."

"But mother and I still love you, father," she ventured shakily. "You have Hever."

"Hever? Love? I spoke of all our plans. That black reptile Cromwell has been elevated to my vacant office of Lord Privy Seal. Traitors, traitors all! Norfolk her judge, the whining bitch Rochford their condemner—no wonder George could never love her or get her with child! And your dear cousin Francis Bryan was only too happy to ride to Jane Seymour and tell her that the queen had been condemned! Damn them all! Rats always leave a sinking ship no matter how grand or important the ship or the fact it might have yet been saved."

"My lord was telling me that we are not to have their bodies to bury," came Elizabeth Boleyn's rasping voice as she looked vacantly at Mary. "The guards were to bury them under the floor of the little church within The Tower where the jailers worship. At least it is a consecrated church though no place for a Howard and a queen. What did you call that church, my lord?"

"Saint Peters-in-Chains, Elizabeth."

"Yes. At least it sounds somehow appropriate. I

pray they will bury their heads with their bodies, so that on resurrection day they will be raised guiltless in His eyes."

"Guiltless, maybe not, my dear, but innocent of the dreadful crimes of which the king sought to brand them. Kingston promised he would see to that as you asked, madam."

"Thank you, Thomas. That mattered greatly to me. And the king will not harm Elizabeth?"

"I told you, no. Elizabeth is declared bastard now, but she is his and he knows it. Tudor is written all over her face."

"But she has her mother's skin and eyes and slender hands, father," Mary put in, and he turned to her again.

Thomas Boleyn refused to sit, but he leaned heavily on the carved mantel and put one still-booted foot on the andiron. "The sandy-haired boy by the gate is your new son," he said suddenly.

"Not so new, father. He will be three this autumn."

"Yes. Well, he looks to be quite a Howard."

"He is a Stafford, father. Not a Boleyn, not a Howard, a Stafford."

He turned his head to one side and looked at her over his arms folded along the mantelpiece. He pivoted his head further and stared at her husband. "My wife has told me repeatedly over the years, I assure you, Stafford, of your loyalty and kindnesses to her and your care of her these last two months. For that I am grateful."

"I do not covet your gratitude in any way, my lord. I did it for the love I bear my wife and her mother."

They faced each other staring over Mary who stood

between them. "I regret, Stafford, that Hever must revert to the crown upon our deaths, now that George is gone. In proper times it would have gone to Mary as the surviving heir or her Uncle James. It is a wonder to me that His Royal Majesty left me Hever even until I die. Sometimes I think he did it for Mary. Do you understand me, Stafford? Hever goes to the crown."

"Mary values Hever, not I, my lord. Wivenhoe will always be enough for me."

"I see. Then would you ever choose to do me any service for myself?"

"For the love I bear your daughter who loves you all too well, my lord, yes."

Thomas Boleyn was the first to break the grip lock of their eyes as he looked toward the door. "Mary has often been foolish, but then so have you, Stafford. No, Elizabeth, I will say this. You had the chance to have much of wealth and lands from the king."

"I wanted nothing from him but my freedom, Lord Boleyn, even as Mary and I want that from you."

"Well, maybe you were right not to trust him. Trust no one. Cromwell did one last favor for Anne when he fetched Mary to her and then he turned on us all. I would ask you for one favor before you go to Wivenhoe."

"My lord, they can well stay in my house as long as they should like to," Elizabeth Boleyn said, rising from her chair.

"Their home is Wivenhoe, wife. They prefer it. He has said it."

"We shall go today then, but we may be back to see Lady Elizabeth. And I assume that your grandchildren are welcome here to see their grandmother. If not, she

676

will be asked to come to Wivenhoe in the summers or whenever she would wish.''

''Oh, yes. Of course.'' Lord Boleyn pointed toward the solar, and Mary feared he would order them from his home instantly. His hand shook as he pointed. ''I would like you, Lord Stafford, to take the king's portrait down from the wall in my entryway and bury it somewhere in the gardens and do not tell me where. Bury it and slice it to ribbons if you would, for us both, for all of us! I should like to put my fist through it again and again, but, 's bones, I have not the strength!''

Elizabeth Boleyn went to him and wrapped her thin arms protectively around him as his dry sobs wracked his shaking body. Staff went to the door and then came back to pull Mary after him. He closed the door to the solar gently.

''I have never seen them like that, Staff. She is comforting him,'' she whispered in the hall as they stood under the big portrait.

''Maybe it will be a new start for them now in the years they have left, Mary.'' He turned and pulled the portrait out from the wall to peer behind it. ''Dirt and dust and wretched bugs,'' he said. He grasped the heavy frame and lifted the painting high off its hooks. ''I almost think,'' he said low to her, ''that he would have softened if we would have begged him to let us stay here and live with them.'' He turned his alert face to hers.

''But he must know we could never do that, my love. Wivenhoe is our home.''

A beautiful smile lit his tired face and his eyes caressed her. ''Then we shall do this last task and gather up Nancy, Stephen, and the lad and be on our way home, my wife.''

They went far out past the knot garden and the beds of tightbudded roses to the pond by the willows. ''Will you fetch me a gardener with a shovel?'' he said to her as he bent over the painting and drew his dagger. She stared down on the rough oil painted surface at the face she had once known so well. Shadows of the willow boughs flitted across the strong, stern features. The narrow eyes seemed to shift and the huge hands were in shadow.

''When Anne was little, she used to be afraid of this portrait,'' Mary thought aloud. ''She said once the hands were too big and the eyes were like father's.'' She turned away and hurried to find Michael, the gardener who had always lived about the grounds at Hever. Michael's face lit when he saw her and he came on the run with his shovel. She sat on the bench near the sundial which would soon be surrounded by the young shoots of mint and dill and watched Michael and then Staff dig. This is where she had been sitting before the labor pains for Harry began, she thought, and Michael was here to help her then. Suddenly reality stabbed at her again. Anne had just drifted off to leave her sitting here alone because she did not feel well enough to tell her how things were going at court. Tears of memory blinded her eyes, for Anne would never laugh and flit about the gardens of Hever again.

She went no nearer as the two men took turns digging a hole under the willow tree to bury the king's head, and her thoughts wandered again. Had sad Meg Roper finally buried her father's head? she mused. Staff always got on so democratically with servants that it amazed her. Why, it was as though Stephen was his best friend.

And then, as she watched them lift the huge frame into its grave and begin to shovel the soil back in, it came to her that her awful past was surely ready to be buried now too. It was as though, through the grief of losing George and Anne, it had gone with them off her shoulders and from her haunted thoughts. "Wait, Staff," she called and dashed to them. "Wait, my lord, do not fill it all in yet. There is something I would add."

She darted through the gardens and into the house past the still closed solar door. She ran up the steps which she had once descended to face the king only to find Staff's dark eyes awaiting her. She shoved the strands of pearls from dear Anne aside and dug under the garnet necklace Staff had given her so long ago at Whitehall. There it was. She had not dared to look on it since the sad death of its beloved giver two years before. It was just as the fair Tudor rose had handed it to her over their chess game so long ago.

Staff and Michael awaited her return, and Michael looked on in surprise as Mary showed Staff the green and white gilded chess pawn in her open palm. " 'Tis a little thing," Michael observed.

"No, Michael, it is a big, big thing," Staff told the puzzled man as Mary dumped the pawn into the freshly turned earth of the grave and Staff covered it.

"I have seen your fine gardens, Michael," Staff complimented the man after the hole was filled. "I have seen them over the years and admired them. Are you wed, Michael?"

The gangly man smiled guiltily and the gap between his teeth showed as it always had. "No, milord. I never did yet find the lass to love and wed with, an' I couldna see weddin' only to raise a passel a young ones."

"A wise man," Staff said seriously and patted the glowing Michael on the shoulder. "I will tell you this, Michael, and I want you to remember my words."

"Oh, yes, milord."

"When the day should come that Hever must be sold, if you do not wish to stay, buy a horse and come to Wivenhoe near Colchester to Lady Mary's home there. We will be expanding our meagre gardens there over the years, and we shall have need of a sure hand like yours. Even if it never happens for years, you remember to come to Wivenhoe to us."

"Thankee, milord," Michael managed, and tears sprang to his green eyes.

"Goodbye for now, Michael. You have always been a true friend to the Bullens," Mary said and found a smile for him inside her bereft, tired mind.

Staff took her arm and they went slowly toward the painted facade of the house through the gardens. "I did not bury the portrait, Mary," he said at last as they went under the iron teeth of the drawbridge. "I cut it out and buried only the frame. The portrait should be for Elizabeth. He is her father nevertheless and it will be a heritage from Hever which she may well never see." He shoved the tightly rolled canvas under his doublet.

"Very well, my Staff," she said, "but do not hang it in my house in the meanwhile."

"I shall hide it in the deepest chest in the cellar, I promise," he said.

As they entered the house, the front door stood ajar to catch the fresh breezes and in a pool of sunlight on the floor, Andrew played with his carved horse and a heavy gold chain. Mary bent over him to examine it. "What do you have, sweetheart?" she inquired and Staff halted on the first step upstairs.

"Staff, it is my father's chest chain with the king's seal. But where . . ."

"I gave it to the lad, Mary. I have no need of it," her father's voice came from the door of the solar. "I have another I shall send your Harry if you like. Leave the boy be. He is having a fine time smashing that wooden horse into it, though he looks at me as though I am some sort of gremlin from a nightmare."

"Thank you for the gift to him, father. He is only a bit shy around, well, strangers. I would be proud to have him know you more over the years."

"There will not be many years, daughter. I can feel it." He nodded toward the dusty rectangle on the wall where the sun never went. "I see the portrait is gone."

"Yes, it is gone," Staff said.

"Then you and I are even, Stafford. You have Mary and you did me a favor freely."

Staff nodded silently, the lower half of his body in the same pool of sun in which Andrew played quietly now. Lady Elizabeth came to the open door of the solar and old, crooked Semmonet leaned hard on her cane behind.

"You will stay for a noon supper before you set out," Elizabeth Boleyn's voice came to them in the silence of the house.

"Yes, of course, Lady Elizabeth," Staff said, his eyes still on Thomas Boleyn as though he were waiting for something.

"We—I wish you well, Mary," her father said then.

"And, of all the plans and dreams and the three fine children, he ensnared us all, and only golden Mary survived," he chanted as though he were in a trance. He looked down jerkily at the boy who played with the shining chain in the sunlight and turned back into the solar.

Mary stared after his back as he disappeared behind the door. For a moment she thought he would come out again young and strong, and ask her what she had overhead, and tell her that she was going to Brussels to the court of the Archduchess. But, no, that was a long dead time ago and there sat her son, hers and Staff's.

"Mother, could you summon Nancy to watch Andrew while we pack to go home?" Mary asked.

"I think his grandfather and I shall tend him in the solar until you are ready to sup with us, my Mary," her mother answered with tears in her blue eyes. Her silver head bent down and she lifted the boy to his feet.

Behind Mary, Staff touched her shoulder, and she turned to smile at him. Then they hurried up the stairs hand in hand to pack.

Afterword

I have long wished to write the story of Lady Mary Boleyn. She is remembered today only in scant footnotes on the pages of English history or in brief mention in volumes on her younger sister Anne, since, as King Henry VIII's mistress, "the Lady Mary went before". Although she is the least noted and remembered of the radiant and rapacious Boleyn clan who sliced through Tudor history like a comet's tail behind their meteoric king, Mary, I believe, emerges as the loveliest, and eventually, the wisest and the strongest of that fated family.

Mary deserves more than a mere passing glance or footnote from history. Used as a pawn in the Tudor and international chess game for power by a ruthless father and two kings, she steps forth from the pages of the past intact and her own woman despite overwhelming odds and indignities. We need only to search for the real Lady Mary between the lines which document her turbulent times to find the whole woman, and, when we do, we will find her also in our hearts.

Several minor characters in this novel such as servants are necessarily fictional; however, the major characters and places are as authentically drawn as history, maps, and records will allow. Quiet, moated

Hever Castle, which becomes almost a character itself in Mary's story, like much else, fell to the king in 1538 when Thomas Boleyn died a year after his wife. At that time, instead of merely taking Hever as was the legal custom, the king arranged a sort of sale and, for an unrecorded reason, made certain that a sum was paid to his long-ago mistress Mary Stafford. Guilt money? Affection money? Money to assure her eldest son was well raised? That is for us to wonder. It does again suggest the magnetism of this nearly forgotten woman.

Henry Tudor and Francois of France died the same year, 1547. Henry had finally been given his male heir through his marriage to Jane Seymour who died bearing the child, but as is fully recorded, it is the Boleyn child Elizabeth who was the greatest Tudor ruler. Mary Stafford's two eldest children served their cousin and queen, Elizabeth I, loyally. Catherine Carey became gentlewoman of the Privy Chamber at the accession of the queen and Henry Carey, 1st Lord Hunsdon, served as her trusted advisor and put down the Catholic Dacre Rebellion in 1570.

Those who were so treacherous to the Boleyns at the last eventually met their own tragic ends: Thomas Cromwell was hanged, drawn, and quartered after falling from power for failing to please his king in the procurement of his fourth queen; Jane Rochford was beheaded with King Henry's fifth queen, Catherine Howard, for acting as her panderer; and the king himself died a gross and disease-ridden man shrieking in his delirium that Catholic priests were waiting to torture him for his ruination of the True Church.

I wish to especially thank Gavin Astor, second Baron Astor of Hever Castle in Kent for his kind correspondence, the use of his own research, and his encouragement to me as I undertook Mary's story. And my gratitude as always to my husband, my travel companion and proofreader.

Throughout the novel, I have employed Tudor sonnets or songs, some of which Mary might have known, to help establish the mood, emotions, and themes of the story. With Michael Drayton's poem, I close these thoughts:

Karen Harper

Sonnet 42

Some men there be which like my method well,
And much commend the strangeness of my vein;
Some say I have a passing pleasing strain,
Some say that in my humor I excel;
Some, who not kindly relish my conceit,
They say, as poets do I use to feign,
And in bare words paint out my passion's pain;
Thus sundry men their sundry minds repeat.
I care not, I how men affected be,
Nor who commends or discommends my verse;
It pleaseth me if I my woes rehearse,
And in my line if she my love may see,
Only, my comfort still consists in this:
Writing her praise, I cannot write amiss.

BESTSELLING ROMANCES BY JANELLE TAYLOR

SAVAGE ECSTASY   (824, $3.50)

It was like lightning striking, the first time the Indian brave Gray Eagle looked into the eyes of the beautiful young settler Alisha. And from the moment he saw her, he knew that he must possess her—and make her his slave!

DEFIANT ECSTASY   (931, $3.50)

When Gray Eagle returned to Fort Pierre's gates with his hundred warriors behind him, Alisha's heart skipped a beat; would Gray Eagle destroy her—or make his destiny her own?

FORBIDDEN ECSTASY   (1014, $3.50)

Gray Eagle had promised Alisha his heart forever—nothing could keep him from her. But when Alisha woke to find her red-skinned lover gone, she felt abandoned and alone. Lost between two worlds, desperate and fearful of betrayal, Alisha hungered for the return of her FORBIDDEN ECSTASY.

BRAZEN ECSTASY   (1133, $3.50)

When Alisha is swept down a raging river and out of her savage brave's life, Gray Eagle must rescue his love again. But Alisha has no memory of him at all. And as she fights to recall a past love, another white slave woman in their camp is fighting for Gray Eagle!

Available wherever paperbacks are sold, or order direct from the Publisher. Send cover price plus 50¢ per copy for mailing and handling to Zebra Books, 475 Park Avenue South, New York, N.Y. 10016. DO NOT SEND CASH.